Praise for the romances of
***New York Times* bestselling author**
Catherine Anderson

"Anderson comes up with another winner by deftly blending sweetness and sensuality in a poignantly written story." —*Booklist*

"Count on Catherine Anderson for intense emotion."—Jayne Ann Krentz

"Catherine Anderson is an amazing talent." —Elizabeth Lowell

"Catherine Anderson has a gift for imbuing her characters with dignity, compassion, courage, and strength that inspire readers."
—*Romantic Times*

"A major voice in the romance genre." —*Publishers Weekly*

"Not only does author Catherine Anderson push the envelope—she seals, stamps, and sends it to the reader with love." —*Affaire de Coeur*

continued . . .

With You Beside Me

A Coulter Family Double

Catherine Anderson

NEW AMERICAN LIBRARY

NEW AMERICAN LIBRARY
Published by New American Library, a division of
Penguin Group (USA) Inc., 375 Hudson Street,
New York, New York 10014, USA
Penguin Group (Canada), 90 Eglinton Avenue, Suite 700, Toronto,
Ontario M4P 2Y3, Canada (a division of Pearson Penguin Canada Inc.)
Penguin Books Ltd., 80 Strand, London WC2R 0RL, England
Penguin Ireland, 25 St. Stephen's Green, Dublin 2,
Ireland (a division of Penguin Books Ltd.)
Penguin Group (Australia), 250 Camberwell Road, Camberwell, Victoria 3124,
Australia (a division of Pearson Australia Group Pty. Ltd.)
Penguin Books India Pvt. Ltd., 11 Community Centre, Panchsheel Park,
New Delhi - 110 017, India
Penguin Group (NZ), cnr Airborne and Rosedale Roads, Albany,
Auckland 1310, New Zealand (a division of Pearson New Zealand Ltd.)
Penguin Books (South Africa) (Pty.) Ltd., 24 Sturdee Avenue,
Rosebank, Johannesburg 2196, South Africa

Penguin Books Ltd., Registered Offices: 80 Strand, London WC2R 0RL, England

Published by New American Library, a division of Penguin Group (USA) Inc. Previously
published in separate Onyx editions.

First New American Library Printing, August 2005
10 9 8 7 6 5 4 3 2 1

Printed in the United States of America

PUBLISHER'S NOTE
These are works of fiction. Names, characters, places, and incidents either are the product of
the author's imagination or are used fictitiously, and any resemblance to actual persons, living or dead, business establishments, events, or locales is entirely coincidental.

The publisher does not have any control over and does not assume any responsibility for
author or third-party Web sites or their content.

❧ CONTENTS ❧

Phantom Waltz

To Steven Axelrod, my agent, who always goes the extra mile for me and has earned my gratitude and respect, and to Ellen Edwards, my editor, who has worked so hard behind the scenes over the years to make my books the very best that they can be.

Last, but not least, to Chris Jansen, Dr. Fred Black's nurse extraordinaire, who has been such a good friend to me. The world would be a much better place if every medical professional had as much heart as you do. Please know, Chris, that you are touching lives and making a difference. Also, by order of decree passed along to me by your brother, Jeff Fretwell, I wish you a belated "Happy Birthday!"

Dear Readers:

Traditionally in romance, the heroes and heroines are physically perfect. That is not to say that those characters are unappealing. I have read hundreds of those books and loved them, I've written a few, and I hope to write and enjoy many more. However, as a novelist, I occasionally get a yen to write something different—a tribute, if you will, to those in our society who are, by birth or unfortunate mishap, left disabled. I have been so blessed as a writer to have an agent and editor, Steven Axelrod and Ellen Edwards, respectively, who have always encouraged me to break new ground. If not for them, *Annie's Song*, a book about a deaf girl, might never have been written.

So it is that, once again, I bring to you, my readers, a different kind of love story, this time about a young woman confined to a wheelchair. I invite you to cast aside all your preconceived notions about what constitutes a great love story and join me in Bethany Coulter's world, where hope for a normal life is only a memory and dreams of romance are long since forgotten . . . until magic comes knocking in the form of a tall, dark, rugged cowboy named Ryan Kendrick.

I would like to thank Dr. Fred Black and his nurse, Chris Jansen, for giving me information and direction in my research. I also salute the many paraplegics who have reached out to others with personal accounts of their disabilities and how paraplegia has affected their lives. I would also like to thank my wonderful husband, Sid, who has never failed to be my anchor in the storm and my bridge over troubled waters.

Catherine Anderson

❦ CHAPTER ONE ❦

Forget chewing nails. Ryan Kendrick was so mad he could have chewed lug nuts. He had a broken-down tractor, and the parts needed to fix it should have been delivered to the Rocking K the day before yesterday. As of this morning, they still hadn't arrived, and Ryan's follow-up calls had gotten him nowhere.

With one shoulder, he butted open the door of The Works, the largest ranch supply house in Crystal Falls. Harv Coulter, a rancher who'd gone bust, had started the business on a shoestring several years back, and the Kendrick brothers, along with many other ranchers in the area, had been patronizing the establishment ever since. Now the huge store was a going concern, well stocked with everything from heavy equipment to fancy western wear, the only problem being that as sales increased, the quality of service seemed to go downhill.

If Harv didn't get his employees whipped into shape, he'd start losing accounts. Delays like this, smack-dab in the middle of spring planting time, were intolerable. Due to late snows, every farmer and rancher in the basin was already behind schedule, and each day of downtime could mean thousands of dollars in lost crop revenue.

Ryan headed for an overhead sign at the rear of the feed section that read PARTS AND REPAIRS, his dusty riding boots beating out an angry tattoo on the concrete floor. When he reached a counter cluttered with parts and catalogs, he shoved aside an air filter, rested his arms on the grease-stained Formica, and settled a blistering gaze on a slender young woman who sat at a computer station near the register.

A long, luxurious mane of sable hair partly concealed her face. Her slender, neatly manicured fingers flew over the keyboard with speedy efficiency. Ryan waited for just a moment. Being ignored did little to mellow his mood. The morning was half over. He glanced at his watch and set his jaw.

"Excuse me," he said. "Is it possible to get some help around here?"

That brought her head up. Ryan went still, his gaze riveted. She had the most beautiful eyes, large, outlined with thick, dark lashes, and so deep a blue they reminded him of the Johnny-jump-up violets that grew wild at the ranch. Normally, he scoffed at the sappy phrases men used to describe women. He'd looked into a lot of eyes and never felt in danger of drowning, or losing his heart.

"I don't usually work the floor, but I can try to help you," she said, her voice as sunny as her smile, which flashed an irresistible dimple in one cheek.

Ryan couldn't stop staring. Her face was small and heart-shaped, with sculpted cheekbones, a pointy chin with just a hint of stubbornness, and a soft, sweet mouth. The tip of her delicately bridged nose was shiny and sported a smattering of freckles, which told him her flawless complexion was natural.

"What seems to be the problem?" she asked.

He started to tell her, but for an instant, his mind went as empty as a wrangler's pocket right before payday, and he couldn't remember why the hell he was there.

He had the strangest feeling, dead center in his chest—a sense of recognition—as if he'd subconsciously been searching for her all his life. *Crazy.* Love at first sight was more his brother's style. Ryan shopped for women like he did for boots, trying them on for size before he settled in for a long-term relationship, and even at that, he'd yet to find a comfortable enough fit to last him a lifetime.

"I, um . . ." He rubbed beside his nose, a habit when he got nervous. A dull ache throbbed behind his eyes. "I'm Ryan Kendrick from the Rocking K," he offered stupidly.

The sweet curve of her lips deepened. "Hi. I'm pleased to meet you. And don't feel bad. I have days like this, only worse. At least you know your name."

He huffed with laughter. "You actually forget your *name?*"

The dimple flashed again. "What works for me is to back up. You're Ryan Kendrick from the Rocking K, and you came in here to . . . ?"

He snapped his fingers. "My parts."

"Your parts?"

He chuckled. "I want to know where the Sam Hill they are."

Pure devilment crept into her expression. "You've lost your parts and think *I've* got them? Most cowboys I know guard theirs like Fort Knox."

Ryan threw back his head and laughed. The tension that had knotted the muscles in his neck and shoulders all morning miraculously vanished.

"I hope you don't have a hot date lined up for Saturday night," she added. "A cowboy who's missing his parts could find himself in a very embarrassing situation."

He nudged up the brim of his Stetson. "Well, now, darlin', that all depends. What are you doin' Saturday night?"

It was her turn to laugh. The sound was rich and musical, and it warmed him clear through.

"I usually avoid cowboys who can't keep track of their parts."

"Go out with me, and I guarantee I'll find mine in damned short order."

"Maybe if you'll give me an order number instead of a hard time, I can help locate the little buggers for you."

Little buggers? Ryan almost corrected that misconception. But there were lines a man didn't step over, and he had a hunch this was one of them. Maybe it was the sweetness of her smile—or that innocent look he'd glimpsed in her eyes—but something told him she wasn't as worldly as she pretended to be.

As he fished in the pocket of his blue chambray shirt, he swept his gaze over her. She was a fragile, slightly built woman, which undoubtedly explained why those eyes seemed to be the biggest thing about her. But despite that, she was temptingly well-rounded in all the right places. *Perfection in miniature.*

Her brown shell top showcased a long, graceful neck, thin but well-defined shoulders, and creamy-white arms that looked surprisingly firm for someone with such a slight build. Beneath the brown knit, small, perfectly shaped breasts pleaded for a lingering look. Minding his manners, he flicked his gaze lower and bemoaned the fact that the counter concealed the rest of her. He was a leg man, and it was a woman's foundation that always swung the vote for him.

Wishing she'd stand up so he could get a look, he handed over the slip of paper on which he'd jotted his order number. While she scanned computer files and tracked down his parts order, they carried on a lively exchange, during which he learned she was twenty-six, had no significant other in her life except a feline named Cleo, and was the baby in a family of six kids. Her five rambunctious older brothers spoiled her rotten and kept things hopping at family gatherings.

Ryan enjoyed talking with her. Even with her attention divided between him and the computer screen, she kept him on his conversational toes. It wasn't often he ran across beauty, brains, *and* a great personality, all in one package.

"So . . . you gonna give me a name to put with the face?" he asked.

"Bethany." Finished with the computer, she leaned back in her chair. "Well, cowboy, time to eat crow. Guess where those parts of yours are."

"Where?"

"En route to the Rocking K. And it's not *our* fault they're late. This is the busy season. Those particular parts are in high demand right now, were on back order, and took two days longer to reach us than they should have."

Ryan had heard that one before, but coming from her, it seemed more credible. He tipped the brim of his hat back down to shade his eyes before returning outdoors. "Hmm. Lucky for me, I didn't raise too much sand, huh?"

"It takes more than a cantankerous cowboy to throw me. Five brothers, remember?" She propped her elbows on the chair armrests, her big blue eyes still smiling. "Have a nice day, and good luck fixing your tractor. Too bad you're not an employee. You could charge yourself time and a half."

By that, Ryan guessed she knew who he was. No big surprise. Practically everyone in Crystal Falls, Oregon, had heard of the Kendrick family. He tipped his hat to her. "Thank you, Bethany. It's been a rare pleasure."

"Any time," she called after him as he walked away.

He had nearly reached the door before he swung to a stop. To hell with walking out. He was thirty years old and hadn't come across a woman who interested him this much in a long time. *Bethany.* She was beautiful, sweet, and funny. The only other women he knew who could take him from pissed off to laughing in three seconds flat were his mom and sister-in-law. No way was he leaving without at least getting her phone number, a date if he could manage it.

"I know this may seem forward," he began as he returned to the counter.

Already back at work, she glanced up from the screen, her thoughtful frown giving way to another warm smile. "You've lost your parts again *already*?"

Ryan chuckled. "Not on your life. I just—" He felt heat crawling up his neck. He hadn't felt nervous about asking a girl out since his early teens. "About Saturday night. I know we were only joking, but on a more serious note, I'd like to get to know you." At her startled look, he added, "Hey, I'm a nice guy. Your boss, Harvey Coulter, will vouch for me."

"Oh, I'm sure you're very nice, but—"

Ryan held up a staying hand. "How about dinner and dancing? We'll go out, have a fine meal, get to know each other a little better. Then we'll cut a rug. I'm hell on wheels at country western, and I know of a great band."

Her mouth curved in a wistful smile. "You like to dance, do you?"

"I *love* to dance. How about you?"

She averted her gaze. Ryan wanted to kick himself for coming on too fast. So much for that legendary charm his brother teased him about. Well, it was too late now. All he could do was go for it and hope for the best.

"I used to enjoy dancing very much." She tapped a pen on the work surface beside her computer, her small hand clenched so tightly over its length that her dainty knuckles went white.

Ryan shoved up the brim of his hat. He did his best convincing with his eyes. "Come on, sweetheart, take a chance on me. We'll have fun. I give you my solemn oath to be a perfect gentleman."

"It isn't that."

"What, then?"

To his dismay, he saw that all the laughter and mischief in her eyes had been eclipsed by shadows. He sensed he'd said or done something to cause that, but for the life of him he couldn't think what.

"If you're worried that you're too rusty to get on a dance floor, I'm easy to follow. Give me ten minutes, and you'll think you've got wings on your feet."

She rolled her chair back from the computer station and folded her hands in her lap, gazing up at him with a prideful lift of her small chin. "Somehow I rather doubt that." Her strained, overbright smile was foiled by the flush of embarrassment on her cheeks. "Don't you?"

It took Ryan a full second to register what she meant. Then he saw that she was sitting in a wheelchair.

He felt as if a horse had kicked him in the gut—an awful, suddenly breathless feeling that made his legs threaten to buckle. It had to be a joke. She was so beautiful and perfect in every other way, the girl of his dreams. There was no way—absolutely no way.

But then his gaze dropped to her legs. The hem of her gathered black skirt came to just below the knees, revealing flesh toned support hose, finely turned ankles, and small feet encased in black slippers. The way her feet were positioned on the rests, one turned inward, was typical of a paraplegic's, and as shapely as her calves were, he could see that her muscles had begun to atrophy.

Sweet Christ. He felt like a worm. His first knee-jerk reaction was to make a polite excuse and get the hell out of there. To *run*.

The thought made him feel ashamed. Judging by those shadows in her eyes, she'd been down this path before and gotten badly hurt, undoubtedly by a long line of jackasses just like him who'd run when they saw her wheelchair.

He'd be damned if he'd do that to her. It was only one date.

Bethany fully expected Ryan Kendrick to make fast tracks or start stammering. That was usually the way it went. Watching his dark face, she had to give him credit; he looked stunned for a moment, but he quickly recovered. Flashing a wickedly attractive grin, he said, "Well, hell, I guess dancing's out. Unless, of course, I can come up with a set of wheels so we can do the wheelchair tango."

Usually men avoided mentioning her wheelchair, and while they groped for something to say, their eyes reflected a frantic need to escape. She always wanted to crawl in a hole when that happened, but Ryan Kendrick's reaction was even worse. If he felt an urge to run, he was a great loss to the stage.

"There are a number of things besides dancing that we can go do." He rested loosely folded fists at his lean waist, frowned, and then started naming off ideas, ending with, "How's dinner followed by a good movie strike you?"

It struck her as alarming. *Terrifying.* He was supposed to be heading for the closest exit. She flirted all the time. A girl had to have some fun, after all. But no man had ever taken her up on it. She didn't know what to say. Every time she looked into his gun-metal blue eyes, her mind went blank. He was *so* handsome, the epitome of tall, dark, and gorgeous. Chiseled features, a strong jaw, jet hair, and oodles of muscle. A dangerous mix. Crystal Falls was a large town, and Bethany had attended different schools than Ryan had. She'd also been a few years younger, so they'd never moved in the same social circles. But as a teenager, she'd seen him a few times at a distance, usually out at the fairgrounds during rodeos, and she'd thought he was handsome even then. He was even more attractive now. Little wonder his name was almost legend and half the women in town fancied themselves in love with him.

"I, um . . ." She shrugged, for once in her life at a total loss for words. If one of her brothers had been present, he would have marked the moment.

Her gaze fell to his mouth. His lips were long and narrow, mere slashes in the granite hardness of his face, yet beautifully sculpted with the muted shimmer of satin. At present, one corner of that hard mouth was twitching, as if he were suppressing a smile.

"Dinner and a movie isn't very imaginative, I know," he said apologetically. "I'll think of something more exciting next time around."

Next time? She wasn't sure how to deal with this. Why was he wasting his time with her? Because he felt sorry for her, maybe? She didn't want his pity.

She should have made certain he saw the wheelchair right away. Then this never would have happened. She couldn't go out with him. Her legs might not work, but her heart was in fine working order, and Ryan Kendrick was a little too charming. With those twinkling eyes and that sexy grin chipping away at her defenses, it would be all too easy to get in over her head.

She smoothed her hands over her skirt to make sure it covered her knees. There had to be a graceful way out of this. "Actually, Mr. Kendrick, the reason I hesitate is because I think I may be busy Saturday night."

He never missed a beat. "How about Friday, then?" He no sooner spoke than he snapped his fingers. "No, Friday won't work. I'm sponsoring a tractor in the mud pulls that night, and I really should be at the fairgrounds."

"Mud pulls?" Bethany immediately wanted to bite her tongue.

His gaze sharpened on her face. "Are you a mud-pull enthusiast?"

She pushed at her hair, then rolled closer to the counter to straighten the work area. "I used to enjoy them very much."

"I'm surprised. Mostly only men like the mud pulls."

She shrugged. "I had strange tastes for a girl, I guess."

"Why past tense? If you really enjoy the mud pulls, I'd love to take you."

He'd obviously never been around a paraplegic. "Oh, I couldn't possibly."

"Why not?"

"Between the parking lot and track, there's an acre of dirt and gravel."

"What's a little dirt and gravel?"

Her pulse started to pound. She swallowed, drew a deep breath, and tried to calm down. He wasn't interested in her that way; he was only being kind. She needed to focus on that, keep her sense of humor, and laugh this off. A little stark reality was called for, apparently. Who better to give him a dose?

"To a walking person, a little dirt and gravel is no big thing," she said slowly. "But my wheelchair tends to bog down on uneven ground, and getting it across deep gravel is difficult."

He gave her a measuring look. "Does it hurt you to be carried?"

"Pardon?"

"Does it cause you any pain when someone carries you?"

"You're kidding. Right? You can't mean to *carry* me."

"Why not?"

Why not? He really didn't have a clue. "The question isn't if it might hurt me, but whether or not your back can take the abuse." She shook her head. "It's very nice of you to offer. Really it is, Mr. Kendrick, but—"

"Ryan," he corrected. "Or Rye, if you prefer. I answer to both. And I'm not being 'nice.' I really want to take you."

"Ryan, then." Searching his gaze, which made her feel as if she'd just swallowed live goldfish, she said, "You're sweet to offer, but you've no idea what you'd be getting into. There are no walkways or bleachers down at that track."

"So? You have a chair, and I'll take a camp stool along for myself."

"No, you don't understand. It's not the seating arrangements that worry me, but that you'd have to carry my chair down there. It's very heavy and awkward to handle, and then you'd have to haul me down there as well." She shook her head again. "No. About the time you got me settled, it'd be my luck I'd need to use the ladies' room, which is clear up at the stadium. That's at least a quarter mile. There you'd be, carrying me and my chair all the way up there, then all the way back. By evening's end, you'd be wishing you never asked me."

"You can't weigh more than a hundred pounds. My back can handle it."

"A hundred and eleven," she corrected, thinking as she spoke that nearly half of that was dead weight, which was heavier and more awkward to handle.

"All of that?" He chuckled, his steel-blue eyes dancing with amusement. "Honey, I lift twice your weight dozens of times a day."

"No, I—"

"It's a date," he insisted. Stepping to the counter, he reached over to push a notepad toward her. "I'll be on your doorstep to pick you up at precisely six o'clock on Friday night. Just jot down your address and phone number."

"I really—"

"Come on," he cajoled. "We'll have fun. It isn't often I meet a lady who enjoys the mud pulls. Where have you been all my life?"

She laughed and tried one more time to discourage him. "I'm really not much on dating. You don't have to do this. Honestly. You're off the hook."

In response to that, he narrowed an eye and shoved the notepad closer. "Full name, address, and phone number. If you won't give them to me, I'll play dirty and get them from Harv Coulter. The Rocking K is his largest account."

Imagining her father's reaction, Bethany smiled. "I should let you go ask him. It might prove interesting. I don't suppose you're a betting man?"

"Sometimes. What's the wager?"

"That my *boss* not only won't give you my address but may run you out of here with a shotgun. Daddy tends to be overprotective of his baby girl."

"You're Harv's daughter?"

"His one and only." With a sigh of resignation, she bent her head and wrote the information he'd requested on the slip of paper. "Don't say I didn't warn you. By evening's end, when you're popping ibuprofen and wishing you had a back brace, I don't want to hear any complaints."

"You won't."

As she tore the top sheet from the notepad and handed it to him, she added, "If something comes up and you need to cancel, Ryan, you can reach me here at the store during the day. I really would appreciate a call. For someone like me, getting ready to go somewhere is no easy thing."

He folded the paper and slipped it in his pocket. "I'll show. Count on it."

She shrugged, hoping to convey that she didn't care one way or the other. "I'll accept any excuse. Even 'my dog ate my homework' will work." She forced a bright smile.

"Friday," he said huskily. "Six o'clock sharp. I'll be looking forward to it."

As he walked away, Bethany heard footsteps behind her. She glanced over her shoulder to see her brother Jake approaching. Dressed in the same ranch-issue faded denim and blue chambray as Ryan, he looked enough like the other man to be related. Tall and lean, yet muscular, her brother had the tough look of a man who'd pitted himself against the elements most of his life.

Jake also had beautiful eyes—a deep, clear blue that was almost startling in contrast to his sun-dark skin and sable hair. At the moment, those eyes were fixed with glaring intensity on Ryan Kendrick's departing back. "What was that all about?"

"What was what all about?" she asked innocently.

Jake gave her a long, questioning look. "As I was coming downstairs, I saw the two of you talking, and it looked like he was flirting with you."

Bethany raised her eyebrows. "Flirting with me? How long's it been since you had your eyes checked?"

His jaw muscle started to tic. "You're paralyzed, Bethie, not dead. And you're a very pretty lady. I know men must flirt with you occasionally."

"So why the scowl?"

"Because that particular man is bad news. You steer clear of Ryan Kendrick, honey. The guy's got a reputation."

Still single at thirty-one, Jake had a bit of a reputation himself. Bethany refrained from pointing that out. "A reputation for what?"

"Loving them and leaving them." Jake stepped over to the counter, opened a parts catalog, and pulled a pen from his shirt pocket. "Don't do any toe-dipping in that particular pond. It's inhabited by a shark, and I don't want my little sister to be his next victim."

§ CHAPTER TWO §

By Friday evening, Bethany was laughing at herself. Ryan hadn't called to cancel, which meant their date for tonight was still on. Against her better judgment and despite all the lectures she'd given herself, she was excited about it—so excited she could barely stand it. For the first time in eight years, she was going out on a date. A *real* date. Not with a relative, not with some friend of her brothers', but with Ryan Kendrick, the most sought-after bachelor in town.

It was absurd to feel excited. It was only a onetime thing, and he had only insisted on taking her to be kind. But, hey. He was taking her someplace really fun, and she intended to enjoy every second of the evening.

Did her hair look all right?

She raced to her bedroom for a final inspection in the vanity mirror. Despite the extreme difficulty of stuffing her limp legs into tight jeans with only her dressing sling to assist her, she had decided to go with the cowgirl look tonight, which had been a little hard to pull off in a wheelchair, especially without a hat or riding boots. Hers were in her parents' attic, buried under a layer of dust.

She turned this way, then that, critical of her reflection. Did the red plaid and denim look silly? In Crystal Falls, most women wore snug Wranglers and western-style tops to events like mud pulls, but they weren't in wheelchairs.

Somewhere in the house, her cat knocked into something. The clattering sound nearly made Bethany part company with her skin. She flattened a hand over her chest and closed her eyes. *Enough*. She had to stop this.

She wasn't so foolish as to hope that Ryan was actually attracted to her. Just the thought frightened her. An evening out, simply to have fun, was one thing, an attraction quite another. That was a can of worms better left unopened.

Taking a deep breath, she opened her eyes and stared hard at her reflection, determined to see herself as others must. She supposed she was pretty, in an ordinary sort of way. Nothing about her was exceptional, though.

The one thing about her that was glaringly apparent was her wheelchair—the bane of her existence and always a part of her life. When Ryan looked at her, that wheelchair was what he would see, not the woman in it. She needed to remember that. She had believed in someone once, putting stock in dreams and thinking her paralysis didn't matter, but in the end, it had been all that mattered.

She would pretend he was one of her brothers. No big deal. She'd never see him again after tonight. She would thoroughly enjoy attending a mud pull again, and that's what she should be concentrating on. She rarely got to do things like this anymore because it was more trouble than it was worth, the hardship falling to friends or family members who volunteered to take her.

She returned to the living room, acutely conscious of the whirring sound her chair made as it rolled over the polished hardwood floors. Once parked, she glanced at the case clock on the mantel. *Six o'clock.* An achy feeling filled her throat. She straightened her shoulders, listening as the pendulum ticked away the seconds. He was just late. If he wasn't coming, he would have called.

And, hey . . . if he didn't show, no skin off her nose. She had a fantastic family, a great job, and interesting activities that kept her on the move from morning until night. She depended on no one for fulfillment or happiness.

Tick-tock—tick-tock. The pendulum mercilessly measured off the passing minutes, and each one seemed to last a small eternity. She leafed through a tole painting magazine, then tossed it back on the coffee table. *Twenty after.*

Oh, well. Like this came as a big surprise? Deep down, she hadn't really expected him to come. It would have been cold at the fairgrounds, anyway. Who wanted to freeze her buns off to watch tractors slide around in the mud?

She moved to a window and gazed out at the side yard where the deepening dusk and an icy chill hovered low over the nude deciduous trees. No buds had sprouted on the branches yet. Because of the high elevation, spring came late for the people in Crystal Falls.

And for some, it never came at all . . .

Bethany knotted her hands into fists and closed her eyes against a rush of scalding tears, hating Ryan for getting her hopes up and hating herself for giving him the power to dash them.

Never again. Maybe it was good that this had happened, serving as a reminder. No wishing on rainbows for her. Better to keep her feet—or in this case, her wheels—firmly rooted in reality.

Ryan glanced at his watch and cursed. Another red light. Why was it that everything slowed him down when he was in a hurry? *Damn.* That old lady in the Chrysler drove at one speed, slow. He smacked the heel of his hand on the steering wheel. Then he grabbed the cell phone out of the flip-down console beside him and punched redial again. No answer. Since they had a date, she was surely at home. Why the hell didn't she pick up? Maybe she had call waiting and was on the other line.

The light finally changed. Ryan rode the back bumper of the Chrysler through the intersection. Then he gunned the accelerator, changed lanes, and swept past the car as if it were sitting still. The engine of the new Dodge hummed as Ryan opened it up on the straightaway.

He'd probably get a speeding ticket, but he didn't give a damn. *Bethany.* He kept remembering those dark, shifting shadows in her eyes when she'd told him she would accept any excuse to cancel. She had expected him to back out, and now he was running thirty minutes late. She would think he'd stood her up.

The doorbell pealed. Bethany wiped her wet cheeks. *Oh, God.* Her face was probably a mess. She considered not answering the door, but that was silly. Besides, it was probably only one of her brothers dropping in to check on her.

She rubbed hard under her lower lashes to make sure there were no mascara drips. Then she finger-combed her hair, giving it a fluff to fall around her shoulders. Not that she cared at this point if she looked nice, but she did have her pride. If, by chance, it was Ryan at the door, she didn't want him to know he'd made her cry.

Dumb. It was forty minutes after the hour. He wouldn't show up this late.

She raced down the hall, braking to a stop well back from the threshold. Leaning forward, she flipped on the porch light, unlatched the special dead bolt her brother Zeke had installed not far above the knob, and opened the door. The first thing she saw was a pair of dusty riding boots. Her gaze trailed up from there as she sat back in her chair, taking in an expanse of lean denim-clad legs.

"Oh!" she said, her heart skittering in a way that made her disgusted with herself. What was it about him, anyway? He put his pants on the same way other men did. He was nothing so special. "I thought it was one of my brothers."

"Nope."

He was taller than she remembered—broader through the shoulders. Standing over her as he was and illuminated by golden light, he seemed to loom. Tonight he wore a faded denim jacket over the chambray shirt, the front plackets hanging open to reveal the muted wool plaid lining. The faint and not unpleasant smell of horses and hay rolled off of him. The black Stetson was in place, its brim tipped forward, shadowing his eyes. As before, those eyes glinted at her, only this time, instead of gunmetal, she was reminded of tarnished silver.

What was she thinking? Tarnished silver? *Brother.* He probably practiced that smoldering look in the mirror so all women within a mile would fall over like nine pins when he smiled. Well, count her out. He was mouthwatering to look at, but so was cheesecake, and cheesecake was a heck of a lot safer.

"You need a peephole," he said, his voice a deep rumble. "It's not safe to open up until you know who's out here, especially when it's almost dark."

He looked and sounded enough like one of her brothers to be a clone, which helped slow her racing heart.

"A peephole at my height? It's a little difficult to identify a man by his fly."

A startled laugh escaped him, the sound a gravelly "humph" that jerked his broad shoulders. "Not so difficult." He grasped the large silver buckle at his waist, tipping it toward the light for her to see. "Mine's flagged with my initials." He turned slightly to display the back of his belt, which was personalized as well. "You can tell who I am, coming or going."

She stared at the lettering on the ornate silver as he turned to face her again. "So I see."

He nudged back his hat, placed a hand on the door frame, and cocked a hip, his opposite knee bending with the shift of his weight. "I'm sorry I'm so late."

His voice rang with sincerity. Bethany steeled herself against it. "I'm sure you had a good reason." No excuse he gave her would be good enough. He was forty minutes late, and he hadn't phoned. In her book, that was unpardonable.

He smiled slightly. "I tried to call. You didn't answer the phone."

"You did?" She'd had him pegged as more imaginative. "How strange. I haven't heard the phone ring, and I've got call waiting."

The long look he gave her made her feel as if her skin was turning inside out. She had a feeling he could tell she'd been crying. His lips tucked in at one corner, deepening the crease in his cheek. It wasn't really a smile, more just a quirk of his mouth, but his eyes came into play, crinkling at the corners to lend warmth to his expression.

"I know I wasn't dialing wrong. I double-checked the number."

An awful thought occurred to Bethany. She glanced over her shoulder. "My cat," she whispered.

"Say what?"

"Shortly before six, I heard her knock something over. I'll bet she bumped the guest room extension off the hook again."

"Ah. Mystery solved."

She started up the hall. "Please come in, Ryan. I'll only be a minute."

She imagined her brothers arriving en masse to check on her because she didn't answer the phone. The very thought made her cringe. It went without saying that Jake would not approve of Ryan's being there.

Once in the guest room, Bethany saw that the phone had indeed been knocked off the hook. As she returned it to the cradle, she lectured herself. Okay, fine. He had tried to call her, just as he claimed, and she'd jumped to conclusions, thinking he'd stood her up. It followed that he probably had a good reason for being late. But that didn't mean she had to let her foolish heart get the best of her again. He was taking her out on a date only to be nice. She would enjoy the evening. No hoping for anything more, no wishing for anything more.

She took a deep breath, feeling better almost instantly. When the evening was over, she'd have a nice memory to treasure, and perhaps he would as well.

This didn't have to be complicated unless she allowed it to be.

When she reentered the hall, he was still standing in the doorway. She saw that he was studying the tole paintings that hung on the entryway wall, compliments of her brother Hank because she couldn't reach that high to drive the nails. "That silly cat. She gets on the nightstand and knocks into things."

He hooked a thumb at the paintings. "You're very talented."

"Thank you, but not really. I've had lots of time to perfect my brushstrokes." She stopped a few feet shy of him and folded her hands. The touch of his gaze warmed her cheeks. "I hope my brothers didn't try to call. They're terrified I'll fall or something. I keep telling them it's silly to worry, that I managed just fine living alone in Portland for six years. I may as well talk to a wall."

"Protective?"

"Horribly. If one of them couldn't get through, he'd notify the others, and they'd all race over here."

He grinned and arched an eyebrow again. "Is that a warning?"

"You might say that. According to them, I'm too trusting."

"And are you?"

"I think my brothers greatly overestimate my appeal. Either that, or there aren't nearly as many wolves on the prowl as they seem to think."

Studying her upturned face, Ryan thought she was pretty damned appealing, and he didn't blame her brothers for being protective. It had been a while since he'd gone out with a woman whose expression was so open. She probably wasn't a very good judge of male character, and she could obviously be very easily hurt. Her eyes were red from crying, her dark lashes spiked with wetness. Knowing he'd been the cause of her tears made him feel like a skunk.

"I really am sorry I couldn't make it on time. I hope you're not mad at me."

"Not at all. I just figured something had come up."

He imagined her watching the clock, then finally giving up on him, convinced he hadn't come because he didn't want to spend the evening with her.

"It's been one of those awful days. Then, to top it off, one of my mares went into early labor. Her first foal, and she had a really rough time."

"Oh, *no*. Is she all right?"

The concern Ryan saw in her big blue eyes looked genuine. Most of the women he dated got their noses out of joint when they learned they'd played second fiddle to a horse or cow, a frequent occurrence in his line of work. "Yeah, she's fine now. Happy as a clam and proud as punch of her new baby."

"That's good. What was the problem?"

"The foal was large and got turned wrong."

"Oh, my. That can be tricky. Did you have to call out a vet?"

To Ryan's surprise, she seemed sincerely interested, yet another rarity. Most women only asked about the goings-on at his ranch to flatter his ego. "I called the vet out to be safe, but as it happened, I got the foal turned by myself. I really am sorry. The mare's sort of special to me.

Shortly after she was born, her mama's milk dried up, and I had to bottle-feed her. We got pretty tight."

It occurred to Ryan that he seldom bothered to explain himself like this. He was a rancher, and things happened. When an emergency came up, making him late for a date, that was just the way it was.

Looking into Bethany's gentle gaze, he found it difficult to take such a hard line. "She was really scared," he heard himself saying.

"Oh, of *course* she was, poor baby, which probably made giving birth even more difficult for her."

Ryan nodded. "I'm sure our ranch foreman, Sly, and the vet could have handled the situation, but I just couldn't bring myself to leave her."

"Please, don't apologize, Ryan. If you'd left her to keep a silly date, I'd feel awful. We assume a big responsibility with our pets."

Pets? Ryan supposed Rosebud was a pet to him, though it was something he never admitted. "She's a very expensive horse."

"Uh-huh, and that's why you stayed, because if something had gone wrong, you would have lost tons of money."

He chuckled and tugged on his ear. "Yeah, there was that, but mainly it was the apron strings tied to my belt loops. I'm her mama."

She laughed at that, her expression softening as if she understood exactly what he meant.

"Why do I get this feeling you like horses?"

"Probably because I do." She leaned forward in her chair. "I have to know. Was it a colt or a filly?"

"A colt."

"What color?" she asked, her eyes sparkling with interest.

"A little sorrel. Cute as a button, all gangly legs and knobby knees, with a big, bulbous nose. And his ears are so gigantic, I swear he's part donkey. But he'll pretty up in a few hours."

"Oh," she whispered, her smile wistful. "He sounds so *sweet*! I haven't seen a brand-new foal in so long, I can't remember when."

The yearning in her expression made Ryan want to scoop her out of that chair and take her to his ranch. As the feeling took hold, he wondered what was happening to him. No woman had tugged on his heartstrings like this in a good long while. Strike that. No woman, period, had ever made him feel like this.

Uncomfortable with the turn of his thoughts, he glanced at his watch. "Well, you about ready?"

"You're running really late, Ryan, and I'll slow you down even more.

If you're one of the sponsors, you need to get there as fast as you can. It might be better if I just stay here. Maybe another time."

"Baloney. You aren't going to slow me down that much, and I won't have nearly as much fun without you."

As he said that, Ryan knew he meant it—maybe more than was wise. What was he thinking? There was no way in hell she could ever fit into his life.

"Where's your coat? It's gonna get chilly out there if the wind picks up."

Obviously eager to go, she wheeled around and buzzed across the entry to a coat tree. She lifted a blue parka from a lower hook and started to poke an arm down one sleeve.

Remembering his manners, he commandeered her jacket. It was more difficult to perform this courtesy with a chair getting in the way, but he tugged and stuffed until he got the garment on her. In the process, he accidentally brushed his hands over soft places. By the time he stepped around to lift her hair from under her collar, his guts were in knots. Those long, dark tresses slipped through his fingers like heavy silk, the strands still warm from her body.

She glanced back. "I need to get my purse. My keys are in it."

"Where is it?"

"I'll run and get it. Watch your toes."

A few seconds later when she returned to the entryway, Ryan scooped her from the chair. She gave a startled squeak and grabbed his neck. Her purse, dangling by its strap from her slender wrist, thumped his arm. "Oh, God, don't drop me!"

Ryan hadn't meant to frighten her. "Easy, sweetheart, I've got you." Even with the parka insulation as padding, he could feel her heart pounding where his left hand curled over her ribs. "Relax," he whispered, his breath stirring tendrils at her temple. "You weigh hardly anything, and I swear I won't let you fall."

Her voice quavered as she said, "I can't catch myself, you know."

He wouldn't have let go for anything. "If something happens and I go down, you'll think you're a basket of eggs. I'm not hurting you, am I?"

"No, not at all. I'm fine. Really."

She looked up, and he got lost in her big eyes. He had no idea how much time passed before he realized he was standing there like a dumbstruck fool.

"It really isn't necessary for you to carry me until we reach the fairgrounds, Ryan. My van's equipped with a lift, and I—"

"We're going in my truck."

"We *are*? Oh, I don't know. It's much less hassle to take my van."

"Sweetheart, trust me. I've got it all figured out. I'll lock up when I come back in for your chair. Is everything turned off, or should I do a walk through before I close up?"

"Everything's off."

He set off down the hall, his boots tapping on the waxed floors. As he turned to carry her out the front door, she cast an anxious glance at the wood ramp over the porch steps. "I hope you're surefooted. That indoor-outdoor tends to get slick on cold evenings like this."

"You'll think I'm a mountain goat. Are you sure I'm not hurting you? You're awfully tense." He flashed her a grin that he hoped might help her to relax. "Clutching my neck like your life depends on it."

"It *does*."

He chuckled at that. As he drew to a stop beside his truck, he executed a smooth maneuver, bending slightly at the knees to open the door, then nudging it wide with his arm. He heard her gasp as he swung her up onto the gray, contoured bench seat. She grabbed the handgrip above the door as if she was afraid she might pitch headfirst onto the concrete when he turned loose.

"I've got you," he assured her again.

Bethany could feel that he did. His hands were locked over her hips. Unlike many paraplegics, she had feeling there. The pads of his thumbs seemed to burn holes through her jeans.

"Steady on?" he asked, lifting a questioning brow.

She felt like a pea balanced atop a totem pole. Big man, big truck—a monstrous burgundy Dodge Ram. The seat seemed a long way from the ground. But then he settled her back so the contours embraced her, which made her feel safer. "Yes, I'm steady on."

He ran his hands under her knees, lifting to reposition her legs, which had flopped as they landed. Her cheeks went hot. That made warning bells go off. She wouldn't feel embarrassed if one of her brothers lifted her legs.

He reached behind her to tug the seat belt across her body. She was about to tell him she could buckle up by herself, but before she got the words out, metal rasped, and the next second, he was adjusting the strap to lie at an angle over her chest. The side of his hand grazed the peak of her right breast, making her nipple tighten. She thanked heaven for the concealing fluff of her parka and wondered, with some trepidation, if she was going to live through the evening.

She might not survive, Bethany decided a few minutes later. Ryan Kendrick was driving in the wrong direction. At the edge of town, he took an exit onto the freeway. The huge Dodge purred to life as he depressed the accelerator and opened it up to cruise at seventy. He turned up the heater to be sure she was warm. Then he flipped on the stereo, filling the cab with the honeyed voice of John Michael Montgomery. It was a lovely, comfortable ride. She just wished she knew where he was taking her.

It was absolutely absurd, but her mind chose that moment to remember every dire warning her brothers had ever given her. That abuse of handicapped women was alarmingly common, that there were sexual perverts who preyed on disabled females, and that she must never forget how helpless she was. Her brothers maintained that it would be sheer madness if she went anywhere with a man without first giving everyone in the family his name, his tag number, and a full physical description, just in case he happened to be a creep.

Typically of her, she hadn't listened to those warnings, and now here she was, going heaven knew where with a man she knew very little about. Even worse, she'd been so afraid of Jake's reaction, she'd told no one about the date.

As Ryan drove, he pulled a cordless Norelco from the console. A second later, the hum of the shaver filled the cab as he began removing his five o'clock shadow. "I hope you'll excuse me. I usually slick up before a date, but this evening I didn't have time. I know I must look like hell and smell like a horse."

He looked and smelled wonderful to her. He also seemed to grow larger by the moment. When he returned the shaver to the console, he drew out some aftershave. While steering with his elbows, he splashed some of the scented astringent into a cupped palm, rubbed his hands together, and then slapped it on his cheeks. She nearly jumped at the loud sound of his palms connecting with his jaws. She'd get a mild concussion if she hit herself that hard. The woodsy, masculine smell of the cologne drifted to her.

Still steering with his elbows and, she hoped, keeping one eye on the road, he returned the bottle to the compartment and removed his hat to finger comb his wavy black hair. After finishing his ablutions, all of which he performed without letting up on the accelerator, he settled the Stetson back on his head, glanced in the rearview mirror, and winked at her.

"This is as good as it'll get. Next time, I'll shower twice. How's that?"

There was that "next time" again. Bethany returned her gaze to the road, convinced that at least one of them should be watching it. A grin tugged at her mouth. If he had nefarious intentions, he was certainly going to a lot of trouble to smell nice before he attacked her.

"I'm not making you nervous, am I? I'm used to doing ten things at once."

"No, you're not making me nervous," she said, still struggling to suppress a smile. "I am sort of curious about where we're going, though."

He slanted her a look, the twinkle in his eyes evident even in the dim light. "It's a surprise."

Everything about him was a surprise. "That sounds fun. What kind of a surprise?"

"If I tell you, it won't be a surprise. What fun would that be?"

He had a point. She hadn't been adventurous in a long while, and no matter what her brothers might say, she meant to enjoy this evening with him. "What about the mud pulls? You're a sponsor, remember, and need to be there."

"I need to make an appearance. We'll still go—*after* the surprise. It's one of those things that just won't keep, and I think you'll enjoy it more than the pulls."

Bethany couldn't imagine what he had planned, but she instinctively trusted him—even when he drove with his elbows. She hugged her waist and stared through the windshield, her vision blurring on the yellow line.

He leaned forward to turn up the volume on the stereo. "Do you mind? This is my favorite song *ever.*"

"You're joking. It's mine, too."

"You like Montgomery?"

She nodded. "I can barely sit still when a song of his is playing."

He swept off his hat, laid it on the console, and then, dividing his attention between her and the road, gazed across the cab at her as if she were the love of his life as he sang the refrain. The song was "I Swear," a beautiful outpouring of devotion in which the vocalist promised on the moon and the stars to be as steadfast as a shadow at his lover's side until death parted them.

Ryan Kendrick had a voice that made her bones melt. When he continued to sing to her, she couldn't resist joining in, even though she sounded like a toad croaking on a lily pad. She had never been able to sing worth a darn. Dancing had been her forte—once upon a memory, a lifetime ago. Now she could only feel the beat of country music and dream.

Just as she found herself dreaming right now that Ryan Kendrick really meant the words he was singing to her. *Idiocy.* What was it about him?

Silly Bethany, spinning dreams. She supposed it was partly that Ryan was so handsome—the tall, dark, dreamy kind of handsome one usually saw only in the movies. That, coupled with the fact that he was so nice, made for a lethal package.

She was almost grateful that there would be only this one evening with him. Otherwise she might be in serious danger of getting her foolish heart broken.

❦ CHAPTER THREE ❦

The "surprise," as it turned out, was taking Bethany to see his new foal. The instant she glimpsed the sprawling brick house perched on a knoll overlooking Crystal Lake, she knew they were at his ranch. Moonlight shone through misty fog that wreathed the trees bordering the clearings, the shimmer of silvery illumination touching everything with magic. In the pastures they passed, she saw oodles of cows with spring calves at their sides, which made her laugh with delight.

"Oooh, aren't they *darling?*"

He stopped for a moment near an outdoor pole light so she could peer through the gloom at the babies. "See that little fella?" He pointed to a sweet baby Hereford with a snow-white face. "I call him Pig. He goes after the tit like you would not believe. Made his mama all sore and then started shoving other calves aside to hog their milk. For nigh on a week, I had to keep him in a pen and feed him with a titty bucket."

A funny look came over his face, and he scrunched his dark eyebrows in a frown. "Sorry," he said softly. "I forget sometimes that not everybody lives on a ranch and hears that kind of talk."

Bethany giggled. She couldn't stop herself. "I grew up on a ranch, Ryan. I'm not that easily offended."

He smiled and visibly relaxed as he shifted back into drive. "You're a sweetheart. I'm sorry, anyhow, for not minding my manners."

As his truck bumped along the gravel road, Bethany gazed dreamily at the lake, which glistened like polished black glass, occasional patches of ice creating frosty islands in the vastness. She couldn't imagine waking up of a morning and being able to feast her sleepy gaze on such beauty while she sipped a cup of coffee. "Oh, my. How lucky you are, Ryan. It's beautiful here."

"I think so. But, then, I was raised out here so I'm probably biased."

She took in the expansive pastures nearer the house, which encircled countless outbuildings and were crisscrossed with white fencing. "You don't need to do this, you know. My chair doesn't handle well on muddy surfaces, and it's bound to be muddy in the stable. We had rain only a couple of days ago."

"If I wait to bring you out, there may not be any new foals. They're still cute later, but nothing beats seeing one right after birth." He flashed a grin, his teeth gleaming in the shadows. "In another hour, that colt's appearance will change." His voice dipped to a gentle, deep tone. "Just relax, honey. Have a good time. The mud won't be a problem."

On a ranch this size, there were probably mud wallows deep enough to swallow his Dodge. "I just don't want you to regret asking me out."

"I'm having fun. A lady who likes mud pulls, horses, *and* John Michael Montgomery. Where have you been hiding all my life?"

Oh, dear. He had no idea what he was getting into. She imagined her chair wheels dropping out of sight in the mud, and him, slipping and sliding as he wrestled to free them from the muck. She swallowed back further protests, though. This was a lovely gesture, and she didn't want to spoil it.

Even with outside lights blazing, she couldn't tell much about his house—except that it looked big enough to hold three of hers. He parked the pickup as close to the stable entrance as possible, unloaded her wheelchair from the bed of the truck, carried it somewhere inside, and then came back to get her. She took a bracing breath when he opened the passenger door.

He quickly unfastened her seat belt and swung her up into his arms.

"Oh, my!"

"I won't drop you, sweetheart."

"What if you slip?"

He chuckled. "It'll be a first. I've carted struggling calves and foals through here when the mud was ankle deep, and I've never gone down yet. It might help if you'd be still, though."

She went instantly motionless, which prompted him to laugh again. "Why do I get this feeling nobody ever picks you up?"

"They don't usually. Not in ages and ages, anyway. I've worked hard to become self-sufficient. I hate inconveniencing people."

"And as a result, you haven't seen a new foal in so long you can't remember when? Forget about being an inconvenience."

He proceeded to carry her with apparent ease into the white clapboard building. As he picked his way down the well-lighted center aisle, he circled several muddy spots in the packed earth, which she eyed with growing dread.

"I wish you'd stop worrying," he told her. "I'm glad for an excuse to check on Rosebud. Sly, our foreman, will come over to look in on her, but it's not the same as doing it myself. Now I won't worry about her while I'm at the mud pulls."

He reached her wheelchair, which he'd left in front of a horse stall. Instead of lowering her into it, as she expected, he maintained his hold so she could look over the stall gate at the mare and newborn foal.

"Well?" His voice rang with pride. "What do you think of him?"

When Bethany saw the horses, she all but forgot the man who held her in his arms. Just as he had described, the foal was all gangly legs and knobby knees, and still so recently born that his nose and ears looked out of proportion to the rest of his body. She laughed in delight. "Oh, Ryan, he's *wonderful!*"

"I thought you'd like him," he said huskily.

"He's going to be gorgeous."

"His sire, Flash Dancer, throws some real beauties."

Rosebud whickered and left her foal to come welcome them. Bethany's heart melted the instant she looked into the mare's gentle brown eyes. "And you must be Rosebud. Aren't you *lovely*. No wonder your son's so handsome."

"Careful. Being a first-time mama, she's a little edgy, and you're a stranger. She tried to take a hunk out of the vet right after the foal was born."

Bethany reached over the gate. "I've never had a horse dislike me yet."

Ryan stiffened, prepared to block Rosebud if she made a threatening move, but the mare only sniffed Bethany's outstretched fingers, then her arm. Apparently satisfied that this new human was no threat, the horse whickered again and moved closer to the gate, nudging Bethany's shoulder.

"I'll be. She does like you."

"Of course. Horses *always* like me." She shared her breath with the mare and stroked her muzzle. "I haven't any clue why, but it's been that way for as long as I can remember."

"Some people are just born with a gift."

"I think it runs in our family. My brothers are amazing with horses. Especially Jake and Hank. You know that movie about the horse whisperer? They're just that good. When I was younger, I spent hours watching Jake work with them. My dad used to say he was like a horse charmer. Different name, same thing. He can work with a wildly uncontrollable horse and have it behaving beautifully in only a few weeks. It's uncanny, almost as if he actually communicates with them somehow."

Watching Bethany with Rosebud, Ryan could believe she had a special gift and that her brothers might as well. Her face fairly glowed as she admired the mare's finely shaped head. Ryan lifted her a bit higher so she could reach over the gate. Keeping one slender arm hooked around his neck, she twisted and arched up to scratch between Rosebud's ears. As a result, her parka drew apart and the plaid-covered peak of one softly rounded breast hovered a scant inch from his nose.

His breath hitched, and his throat closed off. She had no idea she was pressing her nipple so close, and he needed a swift kick for noticing. Even worse, he shouldn't imagine what it might be like if that nipple were bare.

Shouldn't, but did.

She fit comfortably in his arms, her weight so slight he barely noticed it. If they were lovers, he could nibble on that sensitive peak until she sobbed with yearning and begged him to nibble elsewhere. The sweetness of her scent worked on his senses like an intoxicant, the tantalizing mélange of baby powder, deodorant, well-scrubbed skin, and feminine essence making him want to taste every sweet inch of her.

Whoa, boy. What the hell was he thinking? She wasn't trying to entice him. Just the opposite. He recognized "hands off" signals when he saw them, and Bethany's eyes flashed the message every time she looked at him.

"You've spent a lot of time with horses, then?" he asked, forcing his gaze back to her face.

"You're looking at a three-time state champion in barrel racing."

He vaguely recalled that one of Harv Coulter's kids had made a big splash on the rodeo circuit. For some reason, he'd always thought it was one of the boys. "Three-time *state* champion? You're kidding."

"Nope. I was phenomenal!"

He couldn't help but grin at her unabashed lack of humility.

When she noted his expression, she said, "Well, I *was*. No brag, just fact, cowboy. I practically lived in the saddle until I got hurt." Her eyes shimmered. "With five older brothers, I was the world's worst tomboy. I would have slept with my horse if Daddy hadn't put his foot down." She gave Rosebud a final scratch and then lowered herself back into the circle of his embrace to loop both arms around his neck. "Thank you so much for bringing me, Ryan. Even the smell of a stable seems heavenly after so many years. I've missed it."

Her breast now pressed against his collarbone, her nipple only a dip-of-his-chin away. "Don't a couple of your brothers still own horses?"

"Jake and Zeke do, and I'm sure Hank will again someday. On a much smaller scale now that we don't have a ranch, of course. They ride for pleasure. Isaiah and Tucker, my other two brothers, don't live here in town for the time being. They're both away right now, doing their internships."

"Doctors?"

"Vets." She smiled. "They hope to start a practice together here when they finish up. They're both horse lovers as well. Perhaps you can use them when they get their shingle up. It'll be tough until they build a reputation."

"I'll keep them in mind." Ryan frowned. "I'm sorry if it seems nosy, but I have to ask. If two of your brothers still keep horses, why is it you're never around them anymore?"

Her smile remained in place, but the radiance dimmed. "It upsets my mom if I even look at a horse." She glanced down at her wheelchair, clearly expecting him to deposit her in it. When she looked back up, she laughed and said, "Are you going to put me down, or have your arms frozen in this position?"

Ryan was loath to turn loose of her. *Oh, man.* He was in trouble here. He needed to back off, take a deep breath.

What the hell was the matter with him? He'd known men who took one look at a woman and went into Neanderthal mode, but he'd never been one of them. What was more, everything about Bethany's behavior told him she was wary and needed a slow hand. If he moved too fast, he'd scare her off.

The thought hung in Ryan's brain. If he moved too fast? When, exactly, had he gone from taking her out on an obligatory date to making moves on her?

He bent to set her in the chair, acutely conscious as his hands slid away from her soft curves. She felt *right*; there was no other word to describe it.

After she was settled, she leaned forward to grasp her left knee and lift her foot onto the rest. Ryan quickly helped with the other leg. As she sat back and he looked up, their gazes locked, and for a long moment he found it impossible to move or break eye contact. Unless he imagined it, she was holding her breath. He could breathe fine, but his pounding heart was about to crack a rib.

When he finally straightened, his throat had gone tight with an emotion he couldn't and didn't want to name. Judging by the look in her eyes, she felt it as well, and it scared her to death.

As he turned to unlatch the stall gate, he groped for something to say, anything to ease the sudden tension. "You hurt your back in a riding accident?"

It wasn't really a question. Why else would her mother get upset whenever she looked at a horse?

"While I was barrel racing." Her voice was shaky, and the brief silence afterward was brittle. "State competition, my fourth year. I had my eye on the nationals." A melancholy note laced her words. "My horse, Wink, stepped in a hole and went to her knees as she started into a turn. I went over her head, landed on my side over a barrel, and that was that." She brushed at a smudge of dust on her jeans, then pushed at her dark, glossy hair. His fingers itched to touch it. "I was very fortunate. When the barrel tipped, I fell directly in Wink's path and she couldn't stop. With all that weight crashing down on top of me, the injury to my spine could have been much worse."

Ryan glanced at her legs. Worse? Dear God, she was paralyzed from the waist down. It didn't get any worse.

By way of explanation, she added, "Most of the damage was to one side of my spinal cord, and unlike many paraplegics, I have some feeling here and there, which makes my life and daily routine much easier."

Ryan circled that, wondering how "feeling here and there" could make her life easier. Paralyzed was paralyzed. Right?

Apparently noticing the bewildered look on his face, she grinned. "That's a *polite* way of saying it. You'll have to ferret out the rest by yourself."

She was referring to continence, he realized, an ability many paraplegics didn't have.

She glanced around the stable. "How many horses do you have, Ryan?"

"Twenty-three in this stable, close to thirty over at Rafe's place. Working stock, some show. We breed and sell quarter horses on the side."

He moved her chair to swing the stall door wide. "Don't be nervous. Now that she's accepted you, Rosebud will be a perfect lady. I honestly believe I could lay a baby at her feet."

"I'm not nervous."

Eager for more petting, the mare exited the stall.

"Oh, Ryan, how sweet. She really does like me."

It was true; the mare headed straight for her. The new foal wobbled in his mama's wake. Clearly delighted, Bethany leaned forward over her knees to pet him. Rosebud whickered and chuffed, almost as if she were giving permission. Watching the three of them together, Ryan frowned to himself, thinking what a shame it was that this young woman's affinity for horses was going to waste.

"You know, unless I'm mistaken, they have saddles for paraplegics."

In an oddly hollow voice, she said, "Yes, I know."

"Are you afraid to get back on a horse?"

"I honestly can't say. I haven't been on a horse since my accident." She went back to admiring Rosebud's colt. "Probably not. What happened to me, none of it was Wink's fault. She was—*is*—the most wonderful animal on earth."

"She's still around?"

"Oh, yes. Bless my brother Jake's heart, he rescued the poor baby. Took her out to his place and sold her the following week to a local rancher who uses her to work cattle. She's only thirteen and has many a race left in her."

"You say Jake rescued her?"

"Daddy nearly shot her. Silly of him, blaming her." She ran her slender hands the length of the colt's ears. "Wink wouldn't have hurt me for the world."

"I know what you mean. My brother Rafe blamed a horse for the deaths of his first wife and kids, and he ordered the animal to be shot."

"I hear a story in there."

"An old story now, thank goodness. We'd gone north to pick up a stallion we'd purchased." He nodded toward the new foal. "Flash Dancer, this little guy's sire. Rafe took his wife, Susan, and their two kids along. We made a weekend out of it, took in a rodeo, treated the kids to a carnival, that sort of thing. On the way home a hailstorm struck, and the sound of the ice hitting the trailer frightened the stallion. Rafe was following along behind the truck and trailer in the station wagon, and he radioed me in the truck that maybe he and I should ride in the trailer for a while to settle the horse down before he hurt himself." The memories made Ryan's voice grow thick. "Susan grew up here, and she was used to driving in snow and ice. It never occurred to either one of us that she might have a problem."

"Oh, no," Bethany whispered.

"Yeah." Ryan swallowed. "Only a couple of miles farther down the highway, she lost control in a curve, and the station wagon went over an embankment. She and both kids were killed instantly." He rubbed a hand over his face and blinked. "Rafe—he went berserk, trying to revive them. Afterward, he wasn't the same. It damned near killed him. One day he just up and left without a word. Vanished for over two years."

Bethany stared up at him, her eyes huge and stricken.

"Anyway . . ." Ryan shrugged. "I didn't shoot Flash Dancer or sell him, and the story has a happy ending. Rafe met his second wife, Maggie, it was love at first sight, and they've been together ever since, happy as clams." He forced a smile. "I know all about how people can react irrationally when their loved ones get hurt. In Rafe's case, I think it was easier for him to blame the poor horse than to blame himself, which was essentially how he felt, anyway—that it was all his fault."

"Maybe so. Daddy always fretted about me, worrying I might get hurt. Maybe he blamed himself for allowing me to compete. He still goes white around the lips at any mention of Wink."

"That isn't why he got rid of his ranch, is it? To keep you away from horses?" Ryan had heard Harv had gone bankrupt, but gossip was often wrong.

"Oh, no . . . he didn't get rid of the ranch by choice." A distant expression entered her eyes. "Although I'm sure keeping me away from horses was probably his reason for never buying another spread."

Rosebud nudged Bethany's shoulder, then lowered her head for a scratch. Bethany absentmindedly obliged, then finger combed the mare's mane.

"It's just as well since I can no longer ride. Horses used to be such a big part of my life. It was very difficult for me to adjust to the loss at first."

"You say he didn't give the ranch up by choice? What happened?"

"Medical bills." She shrugged. "At first, every doctor who examined me felt sure surgery might get me back on my feet. I was a three-time loser."

Ryan's heart caught at the pain he saw flicker across her face, whether for herself or her parents, he wasn't sure. Until she said, "Poor Daddy. He couldn't let it go, and he went broke, trying to work a miracle for me. A fourth-generation rancher, and he lost his family heritage."

"Some things are more important than keeping a piece of land."

"Absolutely," she agreed. "But we also need to be realistic." Her eyes clouded. "After the first operation, I knew in my heart that I might never walk again. I should have told Daddy and refused to have more surgery. But I was self-centered for a long time after the accident, blind to everything but my own misery. I wanted so badly to walk again, and it never occurred to me that my father was destroying himself trying to make it happen."

"You were awfully young, Bethany. I wouldn't be too rough on myself."

She smiled and threw off the gloom. "How did we get off on this? *Boring*. I don't like to think about those days, let alone talk about them."

That she didn't wish to dwell on it told Ryan more than she could know. Some people talked about their misfortunes to the exclusion of all else.

She cast a wondering glance around her. "This is quite some stable. All spiffy and clean and *huge*."

He followed her gaze. "My *house* is another story."

"A typical bachelor, are you?"

"Not really. Becca, the family housekeeper, comes over with a crew three times a week and supervises while they muck out the rooms. The buildup doesn't get too bad. It's more that I'm such a slob on the days in between. Dirty dishes, socks hanging off the lamp shades. I'm pretty bad."

"It must be nice to be so prosperous that you can afford housekeepers."

"Yeah, it is." Ryan saw no point in lying about it. "It's fantastic, actually." He smiled and rubbed his jaw. "It wasn't always like this. My dad built this ranch by the sweat of his brow. We saw lean years when I was growing up. Rafe and I had to fill in as ranch hands after school and on weekends. It was a family enterprise, and it took the whole damn family to make it back then."

"That's often the way of it. What happened to change things?"

"Rafe and I took over the place and damned near went bankrupt." Her eyes widened, making him chuckle. "Seriously. Dad was off in Florida, living the life of leisure, thinking he was set for old age, and then a string of bad luck hit, the worst of it a forest fire that wiped out over half our herd. Rafe's wife and kids were surviving on steak and milk, two things we had plenty of because we had cows. It was a hell of a mess. Right before we went tits up, we got the idea to sell off some of our land. We parceled off five thousand acres, divided it into lots, and sold sections to developers. We raked in over a hundred and fifty million."

Her eyes went even wider. "Did you say *million*? That's a lot. Is land really worth so much?"

"Yep. I know it sounds incredible, but it's not if you pencil it out. We could have doubled that amount if we'd sold directly to the public instead of to developers. As it was, we got fifty each for Rafe and me, and fifty for our parents, most of which we invested. We're all richer than Croesus now." He winked at her. "When I'm not working my ass off and wading around in cow muck, I count my money."

She laughed at that. "In other words, having a lot in the bank hasn't changed your day-to-day life very much."

"I don't worry about paying the bills anymore. That's a big change."

He shrugged. "And I can blow money when the mood strikes. Mostly, though, I don't have time or inclination. It's a really weird thing, but at the south end of a cow, it's hard to think too ritzy. You know what I mean?"

She laughed again and nodded. "You're right. A cow's hind end has a way of putting things in their proper perspective."

She fell quiet, her face reflecting enjoyment and no small amount of yearning as she stroked Rosebud's velvety nose. Watching her, Ryan burned to get her back in the saddle again. He could almost see the expression that would light up her features.

She bent forward to kiss the mare's forehead. "This has been a wonderful treat, Ryan. I've enjoyed it so much, and I'm so glad you brought me out."

He glanced at his watch. "Speaking of treats, we'd probably better get cracking, or we'll miss the mud pulls completely."

After carrying Bethany back to the truck, he took her chair to a heavily graveled area at the front of the stables. Flipping a switch to activate the air compressor, he used the high-pressure hose at the front of the building to give the wheels a quick wash.

When he joined her in the Dodge, she said, "Okay, confess. You have a paraplegic relative you haven't told me about."

"No. What makes you think that?"

"For a man who's never been around someone in a wheelchair, you're amazingly competent at seeing to my every need."

Glancing over at her as he started the truck, Ryan searched his memory for the last time he'd enjoyed a woman's company so much. He came up blank, which led him to wonder if he was seeing to her needs—or satisfying his own.

❦ CHAPTER FOUR ❦

B*ethany.*
    Ryan had been to countless mud pulls, but never had he enjoyed one so much. Because he was sponsoring a tractor, he and Bethany were allowed to sit in the pits, she in her wheelchair, he on a camp chair. They dined on hot dogs, Coke, and cotton candy, not exactly haute cuisine, but she acted as if it were, saying, *"Yum,"* and wiping drips of relish from her chin every time she took a bite.

Despite the bursts of deafening noise, she made everything seem exciting and special. At one point a tractor lost traction, broke loose, and skidded across the mud toward them. Ryan's heart shot into his mouth. He leaped from his chair, scooped her into his arms, and ran behind the fence. It wasn't until he felt certain she was safe that he realized he'd not only spilled her soft drink all over them, but squashed what remained of her hot dog between their bodies.

Instead of being frightened or upset, Bethany laughed until she was limp.

"Oh, what *fun*!" She shook mustard from her fingers, then glided her tongue over her lip, leaving a sheen on the rose-pink softness. "The *look* on your face when you saw that tractor coming toward us! Oh, if only I'd had a camera."

He didn't know what possessed him, but he dipped his head and licked a blob of relish off her chin. For an instant, she froze, her big blue eyes suddenly filled with wariness.

He wanted to say there was nothing to be afraid of, but maybe there was. He was drawn to her in a way he couldn't understand, and it was happening far too fast. It made no sense. Off the top of his head, he could list a dozen reasons why a relationship between them would never work. But despite that, he felt the pull and was quickly losing his resolve to resist it.

Hoping to make her laugh again, he growled low in his throat, licked at a smear of mustard on her cheek, and said, "Yum. I must still be hungry."

It broke the tension. She laughed and swiped at another spot on her cheek. "Probably! My brothers can eat six hot dogs without even shaking a leg."

"I'll go buy more food, I guess. You're an expensive date, lady."

"Ha. You're a millionaire and getting off cheap."

Ryan was in complete agreement. She deserved better than this, that was for sure. Filet mignon and expensive wine, candlelight and music.

She splayed a fine-boned hand over her chest and groaned as if she were in pain from having laughed so much. In that moment the sounds of the mud pull faded, and he became entirely focused on this woman he held in his arms. Even smeared with condiments, she was so damned beautiful.

He tried to take a mental step back. She couldn't possibly be as lovely as all that. But she *was*. Her nose was small and tipped up slightly at the end, begging to be kissed. A touch of rose accentuated her daintily sculpted cheekbones. Her dark brows formed perfect arches over her eyes, which were big and so incredibly blue, they reached right out and grabbed hold of him.

From the chin down—*don't go there, you jackass*—she was delectable, slightly built but delightfully round in all the right places. Whenever his gaze strayed in that direction, he thought of long nights on silk sheets, the soft glow of candlelight casting an amber sheen on her ivory skin. The image was so clear in his mind that he could almost see her—eyes dark and unseeing with passion, lashes sweeping low, breathing quick and shallow.

Ryan jerked himself back to the moment, disgusted with the way his thoughts were running. After a quick cleanup job with napkins from the refreshment stand, he carried her back to the pits, bought them each more food, and then settled beside her to watch the pulls. Fearful that another tractor might break loose, he nearly moved their chairs behind the fence, where he knew Bethany would be safe, but she would have none of that.

"I don't get a chance to live dangerously often. Sitting down here is fun."

Ryan didn't want anything to happen to her—not on his watch. But he also wanted her to have a good time. He'd swept her out of harm's way once; he could again.

Seeing the sparkle in her eyes made him ache with sadness for her.

What must it be like to have been physically active as she'd been, and then end up confined to a wheelchair? He couldn't imagine it.

During intermission, he pumped her for information. He learned that she'd once loved the wilderness and had frequently gone in by horseback with her brothers to camp at high-mountain lakes, an activity he enjoyed himself.

A dreamy expression came over her face as she shared memories of those rides. "For me, the wilderness was a spiritual experience. I *know*. That sounds really corny, but for me, it was like church. The beauty at daybreak, the muted glow of first light peeking over a ridge, the fantastic colors, the first song of a bird to greet the new day—it's surely God's way of saying good morning."

As if she feared he might laugh, she wrinkled her nose and grinned. He had no urge to laugh, for he felt exactly the same way. "I know what you mean. Nothing makes me feel closer to God than being on a mountaintop. Seeing the sunrise or a gorgeous sunset. An eagle in flight or a deer with a fawn."

Hugging her waist, she sighed and nodded, her expression wistful. Once again, Ryan found himself wishing he could get her on a horse again.

"And *campfires*!" she said softly.

He forced his mind back to the conversation. "Pardon?"

"Campfires. Is anything tastier than coffee boiled over an open flame?"

Her skin—just there, under her ear—would taste pretty damned good. "Nope. Nothing beats camp coffee."

"And, oh, how I loved to huddle around the fire with my brothers at night. We sang songs, ate trout we'd caught for dinner, and then they scared me to death, telling spooky stories about Big Foot and ghosts until we all went to bed."

"And then the fun was over."

"No, that's when it really got lively. They all had one-man pup tents, which are barely big enough for one person, and someone had to make room for me."

"You didn't have your own tent?"

"Yes, but after the stories I was too scared to sleep alone. It became a ritual—the argument about who got stuck with 'the twerp.' They drew straws, and poor Jake always lost. On purpose, I think. He felt responsible for me."

Rafe's wife, Maggie, had a twelve-year-old sister who lived with them. Heidi thought of Ryan as her older brother—when she wasn't entertaining the notion of marrying him someday. He had taken her on a couple of wilderness rides and knew exactly how it went when a young girl got scared at night. Like Bethany's brothers, he'd grumbled, but he hadn't really minded sharing his tent. He wouldn't mind making room for Bethany, either, for entirely different reasons.

"If you took up riding again, maybe you could still take occasional wilderness jaunts," he suggested.

She considered the possibility for a moment. "No, it just isn't feasible."

"Why?"

A blush flagged her cheeks. "I have too many special needs. Most ordinary wheelchairs are terribly heavy, unsuitable for rough ground and much too bulky a burden to take in on a packhorse. There'd be no room left for supplies. On top of that, there are no handicapped facilities in the wilderness."

Handicapped facilities? He hid a smile when he realized she was referring to rest rooms. She amused him and kept him guessing, this woman, sassy and outrageous one moment, then painfully shy about silly things the next.

As Ryan watched her talking, one thought entered his mind repeatedly. *Perfect for me.* She was the lady of his dreams in every way except one; she could no longer walk.

"So what do you do for fun now?" he couldn't resist asking.

"*Tame* stuff. My family is so protective of me since my accident. Anything that involves an element of risk is out." She caught her lower lip between her teeth, yet another gesture he was coming to realize was habitual. "I suppose it sounds pathetic, a grown woman allowing her family to dictate to her."

Ryan hadn't been thinking that at all. He couldn't fault her for being considerate of people's feelings, though he did wonder at the wisdom of it in this particular instance.

"It's just that I hate to worry them. While I lived in Portland, it wasn't as bad. I lived in this totally cool apartment complex for handicapped people. I had oodles of friends, and we all checked on each other all the time. We were always planning group activities, which were a lot of fun because everything there was universally designed, even the swimming pool. When my—"

"Whoa. Back up. What's universally designed mean, exactly?"

She quickly described the complex—how all the bathrooms were spacious to make room for special equipment for paralyzed residents, how all the doorways and halls were wider than usual. "And you should have *seen* the kitchens! Low, extended counters with tons of knee room and accessible work areas so that even someone in a wheelchair could easily cook and reach appliances. I *loved* it. Where I'm renting now, nothing is especially designed for me. My brothers and dad have built me ramps, and I just make do. Everything has to go in the bottom cupboards. Daddy installed turntables so I can reach everything. Even at that, it's inconvenient. All the appliances have to be at the front edge of the counters. The top shelves in my refrigerator are bare. Jake built me a little ramp I can roll onto that makes me tall enough to reach the sink, and Zeke made me a pullout cutting board that's low enough for me."

Ryan had never stopped to think how difficult it must be for someone like her to do things in a regular house.

"Anyway . . . I'm sure that's boring. What were we talking about?" she asked with a laugh.

"How it was easier dealing with your family while you were in Portland."

"Oh, yes. And, boy, was it. I just fielded their questions when they telephoned or came to visit, but the rest of the time, my life was my own. A bunch of us even went skydiving once. I did a buddy jump, of course, so I was in very little actual danger."

The thought made him cringe. He suppressed his dismay and quizzed her about how she'd ended up in Portland, so far from family.

"After my accident and surgeries, I went to outpatient rehab there, decided to take some college courses in my spare time, and ended up going for a bachelor's degree in computer science. I landed a good job in Beaverton after I graduated." She shrugged and smiled. "My family urged me to move home, but I was settled in by then."

"So . . . how did you end up back in Crystal Falls after all this time?"

"Daddy has a heart condition. A few months ago, the doctor ordered him to cut back on his work hours, and Jake had to take over the business. When he called and said he needed help, I couldn't very well say no." She rolled her eyes. "In truth, I think he invented a job for me just so I'd come home, but that's neither here nor there. So far, it's worked out fairly well—except that my brothers sometimes suffocate me by hovering."

That explained why the customer service at The Works had been suffering lately. Her brother had taken over. Ryan knew firsthand how that went. It hadn't been so long ago that his dad had retired. As for her brothers hovering, Ryan could easily picture himself doing the same thing. She did have a disability that made her more vulnerable than other women who lived alone.

"What one hundred percent *safe* activities do you enjoy?" he asked.

"I paint like a fiend." She narrowed an eye. "Sit still long enough, and I may paint you."

He'd seen evidence of her artistic bent. Usually Ryan didn't care for clutter, but Bethany had a flair for making it look nice. Her paintings and doodads, stamped with her sunny disposition, added warmth and charm to her surroundings.

"What else do you enjoy?" he asked.

"Tennis."

"Tennis?" he repeated incredulously.

Her eyes danced. "I have one paraplegic friend so far in Crystal Falls. I met her at the 'Y,' a totally cool lady named Jenny Nelson. We roll around the court together three mornings a week. Mostly we serve to each other and miss. We get a lot of exercise, chasing the balls, and we have fun, ribbing each other about our completely deplorable lack of skill." She thought a moment. "I also swim two evenings a week. I *love* to swim. It gives me an incredible sense of mobility. And occasionally when I visit my folks, I sneak next door to play basketball with the neighbor boys. They're teenagers and think it's totally cool, playing basketball with a crazy lady in a wheelchair."

"*Basketball?*" Ryan couldn't imagine how she managed.

"My chair's self-propelled. I can press the controls with one hand and bounce the ball with the other. It took practice, but I've gotten pretty good. Good enough that I've won a few games." She cast him a mischievous, sidelong glance. "I run over their toes. While they're jumping around on one foot, I race to the hoop and do my wheelchair version of a slam dunk." At his horrified look, she giggled and said, "All's fair when you're playing with a handicap."

"You'd never run over anyone's toes on purpose, you little liar."

"I'm ruthless in competitive situations."

"Uh-huh." Ryan doubted she had a ruthless bone in her whole body.

She gazed at the tractor being hitched to the sled. "I've got ten dollars that says this one wins the competition."

Ryan grinned. "I'd hate to take your money. The winning tractor will be the one I'm sponsoring."

"Want to bet?"

His grin broadened. "You're on," he agreed.

When the mud pulls were over, he owed the lady ten dollars, which she accepted and stuffed in her pocket while grinning at him mischievously. "I did tell you I'm ruthless," she said with a laugh.

By evening's end Ryan had decided he definitely wanted to see Bethany again, as friends if nothing more. Big problem. She apparently liked him and seemed to enjoy his company, but he could tell that she still felt uneasy around him. He'd tried to keep the mood light to help her relax, but there'd been moments when the chemistry between them had taken over, turning a casual glance into a long searching look, a quick touch into a lingering caress. Each time, she'd grown quiet and tense.

What if he asked her out and she said no?

After he parked the Dodge in her driveway beside her gray van, he said, "I can't remember the last time I enjoyed anyone's company so much."

She sat with her arms hugging her waist. In the moonlight slanting through the windshield, he could see a dark splotch on her jacket from the hot dog mishap. "Thank you for inviting me. I had a fantastic time."

Ryan curled his hands over the steering wheel, his grip tightening as tension coiled inside him. Usually after a date, he said, "Hey, this was fun. I'll call you, all right?" And that was it. He couldn't be that casual with Bethany.

He started to speak, then stopped and coughed. Great start. "I, um—" He looked into those big, luminous eyes, and his brain went blank. *Damn.* What was it about this girl that made him bungle everything? He never got nervous or tongue-tied. And he sure as hell never got in a sweat.

"I'd really like to see you again, Bethany," he heard himself say and then immediately wanted to kick himself for sounding so—God, what was the word?—*stupid*, he'd sounded stupid.

In the moonlight her eyelashes cast elongated, spiked shadows onto her cheeks. "That would be nice. Give me a call sometime, and if our schedules jive, I'd love it."

Watching the fleeting expressions that crossed her face, Ryan realized she thought he was just being polite. An awful, sick feeling twisted through his stomach. "I'll do that," he assured her.

When he had her comfortably resettled in her wheelchair in the entryway, he told himself not to complicate matters by kissing her good night. Only there was that sweet mouth, calling to him, and he couldn't resist just one taste. She gave a startled leap when he hooked a finger under her chin. Her eyes went wide when he lifted her face. He searched her gaze for a long moment, trying to read her expression. She looked more surprised than actually afraid. That was a good sign. Right?

He had a feeling she hadn't been kissed in a good long while, a suspicion that was proved correct when their mouths connected. She was so tense and uncertain of how to hold her head that her nose bumped the underside of his. She also had her lips pressed tightly together. With a determined exploration of his tongue, he discovered that her teeth were clenched shut as well.

He drew back, arched his brows, and said, "You straining out bugs?"

"What?"

He immediately wanted to call back the words. She obviously wasn't in the habit of doing this, and making wise cracks wasn't the right tack. He didn't want to embarrass her.

Feeling unaccountably nervous himself, he nudged his hat back and crouched in front of her chair. She watched him as if he were a strange insect she feared might bite. He rubbed his jaw, swallowed, and met her gaze. He tried to remind himself that he kissed other women all the time and thought nothing of it, that he was so well practiced in the art, he could damn near do it in his sleep. Somehow that didn't help. She wasn't another woman, and it was suddenly extremely important to do this right. Perfectly right.

She was too sweet to give her anything less.

"Been a while, has it?" he asked softly.

She laughed and rolled her eyes, her cheeks turning a pretty pink. "Eight years."

"Eight *years*?" he repeated.

"Isn't that pathetic?" She pushed nervously at her hair, took a deep breath, and then met his gaze again. "Maybe we could just skip this part."

Ryan chuckled. "Not on your life. I've been burning to kiss you all evening."

She rolled her eyes again. "I seriously doubt that you—"

He cut her short by grasping her chin. She was so damned beautiful. He knew she thought that all he saw was the wheelchair, but he was far more aware of the woman in it. The front of her jacket lay open, teasing him with glimpses of her figure, the shape of her small but full breasts showcased in the V. Her scent, a simple blend of soap, shampoo, talc, and feminine sweetness, worked on his senses like an intoxicant.

As had happened earlier in the stable, he wanted her, and his thoughts veered off track, making him yearn to peel away the parka and explore the woman hidden underneath it. He didn't know what it was about her. *Something*. He'd felt it the first time he saw her, been unable to chase her from his thoughts all week, and now the feeling had grabbed him by the throat.

He moved in, determined to show her just how hotly he burned. Taking control in a way he never found necessary with other women, he tipped her face to an accommodating angle. When her mouth remained closed, he applied gentle pressure to force it open.

Her lips trembled beneath his—a shy, startled, uncertain surrender, her lungs grabbing convulsively for breath. He shared his own, angling his head to deepen the kiss, dipping into the recesses of her mouth for a taste. *Sweet*. That one word kept circling in his mind. Wonderfully, incredibly sweet. He felt the jolt clear to his boot heels.

Damn. Was he saying good night or hello? He no longer knew or cared. She had the most fantastic, intoxicating little mouth, and her shyness only prodded him, making him want to delve deeper, to taste every honeyed recess. Silk on silk. He brushed his lips lightly over hers, nibbling, coaxing with flicks of his tongue, urging her to relax.

Finally she sighed raggedly, and her breathing changed, the intakes shallow and urgent. He felt her slender fingers grasp the front of his shirt. She sank against him, no longer counting on the chair to support all her weight. She was a welcome burden—a soft, delicate burden that seared his skin at every pressure point. Oh, God. He couldn't believe this, had never experienced anything like it.

He slipped an arm around her, drawing her even closer. All that prevented him from lifting her out of the chair was a purely instinctive reluctance to rush her. Her lips went malleable beneath his. Her mouth opened for him. Her tongue engaged with his in a shy, hesitant dance of touch and retreat. Ryan's head swam.

She moaned, the sound a hushed throb of pleasure at the base of her throat that inflamed him. He moved his hand from her chin to curl it over the back of her head. He needed to be in complete control—to orchestrate her movements, to thrust more deeply, male into female, the urge as old as mankind and so primal, so compelling he was powerless to restrain it. *His*. He wanted to possess her. Learn the feel of her. Lay claim.

His thoughts swirling in a molten eddy, he barely realized what he was doing when he slipped his left hand beneath the parka and settled his palm at her waist. *Softness*. He explored the shape of her, gently probing the thrust of her hipbone through the denim of her jeans. Then he skimmed his fingers upward over her blouse, tracing the line of each fragile rib. She jerked with every pass of his fingertips, her breath catching and becoming a mewling sound in her throat, the soft cries telling him she was as lost to the sensations as he was. One fine-boned hand slipped into his hair, made a fist, clinging to him, the urgency in her transmitting itself to him through every pore of her skin.

Ryan ran out of ribs to trace. His fingertips nudged the underside of her breast, the swollen heat and softness calling to his hand. He imagined the generous softness of her cupped in his palm, knew it belonged there and that the weight of her would feel right, absolutely right, filling the emptiness in him that suddenly clawed at his guts. *Bethany*.

Only by supreme force of will did he resist the temptation. Anchoring his palm on her side, he allowed only his fingertips to touch the beginning swell of her breast—light, coaxing glides that made him yearn to do more. She moaned into his mouth and pressed closer, the invitation explicit, her nipple thrusting forward until he felt the hardened tip graze his shirt, tracing lines over his skin like a red-hot pointer.

With each pass, a jolt went through her, making her slender body jerk. Oh, God, she ached to be touched there. He wanted to take over, to do it for her and do it right, to give her what she so obviously needed. Only when he started to move his hand higher, warning bells went off. He didn't know why, couldn't think clearly enough to examine his reasons for holding back. It would only be a touch, after all, and through the layers of her blouse and bra, which didn't constitute a daring intimacy.

But, no . . . Not now, not yet. He remembered in a flash how this had begun, with her mouth closed against him. In years and life experience, she was a grown woman and a fair mark, but when it came to sex, she was obviously a novice, and he should take it slow.

Ryan knew his limits. One more pass of that throbbing nipple over his shirt, and he was going to lose it. He tried to end the kiss, drawing back marginally. Her hot, eager mouth clung to his, the still shy and inexperienced forays of her tongue gliding lightly over his bottom lip. His guts clenched. He reached up to grasp her face between his hands and forced their mouths apart.

Gazes locked, they stared at each other, both of them breathing raggedly, the reality of how they both felt and what they might have done—what both of them still wanted to do—rising around them like an electrical field. Her eyes were cloudy and confused, the pupils large and liquid black. Looking into those eyes, he knew the exact instant when awareness began to return to her.

Her first reaction, which he also read in her eyes, was shock, quickly followed by dismay that brought an embarrassed flush to her cheeks.

"Wow," he whispered, bending to kiss the tip of her nose, a tender smile playing over his lips as he tried to bring her down gently. She was such an enigma, an intriguing blend of maturity and inexperience. Kissing her had aroused him yet made him feel protective of her as well, forcing him to slow down when what he really yearned to do was speed forward. "That was—something else."

She made an odd sound in her throat. He curled his hands over her shoulders to prevent her from falling because she'd leaned so far forward in the chair. Holding her breath, she stared at him. His own breathing was ragged. He could see the pulse at the base of her throat, a telltale sign that she was as aroused as he was.

She gulped for breath, sat back in her chair, and said in a strained voice, "I think you'd better go now, Ryan." Hugging her waist, she gazed at him with accusing eyes. "Thank you for a wonderful evening. I'll never forget it."

Just like that, he was supposed to leave? After what had occurred between them? He'd never felt like this. Never. There was something very special at work here. Something he'd never even imagined might be possible. How could he turn away from that, no questions asked, and simply walk out?

He rocked back on one boot heel. Still crouched at her eye level, he stared hard into those beautiful, expressive eyes. She was angry, her polite thank-you only a smoke screen. She had enjoyed the kiss, no question there, so he knew that wasn't the problem. He'd lost it for a second, but nothing had happened, so that couldn't be it, either.

"Bethany, I—"

She shook her head and held up a silencing hand. "Don't say anything. Just go. Please."

He pushed to his feet. No mistake. That was definitely anger in her eyes. Over the years, he'd made his share of mistakes with women and been on the receiving end of their anger a few times, but he usually knew what he'd done, at least.

"Honey, I'm—"

"Just *go*," she whispered, her tone fierce. "I mean it, Ryan. I want you to leave. *Now*."

He went. What else could he do?

Once in his truck, he sat in the darkness with his forehead resting on the steering wheel. *Just go*. Oh, God. She was royally pissed, and he hadn't a clue why. Granted, he'd gotten a little carried away, but he'd stopped. You couldn't hang a guy for thinking about it.

He lifted his head and dragged in a steadying breath. *Whew*. The suddenness of it was what had gotten him in trouble. He'd started out trying to refresh her memory on the fine art of kissing, and the next thing he knew, she had been teaching him a few things—like how it felt to lose his head over a woman.

Badly shaken, Ryan drove home, lecturing himself the entire way. He needed to think and be damned sure what his intentions were before he took this an inch farther. A girl like Bethany couldn't be tried on for size and then tossed aside if there was a pinch.

Bethany ripped off her parka and threw it with all her strength. The zipper tab hit the wall with such force that the sound reverberated like a rifle shot. She covered her face with her hands, her chest aching with stifled sobs, her stomach lurching. *Oh, God*. Never had she been so humiliated.

Thinking back over the kiss, she remembered how he'd tried to pull away and how she'd clung to him, begging for more with her mouth and body. She had never felt like that before, had never even allowed herself to get in a situation where she might feel like that. Why put herself through the unnecessary heartache? According to the specialist in Portland, she shouldn't try to have children, and chances were, she'd be unable to enjoy sex. There was also the inescapable fact that most men took one look at her wheelchair and ran in the other direction. Why explore that side of her nature, why open up all those feelings and be forced to deal with them, when she knew they'd probably never have an outlet?

Now, without half trying, Ryan Kendrick had jerked the lid off the Pandora's box of her sexual awareness, making her want things she could never have. No, *want* wasn't the word. He'd made her *ache*, damn him, leaving her aware of needs and yearnings she'd tried to ignore or pretend didn't exist.

She rubbed furiously at her mouth, trying to get the taste of him off her lips. It clung tenaciously, a bitter reminder of how she'd behaved, moaning and trembling and throwing herself at him. She still trembled with yearning. The feeling had hit her like a bulldozer, obliterating her sense of self, sweeping aside her pride.

Never again . . . *never*. If he hadn't pulled away, putting a stop to the madness, there was no telling what might have occurred. He might even have done her the ultimate kindness and made love to her, not because he really wanted to, not because he'd been planning to, but because he felt sorry for her. The poor paraplegic who never got any, so needy that just a kiss had her panting for it. What was a guy to do but give her what she wanted?

Tears stung her eyes. Her face twisted as she fought not to shed them. Just the thought that it could have gone that far made her feel sick. This was exactly why she'd always avoided this kind of situation. Given that she wasn't even sure she was functional in that way, what was the point? She'd only end up getting hurt. Sex was the number one priority for most men, barring all. Her boyfriend Paul had taught her that lesson well, and if she allowed herself to start hoping otherwise, she deserved whatever she got.

She wiped her cheeks. Eight years ago, she'd sworn that no man would ever have the power to make her cry again, and now just look at her. Well, she'd never cry over one again, mark her words. The next time a man—any man—asked her out on a date, her answer would be an unequivocal *no*.

❦ CHAPTER FIVE ❦

A night hawk cawed somewhere along the lakeshore, the sound lonely on the icy wind that blew in off the water. Sitting with his back braced against a lone pine that grew on a slight knoll, Ryan hunched his shoulders inside the lined denim of his jacket. He smelled a storm moving in, though he guessed it might be a couple of days yet in arriving, and his instincts told him it would bring snow. *Typical.* Officially, it was spring, but that meant diddlee squat at this elevation.

He sighed, not really caring if old man winter dumped more white stuff. In Crystal Falls, the occasional late blizzard was expected. The crops were in, but this early on, even a hard freeze wouldn't do that much damage.

The sound of pounding hooves drew his attention. He turned and peered through the moon-silvery darkness. After a moment he made out the silhouette of a horse and rider. Glancing at the luminescent dial of his watch, he saw that it was ten after eleven, late enough to make him wonder who was out riding.

"Howdy-ho!" a feminine voice called.

"Mom? What the Sam Hill are you doing out here?"

Her mare, Sugarplum, decreased speed and fell into a trot, throwing up sandy lake soil with her shod hooves. "When I looked out my kitchen window and saw you under your thinking tree at this time of night, I figured something was up. I thought maybe you needed to talk."

Ryan sometimes wondered if his mother had some sort of maternal telepathy. "What did you do, scan the lakefront with an infrared scope? It's dark. You couldn't have seen me from your window."

"The outside lights are all on up at your place. I could see your silhouette. A man in a Stetson casts an unmistakable outline."

Ryan knew that the ranch foreman, Sly, had been stopping in every hour all evening to check on Rosebud. "How'd you know it was me and not Sly or one of the hired hands?"

"Process of elimination. No one else would be fool enough to sit out here in the freezing cold."

She drew up in front of him and swung off her horse. Leaving the reins to dangle, a method referred to as ground tying in their neck of the woods, she stepped to her saddlebag. Ryan heard glass clink. He narrowed his gaze. As his mother came up the incline, he saw that she was carrying a half-gallon bottle of wine and two goblets.

"Want to share a nip or two with me?"

He ran a thoughtful gaze over her slender figure. Petite and blond, she was still a beautiful woman, even at sixty. "You and Dad fighting?"

She laughed as she sat beside him. Moonlight played over her face, the gentle glow concealing her few facial wrinkles. The gray of her eyes shimmered and shifted like quicksilver. "Your dad gave up fighting with me years ago." She handed him the wine bottle and a corkscrew. "He never wins."

Ryan chuckled as he set himself to the task of opening the bottle. "Only because he pulls his punches, and you don't."

"He also has difficulty articulating when he's furious, which I've learned to use to my advantage. In answer to your question, no, all is fine on my home front."

She braced her forearms on her upraised knees, a waiting goblet clutched loosely in each hand. Ryan popped the cork and filled the glasses she extended.

"That bottle is going to be a dead soldier before I leave," she announced.

"Uh-oh. You feeling a need to tie one on?"

"No, but I think you are. You've been a bit distracted the last few days."

"Distracted?"

"As in staring off at nothing and not answering when we yell your name three times. Tell your mother what's eating you."

Ryan knew he had been preoccupied. Since first meeting Bethany, he'd been unable to get her off his mind. "Nothing's eating me. What makes you think that?" He took a sip of wine, swallowed, and nearly choked. "*Jesus!* What *is* this shit?"

Ann took a taste and grimaced. "It's Hazel Turk's homemade plum wine. Dad says it's got the kick of a sawed-off double-barrel shotgun." She thrust a hand toward him, palm up. "That's twenty you owe to the college fund."

"Ah, Mom, come on. Jaimie's at home in bed asleep."

"Pay up. Two cusswords, ten apiece. Those are the rules. If you don't follow them when he's not around, you'll slip when he is. My grandson is not going to be expelled from preschool for using bad language. Only 'damn' and 'hell' and a few other bywords are allowed, end of subject."

Ryan handed her his wine while he dug in his pocket for his money clip. He peeled off a hundred-dollar bill and traded it for the return of his goblet.

She squinted to see. "This is way too much."

"I'm not finished yet. That gives me eight on account."

"*That* bad?" Ann laughed and stuffed the bill in the pocket of her Wrangler jacket. "Okay, spit it out. I knew you were upset about something."

Ryan took another sip of wine, shuddering as he swallowed. "This stuff tastes like cough syrup."

"I understand that Hazel's wine can give you such a case of the squirts, you don't dare cough. I suppose it could do double duty as a cough remedy."

He gritted his teeth, curled a lip, and stared at the dark liquid.

Ann took a big gulp. "Be brave. Hazel's a dear. Sunday night at the ranchers' association dinner, I want to tell her I drank this and enjoyed it."

Ryan groaned at the reminder of the dinner. He was required to go as well. He'd meant to line up a date, had become distracted by a certain brunette, and completely forgotten. "How drunk do you plan to get? That's what it'll take to enjoy this crap. Besides, if you tell Hazel you like it, she may give you more."

"Oh, my, I hadn't thought of that. Ah, well, I'll just come visit you."

"Thanks." He took another sip. "It tastes better after the first shock."

They both fell to gazing across the lake. While they sipped the wine, they talked about the weather, decided they both smelled snow on the air, and then chatted about Rafe's family.

Ryan was on his second glass and started to feel the tension flow from his body when he finally said, "I met her this week, Mom."

"Ah," Ann said knowingly. Then, "Her, who?"

"*Her.* Miss Right. The girl of my dreams, the one I've been waiting for. I took her out on a date tonight."

"Oh, Ryan, that's *wonderful.* I told you it would happen, sooner or later." She twirled her goblet, watching the crystal sparkle. Then, frowning, she said, "If you just took her out, and she's Miss Right, why on earth the long face?"

"I kissed her, and everything went wrong. She got upset and told me to leave."

"What happened to make her upset?"

Ryan rubbed a hand over his face. "Well, now, there's a question. I was just going to kiss her good night, an old-fashioned, first-date kiss, the kind of thing a guy does on the doorstep. Only things got a little out of hand." He felt a flush creeping up his neck. He and his mother were close, but even so, there were some subjects he felt uncomfortable discussing with her. The particulars about his love life ranked near the top of that list.

Ann's eyes widened. "Wow. It must have been some kiss."

"Yeah, *wow*. I lost it, she lost it." He clenched his jaw, shook his head. "After all the women I've dated, I ask you, what were the chances that I'd run across a half-pint girl with big blue eyes who kisses with her mouth closed, and she'd blow my socks off?"

"One in a thousand, maybe?" Ann studied him, her expression thoughtful. "She kisses with her mouth closed? How old is she?"

"Twenty-six."

"Is she religious or something?"

"No, Mom, not fanatically or anything." Ryan propped his elbows on his knees. "She's just—it's been a while for her, and I suppose you could say she's also a little green."

"At twenty-six?"

"Yeah. I should have handled the situation with more finesse." He drained his glass of wine, then refilled both their goblets. "I sensed that she was wary."

"Wary of you?"

"Yeah, sweet and friendly, but a little standoffish. I think she's been through a bad relationship, gotten hurt. That's my guess, anyway."

"Hmm." Ann shook her head, her expression bemused.

"I think she's as attracted to me as I am to her," Ryan added, "but she's afraid of getting hurt again."

"Ah," Ann said knowingly. "How'd you come up with that?"

"Because when I kissed her, she was right there with me until I pulled away, and then, bang, she looked at me like I'd punched her." He sighed. "Sometimes I think men and women come from different universes. I don't suppose you have any insight to share on the female psyche?"

Ann smiled. "Sweetie, we aren't all designed by the same blueprint." She raised the toes of her boots and slowly lowered them to point downhill again. "Is your bewildering puzzle pretty?"

"Beautiful," he whispered. "She's got the prettiest blue eyes I've ever seen. I swear, they're the biggest thing about her—so brilliant a blue, they put me in mind of Johnny-jump-ups."

"Uh-oh. That's as close to poetic as I've ever heard you get. A bad case, huh?"

He sighed and said, "I just—*yeah,* a bad case. The first time I saw her, I felt thunderstruck. And it's not just her looks. Pretty women aren't scarce in a town as large as Crystal Falls. It was something else—almost a sense of recognition, like I'd been waiting to find her all my life, and there she was. I can't explain it."

Ann smiled sympathetically. "Honey, no one can explain the mystery of love." She grew thoughtful again as she sipped her wine. "You say you think she's been through a bad relationship? How on earth did she manage that without learning how to kiss?"

Ryan's jaw muscle knotted. He stared sightlessly across the lake. "I didn't say she doesn't know how, but that she's out of practice and a little green. I'm only guessing, but I think she was very young at the time she had the relationship and probably a bit of a tomboy. Seventeen, maybe eighteen years old. The sort of thing that never went much farther than handholding and clumsy kissing with a boy who had little more experience than she did."

"And she's never been involved with anyone else since?" Ann asked incredulously.

"She's a cripple."

"A what?"

"A cripple." The word came hard, catching at the back of Ryan's throat. "Not the politically correct term, I'm sure. Paralyzed, Mom, a paraplegic. She was injured eight years ago in a barrel-racing accident."

Silence.

A bitter taste washed over Ryan's tongue. "I don't think men have been standing in line to date her since then. A wheelchair has a way of dampening the male ardor. I don't know who the guy was that hurt her, but he was probably some immature little jackass she knew in high school."

"Oh, *Ryan.*" Ann's eyes darkened in the moonlight, looking like splotches of charcoal in her suddenly pale face. She frowned thoughtfully and gazed across the lake for several seconds. "Not saying you aren't right," she said softly, "but having worked in a rehab center, I'd say it's just as likely that she has faced so many rejections and restrictions since her accident that she's become wary and distrustful. When a woman is found to be lacking countless times by the opposite sex, she protects herself in any way she can, and that might make her seem wary."

"Could be," Ryan conceded. "Going by things she said, I got the feeling that most men run the other direction when they realize she's in a wheelchair." He shrugged. "Hell, to be honest, when I first realized she was a paraplegic, I wanted to run myself, only I'd already asked her out, and I didn't want to hurt her feelings. If I'd started crawfishing, it would have been obvious why." He swallowed and closed his eyes for a moment. "So I took her on a date, thinking it'd only be for an evening, and that afterward I could do a graceful fade-out."

Ann said nothing, which prompted him to continue.

"I got to her house late," he said gruffly. "Rosebud went into labor, and when I tried to call her to explain, her phone was ·off the hook, and I couldn't get through. She thought I'd stood her up, and I could tell she'd been crying. I felt like a skunk. When I told her I'd been held up by a horse, I expected her to be pissed. Instead, she was a real sweetheart about it."

"That's a nice switch," Ann said with a smile. "Most times, don't your dates get miffed if you're late because a horse requires attention?"

Ryan grinned. "You could say that, yes. As in livid. It was an even nicer switch that I had a fantastic time with Bethany. She's bright and funny and interesting. I've taken women out, dropped two or three hundred, and been bored to tears. I took her to the mud pulls, fed her a hot dog, and had more fun than I remember having in ages."

Ann laughed incredulously. "The mud pulls and a hot dog? She must be a very special young lady."

"Yeah, there's just something about her, you know? I've got this feeling. I can't describe it." He flattened a hand over his chest. "This bone-deep feeling. I'd like to explore the possibilities, see if—well, you know—if we can find common ground to build a lasting relationship, but now I doubt she'll give me the chance."

Ann said nothing for a long time, her gaze trailing slowly over his face in a way that had made him squirm when he was a teenager. "I see," she finally said, her mouth twitching as she suppressed a smile. "You're worried about the sex."

Ryan's throat felt as if a cruel hand had closed over his larynx. He swiped at his nose and looked away. "Damn, Mom. Cut right to the chase, why don't you? There are some things a man doesn't feel right discussing with his mother."

Ann laughed. "Since when do we beat around the bush in this family? There are no taboo subjects."

"I can speak frankly with you about almost anything, but this is—well, for me it *is* a taboo subject."

She chuckled again. "So I'm right. You *are* worried about the sex." She bumped him with her arm. "Come on. Loosen up. I may be your mother, but I'm also a retired nurse. You can't hit me with anything I haven't heard a hundred times before, and you may discover that my input is enlightening."

He nodded. "I don't doubt that. It's just that—all right, yes. I am worried about the sex." He felt her gaze on him. "Don't look at me like that. I'm a bastard, and I know it."

"I wasn't thinking that at all."

"Yeah, well, it's what I'm thinking. She's so *sweet*, Mom."

"Good sex is a major concern to most men, and I believe you're normal in that respect." She took another sip of wine. "There's nothing wrong with that."

Ryan relaxed slightly. "I have to admit, it's right up there with oxygen when I'm considering the things I absolutely can't live without. It's definitely enough to make me step back and think twice before getting involved with a woman."

Ann laughed and leaned sideways, bumping him with her shoulder again. "Where did you get the idea paraplegics can't have sex?"

"That's obvious, isn't it? She's *paralyzed*, Mom. No sensation from the waist down. Maybe some men wouldn't care, but I like partners who enjoy that particular activity as much as I do."

"You're making an idiotic assumption. A common one, but it's dead wrong. I know about these things. Whether or not she has feeling in certain places depends on the location and severity of her injury. Some paraplegics, especially women, enjoy normal intimate relationships."

"Really? Are you positive?"

Ann arched an eyebrow. "Is this young lady special enough to continue this discussion?"

He narrowed an eye. "Yeah, you could say that."

"Then, yes, I'm positive. A lot of paraplegic women enjoy active sex lives, not always attaining satisfaction in the same way an able-bodied woman does, but everything being relative, who's to say they enjoy it less? For instance, some of those who can't climax in the usual way experience a phenomenon called 'phantom orgasm.'"

"Phantom orgasm?"

"I liken it to an amputee who can still feel the missing limb. A paraplegic sometimes feels intense pleasure in another part of the body at the point of orgasm."

"That's a far-out concept."

"Factual," Ann corrected. "The body is a marvelous mechanism and compensates when it can. What difference does it make, honey? As long as the girl feels fireworks of some kind, do you really give a hang where they go off?"

Ryan chuckled and rubbed beside his nose. "No. I don't guess I do. Fireworks are fireworks. You *sure* about this, Mom?"

"Absolutely. Do you think I'd say so if I weren't? Even if normal or phantom orgasms are absent, I've heard that paraplegic women are usually fantastic lovers. Because they're handicapped, they're often more willing than an able-bodied woman to go that extra mile to please their partners." She raised her eyebrows and smiled. "When two people care deeply for each other, they aren't afraid to be creative if necessary, and sometimes that's the very nicest kind of love—not perfect in the usual sense, but beautiful because it's extraordinary."

"Hmm."

"It sounds to me as if you're on the verge of falling hard for this young lady."

"Teetering," he admitted. He took another swallow of wine. "Phantom orgasm." He thought about it for a moment. "It'd sure be hell if it happened in her appendix, and she had to go under the knife."

Ann burst out laughing. "Only a man would think of that."

"It's *important*, Mom."

"And you males have a corner on that?" She shook her head. "Back to your young lady. I know it's difficult, but try to be analytical for a moment. You say she really got into it when you kissed her?"

Ryan nodded.

Ann smiled knowingly. "Strange, that. She must have been experiencing a strong physical reaction somewhere. In her elbow, perhaps?"

He chuckled and then grew sober as he recalled the sweet way Bethany had melted against him and trembled with desire when he nearly touched her breast. She had been every bit as aroused as he was. He would have bet his entire financial portfolio on that. "Damn, Mom, you're right. Fireworks were going off somewhere."

"Probably in the usual places. It's a very good indication, at any rate."

Ryan nodded.

"As for her asking you to leave? This is just your mother's take, all right? But I think I know why."

"Why?" Ryan fixed a piercing gaze on her.

"You say you only meant the kiss as an old-fashioned, first-date kind of thing?"

He nodded.

"I'm sure she must have realized that," Ann said softly. "If we're right, and she's already been rejected a number of times, just think how she must have felt, responding that way to you, if it wasn't apparent to her that you were feeling the same way."

Ryan winced and swore under his breath.

"If she hasn't been kissed very many times—which is a fair assumption—then she may not have realized you became aroused as well. When you pulled away, she may have been mortified. I know I would have been." Ann sighed. "I can't say for sure. But if I'm right, she probably hopes she never sees you again."

"Oh, *Christ.*"

"It isn't the end of the world, dear heart. Fences can be mended."

"How?"

"You're your father's son. Trust me, you'll think of a way. If you want to, that is. Unless you're very serious about this girl, Ryan, perhaps you should just stay away from her." She reached over to pat his back. "On the other hand"—she leaned forward to peer at his downcast face—"if she's really the girl you've been searching for, you'd be the biggest fool on earth to let her slip through your fingers. Don't let a wheelchair stop you. If you've got that once-in-a-lifetime feeling, there's nothing—and I do mean *nothing*—that's so great an obstacle it can't be overcome. How's that song go that you like so well? If you have love in your heart, you can move a mountain. Love can make miracles happen, honey."

Ryan exhaled a ragged, pent-up breath. "Do you think I'm nuts, Mom? To be feeling this way about a girl I just met?"

Ann tossed out the remainder of her wine and used his shoulder for leverage as she gained her feet. Her wine goblet dangling loosely from her fingers, she gazed toward the mountains where the Rocking K sprawled farther than the eye could see.

"I think you're a Kendrick," she said softly. "If the tendency to fall in love, hard and fast, is crazy, it's an inherent trait, so why fight it?"

"How does a guy know if it's love?"

Ann frowned thoughtfully. "You just do. It's not something you can explain to someone else—or even to yourself. You just know." She splayed a hand over her heart. "A feeling, way down deep." Her eyes began to dance with twinkling laughter. "Of course, sometimes it's only acid indigestion. So be careful."

"You're a big help."

"You're on your own. Only you know how you feel. Let that guide you."

Ryan watched as she picked her way down the bank. "Hey, Mom?"

"Hmm?" She stopped and looked back.

"Have I mentioned lately how much I love you?"

She smiled and resumed her pace. After stowing her goblet in the saddlebag and remounting Sugarplum, she sat there for a moment, her hands braced on the saddle horn, her head tipped back to stare at the sky. "What did you say this girl's name is?"

"Bethany," Ryan said huskily.

"Ah, Bethany. I like that. It has a very nice ring, coupled with Kendrick."

"I haven't decided to *marry* her yet, Mom. I have a lot of thinking to do before I even decide to see her again."

"Yes, you do," Ann agreed, all trace of levity gone from her voice. "It's entirely unnecessary to say this, I know, but I'll say it anyway. A young woman like that has endured heartache enough. You could hurt her so very easily." She drew sideways on the reins to turn Sugarplum. "Sometimes it's better to simply never know where a feeling may take you than to find out and have regrets."

Ryan gazed after her as she rode off, his mouth tipped in a sad smile.

❦ CHAPTER SIX ❦

It was nine-thirty the next morning, and Ryan had a dozen things to do. Instead he stood at the breakfast bar, staring at the telephone. A glance at his watch told him he'd been at this for twenty minutes, long enough to work out a routine. He picked up the receiver, started to punch in Bethany's number, hung up, and then grabbed the pen by the Rolodex to doodle.

This was a waste of time. He either wanted to call her or he didn't. A fairly simple decision. So why was he standing here acting like a lovesick teenager and getting a crick between his shoulder blades?

Turning to leave the kitchen, he nearly stumbled over the yellow Lab sprawled on the floor near his feet. Because the dog was so often underfoot, Ryan had dubbed him Tripper two years ago when he had appeared on the doorstep, bedraggled and starving. The name had stuck, and so had the dog.

Tripper whined and rolled onto his back for a belly scratch. Smiling, Ryan bent to accommodate him. "I've got to put you on a diet," he said affectionately. "You're getting fat."

Tripper arched his spine to rub his shoulders on the floor. Ryan sighed when he saw how many hairs were coming off on the burnt-umber tile. It seemed that Tripper's fur multiplied as soon as it fell from his coat. Ah, well. Without a dog, life was barely worth living.

He patted Tripper's head and gave the phone a last look. Then he turned away, determined to get on with his day. Moving across the family room to the coat tree, he collected his Stetson, settled it on his head, and stared out the sliding glass door at the large deck, where he loved to relax on summer evenings.

Damn. The slight drop to the deck would be a precipitous barrier for a woman in a wheelchair. If he started dating Bethany and brought her out for visits, he'd have to build ramps and rearrange the furniture to provide wider traffic paths. There were also the bathrooms to consider. They were spacious enough, and because he often housed sickly newborn critters in the bathrooms while he had them on medication, the doorways were plenty wide, but he needed to install bars, at least.

He sighed and rubbed his aching eyes. Tension. If he picked up that phone, there'd be no backing out later. He couldn't do that to her. If he pursued this, he had to know beyond a doubt that what he felt for her was real and lasting.

After grabbing the cell phone and his jacket, he whistled for Tripper and left the house. There was tack to repair, a horse that needed shoeing, and various other chores to eat up his day. He didn't have time to stare at the phone.

Once inside the stable, Ryan approached Rosebud's stall to say good morning. The mare whickered in greeting and came to the gate, flaring her nostrils and looking past Ryan's shoulder as if expecting to see someone else.

Ryan smiled knowingly. "You really took a liking to her, didn't you?" he whispered as he rubbed the horse's nose. "Me, too."

Rosebud nudged his arm and sniffed his jacket. Ryan fished in his pocket for the expected sugar cube. As the mare nibbled the treat from his palm, he petted her, thinking how much Bethany would enjoy this morning ritual.

"You're rotten, you know it?" he whispered to his horse. "Why are all my critters so spoiled, huh? I've got to stop pampering you."

Rosebud chuffed and blew, as if she were telling him what she thought of that idea. Ryan gazed past her, recalling how Bethany's eyes had sparkled last night when she saw the foal.

His throat went tight at the image. When he tried to remember the faces of other women he'd dated, they were all a blur, eclipsed by pixie features and huge, pansy-blue eyes. He couldn't seem to get her out of his head.

He glanced over his shoulder at the depressions left in the dirt by her wheelchair. Farther up the aisle, there were muddy places where she would get stuck if he didn't lay asphalt, and if he did that, he might as well go the whole nine yards with cement pads and walkways outside the stable. Such an undertaking would be costly. But, then, it wasn't as if he'd ever miss the money. He could almost see her buzzing up the aisle, her smile lighting up the gloom. A man couldn't put a price tag on that.

Bethany. He sighed, exhausted. There was no understanding the feelings he had for her. It didn't seem to matter that they made no sense. They simply existed and gained a stronger hold with each passing second.

Bethany dabbed her brush in greenish-black paint to add shadows and definition to the trees in her mountain scene. It was as close as she came to the wilderness these days, re-creating it on canvas. As she painted, she recalled trips she'd taken with her brothers. The scenery, the smells, the sound of laughter on the wind. Oh, how she ached to experience those things again.

Ah, well. This was almost as good, and staying home had its advantages, a hot bath each evening ranking high on the list. Her new bathing sling was wonderful, lowering her into the tub in a reclining position so she could soak.

She added some shading to a drooping fir bough, thinking how lucky she was to have all morning to paint. Other than work and the occasional family obligation, little happened in her life to interfere with her leisure time. She could do what she wished, when she wished, and she liked it that way. She didn't need a man in her life, that was for sure. Why complicate things? She enjoyed living alone with only her cat Cleo to demand her attention. If she wanted to read all weekend, she usually could. If she decided to watch television, she didn't have to fight with an overbearing male over the remote control.

The phone rang. Bethany always brought the portable with her into the hobby room. She leaned sideways to grab it off her craft table, a makeshift work surface Jake had thrown together with shortened sawhorses and a ripped sheet of plywood.

"Hello?"

A deep voice replied, "Good morning, beautiful. You still mad at me?"

Ryan. Bethany's hand tightened on the phone, and her heart climbed into her throat. A flush of humiliation seared her cheeks. Every time she thought about last night, she wanted to die.

"Good morning right back at you," she managed to say cheerfully. "And I was mad at myself, not you. It was a lovely evening, and I had a fantastic time."

He was silent for a moment. "It really was a great evening, and I'd like to do it again."

Bethany squeezed her eyes closed. "I'd love to. Give me a call one of these times, and we'll see if we can't do that."

"This is the call." His voice was laced with amusement. "I'd like to see you tonight."

Tonight? *Why?* So she could throw herself at him again and make a fool of herself? "Gosh, Ryan, I'm sorry," she said tautly. Lying, for any reason, had never come easily to her. "Remember, I told you last week, I'm busy tonight."

"Oh, that's right." He sighed.

"Church and family things."

"You busy tomorrow night, too? I've got a big do I have to attend. I'd love to take you as my date."

"I'm busy then, too, I'm afraid," she said, vastly relieved she needn't lie about that as well. The annual Crystal Falls Ranchers' Association dinner was tomorrow night, and as owners of The Works, her parents were still members. She fleetingly wondered if that was the big "do" Ryan had to attend, then told herself not to borrow trouble.

"Not a problem," he assured her. "I'll take what I can get. What night next week do you have free? I'll juggle my schedule."

Bethany stared sightlessly at the window. "I'm sorry. Monday I have store errands to run that'll keep me busy until late. Tuesdays and Thursdays are my swim nights at the 'Y.' It'll be one thing or another all week."

"Why don't you come out here Tuesday night to swim? I've got a heated pool. Afterward we'll have dinner. I grill a mean steak."

"I swim with my mother. She helps me get dressed afterward. When I'm away from home and all my equipment, I require assistance."

"Ah." Silence again. Then, "What kind of equipment?"

She couldn't imagine why he asked. "All different kinds, mainly transfer gadgets."

"Transfer gadgets?"

"Devices to lift me from my chair and deposit me elsewhere. I can't motivate on my own. Out of my own environment, I find it very difficult to manage."

There, she thought. If that didn't make him turn tail and run, nothing would.

"I'm a great transfer gadget," he informed her silkily. "I'm also multifunctional and come real cheap. All I charge is a smile."

"I would never trust a blind man to pick me up and move me around." Brief silence. "I'm not blind."

"If you come anywhere near me while I'm dressing, you'd better be."

He laughed. "Ah, I see your point. I guess I need to do some shopping."

Bethany's throat closed off, and her pulse began to hammer in her temples. "Why are you doing this, Ryan?" she asked shakily.

"I think that's obvious." She heard a horse whinny, then the sound of water running. She imagined him in the stable, talking to her over a cell phone while he cared for his stock. "I've developed an incurable fascination for a certain lady with huge blue eyes. What're you doing next Friday night?"

"Next Friday?" She reached over to rustle some papers on the table, hoping he'd think she was checking her calendar. "Gosh. I'm busy, I'm afraid."

"How about Saturday?"

"The same. My calendar seems to be full for the next several weeks."

"I see. A brush-off. A very sweet one, but a brush-off, all the same."

Bethany touched her fingertips to her mouth, remembering how it had felt when he kissed her—how she'd all but melted and then clung to him when he tried to pull away. She also recalled Jake's warning, that Ryan Kendrick had a reputation for loving and leaving them. She didn't want to become another name on his list. There was something about him that penetrated all her defenses and left her far too vulnerable. This might be only another flirtation to him, but it wouldn't be for her. She'd end up falling in love with him, and it would devastate her when he decided to move on.

"It's not a brush-off," she assured him. "I really appreciate your thinking of me. I had a wonderful time last night, I'd love to do it again, and I'm very sorry my schedule is so full right now."

"I'll keep in touch. Maybe I'll catch you some evening when you aren't already booked."

"I'd like that. Good-bye, Ryan."

"I hate the word good-bye, especially with a beautiful lady I'm determined to see again. I'll catch you later, how's that?"

"Right. Catch you later."

Bethany broke the connection and let the phone drop to her lap. She bent her head and sat there for a full minute, silently chiding herself. It was so silly to wish for more than she already had, so silly to want more. She had so very much to be grateful for. What was it about Ryan Kendrick that made it all seem so meaningless and empty?

Besides, realistically, what did she have to offer a man who already had it all? She should be grateful that he'd been a gentleman last night. It had been a narrow escape. To put herself at risk again would be foolish. She knew from experience that broken hearts took a very long time to heal.

When Ryan got off the cell phone, he turned from Rosebud's water trough to see his older brother Rafe standing outside the stall. After turning off the faucet, Ryan stepped out, swung the gate closed, and secured the latch.

Arching one jet eyebrow, Rafe regarded Ryan from under the brim of his tattered black Stetson, his mouth tipped in a bemused grin. "That sounded like a no score, little brother. You losing your touch?"

"I sure as hell struck out with that one." Ryan tucked the phone back in his pocket. "It would appear she's going to take some convincing."

"And you'll bother? You usually just move on to better grazing."

"Not this time."

"Hmm. That doesn't sound like you."

Rafe stepped to the stall gate, the lazy shift of his lean but well-muscled body deceptively languid for a man who could move with lightning speed when he chose. Dressed in blue chambray and denim, he stood with his arms resting on the gate, one booted foot bearing most of his weight.

Just then Ryan saw his nephew run up the aisle toward them. In tiny Wrangler jeans, Tony Lamas boots, and a denim jacket, Jaimie was the very image of Rafe except for his big brown eyes, which he'd gotten from his mother. Given the fact that the child wasn't actually Rafe's, the resemblance never ceased to amaze Ryan.

As the two-year-old tried to dart by, Ryan scooped him up in the crook of his arm. "What have I got here? A peck of trouble?"

"Jaimie!" the child chortled.

Ryan lifted the little boy's black hat to see his face better. "I'll be, it *is* Jaimie. What's your mama feedin' you, hotshot? You've grown a full inch since I saw you last."

Always on the run, the child giggled and squirmed to get down. Ryan kissed his chubby cheek, getting a whiff of peanut butter breath, which made him grin as he swung the toddler back to the ground.

Rafe watched the boy run deeper into the stable. "Where's he off to, I wonder?"

"Looking for Sly, no doubt. That old codger attracts kids like honey does bears. Remember how we used to pester him?"

Tripper barked and fell in behind the little boy.

"I remember." Rafe shook his head, his gaze still riveted to Jaimie. "He is growing fast, isn't he? Before I know it, he'll be asking to borrow my truck keys."

Ryan chuckled. "We've got a few more years before that happens, thank God. What brings you over this way?"

Rafe and his wife, Maggie, lived in the main ranch house on the opposite side of the lake, not far as a crow flew, but a distance of about three miles by vehicle.

Rafe inclined his head at the stall. "I thought I'd come see the foal. Maggie was painting her toenails. I thought I'd give her a break. Mom's there, playing with the baby. It's not often these days that Maggie gets any quiet time."

"Mom's there, huh?" It went without saying what that meant. "Then you've heard all about Bethany."

Rafe pretended intense interest in Rosebud's colt. "I heard some."

"Some? In her entire life, when has our mother ever been reticent?"

"Okay, I heard a lot," Rafe admitted with a shrug. "I thought maybe you'd like to talk."

Ryan didn't like the sound of that. He joined his brother at the gate. "There's really not all that much to tell. Her name's Bethany Coulter."

"Any relation to Harv Coulter?"

"His daughter. I met her last week when I went into the store. Asked her out, she said yes. I took her to the mud pulls last night, and we really hit it off."

"You forgot to add that her eyes remind you of Johnny-jump-ups."

Ryan laughed. "There are some things in life you can always count on. The sun will rise of a morning, it'll set at night, and our mother will be talking nonstop every second of daylight in between."

"That's Mom, dependable." Rafe turned to regard Ryan with solemn, steel-blue eyes that seemed to miss nothing. "She says this girl's a paraplegic."

"Yeah. She got hurt barrel racing eight years ago."

A muscle rippled in Rafe's cheek. "How do you feel about that?"

Ryan mulled over the question. "I'm okay with it."

"You're *okay* with it? From what Mom says, you're serious about this girl, little brother. You'd best do better than that."

"I'm a big boy, Rafe. I know what I'm doing."

"I hope so. I'd hate to see you screw up your life."

"Meaning?"

"Meaning you're too tenderhearted for your own good." Rafe swung his hand to encompass the ranch. "All the damned bulls we've got on this place bear testimony to that. If you nurse a sick calf, you develop an attachment, and when it comes time to castrate, you hide it from me."

"I've never hidden a calf from you."

"You most certainly have. Two years back, it was Boomer. You couldn't bear the thought of him ending up on a styrofoam tray, and you locked him in a horse stall. I knew it then, I know it now. I don't know why you keep denying it."

"That is such bullshit. He just wandered in there."

"Oh, yeah? We sure have a lot of calves that accidentally *wander* into enclosures on castration day. Last year it was T-bone." Rafe held out a hand. "Pay up. 'Bullshit' isn't allowed."

Ryan clenched his teeth and fished in his pocket for his money clip. If he didn't get his mouth cleaned up, he'd go broke. As he peeled off a ten spot, he said, "There must be enough in that fund to send the kid to Harvard by now."

"Don't change the subject."

Ryan sighed. "Who in his right mind would name a pet calf T-bone?"

"A softie who was trying to distance himself and not love the damned thing, that's who." Rafe tucked the money into his shirt pocket so he wouldn't forget to put it in the ginger jar when he got home. "And don't tell me you didn't hide him. How else did he wind up in the tack room?"

"He must've followed someone in there, and that person shut the door."

"Someone." Rafe grinned. "You, maybe?"

"Could've been. He was always following me around, if you'll remember."

"All I know is, he never went under the knife."

"He's gonna be a fine-looking bull. Even you can't deny that."

Rafe sighed and bent his head to scuff his boot in the dirt. "No, I can't. He's turned out real nice. Probably all that special feed you give him."

"What special feed? You're letting your imagination get away with you."

As if on cue, T-bone wandered into the stable just then. When the half-grown black bull spotted Ryan, his vacuous brown eyes lighted with eagerness, and he lumbered toward them, chuffing and mooing for his grain.

"Christ," Rafe said.

"That's ten you owe to the college fund." Ryan was still laughing as he went to the feed room to get T-bone his breakfast. When the bull was happily munching grain from a trough, Ryan rejoined his brother at the stall. Rosebud ambled over for petting. Rafe scratched her nose and smoothed her mane.

"You running a ranch around here, or a spoiled-critter shelter?" Rafe asked. "Here's another one of your projects. Hadn't been for you, she never would've survived."

"Nope, and isn't she a beauty?"

After petting the horse a bit more, Rafe smiled. "I wouldn't change you, Ryan. You're a good man. There's no crime in having a big heart. All I'm saying is, just because you feel sorry for someone, you needn't marry her."

"The way I feel about Bethany has nothing to do with feeling sorry for her." Ryan tried to think of a way to explain. "She's fun and interesting, not at all the sort of person who inspires pity. And I haven't said I'm planning to marry her."

"No, but you're thinking about it. I know you."

Ryan bumped the gate with the toe of his boot. "I just met her, Rafe. Don't go jumping the gun."

"Famous last words. With the men in this family, when has time ever played into it? You're talking to the world's fastest operator, remember. What was it before I asked Maggie to marry me, three days?"

"And look how happy you are. I've never seen a man so dopey over a woman."

"Yeah, well, this dope is worried about you, little brother."

"Don't be. I've been around the track a few times. I won't do anything stupid. Trust me on that."

"No one needy has ever gotten a tether on you. I know you, Ryan. You can't walk past a bird with a broken wing. Tie up with a lady in a wheelchair, and you'll never slip free of the rope."

"*Needy?*" Ryan chuckled and shook his head. "I can't wait until you meet her. What are you picturing, a pale and wan invalid? She has a smile to light up a room and a sense of humor that won't quit. You barely notice the wheelchair."

"You'll remember it fast enough when you're stuck at home, playing nursemaid," Rafe warned. "For some guys, marriage to a paraplegic might work, but I'm not sure it would for you. Physical activity is your whole life."

"And my life is so frigging great, God forbid that I should make some changes? You're so wrapped up in Maggie and the kids, you don't know what my life is really like. Maybe I'm the needy one. Did you ever think of that?"

"You?" Rafe gave him a long look. "What's that mean?"

Ryan gestured at the stable. "You kid me about the spoiled-critter shelter I'm running over here. Maybe I'm just lonely." Until that moment Ryan had never focused on his emptiness, let alone tried to articulate the feeling to someone else. Now that he had, it seemed to intensify. "Maybe these spoiled critters are all I've got."

"Mom and Dad live a few minutes away, and Maggie and I are the other direction. You can come over any time you want. You also date regularly. How the hell can you be lonely?"

"Because none of that counts." Ryan hooked his arms over the gate and gazed solemnly at the horses. "You rib me about T-bone. Well, laugh all you want, but that dumb bull, bawling for a carrot at the kitchen window, is sometimes the social highlight of my evenings."

"You're making me feel terrible."

Ryan laughed. "I don't want you to feel bad. I'm just trying to explain. You and Maggie invite me to dinner, and—" He broke off and shifted his weight. "I appreciate being included. And I know you ask me more often than most brothers would, so please, don't think I'm finding fault. It's just that as nice as it is and as much as I enjoy your company, afterward I go home to an empty house. Sometimes the silence is—hell, I don't know—loud is the only word. And I get up in the morning to more of it, I work my ass off, from dawn till dark, and then I work a little longer to put off being alone again. You know what I'm saying?"

A stricken look came over Rafe's face. "Damn, Ryan. Why haven't you said something? We'd love to have you over at our place more often."

"It's a loneliness you can't fill, Rafe. I need a life of my own, a family of my own. And not with the first woman who comes along. I want it to be with someone really special, someone who'll love me as much as I love her, someone who'll need me as much as I need her. Does that make any sense?"

"Of course it makes sense." Rafe bent his head and puffed air into his cheeks. "I've been there. I know exactly what you mean. Before I stumbled upon Maggie and Jaimie, I felt lost. I didn't care if I lived or died—didn't have any reason to care. All I did was worry about how I'd buy my next bottle of booze."

"It's not quite that bad for me," Ryan admitted. "I haven't lost a wife and kids like you did, and I haven't turned to alcohol yet. I'm just lonely. Like at Christmas. I watch you and Maggie, shopping and whispering and hiding Jaimie's presents. That's what it's all about to me—that sense of family and having a greater purpose, and when I see how empty my life is by comparison, I just . . ."

"Feel lost?" Rafe said with an understanding smile.

"Yeah. I guess that word does say it best, *lost*. At heart, I'm a family man. It's what I was raised to be, what I've always imagined I'd be someday, but for the life of me, I've had no luck finding the right lady. Someday has come and gone. I'm thirty years old, I'm not getting any younger, and I was starting to think it might never happen for me."

"Until now?"

Ryan hesitated for several seconds before responding to that question. When he finally spoke, his voice had gone gruff. "Yeah, until now."

Rafe cocked an eyebrow. "You sure, Ryan? You only just met this girl."

"If you're asking me to explain it in rational terms and reassure you, I can't," Ryan admitted. "It doesn't make a lick of sense. I know that." He half expected Rafe to agree with him, but instead his brother only frowned thoughtfully. "One look was all it took. I walked into that store, wanting to take someone's head off. The last thing on my mind was meeting the love of my life. And there she was." A flush of embarrassment crept up his neck. "I know it sounds crazy, but that's how I felt the second I saw her."

Rafe took off his hat and raked his fingers through his hair. Letting the Stetson dangle from his loosely fisted hand, he said, "Maybe we're both crazy, because that makes more sense to me than anything else you've said."

"What does?"

"That you felt something the first instant you saw her." Rafe fixed his gaze on nothing, his expression distant. "I felt exactly that way the first time I clapped eyes on Susan, way back when I was just a kid. Remember that?"

Ryan smiled. "Like anyone in our family will ever forget. You never looked at another girl all through high school and college."

Rafe nodded. "When she died, I didn't believe I'd ever feel that way about a woman again. In fact, I *knew* I wouldn't. That kind of love—the way I felt about Susan—it's a once-in-a-lifetime kind of love, and very few men are lucky enough to find it even once. Then, out of the blue, there was Maggie. I came out of a drunken stupor and stared through the shadows at her, telling myself no woman on earth could be as sweet as she looked. And then that feeling plowed into me. I resented it. I felt as if I was being unfaithful to Susan's memory, even *thinking* along those lines, but I couldn't shake the feeling no matter how I tried. I guess God thought I'd suffered more than my fair share and decided to send me a miracle, because Maggie and Jaimie were exactly that for me, a reason to sober up, two people who needed me as much as I needed them. I think I fell Stetson over boot heels in love with her the instant I clapped eyes on her."

"Did you wonder if you were out of your mind?"

Rafe grinned. "I *was* out of my mind. Remember? I went at courtship like I was killing snakes. The poor girl never had a chance."

"You came to your senses eventually, and it's worked out nicely."

"Yeah. We're happy. Very happy."

"Maybe you should take it on faith that it'll work out just as nicely for me."

Rafe smiled and nodded. "Maybe so."

"One thing's for sure. I've never felt like this before, and it sure as hell wasn't for want of exposure. I've dated so many women, I can't remember them all, and never once did I go over the edge like this. Only with Bethany."

"If this girl is what you want, Ryan, I'll support your decision all the way."

"Good, because she is what I want. I can't explain it. I only know I can't shake it, and it's right. Now I just have to convince her of that."

Still frowning, Rafe said, "Being in a wheelchair, she can't be dating all that often. I'd think she'd jump at the chance to go out with you again."

Ryan huffed and said, "Yeah, well, she's not. Once burned, and all that. She's one blanket-shy filly."

"Blanket shy?"

"You know what I mean. As long as I kept it light, we had a lot of fun, but the instant I let on that I felt a physical attraction, she went all icy."

Rafe mulled that over. "Seems to me there's your answer, little brother."

"What is?"

"Keeping it light. Pretend all you've got on your mind is being good friends. No matter what the cause, skittish women take a slow hand. Trust me to know. I went through the same thing with Maggie. Friendship won't spook her."

"I have a lot more than friendship in mind. Pretending different would be sneaky and—I don't know—it seems sort of underhanded to me."

Rafe chuckled and shook his head. "Man, do you have a lot to learn. Be too direct and honest with women, and they run the other way."

"How do you figure?"

"That's just how it is. Me and Maggie, for instance. We take a walk along the lake nearly every night. Every step of the way, I'm usually thinking about sex. Not her. Last night, it was kitchen tile—which color and pattern would look best when we remodel. Earth tones are coming back

74CATHERINE ANDERSON

in. Should we go with yellows and golds? Whites and greens? On and on. Like I give a rat's ass? I'll love the kitchen however she does it just as long as she's standing in it naked after it's done."

Ryan snorted with laughter. "You are so bad."

"Maggie'd think so, too, so I pretend I'm interested in color choices. I rub her arm and tickle her ear and tell her I'd like tile the same color as her eyes. She's happy as a clam, and once I get her home, I'm happy, too. Call me sneaky and underhanded if you like, but if I were honest, where would it get me? Besides, what's wrong with being friends with Bethany before you become lovers? All really good relationships begin with a strong friendship, so it's not as if you're blowing that much smoke. You want to be friends with her. Right?"

"Sure."

Rafe grinned. "Well, then?"

At a little after seven that evening, Bethany had just completed her bath when the doorbell rang. Thinking it was one of her brothers stopping by to check on her, which they did regularly, she tightened the sash of her pink terry robe, quickly wrapped her wet hair in a towel, and went to answer the summons. To her surprise and intense dismay, Ryan Kendrick stood on her porch.

"You definitely need a peephole," he informed her dryly. "Then you wouldn't make the mistake of opening up to someone you'd rather not see."

His steel-blue eyes glinting with amusement, he nudged his hat back, placed a boot over the threshold, and leaned a shoulder against the door frame. Whether he intended it or not, he had effectively scotched all possibility of her closing the door. Dressed as he had been last night in faded Wrangler jeans, a wash-worn blue shirt, and a lined denim jacket, he looked both wonderfully familiar and dangerous.

Bethany gazed into his eyes, aware of each chiseled feature of his dark countenance. She felt a shiver sluice down her spine. Though she'd just finished brushing her teeth, her mouth went suddenly dry.

He held a white business envelope in one hand which he tapped against his thigh. "I intended to leave this on your door, but your van was in the driveway and the lights were on, so I figured you might be home."

Given the fact she'd told him just this morning that she had plans for tonight, Bethany groped for an explanation. It was, she decided with panicky confusion, a classic case of a lie coming home to roost.

She tugged on the sash of the robe again, reached down to make sure the front was overlapped to cover her knees, and pushed at one end of the towel, which had fallen over her face when she bent her head. "I, um . . . yes. I'm home."

"Is this your idea of a hot date?" He arched an ebony brow, his thin lips tipping in a slight smile, his eyes as sharp and relentless as honed steel. "Taking a bath and washing your hair?"

She hugged her waist, trying without much success to gather her composure. "It was a *hot* bath."

He gave a low laugh. "Well, that's something at least." Without being invited to do so, he stepped in and closed the door. "I wouldn't want you to get chilled," he said by way of explanation as he extended the envelope. "These are pictures of Rosebud's colt right after he was born and a couple that were taken this morning. I thought you might enjoy having a set."

Pasting on a smile, Bethany accepted the offering, her mind screaming one question: *Why is he here?* At a loss for anything to say, she lifted the flap of the envelope. When she drew out the photos of the foal, the uppermost one was so darling she momentarily forgot her concerns.

"Oh . . ." she said softly. She glanced at the next picture down and laughed out loud. "He's so cute. What a struggle, standing up that first time!"

Ryan leaned around to look as well, and chuckled. "I like that horrified expression on his face. Every time I see it, I wonder if he was looking at me."

She came to the third picture. "Oh, my! Crash and burn. He nearly did splits with his little front legs." She sighed and lowered the pictures to her lap. "Thank you, Ryan. How thoughtful. These are a lovely memento."

"Of the evening—or me?"

The faintly challenging note in his voice took her by surprise. Her gaze jerked to his, and the determination she saw there alarmed her.

The distinctly masculine scent of him surrounded her—a tantalizing blend of leather, fresh air, horses, and spicy cologne. He hunkered down, nudged up the brim of his hat, and gave her a long, solemn perusal that made her stomach feel as if she were riding a roller coaster.

"I think we need to talk," he said, his voice a silky rumble.

"About what?"

"About you and me—and what happened between us last night."

His straight-to-the-point manner unnerved her. He was a man on a mission, and she had a bad feeling she was it.

She remembered last night with brutal clarity—how he'd crouched down just this way and kissed her. *Never again*. He was too potently attractive, too charming, too *everything*. She'd be lost if he touched her. Even worse, she had a feeling he knew it as well.

She just wanted him to go away and leave her alone.

As though he guessed her thoughts, his eyes began to twinkle. "That's exactly why we need to talk. I really screwed up last night, and I'd like to mend my fences if I can."

He had screwed up? The way she saw it, she'd been the one who botched it all by getting turned on by a silly kiss and throwing herself at him.

"I, um . . ." He jerked his hat off, raked a hand through his black hair, and scratched above his ear. When he met her gaze again, his eyes reflected heartfelt sincerity. "I had such a good time with you at the pulls. We just clicked. You know what I'm saying? That so rarely happens, finding someone I can laugh with like that. I don't want to muck that up with the other. You know?"

"The other?"

He nodded. "Yeah—you know—the physical thing. I, um . . ." He puffed air into his cheeks. When he met her gaze again, he smiled. "I won't lie and say I'm not strongly attracted to you. That kiss knocked my socks off. But physical relationships are a dime a dozen, and a friendship like the one I sense we can have doesn't happen every day. If I have to choose, and I think it's obvious you want no part of the physical thing, I'll take the friendship."

Bethany's heart clenched. "You want to be friends?"

"You got something against friendship?"

"No, of course not. I just—"

"You just what?"

"I just don't see how that can work."

"Why not?"

A searing heat flooded into her cheeks. How could she tell a man that being around him made her want a whole lot more than an occasional friendly pat on the shoulder? "I'm very attracted to you," she settled for saying.

He smiled again and rubbed his jaw. "Yeah?"

"Yeah. That being the case, friendship becomes a tad difficult to pull off."

"Not true. If we both agree from the start that a wonderful friendship is our focus, and neither of us steps over the line, we can pull it off very easily."

For some people, caring wasn't a decision. If she was around him very much, she was bound to fall in love with him.

"I, um—I'm not so sure I can keep it on a friendship basis," she admitted ruefully. "I'd muddy up the water before we ever waded in, and I can't take that chance. I don't want to get hurt, Ryan."

"I'd never hurt you, honey. You don't hurt your best friend."

The husky sincerity in his voice was nearly her undoing. *His best friend.* A tight sensation banded her chest. "Oh, Ryan, I know you wouldn't mean to. It's just—sometimes things just happen. You may have good intentions, but everything goes wrong. I'd be one of those things. You make me feel so vulnerable."

He sighed and smoothed a hand over his hair. "If that happens, we'll just go with the flow and see where it takes us."

"It can't take us anywhere," she said. "That's the whole problem."

"Why can't it?"

Looking into his eyes, Bethany realized he honestly didn't know. Tears rushed to her eyes, and an acidic burning slid up the back of her throat. With hands gone numb from nervousness, she jerked the towel from her head and lay it on her lap. She knew her hair must look a fright. She didn't care. Let him see her at her worst.

She carefully returned the photos to the envelope, her fingers trembling as she folded down the flap. Wishing with all her heart she could avoid this conversation, she swallowed a lump in her throat that she felt fairly certain was her pride and forced herself to look him in the eye. "I have no feeling in certain parts of my body. You could jab a pin in the calf of my leg, and I wouldn't feel a thing."

His gaze flicked to her terry-draped knees, then returned to her face.

Before she lost her courage, she went on to say, "I'm not sure I can have a normal physical relationship with a man. Chances are, probably not."

"And on the strength of that iffy prognosis, you'll turn your back on life?"

"I haven't turned my back on life. I've just learned to accept that some things may no longer be possible for me. Maybe it's easy for you to go with the flow and see where something takes you. It isn't for me. Chances are, I'll only disappoint you and get hurt in the process. I'd just as soon pass."

"Who did this to you?" he asked so unexpectedly she couldn't school her expression. His lashes swept low, and his smile became a clench of white teeth. "You're so . . . *controlled.* Do you realize that?"

She stared bewilderedly at him. "Controlled?"

"Reasonable. *Calm*. It's not natural, and it sure as hell isn't healthy. Somebody hurt you. It's written all over you. I see it in your eyes every time you look at me. And you know what else I see?"

She shook her head. "No, but I have a feeling you're about to tell me."

"Damn straight. It's worrisome." He leaned closer to peer into her eyes as if there were a crystal ball inside her head. She knew he was teasing, but even so, she had the feeling her heart had become an open book. "I see anger. Deep down where you can't reach, you're so pissed you could take something apart."

A tearful laugh nearly strangled her. "Really. You can see all that?"

"Oh, hey. That and more. You're smoldering and churning like a little volcano about to erupt."

"Has anyone ever told you you're crazy?"

"A few people have made noises to that effect. I ignored them."

"Most women get hurt somewhere along the way, and they don't erupt later in life like volcanoes," she pointed out.

"They don't usually get hurt the way I suspect you did," he countered. "Maybe they get dumped a couple of times before they find the right guy, and maybe they get their hearts broken. But it's not usually over something quite as devastating."

She formed a steeple with her fingers and touched the tips to her lips.

"And you know what else? I'll bet they scream and cry and get angry and unload all the hurt and anger on someone, their moms or best friends. *Someone*. Otherwise, nine-tenths of the female population would be certifiably nuts."

"Are you saying I'm certifiably nuts?" she asked teasingly.

He searched her gaze. "No, honey. Just that you're hurting, and that it'll never go away if you don't talk to someone about it."

"I can't allow that one incident to affect the rest of my life."

"So there *was* an incident." He winked. "Caught you with that one."

"So? My last observation stands. You don't let one incident affect the rest of your life. You move on."

"You shouldn't move on, pretending it never happened, though. Venting and getting it out of your system is the far better choice. You ever try it?"

"Of course, I—" Bethany broke off and stared at him as she remembered back.

"Did you scream and cry?"

"No," she whispered.

"Did you throw things and call him a few vile, filthy names?"

She laughed again, the sound ringing hollowly. "It happened right after the first surgery, and I wasn't supposed to move much. My family was hovering all around me. I couldn't vent, as you call it. Not without upsetting everyone who loved me."

"That sucks." He shifted his weight onto the ball of his other foot and settled his crossed arms on the opposite knee. "I got hurt once. Back in high school."

"You did?"

"Oh, yeah. Like you say, practically everyone gets hurt at least once. It happens to guys, too. Not on the same plane as you did, of course. But at that age, you aren't very philosophical and don't think of how much worse it could be. It just hurts like hell."

For some reason Bethany had never pegged Ryan Kendrick as the type who might have gotten his heart broken. He struck her more as the heartbreaker type.

"Did you vent?" she asked.

He narrowed an eye at her. "If I hadn't, would I be encouraging you to? Of course, I did. And I felt a world better afterward, too." He leaned closer to whisper, "You wanna go find the little creep? I'll smack him for you."

She laughed again and shook her head. "That won't be necessary. It's been eight years. I really am over it."

"Liar." All trace of humor fled from his expression. "Name me one thing you've done to get over it."

She shrugged. "I handled it in my own way. Paul was—"

"Ah-ha. Now we're getting somewhere. The rotten little bastard has a name."

She couldn't handle this. He looked too deep, saw too much. She felt as if she couldn't breathe. She ran shaky hands over the envelope.

"Yes. Paul." The name stuck at the back of her throat and became a huge, dry lump she couldn't swallow. "And he wasn't really rotten, just a nice young man who wanted to have a normal life, and there were no guarantees he could ever have one with me."

"So the nice young man walked out on you."

The memories hurt. Even though she no longer had any feelings for Paul, the sense of betrayal was still razor sharp. She bent her head and flicked a fingertip over a snagged tuft of terry. "Yes."

"And you say he was a nice young man?"

"He really was a nice boy, and he was also only eighteen, which is really young to handle that sort of thing. Looking back on it now, I don't blame him for ducking out." She shrugged and tried to smile. "A lot of grown men might not have handled it as well."

"Don't make excuses for him. You're not his mama."

She rolled her eyes.

"Well," he scolded. "When you've been hurt, you don't make excuses for the jerk who hurt you. That's his mama's job."

"We've gotten a little off track. I was trying to explain to you why I—"

"Not necessary. I can see you're not ready for anything but friendship, honey, and that's fine by me."

"I'm not sure it's fine by me."

"I'm not talking about a steamy affair. Just friendship. Where's the risk in that?"

She brushed at her cheeks. "Maybe. Let me think about it. Maybe."

He touched a fingertip to the end of her nose, then thumbed a tear from under her eye. "What's there to think about? Everyone can use another friend. We could have so much fun together."

She clenched her hands on her lap, so tense that her nails dug into her flesh. Her heart skipped a beat. She feared he might see the longing in her eyes. She searched for something else to focus on and found herself staring at his shirt button.

The front door swung open just then. She looked up to see Jake standing there, his long, denim-sheathed legs braced apart, his eyes a piercing blue as he glanced first at Ryan, then at her. When his gaze came to rest on her face and he saw the tear tracks on her cheeks, his expression went from surprised to furious in one second flat.

"What the hell's going on here?" he demanded, his voice vibrating with rage.

Bethany jumped. Her brother was nobody to mess with when he got his dander up, and nothing got Jake's dander up quicker than a threat to her, real or imagined. She hoped Ryan would have the good sense to stay crouched down. At least then she could be sure Jake wouldn't hit him.

But no. Ryan pushed slowly to his feet. The two men were well-matched physically, both of them tall, bulky through the shoulders and arms, yet lean enough to be lightning quick. Bethany glanced worriedly at her hand-painted terra-cotta flower pots on the floor in the corner of the entry. Then she could only wonder where her head was at. Her brother and Ryan would half kill each other before one of them went down. And she was worried about her pots?

"Hello, Jake." Ryan extended his palm for a handshake. When Jake didn't reciprocate, Ryan kept his arm extended and said, "In answer to your question, nothing's going on. Bethany and I were just talking."

Through teeth clenched so tightly she was surprised he could speak, Jake snarled, "Talking about *what?*"

"The feasibility of our being friends."

Bethany's heart dropped. At that moment she would have tapped Ryan with her toe to get his attention if she'd been able to. *Not the truth,* she wanted to cry. *Don't tell him the truth*.

"Our personalities really click," Ryan said. "We have a great time together."

"That'd better be all that's clicking," Jake said softly.

Ryan finally lowered his arm. He glanced down at Bethany as he returned his hat to his head. The man clearly didn't realize how volatile Jake's temper could be. Either that, or he didn't have the good sense to recognize danger when he saw it. He actually *winked* at her.

"Don't come sniffing around my sister," Jake ground out. "If I can't kick your ass, I've got four brothers who'll be standing in line behind me. Nobody makes her cry and gets away with it."

Bethany wiped frantically at her cheeks. "I'm not crying, Jake. I got a lash in my eye. Ryan was just trying to get it out."

Both men raised their eyebrows and looked down at her incredulously. Okay. So it wasn't the most believable lie she'd ever told. She didn't want 450 pounds of testosterone wreaking havoc in her house.

As if she'd never spoken, Ryan looked back at Jake and said, "As bad as it may look, I did nothing to make her cry. We were talking. That's all. I'll also remind you that she's a grown woman. If she doesn't want me sniffing around, I guess she'll tell me."

"Don't press your luck," Jake said silkily.

"If telling you the unvarnished truth is pressing my luck, one of us has a problem with his temper, and it sure as hell isn't me."

Bethany fully expected Jake to punch him then. To her surprise they just eyed each other stonily, both of them eking every inch they could from their considerable heights, their bodies taut. She finally decided it was a man thing—some mysterious sort of silent communication that took place between bristling males that gave quailing females heart attacks.

Ryan tipped his hat to her, gave Jake another long, smoldering look, and sauntered out the door. Bethany had seen cold molasses move faster.

"Good night, Bethany," he said before pulling the portal closed. "I'll be in touch."

She wanted to say, "Just *go*. Hurry!" Instead she shakily said, "Good night, Ryan. Sorry about this."

He flashed her a grin, winked again, and said, "Hey. Not a problem."

❧ CHAPTER SEVEN ❧

Bethany was so angry with her brother she wanted to shake him. "I can't *believe* you acted like that!" she cried. "You've got no business barging into my house and treating my friend that way."

Standing over her with his fists resting at his hips, Jake scowled thunderously. "Your *friend*?"

"Yes, my friend. I am allowed to have friends, aren't I?"

"Friendship is *not* what that guy has in mind." His gaze dropped to her bathrobe, then jerked back to her face. "Why were you crying? Did he get out of line with you? If he did, I swear to God, I'll break him in half."

Just the thought of Jake and Ryan getting into a fight made her blood run cold. "Ryan Kendrick didn't get out of line with me. Get that thought straight out of your head. What makes you think he'd even want to?"

"Why wouldn't he want to? And if he didn't, why were you crying?"

"Not over anything Ryan did."

Bethany wheeled around and started up the hall. Jake fell in behind her, his boots thumping loudly on the bare wood floor. She stopped to lay the photographs on the hall bookshelf.

Jake spotted the envelope. "What's that?"

"Nothing important." She tossed the damp towel in the general direction of the bathroom hamper as she passed the open doorway. "Just some snapshots he brought over for me."

"Of what?" he asked suspiciously as he snatched up the envelope. A befuddled look came over his chiseled features when he withdrew the photos. "Whose foal?"

"Ryan's." As she continued up the hallway, she explained about their date the previous evening. "He brought me the snapshots as a memento."

"You went out with him and didn't tell me? How many times have I told you never to do that? I also warned you to stay away from him."

"Yes, well, I'm in the habit of making my own decisions. Why don't you do me a big favor, Jake, and get married? That way, you'll have some-one to fuss over besides me. If this keeps up, I'm going to move back to Portland, where I can have some peace."

Jake followed her into the kitchen, looking comically disgruntled, his sable hair ruffled into furrows from his long fingers. "You can't move back to Portland. I need you at the store."

"Baloney. The computer field is flooded with qualified people."

"It's dirty pool, using that as a threat. Think how disappointed Mom and Dad would be if you moved away again."

"It's not a threat, Jake, it's a promise. You have to give me some breathing room. I'm not a child. I don't need you to look after me."

"You're in over your head with Kendrick."

While she put on a pot of coffee, using the ramp that Jake had built her to reach the sink, he rattled off reasons why she should steer clear of Ryan.

She finally broke in to ask, "Do you know that for a fact?"

"Know what for a fact?"

"That he changes women more often than most men do their neckties? Just how often do most men change their neckties, anyhow?"

Jake narrowed an eye. "You're not taking anything I've said seriously."

She flipped on the coffeemaker, then returned the coffee to a lower cupboard. "On a personal basis, do you know anything at all about Ryan?"

"I've done business with him down at the store plenty of times. Judg-ing by the things I've heard, that's as personal as I want it to get."

"Hearsay, in other words." She sighed in exasperation. "Jake, nine times out of ten, gossip isn't true. Forgive me for pointing it out, but you've had a string of girlfriends yourself. Does that make you a heartless womanizer?"

"Don't compare me to Ryan Kendrick. We're nothing alike."

Bethany thought they were very much alike in many ways, but now wasn't the time to argue the point. "True. Ryan's family is very wealthy, and yours isn't. If he even breathes wrong, everyone notices and makes a big deal out of it, whereas with you, no one pays much attention."

"Your point?"

"That maybe he isn't a bad person at all, but a victim of vicious tongues."

Jake pinched the bridge of his nose. "Okay," he said more calmly. "I get the point. I don't know him very well, and there's a possibility all the stuff I've heard is a pack of lies. By the same token, you must admit that you don't know him very well, either, and that the stories may be fact."

"I hate it when you reason with me. I'd much rather fight with you."

He made an odd sound, a sure sign he was about to lose his temper.

"All right, all right," she inserted. "I don't know him well. It's just hard, you know? He seems like a very nice man."

"He's charming, I'll admit, but there's a difference. Some men have no respect for women, Bethany. All they care about is getting them in the sack, and they draw the line at nothing. I don't want you to be his new flavor of the month."

She closed the cupboard door with a bit more force than she intended. "He isn't like that."

"Oh, yeah? And how would you know?"

Before Bethany could stop to consider the ramifications, she said, "Personal experience."

The words cut the air like a knife.

"What do you mean?" Jake asked softly.

Searing heat flooded into her face. She wished she could call back the words, but it was too late for that. "Just what I said. When he brought me home, all in the world he did was kiss me good night. That isn't exactly a hanging offense."

"So why were you in tears, then?"

"Not over anything he did. The rest was entirely my fault."

"The rest?"

She brushed a hand over her eyes. Not for the first time, she found herself thinking that life might have been much simpler if she'd been born with a zipper on her mouth. "It was nothing, Jake. Just a simple, polite kiss at the end of the evening, like I said. It just—well, it got a little out of hand. He's very attractive, I like him, and I haven't been out on a date in a good long while." Exasperated, she threw him a meaningful look. "Is it really necessary for me to spell it out?"

Jake's brows knitted in another scowl. "What are you saying, that you were interested in more, and he passed on the offer?"

"I wouldn't put it exactly like that." She tried to think of a better way to say it, but couldn't think of one. "Sort of, I guess." She sighed and closed her eyes. "In the nicest possible way, yes, he passed on the offer. Are you satisfied now that you've ferreted out all the sordid little details?"

Silence fell over the kitchen, an awful, brittle silence, broken only by the sputters of the coffeemaker and the tick of the wall clock. While she waited for Jake's reaction, she held her breath, not entirely sure what to expect. Even so, she was taken off guard by the huff of sheer outrage that erupted from him.

"He *passed* on the offer? Who the hell does he think he is?"

Bethany nearly strangled on the startled laugh that escaped her. *Jake.* Oh, how she loved him. Of all the reactions she might have predicted, indignation wasn't one of them. She fixed a horrified gaze on his taut face.

"He turned you *down*? I'll kill him. I swear to God, he's a dead man."

She laughed again, this time a little hysterically. "I don't believe you. First you want to break him in half because you think he's trying to take advantage of me. Now you're threatening to kill him because he didn't?"

"Oh, honey." The husky note of sympathy in his voice caught at her heart and brought a rush of tears to her eyes.

In two strides he was across the kitchen. Squatting down next to her chair, he gathered her close. It felt absolutely wonderful to feel his arms around her again, calling to mind countless times in her childhood when he'd held her just this way. *Jake.* He'd always been there to set her world aright. Unfortunately, now that she was older, her hurts ran too deep for easy fixes.

"Oh, God," she whispered raggedly against his shirt. "I never meant to tell you such a thing. I'm really not in the habit of throwing myself at men. Now what'll you think of me?"

"That you're human," he replied, his voice gravelly with affection. "And a very foolish girl for casting your pearls to swine."

"I think that's supposed to be pearls of wisdom among swine, and trust me, wisdom had nothing to do with my behavior."

"Whatever. He's a pig. How *dare* he turn you down. What is he, blind?"

"Oh, Jake, I love you."

"I love you, too, sweetie. You'll never know how much."

She tucked her cheek against his collar to hide the contorted twist of her mouth. As if crying would solve anything. The turmoil of the last twenty-four hours had worn down her defenses, she guessed, and all her feelings lay perilously close to the surface.

He made a fist in her still damp hair and hauled in a shuddering breath. "Ah, Bethie. I told you to stay away from him, and for just this reason. I knew you'd end up getting hurt."

Smiling through tears, she said, "Believe it or not, it isn't really his fault, Jake. Please, don't be mad at him."

"I never get mad, I just get even."

"There's nothing to get even for. Honestly there isn't."

"It just pisses me off that he kissed you in the first place. If he wasn't prepared to take it further, why start something? There's nothing that hurts more than being rejected."

"He didn't reject me. Not really. I thought so at the time, but now I'm beginning to realize it wasn't like that. It was just a good-night kiss that mushroomed out of control, taking him as much by surprise as it did me. He could have been a jerk and taken advantage of the situation, but he didn't."

Jake's hand relaxed, his hard palm and long fingers curling warmly over her scalp. Little wonder she was in perilous danger of falling in love with Ryan Kendrick, she thought. He was very like her brother—big and rough-edged, but disarmingly gentle and wonderful as well. No matter what misfortunes befell her, she would always be rich beyond measure in her family.

"He's really gotten under your skin. Hasn't he?" Jake whispered.

"I'm afraid so," she admitted. "I know it's not smart, that it simply can't be, but my foolish heart isn't listening."

"So what are you going to do now, Bethany?"

She sighed. "Stay away from him. What else? He stopped by this evening to suggest that we be friends and nothing more. On the surface, that sounds really good. We had a fantastic time together last night, and I think we could have a lot of fun. But I'm way too attracted to him for it to work. I'd end up falling in love with him. I know I would."

Jake framed her face between his palms. "Falling in love doesn't always lead to heartbreak, honey. With the right man, it can be a one-way ticket to paradise. If the two of you hit it off that well, who's to say he isn't the right man?"

"Aren't you doing an awfully sudden about-face?"

He cocked a dark eyebrow. "I didn't know the whole story before. The guy takes you out, you have a fantastic time. Then he brings you home, has you where he wants you, and passes on the chance?" He shrugged. "That says a lot for his character, in my book."

"Yes," she agreed wistfully.

"Maybe you should give him a chance. Guard your heart. I'm not saying you shouldn't. But at least get to know him a little better."

"To what end? There are so many counts against me, Jake, so many possible problems. I can't even have children."

"Isn't that a little premature? You work your way up to the kid thing."

"Not me. I couldn't just *sleep* with him without the kid thing and forever being part of the package. That isn't how I'm made."

Jake stared hard into her eyes for a moment. She could almost see his mental wheels turning. "No. Of course not. I don't know where my head went." He sighed. "I don't want you to try to have kids, anyway. Too dangerous. What about those damned blood thinners you take? They'd probably take you off of them while you were pregnant, and you could get another clot."

As if. According to what Doctor Reicherton had told her, she would probably miscarry before clots became a worry. "Oh, Jake. As important as it is, the baby thing is only part of it. He's a *rancher*. His whole life revolves around outdoor activities. Rough ground, fences. How does a wheelchair fit into a world like that? I'd be a big lump, just sitting there in a chair."

"His world can be modified," Jake pointed out. He gestured at the sink ramp. "With all his money, he could remodel his whole house."

"His house, yes. But you can't modify thousands of acres. I couldn't be a real part of his life. And what about—you know—the really big issue?" she asked hollowly.

"Sex, you mean?" Jake's eyes filled with pain for her. "Sweetie, you can't know for sure how that'll go until you give it a try."

Bethany felt as if a hand was squeezing her larynx. "No. But if it went badly, which it very well might, he'd be trapped. Stuck with me."

"You wouldn't be trapping him. He'd be making the decision, not you."

"It'd never work," she whispered, "not in the long run. A guy like Ryan Kendrick? He could have anyone he wanted." She threw up her hands. "It's just *everything,* Jake. No matter what angle I look at it from, all I see is problems. It makes me tired just thinking about it."

"Ah, Bethie," he whispered. "If you really like the guy, why not lay it all out on the table and let him decide? If he cares about you, all the stuff you're worried about won't matter a whit to him."

Managing a strained smile, she sat back and rubbed her cheeks. "I can't believe you're encouraging me to pursue this."

He chuckled and rumpled her hair. Then he rested his hands on her shoulders. In a low voice he said, "Don't take every man's measure by Paul. That's all I'm saying."

Twenty minutes after Jake left, Bethany's phone rang. She raced over to answer. Then, just before she picked up, she thought better of it and let the machine take the call.

"Hello, Bethany, this is Ryan."

She sat back in her chair.

"I just wanted to make sure everything's all right. Your brother was pretty steamed. I hope my being there didn't stir up too much of a hornet's nest. Normally I would've stayed to lend moral support, but he was so upset, I figured that might only make things worse." He paused and cleared his throat. "I guess maybe you're away from the phone right now." Another silence. Then he sighed, and she heard a tapping noise. She envisioned him striking a hard surface with a pencil or pen. "I'd really like a chance to finish our conversation. How's about calling me tomorrow when you have a few minutes? I'll be in and out most of the day, but I can check my messages."

He left her both his home and cell phone number. Then in a husky tenor that tugged at her heart, he ended by saying, "I know you're nervous about seeing me again. Let's talk about that. All right? There's nothing we can't work out, Bethany. *Nothing*. Take a chance on me. That's all I'm asking. I promise you'll never regret it." He hesitated, then said, "No good-byes. Catch you later."

When he broke the connection, Bethany released a pent-up breath, unaware until that moment that she'd even been holding it. *Ryan*. She closed her eyes, his words replaying in her mind. *Take a chance on me*.

Ryan was opening a can of soup for supper when a knock sounded at the side door. Glancing at the copper-framed kitchen clock, he saw that it was after nine. Wondering if there were problems with one of the brood mares, he quickly wiped his hands and went to answer the summons. He couldn't have been more surprised when he saw that his caller was none other than Jake Coulter.

Standing with his booted feet spread apart and his hands shoved in the pockets of his brown leather jacket, Jake stared hard at Ryan for a moment before he stated his business. "We need to talk."

Ryan opened the door wider and stepped back, gesturing for the other man to enter. After moving over the threshold, Jake panned the great room with brilliant blue eyes that reminded Ryan strongly of Bethany's, the only difference being that hers reflected gentleness and sweetness while her brother's were sharp as razors. Jake's attention lingered on the newspapers lying on the ivory carpet beside the teal recliner.

"I was fixing a bite to eat," Ryan said, leading the way into the large adjoining kitchen. "Can I offer you something to drink?"

"What'cha got?"

"Coke, carbonated spring water, beer." Ryan thought about offering some of Hazel Turk's wine as a purgative for what ailed the man, but he resisted the urge. "I've got some hard stuff as well. Name your poison."

"A beer suits me fine." Jake slung his jacket over the back of a chair, then sat down at the oak table. Glancing from Ryan to the adjacent brick wall encompassing the kitchen fireplace, he said, "This isn't what I expected."

"Oh, and what did you expect?"

"Fancier digs, I guess. Nice place, but it's not elaborate like I pictured."

Ryan opened the refrigerator. "We're ranchers, knee deep in cow dung every day. Fancy is for fancy folk or church on Sunday."

Tapping his boot on the tile, Jake said, "Just a good old boy, is that it?"

Ryan took two beers from a shelf and elbowed the door closed. After handing one bottle to Jake, he sat down across from him. Twisting off the cap, he said, "Did you drive clear out here to take shots at me, Jake?"

Jake flipped his bottle cap in the air, palmed it on the descent with a quick snap of his wrist, and then lay it on the table. He took a slug of beer, whistling as he exhaled, and then settled back, his eyes glittering as he met Ryan's querying gaze. "I'm here to talk to you about my sister."

Expecting to be told to stay away from Bethany, Ryan tensed. "So, start."

Jake thoughtfully eyed the gold lettering on the bottle label. "She'll kill me when she finds out I came here. I interfere in her business more than I probably should, and this is definitely sticking my nose where it doesn't belong."

"Nothing you say is going to keep me away from her. Only she can make that call, and I'll do everything in my power to change her mind, even if she does."

A muscle moved in Jake's cheek. "And friendship's all you have in mind?"

The man's eyes were a hell of a lot sharper than mere razor blades, Ryan decided. They cut through him like laser beams. It was one thing to tell Bethany that all he expected was friendship and quite another to get her brother to buy it. "No, friendship isn't all I've got in mind," Ryan admitted. "Just for the record, however, if you tell her I said that, I'll deny it."

"So you flat-out lied to her."

"Whether I lied depends entirely on one's definition of friendship."

"Don't play games. Friendship and intimacy are two different things."

"In your opinion. I'm from another school and believe all relationships need a strong foundation, and the strongest foundation is friendship. This will give Bethany and me something solid to build on later, later being the key word in that statement. She needs time. I understand that, and I'll give it to her."

"Bottom line, you intend to have an intimate relationship with my sister, and you're using the friendship ploy to lull her into a false sense of security."

"That pretty much covers it." Ryan half expected Coulter to come up off the chair when he made the admission.

Instead Jake just nodded. "And then what?"

"I'm sorry? Exactly what is the question?"

"After you seduce her, then what? I don't want her getting hurt, Kendrick. She isn't the kind you can just use and dump, not if you have any decency."

Ryan touched a fingertip to a droplet of condensation on his beer bottle. "I have no intention of using her and dumping her, Jake. I'm in for the long haul."

Jake laughed sourly. "The long haul? Tell me, does that include vows and forever after? Or will you scat when you start to feel bored?"

"Vows and forever after."

Jake didn't attempt to conceal his surprise. "Just like that."

"No, not 'just like that.' I'm in love with her."

"You only just met her a week ago."

"I know exactly when I met her, and it hasn't been quite a week. Time doesn't play into it." Ryan shrugged and sighed. "I can't explain what I mean by that, so don't ask. I just know, is all."

"It's called physical attraction."

"I know what physical attraction feels like. This is more. Laugh your ass off if you want, but this is it for me."

"Are you always so quick to make decisions about women?"

"I never have before. Bethany's different."

"How?"

"She just is." A picture of her face swept through Ryan's mind, and he smiled slightly. "Any man with eyes can see that she's different, Jake." He arched a brow. "Why else would you be here? You know exactly how vulnerable she is. And it scares the holy hell out of you."

"Yeah, it does. I'm afraid you'll hurt her."

"I won't."

Jake relaxed on the chair. "You're really taken with her, aren't you?"

"You could say that. I know you're worried. I sympathize with that. But you've got my personal guarantee it's unnecessary. She'll be in good hands."

"There are things you don't know, things that may change your mind."

"I doubt it."

Jake leaned forward, bracing his arms on his knees. "Humor me and listen. If nothing I tell you in the next few minutes throws you off course, fine by me, but just in case it goes the other way, do her a favor and turn tail right now—before you break her heart. She's been badly hurt once already, Ryan. It took her nearly two years to get over it."

"She still isn't over it. Trust me on that. She still isn't over it."

Jake conceded the point with a nod, took a sip of beer, and then swore under his breath. "So she told you about him, did she?"

"No. Just his name, and only that because I insisted."

"Shortly after the accident, he took up with a girl who'd been Bethany's best friend since kindergarten."

"Sweet Christ." Ryan's stomach clenched. "Her best friend?"

"That's right. In terms of betrayal, it was a double whammy. Before Bethany was transported to Portland for surgery, the two of them went to see her every night at the hospital, acting as if they cared while they were having a thing on the side. Nan got pregnant, and Paul married her in Reno without telling Bethany beforehand. Shame and cowardice. The little son of a bitch did a real job on her. He couldn't bear to look her in the eye and admit what a jerk he was. She had to read about it in the paper. There she lay, trapped on that damned bed, still wearing the promise ring he'd given her, and she came across the marriage announcement in a paper from home. I was there when she found it. She turned as white as a sheet."

"Her best friend? Some friend."

"Exactly. Someone she'd trusted and loved all her life. The worst of it was, the marriage didn't last three months. I'm not sure which hurt Bethany more, Paul's defection or Nan's betrayal. I only know it was the kind of hurt that ran too deep for tears. She just stared off into space with an awful look in her eyes and took off the ring. After that, she seemed—hell, I don't know the word for it. Diminished, somehow, like the life went out of her."

Silence. Ryan pictured Bethany's face again and those big eyes that revealed her every thought and feeling. He sincerely hoped he never ran across good old Paul. He'd plant a fist in his teeth. "I'm not going to break her heart again, Jake. If that's all that's worrying you, rest easy. I'm not perfect and I'm bound to make mistakes, but hurting her that way will never be one of them."

Jake gave him a searching look. "I honestly believe it'd destroy her."

"If there's one thing I can say with absolute certainty about Kendrick men, it's that we're loyal. We don't step out on our women, and we sure as hell don't run like scalded dogs when the going gets rough."

"It doesn't worry you that she may be unable to enjoy a normal sex life?" Jake asked bluntly. "She has no sensation in certain parts of her body that are more or less vital to a woman's enjoyment."

Ryan took another swallow of beer before answering. "I was a little worried about the sex at first. I'll admit it."

"And now?"

"Now I'm not." At the vague answer, irritation flared in Jake's eyes. Ryan struggled to suppress a grin. "My mom's a nurse. I learned some very interesting things from her, namely that lack of sensation isn't a death knell. There's good chemistry between Bethany and me, and that's more than lots of people begin a marriage with. If problems crop up, we'll work our way through them. I'm willing to be inventive if it's necessary."

"Inventive." Jake curled his lip. "And you'll be content with that?"

Ryan sighed. "We're both unattached males around thirty. Can you sit there and tell me good sex with someone you don't love leaves you feeling content and happy afterward, or that you don't wish for more?"

"No, of course not."

"Me neither, and I'm sick to death tired of wishing for more. I feel content and happy when I'm with your sister. Does that make any sense?"

"Yeah, it makes a lot of sense," Jake said.

"The way I see it, if certain things about our personal life don't fit the usual mold, will I really give a shit? If we're happy together and we can please each other, what difference does it make *how* we do it?"

"None, I guess." Jake smiled slightly. "What if she can't carry a child to term? There is a big possibility of that. Her spinal surgeon told her in no uncertain terms she shouldn't have kids."

That took Ryan by surprise. He'd read about brain-dead women who'd carried children to term, and a woman couldn't get much more paralyzed than that. "She can't have kids? Paralysis doesn't interfere with fertility. I've been reading up on it on the Internet. I never saw any mention of that."

Jake shrugged. "Reicherton, her spinal surgeon, said she'd probably miscarry. Special problems of some kind. The point is, that's a possibility. How do you feel about it?"

"I can live with it."

"I'd think a man with all your land and money would want kids of his own."

"Naturally I'd love to, but I'm prepared to adopt if it's necessary."

"Don't pay this lip service. My sister may never have children. If I've got a vote, I'd just as soon she never tried. After her last surgery, she got a blood clot in one of her legs. A real humdinger that left the vein per-

manently narrowed with residual fibers from the clot that interfere with
some little valves in there. They'd probably take her off her medicine
while she was pregnant, increasing the risk of a second clot. We could
have lost her with the last one."

"I certainly won't get her pregnant if a doctor tells me it's dangerous.
But I have to point out that exercise and good muscle tone will greatly
improve a condition like that. If she gets on a good program, she probably won't need medicine."

"Exercise?" Jake sighed and rolled his eyes, the gesture reminding Ryan
so sharply of Bethany that he nearly smiled. "Right. I'll get her started tomorrow. Jogging, do you think?"

"Go ahead. Be a smart ass. I've been reading stuff, like I told you. Did
you know there are treadmills equipped with special harnesses so even
quadriplegics can walk regularly and keep their legs muscles toned?"

"Yes, and they carry price tags equal to the national debt."

"I can afford it," Ryan said softly.

Jake sighed wearily. "So you've thought of everything and still mean
to pursue this."

Ryan chuckled. "Is that what this is about? You were hoping to scare
me off? Save it, Coulter. You're not going to hit me with anything that will
throw me that bad, nothing I won't find a way to deal with. I'll also remind you I've got money out the kazoo. One of the main reasons handicapped people can't lead more normal, active lives is because their
insurance peters out on them, and they've got no financial resources with
which to modify their environment."

Jake narrowed an eye. "What if the state won't approve her as an
adoptive parent?"

"There are private agencies, and as I just pointed out, money isn't a
problem. We'll be able to adopt children, guaranteed."

"How will your family feel about that? Will they accept an adopted kid?"

"My kids will be loved, adopted or not."

"You really are serious about marrying her," Jake mused softly.

"Hell, yes, I'm serious."

After searching Ryan's gaze for a long moment, Jake finished off his
beer. "You got another one of these hiding in there?"

"It's a long drive back to town. You sure you want another one?"

"My limit's two when I'm driving. Yeah, I'll have another one."

Ryan fetched them both a second round. When he was settled back on
his chair again, Jake said, "It appears you've done your homework and
know what you're getting into."

"That's right."

"That being the case, there's only one more thing I want to say to you, Kendrick. Once it's said, maybe we can take a shot at becoming friends."

Ryan shrugged. "So far, I don't much like you, but stranger things have happened."

Jake grinned. "I don't much like you, either, but my sister does. I guess her vote carries the day. I'll back off. No more interference. You'll have an open playing field all the way. Just understand one thing." His smile faded and a dangerous glint crept into his eyes. "If you hurt her—if you cause her to shed so much as a single tear—you'll answer to me. And I promise you, when I'm done kicking your ass, you'll rue the day your daddy looked at your mama with a twinkle in his eye."

❦ CHAPTER EIGHT ❦

It had been nine years since Bethany had last attended a Crystal Falls Rancher's Association dinner, but the event proved to be much the same as she remembered. It was still held at the Ranchers' Co-op Grange, a cavernous hall at the edge of town in which countless tables were set up around a central dance floor. During the meal, the association president competed with the din of flatware clinking on china to give a long speech peppered with microphone whistles and bad jokes that elicited polite laughter from his audience.

While Bethany ate, she exchanged amused glances with her twenty-eight-year-old brother, Hank. Jake's date, a new acquaintance named Muriel, was a novelty. The redhead was pretty in a flashy, voluptuous way, which was undoubtedly what had caught Jake's eye, but her taste in clothes was appalling. Tonight she wore a tight sequin dress that showcased her generous curves in emerald green. The neckline plunged so low that her bosom threatened to spill out onto her plate every time she leaned forward to take a bite.

The Coulter males and Bethany's mother watched in horrified fascination. Bethany could barely keep a straight face. *Poor Jake.* She doubted he'd ever invite a woman to be around his family on the first date again. Bethany and her mom wore dark, modest dresses: Bethany's a jersey, Mary's a lightweight wool.

"Ohmigawd!" Muriel fairly bounced on her chair when she saw the band setting up. "I just *love* live music. Are we gonna dance, Jake?"

Jake's gaze shot like a bullet to his date's jiggling bosom, and his face turned an interesting shade of burnished brown with burgundy undertones. "I think they play mostly country western. That probably isn't your cup of tea."

"Oh, I like all kinds of dancing. Fast, slow, and everything in between."

Jake's smile was strained. "Fantastic."

"Save at least one dance for me, Muriel," Hank inserted, his blue eyes twinkling.

Jake's return glare could have pulverized granite. In that moment Bethany could see why so many people in Crystal Falls believed that her oldest brother was a horse whisperer. His eyes were such a vivid blue in contrast to his dark skin tone, his gaze had a cold fire that almost burned.

Bethany bent her head and pretended intense interest in her steak. The moment Jake looked away, she elbowed Hank in the ribs. "Behave yourself."

"So, tell us, Muriel," Bethany's mother, a matronly brunette with gentle blue eyes and a warm smile, said politely. "How did you meet our son?"

Muriel batted her caked black lashes. The bleary, vacuous expression in her pretty green eyes clearly wasn't entirely due to contact lenses. "Which one?"

Mary cast a bewildered look at her big, dark-haired husband, who sat beside her. Amusement danced in Harv Coulter's azure eyes. He shrugged his broad shoulders, his sharply hewn features softening in a smile as he poured his wife more wine.

"Me, Muriel," Jake whispered. "You just met Hank and my folks tonight."

"Oh." Muriel smiled blissfully and glanced back at Mary. "Jake and I met each other at Safeway. He was squeezing the avocados."

"Ah." Mary cast her eldest son a questioning look. "I see."

"I've never been able to pick out good avocados," Muriel elaborated. "So I asked him to show me how. The next thing we knew, the whole pile came toppling down. Avocados everywhere! When we were finished picking up the mess, one thing led to another, and he asked for my phone number." She winked at Jake. "I doubted he'd really call me. But he did, so here I am."

"I wonder what she was wearing," Hank whispered to Bethany. "I've got twenty that says Jake went blind every time she leaned over."

Bethany touched her napkin to her lips, doing her best not to giggle. "Behave yourself," she whispered again.

"You're no fun anymore," Hank complained.

By the time their meal was cleared away and the band began playing its first number, everyone at the Coulter table was relieved to hear Jake ask Muriel to dance. As the couple moved onto the crowded dance floor, Harv chuckled and said, "I'll bet Jake thinks twice before he goes near a produce section again."

"She's a nice enough girl," Mary said with her typical Pollyanna sweetness. "A bit of a dim bulb, perhaps, but that isn't her fault."

Harv grinned and winked at Hank. "She definitely doesn't hide what little brilliance she has."

Hank, who'd come without a date, excused himself and went to ask a blonde at a nearby table to dance. After watching his tall, dark-haired son walk away, Harv glanced at Mary. "Well, honey? You want to polish my belt buckle?"

Mary frowned. "Are you sure you're up to dancing?"

"The doctor says it's stress that'll kill me, not a little good old-fashioned exercise. I work out every morning. Where's the difference?"

Mary smiled and glanced at Bethany. "Will you be all right, darling? I hate to leave you sitting here all alone."

Bethany waved a hand. "Don't be silly, Mom. I enjoy just watching."

As her parents moved onto the floor, Bethany allowed her smile to slip. She glanced at the empty chairs around the table, resigned to another boring evening. She would have preferred to stay home with her brushes and paints.

Ah, well. She turned her chair to have a better view of the dancers, her fingertips tapping in time to the music. The hall suddenly grew dark and a rotating sphere sprang to life overhead, casting multicolored spirals of light onto the floor. She scanned the crowd. Her folks had vanished, but Jake was as easy to spot as if he were dancing with a beacon.

As the next number began, she saw a tall, dark-haired cowboy stepping onto the floor with a brunette tucked under his arm. The way he moved struck a chord, his loose stride and the fluid shift of his broad shoulders familiar. *Ryan.* Dressed in black with his shirt open at the throat to reveal a V of bronze chest, he cut such a handsome figure that her heart rapped against her ribs.

His hair glinting in the light like polished onyx, he leaned down to catch something the woman said. His face creased in a grin that flashed white teeth. Then he threw back his head and laughed, swinging her in the circle of his arm to face him as they began to dance. They made an attractive couple, he so tall, muscular, and dark, she so dainty and beautiful. The lively western beat required fast footwork, which they executed flawlessly, his black dress boots dwarfing her sassy high heels as he cut a circle around her, then twirled her back into his arms. Bethany knew they had danced with each other many times before.

She concentrated her gaze on the woman, taking in her burgundy silk blouse and skirt, the latter full and swirling gracefully around her shapely legs. When Ryan settled a hand low on the woman's back, Bethany couldn't help but notice how the splay of his fingers stretched to the curve of her hip. Her dainty build accentuated his muscular bulk, the two of them a study in contrasts.

She couldn't believe how it hurt to see him dancing with another woman. And, oh, how that rankled. She curled her hands into fists, then relaxed them when she realized what she was doing. What difference did it make to her if he had come with someone else?

A very beautiful someone else.

An awful, achy sensation filled her chest. She tried to look away and watch the other couples, but her gaze remained fixed on Ryan. Oh, how she wished she were the woman in his arms. She would have given almost anything to have two functional legs so she might dance with him until dawn.

When the song ended and he turned to guide his partner off the floor, he scanned the tables, his gaze gliding past Bethany, then jerking back to settle on her with glittering intensity. Even in the dim light, she saw his jaw clench. He veered toward her, drawing the woman along as he cut through the crowd.

The last thing Bethany wanted was to meet Ryan Kendrick's date for the evening. She considered wheeling away to hide in the ladies' room, but such behavior struck her as being childish. Instead, she forced herself to smile.

"Hello!" she called as they drew closer.

Ryan's firm mouth twitched at the corners then slanted into a grin that made her bones feel in danger of melting. He kept his arm around the woman's slender shoulders as he drew to a stop near the table. "Bethany." His gaze moved slowly over her. "I had no idea you were going to be here tonight."

The woman, who was even more beautiful up close than she'd appeared to be at a distance, beamed a friendly smile, her big, liquid brown eyes revealing no hint of animosity. She glanced expectantly at Ryan.

Catching her look, he said, "Maggie, I'd like you to meet a very good friend of mine, Bethany Coulter. Bethany, my brother Rafe's wife, Maggie."

Heat flagged Bethany's cheeks as she shook hands with Ryan's sister-in-law. "It's a pleasure to meet you, Maggie."

"The pleasure's all mine." Maggie's eyes sparkled with warmth. "Ryan mentioned that you enjoy going to the mud pulls."

"Yes, very much."

"Me, too. Maybe the four of us can go together sometime soon."

Bethany glanced at Ryan. "I'll look forward to it," she settled for saying.

"It's a date, then? That'll be fun. I'll get Rafe's mom to watch the kids, and we'll make an evening of it. Do you like Mexican?"

It took Bethany a moment to register what she meant. "I love Mexican, the hotter the better."

Maggie nodded decisively. "I'm going to like you. Another bean and tortilla fanatic! We found the greatest restaurant. The atmosphere there is absolutely wonderful, very relaxed and friendly."

"Give Maggie a generous helping of greasy tortilla chips with a huge bowl of fiery hot salsa, and she thinks the place has great ambience," Ryan said.

Maggie elbowed him in the ribs. "Don't listen to him, Bethany. The truth is, he wouldn't recognize authentic Mexican or delightful ambience if they ran up and bit him on the leg."

Ryan groaned and splayed a hand over his stomach.

"Poor baby." Maggie's eyes twinkled with mischief. "There's nothing sadder than seeing a big strong man quail with dread at the thought of eating an enchilada." She grinned at Bethany. "He'll take on a thousand-pound bull bare-handed, but a bottle of hot sauce sends him running."

Bethany couldn't help but laugh. Maggie was delightful, and Bethany was completely charmed by the pair's teasing banter. It reminded her of the way she and her brothers needled each other.

Maggie turned and lightly touched Ryan's shirtsleeve. "I'm off to grab my husband before the next song. He promised to dance with me." She turned back to Bethany and extended a delicate hand. "It's been great meeting you, Bethany. Please, make Ryan bring you out to the Rocking K for a visit soon. We'll run off the guys and have a good old-fashioned coffee klatch."

"I'd enjoy that very much," Bethany replied, and sincerely meant it. Maggie Kendrick was an easy person to like.

As she walked away, Bethany looked questioningly at Ryan, who grinned lazily and straddled a chair facing her, his crossed arms resting loosely on its back. After staring at her until she wanted to squirm, he said, "Hi," his voice a husky caress that seemed to wrap her in warmth. "Fancy meeting you here."

"It's a small world, after all, I guess." She thought that sounded stupid and wished she'd said something else. Only what? When he looked at her like that, her brain seemed to freeze.

He nodded, his gaze teasing hers as his mouth slanted into another slow grin. "Too small for you to avoid me. Is that what you're thinking?"

At the moment she had difficulty holding onto a thought.

"Do all men make you so nervous?" he suddenly asked.

"Nervous?"

His gaze dropped to her hands, which were clenched and white-knuckled on her lap. "I don't bite." A heated gleam slipped into his eyes. "Never hard enough to hurt, anyway." He reached out to touch a fingertip to the end of her nose. "What are you doing, sitting here all alone?"

"They'll be back soon. Right now, they're all out dancing."

He glanced at the empty table. "This can't be much fun."

"I'm fine." She shrugged. "My dancing days are over, but that doesn't mean everyone else can't enjoy themselves."

He studied her thoughtfully. "I'll bet you loved it."

"Loved what?"

"Dancing."

Memories. Bethany tried never to dwell on things she could no longer do, but dancing was a tough one, especially when she found herself sitting at the edge of a dance floor. "Yes, I did love it," she admitted. "My dad taught me to waltz when I was about seven, and from that moment on, I was hooked. Whenever we went to a function with music, I drove him and my brothers crazy, begging them to dance with me. I liked all kinds, fast or slow, it didn't matter."

He turned his hands palm up and gazed solemnly at the lines etched there. When he met her gaze again, he said, "Do you miss it terribly?"

Normally Bethany told polite lies, but she found it difficult, if not impossible, to tell him anything but the truth. "Yes, very much." She tried for what she hoped was a bright smile. "There are a number of things I miss a lot."

"Does friendship have to be one of them?"

She laughed. She couldn't help it. "Has anyone ever told you that you're as tenacious as a pit bull once you sink your teeth into something?"

"My mom's words, almost exactly." He let his hands dangle, his broad shoulders lifting in a shrug. "What can I say? I made you a proposition, and you haven't given me your answer yet. Is the friendship on or not?"

"I'm still mulling it over."

"While you mull, can I campaign?"

She laughed again. "You're impossible."

"Just think of all the fun we can have."

The twinkle in his eyes was full of promise. "Doing what?" she couldn't resist asking.

"The possibilities are endless."

"That's a cop-out if ever I've heard one."

"Hey, if all else fails, you can teach me to paint."

At the suggestion, Bethany laughed until tears filled her eyes. She would almost regain her composure—*almost*—and then she'd look at his huge hands and start laughing again.

"I'm offended."

She wiped under her eyes. "I'm sorry. Really. I'm sure you could learn. It's just—" Her voice went thin with suppressed giggles. "Somehow you just don't strike me as the type who'd have the patience for it."

Ryan grinned, thinking to himself that it would all depend on what he used as a canvas. Her flawless ivory skin would sure as hell hold his interest. He'd start by painting the petals of a daisy around her navel and move on from there.

"Honest answer," he said, leaning forward over the chair to hold her gaze. "Right now, this very instant, aren't you having fun?"

Her smile winked out, and a dark, worried look came into her eyes. "Yes."

"Point made. Doing nothing, we have a great time. Just think how much fun we can have if we set our minds to it."

"Probably a lot."

He nodded and pushed to his feet. "Hold that thought."

She was frowning bewilderedly, not to mention looking abandoned and a little lost as he walked away. Knowing he'd soon be back, Ryan smiled as he shouldered his way through the milling crowd toward the bandstand.

Everyone in her family had returned to the table and then left to dance again when Bethany saw Ryan striding back through the crowd toward her. His silver belt buckle flashed in the dim light with every shift of his lean hips. He was so handsome that she allowed herself a brief moment of fancy, pretending he was a stranger who didn't know about her paralysis and was heading her way to ask her to dance. Scotch that. If she was going to dream, why not go all out and dream that she could actually walk?

He sauntered to a stop, gave her a slow, crooked grin that made her pulse skitter, and said, "May I have the next dance, Miss Coulter?"

For just an instant, Bethany felt as if he'd punched her in the solar plexus. Didn't he realize how much she would love to dance with him? Sometimes, if she allowed herself to think about the years of confinement that stretched ahead of her, she felt like a rat in a cage.

"I'd love to," she said flippantly.

"I was hoping you'd say that."

He stepped around to grasp the handles of her chair. As he set off for the front exit, Bethany glanced over her shoulder at him. "What are you doing?"

He flashed her another grin and winked. "Wait and see."

Once in the vestibule, which served double duty as a cloakroom, he started rifling through the coats and wraps hanging on the rod along one wall.

"Are we going outside?" she asked.

"Yep."

"Did you misplace your jacket?"

"Nope."

"Well, if you're looking for mine, it's way down at the other end."

He came up with a heavy black sweater, gave it a long look, and said, "A little big, but it'll do." He turned, advanced on Bethany, and started stuffing her arms down the sleeves. "Your coat would be too bulky for what I have in mind."

"But—this isn't mine."

"I know," he said as he tugged the garment up onto her shoulders.

"Whose is it?"

A mischievous glint entered his steel-blue eyes. "Beats the hell out of me, but we'll have it back before she ever misses it."

"Ryan!" she cried as he wheeled her toward the front doors.

"What?"

"I can't swipe someone's sweater."

He chuckled. "You're not swiping it."

"I'm not?"

"Nope. I swiped it, you're just wearing it."

"Either way! I'm not taking someone's sweater."

"Yeah, you are." He leaned over her to shove open the doors and push her outside. "Relax. What can they do, arrest us for short-term sweater theft?"

Bethany was grateful for the sweater when the frigid night air wrapped around her. "You're crazy. And you'll freeze out here without a coat. Where are we going, anyway?"

"You'll see, and trust me, I won't freeze. I spend so much time out-doors, I'm inured to the cold."

"'Inured?' Cowboys aren't supposed to know such words."

"Beg pardon, ma'am. I'll work on it. Get me a wad of chew, spit between sentences, and scratch where I shouldn't. Goin' to college flat ruint
me."

"I didn't know you attended university. What was your major?"

"Animal husbandry and ag. Got degrees in both." He turned left to
push her along a cement walkway that circled to the back of the building. "Never did figure out why any man in his right mind would wanna
play husband to a bull. Got good marks in female anatomy 101, though."

She laughed at that. "I'll just bet you did."

"When I came home with my sheepskins in hand, I could guess a
woman's measurements at a hundred yards. After all the money he'd
forked out for tuition, the old man was flat impressed."

Bethany grinned, imagining a younger Ryan fresh out of college.
With his looks, he must have been as close to lethal as a young man
could get. "What school did you attend?"

"Oregon State. Most goat ropers go there so they can strut around cam-
pus in their Stetsons and spit fancy. It's a requirement, knowin' how to
spit, and it takes a real knack. Sly, our foreman, can nail a fly at ten feet."

"I was raised on a ranch, remember. I know all about you cowboys. It
has been my observation that you're all full of bull."

"That's right. You have been around cowboys. I guess that means I
should cut the crap?"

"Good plan."

"I never took female anatomy 101. The rest is fact. I have an eye for female curves that won't quit. You, for instance. I could buy you a wardrobe,
from the skin out, and everything would fit perfectly. Any bets?"

"Oh, puh-leeze."

"Women. Why is it they're never interested in seeing a guy show off?"

"Because we're seldom impressed."

"Thirty-two, B. Twenty-one inch waist. You impressed yet?"

He was amazingly accurate, and knowing that he'd looked at her that
closely made her skin tingle. "If you like treading on thin ice, you're doing
well."

He chuckled and fell quiet. To their right was a parking lot. In the
moonlight the cars and trucks resembled shiny-shelled beetles. Above
them, the moon hung like a china supper plate against a backdrop of
midnight-blue velvet sequined with stars. The cold breeze carried the
essence of fir and pine, drawing Bethany's gaze to the mountains that
ringed the basin.

She sighed. "It's a beautiful night. Just look at that sky."

"Nothing quite like it, is there? I've heard Montana referred to as sky country. I figure those folks have never been to Oregon on a clear night."

He wheeled her to a covered breezeway at the rear of the grange. The back doors were propped open, and they could hear the music almost as clearly from there as from inside. The band was finishing the current number. Before they began the next song, Ryan stepped around her chair and leaned down, coming almost nose to nose with her.

"Put your arms around my neck, sweetheart."

"Whatever for?"

He grasped her wrists and lifted her arms himself. "Because," he whispered, "we're going to dance."

"Oh, no, I—"

Before she could complete the protest, he slipped an arm around her waist and plucked her from the chair. Left with no choice, she gave a startled squeak and grabbed onto him. *"Ryan!"*

"It's all right. I swear I won't drop you." He shifted her against him, cupping one big hand over her posterior. "Hold tight. You hanging on?"

For dear life. "Yes, and so are you. No funny business. I can feel that, you know."

"You can?" He slipped his arm from around her waist and moved his other hand down to her rump. Intertwining his fingers, he formed a seat of sorts to hold her hips snugly against his. "I thought paraplegics were totally numb from the waist down."

"Not me. My spinal injury is at L2 and didn't damage all the—" She jumped and gave him a look. "What are you doing?"

He grinned and winked. "My thumb was in a crick. You really *do* have feeling there."

She narrowed an eye. "Yes, and if you do any more wiggling, you'll pay."

"No more. I promise."

"This will never work. I appreciate the thought. It's very sweet, but—"

"Shut up," he whispered.

The first notes of the next number drifted to them, and she realized it was the band's rendition of Montgomery's hit song "I Swear." Tears sprang to her eyes, for the instant she recognized the tune, she knew Ryan had requested it.

"Dance with me," he whispered.

"I feel foolish."

"Who'll see? Only me, and I'm your best bud, so I don't count. Besides, why should you feel foolish?"

"My legs are dangling. My feet will thump your shins."

"Those soft slippers won't hurt my shins," he assured her.

And with that, he swept her into a waltz.

Bethany expected it to feel awkward. As he executed the first few steps, she was rigid with tension, afraid he'd stumble and drop her, or that she was too heavy and he'd exhaust himself.

Instead, it was glorious, and she felt as if she were floating, his strength her buoyancy. *Dancing.* It wasn't really dancing, of course. She kept telling herself that. But it seemed as though it was. *Dancing.* Oh, God. She'd yearned to do this a hundred times over the last eight years, and now she actually was. It gave her the most incredible feeling. Free and light as a bird, caught in the arms of a tall, dark cowboy.

Bethany straightened her arms, let her head fall back, and closed her eyes, wishing the feeling would never end. "Oh, Ryan."

"Good?"

"Oh, yes. Oh, *yes.* You just can't know."

Watching the expressions that crossed her face, Ryan thought he had a fair idea. How must it feel, he wondered, always to be trapped in that damned chair, and now, suddenly, to be swirling in the moonlight?

Damn, she was sweet. Holding her like this was as close to heaven as he ever hoped to get. *Bethany.* A dreamy smile curved her mouth, conveying pleasure so intense he doubted she could put it into words. He imagined making her smile exactly that way while he made love to her, hearing her sigh like that when he kissed her.

Someday . . .

For now it was enough just to hold her like this in the moonlight and see her smile, to know she was happy and that in some small way, he was responsible for that.

By the end of the second number, Ryan's energy was starting to flag. She didn't weigh a lot, but dancing ceaselessly while he supported an extra one hundred and ten pounds took its toll. He hated to return her to the chair, and he wished with all his heart he didn't have to.

Unfortunately, even good things had to end. He made it through a third dance, and then his legs started to give out on him.

She blinked when the music ceased, and he drew to a reluctant stop. The dreamy, slightly befuddled expression in her eyes told him just how much she had enjoyed the dances and that she would cherish the memory long after the evening was over.

"Oh, Ryan." She bestowed a glowing smile on him, her eyes shimmering with gladness and tears. She said nothing more, but those two words conveyed so very much, far more than she probably realized, a gratitude that ran too deep for words, and a bewildered incredulity because he had done something so completely unexpected, simply to give her pleasure.

It was her expression of incredulity that touched him the most. It had been such a small thing, really, lifting her from that chair and taking a few turns around the breezeway. He'd worked harder countless times, and with far less reward. Could there be a sweeter gift than seeing Bethany smile?

She would never spend another evening sitting alone at a table while everyone else danced and had a good time, he promised himself. Never again.

He gently returned her to her chair, which he was quickly coming to realize was a prison without bars. Leaning low, he thumbed a tear from beneath her eye and whispered, "Hey, what's this? I meant for it to be fun, not make you cry."

"Oh, it *was* fun," she said. "I just—" She shook her head and wiped her cheeks. "I'm sorry. This is silly. It's just that I've wanted to dance so many times, and I didn't think I could. That was as close to dancing as it gets. I can't tell you how wonderful it felt." She smiled tremulously. "Thank you, Ryan."

Resting his hands on the chair arms, he held her gaze for a searching moment. "We can have a lot of fun together, you and I. No risks, no expectations, just friendship. I can make it work if only you'll give me a chance."

"I'm tempted," she said with a wet laugh. "You make it so hard to say no."

"Then don't."

She caught her bottom lip between her teeth, her eyes reflecting hesitation and uncertainty. "Let me think about it."

"What's to think about?"

"If I'm around you very much, I'm afraid I'll do something ill-advised and totally dumb, like fall in love with you," she admitted shakily.

Ryan was counting on it.

❧ CHAPTER NINE ❧

The following afternoon on her way home from Bend, where she'd gone to pick up an order of custom-made saddle blankets for the store, Bethany ran into bad weather. Initially, she couldn't quite believe her eyes when a blob of white struck the windshield. The weather forecast hadn't predicted snow.

Within seconds, visibility was reduced to almost nothing. She flipped the windshield wipers onto high and peered at the veil of white ahead of her. Gusts of wind buffeted the stands of fir and pine that bordered the road and swept across the pavement to form shallow drifts on each shoulder.

This couldn't be happening. It was the last of April, for pity's sake, far too late for snow. She slowed down and tightly gripped the steering wheel. She was at a high elevation right now. In a matter of minutes, she'd probably drop out of this into heavy rain. Rain, she could handle. Just as long as she didn't need snow chains, she'd be all right.

Approximately ten minutes passed. The windshield wipers went *swish-thunk—swish-thunk,* the rhythmic sound seeming to mock her as the blades pushed aside the thick buildup of snow. The highway was covered now. *Oh, God.* Her van didn't handle well on ice. Just yesterday over Sunday dinner, her brothers had been talking about getting her a four-wheel-drive SUV before next winter. A fat lot of good that did her now.

After turning on the stereo and switching from CD to FM, she tried to pick up a Crystal Falls radio station. When she located her favorite spot on the dial, a country-western channel that played only hit songs, she listened to the disc jockey's comments on the weather front with growing unease. *A freak snowstorm.* He advised against driving, even in town, unless people had a bona fide emergency. Several multi-car accidents had already occurred on the outskirts of Crystal Falls.

Nervous sweat beaded her face. She felt the rear end of the van lose traction and slip toward the shoulder. She needed to put on traction devices. Big problem. It would be sheer madness to get out of the van. If the vehicle was slipping and sliding, her chair would do the same.

Swish-thunk—swish-thunk. She turned off the stereo to listen. An occasional whining sound told her the back tires were losing their grip and spinning to grab hold again. Squinting to see up ahead, she could detect no letup in the downfall, only snow as far as she could see, forming a white wall. If she lost control and went off the road—well, it didn't bear thinking about.

Positive thoughts, she told herself. If she drove slowly and hugged the center of the road, she'd probably make it fine. It was silly to worry about things before they happened. Right?

Just as she thought that, the van fishtailed on a slight incline. She tried to steer into the skid and regain control, but the vehicle went into a spin. For a crazy instant, the world became a blur, the forested slopes at either side of the road whizzing past the windows like video images on fast-forward. Trees, snow, rocks, and sky. She clung hard to the steering wheel, her only anchor as she was flung sideways by the force of gravity.

Oh, God. The half-formed prayer was cut short when, with a sudden lurch, the van dove off into the ditch with such force that the front bumper plowed into the frozen earth. Bethany's teeth snapped together. The nylon strap that held her in her chair bit into her shoulder. She screamed and tried desperately to regain control of the vehicle, but the hand brake wouldn't work.

The undercarriage of the van jounced over the rough ground. Each time metal struck rock, the noise seemed to explode in the air around her. Through the swirling downfall, she glimpsed a looming blur of gray and white ahead. Still holding hard on the brake, she tried to stop, but the conditions were too slick. The van sped onward, unchecked, until it hit the obstacle, the resultant crunch of metal so deafening that it seemed to reverberate inside her skull.

Her head snapped forward, her face almost hitting the wheel. For a moment afterward, she just stared in befuddlement at the windshield, her one clear thought that the wipers were still working. With each pass, the left blade caught on a spray of gritty mud, making a *swish-scritch* sound that would soon drive her mad. She reached to turn off the wipers and then hesitated, imagining how claustrophobic she would feel, trapped and unable to see out.

And what was she thinking? That was the least of her problems. She'd just had a wreck. A *wreck.* There could be gas pouring from a crack in the tank—or she could be bleeding to death from a cut she didn't know she had. She sniffed the air. If the tank was ruptured, she'd surely smell fuel.

An absurd urge to laugh came over her. She found that vaguely alarming and wondered if she was in shock. The van was tipped at a crazy angle. Her purse and coat, which had been on the passenger seat, now lay on that side of the floorboard beyond her reach. A fine pickle, no question about it.

A rock, she decided. The van had crashed into a rock. Strike that. Any stone that large qualified as a boulder. Craning her neck to see over the dash, she tried to assess the damage. Through the swirl of snow, all she could tell for certain was that the hood looked crunched.

Oh, God—oh, God. She had to *do* something. Only what? All that kept her chair anchored in place were the restraints. If she dared to unfasten the straps, she might topple out of her chair.

Trembling with nerves, she checked her person, paying special attention to her legs because an injury there would cause no pain. As near as she could tell, she was unharmed. *Thank heaven.* She had seen no traffic for at least thirty minutes, so she couldn't count on a passerby to stop and help her.

The van was still running. That was good. Perhaps she'd be able to back out of the ditch and limp on home. The thought no sooner passed through her mind than she heard a hissing sound and saw a cloud of steam shoot from under the van's mangled hood. The engine gave two coughs, sputtered, and died.

Silence. It settled around her with unnerving thickness, broken only by the faint snapping sound of cooling metal.

"Wonderful!"

She rubbed a peephole on the fogged glass to peer out. The snow was already so deep, she could see no asphalt, not even in her skid marks.

"Stay calm." She took a deep breath and slowly let it out. "No major catastrophe here. Just a fender bender and a damaged radiator. No big deal."

Only for someone like her, it *was* a big deal. Like menacing specters looming from the mist, the huge, snow-laden trees that grew along the road bore witness to the remoteness of her location. The woods stretched for miles in all directions. For the first time in her life, she felt intimidated by the wilderness.

At the edges of her mind, panic mounted. An able-bodied woman would be able to climb over the console to get her coat, at least. Without a functional heater, she could very easily freeze to death out here.

With trembling hands she groped in the console, the contents of which were now tossed every which way. Where was her phone? She always kept it in there when she traveled. She cast a worried glance at her purse. After finishing her business in Bend, had she forgotten to return the cell phone to the console?

Yes. Of all the stupid, idiotic, *mindless* things to do.

She thought of all the times she'd harangued her brothers for being overprotective of her. *I'm a grown woman. I don't need anyone to watch out for me.* Those words came back to haunt her now. *I don't need anyone—I don't need anyone.* Pride talking, nothing more. At times like this, her helplessness was pounded home.

Well . . . there was no way around it. If the purse wouldn't come to her, she had to go to it. That cell phone was her only link to help. She couldn't just sit here until someone finally happened along and found her.

Heart in throat, she reached down to disengage the restraint straps that anchored both her and her chair behind the steering wheel. The hasp slipped free. For an instant, nothing happened. Bethany was about to breathe a sigh of relief. Then, with a suddenness that caught her by surprise, her chair flipped sideways, the right arm crashing against the console.

She fell sideways and forward, smacking the dash with her chest. The next instant she lay in a twisted heap on the floorboard, her head wedged against the passenger door, her neck in a painful crick, her useless legs sprawled and anchoring her lower body. *Oh, God.* She pushed and shoved, trying to right herself. The force of gravity fought against her; the van tipped at such a sharp angle that she was almost standing on her head.

Quickly out of breath from her struggle, she rested for a moment, horribly aware that she lay on top of her purse and coat. When her breathing evened out, she ignored the angle of her neck to tug on her purse. What seemed like a small eternity later, she finally wrested it free. She plucked out the phone and stared at it in concern, afraid she had damaged it in her fall. It looked intact.

She dialed the state police, praying as she did that the call would go through. When she heard a female dispatcher's voice, she went limp with relief. She quickly explained her dilemma.

"There are several accidents out that way," the woman said. "In some places, the traffic is backed up for miles both directions. Where are you, exactly?"

Bethany tried to recall the last road signs she'd seen and gave it her best guess. "I can't see a milepost to pinpoint my exact location."

"That's close enough. You're right on the highway, not all that far from town. The problem will be getting a car out there. It may take an hour or more, depending upon officer availability and how long it takes to clear the road. We're dealing with several emergency situations right now, the most urgent ones first."

Bethany stared at the fogged window above her, thinking that her situation was pretty urgent. "I understand. It's just that I'm in a rather difficult spot. You did hear me say I'm a paraplegic? I've fallen on the floorboard, and I'm lying on my coat. I'm not sure I'll even be able to cover up."

"Are you injured, ma'am?"

Bethany was tempted to say yes, just to get some help. It was no fun, lying in a twist with her neck bent sideways. But then she thought of the other people out on the road who'd been involved in accidents, people who might be injured and need assistance they might not get if she lied. "No, I'm not hurt," she admitted. "Just extremely uncomfortable and getting very cold."

"I'll get a car out there as quickly as I can," the dispatcher replied, her voice laced with concern. "Can you hold on for an hour or so?"

Bethany was loath to break the connection. "I'll be right here," she said, forcing a laugh.

After ending the call, she went back to staring up at the passenger door window, which, because it was partially shielded by the angle of the vehicle, wasn't completely covered with white. Looking at the falling snow from this angle was dizzying, making her feel as if she was inside an all-white kaleidoscope. Before long, her van would be completely covered. She just hoped the ditch wasn't so deep that a highway patrolman driving by would fail to see her.

A shiver racked her body. *Cold.* It seeped through the floor, its icy fingers curling around her. She had poor circulation in her legs, which didn't help. She tended to chill more easily than other people.

She set herself to the task of dragging her coat out from under her. *Impossible.* Her rump anchored the wool to the floorboard, and the downward tilt of the vehicle made it difficult to elevate her torso. She pushed and strained and twisted about, all to no avail. In the end, the stupid coat remained under her butt.

Blinking away tears of frustration, she settled for tugging one corner of the wool over her right leg. She told herself that at least the garment protected part of her body.

The seconds dragged. To see her watch, she had to wipe condensation from the crystal face. The dispatcher had said it would be an hour, possibly longer, before an officer could reach her. Judging by how badly she was already shivering, she hated to wait that long.

Ten minutes passed, and Bethany went from shivering to shuddering. She had no idea what the ambient temperature was. Her wool skirt and blouse provided adequate warmth in a heated room, but out here, she may as well have been wearing nothing.

She glanced at the phone. Jake would be at the store. She knew if she called him he'd move heaven and earth to reach her, which was exactly why she hesitated. Her situation wasn't so dire that she wanted her brother to put himself at risk, driving in these conditions.

In the space of five minutes, Bethany felt like a vibrating icicle. She recalled Ryan's swiping the sweater for her to wear last night and wished she had it now. On the tail of that thought, she remembered how strong and wonderfully warm his arms had felt, curled so firmly around her.

Ryan. Bethany blinked and stared at the snow-covered windshield above her. His ranch wasn't far away. Maybe the highway wasn't blocked between here and there.

She grabbed the phone, then hesitated. If she made this call, it would be an irrevocable step. *Friendship.* Normally she wouldn't find that frightening. As Ryan said, no one could have too many friends. But how many women had male friends so handsome that a mere grin could give them heart palpitations?

Stupid, so stupid. It wasn't as if the man was angling for a steamy affair, after all, or even hinting at one. Recalling the gentle way he'd held her last night and the aching sincerity she'd seen in his eyes when he'd spoken to her of friendship, she instinctively trusted him.

Decision time. She could be a total idiot and lie here, freezing to death unnecessarily, or she could take Ryan up on his offer of friendship.

She tried to remember his telephone number and couldn't, so she dialed information. A moment later she was punching in the number to his residence. *Please, be home, Ryan. Please, please, be home.*

Ryan was laying a fire when the phone rang. He brushed his hands clean on his jeans and stepped to the end table to grab the portable from its base. Thinking it was his mother calling again, he bypassed saying hello. "No, I don't want to join you and Dad for snow ice cream," he said with a chuckle. "I'd have to be nuts to go out in this."

"Ryan?" a shaky feminine voice said. "This is Bethany."

She sounded awful, and his heart caught with sudden fear. "Bethany? Honey, are you crying?"

"No, no. I'm just shivering."

The hair stood up on the nape of his neck. "Shivering?"

"From cold. I'm so sorry to call you like this, but I've gotten myself into a bit of a pickle."

She went on to describe her predicament. Ryan tightened his grip on the phone. He glanced out the sliding glass doors at the blizzard in progress. "Dear God, you're stranded in this?"

Her voice quaking in a way that alarmed him, she said, "I'm not hurt or anything. Please, don't get all upset. It's not that big a deal. I think my radiator is bashed. The engine coughed and quit, so I can't run the heater." He heard her take another shivery breath. "I'm sort of—lying in a heap on the floorboard." She laughed shakily. "On top of my coat, of course. Murphy's Law, and all that."

Ryan started to pace. Long, heel-stomping steps muffled by the carpet, his body taut with alarm. "Son of a bitch. Where are you, honey?"

The picture that formed in his mind of her lying on the floorboard sent sheer terror coursing through him. She could be bleeding to death from a cut on her legs and not even know it.

"Have you checked yourself for cuts?"

"Oh, yes. Not a mark that I could find. I'm fine, honestly. Just chilly."

Chilly? She sounded as if she was lying on a vibrating bed. "Where are you?" he asked again.

"You know the Eagle Ridge turnoff? I remember seeing the sign just before I went off the road. That isn't a terribly long way from you, is it? I mean—if it is, the driving conditions are so awful I can just wait for the police. There are wrecks between here and Crystal Falls, but they're working to get the roads cleared and can be here in an hour or so."

There was no way on earth Ryan would let her lie on a cold floorboard for an hour. He knew exactly where she was, and traveling as a crow flew, he could reach her in twenty minutes. "No worries. I'm used to getting around in snow."

"I just—" She broke off and sighed, the sound shrill, shaky, and conveying such weariness, he wished he were already there with her. "Do be careful, Ryan. I'll never forgive myself if you have a wreck, trying to reach me."

"You just hold tight, honey. I'm on my way. I've got blankets in the storage compartment of my snow horse. Rafe and I are members of Search and Rescue. You'll be snug as a bug in a rug before you know it."

After breaking the connection, Ryan left the house at a dead run, tug-ging on his jacket as he went. Seconds later, he threw open the doors to the snowmobile shed, thanking God and all His angels that he and Rafe were always ready for an emergency. He kept a heavy plastic storage trunk on the back of his snowmobile stocked with blankets, emergency food rations, and an extensive first aid kit. He grabbed some bungee cords from a hook on the wall and stuffed them in with the rescue sup-plies. Then he filled the tank with fuel.

In less than five minutes, he was headed for Eagle Ridge, traveling cross country over snow-covered pastureland and through heavily wooded areas where the winter snowpack still hadn't melted.

Bethany huddled as best she could on the floorboard, shivering so hard her teeth clacked. It seemed to her that hours went by before she heard the distant sound of an engine. Her heart leaped with gladness. She craned her neck, trying to see out the window above her, but the snow-fall was so thick, visibility was no more than a few feet.

Finally she heard what could only be Ryan's snowmobile approaching the highway to the north of her. The rumble grew faint, telling her the driver had turned the opposite way. Soon the sounds drifted into silence.

What if he failed to find her? She could no longer see out the wind-shield. What if her van was no longer visible to someone on the road?

Minutes later she heard the snowmobile returning. "Ryan!" she cried. "Ryan, I'm down here!"

When the vehicle finally rumbled to a stop somewhere near the van, she nearly wept with relief. The engine sputtered and went quiet. Then she heard boots crunching on the snow.

"Bethany?"

His voice sounded so wonderful. Before she could reply, the passen-ger door opened and she nearly slid out of the van onto her head.

"Whoa, girl. I've got you."

"Ryan!"

Never had anyone felt so good. Just as she had imagined, his strong arms gathered her close. Bethany clung to his warmth, shuddering un-controllably.

"Oh, Ryan."

She felt him run a hand over her hip. "I'm sorry, honey, but I've got to check you myself to be sure you're not hurt."

She blinked and peered over her shoulder, the oddest feeling of sep-arateness coming over her as she watched him hike up her skirt and run big, brown hands the length of her twisted legs. His long fingers prodded the flesh-colored nylon of her support tights, and she realized he was searching for bone fractures. Normally she would have been humiliated beyond bearing. Her legs lay in an immodest sprawl at awkward angles to her body. Only this was Ryan. Not just any man. Watching the careful way he touched her, she couldn't quite muster a feeling of embarrassment.

He sighed, the sound conveying his vast relief. "You seem okay." He drew her skirt back down, then gently rearranged her legs, keeping one hand cupped over her knees as he lowered them to the floor. "Thank God for that. Huh?" He hunched his shoulders around her and tightened his embrace, pressing his face against her hair. Melting snow dripped off the brim of his Stetson and plopped on her sleeve. She felt the tension ease from his body. "Damn, honey. Talk about scaring the hell out of a fellow. I was so afraid you might be hurt."

Through chattering teeth, Bethany said, "I t-told you I wa-wasn't."

He abandoned his grip on her knees, and she felt him twisting at the waist. The next instant, his heavy jacket settled around her shoulders, the lining still warm from his body. The heat felt sublime.

He reached around her to get the phone and dialed the state police. An instant later he was speaking to a dispatcher. He quickly explained that it was unnecessary now for an officer to be sent out. After ending the call, he tucked the phone into a pocket of the jacket he'd wrapped around her. Then he smiled and gathered her close again. He looked strong and capable, the collar of his shirt flapping in the wind. The ever-present black Stetson was caked with snow.

"I can wear my own coat, Ryan," she protested. "You'll freeze."

"I'm inured to the cold. Remember? And my jacket's already warm. Maybe it'll help to chase the chill off you. We'll use your coat to cover your legs."

As he spoke, he lifted both the coat and her into his arms. Bethany hugged his neck, so glad he was there that for once it didn't alarm her to be picked up.

"One question. What in the *hell* are you doing out on these roads today?"

Against his wet collar, she said, "The weather report didn't predict snow. I went to Bend to pick up an order."

"This is Oregon, remember? And high in the mountains, no less. Never, and I do mean *never*, take a weather report as gospel in this country. The storm front was supposed to pass over north of us, but it changed direction. I've been smelling snow in the air for the past two days."

"You have?"

He struck off up the bank. When he reached the snowmobile, he set her on the saddle seat, then covered her legs with her coat. Bethany grabbed hold of the handlebars to maintain her perch while he dug through a plastic storage compartment behind her. He dragged out two heavy lap robes and a silver insulated blanket, all three of which he wrapped around her, the silver sheet going on last to block the wind.

The entire time he was tucking the blankets around her legs, he lectured her. "The next time you take off on a long trip, you call me, and I'll go with you. There are maniacs out on these roads. What if you get a flat?"

"I can always call for road service."

"Like hell. I've got a friend who's a cop. He lectures women's groups on highway safety. Even if you call for road service, it's dangerous to remain with your vehicle. Psychos look for easy targets, and a lone woman who has car trouble along a deserted highway is one of the easiest targets on earth. You've heard people say to just put a flag on the antenna and lock the doors?"

"Yes."

"Well, that's the worst thing you can do. You're virtually sending out signals to anyone who drives by that you're all alone, broken down, and helpless. Some creep grabs a tire iron, bashes in the glass, and you're next."

"Oh, my."

"Yeah, 'oh, my,' is right." Snowflakes gathered on their faces as his steel-blue eyes met hers. In their depths, Bethany saw more fear than anger. "I don't want anything to happen to you. No long trips by yourself anymore. Agreed?"

"Sometimes I need to go places," she said weakly.

"From now on, you just holler, and I'll go with you. I can always juggle my work to take a few hours off." He sighed, closed his eyes for a second, and then hooked a hand over the back of her head and pressed his forehead against hers. "Damn. I'm sorry. I don't mean to yell. Driving here, I kept thinking of all the things that could happen and praying no one else stopped."

Before she could reply, he was gone. She watched as he collected her keys and purse, then wrested her wheelchair from the van, locked the doors, and climbed back up the bank.

"Is there anything else you'll need tonight?" he asked.

"Surely the road will be cleared before dark."

He put the chair in a carry rack at the rear of the snowmobile and se-cured it with bungee cords. "Take a gander at that snow coming down. The highway will be closed until they can get it plowed, and even after they do, it'll be slick. Where's the point in taking you home when you're welcome at my place?"

"All I've got with me that's important is in my purse. I didn't plan to be away overnight."

"You have enough medication to last you?"

"No. I didn't think I'd be gone overnight and haven't got it with me."

"What all do you take?"

"Just Coumadin, a blood thinner, and a muscle relaxant at bedtime to prevent leg spasms."

He thought a moment. "A couple of glasses of wine will keep your blood thin, and it should work as a muscle relaxant as well. I'll double-check with my mom, just to be sure."

After stowing her things in the storage compartment, he mounted the snowmobile behind her. Sitting sideways as she was, her shoulder butted his chest as he drew her close. After telling her to hug his waist, he started the engine.

"You steady on?" he asked.

"I think so."

"Hold tight, honey. I'll take it easy."

Bethany burrowed her face against his shirt, comforted by the solid warmth of him radiating through the wet cloth. After he got the snow-mobile shifted into gear, he locked a strong arm around her. The vehicle surged powerfully beneath them, and they were off.

Oddly, she felt perfectly safe even when the snowmobile leaned sharply and she slipped on the seat. Ryan had a firm hold on her. The noise of the engine made talking difficult, so she simply hugged him tightly and relaxed. It was heavenly to feel at least marginally warm again.

Traveling cross-country instead of by road, Ryan was able to cut off several miles, and it didn't take long to reach his ranch. For that, he was thankful. However, he could feel Bethany shivering violently. He needed to get her warmed up—and fast.

His dog Tripper came bounding through the falling snow to greet them when Ryan pulled up near the house. He spoke softly to the mutt, but didn't give him the expected ear scratch and pat, choosing instead to gather Bethany up in his arms and hurry inside. He carried her directly to the great room where he'd been about to light a fire when she called. After depositing her on the sofa, he grabbed the portable phone and dialed his parents' place.

His mom answered on the third ring. Ryan quickly related the situation to her. "I need to get her into a hot bath," he concluded. "Can you come over?"

Ann sighed theatrically, the sound drifting faintly to Ryan over the phone line. "Dear heart, have you looked outside? Those are blizzard conditions."

"I realize that, Mom. Just hop on the snowmobile."

"Not when it's snowing this hard. I could drive off into the lake."

His mother could drive the lakeshore with her eyes closed. "Take it slow. I really need you, Mom. Another woman, you know?"

Ann sighed again. "Ryan, dear. This *is* Bethany, the girl who's had your tail tied in a knot for the last week?"

"That's right."

"I see. The same Bethany you've been searching for all your life who has eyes like pansies?"

"What's your point?"

Ann chuckled. "I think a wise man would handle this emergency himself."

Ryan thought she was teasing and laughed himself. "I appreciate the thought, Mom, but there's a time and place for everything. This ain't it."

"Use your head for something besides a hat rack," Ann said with a smile in her voice. "Opportunity knocks. You said you were going with a friendship tack."

"Right."

"So . . . get friendly."

"Mom, I rea—"

"Oops. My timer is going off. I have to run before the cookies burn."

"Mom! Don't hang—"

The line went dead. Ryan stared down at the phone, resisting the urge to cuss a blue streak.

"What's wrong?" Bethany asked, chattering with cold.

Ryan put the portable back in its base. His mother had lost her mind, but somehow he didn't think he should tell Bethany that. Smiling with his teeth clenched was a shade difficult. "Nothing, honey. Just the snow. With the visibility so poor, Mom's afraid to ride over."

"Oh." She huddled inside the blankets, gazing up at him with big, worried eyes. "I see." She waited a beat, shivered, and then said, "I really don't need a hot bath, anyway, though it was nice of you to think of it."

"You're freezing. With such poor circulation in your legs, it'll take hours for you to warm up without one."

"I'll manage."

"Manage?" Ryan scooped her up off the sofa. "We'll manage, all right."

"I can't take a bath, not with only you here to help me."

"Sure you can. I can be a very inventive fellow when I set my mind to it."

Sitting in his upholstered rocker by the fire, Keefe Kendrick studied his wife with narrowed eyes. She was grinning like Lewis Carroll's Cheshire cat as she hung up the telephone. "Annie, are you up to mischief?"

She flashed him a startled look, her gray eyes shimmering. "Mischief?"

He bit back a smile as she walked toward him. "You're not afraid you'll drive off in the lake, and if you've got cookies in the oven, I want some."

She lifted a slender shoulder in a shrug, her rounded hips displayed to mouthwatering advantage by her snug jeans. Even at sixty, his Annie was a looker, with gorgeous legs and perfectly shaped breasts that filled out her red sweater just the way he liked. "Sometimes Ryan needs a push to get moving."

She plopped her plump fanny on his lap and looped her arms around his neck. Keefe knew when his wife was trying to sidetrack him. He cocked an eyebrow. "What're you up to?"

"Hmm." She nibbled his lip. "It's snowing outside. I think snow is *so* romantic. Don't you?" She wiggled her bottom, making a certain part of his anatomy turn hard. "Let's open some wine and make love by the fire."

Keefe seized her bottom lip between his teeth and put just enough force into his bite to let her know he wasn't as dim-witted as she might think. "Annie girl, are you interfering in your son's love life?"

She kissed him, using her tongue with such expertise he nearly forgot his question. "Never. I'm just being a good mother and completely resisting the temptation to interfere. That's Bethany over at Rye's place. *The* Bethany."

Keefe trailed questing fingers up her rib cage. His Annie was one sweet armful. "The girl with the incredibly blue eyes?" he asked huskily.

"That's the one. She got stranded in the storm, and Rye went to fetch her. She's frozen half to death and needs a hot bath. He wanted me to go over and help. Silly boy. Like I'd dream of it. Though a hot bath has interesting possibilities."

Keefe pushed suddenly to his feet. She bleated in surprise as he headed for the bathroom. Keefe's mind was brimming with images of her, rosy from hot water and slick with scented soap. "A bath definitely has interesting possibilities," he agreed with a low growl. "Sometimes, Annie girl, mischief can backfire."

⚛ CHAPTER TEN ⚛

Bethany sat in the bathroom, her gaze fixed on the vanity mirror, lighted by an oak bar of globes that cast glaring brightness over her and everything else. Studying herself in the glass, she decided she resembled a shuddering stick baby with huge eyes and a mop of straggly hair. No wonder Ryan was worried. She couldn't flex her leg muscles like most people to get her blood moving, which meant that half her body had an inefficient temperature-control system.

She rubbed her arms but continued to shiver. Lifting the hem of her wool skirt, she touched her knee and found it was ice cold, even through the nylon mesh of her tights. Oh, how she wished she were at home in her familiar bathroom with all her trusty bathing equipment.

A light tap came on the door. The sound startled her so that she jumped. "Come in," she managed to say in a halfway normal voice.

Her bath attendant entered—all six feet plus of him. Snow-drenched denim skimmed his long, well-muscled legs. With each step he took, his boots rapped the earth-brown tile, the sounds sharp and decisive as he advanced. He'd thrown on a dry shirt, which he hadn't buttoned. The gaping front plackets revealed an expanse of rippling bronze chest, lightly furred with black hair that narrowed to a triangular swath as it descended to his flat, striated stomach.

Her mouth went as dry as dirt, and all she could think to say was, "Hi."

"Hi," he replied, his voice deep and vibrant. The sound made her skin feel as if it were humming. "All ready?"

She'd never be ready. Her mother had helped her dress and undress enough times for her to know he couldn't do this without getting an eyeful.

His gaze as sharp as honed steel, he gave her a thoughtful once-over. From the waist down, she was still fully clothed. From there up, though, all she had on was an oversize T-shirt he'd lent her. Her blouse and bra lay in a neatly folded stack on the vanity, the bra at the bottom so he wouldn't see it.

The only bright spot in this entire miserable mess was that he'd lent her a blue T-shirt instead of a white one. She knew from experience that white T-shirts became transparent the instant they got wet.

"Is it still snowing?" she asked.

"Yeah, it is. Sorry. No letup at all so far. I called Jake, by the way. I didn't want your family to be worried about you. He said he'll go over to feed and water your kitty." He startled her by suddenly hunkering down in front of her. His firm mouth tipped slowly into a grin as he reached up to push a damp tendril of hair from her face. "Honey, I hope all that shivering is from cold and not nerves. You're not afraid of me, are you?"

"Heavens, no." She laughed shakily and then clamped her teeth together to keep them from chattering.

"You sure?" He trailed his fingertip along her cheekbone, coming to a halt at her chin, where he spent a moment tracing the slight cleft with the back of a knuckle. "I've been trying to put myself in your shoes. It's a little difficult. I know this has to be tough, though."

"I'm fine, Ryan. Honestly. I just wish a bath wasn't necessary."

"I have it all figured out."

Uh-huh. He obviously hadn't taken into account that without support bars or a dressing sling, she couldn't even get her panties and tights off without help. At home, she managed by herself with her equipment, and even then, it was no easy task.

"Trust me," he said softly. "Good friends don't embarrass each other."

"I just wish I were h-home, is all. I have everything I need there."

"I'm sorry I don't have everything you need here. I will soon."

"Oh, no. You mustn't start buying stuff for me."

"Why not?"

She knew there were a dozen good reasons, but she couldn't readily think of one. "Because?"

He chuckled. "One of the advantages of having so damned much money is being able to buy things for my friends whenever the mood strikes. Have you any idea how much fifty million earns annually in interest? My tax obligation looks like the national debt."

Bethany couldn't conceive of having that much money. "You poor thing."

He narrowed an eye. "I'm running a business out here, and anything I buy to accommodate the handicapped, namely you, will be a much-needed write-off."

"I see."

"We do have handicapped buyers come out to look at our horses. If I want to buy stuff to make you more comfortable at my ranch, I'll do it, no arguments. All right?"

"All right."

He smiled slightly. "We are going to pursue this friendship thing. Right?"

"I d-don't part with my clothes for just anybody, so I think it's safe to say I consider you to be a very good friend."

That elicited a chuckle from him. "So I can rest my case?"

"Please, don't. The longer you talk, the longer I can put this off."

"There, you see? The situation we have right now is awful. You need a hot bath, and getting you in the tub is a major production, with you all nervous and upset. I'd like to be set up so it's as comfortable for you here as at home. That way, when you need a bath, you can get in the tub by yourself."

"Are you a clean freak?"

"A what?"

"If you're given to sniffing armpits, I may have to reconsider this friendship thing."

He sighed and shook his head. "A smart ass when you're nervous. I should have known."

Guilty as charged. She did tend to crack jokes when she felt uneasy, and right now she felt extremely uneasy.

"Out here, being able to grab a quick bath is a necessity. You've been around animals. Get slapped by a muddy horse tail, and you'll be glad I planned ahead for the eventuality."

Bethany rubbed her arms. "I just wish you were set up for it now."

"I know."

His voice dipped to a husky tenor, and by that she knew he understood how unpleasant this was for her. Somehow, that helped.

She took a bracing breath that shuddered in and out because she was shaking so hard. "Okay," she said, trying to inject some confidence into her voice. "I'm ready. Let's do it and get it over with."

"Will it make you feel any better to know that I called our foreman, Sly, and he's already at work in the welding shop, whipping together some makeshift bathroom bars?"

"He is?"

"When we're finished here, I'll go over to help him. What we come up with won't be fancy, but you'll be halfway comfortable here until morning, anyway."

Bathroom bars? Bethany almost hugged him. She resisted the urge to glance at the commode. Makeshift was fine. Makeshift was *wonderful*. She didn't care if the bars they fashioned were pretty as long as they enabled her to manage that necessity without help.

Still hugging her waist and shivering, she said, "I hate to put you to so much bother, Ryan."

"It's not a bother, honey. We do a lot of welding here on the ranch, and I've got tons of pipe lying around. We'll have something thrown together in just a few minutes." He pushed back to his feet and leaned down. "Hug my neck, sweetheart. Let's get you in that tub. I'm starting to feel cold, just watching you."

Oh, how she dreaded this. There was no way around it, though. "Maybe you could just wrap me in an electric blanket. That'd chase the chill away."

"I don't have one. I'm sorry. I have down quilts on all the beds."

"I could just sit close to the fire."

Much as he had last night, he grasped her wrists and put her arms around his neck himself. "Feel how badly you're shaking? You're going in the tub. You're not catching pneumonia on my watch. Jake would never forgive me."

Jake. Oh, how she wished Jake were there.

"Have a little faith in me," Ryan whispered.

She envisioned him trying to hold her erect with one arm and tugging clumsily at her clothes with his other hand, her body smashed against his the entire while. *Oh, God . . . oh, God*. Her face went hot with shame.

"This will be over before you can yell, 'Hallelujah.'"

She fully expected the usual ordeal she experienced with her mother on swim nights, with him grunting and straining, and her legs flopping every which way like limp noodles. She should have known better. After catching her around the waist with one arm, Ryan straightened as if she weighed scarcely anything. The next thing she knew, she was clasped to his chest, her lower body dangling.

"Oh, God!"

"It's all right, honey. I won't drop you."

He groped under the T-shirt to unfasten her skirt. That accomplished, he divested her of the garment, her tights, and her panties in one fell swoop. She felt his fingertips graze bare skin at the small of her back, but otherwise he executed the maneuver without touching her intimately. The next thing she knew, he was tugging down the hem of the T-shirt and putting her back in the chair.

"There, you see?" He crouched in front of her again to tug the elasti-cized stockings down her calves. "No fuss, no muss. That wasn't so bad, was it?"

It hadn't been bad at all, and the very fact that it hadn't been made her feel trembly.

He grasped her by each ankle to remove her black doeskin slippers and then swept her clothing aside. "Damn, honey, your feet are like ice." He skimmed a hand up her calf. "No wonder you're shaking."

Bethany tugged at the hem of the T-shirt, trying to keep her knees cov-ered. "I can't believe it was so easy. It's always a struggle when Mama helps me."

He slanted her an amused look. "I saw your mom at the grange last night. She's not much bigger than a minute, so that comes as no surprise." After setting her slippers aside, he stood. "Now I'll just pick you up and put you in the tub. If you'll make a fist on the hem of the shirt, it won't float up as I put you in. I brought a clothespin to do anchor duty once I get you situated."

A clothespin? He truly had thought of everything.

As he bent over her, Bethany braced herself, visually aware as he caught her behind the knees with one arm, sensually aware when his left arm slipped between the chair and her back. A big warm hand curled over her side, strong fingers splaying on her ribs just beneath her breast.

"Easy, sweetheart," he said as he lifted her. "I've got you."

He had her, all right. She felt surrounded by vibrant, male strength. Heat radiated through the T-shirt from his bare chest, and coarse, springy black hair rubbed against one of her elbows. He felt so marvelous, she almost took a taste of his sturdy neck. It was the color of caramel, which was right behind chocolate as one of her favorite flavors on earth.

He went down on one knee beside the tub, lifting her over the edge and then gently lowering her into the water he'd already drawn. He kept one arm hooked under her knees to carefully position her legs.

As he had suggested, she grabbed a handful of T-shirt hem so the cot-ton wouldn't float up. "You're very good at this."

"It seems to come naturally." He flicked her another smiling glance as he drew a clothespin from his breast pocket. Brushing her hand aside and grasping the hem of the T-shirt, he gave it a twist to draw the cotton snug around her thighs, then secured it with the pin.

Bethany watched as he turned on the hot and cold water, then shoved a broad wrist under the stream to check the temperature. As he adjusted the valves, he said, "We'll have you warmed up in no time flat,"

She sighed in appreciation and sank a little lower in the water. "Oh, this is lovely." The warm water he was running from the tap curled around her hips. "Thank you so much. I'm sorry to be so much work."

"You're no work. I'm glad to have you here."

The heat was helping her to stop shivering, and her jerking muscles began to relax. Ryan started massaging her legs, his sun-burnished hands striking a sharp contrast to her pale skin. As she watched, she found herself wishing she could feel his touch. She imagined his palms would be slightly rough, the grip of his long, thick fingers wonderfully warm. *Don't go there, Bethany. Friendship. No more, no less.* She couldn't allow her silly female heart to start spinning fantasies and risk ruining what promised to be a good friendship.

He caught her staring at his hands and said, "I thought I might get the blood moving. I'm not hurting you, am I?"

"No. If only you could."

He gave her a bewildered look. Then he winced. "Right. I'm sorry. Stupid question. I just thought—hell, I don't know what I was thinking." He worked his way up to just above her knee, "You can't feel anything at all? Not anywhere? That's so hard for me to fathom. Intellectually, I know it, but on a more instinctive level, I automatically think in terms of having sensation."

Bethany managed a strained smile. "Don't apologize. I'm the abnormal one, not you. And as it happens, I do have a couple of live spots." She touched a fingertip to the inside of her left thigh. "One right there."

He stared at the spot she indicated as if he were committing the location to memory. "Just there?"

"A couple of other places, too. Nerve damage is a weird thing, especially in my case, where the worst damage occurred on one side of the spine. I have sensation in places I shouldn't, and none in places I ought to. Right after I got hurt, our family doctor and a local specialist stood over me, frowning and scratching their heads a lot. I didn't conform to the textbooks and journals."

He frowned thoughtfully. "So you're not completely numb in your legs?"

"Not completely. The numbness is spotty from the point of injury down to the tops of my thighs and grows worse from there until I'm completely numb." She lowered her voice to a conspiratorial whisper. "I have very good feeling in my derriere, for instance, and can detect wiggling thumbs."

She expected him to laugh. Instead, his gaze darted to the juncture of her thighs. "Don't grab me by the hair and shove my head under water for asking. Okay? One friend to another. Are you numb there?"

Bethany wasn't sure how her face could turn so hot when she was still so cold otherwise, but somehow it did.

He immediately backtracked. "I'm sorry. Inappropriate question." He returned his attention to the water faucets, then checked the bath to see how hot it was. "Just curious, is all. You seem convinced you may not be able to have a normal physical relationship. If you've got any sensation at all there, I was just wondering why."

"For starters, I've been told flat-out by my doctor that I probably can't."

"Doctors can be wrong."

"I know, but given his reputation as a spinal specialist, his opinion carries a lot of weight. He's one of the best on the West Coast." Bethany trailed her fingertips over the surface of the water, keeping her gaze carefully averted. "Nerve damage is a strange thing. One nerve may work fine, but another nearby that's vital to the operation may be a dud. A bell with no ding, in other words?"

He chuckled. "Now, there's a way to put it."

"However one puts it, who can say what I'll be able to feel or experience? I can only go by what Doctor Reicherton told me, which wasn't encouraging."

He arched a dark eyebrow. "So you've never—you know—tried a solo flight to check things out yourself?"

Her gaze flicked back to his. "No. I, um—" She shrugged, feeling suddenly uncomfortable. How could she explain that she'd chosen to keep a lid on her sexuality? It made little sense to kindle physical needs and yearnings she might never be able to satisfy. "I haven't dated since my accident, and I guess I never saw much point in checking out the possibilities." She flashed him an impish smile. "Besides, one of my brothers nearly went blind from doing stuff like that."

He huffed with laughter. Then a ruddy flush crawled up his neck. It was his turn to avert his gaze. "I'm sorry. I shouldn't have asked." He tested the water again. "I think that's about hot enough for now. What do you think?"

She thought he felt as uncomfortable with the conversation as she did, which had the odd effect of making her feel more relaxed. "It feels wonderful."

He shut off the faucets, then turned to sit on the floor beside the tub, his broad back braced against the creamy tile that went halfway up the

wall. Lifting one knee to support a loosely bent arm, he settled a twinkling gaze on her.

She walked her fingertips down her thigh, stopping at her knee and
then backtracking. When she glanced back up, he was tugging on his ear-
lobe, a gesture she was fast coming to recognize as a nervous habit. "I
honestly am sorry," he said huskily. "I don't know what possessed me to
ask you such a thing. It's not really any of my business, and it was rude
to pry."

She mulled that over for a moment. "I don't really mind your asking.
I'm just not sure how to answer. It's sort of like living in town and owning a high-powered rifle. If you know you'll never have occasion to use
it, you just lock it away somewhere safe and forget you've got it."

He smiled and nodded. "I can associate with that." He tugged on his
ear again. "So . . . tell me about your family. You and Jake seem very close.
Do you have the same kind of relationship with your other brothers?"

Happy to change the subject, Bethany launched into a brief description of her siblings. "In a large family like ours, it's never easy being the
youngest, and I think it was especially difficult being the only girl. Too
many protectors. Someone was always watching after me. It took a lot of
maneuvering on my part to get away with anything."

"I'm sure your folks appreciated your brothers' efforts."

"Oh, yes. They never had to worry about me much. When Jake went
away to college, there was Zeke to take up the slack, and after he left,
the twins were always breathing down my neck."

"The veterinarians in progress."

She nodded. "Next oldest was Hank, twenty-eight to my twenty-six. He
was just close enough to me in age to be more of a friend than a pain in
the neck. Occasionally he even aided and abetted."

"And your folks? I've met your dad down at the store. He seems like
a nice man. What's your mom like? I saw her from a distance last night.
She looks like a sweetheart."

She is that." Bethany flattened a hand over her waist. "You have to
know her to get the whole picture. She's—what are the words?—a plump
nun in street clothes who just happens to be married and have six kids,
all of whom she'll swear were magically dropped into Daddy's boot during the night while they were sleeping. Sometimes I almost think she believes it herself."

He laughed at the description. "I can tell by your expression that you
love her a lot."

Bethany nodded. "She's a neat lady. Just a little naive. Daddy is from the old school, and he's always shielded her. Me, too, for that matter. He just wasn't quite as successful at the endeavor. If it had been left up to him, I would have been given information about the birds and the bees on a strictly need-to-know basis."

"That birds tweet and bees buzz?"

"Exactly. When we still had the ranch, he went to incredible pains to make sure I never saw the horses breeding." She flashed him a smile. "It caused me no end of difficulty."

"You sneaked to watch," he said with a knowing smile.

"Of *course.*"

He shook his head. "Your poor dad. Raising you must have been a trial."

"For him or me? It can be incredibly stifling when you're daddy's little angel. If I had it to do over again, I would have been sexually active at twelve."

"Twelve? That terrifies me. Heidi's twelve."

"Who's Heidi?"

His eyes shimmered with fondness as he described Maggie's little sister. "She keeps asking me to wait until she's grown so she can marry me. She keeps me on my toes. I love her to death, and I don't want to wound her. At the same time, I don't want to encourage her, either. It's a fine line."

"She sounds darling."

"Yeah." The slash in his cheek deepened as he grinned. "Won't be long before the boys line up at the door. I'll have to go over to help Rafe kick butt."

"I was so crazy about horses as a teenager that I wasn't much interested in boys until I met Paul. Maybe Heidi will be like that."

"Maybe. She wants to barrel race."

"Really?" Bethany's interest was piqued, and she was about to pursue the topic when he broke in with, "Speaking of Paul. How did it happen that you tied up with a kid that age who didn't know squat about kissing?"

"We were young, for one, and Paul was a minister's son and very devout. We mostly just—" She felt suddenly embarrassed and wondered how they'd ever gotten off on such a subject. "We were waiting until we got married."

His mouth hardened. "Too bad he didn't keep his fly zipped with your little friend. What was her name?"

"Nan. How'd you know about her?"

Something dark flickered in his eyes again, and he suddenly became unaccountably interested in the ceiling. "Their marriage was announced in the newspaper as I recall. Not exactly a state secret. Right?"

Bethany's nape prickled. "Why do guys always stare at the ceiling when they lie?"

His gaze dropped back to hers. "You have too many brothers."

"Jake?" she whispered. It wasn't really a question.

Ryan sighed. "You're very lucky, you know. Having an older brother who loves you so much. He'd fight a mountain lion for you, bare-handed."

"He called to talk to you."

He sighed again and said, "Damn. Me and my big mouth. I never meant to rat on him." He shook his head. "And, no, he didn't call. He showed up here Saturday night. We had a nice, long chat."

"Nice? You and Jake?"

"Well, it wasn't nice initially. But he settled down once we talked, and I convinced him my intentions toward you are honorable."

"That we just want to be friends?"

He smiled slightly. "Yeah. The best of friends. He's okay with that. He meant no harm by coming out here, you know. He's just watching out for you. I admire him for that."

"Stick around. Soon your admiration for him will know no bounds."

"I plan to," he assured her.

"Plan to, what?"

"Stick around."

Lying before the fire with his wife clasped in his arms, Keefe felt the tension in her body. After the intense lovemaking they'd just shared, he felt confident her mood wasn't due to lack of sexual gratification.

"What's wrong, Annie mine?" he asked, smoothing a hand over her hair and kissing her brow.

"A guilty conscience," she confessed. "I should have gone over to Ryan's. Normally, not interfering would be all well and fine, but I keep thinking about that poor girl. If she had another woman to help her, she'd feel much better."

"Hmm."

"Do you think I should run over?"

"It's so nice, lying here. A snowmobile ride doesn't sound appealing."

"You don't have to go."

He sighed. "And risk letting my wife drive off in the lake in a snow-storm?"

"I won't drive off in the lake. I know the way blindfolded."

Keefe pushed up on his elbow. "If I stay here, I'll miss getting to meet my new daughter-in-law."

"He hasn't married her yet."

Keefe chuckled. "Yeah, well . . . Ryan always has been slow to do things. He'll get around to it."

"Slow? By whose standards?"

"Kendrick standards. Been me, I would've had her to Reno and back already. Never have understood that boy. He thinks every damned thing half to death before he does it."

Ann hugged his neck. "I'll let you go with me, under one condition."

"What's that?"

"Don't give him any advice."

Keefe scowled. "Why not?"

"Because he's managing just fine on his own, and I don't want him doing anything harebrained, like abducting her."

"I didn't abduct you."

"You pretended we were lost and kept me out in the wilderness for five days. If that's not abduction, what is it?"

"A damned smart move. By the time I got you home, you'd agreed to marry me. I saved myself weeks of frustration." He winked and grinned. "I also did you a big favor. By the time I took you home, you knew that skinny little college boy wasn't so hot, after all. There was also no question in your mind that I could take care of you, regardless of the situation."

"Ah, yes." Ann rolled onto her back, chuckled, and closed her eyes. "You even started a fire with two sticks. Remember that? Later I found out you had a cigarette lighter in your pocket the entire time."

"I also had another blanket in my saddle pack."

"What?"

Keefe leaned over and kissed the end of her nose. "You heard me. I had two blankets."

Ann grabbed him by the ears. "You rotten, conniving scoundrel."

Relaxed from her bath, Bethany toasted in front of the fire while she waited for Ryan to return from the welding shop. From where she sat, she could gaze out the sliding glass doors at the falling snow, which created a pretty winter scene. The lake gleamed like polished black glass, its shores lined with thick stands of towering, snow-laden trees. Dusk had already descended, making everything look misty and ethereal near the ground, the shades of charcoal turning to soot against the sky.

Snuggling deeper in her chair, she savored the quietness, which gave her some thinking time to come to terms with her predicament. Not that this really qualified as a predicament. She'd had a wreck, and now she was stranded here for the night, a situation that had all the earmarks of a disaster for someone in a wheelchair. But so far, Ryan had seen to her every need and managed to do so in such a way that she felt cosseted rather than embarrassed.

Just as predicted, he had gotten her dressed with little difficulty. After lining her chair with a bath sheet, he had lifted her from the tub, set her on the terry, and left. She removed the wet T-shirt, dried off, and put on a fresh one. Then he had returned to help her into a pair of gray sweatpants with elasticized cuffs and a drawstring waist, which had gone on as easily as her skirt and panties had come off. Her oversize ensemble was complemented by a gigantic pair of gray wool socks with red triangular patches at toe and heel.

After getting her dressed, he had pushed her into the great room to sit near the fire, tucked a sofa throw around her shoulders, and then moved some of the furniture to create wider traffic paths. Before leaving for the welding shop, he had fixed her a cup of hot cocoa. Considering the dire circumstances she'd faced less than two hours ago, Bethany felt as if she were caught up in a lovely dream, where nothing was quite as it should be.

Ryan. Thinking of him brought a smile to her lips. How many men would have thought to use a clothespin to keep her T-shirt from floating up? He was so sweet and wonderful.

"Yo! It's me!" a deep voice called out.

Bethany jumped with a start, then turned to see Ryan in the entry. "That was fast."

She no sooner spoke than she realized it wasn't Ryan after all, but a stranger who looked enough like him to be his twin. The man froze in his boot tracks, clearly as surprised to see her as she was him. When he jerked off his black Stetson, the melting snow on its brim sent droplets flying.

"Howdy. You must be Bethany." He brushed at the flakes on the sleeve of his lined denim jacket. "Sorry for dripping on the floor. I tried to shake off outside, but more snow just blew in under the porch overhang."

"You must be . . ."

"Rafe. You met my wife, Maggie, last night."

Bethany nodded. "She's lovely."

"I think so." He finger-combed his hair, the gesture reminding her of Ryan. She'd heard that the Kendrick brothers closely resembled each other, but she hadn't realized until now that they were dead ringers. "I'm sorry for barging in on you." He glanced at her borrowed clothing. "I didn't know Ryan had company."

"Yes, well, it came as something of a surprise to Ryan as well." She quickly related the string of events that had led to her being there.

"You're not hurt, are you?"

"Not even a scratch. It really wasn't much of an accident. The worst of it was all the wrecks, making it difficult for anyone to come get me. Weather allowing, someone in my family will come collect me in the morning."

"I doubt Ryan's in any big hurry to get rid of you. More like, dancing to the snow gods."

"Pardon?"

A ruddy flush crept up his dark neck. He tugged on his ear, yet another gesture that reminded her of Ryan. "Nothing."

Cold air coming in the open doorway curled around Bethany's shoulders, and she drew the throw more snugly around her. Rafe snapped erect, reached to close the door, and then hesitated. "Do you care if I shut it?"

Bethany couldn't help but laugh. "No, please do. I've already been chilled to the bone once today."

"I'm sorry." He closed the door. "I just—well, you know—me being a stranger and all. I thought you might be leery. Leerious, as Sly would say."

Bethany laughed. "I'm not the leerious type."

Even with the jacket providing camouflage, she saw his shoulders relax. "No, I can see you're not. That's good. We don't stand much on ceremony."

"Most ranchers don't."

He grinned, the crooked twist of his mouth once again putting her strongly in mind of Ryan. "That's right. You're no stranger to cows, are you?"

"No, although it's been a long while since I've been around them. You look so much like Ryan, it's astounding."

"People do say we look a little alike."

"A little? You could pass for identical twins."

"Nah. I'm a lot better looking." The corners of his mouth twitched. "Maggie tells me so all the time."

"I'm sure she's speaking from the heart."

"And seeing through rose-colored glasses, to boot."

"We only chatted for a couple of minutes, but she left me with an impression of warmth and sincerity. I liked her immensely."

"I like her a lot myself."

He rested a shoulder against the door. Once again, the way he stood, with most of his weight on one long leg, reminded her of Ryan. He studied her for a moment, his gray-blue eyes seeming to miss nothing. Then he smiled slowly. "Where is Ryan, anyway? I'm surprised he's not joined to you at the hip."

"He's over at the welding shop, wherever that is."

"What's he doing over there?"

"He, um—" Bethany tried to think of a delicate way of putting it. "He's building bars."

"Bars?"

"For the bathroom."

She saw it click. He pushed away from the door, tapping his hat against his thigh. "Well, I guess I'll mosey over that way." He inclined his dark head. "Good meeting you. Maggie says you may come out for a visit. She gets lonely for female company, living so far from town, so I hope you'll do that soon."

"I'm looking forward to it."

He opened the door, started to step out, and then stopped. "I guess I won't mosey, after all. Here comes Ryan now."

Bethany heard male voices and boots crunching on the snow, along with what sounded like a snowmobile coming toward the house.

"Hey, Mom and Dad," she heard Ryan say. "What brings you over this way?"

"You said you needed help," a female voice rang out. "Your father offered to drive me over so I wouldn't end up in the lake."

"I've got it under control now."

"Really? Well, that's good," the woman replied. "We'll just come in and meet Bethany before we leave, if that's all right."

Ryan made a grunting sound and metal clanked. "It's not all right. She isn't dressed to meet a bunch of people, and I don't want her feeling— *Mom,* get back here."

Rafe flashed Bethany a grin and threw the door wide. "Hi, Mom." A petite blonde came stomping into the entry. She fluffed her hair with fine-boned hands to rid it of snow, then offered her cheek to Rafe for a kiss. "Hi, dear heart," she said cheerfully, her large gray eyes flicking past him to find Bethany in front of the brick hearth. "Johnny-jump-ups. No wonder he's been waxing poetic."

Bewildered by the comment, Bethany nodded in greeting. "Hello. You must be Ryan's mom."

"Ann," she corrected warmly as she crossed the room, her right hand extended in greeting. "And you're Bethany, of course. Ryan's told us so much about you."

"He has?"

"All of it good."

Ann Kendrick had a firm handshake and a steady, sincere gaze. Bethany liked her. No artifice, none of the distance that so often erected a wall between strangers. She was simply Ann, dressed in snug jeans, well-worn riding boots, and a denim jacket rubbed white at the elbows. Looking at her, Bethany never would have guessed she was one of the richest women in town. No diamonds, no gold. The only flashy thing about Ann Kendrick was her beautiful smile.

After the handshake, Ann linked fingers with Bethany and sat on the hearth. "You look none the worse for your experience today. I understand you had a wreck?"

"Not really a wreck, more just a fender bender with a huge rock." Bethany was beginning to feel like a stuck recording. "I wasn't hurt."

"That's good. Ryan said you got a bad chill."

Bethany explained how her coat and purse had been thrown to the floorboard upon impact. "I never realized before how much cold air seeps up through the floor of a vehicle until I was lying on one."

Ann sighed. "Well, I'm very glad you thought to call Ryan."

Just then a snow-encrusted Ryan came backing in the open doorway, wrestling and cursing a huge network of piping that refused to fit through the opening. Bethany gaped. How many bars did they think she needed, anyway?

"Dear God," Ann whispered. "He's built you a skyscraper, honey."

Bethany stifled a giggle. It *did* look like a small skyscraper, with a triangular pull-up bar dangling on a chain from the uppermost crossbar.

"Son of a *bitch*." Ryan popped a barked knuckle into his mouth.

"That'll be ten dollars," Ann called out. "I'm keeping track."

Ryan flashed her a glare and muttered under his breath.

"Bring her in through the sliding glass doors," Rafe suggested.

"And then what? If she won't fit through here, she sure as hell won't fit through the bathroom doorway," Ryan said.

A wiry old cowboy with a turkey neck and a face so baked and wrinkled by the sun it resembled a crumpled brown paper sack manned the opposite end of the skyscraper. His droopy tan Stetson looked like an extension of his body, the camel shade of the battered, badly soiled felt almost the same color as his skin. With solemn eyes, he peered through the bars at Ryan. "You reckon she'd fit if we tipped her over?"

"Why is it," Ann mused softly, "that men automatically think that anything difficult is a female?"

Bethany nearly choked on a giggle. "I have no idea. In this case, I'm glad it's a she, though. I'll be getting up close and personal with that contraption."

Ann's eyes danced with merriment as she resumed watching the men.

Waving his injured hand, Ryan stepped back to regard the framework from all angles. The brim of his Stetson and the shoulders of his jacket were covered with snow, and his fresh jeans were wet to the knees. Observing him, Bethany couldn't help but recall that he'd said this would be no bother.

Just then an older gentleman who looked very like Ryan and Rafe appeared outside on the porch beside the wiry cowboy, whom Bethany guessed to be Sly. "What you got the girl figured for, son, a trapeze artist?"

"Enough, Dad. We didn't know how high to make the bars, so we made two. And Sly thought a pull bar would be nice, so we made it tall. Otherwise, all us guys would hit our heads every time—" He broke off and glanced at Bethany. "Every time we went to see a man about a dog," he finished.

Ryan's father grinned through the bars at Bethany. "I'm Keefe Kendrick, by the way. Ain't this a hell of a way to get acquainted with people?"

That was an understatement. She couldn't remember a time when her bathroom requirements had been the main topic of discussion among strangers.

Oddly, after the first wave of intense embarrassment passed, she was able to relax, mainly because everyone else was so matter-of-fact. They all got into the act, finally managed to get the contraption into the house, and then worked together as a team to fit it in the bathroom. The ribbing and laughter ran rampant, and soon Bethany was chuckling right along with everyone else.

"Ya-hoo!" Keefe Kendrick said in a booming voice when the job was finally completed. "Butter my ass and call me a biscuit. I think the damned thing might work, son. Let's have her give it a try."

Bethany threw a startled look at Ryan's father, half afraid he meant for her to try it out right then.

"Come on," he urged.

Oh, God, that was exactly what he had in mind.

"Not for real," Ryan assured her. "We just need to see if the bars are right. If not, I'll run and get the portable welder, and we'll make some quick adjustments."

So it happened that Bethany first tried out her skyscraper while everyone looked on. The triangle pull-up bar proved to be a marvelous improvement on the bars she had at home. She was able to grab hold of it and swing from her chair so easily she whooped with delight. Her audience applauded, and Ryan and Sly beamed with pride for having devised something that worked so well.

"Ryan, this is *wonderful!*"

"You really like it?" he asked hopefully.

"Oh, I *love* it. When I leave, can I take it home with me?"

"No way. That monster is staying put. If you really like it, we'll build you another one for your place."

Bethany frowned. "You don't really mean to leave it here."

"It won't be so ugly if you paint it."

She gave him an incredulous look. "Paint it?"

He winked at her. "I'll spray paint it first, then you can paint little flowers and doodads here and there. It'll pretty right up."

"Painting it would take me days."

"Works for me."

Keefe, who stood in the doorway with an arm around his wife's shoulders, gave the skyscraper a long, narrow look. To Bethany, he said, "If you don't want us fellas bitchin' like a bunch of women about the toilet seat, you'd best remember to wrap that chain around a sidebar after you use it, honey. Otherwise somebody's gonna get his pearly whites knocked down his throat."

Ann smiled serenely. "What are you going to name her, Bethany? Anything that big and homely needs a handle."

Still perched on her throne, Bethany thought for a moment and then swatted the pull bar. "I think I'll call her 'Sweet Revenge.'"

❧ CHAPTER ELEVEN ❧

Everyone had dinner at Ryan's, a family gathering made complete when Rafe drove home to fetch Maggie, his mother-in-law, Helen, and the three kids. Only Becca, the housekeeper-cum-nanny, who had the evening off, was unable to attend. After some good-natured bickering, spaghetti was chosen as the main course with garlic bread, salad, and green beans on the side.

Usually people assumed Bethany couldn't help with meal preparations. In the Kendrick family, everyone was expected to help, including Sly, who was sent over to Ann's house to fetch fresh garlic. Bethany was recruited to prepare the bread. Ryan and his mom put on the spaghetti sauce. Helen was in charge of setting the table, and Maggie and Rafe fixed the salad. Grandpa Keefe and Heidi were assigned baby-sitting duty, a task they seemed to greatly enjoy.

The comradeship reminded Bethany of her own family, and she settled into the Kendrick circle easily, smiling at their teasing banter, laughing when the ragging was turned on her. She found herself wishing that the evening wouldn't end—or, more precisely, that the feeling of belonging didn't have to end.

Ryan. Occasionally their gazes would lock, and the look in his eyes made her heart catch. *You see?* he seemed to be saying. *This can work. It will work, if only you'll give me a chance.*

"Toes!" Bethany warned as she took the bread over to slip it in the preheated oven. "I run over all feet that get in my way."

"You're just hoping to get out of drying dishes," Maggie said with a laugh. "No such luck, lady. We'll take our chances."

The baby awoke and started to cry just then. In the middle of reading a story to Jaimie, Keefe hollered from the great room. "Heidi's talking on the phone. Can someone take care of Amelia? Jaimie and I are to the good part."

"Bethany, can you take care of her? I'm on mop-up detail." Maggie dabbed at Rafe's cheeks with a towel. "Poor baby. Onions do it to you every time."

"I'm not good with babies," Bethany said. "I haven't been around them."

"No time like the present to start," Maggie replied cheerfully. "She may be wet. Her disposable diapers are in the bag there by the sofa."

Bethany went to the great room. Amelia was not a happy camper. Lying on the sofa with pillows plumped around her as bolsters, she was thrashing all her limbs and screaming. Sly stood to one side, gnarled hands at his hips, chin jutted, eyes crinkled as he peered down at her. Judging by the expression on his weathered face, he was more at home with cows. No help there.

'Have you ever changed a diaper?" Bethany asked hopefully.

"Never have much truck with kids 'til they can walk and wipe their noses."

Sly didn't run after making that pronouncement. A true cowboy sauntered, even if he was putting out a fire. Sly did, however, manage to saunter away with amazing speed.

Bethany lifted Amelia from the blankets. The baby's face went serene. She fixed Bethany with big brown eyes and smiled, showing off two tiny teeth.

"Hello," Bethany said softly. She felt inside the little girl's diaper, and sure enough, it was wet. Never having changed a diaper before, Bethany whispered, "Oh, boy. I'm not sure I'm ready for you, Amelia."

Keefe glanced up from the storybook. "There's nothing to it, honey. The diapers have tape tabs. They go on slicker than greased owl dung."

"We have no babies in our family yet, so my experience with them is nil."

"Amy isn't hard to please." He cuddled Jaimie closer and turned the page of the storybook. "If you don't do it exactly right, she won't give a rip."

Bethany's hands trembled as she dug in the bag for a diaper. She kept expecting the baby to start screaming with impatience, but Amelia only gurgled and smiled, as if all the stops and starts were loads of fun.

Heidi returned just as Bethany got the diaper off. She leaned over the back of the couch, her big brown eyes curious but friendly. "Ryan says you were an awesome barrel racer."

Bethany glanced up. "Not bad. I hear you're a barrel racer, yourself."

Heidi wrinkled her nose. She looked very much like her older sister, Maggie, with the same delicate features and a wealth of dark brown hair.

"I'm trying to be. Ryan said that maybe, if I asked you real nice, you'd come out to watch me race and give me some tips."

"Oh, gosh, I . . ."

"Please?" Heidi inserted. "He says you took state *three* times. That makes you an all-time great, practically a *legend*."

"Not quite that good," Bethany said with an embarrassed laugh.

Heidi glanced down at the baby. "You're s'posed to wipe her off now."

"Oh." Bethany felt foolish, having a twelve-year-old give her instruction in diaper changing. There was no help for it. "What should I use to wipe her with?"

"A wipe." Heidi came around the end of the teal sofa to rifle through the bag. She finally located a slender white plastic case filled with disposable cloths. She plucked out one and handed it over. "Haven't you ever done this?"

"No." Bethany dabbed at Amelia's bare bum. "This is my first time."

"You're doing good," Heidi assured her. "You don't have to be so careful, though. Just wipe her off all over, making sure you get in the wrinkles. Otherwise Maggie says she gets all sore. Then you put on powder."

Bethany did as instructed, and soon Amelia was put back together again. The baby chortled happily and kicked her feet, her chubby legs churning beneath the ruffled hem of her cute little red-checked dress.

"We make a pretty good team," Bethany told Heidi as she gathered the baby onto her lap. "When the mud dries up, I suppose I could come out and watch you race the barrels some afternoon."

Heidi's eyes went wide. "You will? For true? *Wow*. Just wait 'til I tell Alice. She'll be green."

Bethany laughed again. "Alice? Another barrel racer, I presume?"

"Yeah, and she's a lot better than me. Now I'll have an edge."

"I don't know how much I can really help you," Bethany warned. "I can't get on a horse and show you anything. Advice can only help so much."

"It'll help me oodles. I just know it! And we don't have to wait for the mud to dry up. Ryan can figure out something."

"Ryan can figure out what?"

Bethany glanced up to see the topic of conversation walking toward them. He leaned down to rest his elbows on the sofa back. "You volunteering me for something, Heidi girl?"

"Only to figure out a way for Bethany to watch me race the barrels. She's worried about the mud."

Ryan smiled at Bethany. "She has a fixation about mud. Not a problem. I can lay out planks, if nothing else. Can you come out next Saturday? That'll be easier than trying to schedule a time after school."

"I have Saturdays off," Bethany agreed. "That would be a good day."

Heidi was so excited, she bounced up and down. "This is *so* cool." She took Bethany by surprise, leaning down to hug her and kiss her cheek. "I was so sure I just *totally* wouldn't like you. But you're so nice, I can't help myself."

Bethany was still laughing as the young girl went racing back to the bedroom to call her friend on Ryan's extension. "Why on earth was she so sure she wouldn't like me?"

Ryan chuckled. "I think she sees you as competition."

"Uh-oh."

He settled a twinkling gaze on her. "You're home free. In the order of importance, I rank well below barrel racing, thank God."

"I'm not a competitor for your affections, in any case."

"Nope. Not in any case," he agreed.

Story time over, Keefe set Jaimie down and watched him scamper away to the kitchen. The child was a pint-size replica of his grandfather, his dark hair and skin earmarking him as a Kendrick by blood.

Bethany's gaze shifted to Ryan. "He looks so much like you."

Ryan gazed after the child, his expression thoughtful. "Yeah, he does. I keep accusing Rafe of hiding in Maggie's woodpile three winters ago, but he swears he wasn't anywhere near Prior, Idaho, when the kid was conceived."

Bethany frowned and shot a startled glance after the little boy. "Pardon?"

"He isn't Rafe's biological son. He was a month old when my brother met Maggie. Not that it matters, one way or another." He held her gaze, his expression suddenly intense. "It's just something I figured you ought to know."

"Not Rafe's?" She shook her head. "I never would have guessed it. He looks so much like all of you guys, and you seem to love him so much."

"We do love him. Bloodlines are important in horses, not people. Jaimie is Rafe's son in every way that matters, and when he's old enough to understand, he'll never feel less a Kendrick than any of Rafe's biological kids. That's the way it is in our family. Right, Dad?"

Keefe tucked in the back of his chambray shirt with sharp jabs of his fingers. "Damn straight. I'd take a dozen more just like him."

As Keefe moved toward the kitchen, Bethany marked the lazy, loose-jointed way he moved, which was strongly reminiscent of his sons.

Someday, when Jaimie grew older, would he walk with that same fluid grace, simply because he'd been raised by these men?

She flicked a wondering glance at Ryan. She'd been so sure he would never in a hundred years be content to adopt children.

A twinkle slipped into his eyes as he steadily returned her regard. She half expected him to say something. Instead he merely straightened and exited the room, leaving her alone with the baby and her confusing thoughts.

Amelia didn't allow Bethany to dwell on those thoughts. Well rested from her nap, she was ready to socialize, and she chortled and thrashed until Bethany focused full attention on her beaming little face. Big mistake. What a beautiful angel she was, all plump and soft and sweet-smelling. Holding her, touching her, and playing with her, Bethany couldn't help but wish for a child of her own. A child she could never have. The doctor who'd done her surgeries had been very clear on that. *Chances are, you'll never carry a child to term. In my opinion, that's a blessing. A woman in a wheelchair has no business having children.*

Remembering those words dealt Bethany a crushing blow to the heart even now. *A blessing.* Never had anyone said anything so cruel to her. She'd been nineteen years old when she had her third surgery. Only nineteen, and a doctor had all but said that she'd never be able to have a normal sex life or a family. When you boiled it all down, what was left? *Nothing.*

Staring down at Amelia's little face, Bethany struggled to shove these feelings away. This was stupid. What was more, it would be embarrassing if anyone saw her looking long in the face. It was just—oh, *God.* Being here in Ryan's home, getting to know his family . . . she wouldn't be human if the thought didn't seep into her mind that this could be *her* home and *her* family.

What was it about him that made her so soft in the head? Oh, sure. His brother had adopted a son, and right now, at this stage of his life, Ryan might think he would be content to do the same. Only it was different for Rafe. He'd already had another child of his own with Maggie, and chances were, he'd have others. Ryan would never be able to have a child of his own with Bethany.

How would he feel about that when he was fifty? A lot of men wanted to sire their own offspring. She suspected it was a man thing, somehow connected with their sense of self-esteem and virility. What Ryan might count as unimportant now could become a major concern later. He was a wealthy landowner with a family dynasty to pass on. When he grew old, wouldn't he want his heritage to go to children with Kendrick blood?

Besides, who was she kidding? As if her inability to have a child was the only problem. Not by a long shot. He spent the majority of each day outdoors, riding, roping, and climbing over rough terrain, and his leisure-time activities were centered on the outdoors as well. A couple was sup-posed to share a life, not exist in different stratospheres.

There was no way she could hope to share Ryan's reality. If she were to go outside right now, she wouldn't get three feet before her chair wheels sank in mud and snow. Ryan would end up having to carry her and her chair wherever she needed to go. Was that what she wanted? To become a burden? *No*. She would want to be a contributing partner in a marriage, not an onlooker.

And on this ranch, an onlooker was all she could ever be.

Standing at the breakfast bar, Ryan glanced her way just then, and their gazes locked. For an instant, Bethany felt as if the world moved away, that they were the only two people in the room.

She was the one who averted her gaze first, and she did so with heart-felt finality. Maybe Ryan could accept her paralysis, but he'd never be able to accept all that came with it—or more to the point, all that didn't come with it, babies of his own and a physically active wife at the top of the list.

What was more, only a very selfish woman would ask it of him.

After a wonderfully congenial dinner around the kitchen table, Ryan put in a video, and everyone adjourned to the great room to watch the movie, a children's film about two dogs and a cat that embarked on a journey through the wilderness to return home. Bethany expected to sit in her chair as she did while watching movies with her own family, but Ryan had other ideas. He scooped her up, deposited her on the reclining love seat, and settled beside her.

After drawing an afghan over them both, he kicked up his footrest and slipped an arm around her shoulders. "Comfortable?"

She was more than just comfortable. It was lovely, being able to snug-gle down on soft furniture like a normal person. "I'm perfect," she assured him.

"Yeah, you are," he agreed, his voice pitched low. Before Bethany could ask what he meant by that, he said, "Have you already seen the movie?"

"No. Have you?"

He glanced at the children, who were sitting at one end of the long sofa with Rafe and Maggie. Like ill-matched bookends, Sly and the delicate Helen sat elbow-to-elbow at the opposite end. "I'd say we've all watched it about twenty times. It's Jaimie's favorite. Sally Field does the cat's voice and Michael J. Fox does the younger dog's."

"Really?" Bethany gazed at Maggie's mother, Helen, whose lovely brown eyes were fixed eagerly on the screen. If she'd already seen the movie that many times, Bethany wondered why she was so anxious to watch it again.

"Helen's one tier shy of a full cord," Ryan whispered.

Sly glanced over and frowned, making Bethany wonder if he had overheard the comment and took exception to it.

Bethany flashed Ryan an appalled look. "What do you mean?"

"Heart attack," he explained softly. "Oxygen deprivation to the brain. She's a darling, just a little childlike."

She gazed at Helen through new eyes. Over the course of the evening, she had noticed that Maggie's mother was strange in a very sweet sort of way. "She's still so young and pretty. What a tragedy."

"Depends on how you look at it, I guess. She'll think more or less like a ten-year-old for the rest of her life, but she's the happiest person you'll ever meet. Fifty-five years old, and she believes in Peter Pan."

Bethany studied Helen a moment longer and decided Ryan was right. The poor thing seemed happy, her eyes shimmering with delight as the movie began. She seemed to be as captivated as the children.

Bethany directed her gaze to the television, hoping to enjoy the movie herself. No easy task. To do so, she needed to block out the caress of Ryan's fingertips on her shoulder. He traced circles on her sleeve, the assault on her nerve-endings ceaseless. Her skin burned everywhere he touched.

Bethany nearly asked him to move his hand a dozen times, only if she did, he would know his touch unsettled her. It was only innocent touching, after all—an absent-minded, repetitive movement of his fingertips on the cotton knit.

Watching the distracted frown that pleated Bethany's smooth brow, Ryan smiled to himself. He knew exactly what was causing that frown and continued to do it without a twinge of guilt. Any young woman who'd never even taken a solo flight was in dire need of a man's hands on her, and in this particular instance, not just any man's hands would do. When the time came, Ryan was determined it would be him who taught her to fly.

He looked across the room and winked at his mother, who was sitting on his dad's lap in the recliner. Ann Kendrick smiled sleepily and cuddled closer to her husband, resting her cheek on his shoulder.

When the movie was over, Bethany couldn't recall much of the plot.

"This has been lovely," Ann said as she rose from the chair. "But now it's time for this old lady to go home to her comfortable bed." She hugged Rafe and his family good night, then circled behind the love seat. After leaning down to kiss Ryan's cheek, she lay a hand on Bethany's shoulder. "It was lovely getting to meet you, Bethany. I hope I'll be seeing a lot of you from now on."

Bethany was trying to think of something to say in response when Keefe sleepily crossed the room to join his wife. He curled a strong arm around her. "Let's go home, Annie girl. You make that bed sound mighty good."

His salt-and-pepper hair gleaming like dark silver in the low light, Keefe dipped his head to nibble on his wife's neck and whisper something as they moved toward the door.

Ann reached up and thumped him on the top of his head with delicate knuckles. "Keefe Kendrick, you stop it. Our grandbabies are here."

"They're all asleep, Mom," Rafe called as he bent over Heidi to stuff her arms down the sleeves of her parka. "And you can forget hurrying out of here like a couple of teenagers. I need help loading cargo."

Helen fluttered behind her son-in-law, nearly bumping into Sly as he lumbered to his feet. "Easy, there, honey," he said softly as he caught her from falling. "No point in wearin' yourself out standin' in one place."

Helen's cheeks turned a pretty pink, and she cast Sly a look as coquettish as any young girl's. The foreman gave her slender shoulder a gentle squeeze and pat, which made her blush even more.

"I just want to help," she explained.

"I'm sure Rafe can think of something for you to do," the foreman said pointedly. "Right, Rafe?"

Rafe smiled. "You can put her shoes on, Helen. That'd be a help."

Keefe reversed directions to assist his elder son. Ryan took that as his cue to get up and start helping as well. While Rafe commandeered the troops at the opposite side of the room, Ryan brought Jaimie over to the love seat and began trying to stick the child's limp fingers into winter gloves. Before long Bethany started trying to help, and within seconds they were both laughing.

"This is like trying to string boots with wet leather laces," Ryan complained. "Damn, Rafe, how come you don't just buy the kid mittens?"

Rafe peered over Ryan's shoulder. "He wants real gloves like mine."

Jaimie mewled in his sleep and snatched his small hand out of Ryan's grasp, which put them back to square one. "Oh, for Pete's sake," Ryan said.

Maggie walked up just then. Unable to help because she was carrying Amelia, she merely observed for a moment, then laughed and shook her head. "Rafe, just stick his gloves in his jacket pocket."

"I don't want his hands to get cold," Rafe insisted as he knelt beside Ryan. "Come here, partner." He gathered his son in the crook of one arm. "Come on, Jaimie boy. Daddy needs you to wake up a little bit."

Jaimie burrowed against his father's chest. "Daddy," he murmured.

Leaving Rafe to handle the gloves, Ryan started trying to stuff Jaimie's feet into his cowboy boots. It quickly became apparent that this would be yet another difficult task. Bethany glanced at Maggie, who just smiled.

"They're overprotective," she said by way of explanation. "No cure for it, so I just let them go."

"I am not overprotective," Rafe informed her. "It's damned cold out there."

"Jaimie isn't very big, Maggie," Ryan put in. "Not much meat on him. And Rafe's right. It's colder than a well digger's ass out there tonight."

Keefe nudged his sons aside. "I swear, it's simple enough to dress a kid."

Everyone gathered around to watch Keefe struggle to dress the limp child. After managing to get one glove on, he rocked back on the heel of his boot, rubbed his jaw, and said, "How's about we just wrap him in a quilt?"

That suggestion was met with enthusiasm, and soon Ryan was seeing his family out. Before leaving, Keefe leaned over to give Bethany a hug. "Good night, little darlin'. You make a mean loaf of garlic bread. I think we'll keep you."

Bethany stared sightlessly at the blank television screen while Ryan was gone. She prayed he kept his distance now that they were going to be alone. If he didn't, she wasn't sure she'd be able to resist him.

When Ryan returned to the great room, he knew the instant he saw Bethany's face that she was tense. He stood near the fire, feet spread, arms folded over his chest. The way he saw it, she'd endured about all the sensual circling and feinting that she could handle. If he was smart, he'd back off. There would be all the time in the world to work on her later if he handled this situation right and made her feel comfortable about returning for future visits.

"You look exhausted," he observed. "I think I'd better get you headed in the direction of bed. Out this far from town, I never know when I'll have unexpected overnight guests, so I keep spare toothbrushes and stuff on hand."

"That's good. I'll be glad for a toothbrush."

He suddenly remembered that she was without her medication. "Damn. I don't remember you drinking much wine at dinner."

"I was afraid I'd get tipsy and embarrass myself in front of your family."

Ryan headed toward the kitchen. "Well, they're gone now. If you get tipsy around me, it's no big deal."

He quickly collected the half-full bottle of wine and two goblets from a cupboard. "You hungry for a bedtime snack?"

He heard the whir of her chair and glanced up to see her coming around the counter to join him. As he set himself to the task of forking pickles from a jar and slicing cheese on the cutting board, he asked, "How's that chair powered?"

"A rechargeable battery. I'll need to plug it into a wall socket overnight."

"Not a problem." He smiled as he popped a piece of cheese into her mouth and then handed her a full glass of wine. He'd happily charge this girl's batteries anytime. "Bottom's up. Two full glasses."

"You needn't tell me twice. I don't want to get any leg cramps."

For some reason, it had never occurred to Ryan that paraplegics might experience pain in their legs. In fact, he had assumed exactly the opposite, that they never felt anything at all, which made him question how many other of his assumptions were wrong. Searching her sweet face, which was smiling ninety-five percent of the time, he realized he was beginning to wonder about a lot of things now that he was coming to know Bethany better, namely how often she smiled when she really wanted to cry.

He remembered watching a movie called *Passion Fish* about a paraplegic woman. The scene that stuck in his mind was of the woman sitting in the kitchen, frustrated beyond bearing by her disability, and suddenly starting to scream. Pulling her hair and screaming at the top of her lungs, with only the walls to hear. Had there been a time when Bethany had wanted to pull her hair and scream? Probably. There were undoubtedly still times when she wanted to.

"Does massage help with the cramps?" he asked.

"I'd have to twist and strain so much to massage out a cramp that I'd end up with back spasms, which are even worse," she informed him with a laugh.

Ryan wouldn't have minded getting his hands on those pretty legs again to give her a massage, paying special attention to that live spot on the inside of her left thigh. That thought had him circling to another even more frustrating consideration, that Bethany might have at least partial sensation in her female parts. Maybe he was all washed up, but it seemed to him that her chances of being able to enjoy sex were good, possibly even excellent, if there were places where she had some feeling.

Thinking of the logistics had him reaching for his goblet. If he hoped to sleep tonight, he needed a good dose of wine himself. Sitting on the love seat with her for nearly two hours had cranked his libido up on high.

He focused his attention on the food and wine, determined not to let his gaze stray to her soft curves. After filling a plate for her, he began eating. Bethany picked up a dill pickle. Instead of biting into it, she touched the tip of her tongue to the end and sucked the juice. Ryan stared, a slice of forgotten cheese caught between his teeth. *Holy hell.* He was in trouble here. Watching her suck on that pickle was enough to send him running for an ice-cold dunk in the lake.

Pocketing the cheese in his cheek, he asked in a froggy voice, "You like pickles?"

"Mmm." She sucked and nipped at it, driving him insane every time she flicked the firm flesh with the tip of her tongue. "Do you?"

Ryan doubted he could taste a pickle. His pulse was slamming in his temples like shod hooves on concrete. "I sure enjoy seeing you eat one."

She went still, her eyes crossing slightly as she looked down her nose. Her cheeks turned a pretty pink, and she plucked the dill from her mouth.

Ryan grinned, experiencing a purely male sense of satisfaction that he'd managed to make her blush. She wasn't as unaffected by him as she tried to let on, and he made her just a little nervous, which was always an encouraging sign. "Don't stop. I find it refreshing to watch a woman enjoy her food." One of his pet peeves was females whose obsession with being thin ruled every aspect of their lives. "So many women are always on diets these days. Why is beyond me, but they act like eating is a cardinal sin. When I spring for filet mignon, I like a woman to dig in and enjoy eating it."

She met his gaze and took a huge bite out of the pickle. It was all Ryan could do not to flinch. He nearly laughed out loud, for he knew very well she'd done it on purpose, expressly to make him cringe. Her eyes danced with mischief. She was such a fascinating blend, he thought warmly, greatly lacking in actual experience with men, yet sharp as a tack and quick to read between the lines. He enjoyed sparring with her.

"I'm your lady, then," she informed him as she chewed, pickle puffing out one cheek. "I enjoy my food. Buy me filet mignon, and I'll devour every morsel."

He laughed at the impish twinkle that lingered in her eyes. "You're on. With what for dessert?"

She raised her finely drawn brows. "I'm surprised you have to ask."

"Chocolate?"

She got a dreamy look on her face. "The richer and more fattening, the better. I crave it like you wouldn't believe."

Ryan wondered if she knew that chocolate supposedly mimicked the feelings a woman had when she was in love. The question no sooner skittered through his mind than she said, "It's a great substitute for sex, you know. Scientifically proven fact."

This time, he did laugh. "You're doing your damnedest to shock me, aren't you?"

She smiled beatifically. "Just testing your mettle. With five brothers, I learned early that it's better to keep a guy on his toes than the other way around. Why? Does it worry you, having a sexually frustrated houseguest? You can always whip up a double batch of fudge."

Ryan Kendrick had a fail-proof cure for what ailed her, and it sure as hell wasn't chocolate.

❦ CHAPTER TWELVE ❦

With two full glasses of wine to relax her, Bethany slept deeply and awoke the next morning well-rested but out of sorts. Some people sang in the shower and threw their arms wide to embrace the day. When she woke up, all she wanted was caffeine, solitude, and absolute silence until the grumpiness wore off. It had been that way ever since the accident, an awful trapped feeling coming over her the instant she opened her eyes and realized her lovely dreams would never again be possible. Dreams of walking and running . . . riding and dancing . . . of being released from the prison that her body had become.

Morning sunlight shafted through the windows, its brilliance nearly blinding because it reflected off snow. The ecru drapes did little to diffuse the glare. Bethany cracked open one eye, groaned, and angled an arm over her face. Even the crackle of the pillowcase linen seemed loud.

Hoping to adjust to the brightness slowly, she inched her arm down. The white walls were whiter than white. There was nothing to break up the monotony, no photos, pictures, or anything. The dresser and bureau were nearly bare, no knickknacks, no scarves or doilies. Motel rooms had more personality.

Men. How could they live like this? Her brothers were the same. Their idea of decorating was to hang a calendar on the wall the first part of January.

Bethany groaned and flopped her arms out from her body like a child about to make a snow angel. Staring at the ceiling, she tried to recall coming to bed. Blurry images circled through her mind. She remembered Ryan sitting beside her after she was settled in, but she couldn't recall what they had talked about. Her only sharp memory was of how his eyes had shimmered in the dim light, a gentle, silvery blue that had given her shivers each time he met her gaze.

Sprawled on her back, she silently cursed her leaden legs, wishing she could turn onto her side to ease the crick between her shoulders. No way. Rolling over required more work than it was worth, tugging and lifting and twisting. Better to just lie there like a beached whale and be content.

Drowsily she studied the patterns in the ceiling plaster, which was also painted a relentless white. How in heaven's name was she going to get out of bed? The door to her room was closed, and though she listened, she heard no sounds to indicate Ryan was up. First thing of a morning, she always needed to use the bathroom. Small problem. Without her bed sling, she was trapped here.

She hated to yell for help and wake him up. Pushing onto her elbows, she glared at her chair, which he'd placed against the wall near an electrical outlet to recharge the battery. It was only about six feet from her, but it may as well have been in the northern reaches of Canada for all the good it did her.

"Rats!" she said. "I *hate* this. Hate it, hate it, *hate* it!"

Seconds later a sharp rap came on her door. "You decent?"

Bethany jerked with a start and blinked. "Yeah. Come on in."

The door cracked open, and Ryan poked his head into the room. Still damp from the shower, his wavy jet-black hair glistened like polished obsidian, and his burnished jaw gleamed in the brilliant morning light, hinting that he'd just shaved. He looked wide awake and nauseatingly cheerful. She detested people who smiled this early in the morning. It made her want to smack them.

"Hi," he said, strong white teeth flashing in a grin. He pushed the door open more widely.

"How did you know I was awake?" she asked crossly.

He hooked a thumb over his shoulder at a white plastic box mounted on the wall near the door. Was everything in his house above floor level white? "Intercom. I've been having my morning coffee and waiting for you to stir." His teeth flashed at her again. "Sounds to me like you're a little grumpy."

Grumpy didn't say it by half. Getting out of bed took bloody forever. Then the drawn-out process of going to the bathroom followed. Like most people, she wanted a cup of coffee as soon as she opened her eyes, and it was generally a half hour before she even saw the kitchen.

He came to stand by the bed. Bethany gazed up at him, detesting the fact that she couldn't get up by herself and had to lie there, waiting for him to help her. "You have bare walls. Don't you get tired of looking at all this white plaster?"

He flicked a glance at the room. "I don't actually look at the walls much."

Like that was a news flash? "Well, you need to decorate. Your house says who you are."

"Uh-oh."

"Uh-oh is right. If your walls are an indication, you have no personality."

He laughed and said, "I'm working on getting a decorator."

"You don't need a decorator. You need—*things*."

"What kind of things?"

"I don't know. *Things*. You know, stuff that reflects who you are."

"I've got mirrors in the bathrooms. They reflect who I am."

"Very funny. Don't you have things that mean a lot to you?" She jerked at the sheet, the corner of which had gotten stuck under her rump. "You need to hang things on your walls to make a statement."

"What do I want to say?"

"That you're someone. That you've lived and had life experiences. Snapshots of your horses, maybe. Pictures of the people you love, at least."

"I got a pair of old boots I'm real fond of."

She glared at him, which made him chuckle.

"Are you like this every morning?" he asked pleasantly.

"Yes."

"Oh, boy." He bent over to tug back the covers, then lifted her into his arms.

She clutched his shirt, still not entirely at ease when he picked her up. "I don't accept any grievances before noon."

He settled her in her chair. "I'll be in the kitchen, sunshine. Coffee will be waiting."

When Bethany joined him at the front of the house a few minutes later, he gave her a wary look. "You cheered up any since I saw you last?"

She rolled to a stop near the counter and rubbed her eyes. Her hair was all tangled, her armpits smelled, and as near as she could tell, the man didn't own a brush, only combs that jerked her long hair out by the roots. She was a creature of habit, with morning rituals that began her day. Here, she didn't even have clean clothes to put on.

"Can I have some coffee?"

He hurried to the coffeemaker and filled a waiting mug. "How do you take it, honey?"

"Strong."

"No cream or sugar?"

"No. Black and straight into the vein will suit me fine."

He chuckled, which earned him another glare. "You want a nail to chew on?"

She ignored the jibe, took the cup of coffee, and went to sit by the kitchen hearth to stare mindlessly at the fire while she tried to wake up. After downing a mug of coffee, she started to feel a bit more human and a whole lot guilty for snapping at him.

"I'm sorry for being so cranky."

Ryan pushed up from the table and joined her at the hearth, resting a boot on the brick as he regarded her. "You weren't so bad that you need to apologize for it. Just a little bristly around the edges."

She struggled to suppress a smile. "You're being polite. Jake says he's seen badgers with sweeter dispositions than I have when I first wake up."

"Yeah?" He shrugged and sighed. "That's a brother for you. Always ready to tell you the unvarnished truth, whether you want to hear it or not."

Bethany burst out laughing.

Jake arrived thirty minutes later. Bethany had performed her morning ablutions as best she could and was enjoying a second mug of coffee when Ryan and her brother came striding into the house, talking and joking as if they were best friends.

Bethany was in no mood for a male bonding ritual. She gave her brother a narrow-eyed look and smiled sweetly. "My goodness, aren't you Johnny-on-the-spot? I'm surprised you found Ryan's house so easily."

Jake flicked a glance at Ryan. His gaze meandered around the room, coming to a halt on the ceiling. "I've had business out this way before."

Ryan cleared his throat and tried to signal Jake with a sidelong glance, which Jake totally missed because he was busy counting ceiling cracks and trying to look innocent.

"Really?" Bethany mused. "What kind of business?"

Jake scratched in front of his ear, glanced her way, and then abandoned his perusal of the ceiling to study Ryan's floor tile. "The Rocking K is always ordering stuff from the store. You know that."

"And that's why you were here before, to deliver an order?"

Jake looked relieved. "Yeah, exactly that. I came out here recently to give Ryan an order. Right, Ryan?"

Ryan shrugged and gave Bethany a wary look. "He gave me an order, all right."

Jake's brow pleated. He looked at Ryan, then at her. His mouth pursed, and a thoughtful expression entered his eyes. "You ratted on me," he said softly.

Ryan held up his hands. "It was an accident, partner. We were talking, and she picked up on something I said. When she asked me point-blank, I didn't want to lie to her."

Jake settled an apologetic gaze on Bethany. "It wasn't any big deal, Bethie. I just wanted to get a few things straight with Ryan. That's all."

"It is a big deal. You're *always* butting into my business. It has to stop."

He shrugged. "It has. I won't be doing it again."

"Why the sudden change of heart? Have I missed something?"

Jake smiled at her. "Nope. I've just realized you probably won't be needing me to watch out for you anymore."

Ryan suddenly leaped into motion. "How's about some coffee before you head back, Jake?"

"Sounds good."

Ryan grabbed a mug from the cupboard. "Nothing like a good cup of java on a snowy morning."

"Nope. Nothing to beat it." Jake joined Bethany at the table. "Am I allowed to ask if you're all right? Or will that be met with resentment, too?"

Bethany had a feeling both men were eager to change the subject, and since she felt she'd made her point, she relaxed. "No, it won't be met with resentment, and in answer to the question, I'm fine. Not even a bruise, and Ryan was the soul of hospitality last night." She filled Jake in on the evening. "He has a really nice family. They all went out of their way to make me feel welcome."

"That's good to know."

Ryan took a chair across from them. He seemed tense to Bethany, but for the life of her, she couldn't think why. It wasn't because Jake was there. Her brother had done an about-face and couldn't have been friendlier had he tried.

The men talked about cattle for a few minutes. Then the conversation drifted to horses, a topic Bethany found far more interesting. As if he sensed that, Jake pushed suddenly to his feet. "Well, sis? You about ready to roll?"

Bethany sighed. "There's no risk in my *talking* about horses, Jake."

Jake grinned. "If you get a bee in your bonnet about riding again, it's not gonna be my hide Dad takes after. I'll let Ryan take the heat."

"I'm not going to start riding again."

Jake met Ryan's gaze. "Never said you were."

Getting back home proved to be the least of her problems. Her specially equipped van was still sitting in a ditch. Jake told her not to worry, that they could do without her at the store until she had transportation again, but Bethany was concerned. She had bills to pay, and she was determined to earn her own way. It could take a day for the roads to clear enough for a wrecker to pull her van to a garage and heaven knew how long after that before the necessary repairs would be done.

Ryan phoned that afternoon and immediately guessed by Bethany's tone that she was upset. When she told him why, he tried to reassure her. "If you need to go somewhere, I can take you."

"No, no. It's just that I hate to miss work for however long it's going to take. It'll make a big dent in my paycheck."

"I can float you a small loan."

"It's not that. Jake will happily give me the money to make ends meet."

"Where's the problem, then?"

She sighed and twisted the phone cord around her finger. "That *is* the problem. Nothing would make my family happier than if I depended on them and didn't work at all. It makes me—" She broke off. "I know it sounds silly, but knowing I may miss work for a week or longer makes me feel panicky."

Long silence at his end. "Panicky about what, sweetheart? You'll be back to work sometime next week."

"And Jake will be standing there with money held out, happy as a clam to be taking care of me."

"What a jerk."

Bethany laughed and closed her eyes. "I know I'm being silly. It's just—I can't explain."

"Try."

"I've worked so hard not to need anybody. It's no big deal to other people, but to me, being independent, making my own way is everything. I know this sounds bad, but my family hovers like a bunch of vultures, just waiting for me to fail. My folks would love for me to move back home so Daddy could watch after me and Mama could pamper me. They'd be pleased if I never worked again, if I just let them do everything. The thought makes it hard for me to breathe."

"And not having your van may enable them."

"Exactly. Without it, I'll lose ground. They mean well. And I love them all so much. It's awful to feel this way, let alone say it aloud."

"I understand. We all need to feel self-sufficient."

"My folks want me back in the nest."

"Well, we won't let that happen, so stop fretting. If they try to put you back in the nest, I'll beat 'em off with a club. How's that?"

She smiled sadly. The very fact that he felt it necessary to offer his support made her feel like a lesser being. "Thank you, Ryan. You're a good friend."

After they broke the connection, Bethany went to a window and stared out at the snow. In Portland, she had never become stranded like this. When it snowed up there, the driving conditions weren't this bad. At least she'd never spun off into a ditch on some stupid mountain road.

She needed her van. It was her freedom. She couldn't even go to the grocery store for bread without it. Until she got it back, she would be a prisoner in her own house and dependent upon other people for everything.

It was nearly midnight that same evening when the peal of the doorbell jerked Bethany from a sound sleep. She fumbled with her sling to get out of bed, her heart pounding with fear. No one in her family would come calling this late unless something awful had happened. *Daddy.* Her first thought was that he'd had a heart attack. *Oh, God—oh, God.* Not her father.

"Damn it!" She jerked at the sling, hating the fact that she couldn't simply hop out of bed and run to the door. When the bell rang again, she wondered if it was one of her brothers. They all had keys to the dead bolts, just in case she ever fell. Why would they lean on the doorbell?

"Coming!" she yelled.

Minutes later she fumbled with the locks, and cracked the door open to peer out. She'd forgotten to flip on the light, and all she could see was a dark, hulking shadow of a man standing on the step. *Ryan?* She'd kill him. Was he out of his mind, coming to see her at this hour?

"You scared me out of ten years' growth."

"I'm sorry, honey. I couldn't get it here any earlier."

"Get *what* here?"

He dangled her car keys in front of her nose. "Your van. She's running again. We used liquid weld to patch the radiator up. Won't last, but it'll work until I can pick up another one at a junkyard this week."

A lump came into Bethany's throat. She opened the door wider to look out, and sure enough, there sat her van in the driveway. Behind it, a dark-colored four-wheel-drive idled, the parking lights casting an amber glow over the snow in her driveway.

"Sly helped me tow her to town." Ryan bent down and kissed her forehead. "Don't want to keep him waiting long, so I'll make tracks. Sorry for dragging you out of bed so late, but I figured you'd be glad to have your wheels first thing in the morning. Now you can go to work."

"Oh, Ryan . . ." Tears gathered in her eyes. "I don't know what to say. You didn't need to do this."

"It was no big thing. We just pulled her out of the ditch with a winch and took her back to my place for a quick fix."

It *was* a big thing. A very big thing. Now that her eyes were growing accustomed to the darkness, she could see how tired he looked. She guessed that he'd worked on the van for hours to get it running.

"I don't know how to thank you."

"Friends don't have to thank each other, honey. It's understood. When you come out Saturday to watch Heidi ride, Sly and I will stick a new radiator in for you. You'll have to go to a body shop to get the grill and hood fixed, but at least she'll run."

With that, he was walking away, and Bethany was left to sit there, shivering in the icy draft, staring after him through tears. *Friends don't have to thank each other.* That man. That big, wonderful, *impossible* man. He was going to make her fall head over heels in love with him, whether she wanted to or not.

❦ CHAPTER THIRTEEN ❦

Just friends. Over the next few days, that became Bethany's mantra. She could never be the woman Ryan needed or deserved, not in bed or out of it. To allow herself to wish or entertain the notion that they could be more than friends would be sheer folly, she told herself firmly. As tempting as the thought might be, it wouldn't be fair to Ryan.

On the following Saturday when she went out to the ranch to watch Heidi ride, she was determined to set the tone of their relationship. The first part of the visit was a snap, for Ryan was busy somewhere else, working on her van. When the radiator was finally replaced and he joined her to watch Heidi ride, she reminded herself not to let gratitude weaken her resolve.

"Thank you, Ryan. What do I owe you?"

He turned a twinkling gaze on her. "Nothing. It was a junkyard special and only cost a few bucks. We have our own engine shop, so it wasn't even much work to slap it in, not with all the right tools to do the job."

"I really do want to pay you."

"Nah." He winked at her. "I'd rather just take it out in trade."

Bethany had heard that expression before. Her cheeks flooded with heat, and she averted her eyes, momentarily uncertain what to say. Then years of experience at verbal sparring with her brothers came to the rescue. "I really hate to rip off a friend. In a trade like that, you'd definitely get the short end of the stick."

He chuckled and said, "You can fix me dinner some night. How's that?"

"How do you know if I can cook?"

"Any woman who enjoys her food as much as you do has to know her way around a kitchen."

The tension between them dissipated then, and she was able to relax. It was easy to joke and laugh with a rancher who had a very spoiled pet bull, an equally spoiled and very plump dog, and was in the process of building a pen down at the lake to save orphaned ducklings from marauding carnivores. Ryan had a wonderful sense of humor, an appreciation of the absurd, and wasn't easily offended when she ribbed him about being such a softie.

When his bull made an appearance, he issued a warning to Bethany. "If T-bone ever starts bawling and slobbering all over the sliding glass door when you're up at the house alone, just toss him a carrot. Make sure you close the door fast, though, so he doesn't get inside."

"That bull gets in your *house*?" Bethany asked incredulously. "Good grief."

"He just wants in the bathroom," Ryan explained solemnly. "He got pneumonia as a baby, and I kept him in there under steam until he got well. He still remembers and can't seem to understand why he's not welcome inside anymore." He scratched his head and frowned. "A man's gotta draw the line somewhere."

A few minutes later T-bone pestered Ryan for a treat. Bethany laughed until tears streamed down her cheeks. The bull butted Ryan, and he nearly knocked him off his feet. In the end Ryan went to the house for a carrot. T-bone was in no mood to take no for an answer.

After Heidi's riding lesson was over and Bethany was making her way back along the planks Ryan had laid out to prevent her chair from getting stuck in the mud, he walked beside her. "You're a fantastic riding teacher," he told her. "Have you ever considered starting an academy?"

"When I can't ride myself?" she asked with a laugh.

"With the proper facilities and a special saddle, you could ride again. 'Never say cain't.'" He flashed her an amused look. "That's Sly's motto, and he brought me up believing in it. 'Ain't nothin' on earth ever gits done sayin' cain't, and that there's a fact.'"

Bethany sighed as she drew up near the van. "Well, not to contradict Sly, but I think we all must accept our limitations occasionally."

"You're a natural," he said softly. "You picked up on mistakes Heidi was making that I've never caught. And she's right, you know. Your name is almost legend in these parts. With some advertising to generate interest, you'd have young people signing up for classes and summer-camp seminars in droves. What's more, you'd love the work. What a waste, you sitting behind a computer."

Bethany smiled. "It's lovely to think about."

"That's a start." He stood aside as she got settled in her van. Then he hooked his folded arms over the edge of her door. "Thanks for coming out. You made Heidi's whole year."

"It was fun. I enjoyed every minute."

T-bone came ambling over just then to butt Ryan in the rump. He laughed and said, "If I bribe you with a barbecued *T-bone* steak, will you come out to watch her ride again sometime?"

"I'd love to." Bethany leaned out to pat the bull's broad head. "Don't listen to him, T-bone. He would never eat you."

Ryan grinned and scratched the bovine's ears. "I sure as hell would. Butt me one more time, and you're gonna be rump roast, T-bone. Makes my mouth water, just thinking about it."

Bethany was still smiling as she drove away. She had enjoyed the afternoon immensely and looked forward to doing it again. However, she didn't expect to see Ryan again any time soon. He owned a ranch some distance from town, she had a desk job, and their paths weren't likely to cross very often.

But Ryan had other ideas. He appeared on Bethany's doorstep that very evening, a boxed pizza balanced on one hand, two rented videos clutched in the other. Did she mind having some unexpected company? He was lonesome.

Bethany couldn't very well turn him away, so she opened the door, never guessing when she did that it wasn't only her home he meant to invade.

Ryan wanted to claim her heart, and set himself to that task. Corny B-grade movies set the mood. They spent the evening tearing apart the plots, criticizing the acting, and laughing at the absurdities while they munched pizza, sipped Coke, and snuggled together on the sofa under the afghan Bethany's grandmother had crocheted. *Just friends*. No searching looks, no kissing, no hint of anything of a sensual nature.

If Bethany's pulse raced when Ryan curled an arm around her, that was her secret. If her heart caught just a little when he brushed his fingertips over her sleeve, that was her problem—or so she told herself.

Actually that was Ryan's plan—to be the proverbial wolf in sheep's clothing.

He became a frequent caller at her house from that evening on. Some evenings he took her out for dinner and then to a movie. On two occasions he accompanied her and her mother to the "Y" on swim night and got soundly trounced when he challenged Bethany to a race in the pool. The girl swam like a porpoise, compensating for her lack of leg propulsion with strong, rhythmic arm strokes. Afterward Ryan was huffing, and he found himself looking at her with new respect, wondering what she must have been like before her accident. Competitive, surely, and incredibly determined. He wouldn't have wanted to enter a rodeo competition against her. She must have been hell on horseback, which explained why she'd been well on her way to the nationals and countrywide recognition as a barrel racer before fate had pitched her a curveball.

Other nights they sat at her kitchen table and played games. She taught him how to play pinochle, which he'd actually been playing for years, but he pretended ignorance because it was cozier that way. He taught her how to play poker, which was also cozy—just not as cozy as it might have been if they'd been betting articles of clothing, which he didn't dare suggest. On the evenings in between, they played other games—Monopoly, Aggravation (he was aggravated, all right), Yahtzee, Trivial Pursuit, and Mexican dominoes. Whatever the activity, they had fun.

Ryan often gazed across the table at her sweet face and wondered how she could fail to see what was so glaringly apparent to him—that they were meant for each other. He loved the way she laughed, tipping her head back and just letting go, the sound almost musical. He loved her indomitable sense of humor. He liked the fact that she played to win and beamed when she outwitted him. God help him, he even enjoyed arguing with her. She had a quick mind and proved to be as stubborn in her convictions as a little Missouri mule, but she was also open to new ideas and conceded a point without any rancor if he was able to prove her wrong, which didn't happen often.

Ryan's favorite nights were when he arrived with videos to watch, whereupon he deposited Bethany on the sofa, snuggled her up under Grandma's afghan, and worked his ass off for two or three hours, trying to seduce her. Casual, seemingly innocent caresses were the ticket, he felt sure, all executed in such an offhand way she wouldn't guess what he was up to—until it was too late.

Ryan the wolf. It didn't take him long to discover a few of her most vulnerable spots, his favorites being the silken nape of her neck and the sensitive hollow beneath her ear, which he tortured mercilessly with feathery touches of his fingertips. He pretended to watch the movies while he waged his assault, of course, but in reality, he was observing Bethany from the corner of his eye and smiling—wolfishly.

When he touched her lightly just under her ear, he could see her pulse leap and then flutter in the hollow of her throat like the wings of a frightened bird. If he ever so casually trailed his fingertips down the slope of her neck and dipped them under the edge of her collar, a rosy blush flooded into her cheeks. He loved the sweet way her breath caught in response to him and how her lips parted on a silent little gasp, her lashes drooping low to veil eyes gone dark with desire. She often gave him searching looks that told him she was suspicious of his motives. He returned her steady regard with the well-practiced innocent look that had served him well with females most of his adult life.

Bethany, an absolutely fascinating combination of wide-eyed innocence and wisdom. Ryan often found himself looking into her startled, big blue eyes and feeling like a low-down skunk for deceiving her.

But he didn't let guilt stop him.

He wanted her—in his bed—in his life. One way or another, he intended to have her. When he wasn't with Bethany, he worked furiously out at the ranch, having his kitchen remodeled, building ramps, and pouring cement walkways until the property was networked, giving her wheelchair access even down to the lake, He also contacted her brother Jake and enlisted his help in tracking down Bethany's mare, Wink, so he could work a deal to buy her back.

When Bethany visited the ranch again, Ryan wanted all the construction to be finished and everything else close to perfect, his aim being to protest her every reservation and argument against marrying him. All his life, he'd heard that actions spoke more loudly than words, and he meant to show her, by the sweat of his brow, how much he loved her and that they could have a wonderful life together, if only she'd give him a chance.

Yet, while Ryan was busily revamping the ranch, Bethany was agonizing over how to break off their friendship. They'd been seeing each other practically every day for over a month now, and it was time for her to face facts. She couldn't make this work. Every time she was with Ryan, it became harder and harder to think of him as only a friend. She had tried—oh, how she had tried—and for a while she had been able to lie to herself. She just wished she could go on lying in order to continue seeing him. He was so much fun, and he always made her laugh, no matter what they were doing. No longer having him in her life was going to half kill her.

But her own needs and happiness weren't the issue. She had to do the right thing, and as difficult as it might be, the right thing was to let him go. It would only become more difficult as time wore on, she knew. With each passing day, her resolve weakened just a little more, making it easier and easier to believe she could fulfill all his needs, when in truth she could never be the wife he needed or deserved.

Foolish, pathetic Bethany. She'd feared from the first that this would happen, and now it had. She was head-over-heels, wildly, crazily in love with him, and she wasn't sure how much longer she could go on pretending differently.

It might have been all right—she might have continued to fool him and herself—if only Ryan had been the type to keep his distance, but he wasn't. He was a hands-on person and very affectionate, always hugging and rubbing and *touching*. Her hair. Her ear. Her neck. Her cheek. He was driving her absolutely mad. Sometimes after he left, she'd lie awake for hours, staring at the ceiling, wondering how it would have felt if he had kissed her in all those places.

Some mornings her brother Jake would stop by her office to ask, "So how's it going with you and Ryan?"

"There is no me and Ryan," she always replied. "We're just friends, Jake. Don't read anything into it that's not there."

Jake invariably grinned when she said that. "Okay, let me rephrase the question. How's it going with you and your *friend* Ryan?"

"Fine."

Jake would frown. "That's it? 'Fine?'"

"There's nothing else to say. We're friends. It's fine. He's very nice, and I enjoy his company, end of story."

On the morning Bethany decided that she had to stop seeing Ryan, Jake asked the same old question again, lingering in her office doorway sipping a cup of coffee:

"So, sis, how's it goin' with you and Ryan?"

Bethany was so depressed, she couldn't muster the energy to go through their usual routine. She just shrugged and said, "All right, I guess."

"Uh-oh. That doesn't sound good. Problems?"

"Not really," she replied, when in truth she wanted to weep every time she thought of how empty her life would be without Ryan in it. How on earth would she fill up her evenings without him? "Nothing I can't handle, anyway."

"Honey, are you feeling all right?" Jake stepped closer to peer at her face. "You've got circles under your eyes."

"I haven't been sleeping very well the last couple of weeks."

Cupping his coffee mug between his hands, Jake leaned a hip on the edge of her desk. "Is something troubling you?"

Bethany wondered what he would say if she told him what the problem was—that his beloved sister, whom he considered to be worthy of canonization, was sexually frustrated and about to lose her mind. "No. A bout of insomnia, is all. I'm sure it'll pass."

Frowning thoughtfully and narrowing his eyes against the steam, he raised his mug to his lips and took a slow sip. "If it continues, maybe you should see a doctor."

Bethany had seen enough doctors to last her a lifetime, and besides that, she really didn't think a doctor could help with her present problem. Given her physical complications, she wasn't even sure Ryan could. What if she was doomed to a lifelong itch, with no way to scratch? Just the thought made her want to scream. She sighed and cleared an erroneous entry on the computer with a vicious jab of her finger on the delete key.

Ryan was in the tack room, replacing a bridle bit, when his cell phone chirped. He sighed and grabbed his jacket off a wall-stud nail to fish the phone out of the pocket.

"Kendrick here," he barked.

"Ryan? Jake Coulter."

Ryan smiled and sank back against the saddler rack. "Hey, Jake. How's it goin'?"

"Not worth a tinker's damn. What the hell's going on between you and Bethany?"

Ryan moved the phone away from his ear. "Nothing." Much to his regret. "What are you talking about? I haven't laid a hand on her."

"I figured as much," Jake said. Long silence. Then he sighed. "Holy hell."

"What does that mean?" Ryan asked cautiously. Jake Coulter was not a man he wanted to tangle with if he could avoid it.

"She's not sleeping," Jake said. "This morning she looks like somebody slugged her in both eyes."

"Not sleeping?" Ryan's scrunched his brow in a worried frown. "She's not sick, is she?"

"Hello. Add it up. She can't sleep, and you say you haven't laid a hand on her. It doesn't take a genius to figure out the problem."

Ryan grinned like a fool. "You think?"

Jake sighed again. "Ryan," he said with exaggerated patience. "Do you remember our conversation when I came out to your place that night?"

"I remember."

"When are you planning to get to the wedding vows and forever-after part of our understanding?"

"I'm working on her."

"Well, if you love the girl, kick it in the ass."

Ryan raised his eyebrows. "Would you repeat that, just for clarification?"

"Don't press your luck. And for the record, you're a dead man if you don't marry her afterward. Clear?"

Ryan chuckled. "I read you. No worries, Jake."

*   *   *

Seducing a woman like Bethany called for careful planning. Ryan preferred to stage the seduction scene at his place. Less risk of being interrupted that way. He didn't want one of her brothers dropping in to check on her right in the middle of everything. He could warn his own family not to come over or telephone, threat of death.

He had hoped to put off bringing Bethany out to see the ranch for another week. Her saddle still hadn't arrived, and he didn't have her treadmill set up yet. But, oh, well. Desperate situations called for desperate measures. Circles under her eyes. Oh, yeah. He'd gotten under her skin. Now all that remained was to reap his reward.

That afternoon Ryan called the store and invited Bethany out to his place for dinner that night. She sounded distracted and weary, and for a moment, Ryan was afraid she was going to turn him down.

"There's something special I want to show you," he quickly inserted.

"Well . . . all right. I've been meaning to talk to you about something. Maybe it's just as well I do it there."

He didn't like the sound of that. "Hey," he said softly. "Is something wrong?"

"Not wrong, exactly. It's—complicated. I'll talk to you tonight. All right? Is six-thirty okay?"

"Six-thirty is fine."

Ryan frowned as he broke the connection. She'd been meaning to talk to him about something? That had "Dear John" written all over it. *Son of a bitch*. He rubbed his brow. The headache he'd been battling since Jake's phone call that morning was growing worse. No worries. He loved her, and he knew damned well she cared for him. If she was thinking about not seeing him anymore, he'd be able to talk her out of it.

He took some ibuprofen, gathered up all his dirty socks and the scattered newspapers in the family room, and then took two steaks out of the freezer to thaw. That done, he made for the shower.

With his aching head shoved under the jets of hot water, Ryan was able to think more clearly, and he began to plan his strategy. He definitely wanted to look sharp, but at the same time, he didn't want to overdo it. He'd be grilling the steaks himself. Nothing too fancy. He should dress accordingly. He decided to wear pressed black jeans, a long-sleeved black shirt, and a pair of black dress boots polished to shine like glass. Women went for black. Why he had no idea, but he wasn't about to mess with what worked. Not tonight.

Did all guys feel sort of sick before they popped the question? His stomach felt like a wet sock being turned inside out. He angled an arm over the tile and rested his aching head on the back of his wrist. He hadn't felt nervous like this over a female in years. After his green wore off and he'd gotten a little experience under his belt, he'd always just figured, "What the hell," and hadn't really worried about how he looked or what he should say.

Falling in love was a real bitch.

She was late. Ryan glanced at his watch. Six-thirty-two, and ticking. *Only two minutes late.* No big deal. It was a long drive from town, and people didn't always time it exactly right. She'd be here.

He paced. Through the kitchen, into the great room. Around the sofa. Past the slider. Quick stop to gaze out at the road. He'd be able to see her coming around the lake long before she got here. Back into the kitchen. He checked the steaks for the umpteenth time to make sure they were thawed. Opened the new low-profile refrigerator to stare at the salad he'd tossed. *Still there, still green.*

He sighed and stepped to the new universal-level sink to scrub the potatoes a little more. Looked out the window again. Where *was* she? *Damn.* His stomach squeezed. He passed a hand over his eyes. He went back over everything he could remember saying to her over the past few days. As far as he knew, he'd done nothing, *nothing,* to make her want to stop seeing him.

He glimpsed her gray van through the trees just then. His heart pitched and did a funny little dance in his chest, making him worry he was about to have a heart attack. He took a deep breath, realized he was sweating, and called himself a thousand kinds of idiot. *Never let them see you sweat.*

He'd wait inside, he decided. If he went out on the porch, he'd look too eager. He no sooner concluded that than he was stepping outside. So . . . he was eager. Big deal. He wanted to marry the girl. She was it for him. No harm in letting her know how he felt.

She parked on the cement pad he'd had poured between the stable and the house. Then she just sat there and stared. Ryan walked down the wheelchair ramp he'd added onto the kitchen porch, then moved along the walkway toward her, wearing a smile that felt carved into his face. He lifted a hand in greeting.

When she finally rolled down her window, he said, "Hi, there."

She fixed him with those huge blue eyes. Her face was so white it looked damned near bloodless. "Oh, Ryan, what have you *done?*" she cried.

Somehow, he didn't think she was any too happy. This wasn't the reaction he'd been hoping to get, to say the least. *Wow* would have been nice. He glanced around, swallowed. It was on the tip of his tongue to explain what he'd done, but then it struck him how stupid that would be. He had obviously built her wheelchair paths all over hell's creation.

"How do you like it?" he settled for asking. "You can even go down to the lake and follow the shore for quite a ways in either direction."

Her face went even paler, accentuating the dark circles under her eyes that Jake had mentioned. "Oh, *God*. What have you *done?*"

Ryan had had a few days in his life when he'd wondered if he wouldn't have been better off never getting out of bed. This was shaping up to be one of them. At the sound of her voice, a horse inside the stable started whinnying and screaming and kicking its stall. Ryan didn't have to go check to see which horse it was. *Hell*. He'd been hoping to surprise her with Wink a little later in the evening. There was such a thing as hitting someone with too much at once.

But, *no*. The horse recognized her voice. *Incredible*. It had been eight years. Eight frigging *years*. Most horses had long memories, but in his recollection, he'd never heard of one recognizing someone's voice after so long.

Bethany glanced bewilderedly toward the stable. "What on *earth* is the matter in there?"

It sounded like the stable was about to fold like a house of cards. Ryan followed her gaze and rubbed his jaw. "It's nothing." He hoped Sly was still around and would do something to settle Wink down. *Fast*. "We have a new mare in there. She gets a little—"

Wink grunted three times and whinnied excitedly. Ryan had never heard the horse make that particular succession of noises before, but he recognized horse love talk when he heard it. His stomach did a slow revolution, and he could only pray Bethany didn't make the connection.

"Wink?" she whispered. She started tearing at the driver's door to exit the van. "Wink!" She fixed a tear-filled, incredulous gaze on Ryan as she extended the lift. "That's my *horse!*"

Ryan thought, Well, hell . . . He puffed air into his cheeks. "Nothing like hitting you with all your surprises at once. I, um . . . bought her back for you."

She moved her chair out onto the platform, set the brake, and then lowered the lift to the pad. "You *what?*"

Just in case she hadn't heard him, he repeated himself.

"You what?" she said again.

Ryan wasn't going to say it a third time. She moved her chair off the lift onto the cement and took off like a shot for the stable. Ryan followed, almost wishing that he could stop her from going inside. But, no. He'd paved the way, so to speak.

At the entrance she braked to a sudden stop, stared for a moment at the wide asphalt alley that stretched, straight as a bullet, the length of the center aisle to the double, cross-buck doors that opened onto the riding arena. Before each stall, a lip of asphalt with a sloped edge extended out, making the hasp of the gate accessible to someone in a wheelchair.

"Oh, *Ryan*," she whispered shakily.

Standing slightly back and to one side, he could see a tear rolling down her pale cheek. About halfway up the aisle, Wink thrust her head out over the stall gate, the whites showing around her eyes, her nostrils flared as she snorted the air. She made the three grunting sounds again and whinnied eagerly. It was clearly a greeting for Bethany alone. Gazing at the horse, Bethany made a low, keening sound, then covered her face with her hands.

"Oh, God, Ryan, why did you *do* this?" She dropped her hands and whirled on him. "Just friends, you said. No risks, no expectations!" With every word, her voice grew shriller. "Jake sold Wink for twenty-five *thousand*. I know Hunsacker wouldn't have let her go for a cent less than that. How much did you pay for her?"

Ryan swiped a hand over his mouth. Instead of feeling like her hero, as he'd imagined he might, he felt like he'd committed a crime. "The money isn't important, honey."

"It *is* important! And don't call me *honey*!"

"Bethany, I—"

"How *much*?" she demanded.

"Thirtyish," he admitted. "That's peanuts, Bethany. I've paid over a hundred for a nice horse without batting an eye."

"*Thirtyish?*" She stared up at him in appalled amazement. "And what does the *ish* stand for?"

"Six.

"Thirty-six *thousand?*" She passed a hand over her eyes. She was shaking. Shaking horribly. "I can't believe you did this. I can't *believe* it! I can't ever pay it back. Not ever."

"I don't expect you to pay me back."

She stared at him with an accusing look in her eyes. Just stared at him as if she'd never seen him before. After what seemed like a small eternity, she spoke, her voice flat and hollow. "It's all been a lie from the very first, hasn't it? You never intended for us to be just friends. You lied so I'd continue to see you."

Ryan thought about lying again. At the moment that seemed like the wisest choice. Admitting the truth didn't strike him as a brilliant move. "Yeah," he said softly. "I sort of lied, I guess. Actually, it depends on how you define love and friendship, sweetheart. Can you really have one without the other?" He shrugged, doing his best to look reasonable. "I don't think so. An intimate relationship without a wonderful friendship isn't love or anything close to it. Been there, done that, and trust me, it has no meaning."

She hugged her waist and sat back in her chair, flinching when Wink kicked her stall door again and shrieked. She closed her eyes, and the muscles in her face drew taut. "I told you from the first, Ryan. I didn't color it. We can never be more than friends. *Never.* And I planned to tell you tonight that even the friendship isn't working for me."

"Why, for God's sake?"

She lifted her lashes and fixed him with those beautiful blue eyes he'd loved since the moment he first looked into them. A deep, vivid blue so clear it could hide nothing, especially pain—the kind of pain that ran too deep for tears and hurt so much, it couldn't be expressed with words.

"I can't be what you need," she whispered.

She circled around him and headed for her van. Ryan gazed after her for a moment. Then he struck out after her. "Bethany, can we discuss this?"

"There's nothing to discuss."

He caught up with her just as she reached the lift. She rolled her chair up onto the ramp, raised it to move inside the van, and then positioned herself behind the steering wheel. He watched in silence as she hit the control to retract the chair lift and bent to fasten the restraints.

"So, you're just going to leave. Is that it?"

"Yes," she said softly, and shut the door.

Ryan hooked his arms over the edge of the window opening and leaned inside. "And I'm supposed to just let you go?"

"You don't have a choice."

When she reached to start the engine, he snaked out a hand and grabbed her wrist. "I outweigh you by a hundred and twenty pounds. That carries the vote."

She threw him a startled look. "Let go of me, Ryan."

"Not until I've said my piece," he bit out.

She twisted her arm free. "Nothing you say will change my mind."

Ryan knew he was about to lose his temper. At the back of his mind, warning bells went off. But he was past caring. "Fine, then!" he bit out.

"Run away, Bethany. It's what you're good at. Right? That's all you've done for the past eight years is bury your feelings and run away."

That got her attention. She turned to look at him, at least. Nose to nose with her, he glared back. "All this time, I figured you for having a backbone. I guess I was wrong. You didn't just lose the use of your legs in that riding accident. You lost your guts."

She flinched as if he slapped her. "That isn't fair."

"Fair? Are we playing fair, here? I'm sorry. I guess I missed it. I'm in love with you, damn it!" He swung his arm to encompass the ranch. "I've busted my ass for damned near a month, revamping my place to show you we can have a life together. Instead of being glad—instead of having the guts to at least give it a try—you're running! The truth is, I scare you to death. Good old Paul, back to haunt us. You're afraid of getting hurt, and you're too big a coward to take that chance."

"That *isn't* true!" she cried. "I'm doing this for you!" Tears rushed to her eyes. "You're just too blind to see it!" Her face twisted, and she cupped a shaking hand over her brow. "I *love* you."

"You have a hell of a way of showing it."

"It's the only way to show it! Do you think I don't want all this?" Her voice went thin. "That it's easy for me to turn my back on it? I want it so bad I can *taste* it! You're offering me *everything*! Everything I ever wanted, ever dreamed of, a life with you, being part of your world! Oh, *God*. Even *Wink*! You even bought my horse back!"

The agony in those words made Ryan's stomach drop. His flare of temper went out like a candlewick, dashed with a gallon of ice water. He was guilty as charged. He had tried to make all her dreams come true. He'd worked and planned and then worked some more, creating a world expressly for her—so she could go wherever she wanted, when she wanted—so she could be around horses and ride again—so she could visit the wilderness whenever she wished.

Looking at it all through her eyes, he tried to imagine how hard it would be to turn his back and drive away if he were in her shoes. He wasn't sure he'd be able to. He'd seen the yearning in her expression so many times—a bone-deep yearning for all the things she'd loved and lost—which was precisely why he'd tried so hard to give all those things back to her.

Yet she was prepared to leave . . . to simply turn her back on all of it, even on the horse that whinnied and called to her now—a horse that still remembered her and adored her after eight long years. It stood to reason that Bethany probably returned the animal's devotion in equal measure.

Yet she was still going to leave . . .

Ryan's throat closed off, and for a moment, he couldn't breathe. There was only one reason she would go when she yearned to stay. She honestly believed it was the best thing for *him*. This wasn't about her at all. It had never been about her. And she was right; he'd been too blind to see it.

"Oh, Bethany," he whispered. "I'm sorry." He hooked a hand over the back of her neck and drew her face to his shoulder. "I shouldn't have said any of that. I didn't mean it."

Her hands knotted on his shirt, and she shuddered as a sob tore up from deep within her. "I—can't—be—what you need, Ryan! No babies. Never any babies. M-maybe never any decent *sex*! I m-might die really young. And I c-can't be a g-good rancher's wife. I'd be a b-burden to you a-and everyone *else*!"

Ryan made a fist in her hair and drew her closer. "Sweetheart, no. Listen to me. Are you listening?"

She made a mewling sound and nearly choked, trying to hold back her sobs.

"I *love* you!" he said fiercely. "If we can't have babies, we'll adopt."

"It's not the s-*same*! Not for a man. And they might not approve me! You should have a f-family. You were *meant* to be a father. Just seeing y-you with T-bone, I knew that. You have so much love to give."

"Sweetheart, we'll have a family. You want a dozen kids? Fine. We can go through a private agency. I've already put out some feelers to find out which ones are reputable. And who says it's not the same? I'll love adopted children just as much as I would my own."

"You say that now. How will you f-feel when you're older?"

"The same. If I can't have babies with you, I'll never have them with anyone. I may be a single father and adopt kids without you, but there's never going to be another woman. You're it for me."

"That's s-silly. You don't mean it."

"Oh, but I do." Ryan turned his face against her hair. "I mean it, Bethany. With all my heart."

"Even if I can't give you good sex?"

"We won't know about that until we try. Maybe it'll be great, maybe it won't. We'll find a way, bottom line, some way that gives us both pleasure."

"Why should you s-settle for that?"

"Settle? Bethany, I *love* you. I've followed a hundred dead ends, searching for you. Not a single one of those women ever meant a hill of beans to me. Just you. I'm not settling, damn it. If I could rope the moon and have any woman on earth I wanted, I'd choose you."

"Aren't you hearing anything I've said? People like me live on borrowed time. Health risks, things we can't prevent! I could get a blood clot next week and die on you. There you'd be, with a dozen adopted kids and no wife to help raise them. *No*! I won't do that to you. I *won't*!"

Ryan tightened his hold on her, terrified in that moment that he'd lose her if he turned her loose. "Then, at least stay with me 'til next week," he whispered raggedly. "Let me have the seven days. Maybe I'll get lucky, and there'll be another week after that, and another week after that. Let me have what there is. Stay with me as long as you can. I'll let you go when God takes you, and I'll be thankful for every second He gives me, but I can't let you go like this."

"You're *crazy*."

"Yeah. You got that right. Crazy about you. Give me what you can. No one has any guarantees, Bethany. No one. We all live on borrowed time. And you know what else?"

"No, what?" she asked shakily.

"You won't die on me. Forget that, lady. I won't let it happen. I'll watch your diet. I'll have you on a treadmill every blessed day, and I'll help you exercise your leg muscles in other ways to prevent blood clots. Plus I'll have you working on this ranch, staying active. You aren't going to die young, not on my watch."

She started to cry again, this time as if her heart were breaking. Ryan slipped his other arm inside the van to loop it around her, then hauled her close against him. He knew he'd won when she stopped resisting him and clung to his neck.

He simply held her for a while, allowing her to cry. He had a feeling these were tears that had been eight years in the making, that she'd held them back for far too long as it was. When at last her sobs began to subside, he ran a hand over her slender back and whispered, "I love you. You can't change that, Bethany. Done deal. And if you run from it, you're going to destroy my life. Can you live with that on your conscience?"

She laughed wetly, the sound muffled against his shirt.

"Give me right now," he urged. "No guarantees. I accept that, and I'll take my chances. Just give me the time you can. Will you do that? *Please?*"

"Oh, Ryan . . . how can I say no?"

"Now you're talkin'."

A shudder ran through her, and she sighed raggedly. "I guess we can give it a try," she whispered. "At least until we see how the sex goes."

Red alert. Ryan tucked in his chin to look down at her. "No trial runs."

She raised her head to stare at him with huge, tear-drenched eyes that made him feel as if he was drowning in wet velvet. "But, Ryan, it might be *awful*. No promises. No commitments. Not until we know."

Though it was the most difficult thing he'd ever done in his life, Ryan grasped her by the shoulders and set her away from him. "No way, lady. If that's all you're offering me, I pass."

She blinked and rubbed at her cheeks. "What?"

"You heard me. All or nothing. No conditions. You either come into this for better or worse, or it's a deal breaker. I want you to marry me."

"But—"

"No buts. When people love each other, really love each other, they take the lemons and make lemonade. I won't settle for less. I want a woman who'll stand by me and stay with me, no matter what."

"You're the one who'll be stuck with a lemon!"

"How do you know? I could be the world's most rotten lover."

She swiped at her cheeks again, looking bewildered. "That's dumb."

"I've had a few complaints." He took a step back from the van. "Mostly not, but there you go. No telling how you'll feel about it. And what's the guarantee that things will remain status quo? Men get hurt and they get sick. A year from now, I could become impotent and unable to make love to you at all. You gonna hightail it then?" He backed up another step. "Thanks, but no thanks. I want promises, and I want commitments. If that's not what you're offering, I pass."

Her eyes turned a dark, stormy blue, and her brows drew together in a scowl. "This is stupid, Ryan. I'm giving you an out."

"Thank you. That's very sweet, but I don't want an out." He braced his feet wide apart, folded his arms, and studied her, smiling slightly. "Well? You going or staying?" He glanced around them. "It's gonna be hell to pay if you go. I never will live all this down, and concrete's pretty damned hard to rip up."

She followed his gaze, finally really looking at the network of pathways he'd built for her. Her eyes filled with tears again, and her mouth started to tremble. "Oh, Ryan . . . I can't believe you did all this for me."

"Only for you, and everyone knows it. Turn me down, and I'll be a joke. The hired hands will be snickering behind my back for twenty years. Are you really gonna do that to me?"

She shook her head, her gaze shimmering as she looked out over the lake. "There are walkways going *everywhere*! I could go and go and *go*."

"Anywhere you want, honey. Just, please, don't go away."

She fixed him with worried blue eyes again and gnawed on her bottom lip. "I'm *scared*."

"Of what?"

"That someday not having your own babies will bother you. That you'll watch television sex and realize how *boring* I am and how much you're missing."

Television sex? He usually changed the channel. Ryan looked at her sweet face and knew he could study it for a hundred years and never get bored.

"You know that lady on the fabric softener commercial?" she asked in a squeaky voice. "The one that rolls over and bounces out of bed with a big smile and puts on her jogging outfit to go running?"

Ryan had absolutely no idea which commercial she was talking about, or how that had anything to do with anything. "Yeah."

"Well, I can't roll over. I'm stuck the way I land. I have to pick up one leg and flop it, then the other leg and flop it. It's more trouble than it's worth."

He grinned. "In bed with me, rolling over will be a cinch. I'll just tuck you up against me, and we'll roll over together."

She wrinkled her nose. "I don't bounce out of bed, either. It's a big, major hassle every morning, and once I'm up, I'll never jog anywhere."

"Sweetheart, what's the point you're trying to make? If bouncing and jogging were real high on my list, would I be standing here?"

"I'm just afraid, Ryan. Someday you'll watch a commercial like that, and you'll feel like I've cheated you and hate me for ruining your life."

Ryan walked slowly back to the van. "Never. I swear it, honey. That'll never happen."

He opened the door of the van then and bent to unfasten the restraints on her chair to push her back from the steering wheel so he could lift her into his arms.

"What are you doing?" she cried.

"I'm making up your mind for you," he said as he swung her up against his chest.

She clutched his neck and gave a startled laugh. "I can make up my own mind, thank you very much."

"Nope. I've got it straight from Sly. 'Never stand around, waitin' for a woman to make up her mind, son. Not unless you're aimin' to put down tap roots.'"

"And what have you decided for me?"

"That you're staying," he whispered. "You're going to marry me, Bethany Ann Coulter. I'm not giving you any outs."

He bent his head to kiss her then, just as he'd yearned to do and dreamed of doing since that first night in her entryway.

He wasn't disappointed. Her mouth was every bit as sweet as he remembered. After her first shy withdrawal, she parted her lips and surrendered that sweetness to him, and just as before, he felt the jolt clear to his boot heels. *Holy hell,* was all he could think. No matter how the sex went, it wouldn't matter.

He could live on her kisses alone . . .

❧ CHAPTER·FOURTEEN ❧

Ryan carried Bethany halfway to the house before he came to a stop. Maybe some men could ignore the shrieks of that poor, damned horse, but he wasn't one of them. He glanced down and saw Bethany gazing over his shoulder at the stable. *U-turn*.

"I think you have some hellos you need to say."

Every step of the way to that horse stall, Ryan told himself there were some things more important than sex, and saying hello to a long-lost love had to be one of them. Wink had been just that to Bethany, one of the great loves of her life. *I would have slept with my horse if Daddy hadn't put his foot down,* she'd told him that first night. Ryan had lost a big chunk of his heart to her then—seeing the love shining in her eyes, sensing her sadness because an intrinsic part of who she was had been stolen from her.

This was important—a reunion after eight years of separation. He could make love to Bethany for the rest of their lives, but this special moment would pass, never to be reclaimed, not for Bethany or for Wink. Ryan had spent thirty-six thousand dollars so it could happen. He wanted both woman and horse to enjoy it. How else would he get his money's worth?

As they approached the stall, Wink started grunting again. Ryan had never heard a horse carry on so. "Listen to that. That's as close to talking as I've ever heard."

When he reached the stall, he thought the mare might climb over the top to reach her mistress. Bethany threw both arms around the horse's neck, Wink swung her head, and the next thing Ryan knew, he was playing catch-as-catch-can to keep hold of his girl.

"Wink!" Bethany cried. "Oh, Wink!"

Clasping her waist to hold her back from the gate so her legs wouldn't be scraped or bruised, Ryan cried, "Bethany, for God's sake, turn loose!"

That wasn't happening. She'd locked onto the mare so tightly, it would have taken a pry bar to break her hold. It got really messy after that, the mare grunting and whickering, Bethany sobbing and raining kisses on Wink's nose. Ryan made a mental note to dunk Bethany in a trough and give her a good scrub before he locked lips with her again.

When the wettest part of the reunion had passed, he gently put Bethany over his shoulder, which made her screech, caught her behind the knees, and unlatched the gate. After carrying her inside, he carefully lowered her onto the fresh mound of hay in one corner of the stall.

"There," he said with a laugh. "Now you two can make happy for as long as you want without me being caught in the middle."

Wink walked over, grunting and making shrill little sounds of greeting. The mare snuffled Bethany from head to toe.

"Oh, Wink. My pretty lady! You're so beautiful." Bethany turned sparkling, red-rimmed eyes on Ryan. "Isn't she gorgeous, Ryan?" She had cried so much, she sounded as if she had a clip on her nose.

Ryan had already looked the horse over good. He raised one of the finest lines of quarter horses in the state and had seen nicer mares. "She's the most beautiful little mare I've ever clapped eyes on." He stepped close to run a hand over Wink's rump, then gave her a pat. "I can see why she was a champion."

"There, you see, Wink? Ryan's an expert, and even he says you're the best." Bethany kissed the horse's muzzle again. To Ryan's horror, Wink rolled her lip back and wiggled it all over Bethany's face. "Kiss, kiss!" Bethany cried, giggling and making smacking noises. "I taught her to do this," she informed Ryan proudly. "She still remembers!"

Ryan sat down beside her. "All I gotta say is, you're washing your face, brushing your teeth, and gargling before I kiss you again."

Bethany rolled her eyes. "Wink doesn't have germs. Don't be such a priss." She grabbed Wink's halter strap and pushed the mare's head toward him. "Say, 'kiss, kiss.' She'll do it for anyone."

Ryan hiked up his arm to avoid the wiggling horse lip coming toward his face. "No, thanks. I draw the line at kissing a horse."

"It's a special trick," Bethany said, looking crushed.

It was special, all right. Ryan sighed, lowered his arm, and let the mare wiggle her lip all over his face. It wasn't quite as bad as he expected, but it wasn't one of his favorite experiences, either.

What a man wouldn't do for love.

An hour later, Ryan found himself eating steak sandwiches for supper in a horse stall. Wink's entrée was sliced apples, which Bethany fed her, piece by piece, as she ate her sandwich. Somehow, this wasn't quite what Ryan had envisioned as a romantic evening.

"This is the most wonderful night of my life," Bethany said with a glowing smile when she'd finished eating. She reached up to stroke her mare's neck. "I never thought I'd see her again, Ryan. Thank you so much."

"You can thank me by riding her again."

Bethany paled. "I'm a little scared."

"Your saddle won't come until next week. That'll give the two of you plenty of time to get reacquainted and bond again. If I were you, I'd probably feel a little shaky about riding her again myself."

"Oh, it isn't that." Bethany rested her cheek against the mare's velvety nose. "What happened wasn't Wink's fault. I've always known that, and I'd trust her with my life. If ever I get on another horse, it has to be her. It would break her heart if I rode someone else."

Ryan had to bite back a smile. She talked about Wink as if the horse were human. "Even though you were almost killed the last time you rode her?"

"Even though," she said with absolute certainty. "When I say it wasn't Wink's fault, I really mean it *wasn't*. Not at all." Her eyes got a distant look in them as she remembered the accident that had left her paralyzed. "She was racing her heart out for me, giving me everything she had to give. It wasn't her fault she stepped in a hole and fell. Afterward, I can't count the people who came by to see me at the hospital just to tell me I shouldn't blame Wink for what happened. They said that when she realized she couldn't stop, she shifted her weight to one side, trying her best not to fall on me. It wasn't her fault that the barrel tipped and threw me directly in her path."

Ryan watched her trail her fingertips along the horse's jaw, her touch so light and loving that she might have been caressing a child. "I don't suppose you can ask for more than that from anyone," he said softly, "not horse or person. Traveling at that kind of speed and stepping in a hole, she could have busted a leg. A lot of horses wouldn't have been watching out for their riders at a time like that."

"No." She smiled mistily. "And it would have been impossible for any horse to stop." She gave the mare another pat. "I know she tried her very best not to fall on me, and that's all I need to know. Why is it that people always want to place blame? Sometimes bad things just happen. The fairground maintenance crew raked the entire arena that morning and packed it with a roller. There shouldn't have been any holes. They're extremely careful about that because some very valuable horses compete in barrel racing events, and they don't want to be liable." She shrugged. "A ground squirrel tunneled up after the area was prepped. I won't say it was an act of God because I can't believe He wanted me to be paralyzed or that He orchestrated the accident, but I will say it was an act of nature— an unforeseeable one that couldn't be blamed on anyone." She wrinkled her nose. "Unless, of course, I want to blame the ground squirrel."

Ryan dusted some hay off his jeans. "Wanna go hunting? We've got ground squirrels aplenty around here that you can use for target practice."

She laughed and shook her head. "I appreciate the offer, but I worked through my anger years ago. I really don't think that poor little rodent tunneled a hole because he was out to get Bethany Ann Coulter."

Ryan grinned. "A very rational way to look at it. Not very satisfying, but rational."

"Looking at it rationally was the only way I stayed sane. Did you know that anger is the easiest emotion for human beings to feel, and when we lose our faculties, it's the last emotion to go? That's why people with dementia so frequently grow violent, because in the final stages, all they have left are unreasoning feelings of rage." Her smile faded, and she looked deeply into his eyes. "I was there once, feeling nothing but rage. I never want to feel that way again. Bitterness and anger affect every part of your life. I just want to be happy and make the most of things. We have to accept and move on. Feeling sorry for ourselves and casting blame only destroys what's left."

"I definitely want you to enjoy life," he agreed.

"For me, that means if I go riding again, it has to be on Wink. Anything less would be a cop-out. Riding her may bring back bad memories and frighten me, but it's something I'll have to do. Choosing to ride another horse would be a betrayal. I can't do that to her. I won't."

"I understand," he said huskily, and he honestly did understand, perhaps better than she realized. Bethany was no coward, and she didn't have it in her to take the easy way out, not when she thought it might hurt the horse that she loved so much. "I only have one question. Feeling the way you do about Wink—trusting her as you do—why are you so afraid to ride again?"

"Because I know I won't be able to use my legs and that it will never be the same. A part of me is afraid that it will be a huge disappointment— that maybe it would be better to dream about riding and tell myself how great it might be than to actually try and find out it isn't all great and never will be again. Does that make any sense?"

"It makes perfect sense. In dreams, there are no limitations. Reality seldom measures up to that. But, Bethany, look at the flip side. What if the reality turns out to be different from before, but just as wonderful in its own way? If you never dare to try, you'll be missing out on that."

"I know." She drew in a deep breath and slowly exhaled. Her eyes darkened with shadows as she met his gaze again. "I'm also really afraid that I may fall. Imagine being in the saddle and not being able to grip with your knees. The very thought ties my stomach in knots."

"You won't fall, honey. You'll be strapped on." Ryan reached out to brush a tendril of dark hair from her face. "We'll take it slow. The first few times, I'll lead you around the corral. You'll get used to it and soon love riding again."

"Oh, I hope so . . ."

"It'll happen."

Ryan meant to see that it did.

Bethany.

When Ryan suggested that they had spent enough time with Wink and should adjourn to the house, her cheeks turned as pretty a pink as June clover blossoms. En route to the van to collect her wheelchair, Ryan chuckled to himself over her shyness. Then he frowned, the realization suddenly striking him that he hadn't had much experience with virgins— as in none, period. Even in college, he'd sought out girls who knew the score. His father would have skinned him and hung his hide out to dry, otherwise.

Ryan sighed as he returned to the stable. Once in front of Wink's stall, he positioned the wheelchair and set the brake, then he stepped in to collect Bethany. She had straw in her hair, and as he got her settled in her chair, the hem of her ruffled blue skirt flipped up, revealing a rent in her hose. The jagged edges of the tear showcased a scrape on her knee.

Ryan hunkered down to examine the abrasion. She immediately started fussing with her skirt, tugging and tucking the folds around and between her legs. He glanced up. Big, wary blue eyes stared back at him. *Uh-oh*. He tried a harmless-looking grin. He never had been very talented at looking harmless.

"What?" he asked softly.

She shook her head. "Nothing."

Like hell. Ryan heaved an inward sigh, thinking that this was exactly why the traditional wedding night had been the butt of so many jokes. It was sort of like going to the dentist. If you thought about it too much beforehand, you got the jitters long before you sat in the chair.

"You feeling a little nervous?"

She shook her head no and then said, "Yes. A little."

Satisfied that the scrape on her leg was nothing to fret over, Ryan framed her face between his hands. Her cheekbones felt fragile under the pads of his thumbs—itty-bitty compared to his own. "You wanna just wait?"

"For what?"

His brain went blank. Good question. Except for marrying her, which he planned to do before the ink on the marriage license could dry, there was no real reason to wait. Unless, of course, he counted the worried look in her eyes. Which he did.

She curled her fine-boned hands over his wrists. "Oh, Ryan, I'm not nervous for the reason you're thinking. Not about making love with you. I've been—" She broke off, and the blush on her cheeks deepened. "I've thought about that part a lot, and I'm looking forward to it. It's just—"

"It's just what?" he pressed.

She smoothed a hand over the buttons of her blouse. "I, um—just sort of, you know, feel self-conscious. You're so . . ." Her gaze flitted over him. "You're so *perfect*. Handsome and superbly fit—the kind of man most women can only dream about."

Ryan's throat went tight. "Thank you. I think that's stretching it a bit, but it's a very nice compliment, and I'm flattered that you feel that way." He searched her expression. "Does that pose some kind of problem?"

"*No!* Not a problem, exactly. It's just that I'm not."

He mentally circled that pronouncement, not entirely sure what she meant. "You're not what?"

"Perfect," she replied, the word barely more than a whisper.

"Oh, honey." Ryan realized then that he'd been trying so hard to play the role of best friend convincingly that he'd failed to let her know how very much he desired her physically. He'd never even allowed his gaze to trail over her figure. Not when she might catch him at it, at any rate. "If you were any more beautiful, Miss Coulter, I'd have a critical case of pneumonia by now."

She looked bewildered. "Pneumonia?"

He chuckled. "From taking ice-cold showers."

She gave a startled laugh and said, "Oh. *Pneumonia*. Of course." A hopeful, slightly incredulous expression came into her beautiful eyes. "Did you really take cold showers?"

Seeing her incredulity made Ryan's heart hurt for her. To him, it seemed such a crime that someone so lovely could reach the age of twenty-six without ever being told how desirable she was. That was a state of affairs he meant to resolve in damned short order. "Dozens of cold showers," he assured her firmly. "I've wanted to make love to you ever since I first saw you. Every single time I was around you, I had to come home and stand under the cold water until I was numb enough to sleep."

He grinned and lowered his gaze to the lush roundness of her small but perfectly shaped breasts. Maybe it was only wishful thinking, but he could have sworn he saw her nipples tighten in response. Encouraged by that, he took visual measure of her tidy figure from there down, his hands itching to curl over her hips, his body aching to feel her softness pressed firmly against him.

When he returned his gaze to hers, her face was pink clear to her hairline, but there was a purely feminine sparkle in her eyes. He decided then and there that from now on he'd do plenty of ogling and make sure she caught him at it.

"I can't exercise certain parts of my body like other people," she confessed shakily. "In those places my muscles have atrophied, and I'm not well toned."

"Does that mean you're going to feel as soft and wonderful as you look?"

She sighed, conveying by her expression that this was no time for nonsense. "I'm just so afraid I'll disappoint you. That you might not like how I look and that I'll be a big disappointment in other ways as well, and that—"

He interrupted her by dipping his head to kiss her. Oh, God, how he loved her mouth, so soft and willing, yet uncertain and hesitant. He wanted to go on tasting her forever, wanted to spend the rest of his life pleasuring himself with her. He'd take this lady, horse slobber and all.

Forcing himself to end the kiss, he whispered, "Sweetheart, would you stop worrying? I think you're beautiful, and my opinion is the only one that counts. It's going to be all right between us. I have this gut feeling, and my gut feelings are seldom wrong."

"Oh, Ryan, I pray you're right. If we can at least have satisfying sex, I'll feel so much better about marrying you. If I can't feel anything, I think I'll *die*."

Wink nudged Ryan's shoulder. He reached up with one hand to rub the mare's neck. "Are you sure that's all you're worried about? You're not afraid I'll hurt you?" Just in case she was embarrassed to admit she felt uneasy on that score, he hastened to add, "This *is* your first time. That's a very natural concern for a woman to have, you know."

She laughed. "I *pray*."

"What?"

"I pray it hurts. That'll be good, Ryan. That'll be *great*."

The very thought made his guts clench. He would have happily hacked off an arm rather than cause her pain. But she was right. He should be praying it would hurt. In this instance, the more discomfort, the more cause to celebrate.

He returned Wink to her stall and battened the gate for the night. Then he pushed Bethany from the stable.

"You want to swing down by the lake?" he asked, thinking he needed to woo her just a bit. "It's beautiful down there at night. The stars twinkle on the water like thousands of diamonds."

"After," she said firmly. "We can go down later."

So much for that tack. When they reached the house, Ryan turned on only a couple of lights and grabbed the remote to flip on the stereo as he went into the kitchen to pour them each some wine. Bethany marveled over the changes in the kitchen, then sat at the opposite side of the counter, her big blue eyes following him nervously.

"Ryan?"

He broke off pouring to meet her gaze. "What?"

"Can we just—" She skittered her fingers down the front of her blouse, dragged in an unsteady breath, and then gulped. "You know—can we just—" She exhaled in a rush. "No big drawn-out thing. Please? I just want to—um—get to the important part. Just this time. I promise. I'm sorry for rushing you, but I need to know."

His heart caught at the shadows of anguish in her eyes. She was about to die of anxiety, and he was diddling around. He set the wine bottle aside, then circled the bar to scoop her up out of the chair.

"You won't have to issue that invitation twice."

As he swung her up against his chest, she wrapped both arms around his neck, pressed her face to the hollow just under his jaw, and whispered, "Tell me again, Ryan. I need to hear you say it one more time."

It wasn't necessary for her to clarify the request. He ducked his chin to press his lips to her temple. "I love you, Bethany, and I'll love you the rest of my life with every beat of my heart."

He carried her to the bedroom. When he set her on the edge of the bed, she bent her head so her hair fell forward to veil her face and then started unbuttoning her top with trembling fingers. She looked so forlorn, sitting there, with her pretty little feet turned all funny, one pointed inward, the other bent over at the ankle.

Ryan ran his hands down her calves, knowing she felt nothing when he touched her there, but allowing himself the pleasure anyway. Through the mesh of her hose, her skin felt cool and wonderfully soft, reminding him of how satiny she was. He kissed the scrape on her knee, which earned him a startled look from her, then he gently repositioned her feet.

When he glanced back up, she was struggling with a button. He pushed her hands away and relieved her of the task.

"Do you mind?" he asked. "I usually like to unwrap my own presents."

She flashed him a bewildered look, which he met with a smile.

"You are a gift, Bethany Coulter. The sweetest, most beautiful gift God's ever given me."

Her mouth went all funny, one corner turning down and quivering. "Oh, Ryan. I forgot to tell you one more really awful thing."

"What?" he asked, his heart catching because she looked so upset. "It can't be that bad. What, honey?"

"I have scars. Terrible ones."

His heart stuttered, then bumped back into rhythm. "Is that all?" He dispensed with the remaining buttons, then parted the front of her blouse and tugged the tails from the waistband of her skirt. "I'll bet your scars are nothing compared to mine. You want to see a scar, darlin'? I'll show you a *scar*."

He rocked back on one heel to unfasten his shirt, then jerked one side loose to reveal a jagged red scar on his rib cage. "I got it from a hay hook. Rafe and I got in a fight when we were kids. I threw something—can't even remember what now—and hit him on the back of the head. When he swung around to come after me, he accidentally gaffed me."

"Oh, *no*." She touched the mark with her fingertips. "Oh, Ryan, that must have hurt so much!"

He chuckled. "It hurt Rafe worse than it did me. He felt so bad, he cried. Dad felt so sorry for him, he didn't even give him a whipping."

Her eyes widened. "Did he whip you boys a lot?"

"Once a day and twice on Sunday, just to keep us in line." Ryan chuckled at the horrified look that came over her face. "Not really. Near as I remember, he took the strap to Rafe once, and that was way back in first grade when he smacked a girl. Kendrick code. No man worth his salt ever strikes a woman, including six-year-old boys."

"Did you ever get the strap?"

"Nope. The only time he ever took after me was when I was eighteen, and then he backhanded me across the mouth." Ryan rubbed his jaw. "Knocked me ass over teakettle, too. The old man carries quite a punch."

"Why did he backhand you?"

Ryan chuckled, remembering. "You want a list? I drove home from town drunker than a lord. Mom took one look at me when I walked in the kitchen and jumped me about taking my life in my hands. I lied and said I hadn't been drinking, which was my second mistake. Then I called her a name in a roundabout way. I never finished the sentence before Dad decked me."

Bethany had clearly forgotten her partial state of undress, which suited him fine. "What on *earth* did you call her?"

Ryan grinned. "I didn't exactly call her anything. I just pointed out that other guys drank, and their moms didn't act like bitches when they got home. I never got much said after 'bitches.' Dad swung, I went down, and when I started to stand back up, he planted his boot in the middle of my chest to inform me there wasn't a man alive who'd ever called my mother a bitch and apologized to her on his feet. If I was smart, I'd talk first and stand up later."

Bethany giggled. "Oh, my. What did you do?"

"I lay there like the intelligent kid I was and told my mother I was sorry from a prone position. Afterward, Dad helped me up, checked my teeth, told Mom to put some ice on my lip, and left the kitchen. He never mentioned it again, and I sure as hell didn't." Ryan smiled, remembering. "I've never spoken to my mother since without showing the proper respect. Bitter lesson, good school. My father isn't a mean man, but he can be a hard one if you cross him, and the quickest way on earth to cross him is to get out of line with my mom."

He peeled her blouse down her arms, doing his damnedest to pretend he wasn't much interested in the view. She was such a pretty little thing, all creamy and soft, with pointy bones here and there for a man to nibble on,

"Where are those awful scars?" he asked, pretending to search for them as he took in the lacy cups of her bra and what they supported. Her breasts were as beautifully shaped as he had imagined and just large enough to fill his hands. Through the lace, he could see the rosy tips peeking out at him. They were hard and thrust against the cloth like little rivets. "I don't see a spot on you that's not perfect."

A flush of humiliation slashed her cheeks. "They're on my back. I had three surgeries, remember."

He started to lean around. "Please, don't look," she said. "I'm self-conscious about them. They're ugly."

Ryan narrowed an eye at her. "Well, there seems to be no help for it. I guess I'll have to drop my trousers and show you what a *real* scar looks like." He reached for his belt buckle. "Tangled with barbed wire. Another story. Rafe was behind that one, too."

She noticed he was about to unfasten his belt and shook her head. "No, no. I—believe you. You don't need to show me."

Ryan arched his eyebrows. "You need to show me yours. There's no room for secrets between us, and I don't want you worrying later that I might see them. Better to get it over with now. Agreed?"

She nodded, but judging by her expression, she was none too thrilled at the thought. He decided to get the misery over with quickly and leaned around to look at the scars along her spine. His guts clenched when he located them, not because the three marks were ugly, but because they represented all the pain she had endured. He wished she might have been spared that unnecessary suffering, yet he also accepted that he, too, would have encouraged her to have the operations on the off chance that the spinal repairs might have helped her to walk again.

Aware that she was waiting for his reaction, Ryan tried to think of something reassuring to say—that the scars weren't ugly, that they didn't bother him, that he would have barely noticed them when he made love to her. All of that was true, but for some reason, the words wouldn't come. So instead, he acted on impulse, bracing himself on one elbow to lean farther around, then slowly trailing his lips the length of each incision mark. Bethany stiffened and arched her spine.

"Oh, Ryan, *don't*."

He finished kissing each scar, then drew back to look up at her. "I love everything about you," he said softly. "Even the slightly imperfect parts. They just serve to remind me of how beautiful the rest of you is."

Her eyes misted with tears. "You don't think they're ugly?"

"Not at all. Nothing about you could ever come close to being ugly."

He grasped the edge of the mattress on either side of her and pushed forward until his nose touched hers. When he continued the advance, she gave a startled squeak and fell onto her back, which was right where he wanted her. He moved his hands beside her shoulders and followed her down. Her eyes crossed slightly as she gazed up at him along the dainty bridge of her nose. He couldn't resist kissing it, then following the slope in a slow ascent to her brow, where he traced the sable arches over her eyes with the tip of his tongue.

"My God, you are so beautiful," he whispered. "I could spend the whole night just tasting you."

She curled her hands over his upper arms, and he could feel her trembling. His heart caught. "Honey, you're not afraid of me, are you?"

"Oh, no."

He bit back a smile. She was so savvy and sassy much of the time that it was easy for him to forget she had absolutely no experience with men. *Down, boy*. Whether she wanted him to or not, he needed to take this slow.

Shifting his weight to lie beside her, he braced up on one elbow and traced the edge of her bra with a fingertip, beginning at one shoulder and taking a lazy journey across the swells of her breasts to reach the opposite strap.

"Do you have any idea how much I want you?"

"As much as I want you, I hope." She cupped a slender hand over his jaw, her dainty thumb trailing lightly along his cheek. Just feeling her touch him made his blood heat. "I tried so hard not to want you, but I couldn't seem to help it." She smiled dreamily. "It got so bad that I couldn't sleep. I just lay there, wide awake, thinking and wishing and wondering. I can hardly believe I'm here with you now and that I'll never have to imagine and wonder again."

Ryan searched her eyes and saw desire, turbulent and hot, eddying in those blue depths.

She nibbled on her lip, a sudden frown pleating her smooth brow. "I really appreciate your being so thoughtful. Going so slow and taking the time to say nice things. But I really don't need you to, if that's why you're doing it. I'm ready for you to—you know—*start*."

Ryan choked back a laugh. "I'm sorry. I don't mean to drag my feet."

"Oh, I'm not complaining! I just—"

"I understand," he whispered, cutting her off by bending his head to kiss her lightly. Against her lips he added, "But, honey, I have to get you ready."

"I'm ready," she assured him.

He settled a hand at her waist and deepened the kiss. *Sweet Christ*. She *was* ready. Her soft, yielding mouth opened hungrily, encouraging him to enter and take. Only a dead man could resist an invitation like that, and he was a long way from the grave.

Between kisses she whispered, "No secrets or games. Right? My body's been as ready as it'll ever get for over a month."

He reared back to search her face. "A *month*?"

She nodded. "All those nights on the sofa, while you were watching the movies? I was thinking about—well, you know—doing *this*."

Ryan struggled to keep a straight face. "You're kidding."

"No, really."

He unfastened the waistband of her skirt. Then he could no longer keep from grinning and started to chuckle as he bent his head to nibble on her neck. "When I was touching you here?" he asked as he nipped her skin. "And here?" He touched his tongue to the hollow under her ear. "And back here?" He leaned around, trying to reach her nape. "Damn, am I good, or what?"

She twisted to look at him. "You did it on purpose."

It wasn't really a question. Holding her gaze, he unzipped the side of her skirt. "Do bears live in the woods? Of course I did it on purpose. I was doing my damnedest to seduce you."

She giggled and closed her eyes. "When we're finished here, remind me to skin you with a dull knife. For now, though, rest assured that your efforts were successful. I insist that you start living up to all those unspoken promises you made to me."

"What promises?"

"That someday you were going to kiss me in all those places—and maybe in lots of other places as well. I've been wondering how it would feel for a whole month. Now I'm ready for you to put your money where your mouth is." She laughed again. "Or maybe I should say, put your mouth where your hands were."

Ryan was more than ready to make good on those unspoken promises. He just couldn't quite believe she was asking, or that he was the lucky man she'd chosen. He'd imagined having to ease her into this, thinking that she'd be shy and a little reluctant. Instead she was impatient, sweetly eager, and as hot as a little firecracker if her kisses were any indication.

Please, God. He wanted to make it perfect for her—an incredible night that would remain in her memory always. She was such a dear heart, He had no idea what she may have imagined while she lay staring at the ceiling in her lonely bed, but he wanted to make her every fantasy come true.

When he drew down her skirt, tights, and panties, she squeezed her eyes closed in embarrassment, clearly afraid he might be disappointed with her. He skimmed his gaze from the lower edge of her lacy bra to the tips of her dainty toes, drinking in the wealth of milk white skin. Every inch of her was absolute perfection, her ribs forming a delicate ladder of descent to an incredibly slender waist that gave way to the ample flare of her hips. Unable to resist the urge, he bent to nibble on the jut of one small hipbone, which made her jerk, gasp, and open her eyes.

He grinned and hooked a fingertip under the edge of her bra. Tugging lightly, he said, "Everything off. I want to see all of you."

With trembling hands, she reached up to unhook the front clasp of the bra. As the lace fell away, her cheeks turned pink, and she studiously avoided looking up at him. "They're not very big. Do you like big ones?"

Ryan was so absorbed with looking his fill that he barely registered the question. The creamy globes of her breasts were small, but exquisitely shaped, each tipped with a delicate, rosy nipple that hardened and thrust eagerly up at him, as if titillated by the searing heat of his gaze. He wanted to touch his tongue to each sensitive peak, to learn the taste of her. But her question still hung between them, waiting to be answered.

He searched her eyes, realizing as he did that for her this was a momentous unveiling, the first time in her adult life that any man other than a doctor had ever seen her naked. Naturally she was unsure of herself. He hadn't had a surplus of self-confidence himself his first time.

"I prefer breasts on the small side," he finally found the presence of mind to tell her.

"You're not just saying that, are you?"

Ryan couldn't help but smile. "No, I'm not just saying that. And as soon as I get you fully on the bed, lady, I've got some promises I need to make good on."

When he leaned over her to turn back the sheets, Bethany's stomach did flips. She didn't know why she felt so nervous, only that she did, and no matter how sternly she lectured herself, it didn't seem to help.

He slipped an arm around her waist, twisted to turn her on the bed, and then gently settled her back against the pillow. Gazing up at him, she thought she'd never seen anyone so handsome. In the dim light his skin looked as dark as teak, and his gray-blue eyes shimmered like moonwashed silver as they trailed slowly over her body.

She realized that her knees were parted and grabbed for the blankets to cover her sprawled legs. Grasping her wrist, Ryan stopped her from taking refuge under the blankets as he situated himself beside her.

"Don't," he whispered.

"But my legs are—"

"For tonight, they're *my* legs." Still wearing his unbuttoned shirt, he shifted his weight to better see her face, releasing her wrist to slide his palm up the inside of her left thigh. "I don't know what angle you've been looking at those legs from, honey, but from my point of view, they're absolutely gorgeous. Hasn't anyone ever told you that?"

"No." Bethany's breath caught again at the feel of his hard, warm palm on the sensitive skin of her inner thigh. "Not that I—oh, my."

"You've got dimples in your knees," he whispered huskily. "The cutest little dimples I've ever seen."

His dark face moved closer to hers—close enough that the warmth of his expelled breath wafted over her cheek as he spoke. He dipped his head to kiss where his breath had already started to make her skin tingle. His lips were silky and touched her like a whisper, blazing a fiery trail to her ear where the tip of his tongue came into play, licking at her lobe and electrifying her nerve endings.

Bethany's eyes drifted partway closed. She grasped his shoulders and dug in hard with her fingers, feeling as if his sturdiness was her only anchor in a world that was suddenly spinning. Oh, God. She loved the way his lips trailed over her skin, so lightly it was like being teased with butterfly wings. And, oh, how wonderful it was to feel his chest graze the tips of her breasts. With every pass, her heart leaped and her breathing hitched. The softness of his shirt was a flimsy barrier over hard, vibrant pads of warm muscle that rippled and flexed each time he moved. *Ryan.* She even loved the smell of him—a tantalizing blend of masculine scents that titillated her senses.

When he trailed his lips to her throat, she let her head fall back and arched, loving the sensations as he kissed and nibbled and suckled her skin. A hot tingling feeling ribboned through her to pool like liquid fire low in her belly, and the funny, achy sensation that had kept her awake countless nights grew so acute she wanted to arch against him like a cat. The inclination became more intense when he traced the shape of her collarbone with the tip of his tongue. Her breathing grew more uneven, the shallow little pants barely reaching her lungs. An unbidden whimper escaped her when she felt his lips moving lower.

A thousand times she had wondered how it must feel to be loved by a man, and a fair five hundred of those times had occurred over the last two months. In the darkness of her room, while she lay alone in her bed, she'd stared blindly into the blackness of night, and wondered, the ache of need inside her making her fantasize and *want.*

How would it feel to have Ryan's hands on her body?

How would it feel if he kissed her skin?

How would it feel to have him suckle her nipples?

Now he was finally about to do it, and she could barely stand the wait. She held her breath, yearning for the heat of his mouth on her breasts.

As he kissed his way downward, he kept to the center of her chest, following the line of her sternum to her cleavage. Bethany's heart started to pound—a resonant pounding that rang in her ears. Her nipples went all hard and were so sensitive that the slight movement of his shirt over the tips made all of her thoughts splinter. He kissed the inside swell of one breast, then he kissed the other. She wished he would just get over there where she so desperately wanted him to be, but he seemed bent on teasing her and building the suspense first.

He kissed little trails toward her nipples, then veered off course, mercilessly tormenting her until she felt sure she would go mad. Each time his jaw grazed her aureole, she jerked and thought about taking fistfuls of his hair to hold him fast.

When she couldn't stand the sweet torture any longer, she did just that, bracing her arms against him when he attempted to move away. He lifted his dark head and stared at the bare peak of her breast, his eyes turning dark and molten. He clearly knew what she wanted. And when he didn't give it to her, as she was praying he might, she could have wept with frustration.

"Oh, God, Bethany, you're beautiful," he whispered raggedly, his hot breath whispering across the throbbing peak to intensify her yearning. "You make me think of strawberries and cream, my favorite thing on earth."

She just wanted him to take a taste. "Ryan . . . ?"

He moved up to take her mouth in a long, deep kiss instead, which wasn't exactly what she wanted, but he kissed her until she couldn't quite remember what she'd been wanting, anyway.

Until his chest dragged over her breasts. Instant recall. "Ryan?"

"What, honey?"

"Would you—" Bethany gulped, wishing he would just get down to business. "Would you kiss me, please?"

He took her mouth again. A deep, tongue-tangling, whopper of a kiss that set her head to reeling. It was lovely. Beyond description. A fantastic, wonderful, soul-shaking kiss that made her heart pound. But it wasn't what she *wanted*.

When he finally broke away to grab for breath, she gulped and said, "Not my mouth. My breasts."

He searched her gaze for a long, pulse-hammering moment. Then he grinned and said, "The waiting is what makes it fun."

"I've had enough fun. Twenty-six years of it."

He chuckled, the sound wicked and laced with purely male satisfaction. "Got you beat. I've been waiting to kiss those breasts for thirty years, and I'm damned well going to enjoy the anticipation." He dipped his head to lap at the V of her collarbone. "I'm going to taste every sweet inch of you and save those beautiful breasts for last."

Bethany nearly groaned. She wanted him to kiss her there so badly that she was trembling. She kept a tight hold on his hair—or tried to, anyway—her mind splintering when the heat of his mouth zeroed in on the underside of her upraised arm and trailed slowly up to the bend of her elbow. She didn't know how he managed it, but he made the most ordinary parts of her body feel like supersensitive erogenous zones.

"Oh, *God.*" She nearly sobbed when he shook her hand loose from his hair and attacked her palm, tracing the lines etched there as if he meant to commit each one to memory. When he drew the tip of her finger into his mouth and she felt that incredibly wet, soft heat drawing on her flesh, she did sob. "Ryan, enough. I can't bear it."

"Sure you can." He licked his way down her finger. "When I'm done with you, you won't remember your own name, and you'll be begging me to kiss those breasts. And when I finally do, the sensations will send you straight over the edge."

"Ah-ah-ahhhh" was all she could get out by way of response. He was nibbling on her wrist bone now. She felt like a smorgasbord laid out for his enjoyment.

He nipped his way back up to her elbow and sucked on it, laving her skin with his tongue. "I'll take your nipples between my teeth," he whispered raggedly, "just like *this.*" He gave her a preview of the delights in store for her, nibbling gently on her arm. "And with each tug of my teeth, I'll make you think you're dying from the pleasure."

She was already dying. He ducked his head under her arm to nibble on her ribs, ascending the ladder of ridges to her underarm, which she might have found embarrassing if she'd still had a clear thought in her head.

"Ryan . . ." she murmured, dragging out each syllable of his name.

He grasped both of her wrists in one big hand, anchored her arms above her head, and then reared back to gaze down at her chest. "Lordy, girl, you're something." His eyes burned with the heat of passion when he met her gaze again. He smiled slightly—the smile of a man who knew exactly what he was about and was savoring every second of it.

"I'm going to kiss them now. Are you ready?"

She'd been ready for ten minutes. She managed to nod. He grinned and then, with an agonizing slowness that made her skin burn with anticipation, he bent his dark head. "Watch," he whispered.

The edict was entirely unnecessary. Her gaze was riveted to his mouth and followed its lazy descent. When his lips came to within an inch of her breast, her nipple went even harder, thrusting upward to meet him. He smiled and blew on the tip. The unexpected waft of steamy warmth followed by the coolness of the air made her spine arch and her breathing stop. She tried to wrest her hands free from his grip, but he tightened his hold.

"Oh, no, you don't. No interference while I do this, lady. For now, you're all mine."

He flicked out his tongue to circle her aureole. Dimly Bethany heard a shuddering pant interlaced with soft whimpers and realized it was her making the sound. He curled his tongue around her nipple. The shock of heat and the silken drag sent a jolt through her that shook the mattress. She sobbed at the white-hot surges of electrical sensation and arched her spine, craving more, *more,* her lungs so emptied of breath that she couldn't speak.

Ryan seemed to understand without her saying the words. He drew her into his mouth, the pull so unexpected and sharp that she cried out. Then he caught her throbbing flesh between his teeth. Red hazed her vision.

She sobbed and cried, "Oh, yes. *Yes.*" She felt him release her wrists, and she grabbed blindly for his shoulders, needing to feel him. She pushed in frustration at his shirt, her body feeling as if it was dissolving into molten liquid with every pull of his mouth. "Oh, Ryan, I love you, love you, *love* you." She tugged frantically at his shirt, finally found bare skin, and reveled in the feeling of touching him. "Yes. Oh, yes. Don't stop. Please, don't stop."

He chuckled and moved to nibble her throat. As he trailed more hot kisses south toward her breasts again, he whispered, "I'll never stop. But I will take occasional detours that will be just as good."

Nothing could compare to—his hot mouth was at her breast again, and whatever else she was about to think fled her mind. *Ryan.* Never in all her wildest fantasies had she imagined it might be this wonderful. Never.

He took one of those detours he'd just warned her about, trailing burning kisses to her navel, which he circled and nibbled, then invaded with his tongue. When he finally met her mesmerized gaze, he arched a wickedly dark eyebrow and asked, "Do you like this?"

She never would have believed that her belly button could be so sensitive, and she *loved* it. She just couldn't find her voice to tell him. There was something incredibly erotic about watching him kiss her there. As though he guessed her thoughts, he desisted his ministrations to look up at her again. His mouth tipped into that crooked grin she'd always found so devastating. It was far more devastating when the cleft of his chin was almost connecting with her navel.

He rose to his knees to finish stripping off his shirt. He was so handsome, he almost gave her a heart attack. She'd glimpsed Ryan's chest a couple of times, and earlier he'd drawn his shirt aside to show her the scar on his rib cage from the hay hook. But just seeing parts of him had in no way prepared her for the sight of Ryan Kendrick, naked from the waist up.

He was the epitome of masculine beauty, his arms, shoulders and chest burnished by the sun to a rich umber, every inch of him sculpted by hard physical labor. Until now, Bethany hadn't believed there was a man alive as muscular as her brothers. Ryan definitely was. His slightest movement set off a chain reaction of ripples. She could have spent hours just admiring the view.

He tossed the shirt on the floor, his grin growing broader as he braced his hands on the mattress on either side of her and moved so his face was above hers again. His gaze twinkling, he glanced at her breasts. "If ever there was a doubt in my mind, I can now say with absolute certainty that I vastly prefer small breasts," he whispered, "You are so beautiful, Bethany. I'm almost afraid to believe you're really here with me."

"Oh, Ryan, I feel the same way, like I'm having a wonderful dream."

He lowered himself beside her, bracing his weight on one arm. He curled a large palm over her ribs and bent to nibble at her lips. While he kissed her deeply, he skimmed his hand down, tracing the curves and hollows of her body, his fingertips setting her skin afire.

She was lost to sensation again, the sound of every breath she drew a muffled rush against her eardrums. Her belly knotted with yearning, the need spiraling down to center low in her belly, where it seemed to radiate heat clear through her. Building . . . building until something inside of her ached and quivered with every pass of his fingertips.

"Ryan?"

"I'm here," he assured her huskily.

His gaze resting on her face, he continued to caress her until she stretched and struggled to undulate her hips. Then he slid a hand down to her pelvis, where he pressed firmly with his palm and began a slow, circular rub that ignited her. She hiked her hips as best she could without the help of her legs, rising mindlessly against the press of his hand in a rhythm as old as man- and womankind. Her breath quickened even more. Her heartbeat became a deafening thrum that made his whispery reassurances seem to come from a great distance. Not that she needed reassurance now. *Ryan.*

He moved his hand from her belly to the apex of her thighs. "Can you feel that, sweetheart?"

Bethany guessed that he was exploring the outer edges of her opening, which she'd already known was numb. The wonderful, dizzying heat of desire fell away, and her stomach knotted with anxiety. She stiffened. "I can't feel anything there, Ryan."

"Nothing?" he asked, his voice ringing with a disappointment so keen that it cut through her like a knife.

"No, nothing, I'm afraid." Her lungs suddenly felt as if they were being compressed by a leaden weight. "Up higher. I have some sensation there."

He touched her clitoris. As gentle as he was, Bethany jerked, startled by how supersensitive that place was. He rubbed the flange of flesh lightly with his thumb, and it felt as if her nerve endings were being abraded with sandpaper. She grabbed for his wrist.

"Oh, Ryan, don't. That sort of—hurts."

He lightened his touch, and when she still didn't release his wrist, he cursed under his breath. "Damn my rough hands. That's the problem."

His hands had felt marvelous on her skin. Hard and sandpapery with calluses, yes, but wonderfully warm and strong. She didn't think they were the problem. It felt more like her nerve endings down there had been damaged. They were so sensitive that even his lightest, most careful ministrations were uncomfortable. She didn't like the feeling but clenched her teeth, determined to make this work. Seconds later, she was hating her traitorous body and wishing she could scream. Instead she willed herself to respond normally to him.

"Easy . . . ," he whispered, and bent his head back down to tease her nipple while his fingertips toyed lightly below. "Just relax, sweetheart. You're so tense. When a woman's tense, this never works. You need to forget everything and just focus on the feelings and on me."

It was impossible for her to relax. The long awaited moment had arrived, and there was too much at stake. It seemed to her that everything was riding on her ability to enjoy this. Her whole future with this man, whom she had come to love so very much. If she failed him now—if she could feel nothing—she was afraid he might change his mind about marrying her. And who would blame him? No man wanted to spend his life with half a woman.

The next pass of his fingertips brought her shoulders off the mattress. She didn't experience pain, exactly, but it was close enough. "Stop, Ryan.

Please. That doesn't feel right. I think the nerves there are damaged or something." She felt his hesitation and rushed to add, "Maybe I have feeling farther up inside of me. Let's just—you know—go ahead and see how it feels."

He resumed kissing her breasts. Bethany knew he was trying to arouse her again, but she was so upset, she couldn't get there again, no matter how desperately she tried.

She felt him tug off his pants and heard his boots hit the floor. The next instant, he rose over her, a dark blur of bronze and ebony. There was an odd crinkling sound, as if he were tearing open foil. Then she felt his hands grasping her hips, and she slid down the mattress slightly.

"I'll try not to hurt you, Bethany mine. Just tell me if you feel any pain, and I'll stop."

She felt the coarse hair on his leg brush against her inner left thigh, and he fleetingly touched her clitoris again, which was now so tender she gasped.

She braced herself, knowing that he was about to push in. *Please, God, let me feel it when he enters me. Please, please, please . . .* In that moment, she could think of nothing she'd ever wanted more. To *feel,* simply to *feel.* If God would grant her only that, she promised herself she'd never ask Him for anything else. For her, that would be everything.

She got an odd feeling—like pressure building way low inside of her. She blinked and brought Ryan's dark face back into focus. His beautiful steely-blue eyes were filled with question.

"Sweetheart, is it hurting?"

Bethany knew then. It was like being slugged right in the center of her chest, a staggering blow that emptied her lungs and made her want to weep.

He was inside her—and she felt nothing but an odd sense of fullness. Absolutely nothing.

❧ CHAPTER FIFTEEN ❧

Ryan held Bethany in his arms until she fell asleep, and then he sneaked from bed to go walking on the lakeshore, his heart breaking a little with every step he took. *Please, God.* The words became a litany, the same words over and over and over. She was so dear, and, oh, how she shined. She was like gentle spring sunshine, his Bethany. Or like a fairy glow of moonlight on water, he thought as he gazed across the lake. Her bright smile. The sparkle in her eyes. She had brought light into his life, making everything seem golden.

"Please, God," he whispered as he reached his thinking spot on the knoll.

He sat beneath the overhanging pine boughs, finding no comfort tonight in the shadows that embraced him. When he gazed at the moon-silvered mountain peaks that loomed like specters over the forests that grew on the opposite lakeshore, all he could think about was Bethany. She'd been as eager for their lovemaking as he had been, responding so readily to every kiss and touch of his hands. She'd been shy at first, but she'd quickly set those feelings aside, giving herself to him so freely and completely, her trust in him glowing in her eyes. Then he had left her hanging.

He braced an elbow on his knee and cupped a hand over his face. He went to church almost every Sunday, and he considered himself to be a decent, God-fearing man, if not a pious and prayerful one. Countless times, he'd gone through the motions of prayer—kneeling, folding his hands, and bowing his head. But he realized now that all those times, he'd never really gone to his knees.

He was on his knees now. He loved that girl so very much. He would have done anything to make her happy. But for all of that, he couldn't give her the one simple thing she needed most, satisfaction in his arms.

Making love to her had been the most wonderful, fulfilling experience he'd ever had, making him feel complete in a way he couldn't begin to express. He'd taken so much, so very much, and in return, he'd been able to give her nothing. *Nothing.*

He'd felt the tension in her body afterward—the kind of tension that told a man he'd failed to bring a woman to completion. *If I can't feel anything, I think I'll die.* Oh, she'd tried to hide her disappointment, hugging him and burrowing her cheek against his shoulder, saying how lovely it had been. But he'd known, and he'd wanted to weep.

Now he was alone. If he cried, that would be his secret.

The tears felt like acid in his eyes. A sob built pressure in his chest until he couldn't breathe. That look in her eyes—oh, God—he doubted he'd ever forget it. Shock, disappointment, and then a terrible despair he hadn't been able to dispel.

His shoulders jerked, and the next instant, he was sobbing. *Please, God.* There in the darkness, Ryan cried like a child for the girl he'd left sleeping in his bed, and he prayed for a miracle, knowing in his heart that if God didn't make this right somehow, he might very well lose her.

The following morning Bethany lectured herself in the bathroom mirror. Time to count her blessings, and they were many. She was in love with the most fantastic man on earth, and he loved her back. That was an incredible blessing. And making love with him last night had been the most beautiful, indescribable experience of her whole life, all of it perfect and wonderful, right up until the last.

What more did she want? She'd enjoyed all of the touching and kissing. That was so much more than she had ever hoped to have. She would be foolish to let the wonder of that be tarnished by her inability to feel the last part.

No way. She would wear a bright smile, and she'd be grateful that God had chosen to give her this much. It was enough. It *was*. If she could grow old in Ryan's arms, she would count herself the luckiest woman alive, and she would not let herself wish for more or feel sorry for herself because there wasn't more.

When she reached the kitchen, he was at the table, nursing a mug of coffee. He pushed another mug toward her and smiled, his eyes lackluster as his gaze moved slowly over her. "Good morning, sunshine."

"Good morning!" she said brightly, which was totally uncharacteristic of her. She glanced out the window. "And it *is* a gorgeous one. Spring may come late in this country, but there's nothing more wonderful once it arrives."

Ryan rubbed his forehead. "Sweetheart, you don't have to do this."

Bethany's face felt so stiff that her smile hurt. "Do what?"

He kept his gaze fixed on his coffee. "Pretend everything's wonderful. I know you're upset—that it wasn't good for you last night, and I'm sorry it wasn't. We can work on it—make it better." He shrugged and flicked her a sad, hangdog look. "I'm sorry I didn't make it happen for you."

She felt as if two fists were twisting her heart in half, and an awful, frightened feeling tied her stomach in knots. Ryan might settle for less than perfect for himself, but it would eat at him like a cancer if he thought it was less than perfect for her.

Bethany didn't generally lie, and she found it particularly distasteful to think about lying to Ryan. But in this instance, she wondered if being completely honest wouldn't do more harm than good. Maybe she was lacking in practical experience, but she wasn't naive. Caring individuals, be they male or female, needed to know that their lovers truly enjoyed being intimate with them. Bethany couldn't imagine how awful she might be feeling right now if the tables had been turned—if it had been Ryan who hadn't found satisfaction in her arms last night instead of the other way around.

The twisting pain in her chest grew more acute, making it difficult for her to breathe. She couldn't bear the thought of losing him. Not now. Not after being with him. Before, as painful as it might have been, she could have turned away for his sake. But now she knew how much she'd be missing. So she hadn't achieved a climax. The rest had been so wonderful—so absolutely *perfect*. She couldn't go back to the empty existence she'd had before—to a life without Ryan. Oh, God, she just *couldn't*.

Not allowing herself to think about the right and wrong of it, Bethany made a snap decision. She'd lie. Before she was with him that way a second time, she'd watch *When Harry Met Sally* again and practice faking an orgasm until she could do it so convincingly that Ryan would never guess it was an act. He'd never look at her like this again, with his heart aching in his eyes. Never. She'd be the best lover he'd ever had, damn it. The very best. Last night, she'd been so caught up in her own pleasure, so overwhelmed by all the incredible sensations she'd never hoped to feel, that she'd given little thought to the things she might do to give him pleasure.

No more. She was no expert on sex, but what she didn't know, she could find out, even if it meant going to a sexual therapist and getting some how-to literature. She'd learn what turned men on, all the little tricks that drove them crazy in bed. No holds barred. Anything. She'd do *anything* to keep from losing him.

"Ryan, how can you say it wasn't good for me? That simply isn't *so*. It was wonderful for me."

He slumped back in his chair and met her gaze. "Sweetheart, let's not go there. All right? Honesty is our ace in the hole. Talking about it openly and working together to find a solution is our only hope. We'll find a way. I promise you. Somehow. It just may take some time." He winked and flashed her a grin that lacked its usual brilliance. "You know what they say. Practice makes perfect."

Bethany felt bile rise up her throat. As long as he felt guilty because she wasn't enjoying it at the end, it would spoil it for him. All along, her greatest fear had been that she wouldn't be able to give him pleasure. Now she knew she could. That, in and of itself, was a miracle. How it had been for her simply didn't matter, not in the overall scheme of things.

"Ryan, look at me." When he met her gaze again, she said, "It was fantastic for me, the most wondrous experience of my life." That much wasn't a lie. "It's true that I didn't feel anything at first. But I did later." She thought fast. "When you moved a little deeper, I *felt* you. What an incredible feeling it was."

Hope came into his eyes. "You did?"

"Oh, *yes*." She hugged her waist, praying he wouldn't notice how her hands were shaking. "I love you so much, Ryan. Being with you that way, it was so beautiful. And I'm so excited because I felt something, there at the end. I'm sure if we'd just kept going a few minutes more, it would have been fabulous."

"Deeper," he repeated. "You felt it when I went deeper? Bethany, that's wonderful." He sat straighter and shifted to face her. "How did it feel?"

Oh, God. She had no idea what a woman felt when a man entered her. She thought of the sensations when he'd kissed her breasts and grabbed for words. "An electrical, tingling feeling." She pressed a palm to her stomach. "Way deep, right here. It's hard to describe."

He laughed softly, and a joyous look came into his eyes. "That'll do." He came off his chair and went down on one knee beside her. After wrapping her in his arms, he buried his face against her hair and held her tightly for a moment. "That'll do, sweetheart," he said huskily. "I can work with that, and we'll get there."

Bethany clung to him and vowed that they would "get there" far sooner than he dreamed. "I love you, Ryan. Please, be happy. I am. So very happy."

Bethany propped her arms on her desk, ignoring the muted click and hum of the computer hard drive perched beside her. To heck with filling out purchase orders. She had more important fish to fry, namely learning all she could about giving a man great sex. There was no listing for a therapist in the yellow pages. Bethany ran her finger down the S's, praying to find *SEX* in all caps. She needed an expert, someone she could pump for information who wouldn't betray her confidence.

"Morning, sis."

Bethany slapped the phone book closed and glanced up from her desk to see Jake standing in her office doorway. "Jake!" She clamped a hand over her heart. "You startled me out of my skin."

He gave her a slow once-over. "How goes it with you and Ryan?"

"Fine. *Great*. He, um—we're doing fine." She was developing a headache that felt as if it might split her skull, but that was beside the point. "I, um . . . how are you?"

"Good." He nodded at the phone book. "Can I help you find something? You were looking pretty intense when I interrupted you. What's up?"

"Nothing. I was just—nothing's up."

He searched her gaze. Then, in a low, soft voice, he asked, "You happy, Bethie? That's all I need to know, that he makes you happy."

There was no mistaking the knowing look in her brother's eyes. She'd told her family that she was going to Ryan's for dinner last night. Jake had probably tried to call her later in the evening to make sure she'd gotten home safely. When she didn't answer the phone, he must have concluded that she was spending the night at Ryan's place. Armed with that knowledge, it didn't take a genius to put two and two together. That was a little embarrassing. But if she meant to marry Ryan, she supposed she would have to get used to it.

"Yes, he makes me very happy," she finally replied. "So happy, Jake. I never thought—well, you know—that I could have a life with him. But he's convinced me I can. You know he bought Wink back for me."

Jake raised his eyebrows. "You're kidding! He did?"

Bethany might have been fooled by her brother's feigned surprise if Ryan hadn't told her that Jake had played a role in locating the mare. "It was so good to see her again, Jake. You just can't know. We spent half the evening in her stall. Ate dinner out there and everything."

"I'll bet Ryan loved that." Jake chuckled. "I'll let you tell Pop about Wink, by the way. He's going to burst a vessel."

Bethany sighed. "Yes, well—maybe I'll wait. Kind of hit him with one thing at a time. It'll probably be a big enough shock when I tell him I'm getting married."

"Oh?" Jake looked surprised again. "This is news."

"Liar. I know you've been talking with Ryan. He told me last night that you hooked him up with the contractors who remodeled his kitchen and that you helped him track down Hunsacker so he could buy Wink back for me."

Jake chuckled. "On that note, I'm heading downstairs to crack the whip."

"Without congratulating me?"

"Congratulations. Just understand, if he doesn't treat you right, you'll be a young widow."

Bethany was still shaking her head when he headed down the hall. She waited a moment, then reopened the phone book, turning back to the list of physicians. There had to be someplace she could go to talk straightforwardly with someone about sex.

"You seen the coffee filters?"

Bethany jumped, slapped the phone book closed again, and glanced up to see Kate, one of the store's employees, in the doorway, holding a coffeepot full of water in one hand. "We have extras filters here in the cabinet."

Bethany hurried over to open the metal door. While waiting, Kate stepped into the office and set the coffeepot on the edge of the desk. After locating the filters, Bethany grabbed a new package and turned to hold them out.

"Thanks," Kate said, reaching over the desk.

A tall, slender woman with lovely features and gleaming auburn hair that hung like a veil to her shoulders, she had always reminded Bethany a little of Cher—a very unpolished and shopworn version. Her heavily made-up brown eyes were bloodshot this morning, and she flashed a strained smile that had "hangover" written all over it. According to Jake, the woman drank heavily and slept with anything in trousers, but she was a good employee who showed up for her shift and came in on her days off when others called in sick. Bethany didn't usually work the floor, which made it difficult to cultivate friendships with the downstairs help, but she'd always liked Kate, sensing she was a warm, genuine person, for all her rough edges.

Kate retrieved the pot of water from the desk. "Too much happy last night," she said in a whiskey-and-smoke voice. "I need a good jolt of caffeine to jump-start the old bod."

"I know that feeling," Bethany said. "Only I don't need too much happy to make me feel that way. I wake up with a dead battery no matter what."

Kate spied the ashtray Bethany kept on her desk for any "no-smoking" offenders to snub out their cigarettes. She glanced over her shoulder at the open door. "Say?" she said conspiratorially. "Would it bother you if I closed that and sneaked a couple of drags? Jake's got a nose like a blood-hound."

"I suppose I can be your partner in crime for one cigarette."

Kate put the pot back on the desk, gave Bethany a grateful look, and closed the door. Smiling as she plucked a pack of Marlboros from her shirt pocket, she said, "You're okay. Thanks. I woke up late, you know? Didn't get my coffee, didn't get my smokes. I feel like I was rode hard and put away wet."

Kate looked that way too. Bethany bit back a smile, watching as the other woman fished in the hip pocket of her skintight blue jeans for her lighter. With a flick, she inhaled gratefully, then exhaled through her nose. "Man, I needed that."

Bethany enjoyed the smell of cigarettes while they were being smoked. It was the stench of stale smoke that turned her stomach. "I tried smoking once."

Kate raised her eyebrows. "I never figured you for the type."

Bethany sat back in her chair, about to launch into a comical account of her brief walk on the wild side in college—or in her case, her brief *roll* on the wild side—with a tight-knit group of female paraplegic friends. As they had all gone through school on special grants for the handicapped, they'd been short on money, so they'd had much more in common than just their physical limitations.

But before Bethany could speak, it hit her like a fist between the eyes that Kate was just the kind of person she'd been praying to find—an expert on sex. And here she was, standing right under Bethany's nose.

"Say, Kate?" Bethany thought quickly. "Are you busy today after work?"

"Why? You need something extra done? I gotta tell you, I have a bitch of a headache. Tomorrow would be a better day for me."

"No, no, nothing like that. I just thought—you know—that maybe we could go have coffee together someplace after work and chat for a while."

Kate frowned. "Have I screwed up? You're not gonna can me, are you?"

Bethany couldn't think of a reasonable explanation for the sudden friendliness so she decided the simple truth was best. "No, nothing like that. I haven't been here very long, and I haven't made many friends yet. Being stuck up here on the second floor most of the time, I can't even get to know the people who work here very well. I've got a problem right now that needs solving, and it's not the sort of thing I'd feel comfortable discussing with one of my brothers. It would be really nice to be able to talk it over with another woman, and I thought maybe you might have a few minutes to spare."

Kate glanced uneasily toward the door. "Jake know about this?"

"No. I'm twenty-six years old. I don't need permission from my brother to have coffee with a friend."

Kate raised her eyebrows. "I didn't figure you for that old." She shrugged. "Sure. Okay. You buyin'?"

Bethany laughed. "I'll even throw in a piece of pie."

"You're on. My stomach should handle pie by then."

After work that evening, Bethany waited in her van. When the other woman finally emerged from the store, she honked to get her attention. Kate waved and broke into a long-legged jog. Once in the van, she rolled down her window, lighted a cigarette, and said, "Way cool. I've never seen the inside of one of these jobbers. You're all set up to roll."

Bethany considered mentioning that no one was allowed to smoke in her van, but then she decided it was a fair trade-off for the information she needed. "Where sounds good? There's a Denny's restaurant a couple of blocks over."

Kate sighed. "I don't suppose I could work a trade, could I? A beer instead of coffee and pie."

"A beer?"

"Yeah. I know a quiet little place we can go."

Bethany would have preferred going to a restaurant. Because she had to adjust her daily dosage of anticoagulant if she drank much alcohol, she seldom imbibed. Kate also liked to party, and her definition of a quiet place might differ greatly from most people's. She hesitated.

"Come on," Kate urged. "Live a little."

Ten minutes later, Bethany was entering a seedy-looking place called Suds. A shotgun floor plan sported a bar along one darkly paneled wall, tables along the other, with two pool tables, end to end, at center stage. Kate pointed Bethany toward a table and stepped up to the bar as if she owned the joint.

"Two Buds, Mike! Hold the head."

"Gotcha!" the bartender called back.

Bethany scooted a chair out of her way and drew up to the table. After withdrawing her wallet, she set her purse on the floor at her feet. The next table over was occupied by two men wearing flannel work shirts and jeans, the sawdust on their clothing earmarking them as mill workers. Bethany paid them little notice as she watched Kate advance toward her with two full beer mugs clutched in her hands.

"I was supposed to buy," Bethany said as Kate set a mug in front of her.

"I'll let you get the next round," Kate assured her as she sat down.

The next round? Uh-oh. Bethany took a sip of beer and smiled. "Mmm. This hits the spot. I didn't realize how thirsty I was."

Kate took a long pull from her glass. White foam mustached her upper lip when she finally came up for air. "God, I've been dying all day for some hair of the dog that bit me. You're a champ, Bethany. I know this isn't your thing."

"I don't know. It's rather nice, actually. I expected someplace a little livelier. You strike me as the type who enjoys large groups of people—with the ratio of males to females making it easy for an attractive single woman to score."

"God, do you have me pegged, or what?" Kate rubbed her temple and sighed. "I'm not feeling up to snuff today. Check in tomorrow night, and you'll see lively." After taking another swig of beer, she leaned forward over her mug as she lit another cigarette. "So—what's the problem you need to talk about?"

Bethany took a big gulp of beer for fortification. "Sex."

Kate shrugged, blew out smoke, and said, "Yeah. What about it?"

Bethany swallowed more beer. "Don't laugh. I'm really in need of some advice. I'm, um—how shall I put this?—a novice, I guess you might say." She patted the arm of her chair. "Wheels have a way of putting a damper on a woman's love life, and I'm only just now starting my first relationship."

Kate narrowed her eyes slightly, the exhaled smoke forming a blue cloud in front of her long, pretty face. "Jesus, honey. That's the saddest thing I've ever heard. Twenty-six years without sex? That sucks."

"Yes, well. I only count the years since puberty. It doesn't seem quite so pathetic that way."

"That's still a long dry spell."

Bethany took another sip of beer and smiled. "I've survived. It was lonely sometimes." She wrinkled her nose. "Oh, to heck with it. You're absolutely right. It sucked."

Kate chuckled. "Hey, without sex, what's it all about?"

"Exactly," Bethany agreed. "Which brings me to my problem. I enjoyed most of it immensely, but toward the end—" She broke off and flapped her hand. "For some paraplegics, the finale isn't all that it should be, and it seems that I'm one of them."

Kate studied her solemnly. "You can't get off?"

Bethany glanced around to be sure no one else could overhear. Then she stared into her beer for a long moment. After taking three huge gulps and wiping her mouth, she said, "Nope, I can't get off. And I really, really want to keep the guy. I love him a lot, and all the rest was really nice."

"Just no bang at the end." Kate sat back in her chair, took a deep drag from her cigarette, and then said, "Shit." She regarded Bethany for a moment. "Well, there's worse things. A lot of women don't get off. They go their whole lives faking orgasm, and they seem to get along fine."

Bethany smiled. "You settle for what life dishes out, I guess, and you learn to be happy with what you have. That's the way I look at it, anyway, and overall, I think I'm very lucky." She shrugged. "I just want to keep it that way. He's the best thing that's ever happened to me, and I don't want to lose him."

"Can't blame you there."

"During my lunch hour, I stopped by the video store and rented *When Harry Met Sally* so I can brush up on my—well, that part goes without saying. But movies and books fall a little short when it comes to giving detailed explanations of how a woman can give a man pleasure. I really, really want to be *good* in bed. As good as I can be, at any rate, given my physical limitations, and I thought you might know a few tricks you might share with me. Like what to wear, for instance. Or maybe some special tips about how to do things he'll really like. I need a crash course."

Kate pursed her lips. "Damn, honey, you don't ask for much. It's a little hard to share twenty years of experience over a few beers."

"I know I'm asking a lot. But I'm desperate. I understand the basics, but I need to take a giant leap from beginner to intermediate, *fast*. I want it to be as perfect and wonderful for him as I can make it. You know? With plenty of added pizzazz to compensate for my failings, so to speak."

Kate sighed. "Can you wear a garter belt and nylons? Most guys really go for those. Meet him at the door wearing that and a lacy black bra. If he's got blood flowing in his veins, his eyes will pop out of his head. If I walked in here dressed that way on a busy Saturday night, I'd have comers lined up out to the parking lot."

Bethany laughed. "That and nothing else?" She'd thought of wearing a lacy peignoir, but nylons and a garter belt had never entered her mind. This was *exactly* what she needed, pointers from a woman who knew the ropes. "I'd feel sort of silly."

"Not for long." Kate winked at her. "Try it, honey. Works like a charm. Guys are weird. If that doesn't work, fix dinner for him wearing nothing but an apron. Just remember to turn off all the burners when he decides he can't wait for dessert."

"Nothing but an *apron?*"

"High heels are a nice touch. Why guys love them, I haven't a clue. I once accidently nailed a fellow in the ass with a spike, believe it or not. He never even broke rhythm."

Bethany laughed so hard at the picture that came into her mind, she had to wipe tears from under her eyes. "Oh, Kate, you're wonderful. Unfortunately, I can't wear high heels."

"Sure you can. You don't have to parade around in them to get his motor purring. Just seeing them on your feet will do it."

Bethany leaned closer. "Another question. You watched *When Harry Met Sally,* right? In your opinion, was that a pretty accurate portrayal of how a woman looks and sounds when she's having an orgasm?"

Kate rolled her eyes. "You're really without a clue. He won't grade your performance, honey. Lesson number one about men. They all want to believe they're God's gift to women. Fake it as best you can, then tell him he's fabulous. He'll walk on water for a week."

Bethany laughed again. She didn't know if it was the beer or if Kate was just funny.

Kate finished her drink and went to get another round. When she returned, Bethany drew a ten from her wallet and pushed it across the table. "The next one's on me."

"Thanks." Kate stabbed the bill with a fingertip, then walked it around in a circle. "I know this is a really personal question, but I'm going to ask. Are you totally—you know—numb down there?"

Heat crept up Bethany's neck, and she glanced over her shoulder again. The two mill workers appeared to be intent on their own conversation, and the bartender was busy cleaning the taps. "Not totally," she said softly. "I have some feeling here and there. It's just—well, spinal injuries are funny. If your nerve endings are impaired, as some of mine are, having sensation in a certain spot doesn't necessarily mean that part of the body will function normally. I have feeling in my buttocks, for instance, but not all the muscles there will flex."

"Hmm." Kate frowned. "How many times have you tried for the big whammy?"

Bethany remembered that horrible moment when Ryan had looked into her eyes and asked if it was hurting. To her dismay, she felt her chin wobble. She took several more gulps of beer. "Only once."

"Only *once*?" Kate rolled her eyes. "Bethany, lots of women don't get off the first few times."

"They don't?"

"Heck, no. I didn't, anyway. I was too uptight, worrying about this and that and feeling self-conscious. Tension and orgasm don't ride double. You know those romances where the couple gets in a huge fight, and the guy muscles the woman into bed when she's still spitting mad?" Kate shook her head. "He kisses her, and she swoons. That's bullshit. At least it doesn't work that way for me. Some guy tries that when I'm pissed, and he'll end up wishing he hadn't. Sex doesn't usually work that way for a woman."

"I really didn't feel that tense until the last when I started worrying about how it would feel. Or, more precisely, if I'd be able to feel it at all. I don't think tension was the problem." She took another long pull of beer. "Afterward—" She passed a shaky hand over her eyes. "I could tell he knew it didn't happen for me, and he was upset. I'm so afraid I'll lose him, Kate. That he won't want to be with me anymore if it isn't good for me at the last."

Kate nodded. "Yeah, that'll do it. Like I said, they got big egos. Most of them can't handle doing a gal who doesn't hit the finish rope. Not for a steady diet, anyway, and that's your aim. Right? To keep him hanging around."

"Right. Oh, Kate, thank you so much for talking to me. You're so *real*. Most people take one look at my wheelchair and freeze up. Sex? The word doesn't cross their lips. They immediately assume I'm a head."

"A what?"

"A *head*." Bethany waggled her fingers beside her ears. "I talk, I smile, I laugh. Anything below the collarbone is distasteful as a topic of conversation."

Kate grinned. "Maybe it's because you never asked them out for coffee to talk about sex. Hell, babe, sex is most people's favorite subject."

Bethany raised her mug. "Here, here. I love you."

Kate's brows drew together. "You drink much?"

"Not a lot. More than I ever have just recently." Bethany swung her mug back to her mouth.

"Well, hell. Who do you talk to?"

"Since moving here, no one. Occasionally with Jake, but not about anything like this. He'd have a coronary."

Kate winked. "I have a feelin' he packs a wallop when he lets the starch out of his collar, but it ain't happenin' around you."

"Exactly. My whole world is starched. With creases." Bethany sighed woefully. "I should have asked you out for coffee a long time ago. Now, here I am with this *man*. Oh, God. He's all my dreams, stuffed into chambray and denim. Just looking at him almost gets me there. *Almost*. That's the story of my life, Kate, a long history of 'almosts.'"

Kate chuckled. "What's his name?"

"Ryan Kendrick."

Kate's eyes widened. "Good Christ. Repeat that. You've slept with *the* Ryan Kendrick?"

Bethany nodded mutely. Apparently, even Kate found it unbelievable that someone like Ryan was interested in her.

Kate grinned and then laughed. "Holy *shit*. You don't mess around, sweetie. Ryan Kendrick? As in so good-lookin', women fall over on their backs like bowling pins and cock up their toes? *That* Ryan Kendrick? The to-die-for *rich* hunk nobody can nail?"

"I never thought I'd be lucky enough to have someone like him fall in love with me. He's *wonderful*. If he isn't happy with me, I'll *die*."

Kate cupped a hand over her eyes, propped her elbow on the table, and laughed so hard her beer slopped. "No *wonder* you're so hooked. He's like—well, *dynamite*."

"Yeah." Bethany swallowed, fixed Kate with an imploring look, and said, "Only with no big bang at the end."

Kate rocked back in her chair and shook her head. "Well, we gotta get a leash on his collar, no question. Isn't just everybody that gets a crack at him." Her smile softened. "You got stars in your eyes, sweetie."

Bethany envisioned Ryan's face and nodded. "I love him so much. I don't care if it's all that fantastic in bed at the end. You know? The first part was a lot of fun. Like, *wow*."

"Been there a couple of times." Kate grew pensive and gave the ten spot another turn. "Bethany, another real personal question. I know the guy's got a reputation for having been around, but that isn't always an indication. You sure he knows what he's doing?"

"Oh, *yes*." Bethany drank more beer. "He's followed a hundred dead ends. A *hundred*. Can you imagine?"

"Ryan Kendrick? Oh, yeah. I can imagine. Poor man. He's like one of them targets at a shooting range. Everybody wants to take a crack. Poor guy has probably had a lot of nasty surprises halfway into relationships when women finally let their true selves shine through."

"Probably. No consolation to me. I about *fainted* when he told me he'd dated so many women. They all had to be better than me. Just the thought scares me half to death. Being compared and all. You know what I'm saying?"

Kate smiled. "You're not exactly dog meat. Not a guy in the store who hasn't looked your way and rubbed his fly a few times."

"Pardon?"

"Christ. Never mind. Like you'd know if Kendrick knows his stuff? I can't believe I asked." She stubbed out her cigarette and immediately lit another one. "You're a sweet kid. Funny. I figured you for being stuck-up."

"You did?"

"Jake acts like you shit golden eggs. Never saw a man so protective of his sister. Must be nice."

"Nice?" Bethany groaned and finished off her beer. She stared at the empty mug, feeling mildly surprised at how easily it had gone down. "You know—I think maybe I just found my poison."

"Holy mother. I can't drive that rig of yours. We'll have to call a cab."

Bethany giggled. "What are you saying?"

"That you're getting a buzz." Kate pushed to her feet, grabbed the ten, and said, "What the hell. We may as well. Only go around once."

When she returned with the beers, she said, "Okay, now we're both relaxed. Got all the starch out of *our* collars. Let's get down to the dirty."

Bethany took a huge gulp of beer and smiled when she came up with a mustache, just like Kate's. "Go for it. I'm all ears."

"Before we talk more about what guys like, let's talk a few minutes about you. I've got a question. Did he try to get you both ways?"

"Both ways? I'm not following."

Kate leaned closer. "You know. Some women can't get off the conventional way. Did he try your hot line?"

Bethany pictured a huge, red phone and burst into giggles. "No, mine's probably been disconnected."

Kate sighed. "Your love button, sweetie. Did he try that?"

"I've never heard it called that before." Bethany sighed and shook her head. "In answer to your question, yes, he tried it. To be honest, I found it very—well, not really painful, but uncomfortable, like all my nerves were exposed. It's hard to describe. The same sort of feeling you get when you bite down on a piece of tinfoil. It made me want to clench my teeth and shudder."

"It can feel that way if you're not into it." Kate got a knowing gleam in her eyes. "The important thing is, you have feeling there."

"That doesn't mean it works properly. Trust me, it didn't."

"It could be that he didn't have the magic touch. Ever think of that?"

Bethany remembered the magic in his touch everywhere else and shook her head. "No. It's more a case of damaged nerves, I think. That isn't his fault, and—"

Before Bethany could finish what she meant to say, the man behind her turned on his chair and said, "If he doesn't know his way around a love button, honey, trade him in for a new model."

"Butt out, Dave," Kate said. "Who invited you into this conversation?"

The man draped his arm over the back of his chair and twisted farther around to give Bethany a long, hard look. "Well, now, if you ain't purdy as a picture."

"Jack off," Kate said.

The man ignored her. He scooted back his chair and pressed his face closer to Bethany's. "Hi, honey. I couldn't help overhearing your conversation. My heart's breaking. Sounds like you've got yourself one hell of a problem."

Bethany blinked and inched her face back. "I'm a little distressed."

He nodded. "What you need is a real man to grease your gears. I'm packin'."

Kate came up off her chair. "Hey, asshole, get out your dictionary. I said, 'Jack off!' Leave the lady alone."

"I'm surprised you recognize one, Kate."

"Stuff it where it'll never again see sunlight." Kate planted her hands on the table and glared daggers at him. "Leave her alone. She's with me."

He gave Kate a long, hard look. "You can't help her. This little gal needs a real man to get her motor running." He returned his bleary gaze to Bethany. "How 'bout it, honey? I'll get you perkin'. Then you can go back to lover boy."

Bethany inched farther away. All she could think of to say was, "I need to use the bathroom."

That seemed to cool his jets. Bethany rolled her chair back and fumbled for her purse. She glanced at Kate as she returned her wallet to the side pocket. "Excuse me." The man blocked her path. "Please. I really need to go."

He sighed and said, "I'll be waiting. Give me an hour. Problem solved."

Bethany's heart was pounding. The effects of the beer had done a vanishing act. That man wasn't taking no for an answer. She cut right, following the signs. She found herself in a long, dark hallway with warped paneling. The ladies' room was the last door on the left.

She was about to reach for the knob when a big hand closed over her shoulder. "My name's Dave, by the way," he said in a slimy voice. Then he leaned down, grabbed the arms of her chair, and turned her to face him. "No one will bother us back here. Let me have a go at that love button of yours."

Bethany stared up at him. His eyes were glassy and hard. He was breathing funny. The smell of his sweat filmed her nostrils, making her feel as if she was breathing olive oil. "Let go of me."

"Ain't touchin' you," he pointed out. "Just your chair. So, arrest me. You want to get off. I want to get off. Let's make some music together."

Before Bethany guessed what he meant to do, he clamped his foul-tasting mouth over hers and shoved a hand down the front of her blouse. She pushed frantically at his shoulders, taking him so off guard that he lost his balance and staggered back, ripping her blouse at the shoulder in the process.

"Fine by me," he said with a laugh. "You want rough? I'll deliver."

A loud, shattering sound of glass startled them both. Dave swung around, as surprised as Bethany. There stood Kate, holding the jagged end of a broken beer bottle in her right hand.

"Take your paws off that girl, you son of a bitch, or I'll make you sing soprano."

Bethany tried to dart into the bathroom, but her chair was just a little too wide to fit. The man's full attention was fixed on the broken bottle now, allowing her the time to get unstuck, back up, and try again. With the second advance, she hit the doorway going faster, and the force of her momentum pushed the chair on through. She swung the door shut, then backed up against it so no one could easily enter. She was shaking so badly that she could barely dig her cell phone out of her purse. She imagined Kate murdering good old Dave, with blood splattered all over the warped paneling. *Oh, God, oh, God.* She shakily punched in the number to the store.

Jake opened a thick parts manual. "I don't know where she went. If she isn't at home, no telling. Have you tried my folks?"

Ryan rested his arms on the parts counter. "I just—hell, I don't know. I figured she'd want to spend the evening with me. How long has she been off work?"

Jake ran a finger down the small print, muttering numbers under his breath. When he found what he was seeking, he glanced up. "About an hour, maybe an hour and a half. You been by her house?"

"I called there." Ryan sighed, unable to shake the feeling that something wasn't right. "I can't figure her just taking off somewhere."

Jake chuckled. "Maybe you weren't as good as you thought."

"Shut up." Ryan rubbed beside his nose. The jibe struck a little too close to home.

The phone rang just then. Without glancing up from the parts catalog, Jake snaked out a hand to answer it. "The Works. Jake Coulter speaking. How may I help you?" He lost his place in the catalog. "What? Where are you?"

Ryan heard a faint voice coming over the line. Shrill, hysterical. He would have recognized it anywhere. He jerked erect, pulse racing. "What's wrong?"

Jake held up a hand. "You're *what?*" He listened for a second. "You *stay* right there. Do you understand me, Bethany? No matter what happens. Get in a stall and lock the door if you have to. I'll be right over."

Jake slammed the phone back into its cradle and came around the counter at a run. "Bethany's in a bar. Some bastard has her cornered in the bathroom, and Kate's about to rip his guts out with a broken beer bottle."

Ryan hit the door of the place called Suds two steps ahead of Jake. As he staggered into the dim interior, he scanned the room for any sign of Bethany. The bartender, a potbellied, sandy-haired guy in a white apron, jerked his thumb toward the rear. "Back there. I done called the cops."

Ryan and Jake scrambled for the rest room sign. It was a toss-up which of them made better time, the only certainty being that they didn't fit abreast when they started down the hallway. Ryan took the lead with an elbow in Jake's gut. If some creep had Bethany cornered, he wanted the honor of killing him.

When Ryan reached the end of the hallway, the scene that greeted him was worse than he imagined. Some woman who looked as if she'd been used hard and smacked for her trouble had a man backed against the wall with a broken bottle shoved against his crotch. She looked prepared to castrate him.

Ryan didn't really give a shit if the guy came out of this with his balls. He tried the ladies' room door, but the damned thing wouldn't open. Jake arrived at almost the same instant. Breathing hard, he flattened his hands on the door.

"Bethany, honey? Open up. It's Jake and Ryan. You okay?"

"Ryan?" she cried from the other side of the door. "Why'd you bring *him?"*

Ryan fell back. If that wasn't a fine how-do-you-do. He was here to save her. She was *his*. Not Jake's. Certainly not that creep's, who was about to lose his reason for being alive. Any man worth his salt looked out for his lady.

Ryan rapped his knuckles on the wood. "Bethany? Open the damn door."

"Is that awful man gone yet?" she asked shrilly. "He ripped my *blouse*."

Ryan glanced over his shoulder. His gaze connected with bleary brown vulture eyes, and he suddenly wondered why the hell he was messing with a door. He turned, advanced, and said to the woman, "I'll handle him from here."

Kate moved back, and Ryan stepped up to take her place.

He might not have laid hands on the man. His mama had raised him civilized, after all. But the son of a bitch looked Ryan up and down, grinned cockily, and said, "Are you the pussy who couldn't get the little lady's rocks off?"

Ryan never remembered exactly what happened after that. Witnesses claimed he grabbed the jerk by his shirt, picked him up, and proceeded to ring his bell by repeatedly slamming him against the wall.

The next thing Ryan clearly recalled, he was in handcuffs. He wasn't sure *why* he was in handcuffs. His knuckles burned, and there was a man in custody holding his face, but Ryan had no recollection of hitting him.

It was all pretty much confusing, actually. The cops brought Bethany out of the bathroom, and every time she looked at Ryan, she wailed, "Oh, God! Oh, God! All I wanted to do was to talk. I never meant for this to happen."

Kate put an arm around her. "Calm down, sweetie. You're twenty-six years old. If you wanna go have a beer now and again, I guess you can."

Ryan decided he didn't like Kate. She was a bad influence. He knew all about bad influences. Over the years he'd gotten into a lot of sticky situations he never saw coming with his brother Rafe. It always started with, "You know what I'm thinking?" And it went downhill from there. Oh, yeah. Ryan knew how easily you could find yourself in a hell of a mess, just because of the company you kept. Not that his brother was bad company. Rafe had just been one of those kids whose nose led him straight into trouble, and being the younger brother, Ryan had always been tagging along right behind him.

Ryan was thinking about that, albeit a little fuzzily, when Jake, who was in no real trouble with the cops, stepped over to the bar. He gave the bartender a long, narrow-eyed look that Ryan immediately recognized as bad news.

In a low, sort of friendly voice, Jake said, "Are you the man who called the cops when he realized a girl in a wheelchair was trapped in the ladies' room with an amorous, unruly drunk trying to bust down the door?"

The bartender might have said yes and gotten away with it. Instead, he puffed out his chest. "What do you think I am, buster, a bouncer? The lady came in, started complainin' to her friend about her sex life, and some guy half my age offered to show her a good time. I ain't touchin' that with a ten-foot pole. Like she wasn't askin' for trouble? My wife likes my face just the way it is."

"She won't now," Jake said conversationally.

And then he hit him.

Shortly after that, Ryan was getting cozier with Jake Coulter than he'd ever wanted to be—in the back of a cop car.

The Crystal Falls city jail had never seen such a ruckus. Ryan could hear his dad yelling clear in the back cell block.

Clinging to the bars like a convicted felon, Jake gazed across the aisle at Ryan. "You think your dad's gonna spring us or join us?"

Ryan pressed his brow against one of the bars and rolled his head back and forth on the coolness. As a substitute for an ice pack, it totally sucked, but it was as close as he was going to get in this place. "My father's jail-bird days are over. He hasn't had any brushes with the law since he married my mom."

Jake listened for a moment. "He sounds a little hot under the collar."

Jake no sooner stopped speaking than Ryan heard his father yell, "What the *hell* is this country comin' to? A girl gets accosted by a drunk, and you arrest her menfolk for takin' up for her? Explain that to me. Used to be, when a man defended a woman, people patted him on the back!"

A low-pitched voice replied, the sound a murmur Ryan couldn't make out.

"He always like this?" Jake asked.

Ryan considered the question. "Nah. Only when he gets royally pissed."

"Then, call the judge!" Keefe roared. "Get the damn bail set! I'm not leaving my boys in the hoosegow all night! You got that, partner?"

Ryan flashed a weak grin at Jake. "Congratulations. You just got yourself a second daddy. Ain't he a dandy?"

They both heard a woman's voice rise over the din just then. "No, Keefe, *please*! I'm all right."

Keefe yelled, "Don't push my wife, you cocky little jackass!"

"Keefe, *please*!" Ann cried again.

A loud crash followed. Jake raised his eyebrows, fixed an alarmed look on Ryan, and whispered, "Holy hell, I think your dad just punched a police officer."

ᔏ CHAPTER SIXTEEN ᔐ

Sly had noticed Bethany's gray van sitting out front when he entered the stable, so he wasn't surprised to hear her talking to her horse. However, he was surprised when he realized she was crying as if her heart would break. With all the Kendricks at city hall, he was a lone soldier at the moment. Sly didn't mix any too good with weepy females.

That being the case, he considered leaving. Turning around, walking out. It seemed like a good plan, but when he reached the doors, the sound of her sobs grabbed him by the scruff of his neck. He stopped and slowly turned back, not entirely sure what he meant to do, but feeling as if he had to do something.

Once he reached the stall gate, he wasn't sure how to let her know he was there. She sat with her back to him, her face pressed against her mare's chest. Sly rubbed his jaw and then said, "Kinda looks like rain. Don't it?"

She jumped as if he'd jabbed her with a cattle prod. Then she hurriedly rubbed her cheeks before turning to look at him. From the first, Sly had thought she was a pretty little gal, but he hadn't really seen why the boy was so taken with her. Now he did. Them eyes of hers were flat something, damned near as big as flapjacks and bluer than blue.

"Sly! I, um—you startled me. I didn't know anybody was here."

He rested an arm on top of the gate. "Just came over to feed the stock. Ryan ain't around to take care of it tonight."

"I know. He's—in *jail*." Her face crumpled. "And it's all *my* fault."

That wasn't the half of it. Could be she hadn't heard about Ryan's daddy yet, though, and Sly wasn't about to tell her. "Well, now, don't take too much blame. That boy's a scrapper, always has been. He come by it kinda natural. Ain't like he just up and caught a bad case of the orneries after he met you."

She wiped her cheeks. As soon as she finished, another big tear spilled out. She dabbed at her nose with a tattered tissue that had more holes than a noodle sieve. Sly dug in his hip pocket for his handkerchief. After checking to be sure it was clean, he opened the gate and stepped inside to hand it to her.

"Here, honey. It's a little dusty but otherwise clean."

"Oh, I—" She stared at the blue bandanna for a second. Then she hesitantly plucked it from his fingers. "Thank you."

Sly hunkered, sifting through the hay while she blew her nose. "I couldn't help but hear you when I came in. Is there anything I can do?"

She took a quivery breath. "I wish there was. I feel so bad, Sly." Her mouth trembled and twisted. "Ryan's mom and dad are going to hate me."

"Aw, now, that ain't likely. This is just one of them things. Been kind of borin' around here of late. You sure enough fixed that."

"I guess I have." She dabbed the corners of her eyes. "All I wanted to do was talk to another woman. What a *disaster*. I was hoping to solve a problem, not create a new one."

"That's how it happens sometimes. The hurrier you go, the behinder you get."

She smiled and nodded. "I definitely didn't solve anything, that's for sure."

Sly searched her face. She looked so lonely sitting there, with only her horse for company. "Don't you have any friends, honey?"

She shrugged. "Dozens up in Portland, just not many here yet. I haven't been back very long, and until just recently, all my time was taken up helping my brother at the store. There's Ryan, of course." She blew her nose again. "I can't talk to *him*. If only Kate would have gone with me for coffee. But, oh, no. We had to go to a stupid bar."

Sly smoothed the hay in front of him. He couldn't help but feel bad for her. "If you got a particular problem that needs solvin', maybe I can help."

"Thank you, Sly. That's very sweet. But it's—well, of a delicate nature, a feminine concern. That's probably not your field of expertise."

"With a name like Sly Bob, there ain't much about females I ain't expert on," he informed her with a wink.

"Sly Bob?"

"Short for Sylvester Bob, last name Glass. Down home, I harkened to Sly Bob."

"Is Galias a Mexican-American surname?"

He cocked an eyebrow. "No, darlin', it's Glass, not Galias."

"I'm not detecting a difference in the pronunciations. How is that spelled?"

"Just like it sounds, G-L-A-S-S."

Flattening a dainty hand over her chest, she burst out laughing, tears spilling over her lower lashes when she scrunched her eyes almost closed. "Just lack it sigh-yoonds?" she repeated, shaking her head. "G-Ale-A-Ayus-Ayus?" When her mirth subsided, she said, "Oh, Sly." She dabbed at her cheeks. "Thank you for taking the time to talk with me. I feel better already."

"I'm glad I lightened your load."

She smiled. "Considerably. So, tell me, how did Sylvester Bob *Glass* get shortened to Sly Bob? Someone didn't like you, or what?"

"Nah. It was the way in them parts, shortenin' boys' names, oft times to the first and middle initials, and my mama didn't like folks callin' me by mine."

Her brow furrowed in a frown, then understanding dawned in her eyes and she nodded. "Ah. I can see why she might have taken exception."

"Anyhow, she took to callin' me Sly Bob, and it stuck. I got teased a lot, and somewhere along the way, I started livin' up to the handle. Bad decision on my part, but it led to lots of interestin' experiences until I was nigh onto forty."

"Then you settled down?"

"Nope. Just got tuckered. Women have a way of flat wearin' a man out."

She rewarded him with another smile. Sly was glad she had at least stopped crying. "I appreciate your offering to lend me an ear. But it's not the sort of thing I can talk to a man about. Especially not *you*. You might tell Ryan."

"I ain't given to talkin' out of school, not to Ryan or anybody else."

"I couldn't ask that of you. I know you're very close to him."

Watching her expressions, Sly got a funny, achy feeling at the base of his throat. There were all different kinds of lonely, and he had a feeling this girl had been nose to nose with most of them. She was also very troubled about something, and unless he missed his guess, it had to do with Ryan. Sly loved that boy like a son. "It won't be the first secret I ever kept from Ryan."

She blushed and shook her head. "No. I just—it's too personal. I'd just—no. I couldn't."

Sly thought for a minute. "You ain't the only one who could use a friend, you know. Here of late, I got me a problem of my own."

Her eyes filled with concern. "You do?"

"Yep. Cain't talk to anybody in the family about it." Sly rubbed a hand over his mouth. "They get wind of this, and I'm liable to get my walkin' papers."

"The Kendricks would never fire you. You're like a member of the family."

"Just goes to show how bad a problem I got, I reckon." He met her gaze. "Tellin' secrets has gotta go two ways. You wanna do a swap?"

"Oh, I don't know. As I said, I'd feel funny talking to you about mine."

Wink stepped over and began pestering Sly for a scratch between the ears. He absentmindedly obliged the mare as he said, "No call to feel funny talkin' to me, honey. There ain't nothin' that shocks this old man."

She went to twisting on the handkerchief, her fingers clenching so hard that her knuckles turned white. "Yes, well, this is about *sex*." She leaned closer to whisper that last word as if she feared someone else might overhear.

"Sex?" Sly chuckled. "Well, now, you are in luck. I might've scratched my head a little on some subjects, but I'm sure enough an expert on that one. I've hung my britches on so many bedposts, I once wore a post hole in the seat of my jeans."

Her eyes widened. "My goodness. Did you really?"

He narrowed an eye at her. "No, not for true. I did wear a white spot, though. Anything you wanna know on that subject, I'm the feller to ask."

"I suppose getting a man's viewpoint might be helpful."

"I qualify on that count. Definitely a man, last time I checked. So what do you say? Wanna swap problems?"

She smiled slightly, then took a bracing breath. "All right. But only if you share yours first."

"Do I got your word you won't never tell? Nary a soul."

"Nary a soul," she agreed.

Sly shoved Wink away and ran his finger under his shirt collar. Then he cleared his throat. His voice went gravelly as he said, "You met Helen, Maggie's mother."

"Yes."

"Well, her and me, we're being friendly on the sly, no pun intended. If anyone finds out, it could cost me my job at the Rocking K. Helen ain't quite normal, you see."

When he finished speaking, she stared at him in stunned silence for several seconds. "Oh, Sly. I don't know what to say."

"Ain't much you can say, I don't guess." He released a pent-up breath. "Unless it's to call me a lowdown polecat for triflin' with her."

"Never that, Sly. I think she's a very lucky lady."

"You don't think I'm doin' wrong?"

"Not if you truly care for her. If you were only using her, then, yes, I think it would be very wrong. But it doesn't sound to me as if that's the case."

"I feel powerful better, just gettin' it off my chest. They all trust me, you see, and in the thirty-odd years I've worked on this spread, I ain't never broken that trust. Keefe and me—we go way back. When he first started this place, I was his right-hand man, and I been here ever since. Stood up for him when he married Annie. Helped raise both them boys." He took off his hat to turn it in his hands. "I tried to keep my hands off her. I knowed she wasn't right and maybe looked at me through a child's eyes, so I tried my damnedest. But the sad fact is, a man don't always choose who he loves. It just up and bites him on the ass."

"Does she love you?"

A burning sensation washed over Sly's eyes. "She thinks I can rope the moon. Could be that's why I love her so. Been a lot of women. None to speak of recent like, but a goodly number in my younger days. Nobody's ever looked at me like that." He tried to think of a way to explain. "When I talk, she listens, all interested like. Follows on my heels like a lost puppy whenever I'm over at Rafe's place. I ain't got a whole lot of schoolin', and lots of folks think I'm dumb. She admires me and thinks I'm smart. That makes me feel real good, and seein' the shine in her eyes when she looks at me, I walk a mite taller in my boots."

Bethany leaned forward to touch his hand. "Oh, Sly. I think maybe you're underestimating Ryan. If I understand how you feel, don't you think he will? He's got a good heart."

Sly enclosed her dainty fingers in his. "He does, at that. But the Kendricks, they're peculiar about their womenfolk. Step over the line in that respect, and they get downright testy." He gave her hand a squeeze. "I don't like sneakin' around, but I cain't see no other way. If they find out, the shit'll hit the fan. I'd marry her, of course. Ain't no way I'll have my Helen hangin' her head. Maybe she ain't real bright no more, but she's as fine a lady as there is."

"Oh, Sly, it goes without saying that you'd marry her. Perhaps that's the solution to this dilemma. Have you considered that? The Kendricks hold you in high regard, and you'd make Helen a fine husband."

"They won't hold me in high regard when they find out I been cozyin' up to Helen. Them thinkin' she ain't right, they're all-fired protective. Chances are, they'll can me. That's the policy here, no messin' with the women. I'd be without a job. How could I care for her? A man's gotta have work in order to do right by a woman, and someone pretty and fine like Helen deserves pretty and fine things. She ain't stupid, you understand. Or retarded, like. She's just slower to get there than other folks."

Bethany bent her head, her dark hair falling forward to hide her face. "I'm glad you told me." She glanced up to smile. "I know my vote isn't worth much, but I think it's wonderful that the two of you have found each other, and I hope you find a way to be together the way you should be."

Sly's voice turned gruff. "Thank you for that. Your vote means a powerful lot to me."

"I'll tell you something else. Just because you have little formal education, that doesn't mean you haven't been to school. It was simply a different kind."

He grinned and winked at her. "I'm beginnin' to see why that boy's been like a pup chasin' its tail since meetin' you. Always did figure him for smart. Just didn't know how smart."

"Thank you, Sly. That's a lovely compliment."

"Sincerely meant. Now, enough about my problem. You gonna tell me about yours?"

After a great deal of hemming and hawing, she managed to do that. Sly scratched his head, after all, and almost wished he hadn't struck this bargain. "Well, now, that there is a whopper. No feelin' at all, you say?"

"Some here and there, but nothing seems to work right," she said hollowly. "I really don't mind that. Just being with Ryan is enough for me. I'm just afraid it won't be enough for him."

"If he loves you, it will. If he don't, you're well out of it. No marriage can work without love, honey, and lots of it. There are always problems. You ain't alone in that."

"I just want to make him as happy as I can. That's all."

Sly could understand that. Nothing made him feel better than to make his Helen smile. "Makin' a man happy is a pretty simple thing. You just follow your nose and find out over time what he likes and what he don't like. As for the other, I can't say I ever seen a woman fake it, leastwise not so's it was obvious. But I can tell you how they go on when they're really likin' it."

She fixed him with a hopeful look. "Can you?"

Sly held up a finger. "I'll be right back."

He had a bad feeling this might call for more showing than telling. He did most things better when he was stone-cold sober, but going on like a woman having an orgasm wasn't going to be one of them. He hurried to the office, fetched his flask, and returned to the stall posthaste.

An hour later when Ryan got home, he spotted Bethany's van. As he walked across the paved yard, he heard what sounded like a coyote inside the stable, gearing up to howl at the moon. *What the hell?* The instant he entered the building, he heard Sly's drawl. He followed the noises to Wink's stall, where he found Bethany and the foreman howling and laughing like fools.

Ryan hung back for a moment. Sly, who looked snockered, sat with his back to the wall, one knee bent to provide himself with an armrest. The foreman watched Bethany throw her head back and make odd noises, then he chuckled, shook his head, and said, "Not like that, darlin'. He'll dose you with pectate."

"Oh, Sly," Bethany said with a discouraged sigh, "will I ever get it right?"

"We're gettin' there," he assured her.

Ryan had seen enough to get the gist of what was going on. It seemed that his failings as a lover had become a main topic of discussion today. If everyone in Crystal Falls hadn't heard the story by noon tomorrow, maybe Bethany could post an add in the *Examiner* to get the word out.

He leaned against the stall gate. "Is this a private party?"

Bethany jumped with a guilty start. "Ryan!" she cried. "You're home."

He nodded. "Rafe called an attorney. First sane thing anybody did all day. The judge finally set our bail. Jake is out, too."

Sly angled him a look. "And your daddy?"

"Nope. The judge said he could cool his heels in there for the night. Punching a cop doesn't go over real well at city hall."

A horrified gasp escaped Bethany. "Your father struck a cop?"

"The guy had it coming. He was going for Dad, and in order to reach him, he shoved my mother out of the way. She hit her hip on the corner of the desk. Bruised her up pretty bad. Dad cold-cocked the little creep."

"Oh, *no*. That's a serious offense, Ryan."

"They'll never make the charges stick. Rafe took Mom to the ER for X rays. The injury is documented, and your dad and two of your brothers were there as witnesses. The cop was out of line." Ryan shrugged. "He got off lucky. If that first punch hadn't knocked him out, Dad would have stomped him."

"That's your daddy," Sly agreed with a nod. "If he hits a man and he don't go down, I'm gonna check behind the son of a gun to see what's holdin' him up."

Ryan moved into the stall and sat beside Sly. He gave Bethany a long look. "Don't let me interrupt. Sounded like you were having a lot of fun."

"Oh, we were about finished. Weren't we, Sly?"

"Yep. I think we was about done, all right."

Ryan smiled. "I don't know which of you sounded the sickest. No offense, but I think you need a little more practice to get it down right, honey. You start that howling and panting around me, and I'm gonna call the paramedics."

Bethany threw an appalled glance at Sly. The foreman pushed to his feet and screwed the lid back on the flask. "Well, I reckon that's my cue to scat." He kissed her forehead. "G'night, honey. If this young whippersnapper gets his ornery up, don't pay him a whole lot of mind. He's all growl and no bite."

"Better that than all howl and no loyalty," Ryan inserted.

"Yep. His ornery's up." Sly slapped his hat on. "G'night."

"Good night, Sly," Bethany called. "Thank you for—" She broke off and glanced guiltily at Ryan. "For all your help," she finished softly.

"Yeah, Sly. Thanks a bunch," Ryan said. When the sound of the foreman's footsteps faded away, he met Bethany's gaze and said, "Start talking."

Her gaze chased away, and her cheeks went pink again. "About what?"

Ryan sighed. She'd been crying. The end of her nose was all red, and she held one of Sly's blue bandannas bunched in her hand. "We can start with the incident this afternoon. Can you explain to me why you chose to talk with some strange woman about our sex life in a public place? And in a *bar*, of all places?"

She fiddled with the handkerchief, tugging up a corner, then tucking it back into the wad. "She wasn't a stranger. Kate works for us. As for the bar, I asked her out for coffee, but she asked if we couldn't go to a quiet place for a beer. She had a hangover and wanted some hair of the dog that bit her."

"A hangover, huh? That should have been your first clue. A *quiet* place? You were damned near raped in that quiet place. I see you went home to change your blouse."

"That's why I didn't go straight to the station. By the time I changed and got there, your folks were inside." She pushed at her hair. "I was embarrassed to face them. It was all my fault—you being there and everything—and I just—" She shook her head. "Now your dad's in jail. Oh, *God*. They'll hate me forever."

"They won't hate you." Ryan drew up his knees to brace his arms. For a long moment he said nothing. "You know, Bethany, the number one requirement for a great relationship is being open with each other."

"No, it's not," she said thinly. "The number one thing is good sex."

"And you feel I didn't give you that."

She looked genuinely appalled to hear him say that. "No. Oh, Ryan, *no*. I'm the one who failed you, not the other way around."

He could see the pain in her eyes—dark, shifting shadows that made him want to hug her. "You didn't fail me, sweetheart. It was fabulous for me."

"No. Do you really think I'm that naive? I wasn't asleep when you got up last night. You were so upset because I felt nothing, you left the house."

Ryan puffed air into his cheeks while he mulled over the situation. "So rather than upset me again, you recruited Sly to tell you how to fake an orgasm?"

"No, of course not. I talked to Kate first. Running into Sly tonight was an accident."

"And after running into him, you asked him how to fake it," he inserted again. "Just how long did you think that would work, Bethany?"

"I don't know. Forever, I hoped." Her lower lip quivered. "I don't want to lose you. If I can't make you happy that way, I'll lose you."

He slapped some hay from his pant leg. "I was upset last night. I admit it. I wanted it to be good for you, and it was really difficult for me to accept when it wasn't."

She fixed him with an imploring gaze. "It *was* good for me. All the parts I could feel. You can't—" She broke off and gave the bandanna a vicious twist. "You can't compare me to other women. Up until you, I had never even been with anyone and had little hope I ever would be. The parts I could feel were wonderful. *You're* wonderful. If I can have just that much—if there's never anything more for the whole rest of my life—I'll feel like the luckiest woman alive." She groaned and lifted her hands. "I don't want to lose you. Please, try to understand. If my pretending to feel would have made it better for you, I was willing to pretend."

Ryan leaned his head against the wall. Wink was munching grain, the sound so familiar that he focused on it for calm. When he finally lowered his gaze back to Bethany, his anger had ebbed. "Promise me something."

"What?"

"That you'll never lie to me again, even if you think it's what I need to hear."

She squeezed her eyes closed. When she finally lifted her lashes, her face had gone pale. "I'm sorry I lied. It's not something I do very often, and I don't blame you for being angry. But try to understand my side. All the wishing in the world won't change my body, and I could lose you over this. The thought terrifies me." She laughed shakily. "Isn't that ironic? One of the main reasons I refused to have a relationship with you in the first place was because I feared exactly this. Now it's happened. I feel nothing. Only it doesn't matter. I want you anyway. And I—if you leave me, I don't know what I'll do."

She bent her head. "I *swore* I'd never do this to you. Clinging and begging. Wanting to keep you, no matter what, even if being with me won't make you happy." Her voice went shrill. "I'm sorry."

Ryan twisted onto his knees and crawled over to her chair. "I'm not going to leave you, honey. And if you try to leave me, I'm going with you. You got it?" He put his arms around her, pressed his face against the curve of her neck, and just held her for a while. "What you said just now—about enjoying all the parts you can feel, about that being wonderful and more than you ever had. I'll remember that. The problem last night wasn't that you failed to make it good for me, Bethany. It was fantastic. So fantastic I felt guilty as hell. You gave me so much, and I couldn't give you anything back."

She clung to him almost frantically, as if she was dangling off the edge of a cliff and he was her only lifeline. "You gave me *everything*," she whispered fiercely. "It was so wonderful, Ryan. You gave me everything."

"Yeah?"

"Yeah."

He pressed a kiss just under her ear. "You willing to go another round? I've been thinking all day about what you said this morning—about me going deeper. Last night, what with it being the first time and all, I was so afraid of hurting you that I didn't go very deep. Who knows? Maybe if I do, I'll find one beautiful little nerve ending that's still alive and kicking in there."

"If not, it doesn't matter. Just having your arms around me is enough, Ryan. Being with you is enough."

Ryan tightened his hold on her, knowing she was right. Never had he loved anyone so much, and if God gave them only this, if holding her and loving her was all he could ever have, it would be enough.

Because, to him, she was absolutely everything.

ᔥ CHAPTER SEVENTEEN ᔥ

Moonlight filtered in through the bedroom window, washing every-thing in silver. Stretched out full length on the mattress with Bethany tucked under his arm, Ryan gazed at her face, thinking how very beautiful she was, her features so delicate they might have been made of porcelain. He traced the shape of her brows with his lips, then trailed kisses down her nose, loving the way her breath caught and how she tightened her hands over his shoulders. He moved to her shell-like ear, nibbling lightly at the lobe.

"What can I do to please you?" she suddenly asked, trying to turn her head and foil his attempt to kiss her on the mouth.

"You please me just by existing," he whispered. "By being here with me. That's all I want, all I need, more than I ever dreamed I might have."

He felt her nose wrinkle against his jaw, a facial gesture that was habitual and always made him want to smile. "Don't be evasive, Ryan. You know very well what I mean. I'm new at this, and you need to be open with me so I can do all the things that turn you on. Do you like garter belts and nylons?"

He smiled in the shadowy gloom. "Kate again?"

"She did mention it's a favorite thing of men."

"Hmm. I like garter belts all right, I guess. But I'm not hung up on them."

"What do you like, then? I really want to know, Ryan. It's important to me to please you."

He just wanted her to lie back and let him devour her. Somehow, though, he didn't think that was what she wanted to hear. "I like you. A *lot*."

She laughed and playfully slugged his arm. "What a cop-out. *Tell* me. There must be things that turn you on. Do you like high heels?"

"Not really. I can't say I like any one thing in particular." He found the hollow beneath her ear and savored the taste of her skin there, thinking to himself that she was as intoxicating as wine, the faint scent of her shampoo making his head spin. "You could make me drool wearing a burlap sack."

"You're impossible."

"I like tight jeans and western shirts," he confessed as he nuzzled the curls at her temple. "The kind with pearl snaps on the breast pockets? There's something about seeing those pearls winking at me that makes my mouth go bone dry."

She giggled and toyed lightly with the hair on his chest. "I'll go buy some immediately. Would you like me to wear just the shirt and nothing else?"

"Sweet Christ." He grew still for a moment. "Would you?"

"If you'd like me to."

"Like isn't the word. Can I go with you to pick them out myself? I like fringe at the yoke, too. That white, shiny fringe. It shimmers and shifts back and forth. That drives me wild."

"I'll definitely wiggle my fringe a lot," she said with a laugh. "Do you like a woman to cook, wearing nothing but an apron?"

"As long as I can untie the sash. Holy hell." He trailed his lips over her cheek, intent on claiming her mouth. "You're driving me crazy. Enough talk. I want you, Bethany. *Now.*"

She held him off by pressing a palm to his chest. "Just a few more questions, I promise."

He sighed. "Only a few."

She looked up at him with those beautiful blue eyes that always made him feel a little short on oxygen. "Do you, um, like fellatio?" Her voice went husky and shy as she posed the question. "I haven't ever done it, but I think—"

Startled, Ryan reared back to stare at her. He'd been with more women than he cared to remember, and never once had he been asked that question in just this way. Only Bethany would call it by its proper name behind closed doors. He suppressed a grin, not wanting to embarrass her. "It's all right, I guess," he said cautiously, half afraid she might scoot under the covers if he gave a more enthusiastic response. "It's not one of my favorite things."

"Oh. Why not? I thought guys really liked it."

He bent to take her mouth in a long, deep kiss. As he broke the contact, he said, "I'd much rather perform that service for you."

She wrinkled her nose again. "I want to do things for you, not the other way around. I didn't do anything to make it nice for you last night."

She was clearly bent on pumping him for information, and Ryan had a feeling he'd better cooperate unless he wanted her to have another tête-à-tête with Kate, the sex guru. He sighed and settled himself beside her again, propping his head on his hand. After winding a lock of her hair around his finger, he said, "I enjoy touching and kissing you. Knowing it makes you feel good makes me feel good."

"I'm very glad because I loved everything you did last night," she whispered, "and I'm sure I always will, but it can't always be only you who tries to please me. I want to be a satisfying bed partner. I never want you to feel like you're missing out on anything."

"That'll never happen. Being with you, making love with you—that was the best it's ever been for me, Bethany. Incredible. *Beautiful*. You can't improve on perfection, not in my book."

"Oh, Ryan, do you really feel that way?"

"I really do. And there's nothing particular I want you to do." He leaned over to kiss the end of her nose. "Except stop talking." He released her hair to move his hand to her breast. After capturing her nipple between his thumb and finger, he gave it a roll, smiling when she gasped and arched at the shock of sensation. He dipped his head to tease the tip of captured flesh with flicks of his tongue, which made her moan and make fists in his hair. "I just want to love you," he whispered. "For as long as I want, however I want. Do you have a problem with that?"

Her only response was a breathless mewling sound. She drew his head closer to her breast, offering herself to him and silently encouraging him to take. It was a request he couldn't refuse.

Forearmed with the knowledge that foreplay might be the only part of this that she could really enjoy, he lingered over her, kissing and fondling every spot on her body where she did have sensation. He wanted to make the prelude as glorious as possible. If he couldn't give her satisfaction, he'd at least give her sensuality and show her how desperately he loved her with every touch of his hands and lips.

Slow, feather-light caresses. Barely perceptible kisses. He used all his experience at lovemaking, putting his own urgent needs on hold while he met hers. *Bethany*. She was so dear. He loved the breathless way she cooed when he found a sensitive place and teased it with the tip of his tongue . . . loved how she tried to press closer to him . . . how she clung to him and cried out his name. *Bethany*. God, how he adored her.

Ryan rolled her onto her belly and kissed a slow trail down her spine, lingering just below her shoulder blades where he knew women were sensitive. From there, he moved to the hollow just under her arm, making goose bumps rise on her satiny skin as he journeyed slowly down her delicate rib cage to her waist, then to her plump derriere. Her buttocks quivered beneath his lips, telling him how intense the sensations were for her.

When he rolled her back over, the shaft of moonlight fell across her breasts and gilded the turgid, pink crests. Smiling, he lay next to her, using his free hand to gently caress her while he lingered over her nipples, tormenting them with light flicks until they throbbed against his tongue and stood at eager attention. Then suddenly laying siege, he nipped them gently with his teeth and drew sharply with his mouth.

"Ryan!" She sobbed his name and arched up. He stayed with her, tasting and suckling until she trembled and he could feel her stomach muscles jerking beneath his palm. At that point his own needs had grown until he ached with urgency. Sliding his hand to the juncture of her thighs, he curled his fingers over her nest of curls to be sure she was ready. His fingertips encountered a slick, wet heat, an age-old welcome to any man.

As he withdrew his hand, Ryan brushed his fingertips over her clitoris. Bethany jumped as if he'd jabbed her with a pin. He froze, his gaze fixed on her face. Last night, he'd failed miserably to give her an orgasm by touching her there, and because it had been her first time, he'd been reluctant to suggest that he try doing it another way for fear of embarrassing her. It was still a little soon to introduce her to that kind of intimacy, but since she'd been the one to mention it first, he decided he might at least bring up the possibility.

"Sweetheart, would you let me try kissing you there?"

She frowned. "You touched me there last night, and it was uncomfortable for me."

"I know, but my hands are like sandpaper. I could be much gentler with my mouth."

She cupped a slender hand over the back of his, as though to protect the spot. "Oh, I don't think—"

"If it's just that you're supersensitive there, doing it with my mouth might make all the difference," he murmured, bending to suckle a nipple as he spoke. Her breath caught at the contact, and she mewled softly again. Between teasing passes of his tongue, he urged, "Please, honey? Say yes. It would make me so happy to give you an orgasm."

She arched up to his mouth. "Will you stop if it's uncomfortable for me?"

"Of course."

"All right," she said breathlessly. "I don't think it will work, but if you want to try, I won't stop you. If you truly want to, that is."

Oh, he wanted to. That sweet, nerve-packed flange of flesh was already swelling beneath his fingertips without his doing anything. Maybe she did have nerve damage there, just as she suspected, and he was tilting at windmills. There was only one way to find out.

He twisted onto his knees and pushed her legs apart so he might kneel between them. She smiled and released his hand. Ryan grabbed the unused pillow next to her and shoved it under her bottom.

"What are you doing?" she asked in bewilderment.

"Just getting you in a better position."

He cocked her knees out so they rested on the ends of the pillow, leaving her open and vulnerable. She cupped her slender hands over the exposed area, clearly self-conscious. They couldn't have that. Ryan lowered himself over her and reached back to tug up the covers to better shield her modesty.

He did his best work under a blanket, anyway.

"I love you so much," he whispered. "Have I told you that recently?"

She giggled. "Not for at least three minutes, you heel."

He bent to take her mouth in a long kiss, smiling at how eagerly she melted into it. *His Bethany*. His heart twisted, and he sent up a silent prayer. *Please, God, let this work. Let me give her pleasure. I'll never miss church on Sunday again, and I'll say a blessing at every meal, and I'll be on my knees beside the bed each night. I'll be the most reverent, faithful man you ever saw, I swear, and I'll give thanks for the rest of my life. Just give me this one thing.*

Not wishing to embarrass her, Ryan didn't head immediately for his mark. Instead he went through all the motions again, kissing her mouth, then all the sensitive places on her body, working his way south the entire while. She held nothing back from him, her response unconditional and given without hesitation. In only a couple of minutes, he had her mewling and quivering with need again.

When he settled his mouth over the spot he'd been aiming to reach, her mewling changed to startled whimpers. He flicked her lightly with his tongue, taking care not to apply too much pressure for fear of hurting her. She made an odd sound at the back of her throat and then gasped in surprise and sighed with pleasure. *Oh, yes*.

He wanted so much to make this good for her. He felt that beautiful little tuft of femininity begin to swell again under the careful ministrations of his mouth, and soon the underlying hardness of her arousal was apparent with every pass of his tongue. He could feel her heartbeat there—her pulse pounding like a trip-hammer.

Ryan cautiously increased pressure then. When she didn't shrink away or cry out, his heart soared and he went for the finish with hard, circular drags of his tongue over the spot. She jerked and arched her spine. She tried to hike her hips. He felt the urgency building within her, and knowing he almost had her there brought tears to his eyes.

"Ryan?" she cried throatily, her voice laced with panic. "This is—I—oh, God, I need you to hold me."

He cupped her bottom in his palms, hooking his thumbs under her hipbones and lifting her up to his mouth. Against her secret place, he said, "It's all right, honey. I'm right here. Trust me, and just let it happen."

"Oh, *God*. Ryan?"

He resumed his assault with renewed determination. Her slender body quivered like a plucked bowstring, and then she sobbed. The next instant she cried out, her muscles jerking and going into spasms as her first orgasm rocked her.

Hallelujah.

For the first time in his life, Ryan Kendrick wept as he brought a woman to climax.

Bethany's bones had melted. She couldn't move, couldn't think, and didn't care. She just lay there in a limp sprawl, dimly aware of Ryan rising over her.

"You okay, honey?"

Her tongue was glued to the roof of her mouth. Her heart was still pounding. He had obliterated her thoughts. Her bones had turned to the consistency of runny pudding. And he wanted to know if she was all right? There was a possibility that she'd died of heart failure and was now in heaven.

"Mmm" was all she could manage to say.

He laughed softly. Then she felt that odd sense of fullness she'd experienced last night, which told her he'd just entered her. "Hold on, sweetheart. Arms around my neck. Come on. I'm going to take you flying again."

Bethany blinked. Arms, go up, she silently commanded. Instead of obeying, her appendages just lay there, limp and useless, one flung above her head, the other out from her body. Ryan's dark face came into focus. His teeth flashed in a broad grin. He dipped his dark head toward hers.

"Come on. Grab hold."

With effort she finally managed to lift her arms and loosely hug his neck.

"There's my girl," he whispered. He reached back to lift each of her legs to vise her knees under his arms. "You ready for takeoff?"

She nodded, wishing he'd just let her go to sleep now. Having lain awake for over a month, she felt so deliciously *relaxed* that she selfishly thought, I won't feel this part anyway. However, she managed to croak, "Ready," before she yawned.

He chuckled and shifted his torso sharply forward, the velvety length of his shaft making firm contact with the one place that had a *lot* of feeling. *Zing*. Bethany's eyes flew wide, and she stared up at him. He flashed her another grin as he made his first, cautious thrust. She gasped and dug all ten fingernails into his shoulders.

"I can make you come this way," he whispered. "Feel that? I'm connecting with *thousands* of lively little nerve endings, honey. It won't be uncomfortable, I promise. Not now."

To her surprise, it wasn't uncomfortable. At least not yet. "Why is that?"

"Because you're aroused, and it's all swollen, which makes it a little less sensitive."

She knew little about that sort of thing and could only trust his word.

"Don't be tense. If it doesn't feel nice, I'll stop." He dipped forward to kiss her. When their mouths parted, he whispered, "Come fly with me."

Bethany expected the friction to be unpleasant. He'd been so careful, kissing her there, but this was different. She felt sure that the rub of all that hardness against her would hurt. Yet instead, his shaft felt like steel sheathed in velvet, and for some reason, wasn't uncomfortable at all. Her breath snagged at the back of her throat when he thrust forward again.

"Tell me if you start to feel tender," he whispered.

With that, he picked up speed, and before she could formulate a thought, let alone articulate it, she was lifting off with him. Her mind spun at the indescribable sensations that rocked her. With every thrust, he was now connecting directly with her clitoris, which sent electrical shocks shooting out every which way to ribbon through her.

"Ryan!" she cried.

"I'm here, honey." His voice had turned husky and clipped. "I'm gonna go deep now. All right? If it even sort of hurts, you tell me, and I'll back off."

He shoved sharply forward with his hips, burying himself to the hilt. Bethany cried out. He stiffened and drew back, his gaze glassy and riveted to her face. "Does it hurt?" he asked.

"No, but I—oh, Ryan, way deep, I can feel you."

"You can?"

She laughed tearfully and locked her hands over his upper arms, urging him forward again. "Oh, *yes*," she cried when he drove into her again. "Oh, Ryan! Yes, yes, *yes*! I can definitely feel that."

He established a hard, fast rhythm then that made further discussion not only impossible but unnecessary. Her moans and gasps of pleasure communicated her feelings with absolute clarity, she felt sure. *Flying*. He was taking her on a private tour of paradise. The building pleasure. The coiling need and urgency. Soaring ever higher. When she crested and plunged over the edge, he stiffened and she felt a white-hot surge pour through her, way down deep.

She arched up as best she could to meet him, her mind splintering as a violent orgasm rocked her body. Definitely paradise, she decided dizzily as the small aftershocks jolted through her.

Ryan Kendrick was the most wonderful man ever to draw breath.

He drew her into his arms and held her with fierce possessiveness when it was all over—hugged her so fiercely that she could almost feel the intensity of his love for her.

"Oh, Ryan," she whispered. She smoothed her hands over his hair, wanting to comfort him. "It's all right. Everything's going to be all right now."

In response he only tightened his hold even more. In that moment Bethany realized just how tormented he'd been about his inability to satisfy her.

She pressed her face against his shoulder. "Oh, Ryan . . . I love you so."

He rested his jaw against her hair, a shudder racking his big body. After a long while, when his breathing evened out, he sighed and said, "Now I wish I'd gone ahead and kissed you there last night. It would have saved us twenty-four hours of sheer hell."

Bethany rubbed her cheek against his skin, loving the feeling of muscle over bone, hard yet forming a comfortable pillow for her head. "Maybe we needed to experience the hell to fully appreciate the heaven. I'm still not normal. I feel absolutely nothing when you first go inside of me."

"It doesn't matter, Bethany," he murmured. "Unless I've been misinformed, you've got feeling where it counts. If given a choice, I think most women would choose to have a clitoral orgasm over a vaginal one."

Bethany grinned against his shoulder. It had definitely been intense— indescribably intense. "I wonder why it didn't feel nice when you touched me there last night?"

He nuzzled her hair. "You were so tense, for one thing. And I think you're right about having nerve damage there, which makes you super-sensitive until I get you really hot." He chuckled, the sound laced with male satisfaction. "That's all right. You asked what things I really like? Kissing you there is my all-time favorite. I think I'm already addicted."

"I'm glad. It was wonderful," she whispered.

"I've been told there's no other orgasm that compares to it."

"By whom?"

Silence. Then a cough. "Never mind. That's not really important, is it?"

"I guess not," she said with an impish grin she hid by keeping her face against his shoulder.

"By shifting forward while I make love to you, I can give you a clitoral orgasm and make you climax with me. *That's* the important thing. It's fantastic for me, knowing you're enjoying it, too."

It *had* been pretty fantastic. Feeling so content and satisfied she could barely keep her eyes open, Bethany pressed closer to him and sleepily whispered, "I love you, Ryan. That was the most fantastic experience of my whole life. Thank you so much."

He chuckled and drew her more firmly against him. "Prepare for a life-time of fantastic, lady. I enjoyed it as much as you did."

Sometime in the darkest part of night, Bethany woke up, realized Ryan wasn't beside her in bed, and reared up on her elbow to glance around. She blinked bewilderedly when she saw him kneeling beside the bed, el-bows resting on the mattress, his big, rough hands clasped in prayer be-fore his bowed head.

"Ryan?" she whispered hoarsely. "Are you all right?"

He glanced up. "Never been better. I was just saying my prayers."

"Your prayers?" Bethany had never figured him for the type of man who got on his knees. Now she wondered why she'd been under that im-pression. Any man as kind as Ryan Kendrick probably had a deep, abid-ing faith that guided him through life. "I didn't mean to interrupt you. I'm sorry."

She lay back, intending to leave him to his meditations. But he low-ered his hands and grinned at her. "No problem. I was done."

A carnal gleam had come into his eyes. He slipped his hands under the covers to lock them over her knees. The next thing Bethany knew, her bottom was skidding over the mattress toward him, the rest of her startled self following.

"What're you doing?"

"Nothin'." He gave her an innocent-looking smile as he positioned her legs, one on each side of him, then slid his hands to her hips to pull her the remainder of the way to him. "Yet, anyhow."

Her most private place bumped intimately against his hard belly. He hooked his arms under her knees, curling his hands over her uplifted thighs.

"Hi," he said softly.

Bethany cupped her fingers over that place he had just laid opened to his gaze. He glanced down at her splayed fingers. "You're gonna have to move those, sweetheart. I got business down there, and they're in my road."

She laughed. "You surely don't mean to—you know—do *that* right now."

He bent his head to kiss the sensitive place on her inner left thigh. Against her skin he rumbled, "Name me one good reason I shouldn't."

"Because my heart may not be able to take it twice in one night?"

His nibbled her skin. "Nah. You won't die from it."

Bethany tried to think of a way she might explain that this was all still new to her, and that she felt a little embarrassed. It had been different when she was aroused and already wanting him. She'd barely been able to think, let alone feel modest. "But, Ryan, you haven't even kissed me yet."

"Hmm." He angled her a look with eyes that were definitely glinting with lust. "You particular about what part of you I kiss first?"

She giggled. "A lady needs a little bit of foreplay to get in the mood."

He arched an imperious brow at her. "I'll tell you what," he said huskily. "Move your pretty little fingers out of my way and prop up on your elbows to watch. You'll get in the mood real fast."

"Oh, I don't think—I'm not going to *watch*."

"Why not?"

She couldn't readily think of a reason, and he didn't give her any time to come up with one. She giggled again when he started nipping at her fingers to make her move them. "How can you switch from saying your prayers to doing this before you even get off your knees?"

"Because I believe with all my heart that the love we have is a sacred gift, and that anything we do to express that love is beautiful."

"Oh, Ryan . . ." Bethany's throat went tight, and she did push up on one elbow then. Being loved by him *was* beautiful—the most beautiful experience of her entire life. He'd kissed her scars. He touched her as if she were a priceless treasure. She felt content as she never had when he held her in his arms. What could be more beautiful or right than that? "I love you so much. So very, very much."

"Then don't hold anything back from me," he whispered against her skin. "I know we've moved fast, but for us, it's the only way. I want to make love to you again, and I want it to be wonderful for you. I can be sure it will be, doing this. It's a miracle, Bethany mine, a gift from God."

It really was a miracle, Bethany thought. A beautiful, wondrous gift. It would be the height of stupidity to let modesty ruin it for her—or for him.

She moved her hand, watching as he kissed his way up her leg. For just an instant she wished she could feel the silky brush of his lips, but she quickly shoved the yearning aside. Seeing him kiss her inner thigh was just as erotic in its way, and it was so wonderful to know she would be able to feel every light brush of his lips when he finally reached his destination.

He finally got there and touched the tip of his tongue to her. Bethany gasped at the shock of hot delight that coursed through her. "Oh, *Ryan*. That—feels—so—*good*."

His hot, wet mouth closed over her, and his tongue flicked lightly at her flesh, gently teasing her sensitive nerve endings until her head was spinning and her blood started rushing.

"You okay?" he rumbled against her.

The movement of his mouth and the thrum of his voice vibrated through her, and she nearly died on the spot. She tried to answer him, but her throat was locked shut, the only sound she could make a soft panting noise.

That was evidently answer enough, for he resumed his gentle assault. He hiked her bottom off the mattress to situate her just so. Every muscle in her upper body snapped taut and jangled. Then she forgot everything. *Lightning bolts.* It was the only way to describe the sensations that jolted through her.

Somehow one of her hands became fisted in his black hair, and the next thing she knew, she was using his hair to pull herself up to a sitting position. He hunched lower to continue loving her. Then he moved up to kiss her breasts.

"Oh, Ryan."

"You dead yet?" he asked with a rumbling chuckle.

"Not yet."

He kissed his way back down to her navel. "Good. Stay with me, sweetheart. I'll take you flying again."

Ryan Kendrick was a man of his word.

She definitely soared.

§ CHAPTER EIGHTEEN §

When Bethany awakened, the morning was too gorgeous for her to greet it with a frown. Sunlight poured in Ryan's bedroom windows, gilding his hair and face. They shared a pillow, which struck her as being symbolic of their lives together from this moment on. He slept with one arm angled up her front, his big hand curled loosely over her left breast. They were both naked, and she reveled in the feeling of all that delicious maleness curled around her.

She sighed, blissfully content. For the first time in eight years, she'd been able to roll over during the night. True to his word, Ryan had tucked her against him several times to switch sides, making it possible for her to snuggle against his back or be cuddled in his strong arms. It had been the most heavenly feeling.

He startled her by suddenly mumbling into her hair. "Will you eat breakfast with me like this?"

"In the kitchen?" She giggled. "Naked, you mean?"

"What kind of fantasy would it be if you weren't?"

"Only if you do the cooking. The oil always splatters when I fry eggs."

"Fruit and a bagel won't splatter." He flicked her nipple. "Imagine my mouth on you there after I've taken a sip of steaming hot coffee."

Bethany's stomach clenched at the thought.

"I'll smear low-fat cream cheese all over you and lick it off," he said huskily. "You can sit naked in my kitchen, skim your teeth over your banana, and drive me out of my mind. You'll never make it out of the house before noon."

She laughed again. "I have to go to work."

"Stay home with me today." He nuzzled her ear. "Go with me to city hall. We'll break my dad out of jail and apply for a marriage license, all in one visit."

"Surely we don't need a license straightaway."

"Yep. I want a ring on your finger, darlin'."

She turned to kiss the bridge of his nose. "Oh, Ryan, you're so sweet."

"No sweet to it. If I don't marry you immediately, Jake'll kill me."

"Don't worry about Jake. I can handle him."

He intercepted her before she could kiss his nose again and settled his mouth over hers. Bethany's pulse started to race. When he came up for air, he replied, "No arguments. You're marrying me as soon as I can arrange it."

"I can't possibly. It takes time to plan a wedding."

His eyes came wide open. "I'd like to keep it simple. No fuss, no muss."

"I used to fantasize about being married at a high mountain lake."

"Now you're talking."

Her heart squeezed. "That's out of the question now."

He rose up to nibble on her throat. "I can get you to a wilderness lake. A beautiful one. In fact, that's how I want to spend our honeymoon, just you and me, at a high mountain lake."

"Ryan, I can't stay at a high mountain lake. I told you, I—"

He laid a finger across her mouth. "I ordered you an all-terrain chair. It's lightweight, so we can pack it in by horseback, and it's guaranteed to go over rocks and small logs. It's due here next week, same day as your saddle."

"You *what?*"

He moved his finger to dip his head and steal another kiss. "Don't frown. You'll get wrinkles."

Bethany scowled anyway. "Even with an all-terrain wheelchair, I'd need special facilities for my personal needs. It's just not feasible for me to—"

"I'm working on that. Mom helped me design an outhouse for you."

"An *outhouse?*"

"Yeah. My dad's been helping me, too. He's more experienced at welding aluminum. It'll be light, have bars, and it all comes apart for easy transport. We're using tent nylon for the top and walls. You'll have all the comforts of home."

She moved her head back to stare at him incredulously. "You're serious."

"Of course I'm serious. We're going on a wilderness ride for our honeymoon. Just you and me, at a gorgeous high mountain lake, just like you loved to do before you got hurt. We'll catch trout for our supper and cook them over an open flame. Make love under the stars. Then I'll tell you scary stories before bed so you'll snuggle up real close when we get in the tent, and I'll make love to you in the sleeping bag. We'll go swimming, too, and I'll make love to you in the water. There's a falls up there. It's so pretty, it'll take your breath, and I'll—"

She burst out laughing. "Make love to me under the spray?"

He grinned. "How'd you guess?"

Bethany relented and took the day off from work so she could be with Ryan. While she enjoyed a third cup of coffee, he went over to the stable to care for the stock. It was such a glorious morning that Bethany threw open the slider to let in fresh air. She was about to shut the screen when the phone rang. Circling Tripper, who snoozed near the end table, she grabbed up the portable.

"Hello?"

"Hey, sis. How are you this morning? Fully recovered from the mix-up yesterday, I hope."

"I'm great, Jake. Better than great, actually."

He sighed. "That's good to hear. I was a little worried when I got the message that you weren't coming in to work."

She explained that Ryan wanted to apply for their marriage license later.

"He doesn't waste any time," Jake observed. "You sure this is the right thing, Bethie? Marry in haste and all that. No need to get in a rush."

"I've never been surer about anything, Jake. I love him so much it hurts."

Long silence. Then Jake said, "Pardon me for bringing it up, but just yesterday weren't you blubbering in your beer, disappointed with the sex?"

"Where on earth did you get that idea?"

"From the bartender."

Bethany's face went hot. She drew the line at discussing the particulars of her love life with her brother. At the same time she understood that he was concerned and needed some reassurance so he wouldn't worry.

"I wasn't disappointed. I was afraid Ryan was." Bethany couldn't think how to explain. "But that's all behind us now. Everything is *marvelous*."

"Marvelous, huh? You sure, Bethany?"

"I'm positive. Please, don't be worried. I love him so much, and he loves—"

She heard something behind her and glanced guiltily over her shoulder. Ryan wouldn't be happy to hear her discussing their relationship with Jake.

Instead of Ryan, it was T-bone behind her. Bethany stared into the bull's vacuous brown eyes, not sure if she should scream or say hello. She glanced toward the sliding glass door, recalling Ryan's warning that T-bone barged in if it wasn't kept closed.

The bull let out a bellow just then that was so loud it seemed to vibrate the walls. "Holy hell, what was that?" Jake asked.

"A bull." Bethany imagined T-bone butting her as she'd seen him butt Ryan. This was no laughing matter. If her chair tipped over, the bull could very easily trample her. "I have to go, Jake. I'll call you back."

"Aren't you in the house?"

"I, um . . . yes," she admitted faintly.

"That sucker sounded close, like he was right on top of you."

He *was* right on top of her. Almost, at any rate. "I'm fine, Jake. I'll call you right back." Bethany broke the connection and tossed the phone on the sofa. "Hello, T-bone," she said shakily.

Long strings of drool hung like shoestrings from the bull's broad muzzle. He nudged Bethany's arm. She half expected him to send her flying with a hard shove, but almost as if he sensed she was different, he was very gentle instead. With a trembling hand, she scratched behind his ears as she'd seen Ryan do.

"I suppose you'd like a carrot. You stay right here, and I'll run fetch you one." And throw it outside, she thought, gulping down terror.

She hurried toward the kitchen. T-bone followed docilely. Once at the refrigerator, she endured wet snuffles while she dug through the vegetable drawer. The bull seemed to like her perfume and the smell of her shampoo. He kept sniffing her ear and hair. She plucked out two carrots and gave him one, hoping to get around him while he ate it.

No such luck. The bull blocked her way, trapping her in the kitchen with him while he enjoyed his treat. When it was gone, he mooed for another. Bethany shivered in the cold draft coming from the open refrigerator as she fed him the second carrot then dug in the drawer for more. Her heart caught when she saw there were only three left. T-bone would devour those in no time at all. What would he do when she had nothing more to feed him?

It wasn't long before Bethany found out. "That's all," she said in a quaking voice. "Time to go now, big guy."

T-bone nuzzled the front of her blouse. When he discovered her armpit and dove his nose in to sniff, she gave a startled laugh. "There's no food in there. That's deodorant, you goofy animal."

T-bone sniffed her chest, giving her breasts gentle nudges. Bethany began to relax. He gave no indication that he meant to butt her. He was only curious. She sighed and began petting him. "Do you like fruit, you big clown?" She moved to the bar and plucked an apple from the bowl. "Here. *Bon appétit.*"

T-bone ate the apple whole. He seemed to love it. Bethany quickly handed him another one, which he also devoured in a couple of chomps. She started to laugh. "How do you feel about bagels and low-fat cream cheese?"

As if she'd rung a dinner bell, Tripper woke up and hurried in. The fat golden Lab sat next to the bull, tongue lolling, brown eyes fixed imploringly on her. She grabbed the bag of bagels and gave the dog one of those. T-bone sniffed the bread but politely turned it down. He loved bananas, however, and ate three.

That was how Ryan found Bethany a few minutes later, holding court in his kitchen with his bull and dog in attendance. T-bone had discovered the marvel of Bethany's skirt and was attempting to learn what was under it. She giggled and shoved at his massive head.

"What is it with the guys around here?" she asked the bovine with a tinkling laugh. "*No,* T-bone."

Ryan leaned his elbows on the breakfast bar and watched her for a moment, trying to imagine the reaction of any other woman he'd ever dated had she been cornered in his kitchen by a bull. Hysteria, surely, and screams to rattle the windows. But here was Bethany, in a wheelchair, calmly petting the huge galoot, as if finding a bull in the house was an everyday occurrence. Ryan had never been more certain that she was the only lady in the world for him.

"Are you spoiling my critters?" he finally asked.

She jumped with a start, then laughed when she saw him there. "Ryan. I'm glad you're back. I have this little problem."

"That's eight hundred pounds of problem, darlin', nothing little about him. I was hoping he'd find himself a love interest and stop hanging around so close to the house. Instead, he's up here trying to make time with my lady the first moment my back is turned."

She flashed him a beaming smile. "No worries. Your lady has eyes only for you. I was afraid at first, but it's almost as if he knows I'm different."

The bull chose that moment to try to get under her skirt from another angle. "He's noting the differences, all right. He's seen Mom a few times, but otherwise, he's never been around ladies much."

"I mean different in that I'm handicapped. You wouldn't believe how careful he's been."

"That's good to hear. I'd hate like hell to have to shoot him."

"Oh, no!" She looked horrified at the suggestion. "Please, don't even *think* it. I'd feel so awful. Just look at how gentle he's being."

Ryan had to admit the bull was being uncharacteristically gentle. He smiled slightly, wondering if those big blue eyes of hers worked on bulls just as they did on men. Over at the stable a moment ago, he'd encountered Sly, who had gone on and on about how special this young lady was. "One look into them big blue eyes, and my old heart flat melted," Sly had told him.

Ryan smiled, recalling the sappy grin on Sly's weathered face. "He sure seems to be taken with you," he told Bethany, not entirely sure if he was talking about the foreman or the bull. "How'd he get in the house, anyway?"

She rolled her eyes. "I forgot and left the slider standing open."

Ryan sighed. "Dumb critter." He stepped around the counter and gave his bull a gentle swat on the rump to get his attention. "Come on, T-bone. Time to go back outside before you decide to take a dump on my floor."

Bethany wrinkled her nose and shuddered. "What a thought."

Ryan got the bull turned, then shooed him outside by brandishing his Stetson. He shut the sliding glass door, feeling sad. Now that Bethany would be around all the time, something would have to be done about T-bone. Ryan couldn't take a chance that the bull might hurt her. Next time, T-bone might get ornery with her. By nature, he was an unpredictable creature.

"Don't even think about it," she said.

Ryan turned to find her sitting behind him. Her big eyes searched his.

"I mean it," she said shakily. "It was my fault he got in, but he was a perfect gentleman. If he's gone the next time I visit, I'll never forgive myself."

Ryan slapped his hat against his leg. "I'm afraid he'll hurt you."

She gazed past him at the bull that still stood on the deck. "You owe him the chance to prove he won't. I'll be careful around him, Ryan. If he gets obnoxious a single time, I promise to tell you immediately. How's that?"

Ryan glanced through the glass, remembering T-bone as a baby. It was a damn fool thing, a rancher turning bulls into pets. He'd named T-bone after a cut of steak, hoping it would serve as a reminder of that, but

T-bone had been sickly, forcing Ryan to care for him, and in no time, he'd started to love the puny critter.

"I'll think on it," he said softly.

"Are you going to be one of those husbands who thinks it's his right to make all the decisions, no matter how I feel or what I say?"

Ryan shot her a bewildered look. "Of course not. This is different."

"That's what they all say." She lifted her stubborn little chin—a feature he'd noticed the very first time he saw her. "If you shoot that bull without just cause, I'll never forgive you. Am I making myself perfectly clear?"

He chuckled. "Are you going to be one of those wives who pokes her nose into my business and offers an opinion whether it's wanted or not?"

She hesitated. Then that chin came up again. "Probably. I was raised on a ranch. It's not as if I know nothing about raising cattle and horses."

"I was hoping you'd say that." He sent his hat sailing toward the coat tree. The Stetson hit the hook, spun, and then settled, pretty as could be. "So when are you going to quit that desk job and help me run this place?"

"You want me to quit my job at the store?"

"If Jake can figure out a way to get along without you, I could really use your help here. There aren't enough hours in the day for me to get everything done. I need a partner, someone I know I can trust. You'd be a damn good stable manager. You know your horses and love them as much as I do."

A gleam of interest entered her eyes. "I couldn't manage the stables, Ryan. I'm in a wheelchair."

"Not a place over there you can't reach now," he reminded her. "I'll have you riding as of next week. You can keep books, give orders, oversee the help, and handle business over the phone, same as I do. Name me one thing you can't do just because you're in a wheelchair."

"I can't do any of the actual work."

"That's not part of the job description. The hands will do the work. Managers manage. That's why they're called *managers*. Even if you weren't in a wheelchair, I'd paddle your fanny if I caught you doing any heavy work. Not my wife. Now that the ranch is doing so well, we hire able-bodied men to help with all that, which is a much better setup. My dad hated it when he had no choice but to count on my mom to do a man's job, and as much as she loves ranching, you'll never see her at the business end of a pitchfork anymore."

"A man's job."

Ryan saw a glint of feminine pride in her eyes, and he rushed to clarify that statement. "You know what I mean. Very few women have the muscle to safely buck hay or lift a struggling calf. It ate at Dad to see Mom doing things that he was afraid might injure her back. She's not a whole lot bigger than you are. It was never a question of respect or equality. She has always been his equal here on the Rocking K, but no matter how you slice it, she's put together differently, with a more delicate bone structure and less muscle to support it. That's all I meant."

A twinkle of laughter replaced the glint in her eyes. "I'll accept that so long as you'll concede that a woman has the brains to figure out a way to compensate for her lack of strength to get the job done if it's necessary."

He grinned. "I won't argue that point. But it's never necessary now."

She relaxed and smiled wistfully. "It's a very tempting thought. I'd love to be a part of all this." She glanced out the slider at the stable. "But what if a mare went into labor?"

"You'd call the vet out, same as I do."

She laughed and rolled her eyes. "You have an answer for everything. The sad fact is, even if I can start riding occasionally with you, I'll be unable to mount or dismount a horse without help. A stable manager who can't ride? I don't think so."

Ryan kept his gaze fixed on hers and struggled not to smile. "We've about got a sling finished for you. All electric."

"What?"

He stepped over and leaned down, bracing his hands on the arms of her chair. "A sling. The seat is made of nylon, and it's tailored to fit. Once you're in the saddle, it unhooks from the pulley ropes, and you can wear it while you ride. When you get back to the stable, you just reattach it to the hooks, and it'll lift you off the horse and onto the chair again."

She stared blankly at him for a long moment. "A sling," she repeated expressionlessly, as if she'd never heard the word. "For the stable?"

"Designed especially for you. It wasn't that difficult. We already have electric slings for the horses. We modified one. My grandpa was a machinist, and Dad inherited his knack for designing gadgets. Mom made the sling seat for you on her sewing machine. All of us ride, and we love it. We know what a joy it'll be if you can get on a horse any time you want."

"Oh, Ryan."

"It was no big thing," he said, half afraid she was getting upset.

She glanced past him at the door. "It's in this stable?"

"Mom's still putting on the finishing touches. It'll be done before your saddle gets here."

"And it works?" she asked softly. "How can you know if it works?"

Ryan realized then that she was afraid to believe him, that it meant even more to her than he'd imagined it might, and she didn't want to get her hopes up, only to have them dashed. "That was Maggie's contribution. She's about your size. Mom fitted the seat to her, and she was our guinea pig. It lifts her on and off a horse, no problem. She made sure not to use her legs, tried to pretend she couldn't. Got her in the saddle, slick as a whistle."

A smile moved slowly over Bethany's trembling mouth. "Can I see it?"

Ryan heaved a silent sigh of relief. "Sure. Right now, if you'd like."

"I'd like."

Bethany couldn't believe her eyes when Ryan demonstrated how the sling worked a few minutes later. She stared up at the ceiling tracks attached to the rafters. She was dreaming, surely. Paralyzed women couldn't buzz out to the stable and hop on a horse to go riding like a normal person.

Ryan Kendrick didn't seem to understand that. Instead he looked at a problem from all angles, recruited his wonderful family to help him, and devised some crazy way to make the impossible happen. She imagined Keefe and Ann Kendrick, along with Rafe, Maggie, and Ryan, all gathered in this stall, puzzling and working, trying to make a small miracle happen for her.

Never say cain't. Ryan had told her he believed in that motto, but this was beyond her wildest imaginings. A stable lift, her ticket to freedom. She'd be able to get on Wink any old time she liked and feel the wind on her face again.

She searched Ryan's beautiful, steel-blue eyes. The love for her that shone in them was impossible to miss.

"I hoped it'd make you happy," he said.

"I'm speechless. This is—well, it's incredible, Ryan. I think I'm dreaming. I'm afraid someone will pinch me awake, and you'll vanish in a puff of smoke."

"Nope," he assured her. "I'm real, and you're stuck with me."

"Oh, I hope so. Forever will suit me fine."

He rubbed his jaw and gazed at the lift. "It just occurred to me that maybe I'm throwing too much at you at once."

"Oh, Ryan, *no*. Aside from Wink, this is the most wonderful gift anyone's ever given me."

"I don't want to push you. We Kendricks—that's a fault we have with the women we love. I don't mean to come over you like a high wind. It's just—well, it sort of runs in my blood, I guess. My dad, with my mom. And you wouldn't believe how Rafe was with Maggie. We Kendricks tend to be a little pushy."

"A little?" Sly poked his head in through the doorway. "Son, you Kendricks are like bulldozers. When you set your sights on a lady, she don't have a chance." He winked at Bethany. "Mornin', darlin'. How you doin' this bright and sunny day?"

Bethany wished she could step over and hug him. Instead she looked him straight in the eye, trying to tell him with her eyes what she couldn't say aloud, that she would never forget last night and that she'd treasure his friendship. "I'm wonderful, Sly. And you?"

"Ain't never been better." His eyes twinkled as he glanced from her to Ryan. "Looks like he got over his orneries, and you lived through the experience. Knew you would, of course. Just like his daddy, that boy. Strike a match to his temper, and he may tear hell out of everything around you, but when the dust settles, ain't a hair on your head gonna be mussed."

Bethany smiled. "He got a little lippy, but I just slapped him up alongside the head and told him to behave himself."

Sly nodded. "Good for you, darlin'. Only way to handle him."

Ryan muttered something under his breath and gave the foreman a narrow-eyed look. "You need something, Sly?"

"Nope." Sly chuckled and winked at Bethany. "I best stop makin' eyes at you. Now his jealous is gettin' up." He started to leave, then stopped and turned back. "Rafe went to get your daddy, by the way. He said if we was to wait 'til you pried yourself away, your daddy would be so het up, he'd act like a rabid badger all the way home."

Ryan chuckled. "We could've sent Mom. She can handle him."

Sly winked at Bethany. "You hear that, darlin'? You watch Annie in action. She'll teach you all you need to know."

Bethany laughed. "Is that right?"

Sly's weathered, sunbaked face creased in a smile. "Damn straight. Ain't a man alive with the guts or wherewithal to tangle with Keefe when he's in a stir. But our Annie will go toe-to-toe with him, one hand tied behind her back."

Bethany raised her eyebrows. "Really? And who wins?"

"Annie," Sly said with a wry chuckle. "Hands down, no contest. Keefe give up on fightin' with her some twenty years back. He just shakes his head and lets her go. Most times, she's right anyhow, so it works out good."

Ryan sighed. "Sly, do me a favor and just shut up. Don't go putting ideas into her head."

"I hate to tell you this, son. She was born with ideas in her head. She don't need me to put 'em there."

Sly left then. Ryan gazed after him for a moment, then laughed and gouged the dirt with his boot heel. "Is he ornery, or what?"

"He's wonderful," Bethany said, and she meant it with all her heart.

When Ryan met her gaze, there was a silent message in his eyes. "You'll never find a better friend. I was sort of upset with him last night, but I'm glad he was here to talk to you."

"He loves you. Do you realize how much?"

Ryan's eyes darkened. "He'd lay his life down for me. Never a doubt."

"Just you remember that," she said softly. "If the time ever comes that he needs you to stand up for him, Ryan, just you remember that."

A bewildered expression crossed his face. "I guess I will. He's like a second father to me." He searched her gaze. "Why do you say that?"

Bethany smiled and shrugged. "No particular reason."

"There is a reason. I know you. Is Sly in some kind of trouble?"

Bethany wanted so badly to betray Sly's confidence then. She believed with all her heart that Ryan would understand the old foreman's feelings for Helen, just as she did, and that he'd fight the whole family on Sly's behalf if need be. But it wasn't her place to open that can of worms.

"Just remember this moment. If ever you doubt him—if ever his honor is called into question—remember this moment and shove your doubts aside. Stand up for him. That's all I'm saying. He's earned that, hasn't he?"

Ryan gazed at the spot where Sly had last stood. "Damn straight. A thousand times over."

Bethany knew then that everything would be all right, that when the moment came, Ryan would stand shoulder to· shoulder with Sly and defend him. That was all she needed to know.

❦ CHAPTER NINETEEN ❦

Later that morning while Ryan did chores, Bethany drove to town to feed and water Cleo. Before returning to the ranch, she stopped by her parents' house. It was time to tell them about the unexpected turn her life had taken. If she waited, her folks were bound to hear about her relationship with Ryan from another source, and she felt they deserved more consideration from her.

Harv Coulter wasn't exactly supportive when he learned that his paraplegic daughter planned to marry a man she'd known for less than two months.

"You're going to what?" he asked when Bethany told him.

Never more than in that moment had Bethany been able to see the resemblance between her father and Jake. Big, dark, and *glowering* pretty much described the pair of them.

She bent her head and fiddled with the gathers in her burgundy skirt, which had been far easier to put on this morning without her dressing sling. She could have asked Ryan to help her dress, of course, and he would have happily obliged her, but her determination to be self-sufficient aside, she'd been afraid such a request might have ended with him putting off his chores again. Every time he touched her intimately, they seemed to gravitate toward the bedroom, which was delightful but not very productive when stock was waiting to be fed. As soon as Ryan got all her equipment moved to his place, she would start dressing the part of a rancher's wife, she promised herself, wearing those snug jeans and fringed western shirts that he liked so much.

When she glanced back up, she was smiling and had to jerk her thoughts back to the issue at hand. She fleetingly met her mother's gaze. Mary Coulter smiled and laid a hand on her husband's shoulder. "Harv, our girl has never been flighty. Hear her out, and remember she's always shown good judgment."

Harv settled a worried gaze on Bethany. "Ryan Kendrick is a scalawag. He flits from woman to woman, never making a commitment. What are you thinking, that you're going to tame him? Marry him, and you'll rue the day."

"He isn't like that, Daddy. Maybe he has flitted a little. He'd be the first person to admit that, actually. What else is a man to do when he's searching for the right person? Jake flits, and you don't call him a scalawag."

Harv tapped the salt shaker on the tabletop. Then he looked helplessly at his wife. "Mary, talk to her."

Bethany's mother looked discomfited. "And say what?"

"Talk sense to her. Tell her how insane it is to tie up with some"—Harv waved his hand—"*scalawag* like Ryan Kendrick!"

"But, Harv," Mary said softly, "Bethany's right. If failure to settle down is an indicator, even our Jake is a bit of a scalawag. And so were you. My parents had a fit when I started going out with you. Remember? Daddy said you were no good, that you'd break my heart. You never did."

Harv propped his elbows on the table and rested his head in his hands. "Holy hell, Mary. That was different, and you know it. I admit, I did a little skirt flipping, but I was looking for you under every single one of them."

Mary beamed and fixed a guileless gaze on her daughter. "Has your Ryan been flipping all the wrong skirts, honey?"

Harv groaned. Bethany swallowed back a horrified laugh. *Finally,* her mother was actually admitting that conception occurred under skirts instead of in boots. She should record this day in the family Bible. "Yes, Mama," she managed to say solemnly. She glanced at her father, who was still holding his head. "I don't know how many skirts Daddy flipped, but Ryan had to flip a number of them before he finally found me."

"Holy hell," Harv whispered again.

"Now, now." Mary bent over her husband and whispered something that made his ears turn red. As she straightened, she patted Harv's hand, then sat down to search Bethany's gaze. "Does he love you, Bethie? When he looks at you, do you feel like he'd wade through a den of rattlesnakes for you?"

"Mama, I think he'd lie down and sleep with rattlesnakes for me."

Mary nodded and squeezed Bethany's hands. "He's the one, then. A woman just knows. Life is riddled with trials. If you know, without a doubt, that he'll stand fast and protect you from any kind of threat, he's the right man."

Bethany nodded. "He'd die for me, Mama. He's so wonderful."

Mary's eyes sparkled. "When are you going to bring him to meet us?"

"I've already met him," Harv said, forcing out the words between clenched teeth. "He's a sweet-talkin', good-lookin', spoiled little rich boy who's been playing fast and loose for so long he's forgotten the meaning of honor."

"That is *not* true," Bethany declared. "He is as honorable as any of my brothers!"

Harv leveled a finger at her nose. "Your brothers would never make promises to a girl they didn't intend to keep. The day I put your hand in Ryan Kendrick's, and he says, 'I do,' I'll eat my jock shorts."

After speaking to her parents, Bethany went by the store to talk to Jake. Her brother was swamped, trying to wait on customers while he filled out an inventory order. Nevertheless he smiled when he saw her.

"I was hoping you might spare me a few minutes to chat," Bethany said with a laugh. "I guess not."

Jake held up a finger for her to wait. He finished helping a customer, asked an employee to cover for him, and then walked with Bethany to the elevator. Once upstairs, they went to his office.

Jake dropped onto a castor chair and propped his boots on the edge of his desk. "It's been one of those mornings. You never phoned me back, twerp. I was a little worried. It sounded like that bull was inside the house."

Bethany smiled. "It was." She went on to explain about T-bone. "Ryan was pretty upset, but I think I've convinced him to see how things go."

Jake sighed and frowned. "Can't blame him for being worried. Bulls can be ornery."

"T-bone is an exception. He's big and clumsy, but he was so gentle with me. We'll see."

Jake glanced at the clock. "So what do you want to talk with me about?"

Bethany gazed at a snapshot of his horses that he had pinned to the wall. *Jake, the horse whisperer.* She knew he hoped to one day purchase a ranch, that it wasn't his plan to run a supply store for the rest of his life. If anyone would understand what she was about to say, Jake would. "I want to talk to you about two things."

"You seem upset."

"Not upset, exactly. I'm feeling a little guilty about a decision I've made. If this will put you in a bind, Jake, please don't hesitate to tell me. All right?"

He lowered his feet to the floor and shifted forward on the chair. "Ryan's asked you to quit the job."

"If you need me here to take up the slack, I won't leave you in the lurch. It's just—well, Ryan's fixed it so I can really be a help on the ranch, and the opportunity is . . ." Her voice trailed away. She'd been about to say it was a dream come true, but that didn't seem fair. Jake had dreams of his own, but he was here, running the family business instead of pursuing them.

"The opportunity is too sweet to resist?" Jake finished for her. He sighed and spent a moment straightening some papers on his desk. "I can do some juggling and get by without you. If that's what you came to ask, consider it done."

"I don't want to be selfish and unfair to you. I'm a member of this family, too."

Jake smiled and glanced around the office. "Thank you for that. But the truth is, I'm helping myself as much as I'm helping Dad. When the doctor told him he had to start taking it easy, he was going to sell the store. It's a going concern, and there are always interested parties. But I asked him to hold off."

"You did? I thought you wanted to buy a ranch."

"I do." Jake grinned and tapped a pen on his desk pad. "And I will. But saving for a few more months will get me better set. I have a good down payment tucked away. Now I'm trying to gather up some working capital. Running the store is allowing me to do that. Dad takes out a monthly income. A certain percentage of the profits are automatically set aside to build the business. The rest is mine, just as if I owned the place. How much goes in my pocket depends solely on how hard I'm willing to work. Most months, I've done well."

Bethany stared at him. "So you asked me to quit my Portland job and move home, knowing you only meant to keep this place a few more months?"

He chuckled. "Before I ever made the decision to call you, Zeke decided to take over the store after I leave. You have a job here for as long as you want one." His smile grew tender. "Those first few months, you helped me hold this place together. Things have smoothed out now. I can get by without you."

"Oh, Jake, are you sure?"

"Go live your life, Bethie. Ryan's offering you the much sweeter deal. When the time comes, I won't hesitate to follow my dream. Why should you?"

"I just don't want to leave if you need me."

He tossed down the pen. "Well, I don't, so pack up and hit the road."

"I'm afraid you're saying that because you think it's what I want to hear."

A suspicious shine came into his eyes. "Eight years ago, I sat beside your bed, night after night. I'd get off work and go directly to the hospital. Remember that?"

She nodded.

"I always laughed and talked and pretended everything would be fine," he said thickly. "You needed me to be strong for you. But lots of times after you fell asleep, I sat there beside your bed and cried like a baby, begging God to give us a miracle. You were only eighteen, and your life had been destroyed."

Bethany lowered her gaze to her lap, her chest squeezing with an awful pain. *Jake*. She hadn't always been asleep when he had cried.

"God didn't see fit to make you walk again, and until now, I was afraid you might never get married and have a normal life. Now, bingo, along comes Ryan Kendrick. He seems to adore you. He's offering you a life I know you're going to love. How do you think I feel about that?"

"Glad?" she whispered.

He nodded. "So glad, Bethie. You've got this wonderful chance to be happy. Really, really happy. *Go*. Don't look back. There's nobody who deserves this more than you."

"Oh, Jake . . . How did I ever get so lucky? Of all the brothers in the world, you're the best."

"Let's not get any sappier than we have to. What was the second thing you wanted to ask me?"

Bethany hauled in a cleansing breath. "I was wondering if you'd mind talking to Daddy for me. He's not at all happy about me marrying—"

Jake burst out laughing. "This is where I play rotten brother. No way."

"But—"

"No." Jake pushed up from the chair. "Dad is Ryan's problem. If he's half the man I think he is, he'll go see our father and do his own talking."

"That's just it. I don't want him to know Daddy's frothing at the mouth. His family has accepted me with open arms."

"And why wouldn't they? Ryan's damn lucky to get you."

"In your opinion. On the flip side, aren't I just as lucky to get him?"

Jake laughed again. "Maybe so, but let Ryan convince Dad of it. My last word, end of subject. I'm not getting in the middle of it."

As she drove back to the Rocking K, Bethany tried not to let her father's reaction spoil her happiness. *Ryan*. She loved him so very much.

Jake had just set her free to go dream chasing. She had every reason to be rejoicing.

Nevertheless, when she got to the ranch and parked the van, her heart felt heavy. Her dad was the best. He'd been there for her all her life, and it hurt that he wasn't standing behind her now.

"What's wrong?" Ryan asked when he saw her face. "Is Cleo all right?"

"Cleo's fine." Bethany gazed past him at the lake, wishing she didn't have to tell him this. But if she kept it under her hat, she'd be setting him up for a nasty surprise when he saw her father. "Oh, Ryan. I went by to see my parents."

He hunkered down in front of her. "Uh-oh. I hope you didn't take it upon yourself to tell them I've asked you to marry me."

"Take it upon myself? They're my parents. Of course I told them."

Ryan shoved his hat back. "Sweetheart, if your dad's anything at all like mine, he's pretty old-fashioned."

"A little. So what?"

"Old-fashioned fathers have set ideas about how things like this should be done. I'm supposed to go see your dad and ask him for your hand. That gives him an opportunity to grill me for a while and make me squirm. If I say the right things, he feels good about the situation. If I don't, he tells me to take a hike."

Bethany gulped. "What happens if he tells you to take a hike?"

Ryan winked at her. "He won't. I'm a slick talker."

"That's one of the things he doesn't like about you."

He threw back his head and barked with laughter. When his mirth subsided, he assured her, "I can handle him, honey. Don't worry. All right? He'll think I'm the greatest thing since the invention of popcorn."

After applying for their marriage license that afternoon, Ryan dropped Bethany off at her house. While she packed some clothes, he drove over to see her father. After a two-minute conversation, Ryan stood on the Coulters' front porch, wondering how in the hell things had gone so wrong.

The man's shouts were still ringing in Ryan's ears as he started toward his truck. *A no-account scalawag?* Nobody said "no-account scalawag" these days. *Damn.* The guy was living in the Dark Ages.

Once in his truck, Ryan envisioned the dejected expression on Bethany's face when he told her how badly this had gone. He slammed his fist against the steering wheel and glared through the windshield at her parents' house, thinking he could buy a thousand just like it and still make change. Who the hell did that old codger think he was?

Ryan nearly started the truck and drove away. But, no, damn it. Instead he climbed back out, slammed the door, and stomped along the walkway to the porch. Up the flipping steps he went, boiling mad. The man was Bethany's father, and for that reason, Ryan would show him respect. But he wasn't about to crawl away with his tail tucked between his legs.

He rapped his knuckles on the door, swearing under his breath. Expecting Bethany's mother to answer as she had before, he strove to school his expression. Then the door flew open, and he found himself standing nose to nose with the old man. Blue eyes like Bethany's shot sparks at him.

"Mr. Coulter, I'd appreciate it if you'd at least hear me out," Ryan began.

"You've got nothing to say that I'm interested in hearing. If my daughter marries you, it'll be against my wishes. That's my last word."

Ryan lost his temper. "No 'if' to it. I *will* marry your daughter. Nothing you can say or do is going to stop me. We're both consenting adults, and it's our decision to make. I'm here only as a courtesy, Mr. Coulter, more for her sake than yours. Your approval is very important to her."

"In one breath you ask for my blessing, and in the next, you inform me you don't really give a rat's ass if you get it. You call that a courtesy?" Harv's face flushed an angry red. "Get off my porch."

"You can make me leave, sir, but what good will that do? First thing you know, I'll be back, asking for her hand again."

"And I'll be saying no, *again*. You're not good enough for her."

"There's not a man on earth good enough for her."

"Amen."

"That established, will you at least give me the benefit of the doubt and trust that I'll do my damnedest to be *half* the man she deserves?"

"Harrumph."

Ryan sighed. "Look, Mr. Coulter, I understand how you feel."

"No, damn it, you don't understand how I feel. And pray God you never do. My daughter isn't like other young women. I don't want to see her go through any more heartache, and you've got heartache written all over you."

Ryan grabbed for patience. "I understand Bethany's got some very special problems and that it's going to take a special man with a lot of staying power to make her happy. I know you're not sure if I've got what it takes. I'm telling you I do, and I give you my word I'll never hurt her."

"I appreciate that. But I've got no way of knowing if your word is good. I know your father, and he's a fine man. But that's no indication you are."

"He raised me, didn't he? It's true I've never stayed in a relationship. I admit that. But it's only because I never found the right woman until now."

"Look, son. It's nothing personal. All right? Our Bethany—if she were like other women, I might be a whole lot more relaxed about this. But she isn't. How are you going to feel a year down the road when the shine has worn off and you're stuck with a wife in a wheelchair? What'll happen to my little girl then?"

"So instead of taking a chance on me, you'll break her heart now? That's what you're doing, you know, breaking her heart."

Harv blinked. "Say what?"

"It's true. She wants you to be glad for her, and knowing you aren't is ruining what should be the happiest time of her life." Ryan met the older man's gaze. "I don't blame you for loving her and being afraid for her. But if she's going to have a normal life, you have to turn loose and let her live it. You can't shield her from everything, not without being the man who hurts her the most."

"I'd never do anything to hurt that girl."

"Then give us your blessing," Ryan said evenly.

Bethany's mother appeared in the doorway beside her husband. She smiled at Ryan. "Consider it given. Tell Bethany her daddy is as happy as a clam, and that her wedding day will be the proudest day of his life."

"Mary," Harv said warningly.

"Go," Mary urged Ryan. "Give her a hug from me." She linked arms with her husband. "I'll take care of the situation here."

"Mary!" Harv said again.

Ryan figured Mary Coulter could handle her husband with no help from him, so he took her advice and headed for his truck. Halfway there, Harv bellowed, "Just understand one thing, Kendrick! The day I find out you've made my little girl cry will be the sorriest day of your life!"

Ryan was laughing when he started the Dodge. He'd never been threatened so much in his life since the day he'd met Bethany. First Jake, now her father. What the hell. He only had four more brothers to go. He shook his head. These folks were so cantankerous, they made the Kendricks seem mild tempered.

Standing in Bethany's bedroom, Ryan peeked in a sack she had just stuffed full of clothing. He plucked out a flannel nightgown. Next he found a Snoopy nightshirt. As soon as possible, he had to take her shopping for lingerie, he decided. Lacy see-through stuff was more to his taste.

She turned from the dresser drawer and caught him frowning. "What's wrong?" she asked with an impish smile. "Don't you like my Snoopy shirt?"

"I'm crazy about Snoopy." He stuffed the shirt back in the sack. "I was thinking about something else."

"You were scowling." A worried look came over her face. "Was there a problem with Daddy you didn't tell me about?"

"He got a little prickly. Nothing I couldn't handle. We have his blessing. That's all that matters. Right?"

"Right." She sighed and glanced around the room. "I have enough stuff to do me. Except for my bathroom sling. Would you mind taking it to your truck?"

"You won't be needing it out there."

"How on earth will I take a bath?"

He grinned and waggled his eyebrows at her. "One guess."

Her cheeks turned a pretty pink. "It's sweet of you to offer, but I'd feel far more comfortable with my sling."

"What fun would that be?" He dipped his voice low and whispery. "When I'm done lathering you up, you'll be so clean, you'll squeak."

Her gaze flitted away from his. "As fun as that might be, I like to do things for myself, and I don't want to depend on you for my baths."

"I ordered you a better one."

Her gaze came chasing back to his. "*Ryan.* What all have you bought me that I don't know about yet?"

"Not all that much."

"What, exactly?"

"You want to be here all night?"

"I'm starting to feel really bad."

"Why?"

"Because you've spent so much money on me. I mean—on the one hand, I know we're going to get married, and I shouldn't feel that way. But on the other, I feel indebted."

"Works for me."

"What does?"

He winked at her. "You feeling indebted. I can think of some fantastic ways for you to work off the debt."

"As your stable manager?"

"Nope. The corporation will pay you a wage for that." He glanced at her bed. "I'm thinking of something more interesting."

She giggled when he started toward her. "Forget it."

"Why?"

"Someone might come. My brothers all have keys."

That stopped him in his tracks. He hooked his thumbs over his belt and slowly skimmed his gaze over her. "We're not even married yet, and already I have in-law-itis. But that's okay. This is Thursday. I have plans for you later."

"What's Thursday got to do with anything?"

A gleam warmed his eyes. "It's your swim night. I have an indoor, heated pool off the back of the house. I'll give you some swimming lessons."

"I already know how to swim. I creamed you doing laps."

"You've never seen my version of the 'breaststroke'."

She giggled again.

"You'll also find ceiling watching a lot more entertaining in there. It's all skylights. When I set you on the side of the pool after I teach you the breaststroke, you'll be able to gaze at the stars while I—"

Cleo began rubbing against his pant leg just then. Ryan broke off to glance down. When he saw who had interrupted him, he bent to scoop her up in one hand. "Damn cat. I was on a roll."

"She's been lonesome. I've never left her alone this much."

"Let's take the pest home with us, then," he suggested.

"I sort of had the impression you weren't very fond of cats."

"I'm not. I hate cats. Did you know she'll eat you if you die?"

"No, sir! Who told you such an awful thing?"

Cleo narrowed her green eyes at him. Ryan squinted back at her. "I know it for a fact. When I was a kid, my grandmother's neighbor lady died, and her cats had almost polished her off before someone found her."

"Maybe the poor things got hungry because there was no one to feed them."

"She fed them." The thought gave him the shudders. "You ever wondered what she's thinking when she squints at you like that? I think she's thinking about having me for lunch with a little A-1 on the side."

"She is not. She's probably just afraid you're going to hurt her. She likes gourmet cat food. No offense, but you probably wouldn't appeal to her."

"You would." He winked at her. "You definitely appeal to my taste buds."

Her cheeks went pink again. "Is that all you think about?"

"Mostly. They say the normal male thinks about it every four minutes."

"You're kidding. You don't, do you?"

"Nah. I think I'm a little undersexed. I go as long as ten minutes sometimes without ever thinking about it." He winked at her again. "You about ready? I can carry green-eyes and one sack if you can get the other one."

"Actually, Ryan, I was thinking I might give Cleo to my mom. Cats are sensitive. She needs a home where she'll be loved and understood."

Ryan stared into the cat's slightly crossed eyes, thinking the poor thing looked a little retarded. "We understand each other, honey." Cleo understood he didn't like her, and he understood she didn't like him. The only reason she rubbed against his leg was to shed on his pants. "And I'll learn to love her, I promise." With his luck, the damn critter would live until she was twenty. "I pretty much like all animals." Except cats.

"I don't know. She's never been around a dog. I'm afraid she won't like Tripper."

Ryan tucked the damned cat under his arm. "She and Tripper will get along fine. He's good with the barn cats over at Rafe's place."

A half hour later, after a harrowing ride from town with Cleo hanging upside down from the truck ceiling for much of the trip, Ryan finally got the squirming, scratching cat into his house. When he turned her loose in the great room, Tripper came waddling over to make friends. Accustomed to barn cats, who weren't afraid of dogs, the Lab never saw the calico's claws coming. He took a swat squarely on the end of his nose, yipped and howled, then ran for the bedroom. Cleo fled in the other direction, leaped at the vertical blinds, and scaled them to gain a perch atop the wood valance, where she arched her back, raised all her bristles, and hissed, looking for all the world like a Halloween decoration.

"Well," Ryan said, "we're off to a great start."

Bethany whirred down the hall toward the master bedroom. "Tripper? Come here, sweetie. Let me look at your nose." From the bedroom, she yelled, "Ryan, he's not in here."

Unless the dog had broken out a window, he had to be somewhere in there. Ryan joined Bethany and executed a search. He finally found the Lab hiding in the bathtub.

"If you aren't the sorriest excuse for a dog I ever saw," Ryan said. "I can't believe you, Tripper. You outweigh that kitty by a hundred pounds."

"Oh, Ryan, his nose is bleeding." Bethany parked sideways to the tub and leaned over to examine the dog's nose. "Poor baby. She really got you good."

Ryan checked the injury. "He'll live. It just smarts a little."

Bethany fixed him with a worried look. "I hope this is no indication of how our life is going to go."

"Don't even *think* that way. Our life is going to be absolutely perfect, sweetheart. Cleo will settle in, and before we know it, she and Tripper will be snuggling together on the sofa."

"Oh, do you think so? She's so easily excited. I worry she'll never like it here. Before I lived in an apartment, and she never went outside. In town, I kept her indoors, too. Now here she is on a horse and cattle ranch."

"She'll be fine. Cats are very adaptable."

A few minutes later, when Ryan tried to pluck Cleo off the valance, the cat yowled, leaped, and dug all four sets of claws into the front of his shirt. "Son of a"—Ryan caught himself just in time, and finished with—"biscuit maker!"

The cat catapulted off of him, hit the floor at a run, and sent stuff flying as she scaled the front of the entertainment center. Once on top of it, she glared at Ryan with gleaming green eyes and hissed.

"I don't think she's adapting very well," Bethany observed.

Ryan smiled. "Sweetheart, she'll be fine. She may sense that you're upset. Ever think of that? If you relax and ignore her, maybe she'll relax, too."

He removed his hat and sent it sailing toward the coat tree. The Stetson missed the hook and fell crown first on the floor. That was not a good omen.

"Oh, *no!*" Bethany cried.

Ryan spun around. "What?"

He followed her horrified gaze to the top of the entertainment center, where Cleo was scratching at the oak as if to cover something up. The hair on his nape prickled. "What the hell is she doing?"

"I think she already did it."

Ryan forgot all about having to donate ten dollars to the college fund and said, "Son of a-aaa-a *bitch!*"

❦ CHAPTER TWENTY ❦

The wedding date was set for Saturday, weekend after next, and the intervening eight days were the most glorious of Bethany's life. *Ryan*. He insisted that she remain with him on the Rocking K, and from the moment she opened her eyes in the morning until he kissed them closed for the last time each night, she had fun. The most wondrous aspect of that, in her opinion, was that even the silly, unimportant things turned out to be unexpectedly wonderful.

The crazy mix of Ryan's household pets, for example. Who would have thought that a very spoiled seventeen-pound feline and an equally spoiled, eight hundred–pound bull would become bosom buddies? Certainly not Bethany. But the following morning was the beginning of what promised to be a lifelong friendship between the two animals.

After having coffee with Bethany, Ryan grabbed his Stetson to head over to the stable to feed the stock. When he opened the door to step out, he paused to flash her a teasing grin. "On the Rocking K, even my wife has to earn her keep, you know. If you want to eat regular, no lady of leisure stuff for you. You'd best show up over there in a couple of minutes, ready to make yourself useful."

Bethany was about to reply when Cleo darted between Ryan's feet to escape outdoors. "Oh, *no!*" she cried.

Ryan dashed out after the cat, Tripper barking excitedly at his boot heels. Bethany hurried out onto the porch. *Cleo*. The poor kitty had seldom been outdoors, and then it had always been in town. She would be terrified out here. Bethany envisioned her small pet dashing off into the woods and getting lost. Cleo was just the right size to become some large, hungry carnivore's lunch.

"Here, cat!" Ryan called in a big, male voice.

Bethany anxiously scanned the yard, looking for a splotch of mottled fur. She didn't see poor Cleo anywhere. "Don't call her like *that*. You'll frighten her."

Ryan shot her a disgruntled look. "How should I call her then?"

In a shrill voice, Bethany called, "Here, Cleo! Here, kitty-kitty!"

Ryan swore under his breath, stomped onto the cement pad, and began calling Cleo in an off-key alto. As much as Bethany appreciated his attempt to achieve the right tone, she thought he sounded like a 220-pound cat killer on the prowl. T-bone came to the summons, bawling stupidly with every step. Bethany felt fairly sure that Cleo would never show herself now.

She wasn't counting on Tripper to join in the search. The plump golden Lab clearly had a score to settle, and now Cleo was on *his* turf. He put his nose to the ground, zigzagged across the yard to a stack of firewood, and began wagging his tail excitedly.

"Ah-hah! She's in the woodpile!" Ryan stomped over. "Here, kitty!" he rumbled as he began moving pieces of wood. With every other breath, he muttered, "Damn cat."

Bethany zoomed down the ramp and hurried over to rescue her poor kitty before Ryan unearthed her. Unfortunately she didn't get there in time. Ryan moved a piece of wood, and there huddled poor Cleo. The frightened feline hissed and yowled, then eluded Ryan's reaching hands by diving between his legs. Bad mistake. She ran straight into Tripper, who was barking excitedly.

When threatened, most cats head for the highest perch available, and Cleo was no exception. It just so happened that, except for Ryan, T-bone was the tallest thing in the immediate vicinity. The cat leaped on the bull's back. Startled to have an uninvited and very prickly creature clinging to his shoulders, T-bone did what any not-very-bright bull would do.

He ran.

Determined to save Bethany's stupid cat, Ryan pursued the unlikely duo, but every time he got close enough to grab Cleo, the cat became frightened and dug in with her claws, which made T-bone run again.

After thirty minutes of fruitless chase, Ryan returned to Bethany, slapping his Stetson against his leg with every step. "I can't get her, honey."

Bethany gazed down toward the lake, where T-bone stood forlornly on the shore with Cleo clinging to his back. The pair looked so silly that Bethany burst out laughing. "I think she's going to stay there. T-bone is the perfect kitty scooter!"

Ryan began chuckling as well. "He's all terrain, too, and goes at a fast clip in high gear." He had worked up a sweat, chasing the bull. He touched a shirtsleeve to his brow. "I'm sorry I couldn't catch her, honey. Now you'll worry all day."

Bethany sighed. "Well, she's safe enough on T-bone's back. Not that she'll stay up there for long."

Famous last words. Come noon, the cat was still riding the bull's broad back while he grazed. Bethany studied the pair, smiling and shaking her head. She wasn't close enough to tell for sure, but it looked as if Cleo was having a nap. Since T-bone had apparently accepted the cat's presence, there was nothing to do but wait for Cleo to get down and come back on her own.

As if he guessed Bethany's thoughts, Ryan said, "She'll get hungry. When she does, she'll come to the house."

No such luck. That night, Bethany had Ryan set out food for Cleo on the woodpile. At some point during the night, the cat must have dismounted the bull in order to eat, for the food was gone in the morning. But when Bethany went out to find her kitty, Cleo was nowhere around.

"She's still riding T-bone," Ryan informed her a few minutes later when she entered the stable. "Sly says the bull came in for breakfast a bit ago, and Cleo was still curled up on his back, pretty as you please. She gave herself a bath while T-bone ate his grain."

Bethany shook her head. "Maybe T-bone's her answer to ranch life. She feels safe on him. Everything here must seem really scary to her. He's big and solid." She smiled up at Ryan. "Sort of like you. I can associate."

Ryan's eyes started to twinkle—which Bethany was quickly coming to realize meant trouble. "Oh, yeah?" He glanced around to make sure they were alone, then leaned down to kiss her. A long, heated kiss that made her head swim. "I want you," he whispered.

Bethany could associate with that as well, which struck her as slightly amazing. After the poolside exploit last night, two more sessions in bed, and a wake-up round that morning, both of them should have been completely sated. "Be good," she whispered. "Sly's here somewhere. We'll get caught."

Ryan flicked the white fringe on the blue western shirt she'd purchased especially for him. "You don't really think I can ignore the way that fringe shifts back and forth over your nipples, do you?" He grazed an already hardened tip and chuckled. "No way, lady."

Since she'd worn the shirt expressly for him, Bethany could only smile smugly, pleased that her efforts had been noticed. Nevertheless, she was startled when Ryan suddenly scooped her from her chair. She shrieked and grabbed hold of his neck. "Not in the *stable*."

"I'll find a private place."

He carried her to the tack room, locked the door, and laid her out on a hay bale. This morning, she wore the shirt and snug blue jeans. He attacked the buttons of her top, saying, "This is where I eat my lunch most days. Tomorrow can you come to work wearing plastic wrap?"

She giggled and then gasped with pleasure when he bent his head to nip gently at her nipple through the lace of her bra. "Ryan, I'm afraid I'll forget where we are and make noise. Sly may hear me."

He grabbed for a length of leather hanging from a nail above them. Still nibbling at her flesh and sending shocks of delight coursing through her, he whispered, "Bite down on that."

She giggled again, and then she moaned, every thought in her head slipping away as he unhooked her bra and touched his hot, wonderful mouth to her bare breast. When he shifted to give her other breast the attention it craved, the cool morning air washed over her moist nipple, making it turn rock hard, which seemed to inflame him when he took it in his mouth again. June sunlight poured in the tack room window to play over them. Ryan mumbled something about barely ripe strawberries, making her whimper mindlessly as he unfastened her jeans. "I'm starving for you. I promise this won't take long."

It took about forty minutes, and she loved every second.

Ryan. She was quickly coming to realize that he was going to be an impulsive, unpredictable, and insatiable lover, the kind of man who could be working intently one moment and then be totally focused on making love to her the next, the only uncertainty being where he might grab her.

After the tack room episode, Bethany didn't really expect to make love again until that night, if then. Ryan had other ideas. Later that morning in the stable office while he was showing her how he kept the books, the phone rang, and Bethany automatically answered because she was sitting closer to it. It was Jake, calling during his mid-morning break to check on her.

Bethany no sooner greeted her brother than Ryan grinned wickedly and started unfastening her blouse. She pushed at his shoulder. When he moved in to kiss her collarbone, she braced the heel of her hand on his forehead, trying to hold him at bay. It was like trying to keep water from rushing downhill.

"This shirt drives me wild," he whispered. "Why should I let this fringe have all the fun?" He drew the cloth apart, unfastened the front clasp of her bra, cupped her breasts in his big hands, and proceeded to drive her half crazy with his fabulous mouth while she tried to carry on an intelligent conversation with her brother.

When Ryan started tugging at her nipples with his teeth, Bethany had to ask Jake to repeat a question. She glanced worriedly toward the door. Ryan chuckled and whispered. "I always plan ahead. It's locked."

That made her feel marginally better—until he pushed her breasts together so he could tease both throbbing nipples at once. The gentle squeeze made blood rush to the tips. Ryan leaned back to observe the swelling process with some interest, his gunmetal blue eyes glinting with mischief. In that moment Bethany wondered how his mother had survived his childhood.

Over the weekend Ryan's parents came to visit. Ann was limping from the bruise on her hip. "The doctor says it'll be a while healing, that I'm lucky I didn't break it. I'm getting too old for bouncing off the corners of desks."

Keefe, who was sporting barked knuckles on one big hand, put an arm around his wife's narrow shoulders and said, "The little son of a bitch will think twice before he pushes a lady again." He winked at Bethany. "He dropped the charges against me yesterday. Got to thinking how it'd look on the front page of the paper and decided his behavior toward my wife had been inexcusable."

"I wonder who put that thought in his head," Ryan mused. "You didn't threaten to call the newspaper, did you, Dad?"

Ann smiled. "Your father is far too direct a man to be that conniving. I threatened to call the newspaper." She glanced adoringly at her husband and held out a hand. "My hero. That'll be ten dollars, please, you ornery old curmudgeon."

Keefe muttered and scowled, but he plucked a ten from his pocket and handed it over. Ann slipped it in her shirt and smiled at Bethany. "Not to worry. I won't let a little bruise keep me from being at the wedding."

This wasn't the first time Bethany had seen the men on the Rocking K getting ten-dollar bills out of their clips or wallets. She looked bewilderedly at Ryan, who quickly explained about the no-cussing rule on the ranch. Bethany thought it was a marvelous idea. By the time she and Ryan were able to adopt, the women would have all the men trained.

On Monday her saddle arrived. Ryan no sooner removed it from the crate than he started putting it on Wink. Bethany's stomach got nervous jitters when she realized he meant for her to go riding straightaway. When he turned and caught her expression, he knelt beside her chair, searched her gaze for a long moment, and then hooked a finger under her chin to lift her face.

"Sweetheart, you don't have to get on her. If all you want is to love Wink and be with her every day, that's fine by me."

Bethany stared at the horse for a long, heart-pounding moment. Memories flashed in her mind of her riding accident, and sweat filmed her face. It had happened so quickly in reality, yet in her mind the events leading up to that split second played out in slow motion. She yearned to ride Wink again. The wanting was so intense, her bones ached. But she was also terrified. No one who'd never experienced what she had could possibly understand how the fear grabbed her by the throat.

"I—um . . ." She squeezed her eyes closed. "Oh, Ryan, I want to so *much*. But I'm scared. So scared."

He caught her face between his hands. "I can get you to the lake for the wedding on a four-wheeler, honey. Don't even think about this as a have-to thing. All right?"

The wedding. Oh, God. Everyone planned to ride horses in to the lake to see them be married. A cold feeling washed over her. She felt all shivery when she met Ryan's gaze.

He swore under his breath and started raining kisses all over her face. "I'm sorry. Jesus, sweet Jesus. I need to be horsewhipped for being such a blockhead. Forgive me."

Bethany curled her hands over her wrists. "I *want* to ride again, Ryan."

He stared hard into her eyes.

"I want to ride again," she repeated. "I just have to gather the courage."

Fifteen minutes later Bethany was strapped onto her horse. She also sweated so badly that it dripped off of her, and she felt nauseous. Terror and bagels didn't mix.

Ryan held the reins. "You don't have to do this. Let's get you down."

"No." Bethany realized she was clinging to the saddle horn like a child. *Oh, God.* The ground looked a hundred miles away. She imagined Wink stumbling and coming down on top of her. She gulped convulsively. "I need to do this. Even if I never go riding outside a corral, I need to do this, Ryan."

He just stood there, holding her horse and staring up at her. "Bethany, honey, please. This is all my fault. Let's get you down."

"No!" She didn't mean to scream at him, but she did. *Screamed.* As if he were her enemy. "Would you stop standing there and do something to *help* me?"

He stroked Wink's neck, trying to calm the mare because her rider was doing just the opposite. In some part of her brain, Bethany knew she needed to get hold of herself. "I need you to help me do this," she repeated shakily.

"What do you need, Bethany? Tell me, and I'll do it."

"*Talk* to me. Make me so I'm not nervous."

The next thing Bethany knew, he was behind her on the horse. The instant his arm came around her, she could breathe again. "I'm right here, sweetheart. Right here with you."

She leaned against his chest and twisted to press her face against his neck. *Ryan.* She felt safe when he was holding her. Absolutely safe. Rationally, she knew he could do nothing to protect her if the horse came tumbling down on top of them. But that didn't matter. Her fear wasn't rational.

She started blabbering. About the accident. How it had happened. How she'd leaned forward and shifted her weight as Wink went into the turn. How they'd been beating their best time, racing with the wind. Then the sudden lurch. The dizzying sensation of flying through the air. *Pain.* A flash of pain so excruciating her brain exploded and went black.

"When I woke up, I couldn't feel my toes. Isn't it crazy that I remember that over everything?" She tipped her chin back as far as it would go and stared at the blue sky above them. "It wasn't my legs I was worried about. I couldn't feel my toes. I remember staring at the sheet and trying to wiggle them. Trying as hard as I could. And—realizing. *Realizing.* My mom and dad were there. Jake grabbed my arms and pinned them to the bed. I remember looking into his eyes and screaming. They didn't even have to tell me. I knew when I couldn't wiggle my toes."

Ryan let Wink's reins fall and wrapped both arms around her. "Forgive me, Bethany. Please, forgive me. You never have to get on a horse again. You can enjoy Wink just as much without riding her."

"That's just it," she whispered against his neck. "I need to ride. I *need* to, Ryan, like I need air to breathe. Don't let me get off. I'll never have the courage to get back on. Keep me on her until this stops."

"Oh, Jesus," he whispered.

"Please," she begged him. "Don't let it end like this. Don't take me down. Just make it better. Please?"

Ryan splayed a hand over her midriff and retrieved the reins. "Sly!" he yelled.

"Yo?" The ranch foreman came into the exercise area. "Whatcha need?"

"Throw open the gate," Ryan ordered.

Bethany watched Sly unlatch the gate and pull it open. Ryan drew Wink around and lunged her out of the corral. Bethany's heart flew into her throat. The ground looked as if it might leap up and smack her in the face. Ryan veered the horse toward the lake. Even though he reined the mare to a walk, the panic she felt was indescribable. She was going to die. Her heart was going to stop. Only it kept beating, and Wink kept going.

After a bit Ryan slowed the mare's pace even more. The breeze that blew in off the lake to kiss Bethany's face was laden with rich, wonderful scents—spring grass and budding wildflowers, pine and fir, and a crispness to the air that came in off the mountains. She relaxed against his hard chest, letting her body undulate with the horse and him.

"Oh, Ryan . . ."

He pressed his face against her hair. "You know, honey, the way I see it, there's only two ways to live life. One way is to protect yourself from all danger as best you can, existing in a safe little bubble. Even then, chances are you could end up getting run over by a bus or contracting some terrible disease."

"What's the other option?" she asked with a shaky laugh.

"You can grab hold of life with both hands, enjoy every blessed minute of it, and take a chance that you may get hurt or killed while you're doing something you love."

She laughed again, the sound still quivery. "No half measures, like having a little bit of fun while you play it safe?"

He nibbled her neck. "That'd be like making love and never having an orgasm. Big-time frustrating."

"Been there, done that. I don't want to live my life that way."

"Then grab hold with both hands," he whispered, and the next thing she knew, she was alone on the horse. He reached up to give her the reins. His beautiful eyes held hers for a long moment. "Live happy, darlin'. You're strapped on, so you can't fall. The only way you can get hurt is if Wink stumbles, and the ground squirrels don't dig burrows along the lakeshore. They stay in the fields where food is plentiful. She seems like a surefooted little lady to me."

Bethany nodded. "She's only fallen with me once, and that wasn't her fault." Even so, once was all it had taken. She closed her eyes and hauled in a bracing breath.

"I'm walking back," he told her. "This being your first time out, it would probably be best if you came up and rode near the stable, where I can keep an eye on you."

Bethany stared straight ahead, so terrified she was trembling. "I, um . . . it's nice, even ground for as far as I can see. Wink responds to voice commands. I'm sure I'll be fine, and—" She broke off and swallowed to steady her voice. "I need to do this, Ryan. First time out, I need to do it by myself for a bit."

She heard him sigh. She didn't dare look at him for fear she'd lose her nerve. "All right," he said. "Go, then. It's flat ground all the way around the lake. I don't recommend that you go too far the first day, but I'll leave that up to you."

Bethany nodded, resisting the urge to ask him to saddle his horse and go with her. It was stupid to feel afraid. The likelihood that Wink might stumble was minuscule. "I, um . . . I won't go too far."

"When you're done, I'll be in the stable. Just ride in and holler. I'll help you off."

Bethany nodded, still staring straight ahead. "If I—um—don't come back in thirty minutes, come find me. Okay?"

"Honey, that goes without saying."

She felt better, knowing he'd come after her if she didn't return in a specified period of time. Heart in throat, she urged Wink forward.

Ryan waited at the stable in a sweat, worrying every second Bethany was gone. When twenty minutes had passed, he saddled up his sorrel gelding and went to find her. She was clear at the opposite end of the lake near his parents' place when he caught up with her. At the sound of his approach, she twisted at the waist and waved, her face beaming, her eyes glowing.

"Oh, Ryan, thank you . . . thank you. This is so wonderful. So *freeing*. I can go places that are impossible in my wheelchair. You've opened up a whole new world for me."

He slowed his horse to a walk beside hers. His heart hurt to see her so happy. "Pretty special day?"

"Oh, *yes*. I don't feel so afraid now. Not entirely at ease yet. But not terrified, either."

"That's good. How's Wink doing?"

"Fabulously. I used to run her a lot, and she loved it. But today she seems content to walk." She leaned forward to stroke the horse's neck. "Maybe we're both just getting old. I think she's enjoying the slow pace."

"Nothing wrong with a slow pace. You can enjoy the scenery."

"That's true. It's so beautiful here, Ryan. You have no idea how very lucky you are to have all this in your backyard. The lake, the forests, and that incredible view of the mountains looming against the sky. It's *heaven*."

"It's your backyard now, too, you know."

She lifted her face to the gentle sunlight. "It *is*, isn't it."

"We're getting married in five days," he reminded her.

"Only five days." She smiled at him. "You getting cold feet yet?"

"Nope. Are you?"

She shook her head. "I've never felt so sure about anything."

He hated to be a wet blanket, but he was worried about her riding for too long. "It'd be best not to overdo the first day. You haven't been on a horse in eight years, and you can't feel what it's doing to your legs."

"Just a while longer. It's so wonderful, I don't want it to end."

Ryan considered their location. "You want to ride all the way around? We've gone so far, I don't think it'll be all that much closer if we double back."

"I'd love it!"

It took half an hour to circle back to Ryan's place. Shortly after their return to the stable, Bethany's legs started to cramp. Ryan carried her to the house. When he jerked off her shoes and jeans, he saw that her feet were bent nearly double in muscle spasms and that the tendons were knotted in her calves and thighs. She lay forward at the waist with her teeth clenched.

As Ryan tried to straighten her legs, she couldn't stifle a scream. He rushed to the phone to call Dr. Kirsch, the Kendrick family physician. The kindly old doctor drove out to the Rocking K. After examining Bethany, he gave her an injection to help relax her muscles.

When the shot started to take effect, Kirsch sat on the side of the bed, holding her hand. "From now on, take it one step at a time, young lady. Tomorrow, no riding. The following day, you can ride for ten minutes. If that goes well, you can add a few minutes to your riding time each day. You have to build up to this slowly, and chances are, even when you've been back in the saddle for a while, you'll still need to take frequent breaks when you go for long jaunts."

"But we're supposed to get married at a mountain lake on Saturday. Ryan planned for us to ride in."

The doctor fixed a questioning gaze on Ryan. "How far is the lake, Rye?"

"About three hours by horseback."

The doctor shook his head. "She won't be ready. Postpone for at least another week, and even then, you'll have to break up the trip, going half the distance one day and half the next."

"We can do that," Ryan said. "Bethany and I can head up on Thursday, go halfway, and camp for the night. It'll be fun."

She angled an arm over her eyes. "I'm sorry, Ryan. I was so excited about being on Wink again, I never even thought about getting leg cramps. I should have had better sense."

The doctor patted her hand. "It's easy to overdo. I don't ride all winter, and the first time I go riding in the spring, I hobble around for days afterward. Every single time, I swear I'll never be so stupid again, but I always am."

"You ride?"

Kirsch chuckled and winked at Ryan. "Why else do you think this bunch out here likes me so well? Keefe doesn't really trust a man unless he smells like a horse every once in a while." He turned back to Ryan. "When you ride in to the lake, take along a pint of distilled white vinegar. If she gets cramps, have her drink two shots, straight. It'll fix her right up."

"Yuck." Bethany shuddered at the thought.

"Nasty tasting and a little acidic on the tummy, but it works in a pinch."

Kirsch went on to carefully question Bethany about her accident and the resultant paralysis. When she'd answered his questions, he said, "Well, young lady, I'll look forward to seeing you again soon. I've delivered all the Kendrick babies. If Ryan has a say, I'll probably be delivering yours as well."

Bethany's face grew pale. She flicked a pained glance at Ryan. "It's very unlikely I'll be able to carry a child to term, Dr. Kirsch. Ryan and I want to try, of course, and we'll hope for the best. But my chances aren't good."

The doctor looked surprised to hear that. Very surprised. "I see," he said. "And why is that? Did you sustain internal injuries I'm unaware of?"

"I, um . . . no. I was badly bruised, of course, but there was no permanent damage. When I had my last checkup, the gynecologist said I was fine."

"Ah. So who said you might not be able to carry a baby to term?"

"The spinal specialist who did my surgeries. He felt my risk of urinary tract and kidney infections would be extremely high, which can lead to miscarriage or preterm labor. There's also a very dangerous condition—I can't remember the name—that he said I might get."

Dr. Kirch mulled that over. Ryan wondered why he was frowning so. "Have you had a history of urinary tract infections?"

Bethany shook her head.

"I see." Kirsch rubbed his chin. "The condition the doctor warned you about was probably autonomic dysreflexia."

"That might've been it," she said. "It's been a long time, but I remember it was a name like that. It sounded really awful when he described it to me."

"It *is* pretty awful," he agreed. "It can cause serious complications at any time during pregnancy or come on during labor. However, it commonly occurs in women with an injury at or above the seventh thoracic vertebra."

"Mine's at L2. But he said there was a chance I might get it."

"What's this condition do to you?" Ryan asked.

"There can be a sharp rise in blood pressure, a severe escalation or drop in heart rate, and there's a risk of convulsions and enlargement of the heart. All in all, it's nothing to mess around with," Dr. Kirsch said solemnly. "There are ways to control it, but sometimes they fail."

"Sweet Jesus," Ryan whispered. "Something like that could kill her." He searched Bethany's face. "It's just not worth it, honey. Not with the risk of another blood clot on top of it. I'd rather we simply never try."

"What's this about a blood clot?"

Ryan quickly recounted to the doctor what Jake had told him.

"There's nothing to say I'll get the dysreflexia stuff," Bethany argued. "And I can be really careful while I'm pregnant not to get a clot. I can stay in bed most of the time with my legs up." She fixed Ryan with an accusing look. "Is that why you've been using protection every time, because of what Jake told you?"

Ryan sighed. "I don't want to take any chances, Bethany. A blood clot might kill you. Jake feels it's unwise for you to get pregnant, and so do I."

She gave him a look that promised she would have a great deal to say about that decision once they were alone.

Ryan glanced at the doctor, then back at her. "We'll settle this later. All right?"

"Just remember what you said about living in a bubble or grabbing hold of life with both hands. That's how I feel about this—that trying is worth the risk."

Cold sweat popped out on Ryan's face. He stared down at her, thinking how dearly he loved her and how devastated he'd be if anything happened to her. He sure as hell didn't want a baby of their own so much that he would put her life in danger.

"I'd like to speak with your surgeon," Dr. Kirsch said. "Do I have your permission to contact him, Bethany?"

"I don't mind if you speak to him, Dr. Kirsch, but I'm sure he'll tell you exactly what he told me—that I shouldn't have children." Her eyes darkened. "He even went so far as to say he felt it was a blessing because a woman in a wheelchair has no business having babies, anyway."

"Hmm." Kirsch shook his head. "What's this doctor's name?"

"Dr. Reicherton. He's up in Portland. You probably don't know him."

"As a matter of fact, I do. We doctors run into each other more often than you might think. Medical conventions and such. Benson Reicherton." He smiled and nodded. "He's a competent surgeon, one of the best on the West Coast."

"Daddy wanted the best," she said. "He was told we couldn't find better than Dr. Reicherton. I never liked him, but he seemed to know his stuff."

Again Kirsch nodded. "Ben's very good. If I had a spinal cord injury and surgery was recommended, I wouldn't hesitate to have him as my doctor. I'd walk a mile to avoid having him as a golfing buddy, though."

Bethany laughed and then suddenly yawned. "You *do* know him."

Dr. Kirsch smiled and winked at her. "I do, at that." He pushed to his feet and collected his bag. "I see that the shot is making you drowsy, young lady, so I'll take my leave and let you rest." He leveled a finger at her nose. "No riding tomorrow. I have a ten o'clock tee time, and if this overprotective fellow of yours calls me off the course over leg cramps, I'll be cranky as a bear."

Ryan followed the doctor from the bedroom. Once at the front of the house, Kirsch scratched his balding gray head. His silver eyebrows drew together in a thoughtful frown. "Something about this doesn't add up. Let me check into it. I'll try to get in touch with Reicherton when I get back to the office."

"You think she can have babies, don't you?"

The doctor glanced toward the hallway. "I don't advise you to tell her that, not until I'm sure. I wouldn't want to give her false hope and then disappoint her. I'm certainly no spinal specialist."

"You're a damned good doctor, though, and I trust your opinion."

The physician smiled. "Thank you. In answer to your question, for what my opinion's worth, this damned good doctor thinks the young lady either misunderstood what she was told or Reicherton gave her incorrect information. Paralysis doesn't generally affect a woman's ability to carry a child, especially not in a case like hers, where the nerve damage is incomplete."

It seemed pretty damned complete to Ryan. "How do you mean?"

"It's a term we use for a spinal cord injury that kills or impairs only some of the nerves. You can take a dozen individuals with a spinal cord injury at the same level and see a dozen different results. Some people may have partial use of their limbs or have feeling where others don't. With an L2 injury like hers . . ." His voice trailed away. "I don't think it should have any bearing on her ability to have children, and unless I'm completely misinformed, there's little or no risk of autonomic dysreflexia. But let me check into it. Could be I'm just an old country doctor who doesn't know beans." He lifted his hand in farewell and stepped out onto the porch. "I'll be in touch."

"What about the blood clot thing?" Ryan asked anxiously.

Kirsch sighed. "I think we can work around that problem. They have some very nice wheelchairs now with adjustable, comfortably cushioned leg rests, kind of like small recliners on wheels, enabling the user to put her feet up whenever the chair is stationary. I also think we can keep the blood thin enough to reduce the danger of clotting without harming the baby."

After bidding the physician farewell and closing the door, Ryan went to check on Bethany. The muscle relaxant had indeed made her drowsy, and she was already asleep. He sat beside her for a while, gazing at her sweet face. The drug had put her so deeply under that her mouth was lax, and a bead of drool glistened on her bottom lip. He smiled and thumbed it away, his heart squeezing at the thought of anything happening to her.

An hour later when Doctor Kirsch phoned back, Ryan took the call in the kitchen. "What did Reicherton say, Doc?"

"A lot of nothing. Basically, this is my take. No doctor can guarantee even a perfectly healthy young woman that she'll be able to bear children. The chance that she'll have problems may be minuscule, but it always exists. The odds against her successfully carrying a child increase substantially if she has special problems or the propensity to have them. That being the case, I won't go so far as to say that Reicherton actually lied to Bethany. However, I do believe he mentioned unlikely complications for a woman with an L2 injury."

"*Why?*" Ryan whispered. "Sweet Lord, *why?*"

"That's a very good question. I keep circling back to his comment to her—that a woman in a wheelchair has no business having babies. I've known Ben for a number of years. I distinctly recall his telling me once that he went into his field because his mother was a quadriplegic."

"How does that relate to what he told Bethany?"

"I'm walking a very fine line here, Ryan. I don't want to speculate and malign the man's professional reputation. As we were speaking on the phone, it occurred to me that perhaps—and I stress the word *perhaps*—his childhood was a difficult one because his mother was severely handicapped. Maybe he hates to see any woman in a wheelchair try to raise children. I only know he said nothing over the phone to justify what Bethany claims he told her. He hemmed and hawed. He pointed out that it's been a number of years, and he didn't have her file in front of him. But essentially he agreed with my prognosis, that unless there are other complications, a woman with an injury at L2 who is continent and has no history of urinary tract infections should be able to bear children without difficulty. Worst case, she may have to deliver by C-section."

A picture of Bethany sobbing her heart out in the van the other night flashed through Ryan's mind, and he closed his eyes, feeling sick. *Never any babies,* she'd cried. Why in God's name had the doctor told her such a vicious lie? Granted, maybe some handicapped women were unable to be good mothers because of their disabilities, but each case was different, and it hadn't been Reicherton's call to make.

"Ryan? You still there?"

"I'm here," Ryan said softly. "Just trying to absorb this. That's all. That girl in there has gone for eight years believing she might never have children. It makes me want to drive nonstop to Portland and rearrange Reicherton's face."

"I'm only guessing. Bear that in mind. And forgive me if it sounds pompous, but I think belated anger over something we can never prove would be fruitless. Why ruin what should be a happy time for both of you? You obviously adore this girl. Enjoy this very special time in your lives."

Ryan nodded and smiled. "You're right. After I wring her neck for not telling me about the autonomic dysreflexia, I'll do exactly that."

The physician laughed. "Now, now. If I were to tell you that having sex might kill you, what would you do?"

"Die a happy man."

"There you are. Don't blame her for making the same choice."

"That's entirely different. She can have safe sex. Having our own baby isn't important enough to put her health at risk."

"In your opinion. Women feel differently sometimes. Having a baby is the most important thing in the world to some of them."

Ryan rested his elbows on the counter. "I hear you, Doc. Maybe instead of wringing her neck, I'll just yell at her for a while."

"Ah, now."

Ryan grinned. "You're invited to the wedding, by the way."

"I'll be there, then. Oh, and Ryan, I want to see the bride in my office. No rush. Call in the morning and set up an appointment for sometime after the honeymoon. I should give her a good going over, get a baseline established for reference during prenatal care."

"I'll get her in to see you, then." Ryan straightened and quickly added, "Hey, Doc? You think, just to be safe, that I should continue to use protection until after you see her?"

Kirsch chuckled again. "Well, now, that all depends. You going to pull a long face if you're hitting the floor for three o'clock feedings in nine months?"

"Hell, no."

"Then, grab hold of life with both hands, as she put it. I honestly don't believe she's at any great risk. I'll take good care of her. Judging by the mutinous expression I saw on that girl's face, you may play heck getting near her again if she so much as glimpses a prophylactic."

"You may be right."

Kirsch cleared his throat. "If I thought there was a need to be cautious, I'd tell you so. I honestly don't. Give the young lady a baby."

Ryan was still grinning when he hung up the phone. He returned to the bedroom, lay down beside Bethany, and drew her into his arms. *A baby.* He'd meant it when he told her he'd be perfectly happy to adopt. But deep in his heart, the thought of making a child of their own had a very special appeal. To see her with a big tummy and know she was carrying his child. To be with her when she gave birth. To watch her cradle a dark, downy head to her breast for the very first time. No matter how much love they might feel, adoptive parents missed out on some of the magic.

Ryan pressed a kiss to her hair and then closed his eyes to dream with her of raising Kendrick sons and daughters on the land where he'd grown up himself. He'd teach them to love these mountains just as he did, he thought sleepily, and one day, they'd take over in his stead to operate the Rocking K.

The thought filled him with a sense of purpose that had been lacking in his life before meeting her. He remembered the morning when he'd told Rafe how lost and horribly alone he often felt, that his pets were all that kept him sane on long winter evenings. He no longer felt that way.

How could a man feel lonely or lost when he held heaven in his arms?

⚘ CHAPTER TWENTY–ONE ⚘

The day after next, Ryan was working in the stable office doing books when it occurred to him that it was nearly eleven and Bethany still hadn't joined him for her daily training session. Not that they usually got much accomplished by way of work. She was proving to have an insatiable hunger for him, just as he did for her, and whenever they were alone in here, they ended up making love at least once, sometimes twice, before lunch.

Remembering the last time, Ryan thought of how beautiful she'd looked, lying naked on his desk, and he burned with a sudden yearning to see her there again. He was about to abandon the books to go find her when he heard Sly shout his name. He leaped to his feet, knowing before he made it as far as the door that something bad had happened.

"Down here!" Sly yelled as Ryan exited the office.

Ryan turned to see the foreman disappear into the stall where they'd connected Bethany's sling. He raced along the center aisle, the thump of his boots on the asphalt only slightly faster than the pounding of his heart. He knew without being told that something had happened to Bethany.

When he reached the open stall and saw her lying crumpled on the dirt beside her horse, Ryan thought his heart might stop. With a quick glance, he determined that she'd attempted to mount the mare by herself, utilizing the sling.

"Jesus Christ!" He pushed Sly out of the way and dropped to his knees beside her, so frightened he didn't know if he was cursing or praying. "Bethany? Oh, dear God."

"I'm all right, Ryan." She suffered his probing hands, telling him over and over that she wasn't seriously hurt. "I just slipped off the saddle, is all. It wasn't far to the ground."

Ryan's fear turned to anger. "What the bloody hell were you doing?" He shot a scathing glance at the foreman. "If she wanted to use the sling, you should have called me."

Sly held up his hands. "Don't jump all over me, son. I didn't know a thing about this until I found her in here."

"It was my fault, Ryan. I wanted to do it by myself."

Ryan wanted to shake her until her teeth rattled. Instead he finished checking her for injuries and then gathered her into his arms, shaking so badly the vibrations made the fringe on her new western shirt jiggle. "Never again," he said fiercely. "Promise me you'll never try to mount her alone again."

She drew her head back to fix him with a mutinous look. "That was the entire point of building the sling, so I could go riding without help."

"That was before. This is now, and if you ever risk breaking your neck again, I'll warm your fanny until you can't sit for a week."

Bethany pushed away to sit up and straighten her shirt. "Don't be silly," she said, brushing straw from her sleeve. She flashed him a bright smile. "I almost did it, Ryan. All by myself. Next time, I'll know not to un-fasten the hooks before I get my leg sheaths buckled. I wouldn't have fallen but for my own stupidity."

Ryan gathered her up in his arms, pushed to his feet, and started to leave the stall to take her to the office. She stopped him by pressing a slender hand to his chest. "Not yet. I want to try again. Just put me in my chair and leave, please. This is something I have to do."

"Over my dead body."

She held his gaze with hers. "I won't fall again."

"You can't know that." He imagined her breaking one of her legs or being accidentally stepped on by the horse. The very thought made his blood go icy. "I meant what I said. Take a chance like that again, and I'll—"

She touched a finger to his lips. "I know I frightened you, and I'm sorry for that. I was afraid of falling myself, which made me so nervous I didn't think everything through clearly." She smiled again. "But now it's hap-pened, and it wasn't as awful as I thought. I fall quite nicely, half of me being limp. It didn't even hurt all that much. Just knocked the wind out of me for a second."

Ryan thought of possible bruises on her legs that she wouldn't be able to feel. His heart squeezed at the flame of pride he saw burning deep in her eyes. *Sweet Jesus, help me.* He knew this was something she wanted and needed to do without anyone's help, that being self-sufficient was one of the most important things in the world to her. But at what price? There was such a thing as carrying pride too far.

"Please, Ryan? Try to understand. I *have* to do this without you. I have to."

He glanced at her wheelchair, which in that moment represented all the reasons why she shouldn't. He almost wished he'd never had his family help him build the damned sling. But, no. He'd built it for just this reason, so she could be free of the chair and all the other constraints in her life. He just hadn't counted on her being so stubborn and taking this do-or-die approach.

Do or die. From the first, he'd always loved the stubborn lift of her small chin. This was who she was. How else could she have become a champion barrel racer? She had probably taken a do-or-die approach to that as well, pushing herself beyond her limits until she became the best. Recalling how she'd trounced him in the swimming race, he suspected she did everything full out. Since that was one of the things about her that he loved, did he really want to change her?

Feeling as if he'd just swallowed ground glass, Ryan said, "Will you let me do just one thing before you try to mount her again?"

"That depends on what it is."

"You'll see soon enough." He forced himself to lower her into her chair. After glancing at the remote control tucked into the waistband of her jeans, he said, "Promise me you won't move until I get back?"

She heaved a sigh. "Don't take very long. The longer I wait to try again, the more nervous I'll get."

Ryan glanced at Sly, who lingered in the open doorway. "Can you lend me a hand real quick, Sly?"

The foreman nodded and followed Ryan down the center aisle to the bunk room, where they sometimes slept when a mare was due to foal. A few seconds later, when both men returned to the stall carrying cot mattresses, Bethany burst out laughing.

"Those should make my landing a little less jarring," she observed.

Ryan smiled weakly as he positioned one mattress beside the mare. As he relieved Sly of the other one, he said, "That's the general idea—to keep you from breaking your stubborn little neck."

"Thank you," she said softly after the padding was in place. "I'll feel better knowing it's there." Then she looked expectantly at both men. "You can leave now." When they hesitated, she smiled. "I won't fall again, I promise. Now, go!"

Ryan gestured for the foreman to follow him, and he left. He only went approximately three feet. Sly drew up beside him. They stared worriedly at the open stall doorway. The hair on the back of Ryan's neck curled when he heard the sling motor start to hum. Where was the harm in her accepting just a little help this first time? he wondered. Once she got the hang of it, he'd happily leave her to do it alone.

He started to step toward the stall. Sly snaked out a hand to grasp Ryan's arm. "Don't," he said softly. "This is something she needs to do by herself, son. You built the damned sling just so's this could happen. Don't spoil it for her."

Ryan knew the foreman was right, but, damn, it was hard to just stand there. Those mattresses weren't that wide. If she fell and missed one of them, she could be hurt. His heart felt as if it was going to pound its way out of his chest. What was happening? Was she on the horse yet? He strained to listen, but he couldn't tell anything by the sounds.

"I *did* it!" she suddenly cried. "I did it, Ryan! Come and just *look* at me. All by myself! I'm ready to ride!"

Ryan and Sly almost ran each other down to reach the doorway. Then Ryan forgot everything but the sight of Bethany. She wheeled Wink around to face them, her eyes glowing, her cheeks flushed with joy. In that moment Ryan caught a glimpse of the feisty, dauntless girl she'd been before the accident. Her hair was a wild tumble of dark, silky curls around her small face. She sat erect in the saddle, looking perfectly capable.

For the moment she was gloriously free, the wheelchair forgotten. The look on her face reminded him of the night that he had waltzed with her behind the grange, and a lump came to his throat. *This* was why he'd bought back her horse, ordered the saddle, and fashioned the sling. So he could see that inexpressible joy in her eyes. He wouldn't spoil the moment for her now by trying to coddle her.

He glanced at his watch. "The doctor said no more than ten minutes today. You're wasting precious seconds."

She snapped the reins and clucked her tongue to get the mare moving. "Out of my way, gentlemen! I'm going for a ride."

Ryan watched her take off down the center aisle. "Take it easy crossing that cement!" He couldn't resist yelling after her. He glanced at Sly. "Christ! I never knew love was such a pain in the ass. Am I going to live through this?"

Sly sighed and shook his head. "Same with kids. You gotta let 'em go. I remember the first time you went riding by yourself. Damn near gave me a heart attack. It ain't easy to turn loose, son, but you have to do it. That's life."

Ryan nodded. He'd told Bethany's father almost exactly the same thing. People had been wrapping her in cotton for far too long. He suspected that was the main reason she'd stayed in Portland, to escape the well-intended but stifling love of her family. He didn't want her to feel that way about him.

Eleven minutes later, Ryan wanted to saddle up Bucky to go find her. Sly stopped him. "She's only running a minute over. Give her a few more to get back. It'll ruin it for her if you go charging to her rescue like the dad-blamed cavalry."

The longest two minutes of Ryan's life passed before he heard the clop of Wink's shoes on the cement outside. He hurried over to grab a bucket from a hook, trying to look busy so she wouldn't know he'd been standing there sweating the entire time she was gone. Sly grabbed a feed bucket as well. Then the two men looked questioningly at each other, wondering what they meant to do next. It wasn't time to grain the horses.

"Hi!" Bethany called gaily as she rode the mare through the front entrance. "It was fantastic! You just can't *know*. And I did it, start to finish, all by myself, you guys. Isn't that phenomenal?"

She wasn't down off the damned horse yet. Ryan swallowed to stop himself from pointing that out.

"I'm so proud of myself." She rode Wink into the stall where her sling awaited. Then as if she had eyes in the back of her head, she stopped both Ryan and Sly dead in their tracks by saying, "Stay out of here. I'll get off of her by myself."

Ryan glanced at the foreman. Sweating as if he'd been hard at work, Sly took off his hat to wipe his forehead with his sleeve. Ryan sympathized. The hum of the sling motor made his guts knot. He bit down hard on the inside of his cheek to keep from calling out precautions.

Seconds passed that felt like multiple eternities strung endlessly together. Finally she yelled, "Okay! I'm off. You can come fuss over me now."

Ryan's knees felt a little weak as he covered the distance to the stall doorway. Bethany was in her wheelchair again and was tugging at the sling girdle to get it off. She glanced up and smiled as the nylon pulled free from under her rump. "We should patent this gadget. We'd become millionaires."

"I'm already a millionaire," Ryan reminded her grumpily. It irritated him to no end that she could be so cheerful when she'd just scared him so badly. "When we're married, half of that money will be yours."

"I ain't rich," Sly pointed out. "Maybe I'll patent the thing. If I had me a big, fat bank account, I just might get myself hitched."

Ryan cast the foreman an amazed look. "To who? Are you seeing someone I don't know about?"

Sly cocked a gray eyebrow, scratched his ear, and then said, "What if I am? I'm of age and then some. I reckon it's not just young fellers who can git bit by the lovebug."

Ryan was so startled by the revelation that he nearly forgot his concerns about Bethany. "I never said it was. I think that's great, Sly. Who's the lucky woman?"

The foreman smiled. "That's for me to know and you to find out. Just know when you finally do that I love the lady."

With that, the wiry foreman left the stall. Ryan turned a bewildered gaze on Bethany. She smiled and sighed. "Isn't that romantic? Sly is in love with someone."

Ryan frowned. "He makes damned good money working for us. He doesn't need millions to get married."

Bethany turned toward the doorway and wheeled out into the aisle. "Come on, Wink. Time to put you back in your stall."

The mare followed her mistress like a dog trained to heel. Ryan stared after the pair for a moment, then hollered for Charlie, one of the stable hands, to come unsaddle and walk Wink to cool her down.

En route to the office a few minutes later, Bethany flashed him a teasing smile over her shoulder. Once inside the small room, she was the one who locked and bolted the door this time. She turned, gave him a sultry look, and flicked the fringe on her shirt with a fingertip. "Hi, cowboy. Did you miss me while I was riding?"

Ryan's pulse hadn't returned to normal yet. As happy as he was that the sling episode had ended well, he still couldn't get that picture of her on the ground at the mare's feet out of his head. "I'm not really in the mood for that right now."

She only smiled and started unsnapping her shirt. "I'm sorry for giving you such a scare. I won't make the mistake of unfastening the hooks until I'm secured to the saddle again. I promise."

Ryan averted his gaze, determined not to get sidetracked. "I think we need to talk about wise choices and the necessity of taking the proper precautions."

He heard cloth rustle, and his eyes were drawn back to her as if they were metal shavings attracted by a magnet. *Two magnets.* God help him. Her bra was unfastened, and both breasts were trying to spill out. One rose pink nipple peeked around the scalloped edge of lace at him. At the sight, the insides of his cheeks sucked fast to his teeth. He couldn't have spit if she'd yelled, "Stable fire!"

"Please don't be mad," she said softly. As she spoke, she grazed her dainty fingertips over the hardening tip of her now bare breast, her eyes beckoning to him. "Come here and let me make you feel better."

Holy hell. She'd gotten a late start at sex, but she was a fast learner. Ryan was across the office before he realized he'd moved. He quickly forgot all about being upset with her. How could a man hold onto a rational thought?

By the following Thursday, when they began their trip to Bear Creek Lake for the wedding, Bethany had conditioned herself daily to the saddle and was ready for an hour and a half ride. She was feeling so happy and optimistic about her future with Ryan that it almost frightened her. Cleo had settled in at the ranch as if she'd been born there, spending her days on T-bone's shoulders and her nights in the house, snuggled in her kitty bed. Bethany had used her new stable sling regularly, mounting and dismounting Wink without any help. Ryan was talking about her opening a riding academy in the near future, not only to train aspiring barrel racers like Heidi, but to work with paraplegic youngsters as well.

It all sounded too good to be true. A handsome, loving, wonderful husband. Being able to have babies. Working full-time with horses. Being free to wander the pathways that networked the property. She felt as if her world had been magnified to gigantic proportions, and she sometimes felt almost giddy. Surely no one could be this happy without something happening to spoil it.

When she confessed her fear to Ryan, he fell back to ride abreast of her, looking so incredibly handsome in the saddle with June sunlight glinting off his breeze-tousled black hair that he made her heart sing. The jingling, almost musical sounds of their camping paraphernalia on the packhorse mingled with the clop of hooves striking rock as they rode along.

"Sweetheart, that's silly," he said. "You *deserve* to be happy. Nothing's going to happen to spoil this for us. *Nothing.*"

Bethany let her head fall back to gaze at the sky. "I know I'm being silly. It's just—oh, Ryan, I'm *so* happy. You know what I'm saying? I've lived so long, always telling myself to be practical, always scolding myself for wanting what I could no longer have. And now, all of a sudden, I'm getting every single thing I ever wished for. Nobody should be this happy. It has to be a sin or something."

He chuckled and leaned sideways on his horse to steal a quick kiss. "Bethany Ann, I can't imagine you committing a real sin, and I'm sure God would agree with me. I've never known a person with a purer heart. I think He sent me an angel."

Her eyes danced with mischief, and she plucked a pinecone from a tree bough to chuck at him. "Angels don't think about what I'm thinking about right now. Let's stop and take a rest under a tree."

Ryan knew what that warm gleam in her eyes meant, and he was sorely tempted to stop. But if they lingered along the trail for too long, it would spoil his plans.

He sighed and reached over to ruffle her hair. "As much as it pains me, I have to pass."

She frowned and pouted her bottom lip. "We're not even married yet, and you're already tired of me."

"Not a chance. There's just something special I want to do this afternoon. When we stop and get our camp set up, will you do me the honor of becoming my wife?"

She threw him a bewildered look. "Today? How can we do that? The minister won't be coming up until Saturday."

"We don't need a minister," he assured her. "Remember telling me that for you, the wilderness was your church? Let's say our private vows today. Just you and me, on a mountain ridge, making our wedding promises to each other with only God as our witness. Who else really counts?"

After thinking about it for a moment, she nodded and flashed him a smile. "I'd love that. I think it would be even more meaningful than the official ceremony."

Two hours later Ryan knelt at the feet of a dark-haired angel in a wheelchair and vowed to love, honor, and cherish her for the rest of his life. As he said the words, he looked into those beautiful pansy-blue eyes of hers and knew that loving her was what he'd been born to do.

When he finished saying his vows, she tremulously followed suit, her eyes sparkling as she whispered each word, promising to love him forever. *Bethany.* She was surely a gift from heaven. To himself, Ryan vowed to be the man she deserved, to spend the remainder of his days protecting her and trying to make her happy. If anyone on earth deserved to be happy, it had to be this woman.

He drew their rings from his shirt pocket. Before he slipped hers on her finger, he held it up to the sunlight. "They say a ring is a symbol of eternity—of pure and everlasting love. I think a lot of people forget that.

I never will. I promise you that." He slipped the ring on her finger and then bent to kiss it. "With this ring, I thee wed."

She smiled as she gazed down at the ring on her finger. Then, after hauling in a deep, shaky breath, she held up his ring to the sunlight. "Whenever you look at this ring," she whispered, "remember I'll spend the rest of my life trying to love you more than I love myself. Because you are who you are, I don't think that will be a tall order." She leaned forward to kiss him. As she drew away, tears sparkled on her cheeks like diamonds. With his help she slipped the ring onto his finger. "With this ring, I thee wed."

Ryan framed her face between his hands as he bent to settle his mouth over hers. A burning desire flowed through him, setting his blood afire. "Now for the best part of a private, mountain ridge ceremony," he whispered as he drew back. "Instead of just kissing my bride, I can seal our vows by making love to her."

Her eyes widened. *"Here?"*

Ryan glanced around and chuckled. "One nice thing about mountain ridges, the neighbors mind their own business and aren't given to gossip." He pushed to his feet, lifted her into his arms, and carried her to a sun-dappled grassy place under a pine tree. After clearing away the needles with the side of his boot, he carefully laid her down and made passionate love to her in the golden sunlight, giving the squirrels something to chatter about.

Afterglow . . . Ryan had heard the term hundreds of times, but the feeling itself was incredible. He held his wife close to his heart, too exhausted to move. Sunshine played over their nude bodies in a warm caress that felt so good he wanted to remain just as they were. Only a fear that Bethany's sensitive skin might burn finally prodded him to move.

The late afternoon and evening played out perfectly. They caught trout for supper from a nearby stream and dined like royalty by a crackling campfire. Ryan was able to find a deep place farther downstream, and just before dusk, they went down to bathe. Big problem. The instant he saw Bethany's bare breasts bobbing so sweetly on the surface of the water, he grabbed her high in his arms, waded to the bank, and made love to her again. They were both a little chilled by the time they finally got out of the water. Ryan dried off his bride, carried her to camp, bundled her in a blanket, and sat with her in his arms by the fire until she felt warm to the touch again. *Touching.* For some reason, that invariably led to more, and he found himself making love to her again, this time on the blanket by the fire. He couldn't get enough of her, and she seemed to share the feeling, always turning eagerly into his arms when he kissed her.

"Listen," she whispered urgently after they got settled for the night in their tent.

Ryan cocked an ear. A moment later he heard coyotes howling.

"Isn't that the most *beautiful* sound?" she said. "Oh, Ryan, just *listen*. The wind whispering in the trees and whining over the ridge. The call of the coyotes to the moon. I never thought I'd hear any of it again. *Never*. Have you any idea how much this means to me, or what a beautiful gift you've given me?"

Ryan personally felt that she was the gift, he the recipient. "I just feel lucky to have found a wife who loves it as much as I do," he told her. "Not everyone does, you know."

She lay on her side, facing him. A coyote howled again. As the sound trailed to them through the mountain darkness, she pressed a kiss to his mouth. Then she sat up suddenly, shoving back the sleeping bag to smooth a hand over his bare flank. "Roll onto your back," she whispered. "I want to make love to you while they call to the moon."

That was a request he couldn't refuse. He turned onto his back. She braced one arm on the sleeping bag beneath them to support her weight. Then she bent her head to trail kisses down his chest toward the triangle of dark hair below his navel. With the light from the fire shining through the nylon wall of the tent, he could see her clearly and guessed her intent. Maybe he was impossibly old-fashioned, but this was something he'd chosen never to let another woman do, feeling it was far too intimate an act to engage in with someone he didn't love. He'd never gone down on a woman until Bethany, either, always choosing instead to use his hand.

His erection was as prominent as a flagpole. All it lacked was Old Glory, flapping in the wind. He smoothed a lock of dark hair back from her cheek. "Sweetheart, you don't have to—"

"Shush," she whispered, and then proceeded to lap at him as she might an ice-cream cone.

It was the most erotic experience of his life. He couldn't say it felt all that wonderful because his shaft wasn't as sensitive as she obviously believed. She was mimicking his technique, which didn't quite cut it for a man. But that didn't matter. Just seeing her love him that way nearly made him lose control.

Ryan caught her by the chin, as pleased with her as he'd never dreamed he might be with anyone. Because she loved him so. Because she would clearly do anything, just to make him happy with her. What she failed to understand was that she was all his dreams, rolled into one, without trying.

"I'm sorry," she said softly. "I don't really know how to do it. Won't you tell me so I can make it nice for you? With practice, I'll get better."

Ryan nearly groaned. *Practice*. One more lap from that quick little tongue of hers, and he would embarrass himself. "I don't know how it's done," he lied. He did know, of course. He had a general idea, at any rate. "No woman's ever done that to me."

Even in the dim light, he saw her eyes fill with bewilderment. "Never?"

"And you're the first I ever kissed there," he said, catching her around the waist to haul her higher on his chest. "That's something special, and I saved it for you."

"Oh, Ryan." She was clearly touched and found that romantic. "For a rank beginner, you're very good at it."

He only smiled. "Thank you. It's important to me to please you."

"So you can understand my wanting to please you."

"You have, honey. If you'd done it any better, I'd be finished right now and snoring. What fun would that be?"

She grinned and relaxed her weight on his chest. What a sweet burden she was, every inch of her so soft and silken. "Liked it, did you?"

He chuckled at the feminine purr in her voice. "So much that I couldn't take any more." He glanced at her mouth and folded his arms under his head. "Kiss my mouth instead." Sensing that she wanted to be the one in control this time, and that she wanted to do things to please him, he whispered, "While you kiss me, rub the tips of your breasts over my chest."

She did exactly as he instructed, and when he felt her nipples turn hard, he forgot about letting her take the lead. *Bethany*. He grabbed her close, rolled to get on top, and made love to her to the forlorn accompaniment of the howling coyotes . . .

Bethany awakened him at dawn. In the time since she'd been staying with him at the ranch, she'd stopped being cranky upon rising, but on that morning he marveled at the drastic change. After he helped her into her chair, she literally threw her arms wide to embrace the morning, tipped back her head to gaze at the treetops, and laughed with gay abandon.

"I feel *alive*!" she cried. "Not just here, not just breathing. I feel so alive!"

Her mood prevailed throughout the morning. When they were once again on the trail, she sang silly songs, reminding Ryan that she wasn't completely perfect, after all. The girl couldn't carry a tune for squat. He was forced to join in just to make it easier on his ears.

"Sixty-seven bottles of beer on the wall! Sixty-seven bottles of beer! You take one down, and you pass it around, sixty—"

"Four bottles of beer on the wall!" he inserted.

"Huh-uh. Sixty-six!"

Ryan was laughing when he heard a large animal tearing through the brush to the left of the trail and spotted a flash of Hereford red between the trees. Seeing cattle up here wasn't a rare occurrence. The Rocking K herds enjoyed an open range and wandered all over these mountains, foraging. But Ryan seldom saw one at a dead run like that.

He reined in his sorrel and listened to the crashing sounds as they grew more distant. "What the hell?"

Bethany had stopped her horse just behind the pack animal. "I wonder what lit a fire under her?"

Ryan frowned thoughtfully. "I don't know. Something tells me I should mosey over and have a look, though. A couple of weeks back, a rancher on up the highway lost two head to poachers." He turned his gelding Bucky and rode back to hand Bethany the lead on the packhorse. "Sit tight for a minute, honey. I'll be right back."

It took Ryan only a couple of minutes to ride through the trees and locate the cow's hoofprints. Following her tracks with his gaze, he spotted a glistening patch of wetness on the low-hanging bough of a fir tree. He swung off his horse to go check it out. When he touched the feathery fir needles, fresh blood came off on his fingertips. He followed the cow's trail on foot for a bit, and sure enough, he soon saw blood on the ground as well. The animal was badly injured.

When Ryan got back to Bethany, he told her what he'd found. "Some idiot must have shot her," he said. "Damn fools. If they can't shoot straighter than that, they've got no business packing a rifle."

Bethany twisted at the waist to gaze behind them. Concern filled her eyes. "Oh, Ryan, how *sad*. If the poor thing's been wounded and she doesn't bleed to death, she's liable to die slowly and horribly from infection or something. We can't just leave her like that."

Ryan agreed. "I can track her," he said. "It's pretty rough terrain once you get off the trail, though. I don't think you should go with me."

"No problem. I'll just wait here."

Ryan smiled. "I think I can do better than this. There's a pretty little meadow just a ways on up the trail. How's about if I let you wait for me there?"

"With food?" she asked.

He laughed and nodded. "I suppose I can dig you out a few snacks."

"That sounds lovely. I could use a little rest, anyway. This way I won't be overtired when we get to the lake."

A few minutes later when Ryan had her comfortably settled in her chair under a tall pine growing at the edge of the meadow, she grinned up at him. "I feel like a princess! All I lack is a soft drink and those snacks you promised me."

He chuckled and went to get a can of pop out of the small cooler on the packhorse, then grabbed the picnic basket, which was brimming with goodies. When he returned to set the provisions at the base of the tree, Bethany said, "Yum." She opened the basket and plucked out the salami and cheese. "It sucks to be you. What a shame you can't join me."

He unstrapped his holster from his hips and handed it down to her. "Just in case," he said. "You know how to use a revolver, I hope."

She accepted the .22, her eyes dancing with devilment. "This isn't a revolver. It's a popgun. And, yes, I know how to use it. I can shoot an acorn off a limb at fifty yards. Is that satisfactory?"

"With or without a rest?"

She raised her small chin. "Without, of course. What do you think I am, a city girl or something?" She glanced around the peaceful clearing. "Why, exactly, do I need the gun? Are the squirrels up here bloodthirsty?"

He chuckled and headed for his horse. "I was thinking more about snakes. I carry it for the occasional timber rattler."

She shuddered and rubbed her arms. "I detest snakes."

Ryan swung up on his horse, watched her rifle through the basket for a knife to slice the cheese, and then said, "Save some of that salami and cheese for me, lady. I may work up an appetite."

"I will." Her expression became more serious. "I hope you find her, Ryan. Good luck."

"Hey, you're lookin' at one of the best trackers this side of the Pecos, lady. What do you think I am, some city boy?"

She pursed her lips. "Where *is* the Pecos, exactly?"

"Beats the hell out of me. But this side of it, I'm the best." He winked at her and grinned as he checked to be sure the magazine in his rifle was loaded. "She was bleeding heavily. It'll be fairly easy to track her. If she's beyond help, I'll finish her off. If not, I'll contact Rafe and give him her location." He patted the cell phone on his belt. "With smoke signals, of course."

She was laughing as he rode away. "Be careful, Tex!"

"Not to worry."

Rather than meander along the trail, he decided to go as a crow flew and save time. As he wove his gelding through the brush that grew in wild profusion off the beaten path, he kept an eye out for sign, hoping to spot where the cow had been shot. She'd been running from somewhere up here, he felt sure.

He hadn't ridden far when the hair on his nape started to prickle. Drawing his horse to a halt, he listened and sniffed the air. The woods had gone eerily silent. Even the wind seemed to be holding its breath. Ryan had been riding in these mountains on a regular basis all his life. He knew every ridge and gully like the back of his hand. When something wasn't right, he sensed it.

And something wasn't right.

At that moment, he was mightily tempted to head back to the meadow and Bethany. He couldn't say why. A part of him thought he was being silly. But another big part of him had the willies.

Then he smelled it. *Blood.* He'd straddled the top rail of a slaughter chute too many times not to recognize the scent of freshly killed cattle. He nudged Bucky forward, his ire rising. What the hell? Had some kids come up here with rifles and used their cows for target practice?

Not far up ahead, there was a water hole—a place where the winter floodwater of Bear Creek had long since wallowed out a wide hollow in the shale and formed a small gorge that was nearly boxed off at one end. In the summer the cattle favored it as a gathering place because trees grew along the lips of the ravine, providing deep pockets of shade below on the banks of the stream.

If some cows had bunched up in that wash, they would have been like ducks in a shooting gallery, easy to pick off with a rifle. With one end of the area almost boxed off, they wouldn't have been able to escape quickly.

Ryan headed straight for the spot. The scent of blood grew stronger. A *lot* of blood. An awful, coppery taste coated his tongue. As he crested the last rise above the water hole, he was prepared to see a number of slaughtered cows. He didn't look forward to it, but he'd looked death in the eye so many times, he didn't expect it to come as a shock, either.

When he saw the carnage, bile crawled up the back of his throat.

Dear God. The cows had bunched up in the gorge, just as he'd guessed. But it hadn't been a sniper that killed them. Never in all his life had Ryan seen such gore. At least ten cows lay dead, some in the stream, others on the banks. The creek flowed red with blood from the mangled bodies.

Something had mauled them.

From a distance, Ryan couldn't tell what kind of animal had killed them. The concentration of cougars was heavy in these mountains because of legislation that had been passed a few years ago, prohibiting the use of hunting dogs. But a cougar didn't usually go on a killing rampage. It snapped the neck of its prey upon impact, then dragged the dead animal off somewhere to eat it.

Ryan dismounted, tethered Bucky to a stump, and slipped his 30.06 pump-action Remington from the saddle boot. The way down to the stream was steep. He slid partway in the loose shale, barely managing to stay on his feet. Once in the gorge, he wasted no time in examining the slaughtered cows. The animal tracks he found in the soft earth near the dead cattle were unmistakably those of a bear.

Ryan could scarcely credit his eyes. Black bears didn't do this sort of thing. They were carnivores, yes, and occasionally killed for sustenance, but as a general rule they tended to be opportunistic creatures, more likely to dine on already dead animals, wood worms, or vegetation, such as berries. Over the years Ryan had heard of bears killing a cow now and again, but never more than one at a time, and always for food.

Yet there was no denying the evidence. Judging by the tracks, this was a large bear. The rare renegade black bear usually turned out to be a young male. An older male seldom attacked without provocation, and a sow generally only got ornery when her cubs were threatened.

A chill trickled down Ryan's spine. That injured cow they'd seen running for her life through the woods had undoubtedly escaped from here. That had been no more than twenty minutes ago. This was all fresh kill, and it wasn't the act of a hungry carnivore, attacking for food. The bear hadn't eaten on any of the corpses. No. It had been in a killing frenzy and had slaughtered these animals for the sheer joy of it.

The thought sent Ryan scrambling back up the bank. *Bethany.* He'd left her sitting in that meadow without any means of defending herself. That .22 caliber revolver would only piss off a charging bear. It certainly wouldn't drop it.

He was panting from exertion and in a cold sweat by the time he reached his horse. Because he knew he had to ride hard to get back to Bethany, he returned the rifle to the boot so he'd have both hands free.

Bethany. She'd been slicing salami and cheese when he left her. A bear could smell food from well over a mile away.

Ryan kicked Bucky hard in the flanks, urging him into a flat-out run. It was rough terrain, and Ryan knew he could very easily injure the horse, riding at such a reckless speed. But he had to. If it came to a choice between the gelding and his wife, he'd sacrifice the horse in a heartbeat.

Please, God. The silent prayer circled dizzily through his mind. He urged Bucky to an even faster pace, terrified that the bear might circle around to the meadow. Bethany was so helpless. She couldn't even try to run.

When Ryan reached the edge of the meadow, he'd never felt such relief in his life. There sat Bethany, beneath the pine right where he'd left her. She spotted him and waved. Ryan slowed his horse. She was fine, thank God. He was close enough now to pick off a bear with his rifle before it could get near her.

As he drew closer, Bethany saw how hard his horse was blowing and called, "Did you find her? Is everything all right?"

"No, I didn't go after her." Ryan scanned the hillsides that encircled the meadow. He didn't want to frighten her, but he didn't want to lie to her, either. "It was a bear, honey. You need to put all the food back in the containers. Seal it up tight. I don't want any uninvited picnic guests to come calling."

"You saw a bear?" She looked delighted. "Way cool. Maybe we'll spot it again. I haven't seen a black bear in aeons."

"Their population has increased substantially over the last few years. They got lumped in on the bill to protect cougars and can no longer be trapped." He drew Bucky to a stop beside Wink and the packhorse. As soon as he dismounted, he drew his rifle from the boot as a safety precaution. He sure as hell didn't want to get caught with his guard down. "I didn't actually see the bear. Just lots of really fresh sign."

When she saw him walking toward her with the rifle cradled in one arm, her smile faded. Her gaze became riveted to his. After a long moment of searching eye contact, she said, "Oh, Ryan . . . what is it?"

He scanned the hillsides again. "I don't want to scare you, honey. But this is no ordinary bear. He's gone berserk."

"What?" Her voice was thin and shaky with incredulous laughter. "How do you mean? Berserk in what way?"

Ryan shifted his gaze back to hers. "You know that cow we saw? She'd been attacked." He gestured with his head. "About a mile east, there's a creek ravine where the cows like to water. Steep shale walls on both sides. Not a box canyon, but almost, making it difficult for them to get out of there fast. The bear must have caught them by surprise. I didn't take time to count heads, but I'd say at least ten are dead."

"*What?* You think a black bear killed ten cows? That's crazy, Ryan. Black bears don't do that. A grizzly, maybe, but not an Oregon black bear."

The hair on Ryan's nape started to prickle again. "He's a big old boy. People go berserk. Why not a black bear?" He leaned his rifle against the tree beside her. "You as good with a pump action as you are with a revolver?"

She was looking over her shoulder at the hillsides. "It's been a long time. I used to be a fair shot with a rifle. No guarantee I can hit anything now."

Ryan nodded toward the weapon. "Keep your eyes peeled while I saddle Wink. We're getting out of here." He glanced at the basket. She'd lain the pistol and holster on the closed end. "Get that salami sealed up in a container. A bear can smell food for a mighty long way. I don't want him coming in on us."

Ryan hurriedly saddled Wink. When he went back to get Bethany, he had to smile. She was doing exactly as he had asked, keeping her eyes glued to the hillsides, one hand curled loosely over the rifle stock in case she had to shoot. She might not be able to walk, Ryan thought, but there was no one on earth he would have trusted more to guard his back.

He bent to lift her from the chair. "I'll get you in the saddle, then come back for the rifle and other stuff."

She hugged his neck as he carried her toward her horse. "You're really worried."

"I've never seen anything like it," Ryan admitted. "It made my blood run cold and scared the hell out of me. The whole way back here, I was praying you were safe."

"Oh, Ryan. I had the .22. I was fine."

He narrowed an eye at her. "That pistol wouldn't have stopped that big old boy. Trust me on—"

"Mrrrhaw!"

The sound came from behind them. Only halfway to the horses, Ryan whirled to see what in the hell it was. When he saw the bear charging across the flat toward them, his heart stuttered to a stop and felt as if it just hung in his chest like a chunk of ice. The animal was huge, and it ran with incredible speed—its fat and fur jolting with every impact of its paws on the earth.

"Mrrrhaw!"

"Oh, my God," Bethany cried. "Oh, my *God*!"

Ryan glanced frantically at the rifle leaning against the pine only a few feet away where he'd left it in order to carry Bethany. If he put her down, he might be able to reach the weapon before the bear caught him. Big problem. There was every chance the animal would stay on course, charging blindly. If so, it would be on Bethany before Ryan could get off a shot. There might also be lag time after he fired. Bears were notorious for taking lead and not going down immediately.

Bethany could be killed.

Ryan had to make a decision, and the way he saw it, he had no real choice. He lay Bethany on the grass right where they were and faced the bear without a weapon.

In those split seconds before the huge animal reached them, his mind spun with disjointed bits of information he'd heard over the years about charging black bears, the most pertinent being that they would sometimes back down if you made yourself look as large as possible and behaved aggressively. He put himself between Bethany and the bear, flung his arms wide, and yelled as loudly as he could. But the bear kept coming.

"Get out of here!" Ryan yelled again. This time he took a couple of steps forward, wondering even as he did if he'd totally lost his mind. "Rrrhaw!" he cried, trying to emulate the bear's ferocious growl.

"Ryan!" Bethany screamed. "Run! Get away!"

The bear was on him then. Ryan felt as if a locomotive plowed into him. His feet came clear off the ground, and both he and the bear went airborne. Dimly he could hear Bethany screaming. *Pain*. His mind washed red with it.

"The rifle!" he managed to yell. "Sweet Christ, the rifle!"

All Ryan's life, he'd been told to play dead in the event of a bear attack. He felt the son of a bitch biting his hip. Felt his bones splintering like chalk under the force of its jaws. How could a man play dead when his body was exploding with such agony? Ryan screamed. There was no holding it back. He screamed as if he were on a torture rack and being ripped apart.

Perhaps he was being ripped apart . . . Pictures flashed through his mind of the mangled cows. *Bethany*. The bear would go for her next. Blind with pain, Ryan forced his body to go limp and rolled onto his stomach, groping for the knife scabbard on his belt. It would be a little like jabbing a hippo with a toothpick, but it was the only weapon he had.

The rifle. The rifle. The rifle.

Bethany dragged herself toward the tree, her gaze fixed on the weapon. She heard Ryan screaming. *Oh, God.* He could have saved himself by running for the gun. But, no. He'd stepped between her and the bear, and now—oh, God—oh, God—now he was dying for her.

No, no, no, no, noooo! She clawed wildly at the grass, dragging herself over the ground one agonizingly slow inch at a time. Useless. She was absolutely *useless.* Dying. Ryan was dying. And she was inching along like a slug on her belly, unable to do anything to help him.

When she finally reached the tree, Bethany felt as if a thousand eternities had passed. She grabbed the gun, managed to sit up, and braced her back against the trunk. Breathing in . . . breathing out. The sound of her lungs echoed against her eardrums. Every swish of her blood was an explosion inside her brain. *Ryan.* She flicked the rifle off safety, jacked in a shell, and threw the butt to her shoulder.

The bear was mauling Ryan. Tossing him around as if he were a rag doll. Every time Bethany started to shoot, she lost her nerve, terrified she might hit Ryan. *Please, God.* She needed a clear shot.

It never came. The bear was in a frenzy. Bethany realized she absolutely had to shoot. She got a bead on the bear, refusing to think about Ryan getting in her line of fire. She hauled in a breath, held it, and squeezed the trigger. *Kaboom.* The kick of the rifle slammed her spine against the tree trunk.

The bear screamed in rage and turned toward her, going up on its back legs. *Mrrrhaw!* The cry was horrible and sounded almost human. Bethany jacked in another shell, sighted in. Before she could fire, the bear took off at a dead run.

Sobbing and calling Ryan's name, Bethany dragged herself toward him. *Blood.* Oh, dear God. She'd never seen so much blood. He was surely dead. She pushed the rifle ahead of her over the ground, knowing she'd need the weapon if the bear circled back. *Ryan.* She loved him so much. Please, God. He couldn't be dead.

When she finally reached him, he mumbled something and opened his eyes. Blue spheres, surrounded by crimson streaks. He smiled at her. "You hit the son of a bitch?"

"I don't know," she sobbed. "Oh, my God, Ryan. You're hurt. You're badly hurt."

"No shit. He got my hip." He blinked and stared hard at her for a moment. "Bethany, I'm—" His throat worked. "Keep the gun close, darlin'. Don't let the bastard hurt you."

That was all he said, and then he lost consciousness.

Praying mindlessly, Bethany managed to sit up. She began checking Ryan, knowing she had to find the worst of his injuries and somehow stop the bleeding. She looked at his hip first. Nearly vomited. Started to cry, then gave herself a hard mental slap. No hysterics. She had to keep her head. Do what had to be done.

She ripped off her shoes to get at her socks. Then she peeled off her blouse and bra. Padding. She had to pad the wounds and tightly wrap them to staunch the bleeding.

While she worked, she prayed, bargaining mindlessly with God. *Just please let him live, and I swear, I'll never come out like this again. My fault. I had no business coming with him into a wilderness area. He would have run for the rifle if it hadn't been for me. Please, just let him live. Please, please, please.*

When she'd done all she could to stop the bleeding, Bethany tugged the cell phone from his belt. She almost lost it when she saw that the case had been crushed. The bear had mangled it while biting Ryan's hip. She tried to dial out anyway. The phone didn't work. It was as useless as she was.

No time to blubber. She had to get help. Use her head. She gazed at the horses. There was no way she could get on one of the animals by herself, let alone lift a wounded man onto a saddle. But those horses were still their only hope.

Keeping the rifle with her, just as Ryan had told her to do, Bethany dragged herself toward their mounts. All three animals were terrified and pranced nervously. As she got closer, she stared at their hooves, praying they wouldn't trample her. *No matter.* She had to get help up here for Ryan. He'd die if she didn't.

Bucky was their best chance, Bethany decided. The packhorse was too loaded down to make good time, and Wink hadn't been on the Rocking K very long. Bucky had probably covered these mountain trails with Ryan many a time, and if set free, he'd know the way home.

Miraculously the gelding stopped prancing the instant Bethany got close to his hooves. Tears nearly blinded her. "You're a good boy," she told him shakily. Before she untied the horse's reins, Bethany sat up and rubbed her bloody arms on his chest, praying whoever found the horse would notice the smears of crimson on his sorrel coat. "I need you to go home, Bucky. Run as fast as you can, boy. Go home."

She jerked his reins free from the stump.

"Go!" she yelled. "Ha! Ha! Out of here. Go on!" She slapped the geld-ing's chest. "Ha, I said!"

Already terrified from the recent bear attack, the horse was skittish anyway, and that was all it took. He wheeled and bolted. As she gazed after the gelding, Bethany sent up a silent prayer that Bucky would head straight for the ranch and that someone would be over at Ryan's place to see him when he got there.

The instant Sly saw Ryan's horse come wandering into the stable with-out a rider, he knew something was wrong. He immediately contacted Rafe.

"We got trouble, son. You best get over here."

Rafe was there within five minutes. He looked Bucky over, saw what appeared to be blood on the horse's chest, and swore under his breath. "Something happened. One of them is badly hurt."

Sly had already deduced that much and had started saddling horses. "You want I should call Bethany's brothers? We're gonna need all the men we can get if we gotta track 'em."

Rafe nodded. "I'll call them, Sly. If you'd finish getting the horses sad-dled, I'd much appreciate it."

"How many?" Sly asked as Rafe turned toward the stable office.

"She's got three brothers living here in town. My guess is they'll all come. Five mounts for us, I reckon, and a spare for Ryan, since his is here." Rafe stopped and sent Sly a hollow-eyed look. "Just pray to God he's alive to need a horse. That's a lot of blood on Bucky."

"Think positive, son. Ryan's a smart boy. Knows them mountains like the palms of his hands. He's okay."

Rafe nodded and opened the door to the office.

The howls of coyotes weren't so beautiful when you were alone in the dark, praying with every breath that the man you loved could hang onto life a while longer. Bethany sat with Ryan's head on her lap. He had re-gained consciousness a few times. Only briefly. A few lucid moments to break up an eternity of aloneness . . .

Each time, all he seemed concerned about was her.

"Bethany," he croaked the first time. "Honey, keep the rifle close and don't go to sleep. One bullet probably didn't kill the bastard, and he may come back."

"I won't sleep, Ryan. Don't worry. I promise you, I won't sleep."

He slipped away from her again. The second time he awoke, he seemed calmer. Or was it only that he was weaker? Bethany's heart twisted, and she wanted to cry as she looked into his shimmering eyes.

"There's a song," he whispered. "Garth Brooks, I th-think. A man wondering if she knows—wondering if he's done enough."

Bethany touched her fingers to his lips and sobbed, unable to imagine what a song had to do with anything. "Save your strength. Don't try to talk."

"Got to. Important." He gulped and stared at the sky. "If I don't wake up, I need to know that you know."

"Know what?"

"How much I—" He closed his eyes. "How much I love you."

He passed out again then. Bethany sobbed and hugged him close, rocking wildly. "I know, Ryan. How could I not? I know . . ."

The next time he regained consciousness, he said, "They'll circle back. Sometimes, they circle back. Keep the gun close and the safety off."

"I will. It's right here beside me. I'll shoot the son of a bitch. Trust me."

His teeth flashed in a weak grin, his face pallid and eerie looking in the moonlight, streaked with dry blood. "I've never heard you cuss. I'll be damned."

"Right now, I could teach you a few dirty words."

He smiled again. "You already taught me a lot, darlin'." He gazed up at her. Then his eyes seemed to lose focus. "It's been good," he whispered. "It was—everything. Understand?"

She nodded. "I know, Ryan. I know how much you love me. Almost as much as I love you, I think."

His face contorted with pain. His lashes fluttered closed. "Bethany?" he whispered weakly.

"What?" she squeezed out.

"I don't think—" He gulped and grabbed for a painful breath. "I don't think I can hold on much longer."

"I'll hold on for you. Rest, Ryan. I love you so. You can't leave me."

The next time he came to, he was weaker. He wasted no time on unnecessary words. "Rafe. My folks. You tell them. We made vows. I want you to have the place."

As if she cared. Tears streamed down Bethany's cheeks. "I don't give a shit about your money, Ryan. Don't even think about that."

"Not the money," he forced out. "The *place*. Heaven in your backyard. You stay, Bethany. You and Wink. With my family. Promise me?"

"You're going to make it, Ryan. You have to. Do you understand? I sent Bucky back. Help will be here soon. Just hold on a little longer."

"Can't," he whispered. "Promise me. You'll stay. Gotta know."

"I promise. I'll stay there, Ryan. With heaven in my backyard. I promise."

He lost consciousness for a long time then.

Bethany kept checking his pulse. It was weak. So horribly feeble. The beats had become so faint, she could barely feel them, and they were spaced an eternity apart. He was losing his strength, his life's blood slowly seeping away.

A terrible stillness came over her as she cradled his head to her bare breasts. *Ryan*. Had it all been a dream, then? A beautiful dream doomed to end, as all dreams did?

The moon was at its zenith when Bethany thought she heard Jake's voice calling her name. She jerked her head up and stared stupidly through the moon-silvery gloom, wondering if she'd nodded off and been dreaming.

"Bethaneeeeeee! Bethaneeeeee!"

Her heart soared with hope. "Jake? We're here! Over here! Jake?"

She saw lights. *Flashlights*. What appeared to be dozens of them, bouncing wildly in the darkness. She hugged Ryan's limp shoulders and rained kisses over his face.

"You made it! They came. Just in time, but they *came*. You made it!"

Even as Bethany said the words, she wondered if she was lying to herself. He was so horribly weak now. As much as she loved him, sometimes love simply wasn't enough.

Nightmares. Bethany dreamed of helicopters. Totally weird. Of Ryan and helicopters? He'd mentioned once that the Rocking K had an airstrip, but he'd never said anything about owning a helicopter. Nevertheless, she dreamed they were flying. She smiled as she struggled toward consciousness. She and Ryan, flying. Just the two of them, lifting off together. Darkness. Confusing lights all around them. The deafening whir of helicopter blades.

In her dreams, Jake was there and so were Ryan's brother and dad. She kept trying to remind them that it was a ten-dollar fine for every cussword, but somehow she couldn't get her brain and mouth to work.

"It's all right, Bethie," she heard Jake whisper. "You did good, honey. It's going to be all right."

Bethany was freezing, yet she felt as if her skin was on fire. She drifted in and out of blackness, deep in an exhausted sleep one moment, jerking awake the next to see swimming faces. Her mom and dad, Jake, and her other four brothers. Everyone she loved seemed to be there.

Everyone except Ryan.

When Bethany finally awakened, rested and lucid, in the middle of the night, only Jake sat by her hospital bed. She gazed solemnly at his dark face for a long moment, remembering all the many times he'd sat with her in just this way eight years ago. Back then, he'd always been the one to tell her the most recent bad news—that she was still paralyzed after her last surgery and she'd probably never walk again. Poor Jake, always chosen to be the bearer of bad tidings. Bethany prayed that wasn't the case now.

"Ryan? Please tell me he's all right," she whispered.

Jake's eyes ached with sadness. "He's still alive," he told her.

Still alive? Not that he was fine. Not even that he was doing fairly well. "What's that mean?" She struggled up onto her elbows and immediately cried out at the pain. Her torso burned at the slightest movement. "Oh, God!"

"You've got a bad burn from sitting all that time in the sun, honey. No clothing to protect your skin. When we found you, you were cooked and flirting with hypothermia as well."

Bethany filed away the information for later and pushed the pain aside. That was a trick she'd learned long ago, how to ignore pain. When it was a part of everyday life for a long while, you had no choice but to live with it. "Ryan. Tell me how he is, Jake. Don't color it. I have to know how he is."

Jake sighed and ran a hand over his rumpled dark hair. "Not good. A crushed hip, three broken ribs, and some very serious wounds, Bethany. He lost a lot of blood. They did a direct transfusion, using Rafe's blood."

Terror washed through her. "But he's—he's here in the hospital now. Right? They'll fix him up, and he'll be fine."

Jake closed his eyes for a moment. When he opened them again, Bethany knew the awful truth before he said it out loud. "He's hanging on, honey. Been a rough night. Touch and go. The doctors—" He shrugged and swallowed hard.

The sight of him struggling to control his emotions told Bethany just how grave Ryan's condition was and made her all the more afraid. "He put himself between me and the bear. He could have run. Tried to save himself. But he protected me."

Jake nodded. "I figured."

"He can't—die. He *can't*. Not now that he's in the hospital." Her voice rose in volume. "He can't *die*. Don't even tell me that! Don't *even*!"

"I'm sorry, sweetie. I'm so sorry. They've done all they can. He's too weak right now to undergo surgery. They have him in ICU. The doctors say if he makes it through the night, he'll be out of the woods."

"If?" Bethany began pushing at the blankets. "Take me to him."

"Bethany, honey . . . you're not in great shape yourself. You shouldn't—"

"Take me to him!"

Evidently Jake saw she meant business. He lifted her from the bed into a hospital wheelchair, covered her legs with a blanket, and pushed her to ICU.

Three days later, Bethany sat by Ryan's hospital bed, staring at his lax features. Still heavily drugged for pain, he slept deeply, unaware of what went on around him. A jagged, angry red cut angled over one of his sunken cheeks. She knew it would leave a scar on his beautiful face, every line of which had been engraved on her heart. Oh, how she wished she could kiss him. Touch him. But she was trapped in her wheelchair and couldn't reach him.

The doctors said he would live, that the danger was past. He'd undergone surgery on his hip. His other wounds would heal with time. He might always have a limp. But he was going to live.

Bethany was so glad. So very, very glad. Over the last twenty-four hours, she had cried enough to cause a major flood.

Ann Kendrick came into the room just then. She stepped around to stand at the opposite side of her son's bed. After touching his forehead in that universal way of all moms, she fixed sad gray eyes on Bethany.

"He'll never understand, you know. It'll break his heart, Bethany, and he may never forgive you. I know my son."

Bethany stared hard at her lap. She hadn't told Ann or anyone else of her decision, but it didn't surprise her that Ryan's mother had guessed. She seemed to be an intuitive lady.

Bethany found the strength to meet her gaze. "Do you understand, Ann?"

Ann's eyes took on a suspicious shine. She stared for a long moment at Ryan. "Yes, I understand," she admitted softly. "He'll probably never forgive me for telling you that. I should probably deny it with my last breath, but, yes, I do understand." She smoothed his black hair with a trembling hand. "If I were in your place, I might do the same thing myself. Kendrick men make wonderful husbands. They love passionately with their whole heart and soul, and they treat a woman like a queen. But as wonderful as it is, being loved that fiercely places a burden of respon-sibility on a woman's shoulders as well, especially for someone like you."

"A terrible burden," Bethany agreed.

"I wish I could tell you he would never again throw himself in the path of danger for you. I know this is as heartbreaking for you as it will be for him. But sadly, I can't. No telling what it would be next time. A frightened horse or a loco steer." She shrugged and smiled tearfully. "On a ranch, you just never know, the only certainty being that he'd jump in to protect you and might get hurt."

Bethany was so relieved that it wasn't necessary to explain her rea-sons. "Oh, Ann, thank you. For understanding, I mean. It's so hard for me to go."

"It's hard for me to let you go without arguing his case, given the fact that he's unable to speak for himself right now." Ann trailed a fingertip over the tray beside Ryan's bed. "If he were awake, he'd tell you how very much he loves you, and that he'd rather be dead than live without you."

Bethany closed her eyes. She knew that was exactly what Ryan would probably say, but hearing Ann say it aloud was worse than merely hear-ing it in her mind.

"Loving him as you do, Bethany, I hope you've considered the prob-lem from every angle and know with absolute certainty that there's no way to work it out. I meant it when I said he may never forgive you. This will hurt him so much. I'm sure you know that." She sighed and shook her head. "Forgive me for butting in. It's your decision to make, and I should just let you make it. It's just that I'm not sure he'll take you back if you should change your mind later. It wouldn't be fair if I let you leave without telling you that."

"I won't change my mind." Bethany tried not to look at Ryan. "The day before it happened, we, um . . . we exchanged wedding vows on Bear Creek Ridge. Just he and I, with only God to hear. One of my promises was that I would try to love him more than I love myself. I'm trying to keep that promise right now."

"Oh, sweetie . . ."

"If I stay on the ranch, the only way I can avoid putting him at risk again is to stay completely away from the animals. That wouldn't be a marriage, Ann. He needs someone to share his life with him, someone who can work beside him and dream with him."

"I know," Ann agreed hollowly.

"All of you tried so hard to make that possible for me," Bethany whis-pered raggedly. "You'll never know how grateful I am. But I just can't do it. I just—can't. All the trying in the world won't make me whole again, and my selfishness almost killed him."

"Oh, Bethany . . ." Ann took a bracing breath. "You're still very upset, honey, and you may not be thinking clearly. Can you give it a few more days? You need time to distance yourself from what happened up there. Time to let the horror of it become less vivid. Maybe then you'll feel calmer and see things a little differently."

Bethany shook her head and wheeled from the room. Ann followed, her riding boots tapping sharply on the well-waxed tile. "If I wait, I won't go," Bethany told her. "I love him so much. It would be so easy to start lying to myself and thinking up reasons to stay. And in the end, I wouldn't go."

"Exactly," Ann said with a humorless laugh. "That's my hope."

Bethany braked to a stop. "Is it really? You weren't on the mountain. You didn't see the bear attack. You're thinking clearly right now. Look me in the eye and tell me you won't blame me if Ryan ends up dead trying to protect me from a danger I might have avoided. Can you tell me that?" Bethany waited a beat. "The truth, and please don't answer lightly. Imagine yourself, standing over his grave. How will you feel when you look at me, Ann?"

Ann's face drained of color. She said nothing, but it was all the answer Bethany needed.

She left Ann Kendrick standing in the hallway and didn't look back. A few minutes later when she exited the hospital, she had never in her life felt so alone.

₰ CHAPTER TWENTY—TWO ₰

Six weeks later, Ryan parked his dusty pickup next to a corral over at Rafe's place. When he exited the vehicle and started pulling on soiled leather work gloves, his father waved from inside the small enclosure where he, Rafe, and Sly were dehorning a hogtied steer.

"Looks to me like you're fixin' to go to work!" Keefe called. "You sure you're ready for this?"

"Can't sit around forever," Ryan hollered back as he limped toward the fence. "I'm getting damned tired of staring at bare walls. Time to rejoin the world of the living."

Keefe strode over to the fence, watching as Ryan struggled to climb up and over the rails. "Still a little sore, I see."

"Nothing that won't get better with use." Ryan swung down inside the corral to stand beside his dad. "Too pretty a day to be inside, that's for sure."

Keefe smiled and squinted at the sky. "Nothing like a summer morning to get the blood to perking. Can't believe it's damned near August. The snows will come before we know it."

Ryan forced a laugh. These days, strained laughter was all he could manage. His heart just wasn't in it. But that would pass. Bethany's four younger brothers had tracked down the renegade bear and killed it. The surgery to repair the damage to his hip had gone very well, and in time, he'd have only a slight limp as a reminder of that day. As for the mess his life was in, the Kendricks were survivors. In time, the pain would subside.

Yep. To hell with her. To hell with everything. He'd move on. Eventually her face would blur in his memory, and he'd forget the color of her eyes. In time, he'd stop hurting.

Time. That was all he needed, a little more time.

"Your mother says you're packing up a bunch of stuff to ship to Bethany," his dad said.

Ryan's guts knotted at the sound of her name. "Yeah. That treadmill, the all-terrain wheelchair, and a couple of other things I've got no use for. She may as well have them."

"Must've been hard, reaching that decision. A final step, cutting her out of your life."

Ryan shrugged. "I don't want to look at the shit. I figure sending it to her is another step toward healing for me."

"Probably wise thinking." Keefe sighed. "I'm sorry, son. I know you're hurting."

"It hurts to cut out cancer, too." Ryan hauled in a deep, cleansing breath.

"That's mighty harsh," Keefe said softly.

"Yea, well, it's how I feel. I'm well rid of her. For better or worse, that was our bargain. First spot of trouble, and she ran out on me. Without a word, Dad. I damned near died for her. I think she owed me a face-to-face good-bye. Don't you? At least a note or something. Screw it. I don't need the aggravation or the heartache. I've come through the worst part without her. I'll get through the rest and be better off in the long run for the loss."

"I hear you." Keefe gazed off at the mountains, His mouth twitched at one corner. "The little bitch."

Ryan stiffened. He stared at the ground for a long moment. "I don't love her anymore," he said evenly. "But that doesn't give you license to call her names."

Keefe's eyes started to twinkle, and he nodded almost imperceptibly. "You're right. It's the daddy coming out in me. She doesn't have that coming. I apologize, son."

Ryan shrugged. "No skin off my nose, I don't guess. If it flips your skirt, go for it."

Keefe rubbed the back of his fist over his mouth. "Nah. I was out of line. She's a sweet little thing. Never did anything to warrant any name-calling."

"Nope."

"Too bad it all came out the way it did."

Ryan shrugged again. Keefe watched Rafe and Sly work for a moment, his eyes still twinkling.

"Take heart, son. You'll find the right woman someday."

"I found her. It didn't work out. That's it for me."

"You'll change your mind when you clap eyes on the right girl."

"Nope."

That was all Ryan said, but the word was a vow.

"You know, son, not that I'm defendin' her or anything, but your mother seems to think she had sound reasons. Listening to her, I can damned near believe it myself. Women." Keefe shook his head. "Sometimes they see things inside out and ass backward, but their hearts are in the right place. They just need a man to get their heads on straight."

Ryan shot his father a glare. "Don't start, Dad. If you're going to switch sides, keep your thoughts to yourself. I don't want to hear it."

"I'm not switching sides. I'll always be on your side. You know that. It's just—"

"That Mom's been working on you?" Ryan finished for him. "I know she feels bad for me and that she hopes I'll go chasing after her. News bulletin. It ain't happening. She made her decision. The day I go chasing off to Portland to kiss her ass and beg her to come back, hell will freeze over. End of subject."

Rafe finished with the bull. As he shooed the animal into an adjoining pen, he spotted his brother and waved. A moment later Rafe sauntered across the enclosure. "Howdy. You're lookin' spry and ready to tangle."

Keefe slipped the cigarettes he seldom smoked from his shirt pocket. He tapped out a Winston, his eyes narrowing as he watched his elder son approach. "His mood just took a downward turn. All it takes is sayin' her name, and he gets prickly as a porcupine."

"Uh-oh." Rafe fixed an amused gaze on Ryan's scowling face. "He's probably just feeling better and getting horny. There's a cure for that, little brother. You can be on her doorstep in less than three hours if you break all the speed limits to get there."

"Jesus Christ." Ryan snatched the pack of cigarettes and lighter out of his dad's hands. The other two men watched him in stunned surprise as he lit up and inhaled. "Back off." He handed back the cigarettes and lighter. "Both of you. I don't need this shit."

Rafe chuckled. "He's hangin' on by a thread to his willpower when he grabs for smokes. Won't be long now."

Ryan had had enough. "Rafe, you're my brother, and I love you. But I swear to God, if you don't shut up, you're going to eat this cigarette, fire and all. Do I make myself clear?"

Sly strolled over. He smiled wryly as he opened his can of snuff and tucked a wad of chew inside his bottom lip. "You sound like a grizzly with a sore paw, boy."

Ryan took another drag from the cigarette, then tossed it on the ground and smothered it out under his heel. "Let's get to work," he said with a snarl.

"You sure you're ready for wrestlin' them steers?" Sly asked. "Next one up is one that slipped past us last year. He's a big old boy."

"I'm here, aren't I?" Ryan threw the adjoining gate wide to shoo in the next victim, a large black steer with wild-looking eyes. Recently brought in off open range, the critter was nervous around humans and ran a circle around the pen, looking for a bolt hole. Ryan settled his hat back on his head. "Well, boys?" he said to the other three men. "You gonna work or stand around with your thumbs up your asses all day?"

Everyone sighed as they resumed work. Sly roped the steer in short order. Rafe jumped in to help handle the huge creature, which didn't take kindly to having a noose around its neck. Nothing out of the ordinary. Half-wild steers never took kindly to being handled.

Ryan grabbed the dehorner. Because he wasn't back to full speed yet after his surgery, he meant to stand aside until his brother and the ranch foreman got the steer hogtied. Unfortunately, the steer had other ideas. It lunged, Sly lost his grip on the rope, and the next thing Ryan knew, the huge animal was charging right for him.

Ryan dropped the dehorner clamp and tried to spring out of the way, but his hip was still weak and it gave under the force of his weight. He staggered and fell. When he tried to scramble back to his feet, he moved too slowly.

"Ha!" Keefe yelled.

With growing alarm, Ryan watched his father jump between him and the charging steer. Keefe waved his Stetson to head off the huge animal. The steer lowered its head and just kept coming.

"Dad!" Ryan hollered. "Get the hell out of the way!"

Keefe stood his ground.

In the horrible seconds that followed, Ryan's brain seemed to assimilate the transpiring events in slow motion. He screamed again for his father to move, scrambling as he did to get out of the way himself. Then it happened. The steer rammed Keefe in the midriff and just kept charging, lifting Ryan's father off his feet and slamming him violently against the corral fence.

In reality it all probably took place in less than a second, but to Ryan, it seemed to take forever. The steer bawled and veered away. Keefe crumpled to the ground, his face ashen, his eyes bulging. He grabbed his chest and fought to breathe.

Sweet Lord. Ryan crawled to his father's side. Frantically, he checked for blood, thinking his dad might have been gored. When he found no blood, he could only deduce that maybe his father's ribs were broken. Keefe was still grabbing futilely for breath. His lips were turning blue.

Rafe and Sly reached them. Rafe fell to his knees beside Ryan. "Dad? Oh, Jesus. Sweet Jesus. His heart. Dad, is it your heart?" Rafe started fishing in Keefe's pockets for his nitroglycerin tablets. When he found the small vial, he tapped a tiny pill onto his palm, then stuck it under their father's tongue. "Try to relax, Dad. Just try to relax."

Ryan moved around to put their father's head on his lap. He imagined Keefe dying. They were so far from town. If the old man was having a heart attack, they'd never get him to a hospital in time. Oh, God. His fault. All his fault. He should never have been in the corral. He knew he wasn't completely back to normal yet. He had no business putting himself in dangerous situations and forcing the people who loved him to take up the slack. Now his dad had jumped in to protect him and could end up dying.

Sly kept the steer away from them while they hovered over Keefe. It seemed as if an eternity passed before the older man finally managed to catch his breath, and then he simply lay there for another eternity, replenishing his oxygen.

"Not my heart," he grated out. "Just knocked the breath out of me."

Relief made Ryan's bones feel watery. He hung his head and spent a moment grabbing for some much-needed oxygen himself. *Damn.* Seeing his dad get rammed like that—it had been the most awful moment of his life. Knowing he'd been the cause of it. Thinking his father might die. Ryan never wanted to experience such feelings again. That awful sense of crushing guilt and a clawing fear that had turned his blood to ice.

When it was all over and Keefe was back on his feet, Ryan was still shaken. He left the corral and went to his truck, unable to stop thinking of how much worse it could have been. The steer might have gored his dad or broken his ribs, puncturing a lung.

Ryan leaned against the fender of his Dodge, shoulders hunched, head hanging, mind racing with so many horrible possibilities. Rafe walked up and laid a hand on his shoulder. "Hey, bro. All's well that ends well."

"He could be dead," Ryan bit out. "And it would have been my fault. I had no business going in the pen. I should have known better than to put other men at risk that way. If you can't cut the mustard, you keep the hell out of the way."

Rafe sighed and patted Ryan's back. "Life is full of risks. Sly's never lost his grip on a rope in all the years I've known him. It was just one of those things. Probably never happen again. We're lucky it didn't go worse than it did."

"Christ," Ryan whispered. "I can't stop shaking, and I think I'm gonna puke."

"It's a bad feeling, I know," Rafe said softly. "Nothing worse than feeling responsible when someone you love gets hurt. Is there?"

"You've got that right," Ryan agreed in a quivery voice that sounded nothing like his own.

Rafe rested his folded arms on the fender beside Ryan's. "Strange how a front-row seat can give you a different perspective on something. Now you have an inkling of how Bethany must have felt."

That brought Ryan's head up. He glared at his brother. "How the hell do you figure?"

Rafe gazed off across the fields. "Nah. You're right. There's no comparison, is there? Five minutes later, and Dad's up walking around, fit as a fiddle. She undoubtedly felt a million times worse." Rafe cut Ryan a hard look. "Probably still does. You damned near died. She kept you hanging on for hours. Imagine it, Ryan. Sitting there all that time, praying you'd live. Naked from the waist up, except for all your blood. Got so cooked from the sun, they had to knock her out with a shot for the pain. While she was holding you, getting baked, I wonder how many times she thought she'd puke? And you know the real kicker? You can look forward to getting better. The hip will heal. You'll get your strength back. You may never be good as new, but you'll come close, and the day will come when you can resume all your former activities without putting anyone at risk. Bethany can't look forward to that. She'll be paralyzed for the rest of her life."

Rafe pushed away from the truck. He didn't say another word. He didn't need to.

Two nights later at precisely half past six, Bethany's doorbell rang. In her pre-Ryan days, she might have felt excited, thinking it was one of her friends coming to invite her to join in an activity. Now she only sighed dejectedly, unable to work up any enthusiasm for company. She didn't want to do something fun. She didn't even want to see a friendly face. She just wanted to be left alone to wallow in her misery.

She hurried through the apartment, which was no easy task because she still wasn't finished unpacking, and she had moving boxes everywhere. She wrestled with the dead bolt, finally got it disengaged, and opened the door until the sturdy safety chain Jake had installed earlier in the week caught hold. Through the crack, she glimpsed a tall, dark-haired man in neatly pressed chinos and a brown sport coat.

"Yes? May I help you?" Though she hadn't yet seen his face, he looked respectable enough, definitely not a punk-with-purple-hair type who might rob her at gunpoint. Even so, she was reluctant to unfasten the security guard. "I'm really not interested in buying anything. Sorry. I just moved in here and—"

The man shifted so she could see his face. She broke off and stared incredulously into twinkling, gunmetal blue eyes.

"Hi, darlin'."

"Ryan?" With shaking hands, she unhooked the chain and backed away to open the door.

Hands in his trouser pockets, his body deceptively relaxed, he rested a slip-on Italian loafer on the threshold and leaned his shoulder against the door frame. Whether he meant to or not, he'd very effectively prevented her from shutting the door again. "You really do need a peephole. It'd save you from opening up to fellows you'd rather avoid."

"Ryan," she said again, her voice shaky.

He looked so different she almost didn't recognize him. Gone were the faded jeans and dusty boots. Every dark hair on his hatless head was perfectly styled. The sexy cowboy had vanished, and a successful-looking city slicker had taken his place.

"If you're here to try and convince me to go back to the ranch, you've wasted the trip."

"Nope. That's not my aim. I never want you to touch a wheel back on the Rocking K."

Her heart sank with disappointment. Stupid of her. Even though she had no intention of relenting, a part of her wished he might at least attempt to get her back. She tried to moisten her lips with a tongue that felt as dry as cotton.

"I'm moving in," he said.

"Oh." Bethany gazed blankly at him for a moment. "What?"

"You heard me. Do I really need to repeat myself?"

Bethany stared hard into his eyes. "I told you, Ryan. It's over. I'm not—"

"Forever," he interrupted. "That's what you told me." He pushed his way on in. "You're mine. No reneging on the bargain. If you don't have a double bed, we'll make do for tonight and I'll buy one tomorrow."

He limped slightly, she noticed. He didn't move as fluidly as he once had, either. He turned to shut the door, then he engaged the dead bolt and the chain. When he faced her again, he flashed that wonderful crooked grin that had always made her heart do flips. The jagged scar on his cheek was still an angry pink, but it in no way detracted from his rugged good looks. Instead it only lent that drop-dead gorgeous face more character.

"I'm not going back with you to the ranch, Ryan. Not ever. If you think by coming here you can convince me, you're wrong."

"I'm not asking you to go back. I understand why you feel we can't live there. Not a problem. We'll live here."

She laughed tremulously. "Right. You're leaving the ranch. Uh-huh. And where's the bridge in Brooklyn you'd like to sell me?"

"No bridge." He rested his hands on his hips. "Where you go, I go."

"No way. You'd shrivel up and die, living in the city. You're a rancher to the marrow of your bones. It'd never work."

"I'll make it work." He moved into her living room and glanced around at the boxes. "It's just as well you aren't unpacked completely. I want to get a house with a couple of acres. Someplace where we can at least keep Wink and Bucky and have a yard for Tripper."

Bethany hugged her waist. "A house? You want to buy a house here?"

He turned to regard her with a no-nonsense glint in his eyes. "Bethany Ann, we can do this the easy way, or we can do it the hard way. I'm here, I'm staying. Nothing you say or do will change my mind. Why don't you just accept what you can't change, and feed me. I'm hungry."

She'd known he loved her. No question. But the realization that he would leave the RockingK , simply to be with her, nearly broke her heart. "I can't let you do this, Ryan. You'll never be happy in the city. You know that. I know that. You'd die an inch at a time."

He shrugged. "If I stay on the ranch without you, I'll die an inch at a time, too. I'd rather die up here with you." He wandered into the kitchen and opened her refrigerator. "Where's the food?"

"I haven't gotten all that many groceries yet."

He sighed and shut the door. Then he eyed her with a speculative gleam. "I'm not really all that hungry for food, anyway. I'd much rather have you."

She held up a hand. "We're not going to hop into bed until we settle this."

"It's already settled." He grasped the lapels of his sport coat to show her his dress shirt. "I even bought new clothes. Decision made. I'm here. I'm staying." He released his hold on the jacket and moved slowly toward her, managing to do the cowboy saunter even in chinos and loafers. When he settled his hands on the arms of her chair, he dipped his head to look deeply into her eyes. "I love you so much, Bethany. Wherever you are—that's where I belong, and that's where I'll be happy. I'll make this work. Just give me a chance to show you."

She could barely see him now through her tears. "Oh, Ryan. You can't *do* this. You were born and raised on that land. It's where your heart is, where your heart will always be. I can't take you away from there."

"You already have," he whispered, and lifted her into his arms.

He swore when he straightened, cursing his bad hip. "I'm still not a hundred percent recovered. But I'm getting there."

"Don't hurt yourself, you big, stubborn blockhead." She hugged his neck, scarcely able to believe how very wonderful it felt to have his arms around her again. She'd lain awake countless nights, longing to feel his embrace, aching with sadness because she hadn't believed she ever would again. "Oh, Ryan. I love you. I love you."

"I know you do," he informed her huskily.

And then he carried her to the bedroom to show her how much he had missed her.

Afterward Bethany lay in his arms, gazing thoughtfully at the ceiling while he toyed with her hair. He honestly meant to stay, she realized. This wasn't a ploy to manipulate her. He simply loved her so much, he had to be with her, and if that meant living in Portland, he was willing to do that. He had absolutely no intention of trying to convince her that she should return to the ranch.

Yet that was exactly what he'd managed to do.

She recalled the promise she'd made to him, about always trying to love him more than she loved herself. How ironic that in the end, it was Ryan who was showing her the true meaning of that vow by loving her so selflessly. Oh, God. He made her feel so miserably misguided and small.

"I'll go home with you," she whispered tremulously. "If you can make it work here, then I can surely figure out a way to make it work there."

"Nope," he said stubbornly.

They spent several minutes arguing. Then they both started laughing. When his mirth subsided, Ryan told her about the incident with the steer. "I understood then, honey. How you felt during the bear attack and why you left me afterward. I'm not in a wheelchair, but in a way, I am physically handicapped right now. I got a very slight taste of how it feels. You aren't afraid for yourself. You're afraid for me, because you know I'll jump in and possibly get hurt again if anything threatens your safety. We can't live like that."

"We can't live like this, either. You aren't cut out for city living, Ryan."

"Sure I am. I've got two bachelor's degrees, for God's sake. I can find some sort of work that challenges me. It doesn't even have to pay all that well. We've got all the money we'll ever need."

They argued a bit more. Then he got up to order some pizza. After the food was delivered, they ate until they were replete, and then he made love to her again. Bethany fell asleep in his arms with a troubled frown pleating her brow, for in her heart she knew that no matter how hard he tried, he'd never be happy living in the city.

The following morning, Ryan woke up to find the bed empty beside him. He stared hard at the sling Bethany had used to sneak out on him and made a mental note to get rid of the damned thing.

Yawning and rubbing his eyes, he bumped his toes on boxes all the way to the kitchen. Next to the coffeepot, he found a note from his runaway bride.

> Dear Ryan:
>
> I can't think how to tell you this, so I'll cut right to the chase. I've left you again. This is never going to work. I lay awake half the night, agonizing over our dilemma. I've decided I'd much rather lose you suddenly while you're doing some damned fool thing to protect me than to watch you slowly lose all your enthusiasm for life, which is exactly what will happen if you stay up here.
>
> Anyway, dear heart, I've gone home. Sorry for doing it this way, but you are being so obstinate, I know talking to you will get us nowhere. Please try not to be too angry with me.
>
> Love, Bethany

Ryan swore when he finished reading the note. Then he went back to the bedroom to throw on his clothes.

It was shortly after noon when Ryan reached the ranch, and sure enough, there was Bethany's van in front of the stable. His temper didn't improve when he discovered she wasn't in the house or any of the outbuildings, which forced him to walk all the wheelchair paths to find her. As chance would have it, he finally found her on the very last path he chose to take, the one that led to his thinking spot on the knoll.

He saw her sitting in her wheelchair under the pine tree long before he reached her. Just sitting there, gazing off across the lake at the mountain peaks with a wistful look on her upturned face. He wanted to be irritated with her. He'd just chased her halfway across the state and back, after all. And this latest shenanigan of hers resolved nothing. He couldn't make her stay someplace where she'd feel afraid all the time, either for herself or for him.

Only how could he stay angry with someone who looked so damned sweet?

"Bethany Ann!" he barked. A guy had his pride, after all. "What the hell do you think you're doing down here? I specifically told you last night that I wasn't coming back here, that we could never make this work."

She didn't even have the good grace to jump. She only smiled slightly and waited for him to reach her. With a bad hip, it was a little difficult to stomp with every step, but he gave it his best shot.

"I've a good mind to turn you over my knee. You run off to Portland, and I follow you. Then you run off and come home when you know very well it's against my wishes. Who in the hell's wearing the pants in this family?"

She glanced at his prissy city-slicker chinos. "Neither of us at the moment."

He swatted his trouser leg. "Don't let the cut of these britches fool you. It's not the damned clothes that make the man. I told you last night that I'd thought it over and decided we'd live outside Portland."

"I've just changed your mind for you."

"You can't make up your own mind, lady. Don't go screwing with mine."

She just smiled serenely. "You know what Sly says. Stand around waiting for a woman to make up her mind, and you'll put down taproots. Your roots are here, Ryan, and they run deep, so this is where we're staying. I was wrong. I realize that now. We're staying here on Kendrick land, and that's final."

Ryan wanted to give her a good, hard shake. Instead he planted his hands on his hips. "You'll be miserable if I make you stay here." He swung a hand to encompass the ranch. "Everywhere you look, there are dangers of one kind or another."

"There are just as many dangers in the city, only different kinds. Remember what you said to me, Ryan? About our having two choices in how we live life—in a safe little bubble where we'll eventually die anyway—or grabbing hold with both hands, enjoying every single second?"

"I remember."

"This is your everything," she said softly. Then she turned shimmering blue eyes to his and tremulously added, "And it's my everything as well. I was wrong to leave. It was a stupid mistake. I thought I was doing the right thing, and I continued to think that until last night when you showed up on my doorstep. It took that for me to realize that there are many different ways to die. Some death isn't of the flesh, but of the heart and soul."

"Oh, honey."

She held up a hand so he'd let her finish. "I was dying inside before I met you. I was slowly suffocating with every breath I took. How can you think that I could be happy in Portland, watching you feel the same way?"

All Ryan's anger dissipated. "I guess maybe you couldn't," he said thickly.

Tears spilled over her lower lashes onto her cheeks. "None of us know how long we've got. That being the case, we shouldn't waste a single day. I want to live every moment we have together as fully as we can. And the only place on earth either of us can do that is right here."

He closed the distance between them. When he leaned down to meet her gaze, she looked up at him with big Johnny-jump-up blue eyes all filled with tears and said, "I want my scalawag cowboy back."

"Your what?"

She smoothed her hands over the shoulder seams of his sport coat. "Don't get me wrong. You make a very handsome city fellow, but I think you're a lot sexier in faded jeans and dusty boots with a Stetson cocked over your eyes. I want my scalawag cowboy back."

Ryan swept her from the chair into his arms. "You got him, darlin'."

He kissed her until both of them felt a little dizzy. Then he turned to carry her up the slope.

"What are you doing? You can't carry me to the house."

"Why not?"

"Because it's silly. Your hip! Just put me in my chair and—"

"What kind of a beginning would that be? I want to carry you over the threshold when we get home."

She laughed in spite of herself. "Has anyone ever told you you're just a little bit crazy?"

"A few people have made noises to that effect. I just ignored them."

With every labored step he took, Bethany gazed back at the lake and the trees and the majestic mountain peaks. She was so glad to be back. So very glad.

Home, he'd said. And he was so very right. Kendrick land, under Kendrick skies. Her man had roots here that ran far deeper than he knew. She'd made the right decision, not just for him, but for herself.

Home. What a beautiful word that was.

⚜ EPILOGUE ⚜

In the Kendrick family Bible, it is now recorded that Ryan Kendrick, son of Ann and Keefe Kendrick, took to wife Bethany Ann Coulter on August 31, in the year of our Lord 2000. What the entry fails to note is that the wedding took place on the shore of Bear Creek Lake that beautiful summer day and was in fact a double ceremony. Also joined in holy wedlock that afternoon were Sylvester Bob Glass and Helen Marie Boyle. The entry in the Bible also fails to note that the younger bride had just discovered she was pregnant and was beaming with happiness.

Present to witness the weddings was a dusty, denim-clad assortment of guests, all of whom rode three hours from Ryan's ranch house to reach the lake by horseback. The Coulter family was well represented, with Bethany's father and all five of her strapping brothers glowering at her groom until he said, "I do."

No bears or cougars made an appearance. Halfway through the ceremony, however, a certain bull named T-bone showed up to witness the marriage. Wary of so many strangers, he stopped a respectful distance away and only mooed once to let his master know he'd found him. Upon the bull's broad shoulders sat a plump calico cat who chose that moment to have a bath.

After the ceremony Mary Coulter smiled sweetly up at her husband and handed him a neatly folded pair of his jockey shorts. Harv laughed, eyed them speculatively, and asked, "Did you think to bring any salt and pepper? I like my crow well-seasoned."

Mary smiled and put her arm around his waist. Zeke, the musician in the Coulter family, struck up a slow, lilting melody on his fiddle. Bethany's parents watched as her new husband lifted her from her wheelchair to sweep her around the sun-dappled clearing in a waltz that was all the more heartbreakingly beautiful because the bride's feet never touched the ground.

"I was wrong about him," Harv admitted. "I can see the love shining in that young man's eyes every time he looks at her."

"And in hers every time she looks at him," Mary whispered. "If it's any consolation, I was wrong as well. Did you see how she looked, riding in today? That girl was born to ride, and because of me, she was denied the pleasure for far too long. I feel so badly about that."

Harv gave her a loving jostle. "We love her, and we were terrified she might get hurt again if we let her ride. She understood that."

"There's such a thing as loving too much," Mary whispered. "I'm glad Ryan came into her life and had the wisdom to see what we couldn't. It's better to let her take risks and enjoy life than to be safe and unhappy."

"Maybe so," Harv whispered. "Just look at how she glows."

Bethany was indeed looking at her husband with love shining in her eyes. Ryan saw it as he turned with her in his arms. She leaned her head back and smiled, putting him in mind of the look on her face when he made love to her.

God, how he adored her. So much that he couldn't begin to express it.

Ryan stopped dancing long enough to tell her in the only way he knew, with a long, deep kiss that probably made the guests wonder if their welcome had run out. He didn't care. Since he and his bride intended to stay at the lake for a week to celebrate their honeymoon, he didn't want anyone to hang around for too long after the ceremony.

"What are you thinking?" she asked.

"That I'm the luckiest man alive."

"Oh, Ryan, I love you so."

Ryan knew she meant it with all her heart. He also knew she couldn't possibly love him as much as he loved her.

He began dancing again. Great swirling steps with his world in his arms, so happy that he wasn't entirely sure if his own feet were touching the ground.

Flying . . . together. In that moment, gazing into Bethany's pansy-blue eyes, Ryan knew the magic would always be there between them, a beautiful, special something that would never die. Some great love stories didn't end happily because there was no ending. They just went on and on, into eternity.

It would be that way for them, a great love story that never ended.

Sweet Nothings

To my husband and hero, Sid, who has filled my life with sunshine. When I think back over the years, I realize that love is an ever-changing journey, and I am so very thankful you are the man who has taken that journey with me. When the way has been rough, you have always been there to steady me. When I've grown disheartened, you've given me the courage to keep trying. In the good times, you've laughed with me and shared in my joy. In the sad times, you have cried with me and given me strength.

In short, you have always been and always will be my everything.

✑ CHAPTER ONE ✑

D *id they still hang horse thieves in Oregon?*
     No, of *course* they didn't, Molly Sterling Wells assured herself.
And she would stop thinking that way immediately. Wasn't that just like
her? Always negative and imagining the worst. No wonder she always lost
courage before she finished anything.

She had enough problems to deal with at the moment without borrowing trouble. She'd been on the way out the door early that morning
when the phone rang, and now she wished she'd just kept walking. As a
result of answering that call, she was now over a hundred and fifty miles
from home, her stomach was growling with hunger, and, to top it all off,
she was hot, tired, thirsty, and hopelessly lost. The next time she got it
into her head to play Good Samaritan, she would think twice.

She had taken so many turns on this gravel country road that she had
no idea where she was, and there were no street signs to tell her. For as
far as she could see, which wasn't far given the hilly terrain, there were
only juniper trees, sagebrush, craggy rocks, and straw-colored grass. This
was only April. Did they get so little precipitation in Oregon, east of the
Cascades?

Accustomed to the lush greenery and cooler temperatures in her rainy
hometown of Portland, she puffed at a damp, curly hank of reddish-
brown hair that had escaped her French braid. Her red Toyota 4Runner
lurched violently just then. She struggled to keep from driving off into the
drainage trench, but the pitching weight of the loaded horse trailer made
steering nearly impossible. She tromped on the brake before she lost control. Sweat trickled from her armpits as she twisted to look out the dusty
rear window.

"*Blast* it!"

Through the front opening of the huge white trailer, she could see
Sonora Sunset. Eyes rolling wildly, the black stallion shrieked in terror.

Her heart ached for him, but there was a limit to one's patience, and after five hours of fighting the wheel, she had reached hers. She wanted to jump out of the vehicle and scream at him. Didn't he understand that she was trying to save his life?

Curling her trembling hands over the steering wheel, she rested her forehead on the back of her wrists. This would teach her not to put any stock in Hollywood films. In *The Horse Whisperer*, a woman had pulled a frantic horse in a trailer halfway across the country with little difficulty, stopping at roadside cafés to eat, staying overnight at motels. What a departure from reality.

She raised her head to stare at the road. *I'm not really lost,* she assured herself. She'd gotten directions to the Lazy J Ranch from a farmer before leaving the main road. She glanced at the dash to gauge the distance she'd driven, and it was right at ten miles, exactly how far the man had said she would come before reaching the front gate. Jake Coulter, the horse whisperer, couldn't be more than a few minutes away. Before she knew it, she'd be handing Sunset over to a Robert Redford look-alike, and her part in this crazy rescue mission would be finished.

As if to express his displeasure with the delay, Sonora Sunset shrieked again, making the trailer rock from side to side and end to end. The bucking motion of the Toyota brought Molly's teeth together in a grind of frustration. Little wonder she was exhausted. She'd been trying to drive the equivalent of a mechanical bull all morning.

She let her foot off the brake and allowed the vehicle to roll forward. *No worries.* After all the near misses she'd had on Interstate 5 this morning, navigating a deserted country road should seem easy.

Narrowly missing yet another rut, she executed a sharp curve and spotted an arched entrance up ahead. Made of freshly peeled logs, it fit the description of the gate that the farmer had given her. As she drew closer, Molly could see the name Lazy J on the crossbeam, the letters bracketed by old horseshoes.

Thank God. She'd finally found Robert Redford.

She swung wide to make the turn onto the rutted dirt road. As she nosed the vehicle through the open gate, she heard the muted sound of a motor and leaned her head out the lowered car window to follow the noise. The road forked up ahead. The last thing she wanted was to go the wrong way and run into a dead end. Backing up a trailer wasn't as easy as it looked.

Sunset didn't like the rougher road surface and lodged a loud complaint. *Just a few more minutes, boy.* They were almost there. According to the Portland trainer, if anyone could help this stallion, Jake Coulter could.

Ker-whump. Molly's teeth snapped together as the Toyota bumped over another deep hole. Dust billowed from under the front tires and hit her squarely in the face. She coughed and squinted. Why would anyone in his right mind choose to live out here? Jake Coulter might be a genius with horses, but he was otherwise sorely lacking in brains.

The road suddenly began a steep ascent that made the Toyota's engine lug under the heavy load. Molly tromped the gas. The engine coughed, and the Toyota lurched. She struggled with the floor shift to grab four-wheel low, breathing a sigh of relief when the SUV labored up the last few feet of hill and the overtaxed engine didn't die.

At the top of the incline, she braked to stare at the little valley below. It seemed to have appeared out of nowhere, a lush oasis at the edge of a desert. Broad expanses of shimmering green grass cut swaths through stands of tall pine, and a sparkling stream ribboned its way from one tip of the valley to the other. Off to the right, she saw a sprawling log home with a green metal roof and two rock chimneys, its rustic design perfectly suited to the forest around it. Maybe Jake Coulter wasn't so dumb after all. *What a gorgeous place.*

The road cut right between the house and a green metal pole building she guessed was a stable. Wide doorways along the back opened onto paddocks, which in turn had gates that led to green pastures fenced with split rails. She saw several horses grazing, the sight so picturesque that the ache of worry in her chest eased. It was a perfect place to leave Sonora Sunset.

Her faith in Hollywood films was restored. All that remained to make the scene complete was for Robert Redford to appear. Though she knew it was foolish, Molly watched for him as she drove the remaining way to the house. After passing the stable, she parked near a corral so she wouldn't block traffic. Then she cut the Toyota engine, pushed at the strands of hair that kept falling over her eyes, and went limp with relief.

She'd done it. Sonora Sunset was safely delivered to the horse psychologist.

As she climbed from the vehicle, the breeze felt lovely against her hot skin, carrying with it the country essence of pine, grass, wildflowers, and a faintly pungent odor she suspected was horse manure. Oddly, the last didn't strike her as being unpleasant, merely earthy, which seemed fitting.

The shade cast by the tall pines and the close proximity of the creek made the temperature at least ten degrees lower here than out on the road. *Horse paradise*. It was so peaceful that she wouldn't have minded staying there herself. For the first time since leaving Portland that morning, she felt safe.

The feeling was short-lived. She jumped with a start when the engine she'd heard earlier roared to life again. Turning, she saw a man off to one side of the house in a stand of tall trees. He was wielding a chainsaw with fluid precision, cutting up a fallen pine. She got a vague impression of tousled sable hair and dark features. Then her gaze dropped, and for the life of her, she couldn't force it back up to his face.

Stripped to the waist, his bare upper torso rippled in a glorious display of rugged strength. Muscle bunched and flattened as he moved, his sun-bronzed skin glistening with sweat. Molly wasn't usually given to gaping at people—she didn't care to be stared at and felt it was rude—but good manners momentarily abandoned her.

He was *beautiful*.

It was an inappropriate description for a man, she knew, but it was the only word that came to mind. His broad shoulders and back angled in a classic wedge to a lean waist, the furrow of his spine forming a shadowy line down to the top of his jeans. Faded denim sheathed powerfully roped legs that seemed to stretch forever. His body was as sculpted and perfect as a carving in seasoned oak. Just looking at him aroused everything within her that was feminine.

The reaction surprised her. Since her divorce, she had sworn off men. Some women enjoyed the game. Others could never quite grasp the rules. She'd learned from hard experience that she fell into the latter category.

As if he sensed her presence, the man suddenly turned to look over his shoulder. When he spotted her, he went stock-still. Even at a distance, his eyes were as blue and searing as laser beams.

A wave of self-consciousness crashed over Molly, and she wished she'd taken the time to dress for a trip to the country. First impressions were important, and Sonora Sunset's life hung in the balance. Her comfortable wedge heels—practical, go-anywhere shoes in the city—were frivolous and inappropriate for this type of terrain. She brushed at her slacks. Beneath her palms, she felt the network of creases her sweaty body had steam-pressed into the twill. There was nothing more unflattering to fat thighs than wrinkled khaki.

The man shifted his gaze to her trendy SUV, then to the huge horse trailer. Over here in this land of macho four-wheel-drive trucks, a Toyota pulling a two-stall trailer clearly wasn't a common sight. An expression of incredulity crossed his dark face.

That made them even. She'd been expecting Robert Redford, and instead she'd got *"I'm too sexy for my shirt."*

Molly assured herself that he couldn't possibly be the ranch owner. Men that young and good-looking were far too preoccupied with flexing their biceps to successfully operate a business.

Using one powerfully muscled arm, he swung up the saw to turn off its engine. After laying the wicked-looking piece of equipment beside the log, he grabbed a dark-brown Stetson and a blue chambray shirt from a nearby stump.

As he walked toward her, he carefully dusted off the hat and put it on, tipping the brim just so to shade his eyes. That struck her as odd. If she were nude to the waist, she'd throw on the shirt first and worry about her head later.

The well-oiled swing of his hips measured off slow, lazy strides that covered an amazing amount of ground with an economy of effort. With every movement, his large silver belt buckle winked at her in the sunlight. She stared at the triangular furring of dark hair that bisected his flat, striated abdomen and narrowed to a dusky line just above his jeans.

As he drew up a few feet away from her, he gave the shirt a hard shake to rid it of sawdust, then shoved one arm down a sleeve. His chest muscles rippled with each movement. Tanned deliciously dark, his skin put her in mind of melted caramel.

"Howdy," he said, his deep, silky voice curling around her like tendrils of warm smoke. "How can I help you?"

He could start by getting his buttons fastened. Her tongue was stuck to her teeth. "I, um . . . I'm looking for Jake Coulter."

He brushed wood chips from the rolled-back sleeves of his shirt. "You've found him. What can I do for you?"

He couldn't *be Jake Coulter,* she thought stupidly. He looked nothing like Robert Redford.

The sheer idiocy of that thought jerked Molly up short. Naturally he looked nothing like Redford. It was just that he was so *young.* Not that she'd ever met any horse whisperers to know how old most of them were. It just seemed to her that they should be fifty or better, with lots of experience under their belts. She guessed this man to be in his early thirties, only a couple of years her senior.

He searched her gaze, his eyes a blaze of azure that looked too deep and saw too much. Molly groped for her composure.

"Is something wrong?" he asked.

Everything was wrong, the man, the situation, *everything*. "No, nothing. You just aren't what I expected."

His wide, firm mouth twitched at one corner as if he were biting back a smile. "Sounds like you've got an· unhappy traveler on your hands."

"Very unhappy." Molly rubbed her damp palms on her slacks. "I, um— I'm Molly Ster—" She caught herself and gulped. If Rodney had the police combing the state to find her, she didn't dare give her real name. "I'm Molly Houston." Where the name Houston had come from, she had no clue. Unless it was because she wished she were in Texas right then. She pressed a hand to her waist. "I—um—"

Um? It was one of her favorite words when she grew tense. At least he was buttoning his shirt. That was good.

Sonora Sunset chose that moment to whinny and kick the doors of the trailer. Molly jumped. Jake Coulter slowly shifted his gaze to the source of the noise. He gave the impression it would take a dynamite detonation to startle him.

When her heart settled back into her chest, Molly swallowed and tried again. "As you can see, I've got horse problems."

He nodded, his eyes filling with questions. "Looks that way."

"A trainer in Port—" She caught herself and cut the word short. The less he knew about her, the better. "A trainer in southern Oregon told me you're a horse whisperer."

His mouth did tip into a smile then—a slow, bone-melting grin that made her insides feel funny.

"I'm sorry," he said. "If it's a horse whisperer you're looking for, I'm not your man. I don't even believe such a thing exists."

Right in the middle of a flutter, her stomach dropped. She'd risked life and limb to get Sonora Sunset here. "But the trainer seemed so *sure* you could help me."

He glanced at the Toyota. His attention came to rest on her hurriedly packed belongings in the backseat and cargo area. A slight frown pleated his thick, sable brows. "I didn't say I couldn't help you, just that I'm no horse whisperer. What seems to be the problem?"

Given the ruckus Sunset was raising, Molly wondered why he would ask. "He, um . . ." She lifted her hands. "He goes berserk when anyone tries to get near him."

Jake Coulter cocked an eyebrow and said, "Ah."

Ah? That didn't strike her as being a suitable response from a man who was supposedly such an expert. "Can you work with a stallion that's to-tally uncooperative, Mr. Coulter?"

"Could be. Depends on the horse."

Oh, God, she was tired. Down to the bone tired. She wanted him to reassure her and say he'd fix everything. Instead he just stood there, studying her thoughtfully. It was the horse that needed help, not her.

"The trainer says he's dangerous," she went on, "that if something isn't done, he may have to be destroyed."

"How long has he been acting up?" He swung up onto the wheel well with the ease of a man familiar with horse trailers and the gigantic, four-legged critters hauled in them. As he looked in at Sunset through the side slats, he asked, "Did this just start or—?"

Sunset shrieked and lunged so sharply away that the conveyance pitched sideways. Coulter grabbed for handholds to keep his footing.

"Holy hell." He directed a smoldering glance at Molly. "Lady, this ani-mal has been whipped."

She wrapped her arms around her waist. "I realize that. I didn't do it, if that's what you're thinking."

"Who did?"

She groped frantically for a safe answer to that question. When one didn't come to mind, she settled for telling the truth. "My ex-husband."

"He should be horsewhipped himself."

Molly thought running Rodney's male pride through a laundry press sounded more satisfying. "This isn't the first time it's happened. It was just never so bad before."

"Lord Almighty, I've seen some mistreated animals in my day, but never anything like this. How could you allow it?"

Molly bristled. "I didn't *allow* it. I had no idea it was happening."

"Your ex has been whipping your horse, and you didn't know it was happening? If this animal is yours, why didn't the trainer notify you?"

She thought quickly. "There were never any marks on Sunset before."

"Even so, the horse must have acted up afterward."

Until this morning, Molly had observed Sunset only from a safe dis-tance. "I never noticed him behaving strangely, and if the trainer did, he never said anything."

He mulled that over for a moment. His gaze still sharp on hers, he fi-nally jumped down from the wheel well. "Does this horse even belong to you, lady?" he asked with lethal softness.

Molly was afraid he'd tell her to hit the road if she admitted the truth.

Without his help, Sunset could end up at a glue factory. "Of course he belongs to me. How would I have brought him here otherwise?"

"Good question." The frown creases between his dark brows deepened as he regarded her. "Do you have papers to verify ownership?"

"Papers? Oh, dear. I totally forgot to bring them."

"He looks like a very expensive animal. If he should injure himself while I'm trying to work with him, I could get my ass sued off."

"I'll sign a waiver," she offered, "absolving you of all liability."

"A waiver wouldn't be worth the paper it's written on if you don't own the horse." He rubbed his jaw, his eyes darkening as he searched hers. Then he cut another glance at the trailer and swore under his breath. "I can't afford a bunch of lawyer fees right now."

He was about to send them packing. She just knew it. Molly listened to Sunset's panicked grunts, and her heart nearly broke for him. She couldn't take him back to Portland and let people who cared nothing about him decide his fate. There was also the very real possibility that Rodney might hurt him again. "I just told you I own the horse, Mr. Coulter. Are you accusing me of lying?"

His jaw muscle bunched, and for what seemed an eternity, they engaged in a visual standoff. She held up her hands in supplication. "Do I look like a horse thief?"

She couldn't read his expression, and her nerves screamed as she waited for him to answer. He glanced at the stuff in the back of her Toyota again.

"No," he finally admitted in a gravelly voice, his mobile mouth tipping into a sheepish grin even as he sighed in defeat. "All right. Let's have a look at the poor fellow." He turned toward her vehicle, suddenly all business. "Are your keys in the ignition?"

Before she could answer he was in the Toyota and cranking the engine. She stepped out of the way as he jockeyed the SUV to get the trailer lined up with the gate. He made backing a trailer look so easy she wondered why she found it so difficult.

"You aren't going to turn him loose, are you?" she asked as he climbed back out of the 4Runner.

He was so tall that he'd mashed the top of his Stetson on the roof of her car. "To get a feel for the horse, I have to unload him."

"If you decide you can't work with him, will you be able to put him back? He's being very difficult. This morning it took the trainer and three stable employees to get him up the ramp."

He drew off his hat to reshape the crown, then settled it back on his head. "I think I can manage. If need be, I'll get my brother Hank to help. He's off in the north section, but I can call him in by radio."

Molly closed her eyes in dread as he opened the trailer doors and extended the ramp. She heard his boots thumping on the wood. Then he said, "Easy, boy, easy."

Sunset whinnied and, judging by the noises that followed, started kicking for all he was worth. Molly opened her eyes partway, half expecting to see Jake Coulter come flying out the back end of the conveyance.

"Easy, boy," she heard him say again.

A second later, she glimpsed Sunset's hindquarters. The stallion nearly danced off the ramp, but somehow Coulter managed to get him going in the right direction again. The thunderous tattoo of hooves on wood made Molly hug her waist and clench her teeth.

Sunset had nearly killed his trainer this morning. She had neglected to tell Jake Coulter that for fear he might refuse to work with the horse. Now she wished with all her heart that she'd been honest.

If the fool man got hurt, it would be entirely her fault.

✄ CHAPTER TWO ✄

As it turned out, Jake Coulter proved to be perfectly capable of handling the stallion by himself. When Sunset tried to rear and strike with his front hooves, the well-muscled rancher foiled the attempt, holding fast to the animal's halter and using his weight to keep him from throwing his head. In a flurry of sound and motion, man and beast spilled down the ramp into the corral.

Coulter was incredibly fast on his feet. When he released the horse, he made for the fence with such speed that all Molly saw was a blur. She released a breath she hadn't realized she'd been holding as he vaulted over the barrier, hat still perched jauntily on his head.

He blotted sweat from his brow with the cuff of his sleeve. "Boy, howdy, you're right. He's a handful."

A handful? A two-year-old child was a handful. The horse whinnied and circled the corral. His hooves kicked up clouds of dust that burned Molly's nostrils. Still hugging her waist, she made tight fists on her white cotton blouse. She'd seen Sunset in action this morning and was afraid he might jump the fence.

Coulter didn't seem worried. He shoved up the trailer ramp and drew the corral gate closed. After securing the latch, he rested his folded arms on a fence rail to observe the horse's behavior. At least that was what Molly guessed he was doing. It put her in mind of the way doctors observed patients after they were admitted to a psychiatric ward, a close scrutiny that stripped away layers and missed nothing.

A thick, suffocating feeling came into her throat. She watched Sunset circling the corral, so sad for him that her bones ached. Maybe horses didn't feel the same way people did about having their privacy invaded.

The shift of his shoulders snapping the chambray taut across his chest, Jake began tucking in his shirt with hard stabs of his fingers. Watching him, Molly got a bad feeling. Her trepidation increased when he jumped up to straddle the fence. "Mr. Coulter?"

If he heard, he gave no indication of it. His gaze was riveted on the horse. Molly stared up at his profile, noting the determined set of his jaw. In the sunlight, his bottom lip shimmered like silk, the only hint of softness in a face that might otherwise have been chiseled from granite.

"Mr. Coulter, you aren't thinking about going in there again, are you?"

He flicked her a look. "How else can I decide if I can work with him?"

"But, Mr. Coulter, he's dangerous."

"A thousand pounds of horse with an attitude problem is most always dangerous. That's what keeps me in business."

"At least get something to defend yourself."

"What do you suggest, a club?" He braced his hands on the rail to lift up and get more comfortable. After watching Sunset for a few seconds more, he shook his head. "If I have something in my hands, he'll think I mean to beat him with it."

"I really wish you'd reconsider," she said shakily as he swung his other leg over the rail. "He almost killed his trainer this morning."

If that gave him pause, he concealed it well. He glanced down, his blue eyes twinkling. "Don't worry, I won't get hurt."

Molly clung to the fence rail, watching helplessly as he lowered himself into the enclosure. Sunset reared and pierced the air with a frantic whinny that held a note of warning.

"Whoa, boy." Coulter set his dusty boots wide apart, his legs slightly bent, the flex of muscle in his thighs visible under the denim of his jeans. "No point in getting worked up."

Sunset was having none of that, not that Molly blamed him. Coulter looked formidable—strong, lightning quick, and prepared for anything. Not even a huge, swift animal like the stallion could hope to escape such an adversary within the confines of a small corral.

Molly knew how it felt to be cornered and helpless. The quivering terror and underlying outrage, the claustrophobic panic that made it nearly impossible to breathe. Oh, yes, she knew.

Sunset wheeled and ran to the opposite end of the corral, then turned to face his tormentor. The whites of his eyes formed crescents over his irises. The muscles in his shoulders quivered with terror.

"You poor, miserable thing." Jake held out his hands so the horse could see they were empty. Tendons and distended veins roped his bronze forearms. "See there? Nothing to be afraid of."

Sunset stood on his rear legs. He screamed wildly and struck at the air, forelegs churning, hooves flashing. When he came down on all fours, his feet hit the earth with such force that Molly could have sworn she felt the vibration.

"Easy." The man was so focused on the horse now that Molly suspected he'd forgotten she was there. "Easy, boy. You're in no shape for this."

Arms still held wide, his lean body tensed to spring if the stallion charged at him, the rancher held his ground while Sunset cut circles around him. He turned to keep an eye on the animal at all times, but beyond that, he didn't move, expending little energy while Sunset exhausted himself.

"You see? I'm not going to hurt you," he said in that same low voice.

Molly dug her nails into her palms and bit down hard on the inside of her cheek, wishing with all her heart that Sunset would stop fighting the inevitable. Why couldn't he understand that Coulter was only trying to help him? Sometimes those who seemed to be your worst enemies in the beginning turned out to be your best friends. Molly had learned that the hard way. Unfortunately, there was no way to impart that bit of wisdom to the horse. He would have to find it out for himself—just as she had.

The horse continued to dart back and forth until he was blowing and stumbling with weariness. His sides looked as if they'd been flecked with shaving cream.

She was dripping with sweat herself by the time the stallion succumbed to exhaustion. Hands locked on the fence, she stared at the horse through a blur of scalding tears. He stood with his rump pressed into a corner of the corral, great head hanging, sides heaving. He was so winded that he looked ready to drop.

She prayed the worst was over, but instead of leaving the corral, Coulter turned slightly sideways to the stallion and bent his head. Keeping his gaze fixed on the ground, he made a slow approach. The horse watched warily but didn't offer to move until the rancher got about five feet from him. Then Sunset grunted and stumbled sideways.

Coulter stopped there. Bewildered, Molly watched him mark the spot with the heel of his boot. Then he backed away, only to approach the line again and again until Sunset showed no reaction whatsoever. Only then did the rancher seem satisfied.

"Good boy," he said, his voice as smooth as warm honey. "We'll get there. But that's enough for today."

He vaulted back over the fence. "I'm sorry about that," he told Molly. "I know it's not easy, letting a stranger do that to your horse."

"What purpose did it serve? You never got close enough to touch him."

Resting an arm on the fence rail, he crossed his booted feet. The breeze kicked back up, molding his light blue shirt to his torso. "It's enough that he knows I could have. On some level, he understands now that I don't mean him any harm." His firm mouth tipped in a grin. "And I learned the same about him."

"You did?"

He nodded. "He's a big old boy and fast as greased lightning. If he had a mean streak, instead of cutting circles around me, he could have tried to run me down. The horse isn't vicious, just damn scared, and who can blame him?"

He walked over to a faucet at the north corner of the corral and began filling a five-gallon bucket. Observing him through the rails, Molly asked, "Does that mean you'll try to help him?"

Instead of answering, he bent to shove the bucket under the fence and then backed away. Sunset eyed him warily. Then he stumbled wearily toward the water. When the horse almost reached the bucket, Jake stepped forward to snatch it away.

Molly clenched her teeth. She watched with growing anger as Jake repeated the process again and again, never allowing the poor horse to drink.

When she could bear it no longer, she cried, "Why are you doing that?"

He flashed her a deadpan look.

"You know he's dying for a drink. Tormenting him that way is cruel."

He moved to the east corner of the corral to slide the bucket under the fence again. "You can't let an overheated horse drink his fill." Once again, he waited until Sunset almost reached the water, then he quickly retrieved the bucket. "When horses get this hot, you have to walk them. Normally I'd lead him around for five minutes and then allow him to have a little water before walking him another five. Since I can't put him on a lead, I'm getting him to move the only way I can."

Molly jerked her gaze back to Sunset. In the heat of the afternoon sunlight, rivers of sweat had begun to crystallize on his lather-flecked black coat. "Oh," she said weakly.

"I'll let him have a little to drink here in another minute." He put the bucket inside the corral again and stepped away so the horse would approach. "Only enough to wet his whistle, though. Then I'll walk him some more. You keep doing that until the horse no longer seems eager to drink. It should be safe then to let him have all the water he wants." He moved forward to reclaim the bucket. "If I let him load up right now, he'll founder or colic. Nine times out of ten, that kills them."

Molly felt foolish, and she hadn't the faintest notion what to say.

A couple of minutes later, Jake finally allowed Sunset to have a bit of water. Then he lured the stallion around the corral again. Molly noticed now that he was checking his watch. When the horse had cooled down, he refilled the bucket and left it inside the corral. He looked thoughtful as he moved to rejoin Molly.

"It appears to me you don't know a hell of a lot about horses," he said conversationally as he rested his arms on a rail. "Can you explain that to me?"

"Just because I've never seen anyone cool a horse off in precisely that way doesn't mean I'm totally ignorant about them." Afraid she might appear tense, she lowered her arms from around her waist. They felt like lengths of stiff hose bracketing her body. "In town, most people board their horses and pay someone for the everyday care." That much wasn't a lie. Rodney and his Yuppie friends boarded their horses, and she knew they seldom did any actual work. "I hired a trainer and was never directly involved in Sunset's daily routine."

In the sunlight, she could see the squint lines that fanned out from the corners of his eyes. His thick, dark lashes cast feathery shadows onto his lean cheeks. "Are you familiar at all with farms and ranches?"

"Farms and ranches?" She sensed her answer was important and that, for reasons beyond her, Jake Coulter might refuse to work with Sunset if her ranch experience was limited. "I've been around them all my life." She thought of the countless times she'd driven past farms and ranches on her way into Portland. That qualified. She'd been around them, right? "Why do you ask?"

He glanced at her wrinkled blouse and slacks. "I'm just trying to get a handle on how much practical experience you have with horses."

Zilch. "I'm no expert, as I said, but I've got enough experience to get by." The trick was in avoiding the beasts entirely, an endeavor she'd been totally successful at until today. "I fall somewhere between beginner and intermediate."

The corners of his mouth twitched. "I see."

Molly was beginning to worry that he really did see, which wouldn't do at all. "Sunset's life is on the line. Without your help, I'm afraid he'll be destroyed."

His gaze moved past her to settle on the Toyota. "It's apparent you need help."

"Well, then? My experience with horses isn't the issue."

"I didn't say it was. It's just that in training like this, owner participation makes all the difference."

"Owner what?"

"Owner participation. I know it may seem like a lot to ask, but one thing I insist upon is that the owners come out to work with their horses several times a week."

Molly felt as if the ground disappeared from under her. She threw an appalled look at the stallion.

Jake raised his dark eyebrows. "Is that a problem? It won't be much help to you if the horse will respond only to me."

For some reason, Molly had likened this situation to dropping her car off with a mechanic. She'd planned to simply leave Sunset here, then come back to pick him up when he was all fixed. "You expect me to— to go *in* there with him?"

"It's a little hard to work with a horse from this side of the fence."

She recalled her vow not to be a quitter this time. But, *oh, God,* she'd never bargained for this.

"I'll take every precaution to make sure you're safe," he assured her. "And I'll always be close at hand in case anything goes wrong. Does that ease your mind any?"

Only marginally. "I, um . . . I live quite a distance away, Mr. Coulter. Driving that far several times a week will be impossible for me."

He glanced at her Toyota again. "Looks to me like you're living out of the back of your car at the moment." He rested his weight more heavily on the fence rail. "It also looks to me like you packed in an all-fired hurry."

She couldn't very well deny the evidence he could see with his own eyes. "I'm sort of—relocating."

"So the distance you'll have to drive won't necessarily be a problem. You can light somewhere nearby."

Her throat had gone so dry that her larynx felt as if it was moving up and down inside a tube of sandpaper. "I suppose that's possible."

He turned to face her, all trace of humor vanishing from his gaze. "That being the case, your working with the horse on a regular basis shouldn't be a problem."

Her courage deserted her, and she almost sold Sunset down the river by blurting out the truth. Just as she parted her lips to speak, she glanced at Sunset. In the slanting sunlight, the blood that beaded his wounds glistened like rubies against black velvet.

Guilt was such a terrible thing, plaguing you every waking moment and then following you into your dreams. Molly remembered the countless nights she'd paced the floors, unable to sleep. Twice in her life, she'd failed people she loved, and they'd both ended up dead. She truly didn't know if she could live with another death on her conscience, even if Sunset was only a horse.

"No, working with him shouldn't be a problem," she said shakily.

"Good." Coulter straightened away from the fence. "I couldn't help but notice that your rig is riding on empty. Can I take that to mean you're short on cash?"

Molly straightened her shoulders. "I'm sorry, but I can't see how my finances are any of your business, Mr. Coulter."

"They'll become my business quick enough when I'm looking to get paid and you don't have the money."

"How much do you charge?"

"Five hundred a week. That covers everything, not just the training, but boarding the horse as well, which can be expensive when you tally up stable wages and feed."

Molly's heart sank. "That seems a little steep."

"You said it best. Horses like that are dangerous, and not just anyone will work with them. I'm damned good at what I do. My services don't come cheap."

"I'm sure you're worth every cent. I don't mean to imply that you aren't." She rubbed her arms, feeling suddenly cold despite the warmth of the day. "How long do you estimate that it may take to get Sunset calmed down?"

"Could take as little as a month, or it may take six. It's impossible to predict. Some horses don't respond at all."

"Oh, *my*."

"I have a good success rate. Most of the time, a horse will hook on with me, but it's always a gamble. Regardless of the outcome, my fee is the same. I can't see my way clear to work for nothing simply because a horse proves to be beyond help."

Molly didn't blame him for that. He couldn't run a ranch successfully on charity. "Actually, Mr. Coulter, five hundred a week will put me in a bit of a pinch. Would it be possible to work out some kind of payment plan?"

He rubbed his jaw. "I hate to sound mercenary, particularly when an animal has been so cruelly abused, but I can't take any jobs on credit right now. Like I mentioned before, I'm just getting this place on its feet. Things are really tight, and I need to see my money up front. I've got only so many hours a day to devote to horse training, and right now, that's paying my bank loans."

Molly had gone to an ATM before leaving Portland, but the machine had stopped spitting cash after the daily limit, giving her a thousand in her wallet, all totaled. She'd spent some of that on gas to get here. She had another eight hundred in checking, the only account available to her right now, but she didn't dare touch it. All bank and ATM transactions could be traced.

If she gave Jake Coulter a small deposit, she might have enough money left over to survive until she found a job, but there was no way she could afford to cough up five hundred dollars a week. Not unless she meant to sleep in her car and scavenge for food until she found work. *If* she found work. Most employers asked to see an applicant's identification, wanted a list of references, and needed a social security number on file. Just in case the police had an APB out on her, she didn't dare give out that information.

Her head was starting to ache, whether from tension or lack of nourishment, she wasn't sure. Not that it mattered. Pain was pain, and this particular brand was whipping her thoughts into a jumble with the brutal efficiency of a wire whisk.

"Well . . . that pretty much throws a wrench in the fan blades, I guess."

"I accept credit cards," he offered.

That was no help. Crazy, legally incompetent women weren't allowed to carry plastic. Oh, how Molly despised Rodney Wells in that moment. "I'm afraid I don't have a credit card."

He drew off his hat to rake his fingers through his hair, leaving thick furrows in the glistening strands of brown. After staring at the ground for a long moment, he gouged the dirt with his boot heel.

Molly could see that he was trying to think of a way he might help her. As much as she appreciated his concern, she could think of no way around the money problem and doubted he would, either. Her heart twisting painfully, she kept her gaze carefully averted from Sunset, afraid she might embarrass herself with tears if she let herself contemplate what might be in store for him.

"It looks as if I've troubled you for nothing," she said, forcing out the words around a lump in her throat that seemed to grow larger by the second. "Thank you for—"

He held up a staying hand, cutting her off in midsentence. When his gaze met hers, she saw that the twinkle of amusement had returned to his eyes, only this time she had the impression that he was laughing at himself and not her. "Can I be totally frank with you?"

Molly had a feeling he was about to speak his mind whether she gave him her leave or not. "Certainly."

"I love horses, and I instinctively like you." His voice dipped to a husky timbre. "I'm not sure I'll be able to sleep at night if I turn the two of you away." He hooked a thumb toward her rig. "I have a real bad feeling you're out of work, out of luck, and almost out of money. Am I right about that?"

Molly tried to smile and failed miserably. "That pretty much covers it."

"Do you even have anywhere to stay?"

A flush of shame moved up her neck. Now she knew how homeless people must feel. "Not at present. I'll stay at a motel until I find a job, I guess."

"With a horse in a trailer? You can't keep that stallion locked up indefinitely."

Molly hadn't thought that far ahead yet. She'd left Portland this morning with only one thought driving her, to deliver Sunset to this man.

Thinking quickly, she said, "Maybe I can pasture him somewhere."

"You can't pasture a horse like that just anywhere. He could kill somebody."

She hugged her waist and shifted her feet, trying frantically to think. It was true; Sunset was dangerous, and pasturing him somewhere wouldn't be safe. Only someone like Jake Coulter could deal with a horse that difficult, and the man charged more than she could possibly afford.

She thought of the fortune that her father had left her. All that money, sitting in the bank, and she couldn't get her hands on a single cent of it. *Oh, God . . . oh, God.* Without Coulter's help, Sunset might be destroyed, and she'd be powerless to prevent it.

She couldn't say why she cared so deeply about a horse. She only knew she felt an affinity with the stallion that defied all reason. Maybe her feelings stemmed from the fact that they'd both been nearly destroyed by the same man, albeit in different ways. If she failed to save the horse, would she be able to save herself?

Struggling to hide how devastated she felt, she thrust out her hand to Jake Coulter and forced a smile so stiff it almost hurt her face. "I'll manage somehow. Thank you, Mr. Coulter. If you'll reload Sunset, we'll be on our way. You've been very kind, taking time out of your busy schedule without so much as a phone call in advance. It's time I let you get back to your work."

He took her hand, his long, work-roughened fingers curling warmly over her wrist. He said nothing, just looked at her. Then he smiled slowly. "Can you cook and do housework?"

That was the last thing she had expected him to say. "Can I what?"

His smile deepened. "I've had an ad in the paper for over a month with little response. If you're willing to work, maybe we can strike a bargain."

He still held tightly to her hand. His grip didn't hurt, but she had a feeling it would be as impossible to escape as a manacle. The pain in her temples sharpened, the sun stabbing her eyes like a pick.

"You want me to be a ranch cook and housekeeper?" She might have laughed, but she was afraid the top of her head might blow off.

"It seems like a perfect solution to me. You're down on your luck, your horse needs help, and I'm in sore need of a cook."

His perfect solution was her worst nightmare. She could cook well enough to suit herself, but she was easy to please. Few men were so accommodating. On top of that, it was a risky thing to do. This ranch was miles from town, and Jake Coulter was a total stranger.

"Cooking really isn't my forte. I can't possibly do it for a wage."

"Sure you can." He winked at her. "Any woman who pulled a horse trailer over the Cascades with that glorified roller skate can do damn near anything she sets her mind to."

He made the idea sound so *reasonable*. And, oh, how tempting it was. She might at least buy Sunset some time. If the horse responded quickly, as little as a few days might mean the difference between life and death for him. "It's a very generous offer."

"Then say yes," he urged. "What have you got to lose? Private quarters come with the job." He hooked a thumb over his shoulder at a small log house farther down the creek. "It isn't fancy, but the roof doesn't leak and it's halfway clean. Just a small two-bedroom. I pay four hundred a week, plus board. I usually offer a fairly decent benefits package, but if you'd rather be paid under the table, that's doable as well."

Under the table? That meant she wouldn't have to give him a social security number. It also meant more money because no taxes would be taken from her wages.

"Come on," he cajoled. "This is the only way I can offset the costs to help you."

"Sixteen hundred a month doesn't quite cover your training fees," she pointed out.

"If you're an employee, I can give you a break on my rates. To make up the extra, you can do outside chores. I'm always shorthanded in the stable."

He expected her to work in the stable? Molly remembered telling him she'd been around farms and ranches all her life. He clearly believed she'd be far more useful than she actually would be.

"I'm not very experienced at working in stables."

His eyes warmed on hers. "Somewhere between beginner and intermediate? Don't worry. I'll show you what needs to be done."

• He had an answer for everything. She stared wistfully at the little log house. It looked so peaceful, a sanctuary along the stream with a forest at its back. This ranch was tucked away from the world. Even from out on the road, it was invisible. If the police were looking for her, what were the chances that they'd ever find her here?

"We can do it on a thirty-day trial," he offered. "If either of us is unhappy with the arrangement at the end of that time, we can back out, no questions asked. How does that sound?"

It sounded marvelous, like the answer to a prayer. She turned a gaze toward Sunset, feeling numb all over and oddly disconnected from reality. *When the going got rough, the new Molly Sterling Wells got going.* The stallion's life was at stake. If she had cookbooks at her disposal, she might be able to get by for a while in the kitchen, and cleaning was a no-brainer. Didn't a day that had begun so crazily beg for a crowning insanity as its finale?

"Don't think it to death," he advised. "Some of life's best decisions are made on the spur of the moment."

"Eventually, if I can work out some wrinkles, I'll be returning to my job. I'm on a leave of absence of sorts." Sunlight stabbed into her eyes again, blurring his face to little more than a dark silhouette with white spots dancing over his features. "Did I mention that?"

"Not a problem. If you'll agree to give me a month's notice before you quit, I'll have time to find a replacement." He grimaced. "Hopefully I'll have better luck with my ad next time around."

Molly felt as if she were about to take a flying leap off a cliff. *Courage.* Maybe he was right, and she was thinking it to death. Being too hesitant had always been one of her downfalls. *"Life is what's happening while you're trying to decide what to do,"* her father had laughingly told her more times than she could count. This man was offering her a way out, not only a job but a place to live, with lodging and feed for Sunset tossed into the bargain.

"All right," she said a little breathlessly. "I'll give it a try. Why not?"

A slow grin creased his dark face. "We have a deal then?"

"Yes, we have a deal."

His smile broadened. "Welcome to the Lazy J, Molly Stir-Houston."

❦ CHAPTER THREE ❦

Once Molly accepted Jake Coulter's offer, she got no opportunity to change her mind. Though the man's fastest speed seemed to be a saunter, he covered ground with amazing dispatch, forcing her to step fast to keep up with him. Before she knew quite how it happened, he'd parked her Toyota in front of the small log cabin along the creek and set himself to the task of unloading her belongings. As Molly scurried back and forth carrying bags, her earlier misgivings came back to haunt her, and one question circled endlessly in her thoughts. *Have I lost my mind?*

Savvy women didn't trust strange men. One had only to read the newspaper headlines to understand how foolhardy it was. Now that she was out of the sun, the pain in her head had eased a bit, enabling her to think more clearly. With clarity came a host of concerns. How could she be sure Jake Coulter wasn't a sex offender or serial killer? If she vanished, no one would think to look for her on a cattle ranch in central Oregon.

As if he sensed her nervousness, Jake didn't enter the bedroom with her when he showed her through the house. Instead he stood in the doorway, blocking the only exit with his considerable bulk. *Wonderful.* The man weighed well over two hundred pounds, every inch of him honed to a steely hardness. If he meant her harm, she would have a devil of a time getting past him.

"Are you okay?" he asked, jerking her away from her troubled musings.

Molly blinked and focused on his dark face, studiously ignoring the impressive span of his shoulders. "I'm fine," she assured him, wanting to cringe when her voice came out thin and tremulous. "A bit of a headache is all."

Feeling stiff and graceless, she turned to take in the room, which was small and held only the essential furnishings. She bent to test the mattress. "What a lovely brass bedstead. Have you any idea what they go for now?"

Stir-Houston? Molly's stomach felt as if it had dropped to the region of her knees. She recalled how she'd nearly blurted out her real last name when she first got here. He had caught the slip, and now he was teasing her about it. That could mean only one thing. He knew she had given him a fake surname.

If he had guessed that much, how much more did he suspect?

He shifted to brace a muscular shoulder against the doorframe, the crown of his brown Stetson brushing against the crossbeam. "More than they're worth?"

Molly gave a startled laugh. Having haunted antiques stores with her adoptive mother Claudia for years, she had a keen appreciation for collectibles. The memories of those shopping expeditions stabbed her with sadness. Not only had she lost her father a year ago, but to all intents and purposes, she'd lost the only mother she'd ever known as well.

"Practically speaking, I suppose brass beds are a little overpriced."

He eyed the mattress. "I'm a nostalgia buff myself, but I draw the line when it interferes with comfort. People back then must have been midgets. When I slept on that sucker, my feet hung over the end, and my ankles banged on the foot rails all night."

Molly could believe it. Jake Coulter wasn't exactly of diminutive stature—a fact that seemed to have taken center stage in her thoughts now that she was alone in the cabin with him. When her therapist, Sam Banks, had encouraged her to let down her guard with men, she felt sure this wasn't the sort of thing he'd had in mind.

She patted the mattress. Then she remembered she'd already done that once and jerked her hand back. If this man was a sex offender, she didn't want to put ideas in his head. "I'm sure the length will do nicely enough for me. I'm not very tall."

His unnerving blue gaze took a leisurely journey from the tips of her toes to the top of her head. "No, I don't guess you are. If a good wind came up, you'd blow away."

"Hardly." Molly pressed a hand to her stomach. In her early twenties, her rail-thin lower body had filled out, adding an unattractive thickness to her waist and hips and eliciting comments from Rodney that she looked pregnant. Not even the safari shirt she wore hid the flaws. "I'm not what you'd call skinny."

His sable brows drew together as his gaze moved over her again. "Nope. More what I'd call pleasingly plump." He let that hang there, then flashed her a lopsided grin that did strange things to her pulse rate. "With the emphasis on 'pleasingly.' "

He turned away, leaving her to wonder what that meant. In her experience, kindly adults used the phrase "pleasingly plump" to describe chubby children. Not that she cared what he thought. She had long since accepted that her body was far from svelte, and no amount of dieting would change it.

She listened to the rhythmic thump of his boots on the old plank floor as he moved through the small house. Casting a glance toward the comfortable-looking bed, she made her weary body move. She found her new employer in the antiquated kitchen. He'd struck a match and was trying to light the pilot on the propane cooking range, once lime green but now yellowed with age. Never having used such an outdated appliance, she stepped closer to watch.

Just as she bent down to peer at the burner, the gas ignited and flame shot toward her face with a startling *ka-whoosh!* She squeaked and leaped away, slapping at her shirt and hair. "Blessed Mother!"

Jake caught her by the shoulders to hold her still. "Are you burned?" He moved a hand over her hair and shoulder. "Molly, answer me."

She clutched her throat and gulped, no longer entirely sure all the heat she felt was due to gas ignition. Everywhere his hand touched, her skin burned. *Red alert.* This man could be dangerous in more ways than one. "I'm fine. I'm sorry. Really, I'm fine." She tried to escape his grasp by wiggling away. "It just went off in my face and startled me. I don't think it actually burned me anywhere."

He gave her hair a final check. "I'm the one who's sorry. I should have warned you. These old gas stoves are bad for that. They even startle me sometimes."

He turned back to test the valves. This time, Molly stood well away, not entirely sure which she most wanted to avoid, the stove or the man. Rings of blue fire leaped to life, making her nerves leap as well. If she had to cook on that horrid old thing, she'd starve.

Apparently satisfied, he turned off the burners and patted the ugly green porcelain with long, sturdy fingers. "She seems to be in fine working order."

He turned on the sink faucets next. The first rush of water was a rusty brown, but it quickly cleared as the flow washed away the pipe sediment. He cupped a hand to collect some water, then bent to taste it. After wiping his mouth, he said, "You'll love the well here. It's artesian."

Molly's gaze was fixed on the old hand pump mounted at one side of the sink. She'd come across a few in antiques shops, but she'd never seen one in a house. "Does that still work?" she asked incredulously.

"Like a charm. When I modernized the kitchen, I was going to jerk it out, but my sister Bethany had a conniption fit." He primed the pump with some water from the faucet, then began working the handle. After only a few tries, water gushed from the spout. He stepped to one side. "Try some."

Taking care not to bump against him, Molly cupped both hands under the flow and bent to drink. Maybe she was only thirsty, but never had anything tasted so wonderful. She gulped greedily for a moment and then remembered he was using muscle power to keep up the flow. Embarrassed, she straightened away, wiping her chin. "I'm sorry. That's absolutely *divine*. It's like drinking from a crystal-clear mountain brook."

He stopped working the handle, his gaze falling to the droplets still on her bottom lip. Feeling self-conscious, she scrubbed her hand over her mouth.

The intense blue of his eyes darkened to a stormy blue gray. "No need to apologize. I don't mind pumping, and water's cheap."

"Not in—" Molly broke off, mentally waving her arms to keep from falling into that one. She'd nearly said water wasn't cheap in Portland. She glanced away, wishing, not for the first time, that she were a more practiced liar. "Not in my hometown."

His dark brows lifted. "What town is that?"

She thought of all the communities that lay along Interstate 5. "Grants Pass."

"Ah." He nodded. "Nice place. My college roommate grew up there."

"You went to college?"

He chuckled. "Us country boys need to have some kind of edge."

Molly had meant no offense. She was just surprised. Jake Coulter didn't have the air of any college man she'd ever known. In his Wranglers and blue chambray shirt, he seemed as earthy and elemental as the wilderness bordering his land, and he sometimes spoke with a lazy disregard for proper grammar. "Which university did you attend?"

"Oregon State. That's where a lot of us country boys go. My twin brothers attended the veterinary school there. My brother Zeke went for his MBA. Hank and I focused on ag and animal husbandry."

"Good grief, you've got *four* brothers?"

"And a sister. That's how I got ornery. I was the oldest of six, and the only way to survive was to get mean." He stepped around her to set the temperature controls inside the ancient refrigerator. "What's your alma mater?"

Another wave of memories washed through Molly, this one leaving her cold and feeling oddly empty. "I went to college only for a short time." That was the story of her life; big dreams, no staying power. "Things happened, and I dropped out."

He glanced over the top of the door at her. "Never would have guessed it. You talk like you've got an impressive education under your belt."

She flashed what she hoped was a bright smile. "I read a lot of books."

"A self-made woman, are you? What line of work?"

Her throat felt as if she'd swallowed drain cleaner, and she glanced longingly at the water still dripping from the pump spout. "Finance," she settled for saying. Given her penchant for tripping over her own lies, it seemed wise to stick as close to the truth as possible. "I work at an investment firm."

"When you're not on hiatus?" he inserted.

"Right. If you've got any discretionary dollars to invest, I'm the person to talk to."

He chuckled and ducked back into the refrigerator, his rumbling voice echoing back at her. "Right now, I don't have a discretionary dime. Buying back the ranch has sucked me dry."

Buying it back? Molly wondered what he meant. Had he owned the Lazy J before? She wanted to ask, but it wasn't any of her business, and she squelched the urge.

When he finally emerged from the refrigerator, the old appliance's motor hummed to life, making the floor vibrate. Molly curled her toes. As he closed the thick, rounded door, she noticed the name Gibson scrolled across the white enamel front.

"The old gal's a marvel. Keeps the milk so cold, your teeth ache."

Molly thought of her shiny apartment kitchen in Portland with its 1200-watt microwave and Jenn-Air cooking range. Her appreciation of old things aside, she preferred having modern conveniences for everyday living, and she sincerely hoped the kitchen at the main house was better equipped. If not, she'd be in big trouble.

He plugged in the toaster to make sure the coils worked. The acrid smell of burning dust and stale breadcrumbs rose to her nose. "Looks like everything in here still works well enough," he pronounced, running a broad palm over the countertop to check for dust. "I cleaned thoroughly when we moved out, but you'd never know it."

As he circled her to leave the kitchen, Molly stared worriedly at the stove. Even with the pilot light on, she was afraid it might explode again if she touched it.

When she joined Jake in the small living room, he was crouched before a camelback trunk. She moved closer to peer in. It was just about large enough to hold a dead body.

Not that she still believed he might murder her. He'd been far too concerned about her after the stove mishap to mean her any harm. Her only lingering worry was that his definition of harm might be entirely different than hers. He was far too charming for comfort, a characteristic that might be inherent, but was far more likely to have been acquired with experience and at great cost to the opposite sex.

She eyed the impressive play of muscle across his broad back every time he moved. In Portland, there were plenty of body builders, but they lacked Jake Coulter's hard edges, looking more like overblown rubber sculptures by comparison. Oblivious to her regard, he set aside some wooly blankets.

"Everything in here was laundered after we moved out. I'm pretty sure it's all still clean." He sniffed a pillowcase, seemed satisfied with the smell, and went back to riffling through the bedding. "This trunk should have protected it."

Molly shifted her weight. "I have my own bedding, Mr. Coulter." She glanced at the jumble of bags on the brown-leather sofa. "It really isn't necessary for you to bother yourself like this."

"The name's Jake, and it isn't a bother. You look tired to the bone." He tipped back his hat to glance up. "I'll just help you get settled in, then be out of your way."

He selected a set of white sheets, three blankets, and two embroidered pillowcases before pushing to his feet. Her gaze snagged on the needle work, a telltale sign that there'd once been a woman in his life. Was he divorced? *Probably*. As handsome as he was, he undoubtedly thought monogamous was the name of a prehistoric dinosaur.

Molly followed him to the bedroom. "I can make my own bed," she protested, wishing he'd leave her to it. "I'm sure you've got a ton of other things you should be doing, and I can manage just fine."

He snapped a sheet over the old mattress. As the linen settled, he said, "Nothing I can't do tomorrow and twice as well. Never came across a chore yet that didn't wait until I got to it."

Molly supposed there was wisdom in that. She was also beginning to understand why this ranch was named the Lazy J. Jake Coulter didn't give the impression that he got in a hurry very often. "I hate to disrupt your schedule."

"Don't believe in schedules." He tucked the sheet on his side, forming a corner far tidier than hers, undoubtedly a result of his having such large hands and the strength to pull the linen tight. "Sure as rain is wet, something always happens to screw them up. It's enough to give a man ulcers if he places too much importance on them."

"Well, you're the boss. If you insist on making my bed, have it your way."

"I will." He winked mischievously, making her wonder if he'd practiced that bone-melting grin in front of a mirror. "I generally do."

Disconcerted, Molly bent to tuck the sheet on her side, then moved with him toward the foot of the bed. They worked well as a team, she decided, and then wondered where that thought had come from.

She watched bemusedly as he unfolded all three blankets. "One will surely be enough," she said, recalling the hot day. "I'll roast."

"Better to kick off than get cold." He began tucking in the blankets at the foot of the bed, the thick pads of his hands barely fitting between the mattress and frame. "You'll be glad of the warmth by morning."

Molly doubted it would get that chilly. "It feels like summer out there right now."

"Don't let it fool you. We'll see snow again before spring makes a debut."

"You're kidding."

"Nope. Just a warm snap. Happens in high-desert climates as spring approaches, freezing one day, hotter than Hades the next." He tossed her a pillowcase. "I won't be surprised if we wake up to frost in the morning."

As soon as the bed was made, he was off again with Molly hurrying behind him to keep up. Once back in the living room, he opened a drop-down metal door sunk into the log wall beside the old rock fireplace. "Looks like you need more wood." As he straightened, he added, "Just as a precaution, make sure you always give this door a couple of kicks before you open it."

Her gaze shot to the wall. "Why?" she asked warily.

"Rattlers. Makes for a nasty surprise when you're half asleep."

"Rattlers?" she echoed.

"They're happy enough to leave if you give them some warning. It's probably not even a worry so early in the year, but it can't hurt to be careful."

"Are you talking about *snakes*?" she asked thinly.

He cocked a dark eyebrow at her. "You aren't afraid of them, are you?"

Of course she was afraid of them. "Rattlesnakes get in the *wood box*?" She peered past him at the metal door. "That doesn't have a latch, does it? Couldn't a snake press against it and come in?"

"Not likely."

When speaking of rattlesnakes, she preferred to deal in absolutes. "But it could happen."

"I suppose."

"Then what stops them from getting in the house?"

"Mostly their good sense. They wind up dead if they get around people. Just give the door a couple of kicks. You'll probably never see one."

She would have a heart attack if she encountered a rattler. She glanced at the tarnished fire tools behind him, wondering if the poker would serve to kill a serpent. When she looked back at Jake, he was tugging on his ear, his expression bemused.

"You've never spent much time in rattlesnake country, I take it."

She pushed at the strand of hair that kept falling in her eyes. "Not really."

"They're reclusive critters. Walk with a heavy tread, make noise. If you go into the woods, find yourself a stick and beat the brush. They'll head for safe ground. I've lived in this country all my life and never known anyone who got bit."

Molly wrapped her arms around herself and glanced worriedly at the wood box again, which prompted him to sigh.

"Would you like me to lay out some rope along the wall?" he asked.

"Why a rope?"

"They think it's another snake and won't cross over it."

"Really? Yes. All right."

He nodded. "I'll have to round some up and bring it over."

"That'll be fine."

His gaze held hers. After what seemed like a very long moment, he smiled. "I honestly didn't mean to give you the willies. Around here, most people take rattlesnakes in stride and don't give them much thought."

"I'll be fine." Molly swallowed, resisting the urge to check behind her for slithering intruders. "Noise. I can make noise. I've never been very light on my feet, anyway. Now my gracelessness will finally serve a purpose."

He continued to search her gaze. She got the oddest feeling he was about to say something and then thought better of it. Finally, he turned and went outside.

Molly stared after him, wishing there were a screen door. With the weather so warm, she'd enjoy a fresh breeze, and she'd be afraid to leave the door open for fear of a snake getting inside. She wasn't sure she could do this.

Rubbing her aching eyes, she once again considered leaving. Only what would become of Sunset? She blinked and stared out the doorway. From where she stood, she could see the stallion in the corral, the bloody stripes on his once beautiful black coat glistening in the sunlight. What kind of person could abandon him?

A loud thump resounded through the cabin. She nearly parted company with her shoes before she determined it was only Jake throwing logs into the wood box.

Exhaustion weighed heavily on her shoulders. She could have collapsed right where she stood. When her employer's looming shape finally filled the doorway, she just stared at him, so depleted of energy that she didn't even feel self-conscious. He brushed back his sagging shirtsleeve to check his watch. "Supper is at six, sharp. Grab yourself a nap, and I'll see you then. Don't bother to knock. We don't stand on ceremony here."

News bulletin of the century. "I can whip up something to eat here," she said scratchily. "I've a few groceries."

He smiled slightly. "Nevertheless, I'll expect you for supper."

She nearly asked if that was an order, then remembered she worked for the man and bit back the question. Sarcasm had its place, and this wasn't it. She had Sunset to think about. If she tested Jake Coulter's patience, he might tell her to leave.

He touched the brim of his hat. "It'll be canned chili and crackers again tonight with antacid tablets for dessert, but joining us will give you a chance to meet all the men. They'll be rolling in shortly, still hung over and grumpy as bears from Saturday night on the town. It'll cheer them up considerably to know we've finally got a cook."

All the men? He made it sound as if an army was due to arrive. For some reason, she had assumed she'd be cooking for only him and his brother. "How many men are there?"

"Nine full-timers. Eleven, counting me and Hank."

"Will I be expected to cook for all of them?"

"Of course."

Molly had never cooked for more than four people in her life. Rodney had always insisted on having meals catered when they entertained because she was so inept in the kitchen. "I can't possibly prepare food for that many men. I don't even—"

"Sure you can. We're a patient lot. You'll get the hang of it with practice." He backed away from the door. "The hired hands stay in the bunkhouse." He hooked a thumb toward a long log building adjacent to the house. "You won't be responsible for cleaning over there, and they've got their own laundry facilities. Your only worry will be to keep their bellies full. They have weekends off. They generally head for town Saturday morning and roll back in here late Sunday afternoon, hungry for supper. After dinner on Friday nights, you'll be free to leave until Sunday evening if you like. Or you can hang around here, your choice. As long as you're back in time to fix dinner on Sunday, it makes no difference to me. Hank and I are usually here. If one of us leaves, the other one tries to stick around. You should never be alone out here."

"That's good to know." Her mind was stalled on the fact that he expected her to cook for eleven people—twelve, including herself. *Oh, God.* She never should have agreed to this.

"Supper, six sharp," he said with another tip of his hat. "Don't forget. We wait for latecomers like one pig waits on another one. We don't dress for dinner, by the way." His grin hinted that he'd just made a joke and found it amusing. "Just come as you are."

❧ CHAPTER FOUR ❧

As Jake walked toward the house, he watched the dust billows that rose around his boots with every step, thinking they resembled miniature mushroom clouds. A fitting comparison. If his suspicions were correct, he had just made a decision that could blow up in his face.

Near the exercise corral, he lifted his gaze to the stallion in the six-foot-high enclosure. Never in all his thirty-two years had he seen a more cruelly abused animal. Those lash marks ran mighty deep. While inside the pen, Jake had visually examined them as best he could, and as near as he could tell, none of them would require stitches, but more than a few would leave scars.

What kind of man could do such a thing?

Resting his elbows on a rail of the pen, Jake rubbed the bridge of his nose, thinking that he needed four ibuprofen chased with whiskey. As a rule, he didn't turn to drink when he felt stressed, but tonight he might make an exception. Sometimes, when a man found answers nowhere else, he could stumble across a few at the bottom of a bottle.

"Holy hell, what happened to that horse?"

Jake jumped at the sound of his younger brother's voice. He whipped around, his thoughts tangling like wet rope as he tried to think how he meant to explain this situation. The prospect was so daunting, he wanted to pull his hat down over his eyes and say he had a headache. It wouldn't really be a lie, given the fact that he had two, one behind his eyes and another taking up residence in the cabin along the creek.

"Howdy, Hank."

"Is that all you've got to say?" Startled by Hank's approach, Sunset reared and shrieked. Hank stopped dead in his tracks. "Ah, Lord, Jake. Where did he come from?"

A tight, choking sensation crawled up Jake's throat. "I'm not real sure where he's from yet. Portland, possibly. Then again, maybe from somewhere down south."

Turning to rest a shoulder against the fence, he watched his brother cautiously close the remaining distance between them. Recently turned twenty-nine, Hank looked enough like their old man to be a clone, his skin tanned as dark as molasses by the sun, his tousled hair lying over his brow like swirls of chocolate. His sweat-dampened T-shirt was smeared with dirt, a result of wrestling with sick calves to give them injections, and the cotton knit clung to his chest like a second skin. His blue eyes fairly snapped as he shoved up the brim of his Stetson to search Jake's expression.

"If you're not sure where he came from, how the hell did he get in our corral?"

"There's a good question."

Hank's jaw muscle ticked. "Looks like somebody whipped the poor bastard."

Jake nodded, noting as he did that Hank had balled his hands into fists.

"Who owns him? Not many things put me in a mood to kick ass, but seeing that sure as hell does."

Jake pointed over his shoulder. "His owner is over at the cabin. Tip your hat before you start kicking ass, or I'll have to kick yours for not minding your manners."

"A lady?"

"Ringer."

Hank's eyes narrowed. "No woman could mark a horse like that, not unless she's built like an Amazon."

"She isn't." Jake almost smiled at the picture of Molly that flashed through his mind. Amazon definitely wasn't a word to describe her. "I guess her to be about five two. It's hard to judge. She's wearing those newfangled shoes with soles as thick as two-by-fours." He curled a thumb over his belt. "Never have figured out what women see in those damned things. Good way to bust an ankle if you ask me."

Hank frowned. "What does her taste in shoes have to do with anything?"

"Doesn't. I was just making conversation."

Hank started to say something, then pressed his lips closed, his gaze sharp on Jake's face. He folded his arms on the fence rail and hooked a boot heel over the bottom rung, spending the next little while watching the stallion.

The silence gave Jake a chance to gather his thoughts, which undoubtedly was Hank's intent. If anyone understood him, it was his youngest brother.

Jake's voice had gone gravelly when he spoke. "I've done a hell of a thing, Hank. You're going to be royally pissed, and I can't say I'll blame you."

Hank shifted, then resettled in much the same position, one hip cocked, one leg thrust behind him. "I can see your tail's tied in a knot about something."

Jake tried to think of a way to cast the situation in a good light. He was tempted to gloss over a few of the facts. Unfortunately, in his book, that would be lying by omission, and he wasn't a man who dealt in falsehoods, not for any reason. He took a bracing breath, slowly released it, and said, "I think the lady stole the horse."

"You think she *what*?"

Jake winced at the loud pitch of his brother's voice. He felt as if cymbals were crashing in his temples. "Given the fact that she doesn't strike me as the criminal type, my guess is she had no alternative."

"There are always alternatives to breaking the law. Why would anyone do such a harebrained thing as to steal a horse?"

"Beats the hell out of me. I assume she had her reasons. She seems like an intelligent woman, and you can tell by looking at her that she's got a kind heart." Jake rubbed the bridge of his nose again. "She claims her name's Molly Houston."

"Claims?"

"The first name fits. I think she plucked the last one out of a hat." Jake thought for a moment before he continued. "She's a puzzle, Hank, one of those people who's really hard to read." In his mind's eye, he once again conjured an image of her, soft and well rounded in all the right places, with whiskey-colored hair, huge butterscotch-brown eyes, and a wealth of flawless ivory skin. All his adult life, he'd gone for tall, long-legged women, barely giving the short, generously endowed ones a second look. But there was something different about Molly—an indefinable something that had caught his attention the instant he saw her. He guessed maybe it was her eyes, so wide and wary and dark with suspicion. He couldn't look into them without wanting to hug and reassure her. "She's a pretty little thing, if you like the type and look past all the camouflage."

Hank shot him another sharp glance. "What camouflage?"

Jake tried to think how he might explain. "Have you ever met a woman who does her damnedest to look homely?"

Hank smiled thoughtfully. "A few."

"That's Molly, only she's fighting a losing battle. It'd take a sack over her head to hide that face." Jake thought of the way she wore her hair skinned back in a braid. "She doesn't bother with a lick of makeup, and her clothes are so baggy they'd fit a woman twice her size with room left over for one small girl." He sent his brother a questioning look. "What makes an attractive woman try so hard to downplay her appearance?"

Hank shifted again, then scratched his jaw. "Beats me all to hell. To avoid attention, maybe? Could be she's timid of men."

Jake remembered how nervous she'd seemed around him and decided that explanation had some merit. "Maybe," he conceded. "Overall, she doesn't really strike me as the timid type, though. It took guts to get that horse here. Most people would have gotten spooked and turned back when they reached the first steep grade."

Hank glanced off at the Toyota parked in front of the cabin and then studied the huge trailer. "Where are you going with this, Jake?"

"Well, now, that's the part you're not going to like, so I'm working up to it."

"Just cut to the chase."

Jake took another bracing breath. "I said I'd work with the horse, and I gave her a job so she can pay my rates."

"You *what?*" Hank's dark eyebrows lifted. "Please tell me I didn't hear you right. A job doing what?"

"Housekeeper and cook. We're looking for someone, and she needs a job and a place to stay. It seemed like the perfect solution."

Hank laughed incredulously. "You hired a horse thief? Jake, this is partly a *horse* ranch. What the hell makes you think she won't steal our horses?"

"I'm not claiming it makes sense. I'm just recounting to you what I've done. I couldn't tell her to go." Jake stared at his palms. "I know I should have discussed it with you first. But I just couldn't turn my back on her. She looked so lost, and I couldn't shake the feeling—hell, I don't know— that we were her only hope, I guess."

Hank just shook his head, looking more incredulous with each passing second. "If she stole that horse, the cops are probably looking for her. You could take the rap for horse theft. That's a serious offense." He jabbed a finger at the stallion. "He looks like a racer to me. They don't come cheap. We're talking grand larceny."

"I've thought of all that."

"We could lose the ranch," Hank pointed out. "Have you thought of that? People won't bring their horses to me if my brother's doing time for horse theft. Right now, the training program is all that's keeping us alive."

Jake couldn't think of a single argument in his own defense. "I know," he said hollowly.

"And you're still bent on helping her? Damn, Jake. How do you know the cops aren't looking for her as we speak?"

Jake swallowed and met his brother's gaze. "I have a feeling about her, Hank. I can't explain it, can't rationalize my way past it. I just couldn't turn her away."

Hank puffed air into his cheeks and bent his head. "All right," he finally said. "If it's something you have to do, there's no point arguing about it. It was your money we invested, not mine. What real say do I have?"

"You know better than that. This is Coulter land. We're partners. My money, your money. I've never made a distinction."

"Until now."

Jake bit down hard on his back teeth and met his brother's gaze dead on. "What the hell does that mean?"

"Just what I said. We've sweat blood to get this place back on its feet." He swung his hand to encompass the land. "Maybe I didn't have the money to match you dollar for dollar, but I worked beside you in the bitter cold to rebuild the house, and I waded through mud and snow up to my ass all winter to repair the fences and tend the stock. Now, first crack out of the bag, you put it all at risk without so much as a word to me?"

Jake winced because everything his brother said was true. "I'm sorry," he said gruffly. "You're right, Hank. I'm sorry."

"Sorry won't pay the mortgage if your ass gets tossed in jail." Hank lowered his arm back to the fence rail and bent his head. "*Damn.* I'm all for doing good deeds, but where do we draw the line? This isn't just any piece of land. We were lucky to get it back. Now you're taking a gamble that could end with our losing it again."

Jake sighed and closed his eyes. "You're right. Guilty as charged. I'm sorry, Hank. I'll tell her I've changed my mind and ask her to leave."

Silence. Jake waited for his brother to speak. When no words were forthcoming, he lifted his lashes. Blue eyes stormy with anger, his mouth drawn into a grim line, Hank was staring at the stallion. When he felt Jake's gaze on him, he shot him a glare.

"That's just great. Dump it all on me."

"I'm not dumping anything on you. You've argued a good case, I know you're absolutely right, and there's nothing else to be done. The ranch has to come first. Like you said, we were damned lucky to get it back in the family."

Hank resumed staring at the horse. After a long moment, he shook his head. "What kind of man can turn his back on that? The poor bastard. Just look at him."

Jake had looked his fill already. The sight was testimony to the depravity and mercilessness of humankind, and it made him feel slightly sick. Even worse, he had a bad feeling that the horse hadn't been the only one to suffer. Molly bore no physical scars that he'd been able to see, but not all wounds were inflicted on the flesh. Straightening away from the fence, Jake shoved his hands in the pockets of his jeans.

At his movement, Hank jerked his head around. "Don't go jumping the gun."

Jake smothered a smile. Not quite four years Hank's senior, he'd always felt much older, undoubtedly the result of being firstborn in a family of five rowdy boys who'd looked to him to set an example. He'd watched Hank grow from a gangly, mischievous teenager into a serious-minded college student, but somehow he'd failed to note his brother's final passage into adulthood. This was no boy who frowned at him now, but a fine young man who did their father and the Coulter name proud.

"Sometimes I just get to wondering what it's all about, is all," Hank said in a low voice. "Other people know where to draw the line. Watching them, it's easy to start thinking that's a smart way to be."

Jake tugged his hands from his pockets and relaxed against the fence again. "If you're bent on it, I'll ask her to leave."

Hank laughed humorlessly. "Nah. I'm as nuts as you are." He looked out over the ranch, his mouth twisting in a sad smile. "When you boil it all down, as much as we love this place, Jake, it's only a patch of dirt."

Jake chuckled in spite of himself. "Coulter dirt. It's special to us in a way no other spread will ever be."

"Only because three generations of Coulters worked it and raised their families here." Hank gazed at the forestland that encroached on all sides. "What do you reckon our great-grandfather would do in this situation?" He slanted an inquiring glance at Jake. "You think he would turn his back on that horse?"

"It's hard to say. I never knew the man."

"We knew Grandpa, and we sure as hell know our father well enough. Remember the time Dad took the quirt away from that cowboy who was beating his horse out at the fairgrounds?"

Jake remembered the incident well.

Hank grinned. "He gave the son of a bitch a taste of his own medicine, and Mom had to bail him out of jail."

"More temper than common sense, that's our dad."

Hank shook his head, his expression growing suddenly solemn again.

"Common sense had nothing to do with it. He was setting a wrong right and teaching the bastard a lesson he wouldn't soon forget."

"What's your point, Hank?"

"That we're Coulters, and with the name comes a responsibility to live up to it." He sighed and shrugged. "To hell with the ranch. If we lose it, we can always buy more dirt, but we can't buy back our decency. Comes a time in life when a man can't turn a blind eye, not if he wants to like himself. I reckon this qualifies." He nodded at the horse. "Neither one of us would be worth the powder it'd take to blow us to hell if we could turn our backs on him."

"I know helping her out isn't the smartest decision I've ever made," Jake admitted, "but it was the only thing I could think to do at the time. She was about to leave, and damned if I could just stand there and let her go."

Hank's eyes crinkled at the corners as he studied the stallion. "You know what they say about wise men making it into heaven. It may not be a smart decision, but no matter what happens, it's probably the right one."

Someone screamed. Molly jolted awake and listened. The sound didn't come again, and she decided she had been dreaming. She started to roll over but was so stiff her joints felt frozen. She blinked, tried to see. There was only blackness. Where was she? She felt like a hunk of frozen meat at the bottom of a freezer. She hugged her arms, rubbed her sleeves. She was so chilled that her flesh felt numb.

Another high-pitched scream rent the air. Startled by the sound, she swung off the bed, tripped over her shoes, and landed in a sprawl on what felt like a dusty wood floor. Her chin smacked a plank, and bright spots exploded before her eyes. For a moment, she just lay there, too stunned to move.

When her head cleared a bit, she ran a palm over the floor, trying to place where she was. The awful scream came again, reverberating in the darkness. It came back to her then. The cabin. Jake Coulter. It was Sunset who was screaming.

Something had to be horribly wrong to make the horse scream that way. She needed to go check on him. Her joints protesting with every movement, she pushed to her feet. How long had she been sleeping? Judging by the darkness, the sun had gone down some time ago, which meant she must have been out for hours.

Waving both hands, she groped her way across the bedroom and spilled gracelessly into the living area. Faint but very welcome moonlight shone through the open front door, creating a pale beacon to guide her.

Once outside on the covered front porch, Molly rubbed the sleep from her eyes and squinted through the feeble moonlight, trying to see Sunset. As if on cue, the stallion shrieked again, the sound laced with terror and panic. She was about to move off the porch when a huge, black shape loomed in front of her. Her heart leaped, and she fell back a step.

"Sorry," a deep voice said. "I didn't mean to give you a start."

The breath rushed from her lungs. "Mr. Coulter?" She strained to see, her eyes burning with the effort. "Is that you?"

"Jake," he corrected.

"Oh, thank *God*," she said, so relieved she didn't care that her voice sounded shrill. "I thought you were a bear."

He chuckled, the sound raspy but warm. "I get as cranky as a bear sometimes. Will that work?"

He moved, and his silhouette vanished. Molly narrowed her eyes, trying to find him in the darkness. "Mr. Coulter?"

"Right here," a deep voice, laced with amusement, said near her ear.

She jumped and clamped a hand over her heart. "Good grief."

He laughed softly. "Can't you see?"

Molly missed the city, where thousands of lights illuminated the night sky. "Of course I can't see. It's black as pitch out here."

"It seems bright as day to me."

"I'm happy for you." Realizing she sounded waspish, she tried to lighten her tone. "It's a good thing one of us can see. Something's terribly wrong with Sunset. Didn't you hear him shrieking?"

"He's fine. As fine as can be, anyway. He ate a little grain earlier, and for the most part, he's settled down. He just got spooked when I walked by his pen."

"Oh. So there's nothing wrong with him?"

"Nothing that time, patience, and a gentle hand won't cure."

She heard paper rustle. Then a clanking sound reached her ears. The next thing she knew, he grasped her by the elbow. "I'll be your eyes until we get some lights turned on." Firming his grip, he set himself to the task of guiding her through the darkness to the doorway. She could have sworn she felt heat radiating from him. "Damn, honey, you feel ice cold," he said, running his thumb lightly over the chilled skin of her arm.

"I got a little cool while I was sleeping."

Once inside the house, he released her to flip on the wall switch. The old floor lamp that stood next to the easy chair by the front window burst to life, bathing the small living area with golden light through its fluted glass globe. Molly blinked, momentarily as blinded by the illumination as she'd been by the darkness.

As her vision adjusted, she saw that he was carrying a quart-sized bowl covered with plastic wrap, a package of what appeared to be Ritz crackers, and a steel thermos tucked under one arm.

"Your supper," he explained. "Can't have you sleeping through meals and losing your strength, not if I mean to work you until you drop."

"Oh. Of course." Molly wanted to kick herself for sounding so humorless and prim. He was kidding around with her, and she should respond in kind. Unfortunately, she never had a clear head when she first woke up, a lifelong condition presently worsened by a tumble off the bed and nerves that felt as if they'd been abraded with sandpaper. "And here I thought you were just being thoughtful."

"That, too," he admitted with dry amusement. "Now that I've landed a cook and housekeeper, I don't want her quitting on me." He brandished the chili bowl. "If I never eat another meal out of a can, it'll be too soon."

Standing there in his rancher garb, he looked even more dangerously attractive than he had earlier. His hat was cocked forward to shade his compelling blue eyes, giving her an opportunity to better appreciate the rest of his face. His firm, narrow lips shimmered in the lamplight like wet silk. Shadows delineated his chiseled features, enhancing their masculine ruggedness. He had a slight cleft in his chin, an angular jaw, and a sharply bridged nose thrusting out from between his thick, sable brows like a blade. Along one side, she saw a slight bump, evidence of an old break.

Her gaze dropped to the collar of his wash-worn shirt, the blue chambray faded nearly to white and forming a stark contrast to the burnished umber of his neck. She'd never met anyone like Jake Coulter. Most of the men in her acquaintance wore tailored suits, her beloved late father included. In the business world, successful men dressed the part.

Oddly, though, despite his humble attire, Jake emanated an air of importance and authority. It was in the way he carried himself, she decided, and in the relaxed, self-confident way he interacted with others. He was the kind of man who would always command respect, no matter what he wore.

She tried to picture him in a suit. Somehow the image just didn't gel. He belonged here, in everyday communion with the land and the wilderness at his back door.

When she met his gaze again, she was dismayed to find that he was studying her as intently as she was studying him.

"I didn't realize you were so *tall*," she blurted stupidly.

He flashed her a slow grin. "And I didn't realize you were so short. The heels, I guess. They must tack on a few inches."

"I'm only a little shorter than average."

His grin broadened. "If you stretch? What are you, about five two?"

"Three." Heat gathered in her cheeks. She'd been teased unmercifully in high school about being short, and it had been a sore point with her ever since. She folded her arms at her waist. "If there's a height requirement for the job, Mr. Coulter, just say so, and I'll gather my things."

"No height requirement." He gave her a long look that made her toes curl. "I never take anyone's measure in inches. Your legs reach from your ass to the ground, same as mine. I reckon that'll do."

Once again she had the feeling that he was looking too deeply into her eyes, that there was nothing she could hide from this man. She wanted to break the visual contact but couldn't. Finally he shifted his attention to her mouth, his irises turning a molten blue gray. She glanced nervously away, feeling uncertain and confused. He was looking at her mouth as if—

She cut the thought short. Handsome men like Jake Coulter were never attracted to women like her. It was silly to even entertain the notion. She probably just looked a fright, with her hair all mussed and her eyes bleary with sleep.

"Thanks for bringing me dinner. It was very thoughtful."

She held out her hands to accept the bowl. He smiled and moved past her. After reaching around the wall to turn on the overhead kitchen light, he proceeded to set the food on the round wooden table in the adjoining eating area. "I'll keep you company while you eat. I need to talk with you."

Molly's stomach knotted. What did he need to talk to her about? His tone brooked no argument, but she decided to give it her best shot, anyway. "I'm not at my sharpest when I first wake up. Maybe we should save it for later."

"It's bad for the digestion to eat alone."

During her marriage, Molly had taken most of her meals alone. Rodney had been far too busy with his many girlfriends to spend much time with his wife. "I'm used to it."

"Is that so?" He set the thermos beside the bowl, then glanced over his shoulder at her. "A pretty lady like you shouldn't be."

Pretty? Her face went hot again. She hated it when men gave her compliments. She knew they didn't sincerely mean them, and that had the perverse effect of making her feel worse about herself instead of better.

She looked at her watch. It was almost eight o'clock.

When he noticed her checking the time, he said, "You won't turn into a pumpkin. Come sit down and eat your supper. This way, I can take the dirty dishes back with me and throw them in the machine."

He turned from the table to catch her shivering and rubbing her arms. His gaze shot past her to the open front door. "While you dig in, I'll start a fire. The night air in this country has quite a bite when you're not used to it."

Molly started toward the kitchen, only to collide with him as he moved toward the door. She came up hard against his chest and was almost knocked off her feet. He caught her by the shoulders.

"Are you all right?"

"I'm fine," she assured him, trying to step away.

"I'd forgotten how small this place is." He maintained his grip on her upper arms. "You can't cuss a cat without getting hair between your teeth. Hank and I were always mowing each other down when we stayed here."

He hadn't mowed her down, exactly, but if he didn't turn her loose, she couldn't say how long her legs would hold her up. Her skin felt electrified where his hands touched, the feeling radiating out to sensitize nerve endings she'd forgotten she had.

"What's this?" he asked, lifting one hand to cup her chin. "Did you take a fall?"

Molly was about to say no when his thumb grazed a tender spot, calling to mind her headlong plunge to the floor. "I, um—yes, sort of. Nothing serious. I didn't realize I'd hurt myself."

He lightly traced the spot again. "It's only a small scrape, but it may leave a bruise." He moved his thumb up to her mouth. The slight drag on her sensitive flesh made her breath hitch. "Your bottom lip is a little swollen as well."

She couldn't move, couldn't think. Even after he lowered his hand back to her shoulder, his gaze lingered on her mouth as if he were thinking about kissing her. She was afraid she might faint if he did.

CHAPTER FIVE

Jake Coulter was a man who knew his business with the ladies. Molly could tell that just by looking at him. When he kissed a woman, he'd take control. No clumsy groping, no hesitance, just masterful hands and lips, taking possession. She balled her hands into fists, appalled by her thoughts. Even worse, what if he saw them in her eyes? This wasn't like her. She barely knew him.

She shivered again, only this time not from the cold. His grip on her upper arms tightened, the strength in his hands compressing her shoulders slightly. He felt capable of lifting her clear off her feet. Molly fleetingly wondered how that might feel.

On her wedding night, Rodney had carried her over the threshold, but that had been ten years and thirty pounds ago, and she could barely remember it now. He'd bumped her head on the doorframe. She did recall that much. And he'd put her down the instant they got inside, more interested in drinking champagne than in making love with his bride.

The memory brought a pang of nearly forgotten hurt. Her honeymoon had ended quickly, mere hours after her wedding. She'd looked forward to an incredible evening—romance, soft music, and passionate lovemaking. Instead, she'd surrendered her virginity to a fumbling drunk who'd collapsed on top of her afterward and snored in her ear. Her marriage had gone downhill from there.

And therein lay her problem with Coulter, she decided. So many good years were gone, stolen by a man who'd never loved her or even wanted her. Deep down, in a purely feminine corner of her heart, she felt cheated.

She was almost thirty, and though that was still fairly young by many people's standards, she couldn't shake the feeling that time was running out.

What was it like to receive a magical kiss in the moonlight?

How would it feel to be swept off her feet?

She could go to her grave without ever experiencing passion. She could do without the love poems and being serenaded at her bedroom window. If nobody ever climbed the trellis to profess his undying devotion, she could live with that as well.

But, damn it, before her ovaries became atrophied, she wanted someone besides her father to tell her she was beautiful and to give her flowers. Just *once*. Was that so much to ask?

"I guess it depends on what you're asking."

Molly blinked. Jake's face was cast into shadow by the glow of light from the kitchen. "Pardon?" she asked, praying that she hadn't been thinking out loud.

"Is what too much to ask?" he repeated.

She blinked again, clamped her mouth closed. She had mush for brains. "Nothing. My mind must have wandered. I told you, I'm not very clearheaded when I first wake up."

He rubbed his hands up and down her arms. "Let me get that fire started."

He had already started one and just didn't know it.

Molly gulped. *Oh, boy*. This was not good. How could she work for a man when she remembered him without a shirt every time she looked at him?

As if Jake Coulter would ever even give her the time of day. What on *earth* was she thinking? She had pasty white skin, saggy boobs, a thick waist, cottage-cheese thighs, and so many dimples on her buttocks, they resembled oversized golf balls.

She made her way to the table. *Enough*. She was finished with men. Absolutely, totally, forever finished. When she regained control of her money, she'd buy her own darned flowers, thank you very much. A whole bathtubful, if she wanted. The male of her species could take a flying leap.

She sank gratefully onto a battered old chair, her heart racing as she tried to focus on the chili. She was acutely conscious of the sounds Jake made across the room, the clunk of firewood, the crinkle of newspaper. Within seconds, he had a fire laid.

He took a kitchen match from the box on the mantle, and with one quick snap of his wrist, struck it on the side seam of his Wranglers. Molly had never seen anyone light a match on his pants. She tried to picture herself doing it that way and decided she'd either freeze to death for want of heat or set herself on fire.

Fascinated, she observed him while he worked, admiring the way he crouched so comfortably in front of the hearth. Everything about the man, every movement he made, was deliciously masculine.

Deliciously? The word hung in her brain. She was more exhausted than she realized, she decided. Her body was awake, but her brain was still in a partial dream state.

As if he sensed her eyes on him, Jake glanced her way. Molly turned her gaze back to the chili. With trembling hands, she peeled away the plastic wrap. The sharp, hot scent of the spicy beans and ground beef wafted to her nostrils.

At the best of times, she wasn't overly fond of chili. Canned or home-made, it was usually greasy, and fatty foods didn't sit well with her stomach. Neither did she care much for meat. Her mind always conjured images of the poor animals that had died to supply her with sustenance.

Somehow she didn't think that sentiment would be met with enthusiasm on the Lazy J. Raising and selling beeves was a part of Jake Coulter's livelihood.

"Is something wrong with the food?"

Molly threw him a startled look. He was still crouched before the fire. Amber light flickered over his face, limning the hard planes and chiseled sharpness of his features. His eyes gleamed in the dancing illumination like sun-washed silver. In that moment, she decided he had the visage of a wicked angel. She would do well to remember it.

"No, *no,* nothing's wrong with it." She wadded the plastic wrap in her fist and dug in hard with her fingers. "I'm just not quite awake yet."

He chuckled and nodded at the thermos. "There's milk, fresh from the Guernsey this morning and chilled to a turn. Maybe that'll open your eyes."

Oh, it would open her eyes, all right. She'd drunk 2-percent as a child, then switched to skim as an adult because of her weight problem. She'd never tasted raw milk in her life. She doubted she'd like it very well. The pasteurized whole milk she'd sampled in restaurants always left a waxy film in her mouth.

But Jake Coulter was watching, and Molly had learned that it was always best to go with the flow. People who made waves usually got swamped in their own wake.

She unscrewed the little tin cup from the thermos. The light green lining was stained brown from countless servings of coffee. Not really dirty, she assured herself, just stained. She twisted off the stopper and poured some milk. Her stomach lurched. There were little floating particles on top. Cream, more than likely, but that didn't ease her mind. She thought of the high fat content and had to force herself to take a sip.

Just as she expected, the milk left a coating inside her mouth. She swallowed and determinedly took another gulp. Hadn't Jake heard about bad cholesterol? Molly religiously read food labels as she made her grocery selections.

"How is it?" he asked.

"Oh, it's—" She cleared her throat. A string of something slimy dangled from her uvula. "It's lovely. I've never tasted raw milk."

His dark eyebrows lifted. "A dyed-in-the-wool farm girl, huh?"

Too late, Molly realized her mistake. Someone who'd been around farms all her life would have tasted raw milk countless times. "I'm just calorie conscious, is all. Skim milk is only eighty per cup."

He pushed easily to his feet. The firelight threw his shadow across the room, the outline of his Stetson nearly spilling onto her toes. He strode slowly toward her, every tap of his boot heels making her nerves jump. *Oh, God.* She really, really wished he would stop looking at her like that.

"I hope you're not dieting," he said matter-of-factly.

Molly flashed him an incredulous look, which he met with that twinkling gaze she found so unsettling.

"Let me guess. You don't conform to all the weight charts for a woman your height, so you think you're overweight." Without waiting for her answer, he shook his head and added, "Those damned charts are for women with average builds, and trust me, honey, yours isn't average."

Was he toying with her? Maybe that was it. To some men, the thrill of making a conquest was everything, and they'd sleep with just about anyone to stroke their egos. Well, if that was his game, he could count her out.

He kept coming. *Tap, shuffle . . . tap, shuffle.* He had the cowboy saunter perfected to an art, she'd give him that, his long legs lazily marking off strides, his lean hips shifting loosely. She tried to avoid his gaze, but the closer he came, the harder it was. His shadow finally fell over her.

She flicked her gaze to his, couldn't look away. No maybe to it, the man had a gleam in his eyes. Was he *trying* to make her nervous? There was an alarming thought, and now that she came to think of it, that made perfect sense. This afternoon, she'd sensed that he was suspicious of her story. If he'd come over to pump her for information, he would be able to dig more out of her if he kept her rattled.

"You don't warm up to men very easily, do you?" he said, his deep voice laced with humor as he circled the table to take a seat across from her. "Are you this way with everyone, or is it just me? I can't recall ever making a lady so tense."

Maybe all of them had been brain dead, Molly decided. "I'm not nervous. What makes you think that?"

He smiled and nudged his hat back to study her. "You're not afraid of me, are you?"

"Why would I be afraid?"

He rocked the chair back on its hind legs and hooked his thumbs over his belt, which made him look all the broader through the shoulders. "We're a long way from town. It just occurred to me that maybe you're worried. You don't know me from Adam. If I had any meanness in mind, you could be in a peck of trouble."

Molly tried to moisten her lips, struggled to swallow. Her mouth was dry as dirt. "Thank you so much for pointing that out. Now I have something new to worry about."

He laughed sheepishly and bent his head. There was a piece of hay stuck to the crown of his hat. When he glanced back up, his eyes were warm with a mixture of amusement and regret. "I only brought it up because I don't want you feeling uneasy. My mama will vouch for me if you want a character reference."

"Your *mother*?"

"You bet. Nobody knows a man better than his mama. She'll tell you I'm a gentleman, for all my rough edges. If I'm not, just let her know, and she'll snatch me baldheaded."

Molly smiled in spite of herself.

He winked and grinned. "Don't believe anything else she says, however. Like most moms, she keeps a list of my faults, which she's willing to share with almost anyone who'll listen."

"How long a list?"

"Pretty damned long. I think she's been keeping notes since I was about five. I'm one-track minded, bullheaded, quick to lose my temper, and in sore need of some polish, according to her." He winked at her again. "She's fond of saying that I think tact is what the teacher sat on. I keep telling her that being direct is a virtue. I may not have much talent for beating around the bush, but at least people know where they stand with me."

"That's good to know."

"I'm glad you think so, because I don't plan to beat around the bush with you, either."

Molly's heart did a funny little jig at the base of her throat. She felt as if she were about to choke on a lump of vibrating Jell-O. "I'm afraid I'm not following."

"You will be soon enough." He gave her another long, searching look. His jaw muscle started to tick. "I know you stole the horse, Molly."

She was going to have a heart attack. "Why on *earth* do you think that?"

His lashes dipped low over his eyes, but even so she glimpsed a glimmer of impatience. "I don't think, I know. There's no point in trying to snow me. Save yourself the effort."

She had no idea how he'd found out, but there was no doubt that he knew. She could almost hear the key turning in the lock. "H-have you already turned m-me in?" she asked, her voice quivering like a reed whistle.

As quickly as it had come, the impatience left his eyes. "Do I look like the kind of guy who'd turn a lady in?"

"Yes."

He chuckled and scratched his temple. "I have no intention of turning you in. You have my word on that."

Molly's heart was still jumping in her chest. "How did you find out?"

The corners of his mouth twitched. "You're a lousy liar."

"No, really." She glanced nervously toward the door. "I need to know. Have the police been here? Is that how you found out? I *knew* it was a mistake to stop at that rest area. With Sunset kicking up such a fuss, people were bound to notice me."

He sighed and crossed his arms. "No cops have been here, Molly. You're perfectly safe. No one has tracked you down." He paused for emphasis. "Not yet, anyway. But how long will that last, do you think? You can't steal an expensive animal like Sunset and hope to get away with it. This is the electronic age. Law enforcement communication is lightning fast. They're going to find you, the only question being, how soon."

She was going to be sick. What he said was true, and she knew it. If she stayed in one place, they would find her sooner or later. She clamped a trembling hand to her midriff. Bile rose up her throat.

"I suppose you'd like me to leave." She sat straighter on the chair. "That's fine. I understand. You don't want any trouble, and I can't blame you." She dropped the ball of plastic wrap on the floor and grabbed the edge of the table to stand up. "Luckily, I didn't unpack anything. It won't take me long to load my car back—"

He sat forward in the chair, the front legs smacking the floor so sharply that she jerked. He snaked out a hand to capture her wrist. "You're not going anywhere," he said softly. "Get that thought right out of your head."

His grip was like steel, the press of his fingers relentless. Molly stared into his eyes, a dozen horrible thoughts circling through her mind. The one that finally gained front stage was that he meant to keep her there against her will.

"Sit down," he said softly.

She sat. Gaped at him. Struggled to breathe.

He lightened his grip on her wrist, his gaze still locked with hers. As his fingers relaxed, she thought about jerking away and running. But then she remembered how quickly he had moved that day in the corral. He'd be on her before she took two steps.

"Now I've frightened you."

Molly gulped back hysterical laughter. She almost said, "Go to the head of the class."

"I'm not going to harm you, Molly," he said, his voice husky with sincerity. "I only want to help you."

"Oh." Her heart fluttered back down to where it belonged. Sort of, anyway. He wouldn't be the first man to lie to her, and she had no idea if his word could be trusted.

"I don't know what led you to steal the horse," he went on. "I can only guess. But whatever your reasons, they won't matter a whit when the police finally find you. They'll toss you in jail and throw away the key."

Actually, they'd probably take her back to a clinic, but why split hairs? Though she had eventually benefited by her stay at Haven Rest, the place had been a jail of sorts.

She wondered what her therapist, Sam Banks, would say if he could see her now. He wouldn't be pleased. Stealing that horse had not been a smart move.

Molly bent her head, stared numbly at the scarred tabletop. She would *not* have regrets. No matter what happened, she'd made the best decision she could at the time, and it was pointless to start second-guessing herself now.

"I think you desperately need a friend, honey," Jake said, his voice pitched to barely above a whisper. "Won't you trust me?" He slowly trailed a fingertip over her wrist bone. "Tell me what happened. I'll help you get things straightened out."

The starch went out of Molly's spine. She was relieved that he didn't intend to do her any physical harm, but this was almost as bad. She couldn't tell him what had happened. He'd never believe it, for one. It was all so insane, she could scarcely believe it herself.

No. If she told him her story, he'd automatically assume she was crazy, like everyone else. A woman's husband of ten years didn't have her committed unless there was truly something wrong with her. Right?

Wrong. If a man was trying to cover up a murder and gain control of a large inheritance, he'd do almost anything. Only who was going to believe that? Certainly not Jake. It sounded like something straight out of an Alfred Hitchcock thriller. The fact that her own mother had turned against her made it look even worse.

When Molly just sat there, close-lipped, Jake sighed and released her wrist. "All right," he said as he sat back on his chair. "You're not ready to talk yet. I can see that, and I won't press you. But know, even as I say that, Molly, sooner or later you're going to have to. If you wait until the cops are slapping cuffs on you, it may be too late for me to do anything."

"You can't do anything now," she managed to squeeze out. "Nothing."

"There are animal protection agencies I can call. One look at that horse, and they'll be up in arms. If we report this right away, I'm sure they'll intervene on your behalf with the police. Horse theft is against the law, no question about it. But if you did it to protect the poor animal, it's understandable, and they'll go to bat for you. I know they will."

Molly just stared at him.

"Won't you please call them?" he urged. "Or let me call them for you? I realize you're frightened of something, and I'm sure you've got good reason to be. But you can't let that cloud your judgment. You'll only dig yourself a deeper hole by waiting."

"Where were the animal protection agencies this morning?" she wanted to scream. Rodney had threatened to return to the stable with a gun and kill Sonora Sunset, and all the trainer had gotten was a stupid voice mail message when he'd tried to call the Humane Society. The police hadn't been any help, either. They had no facilities to board abused animals, they'd told the trainer. If the owner of the horse returned with a gun, they would send out an officer, but other than that, there was nothing to be done until the Humane Society returned the trainer's call.

Molly was in up to her neck *because* of the blasted agencies. They'd failed Sonora Sunset when he needed them most. Rodney had flown into a mindless rage because the horse had lost a race. When the trainer called Molly out to the stable and she'd seen how cruelly her ex-husband had whipped the stallion, she hadn't doubted for a minute that he might return with a gun to finish him. What should she have done? Let the horse be shot?

She hadn't been able to *do* that. No matter what the cost to herself, she just hadn't been able to do that.

It was too late for the animal protection agencies to step in now. She was a recently released mental ward patient, still on probation and under a doctor's care, and she'd stolen a sixty-five thousand dollar horse. How would that look? By the time Rodney finished putting his spin on it, Molly knew exactly how it would look.

"Is it your ex?" Jake asked. "Is that who you're afraid of?"

"Yes," she said hollowly.

He sighed and passed a hand over his eyes, then rested his arms loosely on the table. "There's no reason to be afraid of him now."

"You don't know him."

A glint came into his eyes. "I know this. The bastard won't lay a hand on you. He'll have to go through me first. If I can't kick his ass, there'll be ten men standing in line behind me to do the honors."

He thought Rodney might beat her? Molly nearly corrected that misconception, but by doing so, she would be paving the way for him to ask more questions she didn't wish to answer.

The threat from Rodney wasn't physical. It had never been physical. Given Sunset's deplorable condition, Molly could see how Jake might think so, but in actuality, what Rodney would do to her would be far worse. If he found her, he would strike blows with treachery and lies.

Molly would never underestimate her ex-husband again. *Never.* She had hoped to find temporary sanctuary on the Lazy J, but now she saw that staying here wasn't an option. Jake Coulter knew just enough to be dangerous. She couldn't take a chance that he might take matters into his own hands and call the authorities behind her back, believing that would be best for her in the long run.

She'd saved Sunset from taking a bullet. Now the horse was safely in Jake's possession. That was the best she could do for him.

❦ CHAPTER SIX ❦

J̌ake was about to plant a boot on the bottom step of his front porch when he hesitated and glanced back through the darkness at the cabin. He couldn't forget the frantic expression he'd seen in Molly's eyes. At times during their conversation, she had put him in mind of a caged animal searching desperately for a way out. Now that he'd left her alone, he was afraid she might run.

What would happen to her then? Jake suspected she was fleeing from an abusive ex-husband who flew into maniacal rages. If Sunset's deplorable condition was any indication, the man was downright dangerous. What might happen to Molly if the bastard caught her off alone? It didn't even bear thinking about.

He shifted his gaze to her Toyota, which was still parked near the porch of the cabin. He smiled thoughtfully and swung back around. Fearing that the horse might raise another ruckus, he kept well away from the corral as he stealthily retraced his steps.

"What the hell is that?" Hank demanded when Jake entered the house later.

Stepping down into the great room, Jake glanced at the object he held in one hand. "What's it look like?"

Hank, who'd been reclining on the couch with a cold beer, sat forward on the cushion and frowned. "It looks like a rotor."

Jake tossed the object in question on the burl coffee table he'd built a few months back. "If it looks like a rotor, I reckon that's probably what it is."

"Where'd it come from?"

Jake swept off his Stetson and tossed it on the table as well. "The same place most rotors do." He thrust his fingers through his hair, combing away the ring left by his hat. "Out of a distributor."

Hank narrowed an eye. "Whose?"

"Take a wild guess."

Jake struck off for the kitchen. After the day he'd had, that ice-cold beer looked mighty good.

Hank leaped up to follow on his heels. "You *didn't*."

Opening the refrigerator door of the old avocado-green side-by-side he'd borrowed from his parents, Jake said, "I had to do something to be sure she stayed put."

"I thought you gave her a job, that she was going to stay on here and work for us."

"That changed."

"When?"

"When I told her I knew she'd stolen the horse."

An amazed look passed over Hank's dark face.

Jake rushed to add, "I figured she'd feel better if everything was out in the open. Needless to say, it sort of backfired." He plucked a bottle of beer off the top shelf, bumped the door closed with his hip, and tossed the bottle cap into the trash under the sink. "I was afraid she'd try to skedaddle, so I fixed it so she can't."

A slight smile touched Hank's mouth. Jake chugged some beer to wet his throat, then eyed his brother as he wiped his mouth with the back of his hand. "Go ahead and spit it out. I can see you're about to choke on it."

Hank shook his head. After taking a long pull from his beer, he took a seat. The homemade chair he chose was the one that wobbled, compliments of an overlong leg that no one had found time to shorten. He shifted to balance his weight.

"I know tampering with her car was a chicken-shit thing to do," Jake confessed. "But I couldn't think of any other way to keep her here. Just the thought of letting her leave scares the ever-loving hell out of me."

"I can't say as I blame you there," Hank agreed. "Whoever whipped that horse has a screw loose. I'd hate for him to take after a woman like that." Rocking the chair onto its back legs, he fixed Jake with an inquiring look. "She's going to be royally pissed when she discovers her rig won't start, you know."

"She'll only be pissed if she realizes I'm responsible."

Hank's eyes filled with amusement. "Did you put the distributor cap back on so she can't tell anything's missing?"

Jake's only response was a grin.

"It'll be just your luck that the lady's an ace mechanic."

"Not a chance." Chuckling, Jake straddled a chair to face his brother. "She's probably never even checked her own oil."

Jake no sooner spoke than a loud crash came from the front of the house. It sounded like someone had just thrown open the front door with such force that it smacked the interior wall. He cocked an ear. Hank threw a bewildered look over his shoulder. A fast click of footsteps in the hallway reached their ears.

"Where are you, Jake Coulter!" a high-pitched voice cried.

Hank's eyebrows shot clear to his hairline. "Uh-oh."

Jake was just pushing up from the chair when a small bundle of furious female barreled into his kitchen. Hands doubled into fists, she stopped just inside the archway, braced her feet wide apart, and flashed him a fiery glare.

"Where is my rotor?" she demanded.

"Your what?" Jake tried.

"My *rotor*!" she cried again. "How *dare* you remove it?" She took a threatening step closer. "Tell your mother to add arrogant to that list of faults. You had no right to disable my vehicle. No *right,* do you hear?"

She was shaking. Shaking violently. It occurred to Jake in that moment that she was far more upset than the situation warranted. Granted, he had stepped over the line. But even so, no permanent damage had been done.

He looked deeply into her eyes, and behind the glitter of outrage, he saw panic, the same kind of panic he experienced whenever anyone tried to hold him down. At those times he lost all sense of reason, started to feel as if he couldn't breathe, and fought like a crazy man to get away.

"Molly, keep your perspective," he said, injecting a soothing tone into his voice.

"Perspective?" She grabbed for breath. "You stole my rotor, and now you accuse *me* of losing *my* perspective? You're attempting to hold me here against my will."

"Those are pretty strong words."

She fixed him with a virulent glare. "I want my car part."

"All right." He held up his hands. "Just calm down."

"I'll calm down when you return my rotor, and not before!" She took another step toward him. "I mean it! You hand it over!"

Jake had a bad feeling he was about to be taken apart by a pint-sized whirlwind. She looked ready to put out her claws and go for his eyes. Under other circumstances, he might have thought the situation humorous. But there was nothing funny about that look in Molly's eyes. The lady wasn't merely angry or upset. She was frantic.

He was about to assure her that he would return her rotor posthaste when she spun and started opening drawers. "No one keeps me where I don't want to stay. *No one!*"

She jerked so hard on the junk drawer that the rollers parted company with the runners. With the handle still hooked over her fingers, the drawer dived toward the floor and smacked her across the shins. She cried out in pain. Stuff spilled everywhere.

For a moment, Jake could only stare stupidly at a foil condom package that had landed at his feet. Where in bloody hell had *that* come from? He threw an accusing look at his brother, who shrugged, denial implicit in the gesture. Jake could only conclude that one of the hired hands must have stuck it there. *Fantastic.* Now Molly would think they were a bunch of sex fiends who had olive-oil orgies in the kitchen.

But Molly didn't see the condom. She had eyes only for the rotor, which wasn't there, and she continued to search for it with a single-mindedness that Jake found alarming. She dropped that drawer and jerked open another one.

Hoping to save her shins and his kitchen, Jake stepped forward to grab her arm. At his touch, she turned and planted a knotty little fist directly over his solar plexus. His breath *whooshed* from his chest. For a second, all he could do was hunch his shoulders and gasp like a landed fish while he stared at her in stunned amazement.

"Don't *touch* me!"

Okay, fine, he wanted to say, but the words wouldn't come.

"I want my rotor. You hand it over, or else!"

"I will, Molly," he finally managed to croak. "Just—give me a minute."

"I want it now! Or I swear, I'll steal a truck. Turn me in for that, why don't you?"

Bent forward to hold his belly, he rasped, "We don't leave keys in our vehicles."

"I'll hot-wire one!"

Hank sat back, clearly enjoying the show. "Never checked her own oil, huh?"

Jake shot a glare at his brother. "Shut up, Hank," he said weakly. Grabbing for another breath, he returned his gaze to Molly. "I'll give you the rotor. But first, you've got to calm down."

She thrust her arms down to her sides. "Now! I want it right now!"

Jake cleared his throat, straightened. He started for the archway that led into the great room. En route, he tried to reason with her. "You really shouldn't leave, Molly. At least you'll be safe here. If trouble catches up with you, there are eleven men on the Lazy J to watch out for you."

"I'm sick to death *tired* of being told what to do! And I don't need a bunch of arrogant, overbearing males to watch out for me."

At the back of Jake's mind, he knew he'd be wise to keep his mouth shut, but who had ever accused him of being wise? "Pardon me for pointing it out, but physically, you're no match for a man. If your ex-husband catches you alone, what the hell are you going to do?"

"That's my concern, not yours. Just give me my rotor."

Jake reached the coffee table and stared blankly at its surface. No rotor. He knew damned well he'd put it right there. So where in the hell had it gone? One word circled repeatedly in his brain—*shit.*

"It's gone." He knew before he spoke that she wasn't going to believe he hadn't hidden it. "I put it right here, I swear to God." He bent to look under the table. "Where the hell—?"

"Don't give me that!" she cried.

Jake straightened and held up his hands. "Molly, I swear on all that's holy that I left it right here." He walked around to look under the couch. *Holy hell.* "Hank?" he yelled. "Did you take the damned rotor?"

Hank sauntered into the archway, leaned a shoulder against the frame, and flashed a lazy grin. "Why would I take the damned rotor? I've got my own damned rotor."

"This isn't funny," Jake warned.

His brother crossed his ankles. "Depends on your viewpoint, I guess. I think it's hilarious." Molly turned and let out a hiss so sibilant it sounded venomous. Hank nodded politely. "I'm pleased to make your acquaintance, too. I'm Hank, by the way." His grin broadened. "The arrogant bastard's little brother. And just for the record, arrogance is only one of his many shortcomings. Bad manners rank high on the list, to my way of thinking. He could at least introduce us properly."

"I just want my rotor," she cried.

Hank glanced at the table. "He really did put it right there. I can't think where it went, unless it grew legs." His gaze fell on the Stetson. "You look under your hat, Jake?"

Before Jake could do that, Molly descended on the coffee table. She jerked the hat up by its crown, scrunching the carefully shaped felt with angry fingers. Jake winced. Stetsons didn't come cheap, and he wasn't a rich man.

Sure enough, there lay the rotor.

She dropped the Stetson and grabbed up the engine part. Pressing it to her waist, she hurried from the room as if the hounds of hell were at her heels.

Jake stared after her, feeling ashamed on the one hand, but still very concerned about her on the other. Now that she had her car part, she'd undoubtedly leave as quickly as she could, the only question being where she might go. Earlier that day, she'd told him she had very little money. How long would it last? And what would she do when it was gone, pull off to the side of the road somewhere and sleep in her rig?

The stallion started to scream just then, the shrieks rending the night and drifting faintly into the house. In his mind's eye, Jake saw Molly scurrying past the horse's pen, her footsteps carrying her inexorably toward the cabin and freedom. It would take only a few seconds to put the rotor back in her rig. She could be gone in five minutes.

Still standing in the archway, Hank said, "What're you going to do, Jake?"

At the question, Jake came back to himself, visions of Molly being beaten circling through his head. He grabbed his hat. Without bothering to reshape the crown, he shoved it on his head. "I guess I'll go talk to her. If I can get her calmed down, maybe I can convince her to stay."

"Talking. Hmm." Hank nodded his approval. "There's a good plan. Too bad you didn't think of it *before* you stole her rotor."

Caught midstride by the dig, Jake stopped and looked back at his brother. "You know, Hank, one of these times someone's going to take exception to that smart mouth."

Hank smiled. "You reckon?"

Jake found Molly sitting on the front porch of the cabin. Arms locked around her bent legs, face pressed to her knees, she was shaking like a leaf. Jake was somewhat encouraged by the fact that the rotor lay beside her on the step. He hoped that meant she was no longer in a big rush to leave, but he thought it more likely that she was simply too upset.

When he stepped close to grab the engine part, she flinched and jerked her head up to stare at him. In the moonlight, her face looked as white as fresh snow and her eyes were huge glistening spheres of amber, reflecting emotions that made his heart twist. She'd been wary of him before; now, thanks to his idiocy, she was downright spooked.

He stood there for a moment, groping for the words to apologize. Unfortunately, he'd never been a glib talker. That was a failing that grew worse when he got upset, and he was plenty upset right then, mainly with himself. Of all the damned fool things for him to do, this latest took the prize.

Words failing him, he strode around to the front of her rig, lifted the hood, and set himself to the task of setting a wrong right. After he finished, he wiped his hands on his jeans and retraced his path to the porch, dreading the conversation yet to come. He owed her a heartfelt apology, and he needed to make it convincing.

When he sat beside her on the step, she inched away and hunched her shoulders. The posture was so defensive he felt a little sick. This was his fault, entirely his fault. The Lazy J was remotely located. Under the best of circumstances, any female with brains would be uneasy, and thanks to him, these were far from the best of circumstances.

He stared off into the darkness, wishing he knew what the hell to say. When nothing brilliant came to mind, he fell back on childlike simplicity. "I'm sorry for what I did."

No answer. She just huddled there, shivering. She looked so small and alone that he wished he could hug her. The yearning came over him so suddenly and with such sharpness that it gave him pause. What was happening here? He'd always liked women and enjoyed their friendship, but this was the first time he'd ever experienced such fierce feelings of protectiveness for a female outside his family.

"I've got a bad habit of acting before I think sometimes," he went on cautiously. "If you want to leave, you're free to go. I'll even help you load back up."

Still no answer.

He sighed and rubbed his eyes. *Damn.* "You're right. It was arrogant of me to think I know what's best for you. If I could take it back, I would."

"Me, too," she said in a quivering voice. "I can't believe I hit you. I've never hit *anyone*. Never! I can't believe I did it."

Jake suppressed a smile, relieved that she was at least willing to talk to him. "No real harm done."

She straightened and extended her arms in front of her, elbows resting on her knees, hands knotted into small fists. "I can't stand to feel trapped. It makes me crazy."

He wished he could coax her into telling him more, but he erred on the side of caution and filed away that tidbit of information for later. "No one likes to feel trapped."

She rubbed her arms, making him wish he had a jacket to give to her. "I was irrational, out of control. I don't know what came over me."

In the moonlight, her eyes were huge splashes of luminous darkness, her pale face framed by a fiery nimbus of rebellious curls that had escaped her braid. Jake ached to cup her chin in his hand and trace the fragile line of her cheekbone with his thumb. Even without makeup, she was lovely, and it saddened him that she didn't seem to know it.

"Only crazy people do crazy things," she said hollowly.

"Well, then, I reckon we're both nuts. Stealing your rotor to keep you here wasn't exactly a rational move."

She flashed him a startled look, her eyes bright with unshed tears. "At least you didn't become physically violent."

On a comparative scale, Jake figured his had been the worse offense. She hadn't really hurt him, after all. "Don't worry about it, Molly. I had a punch or two coming, and I'm none the worse for it."

"I still shouldn't have hit you. You must have thought I'd lost my mind." A haunted look came into her eyes. "Who knows? Maybe I have."

Resting his arms on his knees, he let his hands dangle and listened to an owl hoot into the night. Somewhere out in the darkness, a small rodent was probably scrambling for safety.

"I'll accept your apology if you'll accept mine," he said huskily. "I never meant to upset you like that. I just wanted to help." He waited a beat. "I knew you'd probably take off. I was worried about what could happen to you."

"Nothing will happen if I'm careful not to let anyone find me."

"They're bound to find you eventually, Molly. You can't run long enough or far enough to avoid the cops forever."

"I know that." She rubbed her forehead as if it hurt. "All I need is seven months."

He mentally circled that. "Why seven months?"

"A certain difficulty in my life will be over then," she told him. "After that, I'll still be in big trouble for stealing the horse, but if I act quickly and play my hand right, the consequences won't be too terrible. Unless, of course, he can somehow petition the court for another year."

Jake realized she was talking more to herself than to him and revealing things she didn't intend to in the process. Unfortunately, the information made little sense to him. "Petition the court for another year of what? I'm not following."

She groaned. "I know you're not. I'm sorry. Just take my word for it, all right? I can't contact the authorities about Sunset for seven months. If I do, he'll find me, and if he does, my goose is cooked."

"Then stay here for that period of time," Jake encouraged. "Seven months isn't so terribly long, not in the overall scheme of things."

She threw him an accusing look. "And have you call the Humane Society behind my back, thinking you know what's best?"

Jake knew he had that coming. "I give you my word I won't do that. Not without your knowledge and permission."

"And I'll never give it."

"Why, Molly? Can't you tell me just that much? Getting the animal protection agencies involved and on your side would be a smart move."

She shook her head and shivered again. "Not for me, it wouldn't."

"*Why?* Two heads are better than one. Tell me what's got you so frightened. Maybe together we can find a solution."

A closed look came over her face, and she shook her head again.

Jake puffed air into his cheeks. Calling the Humane Society was the best thing to do. Why the hell couldn't she see that? No court in the land would send her to jail for stealing that horse to protect it.

"At least do this much for me," he said softly. "Stay on here. Don't take off to parts unknown where you'll have no friends to turn to."

When she started to shake her head again, Jake quickly added, "I won't call the Humane Society, Molly. I swear it. I won't call anyone unless you ask me to. You can stay on, just as you planned. No questions, no pressure. The job is still yours."

She fixed huge, frightened, and very uncertain eyes on him. "How do I know you'll keep your word? That you won't call someone behind my back?"

Jake had always prided himself on being a man of honor, and the question stung for an instant. But the fear he saw in her eyes made it impossible for him to feel offended. She had no way of knowing what kind of man he was, after all. Evidently, she had a great deal to lose if she trusted him, and he stood to lose nothing if he betrayed her. Aside from the Lazy J, which was a family heritage he'd once believed forever lost, Jake had only one possession that he truly treasured.

Straightening one leg to raise his hip, he reached into the front pocket of his Wranglers and drew that possession out. Holding it up by the heavy gold chain, he said, "This is my grandpa's watch. Right before he died, he gave it to me. I've carried it with me ever since." He gazed at it for a moment then smiled ruefully. "It broke some time back. I know I should get it fixed, but I can't bear to let a jewelry shop send it off for repair. I'm afraid it might get lost."

He lifted Molly's hand, lowered the watch onto her palm, and curled her fingers around it.

"What are you doing?" she asked thinly.

"Putting it in your safekeeping," he said huskily. "When you leave the Lazy J, I'll expect you to return it to me. Until then, consider it collateral against my word. If I go in default, it's yours to keep."

She unfurled her fingers, tried to press the watch back on him. "That isn't necessary."

He waved her hand away. "No. You keep it. As insurance. Aside from this ranch and the people I love, there's nothing I value more than that watch. If I go back on my word, it's yours."

Jake pushed to his feet and gazed at the starlit sky for a moment. He thought of that little rodent again, pictured it scurrying madly for safety and possibly making a fatal wrong turn in its panic. The night owl was still calling, ever ready to dive down and seize its prey. The rodent's only hope was to stick tight and keep its head down.

"You can go or stay, Molly. I hope you'll choose to stay. I'm sorry for trying to make that decision for you." He glanced down at her. "If you choose to haul ass, don't forget to leave the watch on the table. If you take it with you, it'll break my heart. When you read the inscription, you'll understand why."

He left it at that, forcing himself to walk away. With every step, the realization was driven home to him that he was leaving a chunk of himself behind, and that it might be gone come morning.

As irrational as he knew it was, he wasn't sure if he was thinking of the heirloom watch or the woman who clutched it in her trembling hand.

§ CHAPTER SEVEN §

To stay or not to stay, that was the question. Molly paced a circle around the old leather sofa where her bags of belongings lay in helter-skelter piles. She didn't know whether she should return them to the Toyota or start unpacking. Dust burned in her nostrils, a reminder of the cleaning that would have to be done in the cabin before she could put her things away. If she was going to stay, she needed to get started.

Could she trust Jake Coulter? That was the real question she needed to address, and whether or not she stayed would depend entirely upon the answer.

She gazed down at the old timepiece in her hand. The inscription inside the gold cover read, *"Forever, Matthew, my love, June 6, 1873. Hattie."* By the date, Molly knew the watch was a family heirloom, passed down to Jake's grandfather by his father before him. Little wonder Jake treasured it. If the watch went missing, something truly priceless would be lost to the entire Coulter family.

Molly closed her hand over the gold, now warm and slick from her sweaty palm. Jake had entrusted this into her keeping. If he had that much confidence in her on such short acquaintance, why couldn't she have just a little in him?

She thought of Sam Banks, her therapist, and wished with all her heart that she could phone him without running a risk of her call being traced. During her stay at the clinic and over the last five months since her release, he'd been her sounding board and only steadfast friend, someone she could contact, day or night, if she needed to talk. Though he tried never to pontificate, choosing instead to let her reach her own decisions, he always managed to guide her in the right direction.

What would he say to her now?

Molly closed her eyes, the memory of his mellow voice whispering in her mind. *"We shouldn't stereotype people,"* he'd once told her. *"Give each individual a chance to prove him- or herself before you pass judgment. Giving your guarded trust is never a mistake, Molly, not if you're smart about it."*

Another time, when she had expressed a concern that she was a terrible judge of character, Sam had popped back with, *"Why is that? Because you trusted and believed in people, and they betrayed you?"* Since that was exactly the reason, Molly hadn't been able to think what to say. Not only Rodney had betrayed her, she had reason to believe her father-in-law, Jared Wells, who'd been her dad's partner and best friend, had taken part in the scheme as well. There was even evidence to implicate Claudia, the only mother she'd ever known. What was she supposed to do with that?

Toward the end of that counseling session, Sam had presented her with a question that seemed particularly appropriate to ask herself now. Along with everything else, was she going to let her marriage to Rodney rob her of the ability to trust?

The very thought made Molly tremble with outrage. Her ex-husband had taken so much from her already, so very much—her youth, her peace of mind, her liberty—and, she suspected, even her father. Was she going to let him continue to ruin every aspect of her life? *No, damn it, no.*

Even as determination filled her, she felt a dark cloud of hopelessness move over her. In only seven more months, she would have reached the finish line. Rodney would have lost her power of attorney. She would have been able to walk back into Sterling and Wells to take her rightful place behind her father's desk. She would have then had the financial resources to hire legal representation and stonewall Rodney if he tried to pull any more fast ones in court. She'd been so close, so very close, to regaining her independence. Now, in one fell swoop, she had jeopardized everything, even her plan to avenge her father's death.

Now, thanks to her stupidity, Rodney could get the upper hand again. He would put his spin on the horse-theft incident, holding it up before a judge as irrefutable proof of her emotional instability and legal incompetence. Even Molly had to admit that stealing a sixty-five-thousand-dollar racehorse was a crazy thing to do, and she would have a devil of a time convincing a judge she'd had good reasons.

Sam Banks had warned her. *"Keep your nose clean, Molly,"* he'd cautioned her repeatedly. *"Whether you like it or not, whether it's fair or not, you're living under a microscope right now."*

Since her release from the clinic, she'd lived like a goldfish in a small glass bowl, thinking twice and sometimes thrice before she did anything. Other recently divorced women could quit their jobs, move to exciting new places, go back to school, or start new careers. On a whim, they could bleach their hair, dress like teenagers, go on crash diets, or engage in tawdry affairs. No one cared if their choices were based on sound judgment or if they were even rational. But Molly didn't have that freedom. Before she did anything, she had to think of how it might look to a judge.

In a perfect world, Rodney's power over her personal life should have ended the day her divorce was final, but no world was perfect, least of all hers. The very fact that Sam had helped her obtain a divorce while she was still in the clinic could work against her. Rodney would argue that she'd been incapable of making wise choices, hadn't understood what she was doing, and that her doctor had made a grave error in judgment. He would also claim that she still needed someone, namely him, to look after her and her business interests. Further strengthening his hand was the fact that her adoptive mother, an MD and something of an expert witness in her own right, might testify against her in court.

Molly wasn't sure what motivated Claudia, whether she was involved in the scheme to take over the firm, or if she was merely doing what she honestly believed was best. Molly only knew that her mom had joined ranks with Rodney to have her deemed legally incompetent and had later signed the necessary forms to have her committed. Molly had seen Claudia's signature on the papers herself.

It had been the most heartbreaking revelation of her life.

In the end, it hadn't really mattered what Claudia's intentions had been. The result was that Molly had been stripped of her rights. Individuals who were deemed legally incompetent in a court of law were treated like children in many ways until the mandate was reversed. The court appointed a person to act as their legal guardian. If they had money, they were often denied access to the funds and were allotted only a monthly stipend to cover basic expenses. Their driver's licenses were frequently revoked. They weren't allowed to have charge accounts. If they owned firearms, the weapons were removed from their possession. Their signature on a legal document was worthless unless the court-appointed guardian agreed to co-sign. In many ways, they became nonpeople who could make no decisions for themselves and whose protests went unheard.

In Molly's case, the situation had been even worse because her husband and mother had had her committed, not only calling into question her judgment but casting doubt on her sanity as well. First she'd been stripped of her rights; then she'd been locked up.

At the clinic, Sam Banks, the doctor whom she'd initially seen as her enemy, had turned out to be her knight in shining armor, transforming what might have been a nightmarish imprisonment into a time of healing. He had listened patiently to her outlandish story and had begun to believe her when no one else did. Eventually, he had fought in court to help her get a divorce, telling the judge that it had been her dysfunctional relationship with her overbearing husband that had caused all her problems in the first place.

In a world that had turned viciously against her, he'd been her only ally.

Until this morning, she had followed Sam's advice to the letter, refraining from any behavior that might cast her in a bad light. But now she'd totally blown it, jeopardizing all her plans and putting herself at the mercy of strangers she wasn't sure she could trust.

Unfurling her fingers again, she gazed solemnly at the watch Jake Coulter had given her. In the firelight, the aged gold case seemed to gleam with inner warmth, much like the man who had placed it in her hand. He was a strange one, she thought with a faint smile, forceful and overbearing, yet seemingly gentle and kind as well.

He'd thrown her a lifeline, whether he realized it or not, providing her with a perfect place to lie low for a while. The chances that anyone would think to look for her on a ranch were minuscule. If she stayed on here and took precautions, it was entirely possible that she could ride out the clock until the entire year of probation elapsed, gaining strength each day for the inevitable battles she would face when she returned to Portland, not only to vindicate herself, but to seek justice for her father's death.

In just seven more months, her power of attorney would revert back to her, and she would be legally free of her ex-husband and her mother. If she acted quickly when that day arrived, she could get a good attorney on retainer and reclaim control of the firm before Rodney had time to appeal to the court for an extension. Only seven more months. If Jake Coulter's word was good, she could surely hole up here for that long.

Slipping the timepiece into her pocket, Molly approached the plastic bags that held her belongings. She'd fallen in love with the Lazy J at first sight, thinking it was the perfect place for Sunset to recuperate. Why not remain here herself? It was a beautiful and peaceful setting, so far removed from her usual surroundings that it gave her a sense of separateness and safety. This quaint old cabin was growing on her as well, its air of timelessness soothing her in a way she couldn't define.

Decision made, Molly went to work. Since she'd slept most of the evening, she could afford to stay up late. Thanks to Rodney, she didn't have much by way of household goods to put away. If she got right to it, she'd be finished unpacking inside of two hours.

As she washed out kitchen drawers and set herself to the task of putting her cooking utensils away, Molly recalled her rampaging attack on Jake's house. She still couldn't believe she had behaved so badly, and then, horror of horrors, she'd capped it all off by slugging the poor man.

An unbidden grin tugged at her mouth. The look on his face had been priceless, and for just a moment, she'd felt so *free*. Though she wished now that she could undo the incident, she had to admit that a perverse part of her had enjoyed being wildly out of control for a few minutes. What did that tell her?

Sam would probably say she'd been releasing long-suppressed rage, and Jake Coulter had just been standing in her line of fire. He would then advise her to find healthier, less objectionable ways to vent her feelings in the future.

Well, punching a pillow had never given her a rush like she'd felt this evening, and there had never been a sense of closure, either. She had experienced that with Jake. He had apologized and so had she. That felt nice. Instead of trembling with helpless anger when she thought of him, she actually wanted to smile. *"I'm sorry for what I did."* Such simple words, uttered with husky regret. In ten years of marriage, a sincere apology had never passed Rodney's lips.

Satisfied with the order of the kitchen drawers, Molly turned her attention to wiping out the cupboards. Tomorrow she would begin cleaning Jake's house. She had gotten off to a rocky start, but she would make it up to him.

Though she'd taken no time to admire it, he had a lovely home with an impressive, log-wall interior, beautiful oak floors, and an eclectic collection of handmade furniture, fashioned from logs. She would sweep and scrub and polish until the place shone. She'd also do her best to put tasty, wholesome meals on his table. He'd not be regretting his decision to hire her.

She just hoped he had some cookbooks.

Finished in the kitchen, she moved to the bedroom. As she hung her slacks and tops in the closet, Molly worried her bottom lip. Her wardrobe wasn't exactly suitable for ranch life, but she'd have to make do.

She turned to grab another sack, thinking it contained only underclothes. The corner of something hard poked through the bag and touched her leg. She thrust in a hand and drew out a folding picture frame. Sadness clutched at her even before she looked at the two photographs, one of her best friend Sarah, the other of her father. Molly studied their faces, her feelings of regret and shame still sharp. It had been well over ten years since Sarah's death and eleven months since her father's, but the hurting never stopped.

She set the frame on the nightstand, turning the pictures toward the bed so they would be the last thing she saw when she went to sleep. Reminders of grave mistakes helped a person never to make the same ones again. Seeing her father's smiling likeness also reminded her that she had a far more important mission to accomplish than merely getting her affairs back in order. Her father was dead, and if her suspicions were correct, Rodney Wells had pulled the trigger of the gun that killed him.

She couldn't let that slide, she thought, knotting her hands into aching fists. If it was the last thing she ever did, she would make Rodney pay. Only then would she be able to lay her father to rest and move on with her life.

From outside, she heard Sunset whinny, the sound forlorn. She stepped to the window and swept aside the lace curtains to push up the bottom sash. Crisp night air, redolent with the scents of nearby forest and rolling grasslands, flowed in around her, the chill a sharp contrast to the fire's warmth that caressed her back. Down along the creek, frogs raised their voices to the moonlight, the melodic cacophony underscored by the rhythmic hiss of irrigation sprinklers in the fields.

Molly dragged in a deep breath, marveling at how different it smelled here. Off in the distance, she heard a coyote baying at the moon. From up near the main house, a dog barked in response. The unharmonious duet prompted Sunset to neigh again.

Though Molly squinted to see through the darkness, she couldn't make out the horse. Nevertheless she leaned out the window, hoping Sunset might be able to see her.

"I'm here, boy. You're not all alone. I'll leave my window partway open so I can hear if you need me. No one's going to hurt you ever again. I promise."

The stallion grunted and whinnied softly, almost as if he was comforted by the sound of her voice.

I did the right thing, she thought. *No matter what happens to me, I did what had to be done, and that's the end of it.*

"Molly?"

The masculine voice slipped into Molly's dreams. *"Molly, can you hear me?"* She struggled to wake up, afraid if she didn't that they'd give her another injection. No more. Please, no more. She had to talk to them, make them believe her. She couldn't do that when her head was muzzy. She wasn't crazy. Had to tell them. Not crazy. No more shots.

"Molly!"

Molly jerked awake. For a moment, she stared blankly at the knotty pine ceiling, uncertain where she was. Then the events of yesterday slammed into her brain.

Rap—tat—tat. The sharp, rhythmic report sat her up straight. She rubbed her eyes, squinted against a shaft of blinding morning sunlight, and groaned. Someone was knocking on the door. *Jake Coulter? What time was it, anyway?*

Blearily, she glanced at her watch, decided it had to be wrong, and stumbled from the bedroom.

"Coming!" she yelled. Once in the living room, it occurred to her that she shouldn't assume it was her new employer at the door. There was still a very real possibility that the police might find her. She stopped dead in her tracks. "Who is it?"

"Jake."

Recognizing his deep voice, she fumbled with the dead bolt. The apparatus rattled like a bunch of aluminum pots as it disengaged.

A tall blur of blue stood on the doorstep. Even half asleep, she felt her stomach tighten at the sight of him. "What time is it?" she managed to croak.

"Six," he informed her in that deep, silky voice she remembered so well, "and we're running late."

Molly pushed at her hair. *"Late?"*

He gave a low chuckle. "Yes, late."

She looked at her watch again. "How can we be running late when it's only six in the morning?"

He chuckled and stepped inside, thrusting a large mug of coffee under her nose. "I brought you some morning wake-me-up."

She took the proffered cup with undisguised eagerness. Not even six-feet-plus of well-muscled male was enough to wake her up without the help of a strong jolt of caffeine. She slurped a little into her mouth and swallowed before saying, "God bless you."

He gave another low laugh. "I wasn't sure if you had the makings for coffee over here. I can't get my eyes open without it."

Molly's eyes were coming open with record speed. "My goodness, it's certainly *strong.*"

"I usually have time for only one cup, so I try to make it count."

A spoon would have stood straight in the stuff.

She took another sip, then cradled the mug in her hands. Jake moved inside and closed the door. Without considering how it might look, Molly retreated a step, then wanted to kick herself for acting like an idiot. She wasn't sure why this man unsettled her so. She only knew that he did.

This morning he wore clothes identical to those of yesterday, the only difference being that the blue chambray shirt and jeans looked freshly laundered. Beneath the brim of his Stetson, his sable hair was a shade darker with dampness from his shower, and he was freshly shaven, his jaw shiny and red from scrubbing, the woodsy scent of his cologne mixing nicely with the earthy smells he brought in with him from outdoors.

He smiled as he gave her a head-to-toe once-over. "Do you always sleep fully dressed?"

She glanced down at her wrinkled attire. Heat rose to her cheeks as she forced her gaze back to his. "Only when I'm so tired that I fall asleep before I realize what hit me." Feeling painfully self-conscious under his unwavering regard, she switched the mug to one hand and pushed at her hair again. Her braid had come partially undone, and a rippled shank of brownish red hung forward over one eye. "I'm sorry. I must look a fright. I stayed up late unpacking."

"You look fine." His warm gaze trailed slowly over her face. He had a way of looking at a woman that made her feel beautiful, a talent she felt sure had served him well over the years. "A little sleep rumpled and tired, but you had a rough day yesterday."

Determined to remain immune to his well-practiced brand of charm, she tried to blink the bleariness from her eyes. A yawn tried to crawl up her throat. She swallowed it back.

He shoved back his sleeve to check his watch. "I apologize for rousting you out at this hour, but here on the Lazy J we get up with the chickens. I was hoping to give you a walk-through over at the house and discuss your job duties before I start my day. I usually head out pretty early."

Molly lost her battle with the yawn and blinked again. "Don't apologize. It's my own fault for staying up so late. Can you give me a few minutes? I need to grab a quick shower and get my eyes open. Then I'll be over."

He nodded. "Not a problem. I have milking to do and eggs to gather. How does thirty minutes strike you?"

She stifled another yawn. "Make it thirty-five, and you've got a deal."

He grinned, the flash of his white teeth almost blinding. "Thirty-five, it is."

He started to leave, then turned back, his hand coming to rest on a length of rope tucked over his belt. "I almost forgot." He tugged the hemp free and dangled it before her nose. "I promised you a snake deterrent." He stepped around her to advance on the wood box. After arranging the rope in a half circle on the floor, each end touching the log wall, he made his way back to her. "That should do it."

Molly glanced dubiously at the rope. "That really works?"

"No snakes will get in the house and crawl over that rope, guaranteed."

A short length of rope seemed pitifully inadequate to her, but he had to know a lot more about it than she did. "Thank you. Having it there will ease my mind."

"That's the whole idea, easing your mind." He opened the door. "Sorry to run, but I've got chores. I'd best get to them."

Sleepy-eyed, she watched as he stepped back out onto the porch. After the door crashed closed, she dropped onto the old leather easy chair to finish gulping down the coffee. Thirty minutes? That was barely enough time to prop one eyelid open. She groaned and rubbed her face. It had been too long since she'd had to get up early for work. Her body was in shock. For the last five months, she'd been restricted from taking a job, so she'd staved off boredom by volunteering at the hospital pediatric ward in the afternoons. Reading *Winnie the Pooh* aloud and bending flexible straws into imaginative shapes hadn't kept her in shape for the rigors of real employment.

Getting up with the chickens was really going to suck.

Thirty minutes later, Molly knocked on the front door of the house. With every breath she exhaled, foggy puffs of steam formed. She glanced at a big, clock-faced thermometer mounted on a railing beam to her right. *Thirty-five degrees?* She shuddered, wishing she'd had the good sense to grab her parka. The sleeves of her loose cotton top clung to her skin where she'd failed to get completely dry after her shower, and she'd braided her hair while it was still wet. She felt like a human icicle.

From inside, she heard voices. Then came the sharp tap of boots on the interior oak floor. She expected to see Jake. Instead, a wiry older man with thinning gray hair and friendly green eyes opened the door. "Howdy!" he said warmly. "I reckon you must be Molly." He thrust out a gnarled hand that looked none too clean. "I'm Levi."

Molly grasped his extended fingers, expecting the usual polite shake. "I'm pleased to meet you, Levi."

"Not as pleased as I am." He proceeded to raise and lower her arm as if it were a pump handle. "I understand you're one hell of a shade-tree grease monkey."

"One hell of a—?" Molly broke off, swallowed, and revised that by saying, "You understand I'm a what?"

"A mechanic." Instead of stepping back so she might enter the house, Levi joined her on the porch and shut the door. "My Mandy has a perplexin' hitch in her get-along."

Molly was beginning to wonder if they spoke the same language.

He grasped her elbow and turned her about-face. "Runnin' rough as a cob, like as if there's water in her gas tank. No crack in the block, though, and the fuel checks out fine. I changed all the plugs, and that didn't help." He led her down the steps. "Threw in a new fuel pump, and that didn't help, either. Jake, now, he's a fine mechanic. Most times, he can fix what's broke. But he hasn't had time to spare all week."

With Molly firmly in tow, Levi walked to a battered brown Ford pickup with rusted rims and a bumper wired on with coat hangers. He slapped the front fender. "She don't look like much, but we're old friends. Can you tell me what's ailin' her?"

This was her first day on the job, and she didn't want to be late meeting Jake. But when she looked into Levi's worried green eyes, she couldn't tell him no. "Well," she said hesitantly. "I suppose I can take a look."

She stood back as he climbed into the pickup and started the engine. The resultant roar nearly split her eardrums. Black smoke puffed from the rattling tailpipe. After the initial explosion of noise, the engine settled into an erratic pattern of sputters, coughs, and vibrations. Molly tipped her head. "That sounds like a timing problem."

"No kidding? Can you fix her?"

Molly stared at him incredulously. Most men smirked at her mechanic skills. Women had their place, and under the hood of a vehicle definitely wasn't it. "I, um . . ." She knew she should put him off until later, but his expression was so imploring she didn't have the heart to do it. "I suppose I can try. Do you have a timing light?"

Levi spilled back out of the cab, amazingly spry for a man who looked to be well past sixty. His red cotton work shirt was spotlessly clean, the sleeves rolled back to a precise three-quarter length. "Honey, there's not much by way of mechanic tools we don't got. Mainly we're lackin' in know-how." He flashed her a smile. "It's glad we'll be to have another decent mechanic on the place."

How long could it possibly take for a woman to shower and dress?

Jake sighed and stepped to the stove to pour a third cup of coffee, a rarity for him. Here it was, seven fifteen, and he hadn't even started his day yet. When Molly finally showed up, they would have to come to a clear understanding, namely that he expected her to be prompt.

"What's got you in such a grump?" Hank asked when he stepped in from outside. "You look like you could chew bolts and spit out buckshot."

"Molly's forty-five minutes late. I told her yesterday that we aren't much on schedules around here, and I guess she took it to heart."

Hank chuckled. "She got waylaid."

"By whom?"

"Levi. He's got her working on his pickup."

"You're not serious."

Hank grabbed some crackers from a plate. "If you want to chew her ass, now's a fine time. She's head-down under the hood, with nothing but cute fanny poking out."

Hank's description titillated Jake's imagination. He set his mug on the counter and strode through the house to the front door. When he stepped onto the porch, he saw that Hank had called it right. Molly's body was angled head-down over the battered grill of Levi's pickup, the seat of her denim jeans pointing skyward. There was more of her than just fanny showing, but that was the part of her that caught and held the male eye.

Nice. As he ran his gaze over those sweetly plump contours, Jake wished, not for the first time, that the lady would wear some clothes that came close to fitting her.

Molly chose that moment to wiggle her butt, providing a display of feminine roundness that resulted in a swift arch of Jake's eyebrows. On second thought, he wasn't sure snugger britches would be a good thing. As it was, Benny was lingering in the doorway of the stable, his blue eyes fixed on Molly's upturned posterior, a vacuous expression on his craggy face. Standing behind him was Jake's youngest hand, Danno, a redheaded twenty-year-old with more testosterone and freckles than brains.

As Jake descended the front steps and started across the yard, he shot both hired hands a warning look that jerked them to attention. Benny, the older of the two at thirty-six, ran a finger under the red bandana at his throat, collected himself, and swung around to return to the stable, only to collide with Danno, who suddenly decided to head out. In a tangle of arms and legs, they looked as though they were doing the tango for a moment.

Jake released a sigh. Nope. Snug britches on Molly would not be conducive to labor output. As he made his way across the remainder of the barnyard, he assumed a scowl, which he felt was deserved under the circumstances. Just because the lady had a world-class ass and more curves than a road atlas didn't mean she could keep him waiting for forty-five minutes without hearing about it.

As he drew up at the fender of the truck, Jake cast a grinning Levi a narrow-eyed glance. Raising his voice to be heard over the now smooth purr of the engine, he said, "I hired this woman to cook and clean, not work on trucks." He glanced at his watch. "We had an appointment forty-five minutes ago."

At the sound of Jake's voice, Molly gave such a start she dropped the timing light, rapped her head on the raised pickup hood, and almost fell off the bumper. Levi caught her from toppling with a hand on her rump, which made her jump as if he had goosed her. In a borrowed denim jacket that was several sizes too large, she looked too cute by half as she teetered on her dented chrome perch and grabbed for balance.

"Mr. Coulter!" She fixed huge, butterscotch-brown eyes on him. "Has it really been forty-five minutes?"

He struggled not to smile. It was a little hard to stay mad when she looked so horrified. "It certainly has, and I have work to do."

She clamped a greasy hand over the smarting spot on her head. "I didn't think I'd been out here that long. I knocked on the door precisely at six-thirty. Honestly."

Since it was her first day and he knew Levi, Jake decided to go easy. He assured himself that his decision to be lenient had nothing to do with the worried, apprehensive look in her big brown eyes. What in God's name had happened in her life to give her such a low estimation of men? He wasn't going to fire her for being a few minutes late.

Softening his tone, he said, "Hank told me you got waylaid." He glanced at his hired hand. "Levi tends to come on like a high wind sometimes." He took the sting out of what he said next by giving her a teasing wink. "I'll let it go this time. Just don't let it happen again, all right?"

She gave the crown of her head another rub, then grimaced as she lowered her hand and saw the grease on her fingers.

"You about finished up?" Jake asked. "Sounds like she's running better."

She reached for a grease cloth lying over the radiator cap. As she wiped her hands, she said, "It was only the timing." She flashed a sweet smile at Levi. "She needs a lot of other work done, though. The points should be replaced, and that liquid weld you put in the radiator won't last. You might call around to some junkyards, Levi. If you can find a radiator, I'll be happy to help you put it in when I have a day off."

"You're an angel, Miss Molly. I'll get right on finding one."

The elderly cowboy offered her a hand down. Jake observed the inter-
action between the two, Molly hesitant and uncertain, the old man oblivious to her shyness. Levi Trump had never met a stranger. Though she still
seemed tense, it appeared to Jake that his housekeeper was already well
on her way to making friends with the old codger. Unless he missed his
guess, Molly needed a friend, and for all his rough edges, Levi would be
a fine one. He was old enough to be safe, yet young enough to remember being on the shy side of thirty with more problems than solutions.

Jake glanced at his watch again. Molly's cheeks went pink. "I'm ready."

"I certainly hope so. The day's half over." Glancing at Levi, Jake said,
"I thought you and Shorty were supposed to be changing hand lines."

"We're headin' out straightaway." Levi plucked the grease rag from
Molly's fingers. "I thank you kindly for fixin' Mandy, honey."

"It wasn't any big deal." Molly's cheeks turned a deeper pink as she
peeled off the jacket and returned it to the hired hand. "I was glad to do
it."

Hooking the jacket over his shoulder by a thumb, Levi nodded and
winked at Jake. "Thanks for the loan of your cook, boss. Though I gotta
point out, maybe you hired her for the wrong job."

Jake listened to the purr of the engine for a moment. "Maybe so."

He swung a hand, indicating that Molly should precede him to the
house. She set off, affording him a pleasing view of her backside as she
walked. The breeze picked up, molding the loose folds of her cotton top
to her body, showcasing a slender waist and full hips that could easily
make a man go cross-eyed if he admired the action for too long.

"I really was at the door by six-thirty, just as agreed," she said over her
shoulder, "but Levi caught me before I got inside."

"At least Mandy's fixed. He's been pestering me all week to have a
look at her, and I haven't had time." Lengthening his stride, Jake drew
abreast of her as they reached the porch. "So tell me, how did a pretty
girl like you become an ace mechanic?"

She rolled her eyes, whether at the compliment or the question, Jake
wasn't sure. "I can thank my father for what little skill I have. He was into
antique cars and did all the refurbishing himself."

Jake took her arm as they went up the steps. Her hip bumped against
his thigh, and he felt her stiffen. "So you developed an interest in old cars
and learned a lot about engines in the process?"

"Actually, I didn't enjoy working on cars all that much. I think I knew,
even as a teenager, that I might end up single, and just in case, I wanted
to have rudimentary mechanic skills."

Jake shot her a sharp look. "Why was that?"

"It can be tough for a single woman if she knows nothing about cars."

Jake released her arm as they gained the porch. "No, I mean why did you think you'd end up single?"

"Do you think that I suddenly woke up a plain Jane yesterday morning?"

Jake looked deeply into her beautiful eyes, and his heart caught at what he didn't see there. No laughter, no hint that she was joking. She honestly believed she was plain.

Try as he might, he could make no sense of that. Granted, she wasn't Jake's usual type, but there was no denying that she was pretty. How could she possibly look at that face and not see what everyone else did?

Had someone told her she was unattractive? All too often, one's self-image was formed by the cruel remarks of others. If Molly had been told she was plain, she would see a plain woman when she looked in the mirror. It was as simple and as heartbreaking as that.

He absolutely could not tell this woman she was pretty again. This was her first day on the job, and she was the only female on the ranch. If he paid her too many compliments, she might think he was coming on to her. A man in a position of authority had to be careful what he said and did when dealing with a female employee.

There would be no misunderstandings of that nature, not if he could help it. After showing her through the house and explaining her duties, he would give her the list of groceries they needed, write a check for the purchases, supply her with a vehicle, and leave her to manage the rest on her own.

❧ CHAPTER EIGHT ❧

Eight hours later, Molly entered the pantry and stared at a collection of small coolers on the top shelves. They were a variety of colors, none large enough to hold much more than a six-pack of soda pop and all sporting ground-in dirt. Why on earth were they taking up kitchen storage?

She didn't have time to worry about it. Going into town for groceries had taken up most of her morning. She'd spent the afternoon cleaning and doing laundry. Now it was almost five. She didn't want to be late getting dinner on the table.

Throat constricted with nerves, she went to get the vegetables. The amount needed to fix a stir-fry for twelve people was amazing. Feeding so many, she would have to go shopping for fresh produce every few days.

She was pleased that there was an industrial range with a nice grill and a gigantic oven. There was also plenty of commercial-sized cookware. She wouldn't have the added headache of having to use three or four pots to fix enough of one thing.

She worried her bottom lip as she began peeling carrots. She'd never been a blue-ribbon cook. This teriyaki dish was one of her personal favorites, and she was adding chicken because she figured they'd all like meat. She wanted to start out with a meal that everyone enjoyed. First impressions were important.

Oh, *God*. Why had she agreed to take this job? Rodney had hated her cooking. Now, here she was, trying to feed eleven men. *Hello, Molly. Are you out of your mind?*

As soon as she got the vegetables rinsed, she had to get the rice on the stove. She glanced at the wall clock. Yet another of Jake's creations, its case was a four-leaf clover made of horseshoes, the hands fashioned with antique nails. It was unique and suited the rustic log house perfectly, as did the old Jack Daniel's barrel that served as a sink vanity in the downstairs bath. Molly had never seen a home built by its owner from the foundation up. The plank doors and rudimentary detailing in every room created a delightful pioneer simplicity that made her feel as if she'd stepped into the past.

The clock said ten after five, leaving only fifty minutes if she meant to serve dinner at six. Looking at that silly clock soothed her frazzled nerves. Jake Coulter seemed to be a simple man with simple tastes. He would be happy with anything she cooked as long as it was edible. It was dumb to get in a dither.

Jake was starving and figured his hired hands were as well. They'd been out of bread for sandwiches that morning, so they'd all worked straight through with only crackers and peanut butter for lunch. When men did hard physical work, they needed plenty of grub to keep their strength up.

The house smelled divine when he stepped inside, the mix of scents sharp, rich, and mouthwatering. Not wanting to mess up the clean floors, he wiped his boots on the entry rug. As he made his way through the great room, he was pleased to see that the burl tables had been polished. Envisioning the buildup of grime that had accumulated throughout the house, he felt as if a thousand pounds had been lifted from his shoulders.

Man, this was terrific. To have a woman waiting when he came in after a hard day, to have his home all spiffed up and shiny, to know he probably had clean socks and shorts for tomorrow. It was enough to make him think about getting married. Not that he believed a woman's place was in the home, or that her sole purpose in life was to see to his needs. But it sure was nice for a change. Ordinarily he dragged in, so tired he could barely blink, and it was his responsibility to cook or heat something up.

Just outside the kitchen, he stopped to hook his Stetson over one of the dowels he had sunk into a log to create a coat rack. Then he followed his nose toward all those fantastic smells. *Food*—the hot, tasty, homemade variety.

"I've died and gone to heaven," he said as he stepped through the archway. "Something sure smells good."

Molly jumped at the sound of his voice and whirled from the stove, making him wish he'd thought to holler out a warning as he entered the house. Startled while stirring the contents of a pot, she'd slopped what looked like broth over the front of her blouse. She plucked at the cotton, trying to tug the searing wetness away from her skin.

"Damn." Jake hurried across the kitchen to grab the dishcloth. Anchoring her with one hand on her shoulder, he dabbed at her blouse. "Are you scalded?"

"No, no. It just stung a little."

She caught his wrist, her cheeks flooding with color as she met his gaze. Without fail, her eyes always reminded him of butterscotch, his favorite flavor on earth. He wanted to think that he was only hungry, but deep down, he knew that wasn't the problem. There was something about this lady that appealed to him in a way he couldn't define, let alone understand.

Tossing the rag back in the sink, he retreated a step. "I didn't mean to startle you. Working outside all day, I get in the habit of talking loud, and I forget to turn down my volume when I come indoors."

"No worries." The smile that touched her lips didn't reach her eyes. "I knew you'd be coming in to eat soon. I don't know why I reacted that way. Being in a new place, I guess."

Jake had a feeling it didn't take much to startle her. Even the way she stood suggested brittle tension, her softly rounded shoulders rigid, her body taut. Whenever he looked at her, she had trouble keeping her hands still, her nervous fingers tugging at her blouse or toying with the buttons.

Normally, Jake might have wondered if she was afraid of men, but after their confrontation last night over the rotor, he found that difficult to believe. She'd stood toe-to-toe with him, ready to do battle. He'd known very few women with the courage to take on a full-grown man.

She was a puzzle, this lady, anxious and painfully unsure of herself in many ways, yet at the same time displaying strength and courage that a lot of people lacked. The contrasts fascinated him—and tugged at his heart.

She splayed a hand at the base of her throat, her fingertips doing a fluttery little dance over her collar. Tendrils of curly hair had escaped her braid to frame her face with wisps of amber. To his delight, he saw that she'd tied a kitchen towel around her middle to serve as an apron, cinching in her smocklike top to show off her figure. And what a figure it was. The lady was stacked. She had delightfully generous breasts, a proportionately slender waist, and ample hips that made him contemplate the pleasures to be found with a woman who was soft all over.

If she were actually his wife, he'd sample her first and save supper for later. Much later.

Uncomfortable with that train of thought, he turned his gaze to the long plank table. It was a patio-style affair with cross-buck legs that he'd thrown together with scrap lumber and shined up with several coats of polyurethane. Nevertheless, she had set it all fancy with water glasses and wine goblets at every place. At the center of each plate, paper towels, folded into pretty, pleated fans, stood at attention. Jake stared, wondering how long she'd worked to make all those itty-bitty creases.

"I know." She waved a hand. "It probably looks silly. I didn't realize there were no napkins until I was already back from town."

Jake had never seen paper towels look prettier. "When you work with horses and cows from dawn 'til dark, a little bit of fancy at the end of the day is kind of nice."

"Not very fancy, I'm afraid. Next time I'm in town, I'll buy some napkins. Rings as well. A meal tastes so much better if it's pleasing to the eye."

Jake couldn't afford linen napkins or rings. At present, he was still operating in the red. "Paper towels are fine. Are we having wine?" He wondered how much she'd spent on that.

"Just some inexpensive white zin."

He cued in on "inexpensive" and gave her marks for being perceptive. "That'll be a treat." Afraid she might grace the table with wine he couldn't afford every night, he quickly added, "Just don't make it a habit."

"Oh, no. I just—" Her fingertips flitted down the line of buttons on her blouse. His quick reaction with the dishrag had saved the cotton from staining, he noticed. "This is the first dinner I've fixed here, and I want it to be special."

Just having her there made it special. Her smile was so sweet and hesitant, the appeal for approval difficult to resist. It seemed to him that the kitchen seemed cheerier with her in it—brighter, somehow. He panned the room, taking in the shine she'd put on everything. He could see his reflection on the front of the old side-by-side.

"Just getting a home-cooked meal will be special." He glanced at the large pot on the stove. "What's cooking?"

"It's a surprise."

"Well, I'm hungry enough to eat the south end of a northbound jackass." He stepped over to the sink to wash up. "Don't keep me in suspense too long."

Molly spent the next few minutes dishing up the rice and stir-fry. While she worked, several more men filed in. When she turned to serve the meal, all but one place at the end of the long table had been taken. The men all sat straighter as she advanced on them with the huge bowl of rice in her hands.

"This is Molly," Jake said by way of introduction. "Starting at my left"—he pointed a finger—"that's Skeeter, Preach, Shorty, Benny, Danno, Tex, Bill, and Nate. You've already met Levi and my brother Hank."

Molly scanned their faces, which ranged from young to very old. Except for Levi, who wore a red shirt, they were all dressed in chambray and denim. In the sea of variegated blue, their features blurred, and she promptly forgot their names. The only person who stood out, aside from Hank and Levi, was the redheaded youth named Danno, who had so many freckles she could barely make out his hazel eyes.

"I'm pleased to meet all of you." She turned to fetch the serving bowl of vegetables and chicken. "I hope you enjoy. This is one of my favorite dishes." When no one moved to dig in, she added, "I'll pour milk for those who want it, and wine for those who'd like that. Meanwhile, feel free to dish up."

"Where's the bread?" Danno asked.

Molly glanced at the table. "I, um . . . didn't plan to serve bread, Danno. We have rice."

"Rice?" Danno squinted into the bowl. "It's funny looking. What did you do, douse it with soy when you cooked it?"

"It's brown rice." Jake began dishing food onto his plate. "They say it's healthier than white. Try some, Danno. It's a great substitute for potatoes."

"Even with potatoes, we always get bread," Danno complained.

Molly could see the young man wouldn't feel fed until she gave him bread, so she hurried into the pantry. "I haven't any dinner rolls. Will this do?"

Danno's eyes brightened as he grabbed the end of the loaf bag. "This'll do fine." He drew out four slices then scanned the table. "Where's the butter?"

Molly stepped to the refrigerator and plucked out the butter spray, which was a flavorful substitute, calorie free, and contained no fat. "Here you go."

Danno took the spray bottle, stared at it for a long moment, and then said, "What the flipping hell?"

Every head at the table swiveled to stare. *Silence.* Molly licked her lips. "It's, um, butter spray. It's very good. You can't believe it's not the real thing."

Danno frowned. "What happened to the regular butter?"

"I didn't buy any."

Danno flashed a glance at Jake. "When did we start buying butter?"

Jake spooned out some vegetables and chicken onto his rice. "This is Molly's first day, Danno. I didn't have time to show her how to make butter."

Molly threw a startled look at her boss. He expected her to *make* butter? Jake glanced up. "We have an electric churn. It's no big deal."

Molly wasn't particularly interested in learning how to make butter. She liked her unclogged arteries and wanted to keep them that way. There were also a few older men at her table who needed to watch their cholesterol. No one was having a heart attack on her watch, not if she could prevent it.

Brave thoughts. In reality, she knew she would make butter until it came out their ears. Anything to please them. She needed to keep this job.

As she made her way around the table to pour the wine, Danno sprayed his bread, scowling gloomily. When he finally took a bite, he snarled a lip and asked, "Do we have any jelly?"

"Oh, yes." Though she couldn't imagine anyone's wanting jelly with zesty stir-fry, Molly hurried back to the fridge. She was starting to feel as if she were in a footrace. When she handed Danno the small jar of Simply Fruit, he studied the label before removing the lid and then scooped out nearly all the jar's contents onto his bread. He folded one slice lengthwise over the oozing preserves and stuffed the whole works into his mouth. "Mmm."

Molly decided then and there that she'd better buy less expensive jam from now on. If Danno was any indication, these men were into quantity, not quality.

By the time she took her place at the foot of the table, she had begun to suspect that her first meal at the Lazy J had fallen short of expectations. She unfolded her napkin, noting that Jake was the only other person who'd bothered to spread his over his lap. The other men had set their paper towels beside their plates. She waited expectantly for someone besides Danno to sample the food. Just as expectantly, her diners stared back at her.

It struck Molly then that they were waiting for her to take the first bite. "Oh, please, don't wait on me," she said, feeling more nervous by the second. "I'll be up and down all during the meal." Determining that no one at her end was going to pass her the rice, she came up from her chair to reach for the bowl herself. The contents were nearly gone. "Just enjoy your food."

Waiting in an agony of suspense to see their expressions when they tasted the stir-fry, Molly forgot all about the rice bowl she held in her hands.

Jake finally took a bite, glanced pointedly at his men so they would follow suit, and said, "Mmm, this is delicious, Molly." He flashed her a smile as he lifted his goblet. "The white zinfandel will set it off perfectly."

Following his older brother's example, Hank started shoveling food in his mouth. When he tried his wine, he graced her with a broad grin. "First time we've used the crystal. It was a housewarming gift. Our sister Bethany and her husband Ryan got Jake a whole set."

"It's lovely." Molly had been pleasantly surprised to find the fine glassware in one of the cupboards, and she'd wondered about it at the time. Jake didn't strike her as a man who spared much coin for anything that wasn't essential.

As though he read her mind, Hank grinned and added, "It's impractical as hell." He winked and extended his pinky as he took another sip of wine from the fluted goblet. "Ryan's a rich boy. I feel downright highfalutin."

Molly searched Jake's dark face. His expression as he applied himself to his meal was unreadable. Despite his seemingly sincere compliment on the food, she couldn't shake the feeling that he wasn't entirely happy with what she had served. A knot of dread formed at the pit of her stomach. If she lost this job, Sunset was doomed and so was she. Just thinking of the possibilities made her stomach tighten with anxiety.

"This wine *is* good," the sandy-haired man called Shorty said. He settled questioning blue eyes on Molly. "My partner is waiting on the porch. His name's Bartholomew, Bart for every day. If you've got any leftovers tonight, he'd surely appreciate them."

"Your partner is out on the porch?" About to dish herself some rice, Molly set the bowl aside and pushed up from her chair. "There's no need for him to wait out there, Shorty. We'll make room at the table. He can have my place."

Jake's head snapped up. "Bart's a dog, Molly. I asked Shorty to keep him outside from now on. I didn't think you'd appreciate him tracking up the clean floors."

Shorty bent his head, but not before Molly glimpsed the resentment in his eyes. Clearly, Bart had been allowed to come inside until now.

Though she'd never been around dogs very much because her father had been allergic, Molly didn't want to make any unnecessary changes in the usual ranch routine. She stepped over to open the back door. There on the steps lay the ugliest, shaggiest, dirtiest creature she'd ever clapped eyes on. His right flank was partially bald. One blue eye shone up at her with suspicious curiosity, the other clouded with white and angled off in the wrong direction.

"Hello, Bart." The greeting was all the invitation the dog needed. He rose and moved over the threshold into the kitchen. As she watched the canine make his way toward Shorty, Molly saw that he was carrying a front foot. "Oh, no, he's hurt!"

All the men turned to look as Shorty bent to examine the dog's paw. "Another damned foxtail," the old hired hand pronounced.

"Where in hell did he pick up a foxtail?" Levi asked. "Kindee early in the year for 'em, ain't it?"

Shorty patted the dog's head and softly told him to lie down. As he turned to resume his meal, he said, "Leave it to Bart. If there's a foxtail within a hundred miles, he'll find the dad-blamed thing."

Molly returned to her place, her attention fixed on the dog. Bart whined softly and began licking his paw, clearly in discomfort from the sticker lodged between his toes. Her already nervous stomach knotted with sympathy.

"Shouldn't someone pull out the foxtail and disinfect the sore?" she asked.

Shorty nodded. "I'll get right on it, soon as supper's done."

It seemed to Molly that the dog's foot should come first, eating later, but she refrained from saying as much. It was important that she get along with everyone, and offering her opinion where it wasn't wanted was no way to gain popularity. "Is Bart accustomed to having his dinner while everyone else is eating theirs?"

Shorty raised his gaze and nodded. "Yes, ma'am. Nothing special. Just whatever the rest of us are having."

Molly glanced incredulously at the dog. "Surely he won't like stir-fry."

"Neither do we," Danno inserted, "but we're eatin' it."

"Danno," Jake said warningly. He smiled at Molly. "Don't pay this young whippersnapper any attention. The rest of us think your stir-fry is wonderful."

Levi seconded that. "Yes, ma'am. Damned good grub."

The dark-haired, craggy-faced man named Preach lowered his wine glass to say, "It's got my vote."

At the rate the rice and vegetables had already disappeared, Molly doubted there would be anything left for poor Bart, so rather than resume her seat, she went to put on more rice. She could scramble some eggs to mix in with it. That would do as Bart's dinner for tonight.

"What are you doing now, Molly?" Jake asked. "You haven't even filled your plate yet."

"First, I want to put on a little extra rice for Bart. We can't have Shorty's partner going hungry."

Behind her, Molly heard a chair scrape the floor and the ensuing thump of boot heels. She glanced around to see Jake at her end of the table, scooping what remained of the rice onto her plate.

"I can do that."

"Not if it's all gone, you can't." He flicked her an amused glance. "It would seem that your stir-fry is a hit."

Molly looked away, afraid her expression might reveal how pleased she was. Aside from Danno, everyone else seemed to like the food. That wasn't a bad success ratio.

After putting the rice on to cook, she reclaimed her chair, fully intending to partake of the meal even though she had little appetite. She'd taken only one bite when Bart whined. She glanced down to see the dog chewing on his paw. Her heart caught with pity. It seemed cruel to just sit there, ignoring the animal's distress.

Gazing the length of the table at her employer, Molly cautioned herself not to interfere in what was clearly the established order of things. Shorty would see to the dog in good time, and Bart would survive until then, she assured herself. It wasn't her place to say anything.

She had nearly convinced herself when Bart whined again. That did it. She couldn't just sit there, pretending not to notice.

"Please, excuse me for a moment," she said politely, as she left the table to go to the downstairs bathroom.

Jake sighed as he watched Molly leave the room. At last count, she'd taken only one bite of food. Never in all his days had he seen anyone so tense. As if her life hung in the balance, she'd watched the men's faces while they ate, and she'd grown downright pale when Danno criticized the meal. Jake ached to tell her that he had no intention of firing her. Cooking for so many was no easy task, and he fully expected her to make a few blunders while she was learning the ropes.

He was relieved when she returned to the kitchen only seconds later. His feeling of relief was quickly replaced by apprehension when he saw that she carried a bottle of hydrogen peroxide, cotton balls, and tweezers. She clearly intended to remove the foxtail from Bart's paw.

Jake glanced worriedly at Shorty, wondering how the old man would react. It was an unspoken law with many cattlemen that a man's dog was to be touched, fed, and given commands only by its owner. Those individuals believed that a canine's loyalty to its master was diminished by outside influence. Though Jake disagreed with that school of thought, he respected Shorty's right to believe whatever he chose. The old hired hand loved Bart and treated him kindly. That was all Jake really cared about, that the dog never suffered for his master's eccentricities.

Unaware that Shorty allowed no one else to mess with his dog, Molly knelt beside Bart and began cooing softly. The canine, as unaccustomed to women as he was to friendly overtures from strangers, responded with low, warning growls. Instead of seeming alarmed, Molly only cooed more sympathetically.

Warning signals jangled in Jake's brain. He had a very bad feeling that his cook knew very little about dogs. Ordinarily that wouldn't have posed a problem—but Bart was no ordinary canine. Cattle dogs were as different from their domestic cousins as night was from day.

"I don't blame you a bit for feeling grumpy," Molly murmured consolingly to the disgruntled blue heeler. "There's nothing worse than having a hurt foot, is there? Well, don't worry. I'll have that nasty old foxtail out in two seconds, and you'll feel better."

Shorty stopped chewing, pocketed the food in his cheek, and bugged his eyes at Jake. Hank threw his brother an anxious look as well.

"Careful, Molly," Jake warned. "Bart is surly, and he snaps sometimes."

"Oh, surely not," she replied. "He seems like such a sweetheart."

The dog's growls didn't sound very sweet to Jake.

Shorty turned on his chair to fix Molly with a disapproving scowl. "Just what're you up to, missy? He's my dog. I'll take care of him."

Soothing Bart with gentle strokes of her slender hands, Molly glanced up and smiled, her big brown eyes shimmering in the overhead light. "I thought I'd get this foxtail out for you, Shorty. Go ahead and enjoy your meal while it's hot. I'm not all that hungry, and I don't mind the interruption."

The elderly man's shoulders stiffened. "Bart don't take kindly to bein' pestered by strangers. Don't you hear him snarlin'?"

"Oh, those aren't snarls." Molly bent to cluck her tongue at the growling dog. "He's just talking to me. Aren't you, Bart? Yes. You're telling me all about it, aren't you? Poor baby. I know how it must hurt." She ran a fingertip along the dog's muzzle, apparently heedless of his sharp incisors. In a singsong, baby-talk voice, she said, "I'd be grumpy, too. Yes, I would. Your little paw is all swollen. I'll bet that foxtail has been in there all day. *Ouch.*"

By no estimation was Bart's paw little. The blue heeler was large for his breed, a variation from standard that had made Jake question his bloodlines more than once. More alarmingly, the dog's bared teeth weren't small. Molly could be badly hurt if Bart decided to bite her. "Molly, maybe you'd better let Shorty take care of that," he tried.

"Really, I don't mind," she insisted. "It'll only take me a few seconds."

Shorty had completely reversed his direction on the chair to stare at their new cook. The old man was clearly amazed that Bart hadn't already tried to take her arm off. "I'd listen to the boss and back off if I was you, missy. Bart's been known to bite on occasion."

Molly gave the dog a measuring look. Then her mouth curved into a beatific smile. Jake had known a lot of women who pretended to be sweet and caring, only to discover later that they were hell on wheels. With Molly, however, he didn't believe it was an act. As hokey as it sounded, even in his mind, she fairly glowed with goodness. You simply couldn't look at her and doubt that she had a kind heart.

"He won't bite me," she assured Shorty. "He's just feeling out of sorts. And who wouldn't?"

With that pronouncement, she proceeded to lift Bart's paw onto her knee and go fishing with the tweezers. Shorty gaped. The dog growled more ferociously, but to no avail. Molly ignored the warnings. Jake pushed up from his chair and moved closer.

Instead of sinking his sharp teeth into Molly's tender flesh, the dog only whined, cast a resigned look at his master, and licked Molly's wrist. Jake relaxed and winked at Shorty, who looked as if he'd just swallowed a sock.

"I don't gen'rally let strangers touch my dog," the hired hand said.

"That's very wise," Molly observed, flashing the old man a quick but understanding smile. "You just never know who might do something despicable. I read in the paper just last month about some man who went around poisoning dogs at the city park. Isn't that terrible? He put arsenic in bits of ground beef. I can't imagine anyone's doing such a heartless thing, but there you are. For Bart's sake, you need to be cautious."

Shorty looked helplessly at Jake. Then he sighed and slid off his chair to crouch at Molly's elbow. After watching her gently probe for the foxtail, he grinned and said, "He's taken a shine to you, no question." After watching her work a minute longer, Shorty added, "I've always heard tell dogs can sense things about people that we can't—like as if they can smell the goodness or evil in a person. My mother was a firm believer in that. Had herself an old coon dog that didn't take up much with strangers.

When that old hound liked a man, my ma trusted him with her life." Shorty reached to scratch behind his dog's ears. "I reckon old Bart is givin' you a real high recommend, Miss Molly. A real high recommend, indeed."

Molly's cheeks went pink. She glanced wonderingly at Bart. "I like you, too, punkin. If you had a bath, you'd be a very handsome fellow." She touched the bald patch on the dog's flank. Then she resumed probing for the sticker. "What caused him to lose his hair there, Shorty? Was he injured somehow?"

Shorty sighed. "One time while I was inside paying the tab at a gas station, I left him in the back of my truck. When the attendant tried to put fuel in the tank, Bart took exception and raised a ruckus. By the time I got back out there, the dad-blamed fellow had doused him with gas. I didn't know it happened until I saw him shiverin' and bitin' at himself later. By then, he was burnt pretty bad, and the hair never grew back."

Molly's eyes darkened with shadows. "Oh, how *awful*. Why would anyone do something so mean?"

Shorty shook his head. "Like I said, Bart can be ornery sometimes. Maybe he snapped at the fellow."

"That's no excuse, and Bart isn't ornery," Molly protested. "He's a doll." She made kissing sounds near the dog's nose. Moments before, Jake would have worried for her face, but the bedraggled canine clearly recognized a bona fide sweetheart when he met one. "There!" she finally cried triumphantly. "I got it, Bart." She held up the tweezers for the canine's inspection. "Now, doesn't that feel better, sweetie?"

Bart bypassed the tweezers to lick Molly's face, which made her sputter and laugh. "Oh, dear, you have bad breath. The next time I'm in town, I'll get you a toothbrush and some dog toothpaste. We'll take care of that little problem."

Shorty's eyebrows arched toward his balding pate. "Dog toothpaste? I've never heard of such."

Molly set aside the tweezers and peeled Bart's lip back to examine his teeth. "Just *look* at that tartar buildup. No question about it, he needs better oral hygiene, or he'll get cavities soon." The men at the table exchanged amazed glances as she went on to say, "The toothpaste comes in doggy flavors. I've seen it advertised on television. Bart will love it."

Shorty looked none too certain about that. "Hmm. Well, I'll be. I never knew there was folks who brushed their dogs' teeth."

"We brush ours," Molly pointed out.

"Seems like a lot of fuss for nothin' when a good bone'll do the job."

"I'll get him some bones, too." Molly dabbed between Bart's toes with the antiseptic. Then she glanced up at Jake. "I'll pay for everything. No worries."

For once, the farthest thing from Jake's mind had been his concerns about money. He was far too fascinated, watching Molly interact with Shorty and the dog. On a good day, it was a toss-up who was the more difficult to get along with, the canine or the old man. Yet she had won them both over without half trying.

"I can brush his teeth for him every day if you'd rather not be bothered, Shorty," she offered. "I know you're busy, and I won't mind taking the time to do it."

Shorty thought about it for a moment and then nodded. "I reckon it can't hurt. I'd hate like heck if his teeth went bad. False chompers for a dog would cost dearly."

Molly gave a startled laugh. "I bet they would, at that." A fond warmth crept into her eyes as she regarded the old man. "If such a thing existed, you'd get him some, though. Don't tell me you wouldn't. When it comes to this dog, you're a softie. I can tell."

"I reckon I would," Shorty agreed. "He's gotta be able to eat, don't he?"

Jake resumed his seat to finish his meager meal, incredulous but pleased that Molly was already making friends with his men. There was something about the lady that made a man go a little soft in the head the instant he looked into her big brown eyes.

His grin broadened when he glanced at Bart. Whatever that indefinable quality was, it seemed to have the same effect on canines as it did on men.

❦ CHAPTER NINE ❦

When the meal was over, Jake rolled up his sleeves to help Molly clean the kitchen. The instant she realized his intent, she got all flustered, her cheeks turned a pretty pink, and she tried to take the rice bowl out of his hands.

"I can do this, Mr. Coulter. You worked hard all day, and cleaning the kitchen is my job."

Just once and of her own accord, Jake wanted to hear her address him by his first name. Keeping a firm grip on the serving bowl, he said, "You worked hard today, too. The house looks wonderful. Did I mention that?"

Her eyes went all sparkly with pleasure. "I barely skimmed the surface. I'll do some deep cleaning tomorrow."

"Nevertheless, I know you put in a hard day, and I really don't mind helping you clean up. That way, the work will be over more quickly for all of us."

She finally relinquished the bowl. "It has been a long day. Everything being new, I've been slow. I'll get a routine worked out soon, I'm sure."

Jake could hope. She'd bounced up and down so much during supper that she'd eaten hardly anything. Not that there had been much food left to put on her plate. He and his men had taken only a small portion each, but there had been barely enough to go around, even then.

How could he tell her that she needed to cook in much larger quantities? She'd done her best, and she was obviously so worried about her performance that he was afraid any criticism, no matter how kindly intended, might do more harm than good. Given the fact that gentle deliveries weren't his specialty, that presented one hell of a problem.

He had enjoyed the meal, such as it was. But he worked long and hard, and so did his men. They burned off calories almost as fast as the food went into their mouths. Stir-fries were fine as an occasional main dish, but she needed to add more protein, fix several rich side dishes as well, and make sure there was a lot of bread and fresh butter on the table. Otherwise he and his men were going to be hungry all the time.

At least no one but the dog had been rude enough to lick his plate.

Mulling over the problem, Jake set himself to the task of rinsing dishes and putting them in the dishwater. While he worked, Molly flitted around him, clearing the table, washing the counter, polishing the stove, and putting things away. Jake had always been a stickler on kitchen tidiness, but he'd never cleaned up quite as thoroughly as Molly did.

She was so tense she seemed to have trouble staying focused. She kept forgetting where she had laid the dishcloth. She wandered around, opening cupboard doors to stare blankly into them while she muttered under her breath. Jake could only hope she started to relax around him soon, or they were both going to have nervous breakdowns.

When the kitchen was spotless enough to suit her, he glanced out the window, saw that night had fallen, and offered to see her home. He hoped he might find an opening during the walk to tell her she had to start fixing more food.

"Oh, you don't need to walk me," she protested. "I know the way."

"It's dark out there. With your poor night vision, you could take a wrong turn and get lost."

She laughed. "My night vision isn't *that* poor."

Acutely aware that she felt uneasy with him, Jake might have let her go home unescorted if he hadn't recalled her reference to bears last night. She was clearly out of her element in this rural setting, and he didn't want her to grow frightened out there, alone in the dark. He led the way from the kitchen, stopping just beyond the archway to collect his hat. "I'll rest easier if I see you to your doorstep."

Hank, crouched before the wide rock fireplace, glanced up from rumpling newspaper. "Best let him walk you, Molly. I spotted cougar track along the creek last week. It's a worry when they come in so close to the house."

Molly paled. "Cougar track? Oh, dear."

Jake wished that Hank had kept his mouth shut. The actual danger of a cougar attack anywhere on the ranch was fairly minuscule. "Don't listen to him, Molly. Cougars seldom bother humans."

"Bull. Wasn't that long ago a cougar attacked a little boy standing in line at a municipal swimming pool."

"That wasn't in Oregon," Jake reminded him.

"Like cougars know what state they're in? What about the cat outside Lakeview that attacked the mail truck? That was in Oregon."

"That happened quite some while back, and for all we know, it was nothing but a story. I never saw mention of it in the newspaper."

Molly fixed Jake with a worried look. "If there's a danger, please don't keep it from me. I'd rather be a little nervous and take precautions."

Jake didn't want her jumping at shadows. "Cougars rarely attack people."

"That poor lady jogger in northern California probably told herself the same thing," Hank inserted. "All they found were pieces of her jogging outfit."

"Oh, how *awful!*" Molly shivered and rubbed her arms. "What a terrible way to die."

"Not so bad, actually. The cougar probably snapped her spine upon impact." Hank nodded sagely. "That's how they make a kill." He snapped his fingers. "Just like that. They tracked the cat down. She only weighed eighty pounds, just a young female with cubs. The cougar along our creek is a big old fellow. I could tell that by the prints."

Jake glared at his brother over the top of Molly's head. "Are you finished having your fun, Hank? You've frightened Molly. Now she'll be nervous every time she steps outside."

Hank angled a mischievous look at Molly. "Have I scared you, Molly?"

"No. Not really. I just—" She rubbed her arms again. "My goodness! Where I live, cougars aren't a problem."

Jake could believe that. He had a hunch she came from Portland, and the only cougars in the downtown areas were probably stuffed. "They aren't a problem here, either."

"Yes, they are, and growing to be more so each passing year," Hank protested. "They're way overpopulated and easily habituated to humans, so they get bold."

Jake was going to kill his brother before any cougar got a chance. While Hank was still spouting alarming facts about cougars, he hurried Molly from the great room.

"Have a nice walk, you two," Hank called, a twinkle in his eye.

The instant they stepped onto the front porch, Molly came to a dead stop and pressed closer to Jake. Darkness and the chill night air curled around them. He felt her shiver. When he glanced down, he saw that she was peering owlishly toward the steps. Her wariness of him had apparently been shoved from her mind by a greater fear, namely big-toothed predators.

"Can cougars really jump from heights of sixty feet?"

Even as she spoke, she tucked herself more snugly against his side.

Jake slipped an arm around her. "Don't listen to Hank. He's twenty-nine, going on sixteen. Telling spooky stories to a pretty lady makes him feel macho."

She laughed nervously. "You didn't answer my question. Can they?"

Jake sighed. "Yes. According to the statistics I read, they can. I've never seen it myself. You have to remember that those statistics are the most impressive ever documented, the feats of supercougars, in other words. Around here, the cougars are all wimps."

An owl hooted, and she nearly jumped out of her skin. She nudged her shoulder into his ribs, getting as close as she could without joining him inside his Wranglers. He tightened his arm around her. She stiffened slightly but made no offer to pull away.

As they started down the steps into the deeper darkness, she craned her neck to see through the shadows. She felt so good, snuggled up against him, all feminine softness and intriguing curves. Every time he flexed his splayed fingers on her side, he felt her flank muscles quiver, creating images in his mind of how she might quiver if he touched her in other places.

When she moved just right, one of those places grazed the knuckle of his thumb. Never in his recollection had the weight and heat of a woman's breast felt so tempting. He wanted so badly to cup that generous softness, to learn the shape of her, to capture her nipple and give it a tug, to hear her breath catch.

Holy hell. He was going to murder Hank when he got back.

He'd been too long out of a relationship. That was the problem. Since starting up the ranch, he'd had no time for a social life, and now his body was telling him about it. That was all it was, he felt sure. He liked tall, leggy females with figures his mother likened to Barbie dolls, not short, sweetly plump women who could kiss his navel without having to bend much at the knees.

Now there was an interesting possibility.

One he had no intention of exploring, of course.

This was not good. Molly, with her big, vulnerable brown eyes, wasn't his type. She had hips. And, hey, the women he dated *always* wore acrylic nails—long, wicked, blood-red claws. He hated them, but that was beside the point.

So, what was the point?

With Molly pressed so temptingly against him, Jake honestly didn't know. He only knew she reminded him of his mother in little ways. Jake loved his mother as much as the next guy. She was one of the dearest people on earth and still beautiful even in her late fifties. It was just one of those things that only men understood, he guessed. When it came to carnal pursuits, anything that put you in mind of your mom was to be avoided.

Molly definitely reminded Jake of Mary Coulter. They each had big, guileless eyes and smiles to light up a room. They also had similar builds, both of them short, curvaceous, and soft. They were the kind of women who were made to cuddle children close.

They were also the kind of women who bore lots of children because their husbands couldn't keep their hands off them.

What was he *thinking*?

Suddenly narrow-hipped, long-legged, big-busted women no longer seemed very appealing. He wanted short and soft and—*don't go there, Jake.*

With some women, acting on an instant attraction was fine, but Molly wasn't one of them. He could see her heart in her eyes, and a bruised, wounded heart it was. He would never forgive himself if he hurt her, and he'd never been a staying kind of man. He liked to think that was because he hadn't met the right lady yet, but what if he was wrong? And what was to say Molly was the right lady?

"Thank you for walking with me." She glanced worriedly upward as they passed under a tree at the edge of his yard. "I really appreciate it."

Jake was so damned tempted to play this up, but he wasn't a hormonal teenager, and fear had long since ceased to be a tool of seduction.

"Molly, no cougar is going to attack you around here. Do you really think I would neglect to tell you if I thought it was a possibility?"

She fixed a big, worried gaze on him, her eyes luminous in the moonlight. "Hank seems to think it's a possibility."

"Hank is an idiot." Jake winced. "Not an idiot, exactly. An opportunist might be a better description. He played the cougar thing up because he knew I was walking you home. He thought he was doing me a favor." He remembered his vow not to pay her too many compliments. So much for that plan. "You're a very pretty lady, and just look at you now, melting over me like a pat of butter on a biscuit."

She snapped erect. The worried look in her eyes vanished. "He was matchmaking?"

Jake mourned the loss of her softness pressed against him, but he relinquished his hold on her waist. "He didn't mean any harm. He's a big tease and doesn't take much of anything too seriously."

Molly folded her arms. "You and me? If that isn't beyond silly."

And what was so silly about it?

He could kiss her silly. What would she have to say about that?

She picked up her pace, leaving him to step fancy in order to catch up with her. Ahead of them, a knee-high shrub grew at the edge of the patchy lawn, and Molly was headed straight for it. He grabbed her elbow just before she ran over the top of it.

"Bush dead ahead," he said as he steered her around it. "How do you navigate at night, girl? Bats are blind, but they have radar."

"I wish I did. Is it always so dark in the country?"

Jake switched hands on her elbow and slipped his right arm around her waist again. This time she jerked as if he'd stuck her with a pin. He almost released her. When she wasn't afraid, the lady obviously didn't appreciate being touched. No matter. He didn't want her to trip over something in the dark and get hurt, which was exactly what might happen if he turned her loose.

She stiffened away from him as they walked, trying without success to keep distance between their bodies. Jake firmed his hold on her and set an even pace, measuring his strides to accommodate her much shorter legs. She fit nicely against him, her soft fullness molding to the hard planes of his body. He liked the way she felt and, once again, he found himself wishing he could explore all those plump places.

He looked up at the sky and said, "Will you just look at that?"

It was a corny, shopworn line, but it worked. She glanced up, sighed in appreciation, and relaxed against him. "Isn't that *incredible*? I never realized there were so many stars."

"Out here, you can see them better, is all. No city lights to dim their sparkle." Jake didn't add that he was far more captivated by the sparkle in her eyes.

Sunset whinnied at their approach, the sound less panicky than yesterday, but not exactly a herald of welcome yet. "Did you stop to visit with him today?" Jake asked.

Molly laughed, the trill decidedly edgy. "I said hello before I went grocery shopping and again when I got back, but I wouldn't say we had a visit. He goes the other way when I get close and stays in the corner until I leave."

Steering her with a slight pressure of his hand, Jake detoured toward the corral. Sunset shrieked and reared. Moonlight glanced off the shiny sections of his black coat where he'd sustained no injuries, and his mane lifted in the breeze, flashing around his arched neck like tarnished silver.

"Did he act up like this?"

She shook her head. "No. He just grunted at me and danced around a little. I think he was afraid I might go inside with him."

Jake wondered if she saw the significance of that. If the horse didn't shriek and rear at her approach, it was a very good sign. After watching Molly with Bart earlier, he wasn't surprised to discover that the stallion instinctively trusted her. Some people had a natural gift with animals.

Jake had a way with animals himself. It was a talent that had served him well, enabling him to make good money training horses. Sunset hadn't warmed up to him yet, but it was early on, Jake was a man, and the memory of the whipping was still fresh in Sunset's mind. Jake had every confidence that he would begin to make headway in a few days. He just had to be consistent and patient.

Once at the fence, he opted to keep his arm around Molly. She was shivering slightly, whether from his touch or the chill air, he couldn't say. Just in case she was cold, it seemed only gentlemanly to share his body heat, since he hadn't thought to bring a jacket.

He smiled to himself. The truth was, he liked having her close. She felt so right, which made no sense at all. He was a lofty man. The top of her head didn't quite clear his shoulder even when she was wearing three-inch heels. In sneakers, she was definitely what he would term vertically challenged.

He'd never seen so many curves packed into sixty-three inches.

Beneath his palm, he could feel the ladder of her ribs, the generous overlay of soft flesh and silky skin supple and warm. As near as he could tell, there wasn't much unneeded padding there, only enough to make her feel lush.

Why in the hell was she on a diet?

"What is it?" she suddenly asked. She peered through the gloom at Sunset. "Is something wrong with him?"

Realizing that he'd betrayed his thoughts by tensing his body, Jake forced himself to relax and turn his mind to safer things. "He's fine." He glanced down. "Can't you see him?"

"I can see him—sort of. Not very clearly, though."

Jake stooped down, making a show of getting at her eye level. "Is the light worse down here or something?"

She laughed and inched her face back from his. "I doubt it's any worse down here than anywhere else."

Jake thought the view was a hell of a lot prettier down there. Her lips were only inches from his. Never in his memory had he wanted so badly to steal a kiss. That mouth. Naked of any lipstick, it was a natural pink and shimmered in the moonlight, the pout of her bottom lip begging him to take a taste.

If she'd been any other woman, Jake would have acted on the urge. At thirty-two, almost thirty-three, he'd been around the block more times than he could count, and with maturity, he'd lost any hesitance with the ladies that he might have once had. A friendly kiss meant nothing. If it led to more, that didn't usually mean much, either. He dated women who knew the score. As long as he gave as much pleasure as he took, he owed them nothing more than that, and they expected nothing more.

Molly was different, though. He'd sensed that the first time he saw her, and his feeling hadn't changed since, except to grow stronger. She was well past the blush of girlhood. In her eyes, he saw wisdom that had been hard earned through painful experience. But, for all of that, she was vulnerable. When he kissed her—if he kissed her—nothing about it would be simple.

He straightened and spoke to the stallion. Sunset whinnied and pranced nervously at the louder pitch of Jake's voice.

"When will you start working with him?" Molly asked.

Jake glanced down, wondering if she could see his face clearly. "I'm working with him already." He resettled his hand on her side, noting as he did that she didn't jerk or stiffen this time. "Several times today, I got in the corral, sat in one corner, and stayed until he stopped feeling nervous."

"That's what you call working with him?"

"It can't happen overnight, Molly. And, yes, the way I train, that's working with him, maybe the most important part. I don't like to force my will on an animal. It can be done. Easily, I might add. But what's gained? Sunset already knows he's at a disadvantage, that I could use hobbles and twitches and do anything I wanted to him. Shall I drive the point home to him yet again?"

Her expression softened as she studied the horse. "So instead you're letting him get used to you slowly."

"Exactly. He's been terrorized enough. This time, we'll do it the easy way, in small increments, until he isn't so afraid of me. That can only be accomplished by repeated exposure. By hanging around his corral, I'm desensitizing him to my presence. When I can approach without setting him off, it'll be time to move on to the next step."

"What will that be?"

Jake searched her eyes, which glistened up at him like twin measures of expensive Scotch shot through with moonlight. "The first step will be to move in closer yet. When he accepts that, closer still, until he gets used to me and welcomes the touch of my hands."

"And then?"

"I'll doctor him, even if he no longer has any open wounds."

"Why will you do that?"

Jake thought a moment, trying to come up with the words to explain what he did instinctively. "Because, healed or not, the wounds will still be there."

She made a slight sound at the base of her throat and nodded. Her sadness for the horse rolled off her in waves, filling Jake with a melancholy that made him ache.

"With a person, you can accomplish quite a lot with words, but all a horse understands are a few basic commands and tone of voice. You have to communicate with him in other ways, mostly by your actions. I need to tell Sunset that I'm sorry about what happened to him, that I know all the pain he suffered, and that I want to make him better."

Tears glistened in her lovely eyes. "I wish I could tell him that, too."

Jake tightened his hand over her side. "You already have, honey. By bringing him here, you told him. Somewhere in all his confused thoughts right now, I think he understands that you're the one who saved him. When he's ready, I won't be surprised if he trusts you more than anyone else."

"What makes you think that?" she asked tautly, sounding none too pleased by the prospect.

Jake bit back a smile. "You say he didn't shriek and act up when you stopped to visit him today? That he just grunted and danced around a little?"

"Yes."

"That means he's not as afraid of you as he is of me, that on some level he already trusts you. He probably senses that you care about him. At least, that's my guess."

"Oh, do you really think so?"

Her expression was such a mixture of hope and dread that Jake couldn't help smiling again. "I really do. To be gifted with that kind of trust is a very special thing. I hope you'll appreciate what an honor it is, and that you'll use it to help in every way that you can."

"How can I do that?"

"You can start by spending time with him every day. Just hang around his pen for a half hour or so and talk to him. It doesn't really matter what you say. Your tone of voice will convey your feelings. Let him know you care about him and that you're here for him. He's very frightened right now."

"Yes," she agreed faintly. She straightened her shoulders and stared through the darkness at the nervous stallion. "He sort of scares me."

Sort of? Jake thought that fell short.

"He's so big, and he gets so violent when he's frightened," she added. "I'm not sure I'm the right person to help him."

"In time, that'll change. You'll feel more comfortable with him soon."

"Oh, I don't know. I'd much rather just watch you work with him."

"And accomplish what? Every time that whip cut into him, his pride and dignity took a blow, and the hurt of that will never heal until it's acknowledged and an attempt is made to soothe it away. As his trainer, I can get him partway there, but someone who loves him will have to take him the rest of the way."

Her uplifted gaze went suspiciously bright again. After taking a shuddering breath, she swallowed, looked away, and said, "I don't love him. Not really. I just feel sorry for him."

Jake didn't believe that for a minute. The very fact that she'd stolen the stallion to protect him told Jake her feelings ran deep and strong, that she felt far more than just pity, even if she hadn't realized it herself yet.

"We'll see how it goes. One peculiarity about horses and most other animals is that they choose their masters. We buy them and claim ownership, but the heart of a creature can't be owned. Sunset will choose who he'll love, and if that turns out to be you, you won't have a hell of a lot to say about it."

"In other words, he'll be my horse whether I want him or not?"

"I'm afraid so."

Jake studied her profile, thinking to himself that Sunset might not be her only conquest. Something was happening inside him. He felt it every time he looked at her. He had the strangest feeling that this was absolutely right—that he'd been waiting for her all his adult life. It was a feeling that grew stronger each time he was with her.

"I'm so glad I brought Sunset here."

"I'm glad you came," he said huskily.

"I'll do my best with him," she promised hesitantly. "Even though I'm nervous with him, I'll try."

Jake already knew that. The lady wasn't lacking in backbone. In fact, he'd venture to say that she had no idea how strong she actually was.

"It'll be a long, hard haul," he warned. "But nothing worth doing comes easily."

"Sunset is worth it." A distant look came into her eyes. "I wish you could have seen him the way he used to be. He was magnificent." She smiled sadly. "He had a dauntless spirit, and you could tell just by looking at him that he'd been born to race. He ran his heart out for Rodney. Literally ran his heart out."

Rodney. Finally, the bastard had a name.

"It's so sad, seeing Sunset the way he is now," she whispered. "He loved Rodney so much, and he tried so desperately to please him, but nothing he did was ever good enough." She rested clenched fists on the fence rail. "When you try that hard, when you give someone your very best and it's never good enough, it does something to you. Way deep inside, it does something, and you're never the same again."

Jake's heart caught. He knew she wasn't speaking only of the horse. There was too much pain in her voice.

"Rodney was never satisfied with anything. I think that broke poor Sunset's spirit long before the whippings did."

Jake wanted to put his arms around her, gather her close. She looked so sad, and so very, very lost.

With the echo of her words still circling in his mind, he knew he couldn't possibly criticize her performance in the kitchen. She'd tried her best, giving him all she had. He would be damned if he would tell her that, once again, her best hadn't been good enough.

A few minutes later, Molly slid home the bolt on the cabin door. From outside, she could hear the tap of Jake's boots on the planks as he crossed the porch and descended the steps. When the sounds faded away to silence, she turned to lean against the door. *Exhaustion*. It seemed as if an eternity had passed since six that morning, and she'd spent every second in high gear.

Passing a hand over her eyes, she went into the bathroom to prepare for bed, her weary joints protesting with every step. In the harsh light cast by the ceiling fixture, her reflection in the mirror looked pale and haggard. She avoided looking at her face as she loosened her long hair from the braid and began her nightly brushing ritual. Not that shiny hair mattered to her anymore. She'd long since stopped wearing hers loose. It was so wildly curly and uncontrollable that it overwhelmed her features.

Five strokes into the brushing ritual, Molly heard a knock at the door. Laying the brush aside, she moved back into the tiny living room. It hadn't been far from her mind all day that the police might still find her here. "Who is it?" she called, her nerves jangling.

"Jake."

There was no mistaking that deep voice. Molly hurried over to unfasten the dead bolt, wondering why on earth he was back. As she opened the door, she voiced her first concern. "Has something gone wrong with Sunset?"

"No, no, he's fine. I just—" A looming silhouette in the darkness beyond the threshold, he broke off from speaking to stare at her.

Molly peered up at his shadowy face, trying without success to read his expression. "Yes?" she prompted.

"I'm sorry. Your hair. I've never seen it down."

Her hand flew to the cloud of curls over her right shoulder. "Now you know why."

"I almost didn't recognize you."

She pushed at a thick hank. "Probably because you can't see me."

"I can see you fine." He leaned a shoulder against the jamb, bringing his face into the spill of light from the old floor lamp by the front window. His blue eyes moved slowly over her hair, then came to rest on her face. "My God. Do you have any idea how beautiful you are?"

Molly had to resist the urge to look over her shoulder to see if someone else was in the room.

He nudged up his hat, his gaze still fixed on her face. "Being your boss and all, I promised myself not to do this. But, *damn*. Talk about hiding your light under a bushel. All that glorious hair, and you keep it in a braid? I could get drunk just looking at you."

Molly gave a nervous laugh.

"Your hair is the exact color of Scotch whiskey." He continued to study her. "Very expensive Scotch whiskey," he added.

Molly touched a hand to the side of her head. Some people had the occasional bad-hair day; she'd had a bad-hair life. In the early years of her marriage, she'd made the mistake of getting it cut short, and she had looked like an overweight, female version of Bozo the Clown. Rodney had threatened to divorce her if she ever went near a beauty shop again.

Jake whistled softly. "Damn. I do have eyes in my head, and I realized you had fine features. But I had no idea you were so pretty."

Molly wondered if she'd fallen asleep on her feet and was having a crazy dream. "Um . . . what do you want, Mr. Coulter?"

"Damned if I can remember."

He didn't seem in any great hurry to regain his memory. He just continued to lean against the jamb, studying her.

"I hope it wasn't important."

"I'm sure it was or I wouldn't have come all the way back over here." He smiled suddenly and shook his head. "It'll come to me in a minute." He pushed erect and moved into the house, closing the door behind him. "I'm sorry for gaping. The transformation is just so startling."

Molly pushed at her hair again. "It's startling, all right. Needless to say, I never wear pink. Can you imagine the clash?"

He smiled slightly as his gaze moved slowly over her. "You'd look fabulous in pink. You really hate your hair, don't you?"

"Hate is too mild a word. I detest it. You're very kind to say it's the color of whiskey. I've always likened it to red mud."

He chuckled. "I think you're your own worst critic, Stir-Houston, and wouldn't believe you were pretty if they crowned you Miss America."

"You'll never see me in a bathing suit contest. All those spotlights, glaring on my white thighs? The judges would go blind."

He shook his head again. Then he snapped his fingers. "I remember why I came back. Do you have an alarm clock? I can lend you one of ours."

"I have one."

"Good, good." He hooked his thumbs over his belt, his gaze still moving over her as if he couldn't quite believe the change. "Well . . ." He took a backward step toward the door. "I'd better make tracks so you can get some sleep."

"Morning will come early. Up with the chickens, and all that."

A moment later, he was gone, and Molly was left to stare at the closed door again. Bewildered, she touched a hand to her hair. Then she threw the dead bolt and returned to the bathroom to finish her nightly ablutions.

When she resumed her position in front of the mirror, she couldn't resist taking a long, hard look at herself in the glass, something she seldom did since her divorce. *Beautiful*? She trailed a fingertip down the bridge of her nose, then traced her cheekbone. It was the same old face staring back at her.

As she studied her reflection, Molly got the oddest feeling she didn't know the woman who stared back. It happened to her a lot lately, which was why she seldom gazed at her reflection overlong these days.

Her features seemed to blur, their definition becoming less distinct with every beat of her heart. She stared, and kept staring, her pulse slamming in her temples. Mud red and serpentlike, the strands of her hair seemed to undulate and slither, curling ever tighter over her face.

No more, Molly.

She flattened a hand against the glass, her breathing ragged, her body filmed with sweat. A singsong voice in her head whispered, *"Molly, Molly, where have you gone?"*

The horror of it was, she no longer really knew. "Beautiful," Jake Coulter had called her. *Lies, all lies.* Molly Sterling Wells was not beautiful. She had it on good authority that she was, in fact, ugly, so ugly that her husband had found her repulsive and turned to other women in the early days of their marriage.

Molly cupped her hands over her face, hating Jake Coulter for doing this to her. Was he only being kind? Or was he amusing himself with her?

She had no idea what his game was, but she did know one thing.

She didn't want to play.

Sleep didn't come easily to Molly that night. She slugged her pillow into a lump and then slapped it flat, unable to get comfortable. She tossed, turned, and lay on her back in a sprawl. Then she tossed and turned some more. The sheets caught around her legs, confining her lower body like a straightjacket. She detested the feeling and kicked free, only to shiver when the cool air washed over her.

When at last she drifted into a restless slumber, she began to dream, the images coming in confusing, disjointed cameos.

It was late evening, and Rodney, sitting at the edge of the bed, drew open the nightstand drawer. He took out a magazine and opened it to stare, glassy-eyed, at pictures of nude women.

"Why do you do that?" Molly asked tautly. She glanced at the glossy photographs. The women were beautiful, and their bodies were perfect. "Aren't I enough for you?"

"I need visual stimulation, is all. A guy has to charge his batteries somehow." While he continued to look at those other women, he began touching himself. When he was sufficiently aroused, he turned off the light and took her into his arms. "Unfasten your gown and give me some sugar, darling," he whispered. "Push the tops up with your hands. I like sweet little firm ones."

He drew her into his mouth and made loud, wet sucking sounds. Molly wanted to die because she knew he was pretending she was someone else. That was why he turned out the lights, so he wouldn't have to look at her. It went on and on. With each pull of his mouth, she shuddered and felt as if she might vomit. Her skin felt as if it was turning inside out.

He suddenly caught her nipple between his teeth, biting down hard enough to make it hurt. Then he spit her out, as if the taste of her was vile. "It's like sucking on a cow teat."

Molly tossed in the bed. *Dreaming*. This wasn't real. She was free of him now. It wasn't real. She needed to wake up. Only she couldn't, and the dream changed.

She was dressing for work, and Rodney came into the bedroom.

"If you don't do something soon, your tits will be hanging to your knees. I'll pay for the surgery. Don't mention it to your folks, and just get it done. Don't you love me? Don't you want to please me?"

She had done nothing but try to please him. She walked the way he wanted, dressed the way he wanted, talked the way he wanted, laughed the way he wanted, even thought the way he wanted, all to save a marriage that hadn't been worth saving. She didn't know who she was anymore, except that she was Rodney's wife. Now he wanted her to let some surgeon hack away at her body. Breast augmentation, a tummy tuck, thigh liposuction. The list of his complaints went on and on. The thought of doing it made her feel frantic. Her body was all she had left—the only thing about her that was still Molly. And now he wanted her to change that, too.

Maybe she wasn't beautiful. Maybe she wasn't desirable. Maybe she was just plain ugly. But it was her body, not his. If she had surgery, he would own her. She'd be the object that Rodney Wells had created.

"I'm not having surgery, Rodney."

His eyes glittered. "Yeah? Well, maybe I don't want to spend the rest of my life married to a fat cow. I love you, Molly. But that's too much to ask of any man. You could have it all fixed. If you refuse, it's the same as telling me to hit the road."

She deliberately chose a dress she knew he despised and drew it off the hanger. "So what's keeping you? Go, Rodney. I no longer really care."

"You don't mean that. No other man will ever want you. Then what'll you do?"

"Die a happy woman."

The scene changed.

She was lying in bed, and she was sick, so horribly sick. "No more pills, Rodney. They make me so dizzy and nauseated. Please, no more pills."

He gently lifted her head. "Darling, don't be difficult. I'm trying to help you. Swallow them down. There's a good girl."

In a dizzying swirl of blacks and grays, she felt herself falling.

Then Rodney was there, kneeling beside her on the floor, his face drawn with worry. "Oh, darling. Oh, dear God. How long have you been lying here? Molly? Molly, can you hear me?"

She tried to answer, wanted to answer. But her tongue seemed discon-

nected from her brain. The pills. They were making her sick. She knew that for sure now. But she was too doped to tell him.

He carried her to bed. Vaguely she was aware of him shaking out medication onto his palm. She clenched her teeth, determined not to swallow the pills this time. No, no, no. They were the problem. Why couldn't he see what they were doing to her? Yes, they helped her sleep. But she woke up violently ill, and she couldn't think clearly.

The shadows swirled again.

Rodney was sitting on the mattress beside her.

"Darling, I have some papers I need you to sign from the firm," he told her as he propped her up in bed. He put a pen into her hand. "Hold on to it, love. There you go. There's my good girl."

She tried to see the documents. Her vision was so blurred it was impossible. She could barely bring Rodney's face into focus. Her father had told her never to sign anything until she read it. Now he was dead, and he'd left her his half of the firm. She had to be responsible—a good businesswoman, as he'd raised her to be. She could remember telling Rodney that. She wasn't sure when, but she distinctly remembered telling him. So why did he persist in trying to get her to sign these papers?

"Sign the damned things!" he raged. "I'm your husband, goddamn you. I've had it with this absurdity. Sign the fucking papers!"

Molly thought he was going to hit her. Never in all the ten years of their marriage had Rodney lifted a hand to her. But now he stood over her with a raised fist. She tried frantically to focus, but she saw two of him, then three. Which of those upraised fists would strike her? Looking up at him and struggling to clear her vision, she no longer believed she knew her husband. The veil of kindness had slipped, revealing a monster underneath.

"If you can't trust your own goddamned husband, who can you trust?" he raged.

Fear turned Molly's blood to ice. She could trust no one, absolutely no one. She realized that now.

Now, when it was too late.

§ CHAPTER TEN §

Jake Coulter wasn't an easy man to avoid. The next morning, after cleaning up the breakfast mess, Molly went into the utility room to familiarize herself with the milk separator. She'd barely had time to look it over when she heard a floorboard creak behind her. She turned to see her new boss in the doorway. Dressed in what she was quickly coming to think of as rancher garb, chambray and faded denim, he looked absurdly handsome, his sun-darkened skin and sturdy shoulders showcased to best advantage by the wash-worn blue cloth.

"Need some help with that?" he asked lazily.

Just the deep timbre of his voice made her nerves hum. "I think I can figure it out."

He moved to stand beside her. "You pour the milk in this reservoir, and then you just flip the switch. The machine does the rest, filtering the separated milk into that reservoir and funneling the cream out here. It beats skimming it off with a ladle."

"That sounds easy enough." Molly hefted the five-gallon bucket. It was heavier than she expected it to be. "My goodness, the poor cow, carrying all this around."

Jake chuckled and helped to steady the bucket. "I've thought the same thing myself a time or two."

Acutely aware of his nearness and the fact that his left hand grazed her side, she concentrated on getting the milk poured so she could move away. She put the empty bucket in the deep utility sink to wash later. "Thank you for showing me how to run this thing. I know you're busy."

"Not a problem. I'll show you how to use the churn as well. It'll be nice not having the cream go to waste. I haven't had time to make butter in days."

"Are you sure you have time right now? I honestly do think I can manage by myself."

"No point in that when I can show you how it works in two minutes flat."

Two minutes stretched into an hour, and Jake was still there, helping Molly wash up and sterilize the equipment. He talked almost nonstop the entire time they worked, revealing an amazing talent for carrying on a one-sided conversation. Molly wondered if that was due to his having worked alone so much. She imagined most ranchers spent much of the day with only animals for company.

"How did you learn to separate milk and make butter?" she asked.

"I grew up out here. Not in the same house, of course. The family place burned to the ground about five years ago, so I had to rebuild. But the remoteness of the location hasn't changed. Imagine having to drive clear to town to keep milk in the fridge for six kids. My folks got a milk cow, and the rest just followed."

"I thought—" Molly glanced wonderingly out the window over the sink at the forestland that bordered the yard. "I thought you were just starting up this ranch. You said something once about getting it back, but I figured I misunderstood."

"No misunderstanding. My father went bankrupt and lost the Lazy J about nine years ago. The man who bought it didn't insure the dwellings, and when the house burned, he couldn't afford to rebuild. His family of five had to live in the cabin, which was tough. The price had bottomed out on beef as well, and he never really recovered financially. When I made him an offer late last summer, he jumped at the chance to sell."

His eyes darkened as he spoke, telling Molly far more than he probably realized, that he loved this piece of land. It was more than just a ranch to him; it was his heritage. She glanced back out at the trees, scarcely able to imagine the history that must exist for him in every blade of grass. "You played in that yard as a little boy?"

He grinned. "I was born out here, so, yeah, that was my playground."

Molly threw him a questioning look. "Born out here. Your folks were living here at the time, you mean?"

"No, I mean I was actually born here. My dad was out working cattle, and he didn't get word that my mom was in labor in time to take her to town. He had to deliver me."

Molly pressed a hand to her waist. "Oh, my."

He shrugged. "My great-great-grandfather started the ranch, and four generations of Coulters, including my own, were born on this land. After surviving my debut into the world, my mom decided hospitals were for the birds, and for the next five kids, my dad and a midwife attended the births."

Molly could not imagine having a baby at home. Not that she'd ever have the chance to make the choice. Rodney had promised her babies, but, as with everything else, he'd never carried through. Raised as an only child, she'd always yearned to have a large family. Accepting that she would never have even one child, let alone a half dozen, was one of the heartbreaks of her life, right up there with the grief of losing her father.

"What?" Jake asked softly.

Molly realized her expression had turned glum. She forced a bright smile and shook her head. "Nothing."

He searched her gaze for a long moment. Then he returned his attention to the dish washing. "It'll happen. You're young yet."

Molly gaped at him. She couldn't believe he'd guessed her thoughts. He flicked her an amused look. "One kindred soul recognizing another," he said by way of explanation. "I want children, too. Being the oldest of six kids, with all of us boys so close in age that our mom barely had time to take a breath in between, I've always wanted a large family." A dreamy look came into his eyes. "My little sis gave birth just last week. A little boy. I can't tell you how I felt the first time I held him. It made me want one of my own so bad, I damned near got tears in my eyes."

"You?" she asked incredulously.

He threw back his dark head and laughed. When his mirth subsided, he said, "Yes, me. Why does that surprise you? Don't most people want kids someday?"

"Most men don't. Not really. I think they only say they do because it's what women like to hear."

That prompted him to laugh again. "I'm not touching that with a well-charged cattle prod. I'll only say that I must be an exception. I want kids. I can't tell you how much."

Molly had heard that refrain before. Suddenly tense, she busied herself reassembling the churn. The scattered parts were a puzzle, and when she grew stumped, he reached over to help. Her throat going tight with emotions she couldn't and didn't want to name, she stared at his forearm, watching the play of tendon each time he flexed his wrist, fascinated by the way the light glistened on the silky dark hair that furred his wet, sun-bronzed skin.

"See?" he said softly after reassembling the churn. "Right when everything seems hopelessly jumbled, something happens and it all falls into place." He winked at her. "After a divorce, lots of people feel defeated and finished, Molly. It's natural, and in time, you'll heal." With a damp fingertip, he touched the tip of her nose. "Right when you least expect it, some fellow is going to come along. He'll take one look at you, and he'll be a goner."

Molly no longer believed in true love and forever after. Aching in places she had refused to acknowledge for years, she stared up at his dark face. *Wishing . . . wishing.* The rumbling timbre of his voice suffused her with warmth, and the feeling frightened her half to death.

Dipping her chin to break eye contact, she summoned a chirpy voice to say, "Well, this is done. I suppose I'd better get to work. I haven't had time to make out a list of things to do yet, but I think it may be taller than I am when I'm finished."

"Forgive me for pointing it out, but that's not saying much."

"It isn't nice to tease people about their shortcomings."

"Lack of height in a woman isn't a shortcoming. A lot of men think it's attractive. I think it's attractive."

He pulled the sink stopper. The water made a gurgling sound as it spiraled down the drain. Molly struggled to focus on that noise. It was real. Jake Coulter wasn't. He was just a wish in her foolish female heart that could never come true.

"Before you get started on cleaning, we need to go over how we do lunches." He led the way to the pantry, stepping aside at the doorway so she might enter first. Waving a hand at the small coolers on the top shelves, he said, "On a ranch, it's not always possible to come in for lunch at a specific time. It's more practical to pack the midday meal in coolers so we can eat in the field—or wherever else we happen to be. We keep small packs of blue ice in the freezer. It keeps the food cool, even on a hot day. I know it'll be a pain, fixing both lunch and breakfast so early, but on the plus side, it'll free you up during the day to do household chores and get in some extra work outdoors."

"Ah. I wondered what all the coolers were for. I thought someone here on the ranch owned shares in Coleman."

He laughed. "They make handy lunchboxes. You can toss them in the back of a pickup or strap them on a horse, no fuss, no muss."

That explained why all the coolers sported ground-in dirt. Molly decided she would scrub them down with abrasive cleanser and do her best to keep them clean from now on.

"What sort of things do you like for lunch?"

"Sandwiches, chips, snack cakes. Nothing fancy. Just make sure you give each man plenty. They work their tails off."

Molly made a mental note to pack two sandwiches in each cooler. Believing that their conversation was concluded, she started to leave, but he blocked her way with his considerable bulk, bracing one arm against an adjacent shelf and leaning slightly toward her. It seemed to Molly that the log walls moved in closer and the air went thin.

"Was there something more you wanted to tell me?" she asked.

His unnerving blue eyes trailed to her hair. "You're wearing a braid again."

"Yes. Is that a problem?"

"No. It's a nice, tidy style for the kitchen." A mischievous twinkle slipped into his eyes. "But when you're not cooking, I hate to see you hide something so beautiful." He reached over her shoulder to grasp her braid and draw it forward, his strong fingers sliding to its end, which lay over her breast. Moving his thumb back and forth over the elastic band, he smiled slowly. "I keep thinking how you look with it down."

The brush of his knuckles over the crest of her nipple made her stiffen. Uncertain if the contact was intentional, she pushed his hand away and made a fist over the braid herself. "Long hair worn loose in the kitchen is unsanitary."

He shrugged and trailed a fingertip lightly along her jaw. "Maybe, but you'd sure be a glory to look at."

Before she could think of a response, he turned and exited the pantry. Molly stared after him, still clutching her braid. When she felt sure he was gone, she touched a hand to her cheek, feeling oddly off balance, much as she had as a child after jumping off the merry-go-round. *"A glory to look at?"* On the one hand, she wanted to laugh, but on the other, oh, how she wanted to believe him.

Jake. Over the next few days, it seemed to Molly that he was there nearly every time she turned around. When she arrived at the main house each morning, he was waiting for her in the kitchen and insisted that she join him for a cup of coffee before they began their respective chores.

During those impromptu coffee klatches, he plied her with friendly questions in an obvious attempt to become better acquainted with her. Given the fact that he was true to his word and never pressed her for damning information about her past, Molly didn't really mind. She worked in the man's home, after all, and it was understandable that he wanted to learn all he could about her.

"Do you enjoy any sports, Molly?" he inquired one morning.

"I used to love golf and played nearly every Saturday with my dad," she replied easily. "I was never very good, I'm afraid. But we had a lot of fun."

"There's nothing wrong with being mediocre if you enjoy the game."

Mediocre had not been good enough for Rodney. Golf was a wealthy man's game, he believed, and one's skill was a reflection of one's breeding. Her amateur performance on the course had been an embarrassment to him.

"Yes, well, I wasn't that passionate about it, I guess. When I grew older, I lost interest and didn't care to play anymore."

"When you grew older? After you were married, you mean?"

A cold, empty feeling filled Molly's chest. "Yes, after I was married."

Another morning, he said, "So, tell me, Molly, what's your favorite time of year?"

"I'd have to say autumn."

"Ah." He smiled and nodded. "That is a gorgeous season."

"I *loved* the brilliant colors on the hillsides and the crisp chill in the air." She felt a little embarrassed, but added, "Most of all, though, I loved the holidays—the anticipation, the get-togethers, and all the decorations."

He smiled as though he shared that sentiment. "Which holiday season is your favorite?"

"Hmm, that's a tough one. I enjoyed Halloween and Thanksgiving a lot, but I think Christmas was always most special."

"We usually have snow here by Christmas. There's nothing more beautiful than cheery lights reflecting off the snowdrifts."

A picture flashed in her mind of his house, twinkling cheerfully inside and out with Christmas lights. She saw Jake at center stage, crouched before a gigantic tree with a dark-haired little boy at his side. In that moment, it was all too easy to imagine herself as a part of that homey scene. She quickly shoved the image from her mind.

Another morning he was sitting at the kitchen table reading a novel when Molly walked in. "Good book?" she asked as she peeled off her green parka.

He tossed down the paperback. "A whodunit. Nothing spectacular. The plot is pretty thin."

"Ah, a mystery buff, are you?"

He nodded. "Do you like to read?"

"I used to have my nose in a book all the time."

He grinned. "What was your genre?"

Her cheeks went hot. She hung her coat on a dowel and moved into the kitchen. "I was crazy about historical romance in my younger days."

"Ah." A mischievous glint warmed his eyes. "Romance is what brought us all to the dance. What made you stop reading it?"

She wrinkled her nose. "Rodney felt that my reading love stories gave me unrealistic expectations of our relationship."

The amusement in his eyes became more pronounced. "Sounds to me like good old Rodney was afraid he wouldn't measure up."

That was an understatement. Uncomfortable with the conversation, Molly bypassed having coffee and dove into the breakfast preparations. As she began peeling apples for the bowl of fresh fruit that she served without fail each morning, Jake came to lean his hips against the counter.

"Can I ask you something?"

Molly had become accustomed to this question-and-answer game. "Sure. Fire away."

"Why do you always refer to yourself in the past tense?"

She stared at him, bewildered, an awful, cold feeling clawing at her chest. The kitchen had gone unnaturally bright, the overhead lights glaring, the bits of chrome on the appliances flashing with blinding brilliance.

His voice sounded far away as he added, "I really enjoy hearing about the things you used to enjoy. Don't misunderstand me. But I'd also like to know who you are right now."

"Who I am now?" she repeated stupidly.

"Yes, now. I know that you used to love to read and enjoyed playing golf. But what interests you now?"

"I'm the same person. I haven't changed."

"How long has it been since you read a romance?" he asked softly.

It had been nine years, but Molly couldn't bring herself to admit that. "A while," she settled for saying.

"How long has it been since you played golf?"

Her only answer was a shrug.

His expression grew concerned. "How long were you married, Molly?"

Pain lanced through her skull, and the cold feeling in her chest moved through her whole body. *Where are you, Molly? Where have you gone?* That frightening little voice that had taunted her so many times when she looked in the mirror was now a singsong in her mind as she looked into Jake Coulter's eyes. In those blue depths, she glimpsed dead dreams, and she wanted to run from him. Big problem. His ranch had become her only sanctuary.

"Why are you asking me all this?"

He searched her gaze. "Because I want to know you better." He folded his arms loosely across his chest. "Not who you used to be, but who you are right now."

She shook her head. "That's silly." Her voice sounded hollow even to her. "I'm the same person."

"Are you?" He let that hang there for a moment. Then he whispered, "Molly?" He said her name softly and reached over to cup her chin in his hand. Jerked from her confused thoughts, she stared up at him with growing dread, unable to shake the feeling that he was parting curtains in her mind that she might never again be able to close. "I'm sorry, honey," he said huskily. "I don't mean to upset you."

How could he hope not to upset her when he was asking such disturbing questions? *Who are you, Molly?* She no longer really knew. It was as if something inside her—a very vital something—had been obliterated. A few mornings ago, he had told her that everyone felt this way after a divorce and she would get over it in time. But she didn't think so. There were no bleeding wounds within her to heal. There was only emptiness—an awful emptiness.

He trailed his thumb over her cheek. "I'm sorry," he whispered. "Forget I said anything."

He pushed erect and glanced at the clock. "I'd better get cracking, I guess. The cow won't milk herself."

Listening to the sharp tap of his boot heels on the oak floor, Molly let the partially peeled apple slip from her numb fingers. The fruit fell into the bowl with a soft plunk and rolled onto its side. In the time that she'd stood there holding it, the ripe pulp had already begun to turn brown in places. Intellectually, she knew that the discoloration was a chemical reaction of some kind that occurred when the fructose was exposed to the air. Emotionally, she likened it to the first stages of rot. If left exposed for too long, all that was good and sweet and wholesome within the apple would turn sour.

Jake paused at the back door to turn on the radio. When the reception came in, he tuned in to a station that played popular oldies. As it happened, that morning they were doing an 1980s top-hits countdown. The very first song was an almost-forgotten favorite of Molly's from her high school days.

When she heard Jake step out and close the door, she stared woodenly at nothing, her eyes filling with tears. It had been eight years since she had listened to that song.

That afternoon when Molly went out to spend her obligatory hour with Sunset, she saw Jake in the adjoining pasture, working with a baby horse. Over the course of her stay so far, she'd noticed that he rarely worked with the cattle, choosing instead to devote the majority of his time to the training program.

A smile touched her mouth as she watched him rub a saddle blanket over the young animal's body. Most people would have done it a couple of times and been done with it. Not Jake. He repeated the process again and again, flapping the blanket near the foal's head occasionally, which startled the little fellow.

Some fifteen minutes later, Jake vaulted over the split-rail fence and came striding toward her, the thick wool hooked over his thumb to ride his shoulder.

"What was that all about?" she called.

He grinned. Even at a distance, his eyes were a blaze of blue. "That was blanket-flapping 101."

She laughed. "I see."

Drawing ever closer with those long, seemingly lazy strides of his, he said, "Having a man chase you with a blanket can be a pretty scary proposition."

Molly could well imagine that it might be, especially if that man could move as swiftly as Jake Coulter could. She turned her gaze back to the foal, which was now romping in the grass, delighted to be free again. "So you're teaching that little guy not to be afraid?"

"You got it." He joined her at the fence and drew off his hat. His dark hair was depressed where the band had rested. He raked his long, sturdy fingers through the chocolate-colored strands, then resettled the Stetson on his head. "All creatures are instinctively afraid of some things." He turned a thoughtful gaze on her. "The only way to overcome fear is to face it repeatedly until the thing that frightens you no longer seems scary."

Molly averted her gaze. Though she knew him better now, she still couldn't shake the feeling that he read more in her eyes than she wished him to sometimes. "That's an interesting thought."

"A true one."

She nibbled the inside of her lip. "Fear isn't always unfounded. Sometimes the things we fear will do us great harm if we don't avoid them." She immediately wanted to call the words back. That feeling intensified when she met his gaze again. He was studying her with a thoughtful frown.

"And sometimes," he said softly, "there's nothing to fear at all. If you're afraid of something and don't face it at least once, how can you ever know if your fears are real or only imagined?"

Molly straightened away from the fence. "Good question." She hugged her waist and stared hard at Sunset. Hoping to change the subject, she said, "He's growing more at ease with us. Have you noticed?"

A hint of a smile played at the edge of his hard mouth as he joined her in regarding the stallion. "He still gets antsy when I enter the pen. The courtship period isn't over yet."

"The courtship period? Is that what you call it?"

His twinkling gaze met and held hers. "Moving in, backing off. Much of horse training is a courtship of sorts, slowly overcoming shyness and fear to build a relationship of trust. Sunset would just as soon pass, but he's cornered and doesn't have a choice. In time, he'll come to realize I'm more stubborn than he is and accept the inevitable."

Molly felt cornered as well, and she quite often got the feeling that he was playing the same game with her. *Moving in, backing off.* Only to what end? He was a handsome, virile man who could have his pick of beautiful women. Why would he waste his energy on someone like her?

She wanted to tell him that her situation was nothing like Sunset's, that she was free to leave anytime she chose, but even as the thought slipped into her mind, she knew it wasn't true. She was trapped here for now, held fast by the velvet manacles of safety that she could find nowhere else.

She glanced at her watch. "My goodness. I didn't realize the time. I need to get dinner started."

"And I've got two more horses to put through their paces before I quit for the day."

"I guess we'd both better get back to work."

As she struck off for the house, Molly could feel the heat of his gaze on her. Her back tingled, her butt tingled. She wanted to whirl around and tell him to stop staring. Instead she hurried up the steps, anxious to escape into the house. At the doorway, she threw a searing look over her shoulder, only to find that her target had vanished.

He hadn't been watching her at all. It was only her imagination.

As she let herself inside, Molly wondered if everything else was her imagination as well. Maybe she was making mountains out of molehills, reading hidden meanings into things he said and did that he never meant to convey.

That was it, she decided with some relief. That *had* to be it. Jake Coulter was so far out of her league, it was ludicrous to think he would ever even give her a second look, let alone plot ways to seduce her.

Of an evening, when Molly finished her work for the day, Jake always walked her home. That night, Molly vowed to walk at a fast clip. Whether it was all her imagination or not, this man did things that made her nervous. He seemed to look too deep and see too much. She was a woman with secrets she didn't dare reveal. She needed to be careful, and the most surefire way to do that was to keep her distance.

To her dismay, he veered right toward the creek instead of walking her directly home. "Where are we going?" she asked.

His teeth gleamed blue white in the moonlight when he smiled. "I thought it might be relaxing to take a little stroll."

That was the last thing she wanted to do, but his firm grip on her elbow brooked no argument. "I hope you don't plan to stroll too far. I'm tired tonight."

"You'll rest better for the dose of fresh air."

Once at the stream, Molly was so charmed by the tenebrous beauty that she forgot to feel tense. A breeze whispered in the lofty pines, the sound surreal and melodic. Moonlight shone through the swaying boughs in misty beams, making the water look like molten silver spilling over the rocks. Near them, the frogs, frightened by their presence, had grown quiet, but farther downstream, their voices were still raised in a raucous cacophony.

"Why do you reckon frogs croak?" Jake suddenly asked.

Molly suppressed a smile, wondering how it was that this man could so easily work his way past her defenses. She'd been so determined not to talk with him tonight, and now here she was, about to engage in a conversation about frogs, of all things. "I have no idea. Maybe they're conversing with each other."

He listened. "You think the ones with shrill voices are lady frogs?"

Resisting the urge to laugh, she cocked her head to listen. "Maybe."

"Could be the fellas are whispering sweet nothings in their ears, and that's a lady frog's way of tittering."

She giggled. She couldn't help herself. "Sweet nothings? That croaking doesn't sound very romantic to me."

"Maybe it all depends on who's talking and who's listening."

Molly sighed and hugged her parka closer. He glanced down. "You cold, honey?"

"Only a little."

He startled her by slipping an arm around her waist. "I've got plenty of heat to share."

He did, at that. The warmth radiating from his big body curled around her. Molly's pulse accelerated. Try as she might, she couldn't relax against him. He was too—*everything*—too big, too strong, too handsome, too charming. From the first, he'd sparked her imagination and made her want things she had no business wanting.

"What are you thinking?" he asked.

"Nothing, really."

He glanced down at her, his eyes glistening in the moonlight. "Nothing, Molly? Or just nothing you want to share with me?"

She drew away from him and cupped a hand over her mouth, pretending to yawn. "Excuse me. I must be more exhausted than I realized. Do you mind if we head for the cabin now?"

He smiled slightly, his indulgent expression conveying that he saw right through her. "Not at all." He grasped her elbow to guide her up the bank. "Watch your step going over these rocks."

Molly was about to say she could see just fine when she caught her toe and stumbled. He stopped her from falling with an arm around her waist, his big hand splayed over her midriff. Her breath trapped at the base of her throat, and she jerked her head up to look at him. He slowly drew his arm from around her, his expression, concealed by the shadow of his hat, unreadable.

Unsettled by his touch, which had come perilously close to the underside of her breast, Molly gathered her composure and struck off again, acutely aware of his grasp on her arm. Her hip occasionally bumped against his thigh as she hurried along.

"You racing to put out a fire?" he asked.

They reached the front porch of the cabin just then, saving her the need to reply. She pulled away from him and moved hastily up the steps. At the top, she turned, thinking to thank him for walking her home. She nearly jumped out of her skin when she found him standing right behind her.

"Oh!" She pressed a hand over her heart. "You startled me."

He chuckled. "It doesn't take much. Correct me if I'm wrong, but I think I make you uneasy."

"Don't be silly, Mr. Coulter. Why would you make me uneasy?"

"The name is Jake."

"I know what your given name is."

"Then why won't you use it?"

"You're my employer."

His dark face creased in another grin, the lines that lashed his lean cheeks looking as black as ink in the eerie light. The smell of leather, hay, and man surrounded her. She shivered and rubbed her arms.

"My other employees call me Jake."

"That's their choice. I prefer to keep things more businesslike."

"Because it makes you feel safe?"

Molly couldn't think what to say, which elicited another smile from him. "No question about it, I definitely make you uneasy." He ran his gaze slowly over her face as though searching for answers in her expression. Molly could only hope he found none. "Why is that, Molly?"

She moistened her lips and swallowed. "I'm not sure. Post-divorce jitters, I guess."

He toed a board of the porch, then settled his hands at his hips. "Was Rodney ornery with you?"

She just stared at him.

"Behind closed doors, I mean." He cupped her chin in his hand. "Is that why I make you nervous, because you never knew what to expect from him?"

"Rodney was never physically abusive to me. As for why you make me nervous, it has nothing at all to do with that. I don't even think of you that way."

He rubbed his thumb over her bottom lip, his mouth tipping into a thoughtful grin. "You don't, huh?"

"No, of course not."

He lightened the graze of his thumb, treating her to a soft caress that set her lip to tingling. "Maybe you'd better start," he said huskily.

Speechless, Molly gazed after him as he loped down the steps and struck off into the darkness. Her night vision being what it was, he was a shadow one moment, then gone the next.

Taking a deep breath and exhaling slowly, she closed her eyes and chafed her arms again, feeling cold in a way that went deeper than the flesh. The night wind gusted in under the porch overhang, its whisper seeming to say, *Molly . . . Molly . . .* " She curled an arm around the support beam at the top of the steps and pressed her forehead against the wood. *"Molly . . . where are you?"* She shuddered and clenched her teeth. Maybe Rodney had been right all along, and she was crazy. Normal people didn't hear voices in the wind.

She pressed closer to the beam, needing the support and finding comfort in the solidness. It made her think of Jake, of how sturdy his big, lean body felt when he drew her against him. A tight, suffocating feeling welled in her throat. She wrapped both arms around the log and clung to it, wishing with all her heart it could hug her back.

❧ CHAPTER ELEVEN ❧

"Is any of that rice and eggs that Molly made for the dog left over?"

His mouth filled with crackers, Jake whipped around to locate his brother in the gloom. It was four o'clock in the morning, and he hadn't expected anyone to be up and about yet. They usually got off to a slow start Monday morning. The hired hands were never completely recovered from their Saturday night festivities, and he and Hank were usually exhausted after doing all the work themselves over the weekend.

"What are you doing up so early?" Jake asked. "I figured you'd sleep in."

Padding on bare feet, his brother came into view, his dark hair rumpled, his chest bare. His jeans were zipped, but he'd left them unbuttoned. "Who slept? Supper last night was deserving of Levi's cowboy blessing."

Jake hated to bite on that one. "What's Levi's cowboy blessing?"

" 'Three beans for four of us, thank God there ain't no more of us.' "

Jake chuckled. "It wasn't *that* skimpy."

"Pretty skimpy. If God had meant peppers to be stuffed, He'd have made them that way. And what the hell kind of soup was that she fixed?"

"Minestrone."

"It was so thin, I could've drunk it with a straw. I'm starving. I tossed and turned all night."

Jake shoved the jar of peanut butter along the counter so his brother could help himself. "She's trying. Did you notice Bart last night? Yesterday afternoon she gave him a bath and doused him with aftershave. He smelled so pretty I damned near kissed him."

Hank chuckled. "I happened by the house while she was bathing him. The bathroom looked like a hurricane had struck, and she was wet from head to toe."

"She sure is a sweetheart."

"No argument there," Hank agreed. "But her being sweet doesn't put food in our bellies, Jake. You have to talk to her. In all your life, I've never known you to pull your verbal punches." He grabbed the table knife and piled peanut butter onto a cracker. After popping it into his mouth and chewing a couple of times, he swallowed and said, "Now, suddenly, you're Mr. Tact. You've picked a hell of a time to become a diplomat."

"It's not easy, learning to cook for so many. She'll get the hang of it soon."

His expression thoughtful, Hank popped another cracker into his mouth. "You really like her a lot, don't you?"

Jake considered the question. "Yeah. Yeah, I do."

"Are you getting serious?"

Again Jake took a moment to consider before answering. "As serious as I've ever felt," he said softly. "She grows on a fellow. You know? With some women, the better you get to know them, the more unappealing they are. But Molly is sweet all the way through. Her brushing Bart's teeth, for instance. He isn't exactly cooperative, but she does it anyway. And she's always doing other little things, just to be nice. Sewing on buttons, mending jeans, putting little surprises in our lunch pails. I've never asked her to do any of that stuff. She takes it upon herself."

"The carob-coated raisins were a surprise, all right."

Jake sighed. "It's the thought that counts. She wants us to eat healthy. You can't fault her for that."

"I'm not faulting her. I'm just hungry." Hank grabbed another cracker. "Hot cereal and fruit for breakfast just doesn't cut it." He glanced over his shoulder. "Is that why you haven't turned on the lights, because you're afraid she might see and realize you're up, raiding the kitchen?"

"I don't want to hurt her feelings. Being a little hungry for a few more days won't kill us."

Hank shoved another cracker in his mouth. "Speak for yourself. I wonder where she's from?"

"My guess is she's from Portland."

"Portland?" Hank had been up that way a few months ago. "Oh, man, I hope she doesn't serve us any of that field-green salad shit."

"What is field-green salad?"

"Just like it sounds, greens out of a field. Dandelion leaves and stuff."

"You're kidding."

"It's all the rage in the nice restaurants up there. City people. There's just no figuring 'em." Hank shuddered and shook his head. "They charged me eight bucks for that crap. I'm telling you, we could make a fortune. Just turn them out to graze and charge by the head."

"Eight bucks for field greens?"

"Everything on the menu cost separately."

"À la carte," Jake inserted.

"À la highway robbery, more like. My supper cost me over thirty dollars, and all I got was a tiny piece of prime rib and a bunch of what cows eat. No bread, no spuds. I damned near starved to death."

Jake chuckled. "Now you're sounding like Danno."

The back door opened just then, and both men gave a guilty start, afraid the new arrival might be Molly. Instead, Levi poked his head in. "Howdy." He stepped over the threshold and softly closed the door. "What're we havin' here, a convention?"

Jake sighed and shoved the jar of peanut butter along the counter to his hired hand. "We're just filling our empty spots, Levi. If that's why you're up early, help yourself."

Later that morning, Jake gathered his men in the stable to line them out for the coming week. Usually they sat around the kitchen table on Monday morning, and he assigned each man his chores over coffee, but he'd been anxious to get them out of the house today. Judging by their disgruntled expressions, their time off hadn't sweetened their dispositions any. Jake feared they were about to mutiny, and he didn't want Molly to see the fireworks.

"What the hell were those things she fed us for breakfast?" the gangly, ever-hungry Danno asked.

"Crêpes," Hank supplied. "Fancy French pancakes."

"The French can have 'em."

Jake sighed, took off his hat to stare blankly at the inside of the crown, and then returned it to his head. "Gentlemen, let's all practice a little patience. That was a real pretty breakfast she served. Just think how hard she worked, cutting all those strawberries into flower shapes."

"Those pancakes were so thin, you could read the newspaper through them, and each of us only got four." Preach, the quiet one of the bunch, scowled at his boss. "I'm so hungry, I could eat frogs while they're still hopping. Pretty doesn't fill a man's gut."

Nate, a nice-looking twenty-five-year-old with a winning smile and a penchant for teasing, laughed and inserted, "If pretty filled a man's gut, Preach, we'd just toss Molly on the table and forget about food."

Just that fast and Jake was mad. He fixed Nate with a glare. "Any man who lays a finger on the lady will answer to me. Is that understood?"

Nate raised his eyebrows. "I guess that's plain enough."

"You keep a civil tongue in your head when you speak to her, and do it with your goddamned hat in your hand."

Hank touched his brother's sleeve. "Hey, Jake, he was just joking."

Jake shook his arm free. "There are lines we don't cross on this spread, and that's one of them. She's a lady, not some Saturday-night bar floozy, and she'll be treated with respect by every last one of you, or I'll know the reason why."

Nate's brows arched higher. "Kinda touchy this morning, aren't we, boss? I'd never get out of line with a lady, and you know it."

"Make damned sure you don't."

Even as the anger roiled within him, Jake knew he was overreacting. Nate's remark had been a little off-color, but he'd meant no real harm. He took a deep, calming breath, wondered what the hell was wrong with him, and tried to soften his expression. "Molly is pretty, and we wouldn't be men if we failed to notice that." He scanned the group, offering no quarter with his gaze. "Just mind your manners when you're around her, and you'll have no problem with me."

All the men nodded.

Jake grabbed his clipboard, gave his notes a quick scan, and began assigning the men their jobs for the week. When the last hired hand had sauntered away, Hank gave him a pointed look and said, "Pardon me for pointing it out, but no matter how much you like Molly, you did hire her to do a job. If she's not cutting the mustard, you either have to get her straightened out or can her ass. The men have to eat."

Jake bit down hard on his back teeth. "I'll handle it."

"When? We're all starving."

"You won't waste away."

"Maybe not, but my work has been off, and it will be again today. After a breakfast of see-through pancakes, you can bet she packed us piddly-ass lunches again, only two sandwiches each, and those with fat-free mayo." Hank made a face. "Where does she buy all that whole wheat crap? Those chips taste like sawdust."

"I think she gets them at a health food store."

"Well, I hate them. We all do. Even Bart won't eat 'em."

"I *said* I'll handle it."

Jake heard the front door of the house open and close just then. He leaned around to look out the stable doorway and saw Molly coming down the front steps. Once she gained the ground, she fetched a huge, gnarled limb she'd evidently left leaning against the porch. As she cut across the yard toward the creek, Jake gazed curiously after her.

"Great," Hank whispered. "See-through pancakes for breakfast, and now she's taking a morning stroll. If she's going out to pick field greens, I quit."

"You can't quit. You're part owner."

"I haven't kicked in any money. All I'll be out is sweat."

Jake sighed, his gaze still fixed on their cook. Dressed in baggy jeans and a loose, white cotton blouse, she looked adorable in spite of herself. She tiptoed daintily over some stones to get across the stream, then set off toward the woods, swinging the tree limb at the brush as if it was her aim to flatten it.

"What the hell is she doing?" Hank asked.

Jake watched Molly for another few seconds. "I have no idea."

"Whatever she's doing, she's going at it like she's killing snakes."

Snakes? Jake remembered the conversation they'd had about rattlers that first day. He groaned. "Oh, *damn*."

"What?" Hank glanced back at him.

"I think she's beating the brush for rattlers."

"What?" Hank stepped to the doorway to get a better look. His shoulders jerked with laughter. "Who in God's name told her to do that?"

"I did."

"You're joking."

"I didn't mean for her to do it that way." Jake watched Molly whack a sage bush. He chuckled and shook his head. "But I did tell her to beat the brush." He observed her a second longer. "Well, hell. After putting the rope in front of the wood box, I kind of hoped the snake issue was put to rest."

"You put a rope in front of her wood box? What for?"

"As a snake deterrent."

Hank narrowed an eye. "That's an old wives' tale. It doesn't work."

"I know that, and you know that, but she doesn't. It eased her mind, mission accomplished."

Hank resumed watching Molly. His dark face creased in a mischievous grin. "You reckon we'll have any brush left when she's done?"

Jake slapped his brother's gut with the clipboard. Hank's breath rushed from his chest as he grabbed hold of the notes. "Where you going?"

Never breaking stride, Jake called back, "To show her how to beat the brush and have a talk with her about her cooking."

"Tell her we like spuds, and lots of 'em!" Hank yelled after him.

Jake groaned and nodded. This was one chore he was not looking forward to. Just as he reached the creek, he heard Hank holler, "Homemade biscuits, too!"

Sunlight streamed through the boughs of the ponderosa pines, the shafts of light filled with motes that shimmered like pearl dust in the morning glow. The vanilla scent of tree bark, the musk of sage, and the moldiness of the forest floor, carpeted with countless layers of decaying needles, filled Molly's nostrils. She hauled in a deep breath, thinking how absolutely glorious the morning was and how blessed she was to have a moment to enjoy it.

As she moved deeper into the woods, she felt as if she'd stepped off into a fairy tale or traveled back through time to the pioneer days. Indulging in a rare moment of fancy, she recalled the countless Indian romances she'd read during her first and only year of college. This was just the sort of setting she'd always imagined when she read about a beautiful, fair-skinned heroine coming face-to-face with a dark and dangerous half-breed warrior.

She grinned and was about to whack another bush in her path when a branch snapped behind her. Her heart shot into her throat, and she whirled around with the limb raised high.

"You gonna thump me with that thing, or is it safe to come closer?" a deep voice, laced with amusement, inquired.

When Molly recognized Jake moving through the trees, she released a pent-up breath, touched a hand to her throat, and let the limb sink to the ground. "Mr. Coulter, you frightened me half to death. I thought you were a cougar."

His twinkling blue eyes narrowed on her face. "I told you it's fairly safe to take walks during the day."

"The key word being '*fairly*.'" She glided her fingertips down between her collarbones as her heart slid back into its proper place.

"The way you're swinging that club, no cougar in its right mind would dare take you on. You look downright fearsome."

He was the one who looked fearsome, so tall and dark, his shirt stretched taut over his broad shoulders, the faded denim of his Wranglers sheathing his long, powerfully muscled legs. Molly tried to imagine him in nothing but a loincloth and moccasins. The picture that leaped to mind was enough to give her arrhythmia.

It was silly in the extreme for her to think about him in that way, of course. But for some reason, she couldn't seem to help it.

"What?" Jake asked, his gaze still searching hers.

She realized she'd been staring. "Nothing. I'm just surprised to see you out here. I thought you were working."

"I'm never too busy to take a walk with a pretty lady."

That was a big part of her problem with him, she decided. He not only acted as if he thought she was pretty, but he said so, making it difficult for her to keep her perspective.

Molly wondered why he had followed her. "If you're upset because I'm taking a break, I only meant to be gone for a few minutes." She glanced at her watch. "I started work before five, and it's half past eight. I thought I'd take a short walk. I guess I should have checked with you first to make sure that's allowed."

For what seemed to her an interminably long while, he looked deeply into her eyes. Then his hard mouth tipped up at one corner in a smile.

"I'm not here to jump you about taking a break, Molly."

"Oh." She fiddled nervously with the buttons of her top, then pressed a hand to her waist. She really, really wished he'd stop looking at her that way. "Why, then?" She thought quickly. "I know the crêpes were a little tough. I'll do better next time."

He nudged up the brim of his hat. The better to stare at her, she guessed. A shaft of sunlight filtered down through the tree boughs, playing over his burnished face.

"Why do you immediately assume that I came out here to chew your ass about something?" he asked softly.

Molly considered the question. "Because I can't think of any other reason you might have followed me."

He shook his head, his smile broadening, yet not seeming to reach his eyes, which she could have sworn looked sad just before he glanced away. He spent a moment gazing off into the woods, his expression thoughtful.

"Maybe I came out here to tell you those were the best damned crêpes I ever ate. Did you think of that?"

"I thought they were a little tough."

"They were delicious," he corrected. "Everyone cleaned his plate."

"They were probably just being polite." Nervous beyond measure, she dug the sharp end of the tree limb into the ground. "If you didn't follow me to complain about the crêpes or chew me out for taking a break, why are you here?"

"I came out to take a walk with a pretty lady." The slashes at each corner of his mouth deepened as he smiled this time. "You don't mind having some company, do you?"

"Oh, no, I don't suppose I—"

She broke off when he stepped forward, grabbed the limb from her hand, and tossed it into the brush.

"That's my snake stick."

"How big do you think the snakes are hereabouts, the size of pythons? Beating the brush with a limb that large will wear you to a frazzle." He bent to pick up a skinny branch. "This is more the thing."

"That isn't big enough to kill a snake."

"Killing a snake isn't your aim. You just want to warn them away." He grabbed her by the hand and set off at a much faster pace than she'd been going. His palm and fingers felt incredibly hard and warm, wrapped around hers. As they walked, he tapped the bushes, rather like a blind person might a cane. "That's all you need to do," he said as he handed her the branch. "Every rattler for a mile will feel the vibrations and clear out. If you're walking through really thick brush, you can get a little more ambitious and occasionally whack a bush. Keep an ear cocked for any buzzing sounds and watch where you step. You'll probably never see a snake."

Molly cast him a dubious look. He laughed and chucked her under the chin. "Trust me, all right? There's no need to bludgeon every bush you see."

"Hmm."

He rubbed his thumb over her knuckles, sending zings up her arm. Molly whacked a sage bush, using a little more force than he claimed was necessary.

"Just in case," she said by way of explanation.

"Go ahead. Wear yourself out. You'll never want to come walking again. Your arms will be sore for days."

She decided her arms *were* getting tired. She followed his example and began tapping the bushes. "Are you sure this is enough?"

"Positive. Rattlesnakes aren't deadly, you know. If you're unable to get antivenin, their bite just makes you all-fired sick. Occasionally, someone has secondary complications and dies, but a healthy adult usually doesn't."

"If the bite doesn't kill me, the heart attack will."

He chuckled. "You're really afraid of them, aren't you?"

"I'm the biggest chicken you've ever seen when it comes to snakes. Even the garden variety makes me hyperventilate. I'm not at all afraid of spiders, though, and when I was small, I caught a mouse and made a pet of it, so they don't frighten me, either. Just keep snakes and all things slithery away from me."

He gave her fingers a squeeze. A friendly gesture, nothing more, Molly assured herself. If tingles raced up her arm, that was her problem. She wished he'd let loose of her hand so she could think straight.

"You know how to tell a ponderosa pine from a lodgepole?" he suddenly asked.

Molly stopped thumping the dirt to glance at the trees around them. "The bark of a ponderosa is the color of cinnamon, and the bark on a lodgepole isn't?"

"Not all ponderosas turn cinnamon. A lot of them are plain old brown."

"How do you tell then?"

"The needles." He reached up to grab a cluster and held it before her nose. "A ponderosa has three per cluster, a lodgepole only two."

"Ah."

He flashed her a grin that sent electrical heat ribboning through her. "You know how to tell a juniper with your eyes closed?"

She thought for a moment. "No, I can't say as I do. By its smell?"

He nodded.

"What do they smell like?"

"Cat piss."

Molly burst out laughing. "Not really."

His dancing gaze met hers. "Honey, would I lie to you?"

Molly was still trying to think of a response when he launched into another spiel about wildlife, telling her a host of different things about the golden-mantled squirrels they saw, then moving on to skunks, mule deer, and lastly, black bears.

"If I see a bear, I should raise my arms and talk to it?" she asked incredulously. "Is there any particular topic of conversation they favor?"

He narrowed an eye at her. "You want to learn this stuff or not?"

"Yes, absolutely."

"Then stop with the sarcasm." He squeezed her hand again. This time, she assured herself he only did it to let her know he was kidding. "Bears have very poor eyesight," he went on, "and if you're downwind of them, you need to let them know you're not another bear. Lifting your arms makes you look larger, and talking helps to distinguish you from other animals. Hold your ground, make eye contact, and say, 'Yo, bear! How you doin' today?' "

"And that'll make it go away?"

"Most of the time. There's the rare fruitcake black bear, of course, but they're few and far between. Grizzlies are another story, but we don't have any of those around here."

"For future reference, what should I do if I ever meet a grizzly?"

"Be extremely polite."

The reply caught Molly off guard, and a startled giggle lodged crosswise in her throat, making her snort. Heat seared her face. "Excuse me. I haven't done that in *years*."

His gaze was warm when it came to rest on her face. "Don't apologize. I think that's the first time I've ever heard you cut loose and really laugh."

"That was a *snort,* not a laugh. I used to do it a lot until I broke myself of the habit."

"Why did you break yourself of it?"

"Because it's—" Molly was about to say it was unladylike, but as the words formed in her mind, she heard the echo of Rodney's voice. *"Don't ever laugh like that in front of my friends again. It's humiliating to have your wife snort in public like some fat, old sow."* "My husband found it annoying, and I just broke myself of it, is all."

He frowned slightly. Then he shrugged. "Each to his own, I reckon. I happen to think it's a very cute laugh."

"You think the way I snort when I laugh is *cute?*"

"It's more a feminine snicker than a snort."

He drew her between two trees, then around a thatch of sage. Watching him from the corner of her eye, she admired the easy way he moved, his shoulders shifting slightly with each swing of his lean hips. He was surefooted, the heels of his boots connecting solidly with the ground each time he stepped.

"What really bugs me is phony-sounding laughter," he said, picking up the thread of their conversation. "I hate it when women shriek really loud when they laugh. The sound sends shudders up my spine after a few minutes."

Molly had heard women laugh that way and knew exactly what he meant. "Well, rest easy. I never shriek."

He slid her a sidelong glance. "Never? Some men might take that as a challenge."

She flashed him a startled look. The suggestive gleam in his eyes turned her brains to mush. Unable to come up with a response, she decided to pretend the comment had gone straight over her head. She sighed and glanced around them. "Oh, *look*! What lovely flowers."

He led her to the deep pink blooms. "These are early maiden pinks," he said as he bent to snap a stem. When he straightened, he tugged on her hand to pull her closer and held the blossom to her cheek. "Just as I thought," he said huskily. "Pink doesn't clash with your hair." He tucked the flower stem behind her ear. "You'd look beautiful in it."

"I've found that neutral shades go better with my complexion."

"Neutral meaning shades of white, brown, and beige?" He drew her back into a walk. "You have a complexion like cream, lady. You could wear any color. I think you've got the prettiest skin I've ever laid eyes on."

Molly decided it was time to put a stop to this compliment business before she did something totally stupid, like start believing him. "Jake, I really think—"

"I'll be damned. Let me clean my ears out. Did you just call me Jake?"

She released another sigh. "About the 'pretty' business."

"What about it?"

"You're very kind, but I don't feel comfortable with your paying me compliments constantly."

"I haven't done it constantly. A few times, at most."

"It's just that I'd rather you didn't."

"Why? If it's because I'm your boss, that's really not fair. I do have eyes in my head, and it's a little hard not to notice what's right in front of my nose. It's not as if I've let it interfere with our working relationship."

"I never meant to imply that you had."

"Then what's wrong with me saying you're pretty?"

Molly pressed her lips together, trying to think how she might explain. "It has nothing to do with your being my employer. *Nothing*. It's just that I know you're only being nice, and I find it more embarrassing than flattering."

Silence. They covered several more feet of ground before he finally spoke. "You think I'm only being nice?"

She wished now that she hadn't said anything.

In a gravelly voice, he asked, "Who told you that you aren't pretty, Molly?"

"It wasn't necessary for anyone to tell me. I look in the mirror on a daily basis."

"You must not look very hard. You're a beautiful woman, and I'm not the only man on this ranch who thinks so."

She rolled her eyes. "Oh, please."

"You don't believe me."

"Of course I don't. You're either very kind or very blind. I know I'm not much in the looks department."

"Not *much?*"

He suddenly stopped walking. With her hand enfolded in his, Molly was jerked to a stop when she reached the length of her arm. Startled, she swung around to look at him, her snake stick held aloft in her free hand.

"You going to hit me with that?" he asked softly.

"Good grief, no." She lowered the branch. "Why would I do that?"

"Because I'm going to do this."

He tugged hard on her hand. Molly wasn't expecting to be jerked off balance, and she tumbled against his chest. He locked his strong arms around her and dipped his head. The next instant, he was kissing her. He didn't ask; he just took, his wonderfully firm, mobile mouth staking claim.

It was—*oh, God*—it was—she couldn't think clearly. Her heart turned a somersault, her nerves leaped, and her legs went watery.

His mouth was hard and moist and hot and hungry. He grasped the underside of her jaw, pressed in at the joints, and forced her teeth apart. Then he plunged deeply with his tongue, tasting her as if she were a culinary delight and he was a starving man.

Molly tried to breathe, couldn't. Tried again to collect her thoughts, and had no luck with that, either. His chest grazed her breasts, and her nipples went instantly achy and taut, eliciting a moan from deep within her.

"Sweet Christ," he whispered when he dragged his mouth from hers to grab for air. His eyes were molten on hers, his breath, scented with coffee, wafting over her face. "Where's your stick? I think you better whack me with it before I take this any further."

Molly had no idea where her stick had gotten off to. As for taking this any further, it was complete and utter madness. She intended to tell him exactly that, but all she managed to get out was a bleep before his lips settled over hers again. This time, he closed his hand over her braid to tip her head back and hold her still. Then, with a deft twist of his fingers, he stripped the elastic band from her hair, loosening the tresses and gathering them in his fist.

"You're *beautiful,*" he whispered fiercely against her lips. After kissing her until every rational thought in her head went flying again, he intensified the assault by bending his knees to bring his pelvis hard against hers.

She moaned into his mouth. Her legs would no longer hold her up. He angled an arm under her rump and drew her hard against him. She could feel his arousal, pressing in where she was most sensitive, the upward drag of denim and man sending jolts of pure pleasure zigzagging through her.

In all her life, she'd never wanted anything like he made her want him. It came over Molly like a landslide, crushing the breath from her, making her mind spiral wildly. She wanted his hands on her, his mouth at her breasts with the same hungry urgency with which he now took her lips. Oh, how she *wanted*.

She ran her hands over his shoulders, glorying in the pads of vibrant muscle and flesh that rippled under his shirt. She dug in hard with her fingers to resist her urge to tear at the chambray to feel his bare skin. *Jake, with the laser-blue eyes.* She couldn't believe he was kissing her. Things like this never happened to Molly Sterling Wells.

No man had ever jerked her into his arms and devoured her mouth.

No man had ever run his hands over her back and up her sides to feverishly touch her breasts.

When he thumbed her nipples through the layers of her clothing, the shock of each pass made her whimper.

He abandoned her mouth to trail kisses down the column of her throat, his teeth and tongue doing wonderful things to her skin, making it go hot and cold at once. Between her legs, she was wet, the folds of her flesh throbbing, her opening quivering in grasping spasms for the hardness that ground against her.

She *wanted* him.

As if the sheer force of her yearning was transmitted to him through the pores of her skin, he suddenly tightened his arms and lifted her off her feet. Startled, Molly cried out and clung to him as he moved to a tree. Pressing her back to the trunk, he sandwiched her between his hard body and the rough bark, his hungry, persuasive mouth trailing kisses down her neck.

"Molly," he whispered, "put your legs around my hips."

She sobbed, driven by a tidal wave of yearning to do as he told her. When she locked her thighs around him, he pushed her higher against the tree. Dimly Molly realized that he was supporting her weight with the press of his lower body. He put his now unencumbered hands to quick use, cupping her breasts in his hard palms and shoving upward until her tight nipples thrust turgidly against her clothing, becoming easy targets for his mouth.

He caught one hard tip between his teeth, nipping lightly and tugging. A shock of sheer delight zigzagged through her, and she cried out, her clutching hands knocking aside his hat and threading through his thick hair. He responded by drawing her nipple, clothing and all, into his hot mouth.

The sharp pull shattered Molly, the sensations making her muscles quiver and jerk as though she were a marionette on strings. She tightened her fists in his hair and felt as if she were melting in the rush. "Jake?"

He moved up to kiss her eyes closed, his deep voice pitched to a soothing whisper, his silken lips tracing the arch of her brows. "Dear God, you are so beautiful, Molly. If you ask me to stop, I will. But please don't. Please don't."

She felt his clever hands unfastening the buttons of her top, felt his work-roughened fingertips separating the placket.

Dapples of sunshine played warmly over her face and upper chest, a sharp contrast to the cool caress of the morning air. She stiffened, feeling suddenly self-conscious because she knew he was about to bare her breasts and would be able to see every flaw in the unforgiving brightness.

"Cow teats," Rodney had called them.

Even now, the memory made Molly cringe. Her eyes snapped open, her blood running cold as she stared at Jake. Sunlight glanced off his thick, sable hair and played over his strong jaw. He was so handsome, far better looking than Rodney in every way. *Oh, God.* What was she thinking? If she wasn't good enough for Rodney, how could she hope to measure up to Jake's expectations?

She imagined the look that would come over his dark face when he saw her saggy breasts and white, flabby thighs. An awful, chilling shame swept through her, and she knew she couldn't go through with this.

Couldn't, absolutely couldn't.

Just as he was about to tug her breasts free from the cups of the bra, she grabbed the front plackets of her top and jerked them together. Startled by her sudden resistance, he flicked a passion-hot gaze to hers, his features taut.

"What is it?" he whispered.

Holding tightly to her blouse, Molly let her head fall back. "I—I don't—want to do this. I don't know what came over me. I really don't want to do this."

She could feel his gaze on her face and knew he expected more of an explanation. What was she supposed to say, that she was embarrassed for him to see her, afraid he would turn away in disgust as Rodney had countless times?

Scalding tears burned at the backs of her eyes. "I'm sorry, Jake. So sorry. If you think I'm a tease and hate me, I won't blame you. But I—just can't do this. I'm sorry."

She felt the tension go out of him. She half expected him to step back from the tree and let her fall. If he had, she wouldn't have blamed him. A mature woman didn't lead a man on and then, for no apparent reason, turn him off cold. It was cruel and inexcusable.

Instead of jerking away and letting her fall, Jake continued to hold her against the tree trunk with the press of his hips. She heard him grab a deep, ragged breath, then *whoosh* like a blowing whale.

"I'm sorry," she repeated shakily.

He took several more breaths. Then he cupped her face in his hands and forced her to look at him. His eyes were the color of molten steel, their usual clear blue now cloudy with turbulence. He looked furiously angry, but Molly knew by the gentle press of his fingers on her skin that, for reasons beyond her, his rage wasn't directed at her.

"Don't apologize," he whispered, his voice gravelly. "What have you done to be sorry for?"

"I shouldn't have let things go this far."

He chuckled and pressed his forehead against hers, his eyes and dark features blurring in her vision. "I don't think you were entirely responsible for that." He straightened to let her slide down the tree. When her feet connected with the ground, the heels of her canvas sneakers were angled up onto the gnarl of a root, giving her added height and putting her face closer to his. "As I recall," he went on, "I was the one who jumped you, not the other way around."

Molly tried to return his smile, but her trembling mouth refused to co-operate. He murmured something unintelligible and dipped his head to nibble lightly at her bottom lip, his thumbs tracing her cheekbones. With the first brush of his firm, silken lips over hers, she lost her ability to think clearly again and abandoned her hold on her blouse to make tight fists on his shirt.

"Dear God," he whispered. "I've never felt like this. What's going on here?"

Molly didn't know what was going on with him, but she felt fairly sure she had lost her mind. When he drew away, the smoldering heat in his eyes left her in no doubt that he felt the same way, which struck her as being even more incredible. He *wanted* her? She was so tempted to ask him why. What could a man as handsome as Jake Coulter possibly see in someone like her?

"I think I'd better walk you back now," he informed her huskily as he bent to retrieve his hat. "Otherwise I may break my own cardinal rule."

"What's that?"

He dusted the Stetson on his pant leg, then positioned it just so on his dark head, his eyes twinkling as he regarded her. "Thinking no means maybe."

He moved back to her, his gaze dropping to her still unbuttoned blouse. When he reached toward her, Molly pushed his hands away. "I can do it," she insisted.

He watched her fumble with the buttons for a moment, then he reached to lend assistance. "I undid them. I guess I can help put you back together."

Molly was trembling so badly that she finally gave up and allowed him to finish the job. Her nerves leaped with every brush of his knuckles against her chest, and her breasts ached for him to touch them again. She swallowed, hard, doing her best to avoid looking at him.

His hands stilled on the last button. "Molly?"

He said her name softly, but his tone was no less compelling for all that. She glanced up. The instant their gazes met, she knew she couldn't have looked away if her life depended on it. The tenderness she saw in his eyes nearly brought tears to her own.

"You're beautiful," he told her softly. "From the top of your head, to the tips of your toes, you are absolutely beautiful, and if anyone ever told you differently, he was a damned liar."

❦ CHAPTER TWELVE ❦

Hank was still in the stable when Jake returned from the woods. A quarter horse mare was about to foal, and Hank had volunteered to stay close all day to watch her.

"How's White Star doing?" Jake asked.

"Pretty good." Hank closed the gate of the foaling stall farther up the aisle, then came to join Jake at the front doors. "She's dropped a little more. To be on the safe side, I just rewrapped her tail. She hasn't passed the cervical plug yet, though. My guess is, it'll be another day or so."

"Is she feeling pretty restless?"

Hank nodded.

"That's always a sign. We'd best continue to keep an eye on her. We don't want her to surprise us."

"How'd it go with Molly?" Hank asked.

"It didn't."

"What do you mean, it didn't? You talked to her, right?"

"No." Jake hooked his arms over the gate of a front stall and gazed somberly at the buckskin mare within the enclosure. "I just couldn't do it, Hank."

Hank came to stand by him. After getting settled, he asked, "What happened?"

Jake rubbed a hand over his face and blinked. More had happened out there than he'd ever intended. "The minute she saw me, she started trying to guess what I'd come out there to jump her about." He glanced at his brother. "I think her ex-husband did a four-deck shuffle with her self-esteem. It's damned near nonexistent. I couldn't bring myself to deal it another blow."

Hank's mouth tightened.

"What am I going to do? I know I need to talk to her, but when I try,

I think of the paper towels, folded all pretty, and about her chasing Bart around the kitchen with the toothbrush."

Hank smiled ruefully. "I was more impressed with the strawberry flowers on my see-through pancakes. *Those* took time and effort."

"You're a big help."

Hank chuckled. "I was just trying to commiserate." His amusement faded, and he chafed his palms. "I know what you're saying, Jake. She may not be hitting the mark, but she's no slacker. She's worked her fanny off. Have you found little sacks of perfume stuff in any of your drawers yet?"

Jake tugged up the neck of his T-shirt to give it a sniff. "No wonder I smell like a French whore. I thought it was the laundry soap or something."

"Nope. Bart's not her only victim. She's making us all smell pretty."

"I don't guess that'll kill us." Jake's voice went oddly thick and scratchy. "To criticize her performance when she's trying so hard—I don't know—when I look into those big brown eyes, I just can't do it."

Hank rotated his shoulders and then resettled his weight against the gate. "Maybe you need to try a totally different tack."

"Like what?"

"Instead of criticizing her cooking, how's about if we just pitch in and show her how we'd like it done?"

"That'd be the same as saying she can't cook for shit."

"No, it wouldn't. We like most of what she fixes. There's just not enough of it. The trick here is to be subtle. Just go in before mealtimes and say you want to show her how to fix some ranch-style dishes that all of us particularly like. She's a quick study. She'll notice how much more you cook. One problem solved. And she'll learn how to fix a few new things, like pan gravy and country biscuits." Hank warmed to his subject. "I can catch her before she fixes lunches a couple of mornings. Say I've got some slack time and want to help."

"Slack time at five in the morning?"

"She may be a little suspicious, but that's better than openly criticizing her."

"Do you really think helping her in the kitchen is the way to go?"

Hank nodded. "She hasn't been packing us nearly enough lunch. I'll just grab the real mayonnaise and make each of us four sandwiches instead of two. She'll notice the increase, and when the coolers come back empty, she'll realize we need more food. It'd also help if you could take her grocery shopping at least once. If I have to eat another health-food corn chip, I'm going to barf."

Jake considered the suggestion for a moment. "You know, it just might work."

"It *will* work if you handle it right," Hank assured him.

Jake passed a hand over his eyes. Then he nodded. "All right. I'll try it. It'll mean taking time out of my day to work in the kitchen with her, though."

"Like anybody will bitch? We can all take on some extra chores for a few days and cover for you. Anything to get more food."

Jake felt as if a thousand pounds had been lifted off his shoulders. At least one of his problems with Molly was on its way to being solved.

Hank shifted his stance to look Jake full in the face. "Something else is worrying you. You going to tell me what?"

Jake tensed. "What makes you think something else is wrong?"

Hank searched Jake's eyes. "Come on, Jake. We're brothers. You can't bullshit me."

Jake glanced away. "It's personal."

"You're downright sick about something. If you can't talk to me, who the hell can you talk to?"

"No one," Jake replied gruffly.

"Ah, so it's about Molly. Never let it be said that you're a man to kiss and tell. Is that it?"

Jake shot his brother a warning glare and straightened away from the gate. Without another word, he turned and left the stable. There were some things he simply couldn't share, not even with his brother. Secrets of the heart were personal things, and Molly's belief that she was ugly was exactly that, a secret of the heart.

Jake decided to put the problem with Molly on a back burner and just let it simmer for a few days. He needed time to think. She needed time to get over their encounter in the woods. It seemed best, all the way around, to back off and see how things cooked up when he wasn't stirring the pot.

Good plan, bad situation. The minute he stepped into the kitchen that evening, Jake knew it wouldn't work. Molly took one look at him and turned an alarming shade of vermilion.

Jake hoped it was a passing thing. He sat down to eat, doing what he thought was a credible job of pretending nothing was wrong. Molly took her usual place at the opposite end of the table and proceeded to ignore him in a very *loud* way.

"So, boss, how'd it go today?" someone asked to dispel the tension.

"Pretty good. How'd it go for you?"

Silence. Expecting a reply, Jake glanced up to find every head at the table turned toward Molly. Following the gazes of his men, he saw that his cook-cum-housekeeper was dishing a veritable mountain of rice onto her plate.

She suddenly froze, staring at the spoon in her hand as if she wasn't quite sure how it had gotten there. Then she shifted her gaze to the amount of rice she'd served herself, and her cheeks went pink again. She glanced up and saw everyone staring at her. The flush spread over her whole face, deepening by degrees to a brighter pink.

"I'm sorry. I was woolgathering," she explained in a taut, hushed voice. She started scooping rice off her plate back into the serving bowl. "My goodness. What on earth was I thinking?"

Jake knew exactly what she'd been thinking. Evidently his men realized something untoward had happened between him and Molly as well. Nine pairs of accusing eyes turned toward him. Despite the fact that they complained loudly behind Molly's back about the amount of food she prepared, they had all clearly come to care about her and were almost as protective of her as Jake was.

Not that he blamed them. She fussed over everyone like a little mother hen, a fact that was driven home to him as he glanced around the table. The sleeve of Shorty's shirt sported a neat line of stitches where she'd mended a rip. At her insistence, Levi wore a Band-Aid over one eyebrow to cover a small scratch he'd gotten while working with barbed wire. Tex smelled strongly of the wintergreen she rubbed on his shoulder each evening to ease the pain of his bursitis. Bill, who could rarely afford a barber because he paid so much in child support, had a tidy new haircut. In short, there wasn't a man in the group who hadn't been a recipient of her kindness in some way. Even the dog's life had improved since her arrival.

His mouth full of gooey rice, Jake struggled to swallow. After a moment, he chanced another glance at Molly. Head bowed over her plate again, she was hacking at a piece of chicken. Since she seldom ate meat, that was, in and of itself, an indication of how upset she was.

So much for putting the problem on a back burner.

He knew he had to talk to her. Some things could be let go, some things couldn't, and this obviously fell into the latter category.

Avoiding Jake's gaze, Molly flitted busily around him as they cleared the table and rinsed the dishes to put them in the machine. When ad-dressed, she murmured a clipped reply, but no unnecessary exchanges took place.

"I can see myself home tonight," she informed him when the kitchen was in order. She stepped over to grab a flashlight lying on top of the side-by-side. Then, without so much as a backward glance, she left the kitchen, pausing just beyond the archway to fetch her parka. "It's really not that far, and I'm not worried about cougars anymore."

Jake guessed cougars had taken second seat to a greater danger, namely him. Following her to the coat rack, he got his Wrangler jacket. He left his Stetson hanging there. Some maneuvers were best executed while a man wasn't wearing a hat.

Molly gave him a startled look when she saw him donning his jacket. "I said I can see myself home."

"I heard you." Jake stepped over to help her with her parka. He felt her flinch when he ran his fingers under the collar to tug out her braid. "What you can do and what you're *going* to do are two different things."

Before Jake could say more, she was off, making a beeline through the great room for the front door. Once on the porch with the door closed behind them, she turned to confront him. Lifting her small chin to a defiant angle, she fixed him with big eyes that shimmered in the moonlight that slanted in under the porch overhang.

"Molly, I know you're very upset with me," he tried. "Can we talk?"

"I'm not upset with you," she said, her voice quivering. "I'm upset with myself. There's a big difference."

"Why are you upset with yourself?"

She flipped on the flashlight. "I really don't want to discuss it, Jake. I'd like to pretend this morning never happened."

He thought he glimpsed tears in her eyes just before she whirled away to descend the steps. Jake gazed after her for a moment. If the erratic bob of her flashlight beam was any indication, this was going to get worse before it got better. He sighed, shoved his hands into his pockets, and went down the steps three at a time. When he hit level ground, he kicked into high gear, lengthening his strides to catch up with her.

When she heard his footsteps coming up behind her, she spun around. This time, when she spoke, her voice went from quivery to downright tremulous, every intonation shrill. Jake knew by the sound that she was trying to hold back tears and was going to lose the battle.

"Would you leave me *alone?*" she cried.

"I think we need to talk."

"We do not need to talk. To what end? So you can try to convince me I'm beautiful and make me feel less ridiculous?"

"Ridiculous? *Why?* I'm the one who started it, not you. If anyone should feel ridiculous, it's me."

The flashlight beam cut a wide arc around her feet as she swung her arm back and forth against her leg. "I don't want to talk about this. Right now, I don't even want you *near* me. Can't you see that?"

He could see it, all right. The question was, why? The panic in her eyes told him that flight might be her next course of action. They had to get this settled between them. If he left it until morning, she might be gone.

"Why don't you want me near you?" he asked. "Can you tell me that?"

"It's obvious, isn't it?"

"Ah, Molly," he said hoarsely, "what in God's name has he done to you?"

Her chin came back up, only a slight quiver of her lower lip giving her away. Her eyes were huge splotches of moon-touched amber in her face, and all Jake could see in their depths now was pain. Pain that ran so deep, it went beyond tears.

He took a step toward her, wanting nothing more than to gather her up in his arms.

"Don't!" she said.

"Don't what?"

"Just *don't*," she said again. "I know you feel badly, and it's very sweet of you to want to make me feel better. But that will only make it worse."

"What?"

She made a low sound of frustration and squeezed her eyes closed. "What's your game, Jake? Whatever it is, I don't want to play."

"I'm not playing a game, Molly. Why would you even think that I am?"

She fixed him with an accusing glare. "Because this doesn't make an iota of sense, that's why. We're both mature adults. Can't we simply move past this and forget it happened?"

"But it did happen."

"Yes, unfortunately." She sighed and tipped her head back to stare at the sky. "You know what I think the problem is? You're too nice for your own good, and mine as well."

"Thank you for that much, at least."

She laughed softly, the sound totally lacking in humor and laced with bitterness. "Misguided, but nice."

"Ouch."

She sighed and met his gaze. "I'm sorry, but it's true. You shouldn't go around kissing women to make them feel good. It's dangerous."

"Ah, I see. I should kiss women to make them feel bad?"

She rolled her eyes. "Don't be deliberately obtuse."

"Ouch, again." Jake bent his head and rubbed his jaw. "Molly, I think we need to back up and clarify why I kissed you to start with."

"What's to clarify? You paid me a compliment, I didn't believe you, and in some misguided desire to make me feel pretty, you kissed me to drive home the point. Unfortunately for you—and for me—it backfired. You found yourself being attacked by a horny divorcee, you didn't want to hurt my feelings by pulling away, and things got out of hand." She sighed and drew an arm from around her waist to push at a tendril of hair that had escaped her braid. "Thank God I came to my senses."

Jake was beginning to wish now that she hadn't. They might have avoided this if only she had let passion run its course. She wouldn't be hunching her shoulders to hide those gorgeous breasts right now, that was for damned sure.

"For the record," she went on, "I don't blame you for any of it. I know men are easily aroused, especially if they've been working hard like you have for months on end and neglecting their physical needs. I was all over you. There was friction between our bodies. You couldn't control your physical response to that, and it went downhill from there. It was just—" She broke off and shrugged. "It was an unfortunate mess, is what it was. I'm very sorry it happened, and now I just want to forget that it did."

"So you have it all figured out, do you?"

She avoided looking at him. "Mostly. Your following me out here is a little baffling. I'm afraid you've got some harebrained notion that you can kiss me again and make it all better. Not a good plan."

"Why not?"

"Because you're—" She sighed and waved a hand as if to erase the bad start. "Never mind."

"Because I'm what?" he pressed. "I hate half-finished sentences."

"Too attractive," she muttered.

"Pardon?"

"You heard me."

"You find me attractive, Molly?"

She narrowed her eyes. "No, I think you're a real dog. What exactly do you think this morning was about? Do you think I react like that to every man who kisses me?"

Jake folded his arms to keep from touching her. "I hope to God not. I'm the possessive type."

She rolled her eyes again. Then she turned and struck off, calling, "I'm going home now, end of discussion."

Jake set off after her. As he drew abreast, he said, "I've let you have your say. It's only fair that you let me have mine."

"Talk fast. When I reach my door, I'm going inside, and you're not invited."

Jake reached out to grasp her arm and slow her pace. "First of all, I don't kiss women to be nice. I never have, I never will, and I didn't today. I kissed you because I've been wanting to ever since I first met you."

"Oh, *brother*."

"I didn't interrupt you with sarcastic asides. Don't interrupt me." He drew her to a stop and turned to study her pinched face. "Secondly, I resent the implication that I am so easily aroused and so sexually deprived that any warm body will do."

She threw him a startled look. "I never meant it like that."

"It's a damned good thing because I don't sleep with just anyone."

"Oh."

"Contrary to the belief of some, not all men's decisions are made for them by what's behind their fly. Good Christ." He hooked a thumb toward the woods. "I don't know what the hell happened out there. Spontaneous combustion might best describe it. I only meant to kiss you, and the first thing I knew, I had you up against a tree."

"Don't remind me."

"How do you think that makes me feel? I generally try to treat women with respect. I've only known you for a little over a week, and there I was, going for it. And in broad daylight, no less."

"Must you give me a blow-by-blow replay? It wasn't one of my finer moments, either."

He ignored that. "I have nothing against nature and daylight. Don't get me wrong. But we were no more than a stone's throw from the house."

She cupped a hand over her eyes. "Oh, *God*."

"Anybody could have come along, and there we would have been."

She groaned again.

"I totally lost it."

"Me, too," she said faintly. "I'm so sorry. It was my fault."

"Your fault?" He nudged her hand from her eyes, caught her by the shoulders, and leaned down to put his face before hers. "It wasn't anybody's fault, Molly. It just *happened*. You're a beautiful lady, and you're one sweet armful. I've never been hit so hard and so fast by a kiss in my life."

"There you go again."

"There I go with what again?"

"Saying I'm pretty. You really need to stop doing that."

"Why? You afraid you may start believing me? Why not? You believed Rodney."

"Let's leave Rodney out of this."

"We can't leave him out of this. It's his lies that are causing us problems right now." She started to speak, and Jake laid a finger across her mouth to silence her. "Molly, do you trust me?"

She wrinkled her nose.

"Forget about what happened this morning," he urged. "Before then, did you trust me?"

"I'm here, aren't I?" she said against his fingertip. "If I didn't trust you, I'd be long gone."

"Good. Then will you give me fifteen minutes?"

She blinked and peered up at him owlishly. "To do what?"

"I want to introduce you to someone."

"To whom?"

"It's a surprise. Will you give me the fifteen minutes?"

"I suppose," she said hesitantly. "But only if you promise to behave yourself."

Jake turned her toward the cabin, taking a firm grasp on her arm to draw her along. Flashlight beam bobbing in front of her, she cast him a bewildered look. "I thought you were going to introduce me to someone."

"I am."

They reached the porch, and Jake hustled her up the steps as fast as her shorter legs would allow. He shouldered open the door, reached inside to flip on the lamp, and nudged her into the cabin ahead of him. After closing the door, he glanced at his watch and then shoved it under her nose so she could see the time.

"Fifteen minutes," he repeated, "and your complete trust. I promise you won't regret this."

"I'm already regretting it," she said when he grabbed her arm again to guide her toward the bathroom. "What are you doing? There's no one in there for me to meet."

He pushed her ahead of him into the dark enclosure. "There is now." He flipped on the overhead light. Blinded by the brightness, she narrowed her eyes to see. Before her vision completely cleared, he had her standing before the mirror and was unfastening her braid. When she reached to stop him, he stiffened his arms against her and said, "Trust. Remember?" After loosening her plaited tresses, he said, "Stand right there. Don't move."

"You're making me very nervous."

Jake jerked open the door of the small linen closet. Inside were towels that he'd left at the cabin for guests. He bypassed all those at the top to tug a pink one from the bottom of the stack. Next he fished through the toiletries lying on the shelf above, locating a brush with strands of whiskey-colored hair caught in the stiff bristles.

As he stepped up behind her, he smiled at her in the mirror. "I don't mean to make you nervous. Just bear with me a second. All right?"

Setting the towel on the edge of the sink, he dispensed with the flashlight, then drew off her parka and tossed it aside. That accomplished, he began brushing her hair. It felt like silk as it ran through his fingers, the curls clinging to his hands, exhibiting far more friendliness than their owner ever had. He caught her bewildered expression in the glass.

"There's a method to my madness."

Her eyes darkened as she stared at her reflection. "I can't do this," she said shakily. "I really can't do this."

Jake heard the note of panic in her voice. He sharpened his gaze on her face, which had drained of color. Perspiration glistened on her forehead.

Then he looked into her eyes. Never in his life had he seen anyone who looked so hopelessly lost. His hands stilled. Where his wrists rested against her shoulders, he felt the shallow, rapid pace of her breathing. "Molly?" he whispered. He glanced down and saw that she was gripping the edge of the sink with such force that her knuckles had gone white. "Sweetheart? What's wrong?"

He felt a shudder move through her body. Her frightened gaze sought his in the mirror. "I can't do this. I know it's stupid, but—" She broke off and squeezed her eyes closed. "I just can't, is all."

Jake set the brush aside and gripped her firmly by the shoulders. "What's stupid?"

"Nothing," she said faintly.

"Molly, tell me," he urged.

"You'll think I'm crazy."

He ran his thumbs in a circular massage over the knotted muscles in her shoulders. "No, I won't. I swear. Tell me."

"It's just—" Her face twisted, and she dragged in a shaky breath. "When I look in the mirror, I can't find myself anymore. The person in the glass—she's someone I don't know."

Jake rested his cheek atop her head. Pain twisted through his chest, hurting so much it almost took his breath. "Is that all?" He forced himself to chuckle. "Honey, we all feel that way sometimes. It's natural."

"This is different," she insisted. "I'm empty inside. The person I used to be isn't there anymore."

Jake sighed and slipped his arms around her waist. The fact that she didn't try to pull away told him how very upset she was. "That isn't so," he assured her. "You're in there, honey. Trust me on that. You're just feeling lost and confused right now." He studied her pale reflection, smiling slightly as he took in each lovely angle of her face. In that moment, he realized that every feature had been indelibly engraved on his heart. "I see who you are all the time, in countless little ways, and so does everyone else. You've got the kindest heart of anyone I know. If you don't believe me, just ask Bart. He's never had it so good. Or get Sunset's opinion. He can tell you a few things about yourself, namely that you've got more courage in your little finger than most people do in their entire body."

Her lashes lifted, and she fixed him with a question-filled gaze. "I'm not courageous."

"You rescued that stallion and broke the law to do it. Trust me, honey, that's courageous."

"I had no choice. Sunset could have ended up dead."

"A lot of people wouldn't have cared, not so much they would have been willing to put their bacon on the plate. No matter how you circle it, that took guts."

Faint touches of color rose to her cheeks. Jake smiled at her in the glass. Bending down to put his face beside hers, he whispered, "All your fine inner qualities aside, I'd like you to see the Molly I do. I don't think you've really looked at her before. Or it's been a very long time since you did." He caught her chin on the crook of his finger and lifted her face to the light. "Feature by feature, I want you to really look, Molly. Forget everything anyone else ever said to you and really *look*."

Her gaze shifted to her own face.

"You have the most beautiful hair I've ever seen." He lifted a mass of curls on his palm and turned them to catch the light. "Just look at how they shimmer. Have you ever held a glass of Scotch up to a flame? Your hair is like that—the color of whiskey shot through with firelight." He kept turning his wrist until she joined him in staring at the play of light on her hair. "*That* is beautiful, Molly. Don't you agree?"

Her throat worked as she swallowed. "The way you're moving it in the light makes it look pretty," she conceded.

"This is nothing compared to how it catches the light when you wear it loose and you move your head. It's like looking at swirls of liquid fire."

He let her hair slip from his palm and resumed studying her face. "Now your eyes," he said with a grin. "Just look at those eyes."

She did as he suggested.

"They're almost exactly the color of your hair, and they sparkle so pretty. From the moment we met, they captivated me. That was the first thing I noticed about you, your beautiful eyes."

Those eyes filled with bewilderment now. "You noticed my eyes?"

"I definitely noticed. Even with no liner or shadow to make them stand out, they're heart grabbers."

A flush touched her cheeks. "This is silly."

Jake glanced at his watch. "I've got ten minutes left to be silly." He turned her face slightly. "Now the nose." He couldn't help but smile when he looked at it. "It's small and perfectly straight, except for right at the tip where it turns up just slightly. How could anyone find fault with a nose like that? Mine is twice that large and crooked to boot."

"It isn't crooked."

He grinned and narrowed an eye at her. "We'll argue that point later. For now, we'll move on from that perfect nose to those sculpted cheekbones." He ran a finger along the hollow of her cheek. "I've heard that movie stars get their back molars yanked out to achieve that look."

"You're kidding."

"Would I lie to you?" He ran his thumb over her bottom lip. "And look at that mouth, would you? Not a trace of lipstick, and it's such a pretty pink. That second night after I met you, I wanted to steal a kiss so damned bad I ached."

"You did?"

He chuckled. "I'm damned glad now that I didn't. I got myself in enough trouble this morning."

She bent her head, her dark lashes feathering over her cheeks like spider etchings. "It's not just my face, Jake. It's the rest of me."

"I'm getting to that."

She threw him an appalled look. "Oh, no, you're not."

He winked at her. "No bare body parts, I swear. I just want to show you something."

"What?"

He reached around her to unbutton her blouse. She grabbed his wrists. "You said no bare parts."

"And I'm a man of my word. Relax." He unfastened the second button, then a third and fourth. "I just want to tuck your collar under and open the front."

"That's baring parts."

"Then I see bare parts downtown all the time," he challenged. "Women wear tops cut this low every day."

"They aren't me."

"No, but they probably wish they were." He directed a pointed glance at the bountiful display of cleavage above the V of her blouse. "Your breasts are beautiful, Molly."

"They're big and floppy," she informed him in a faint voice.

"Flop them my way and see what happens." He draped the towel over her chest to form a scoop neckline. "There," he whispered. "Get a load of that."

She looked up and went still. Jake smiled. "Where's the clash?" he asked. "Pink is your color, lady. Just look at how it makes your skin glow." He trailed a fingertip along the edge of the towel, acutely aware of the way she shivered at his touch. "If that isn't flawless, nothing is," he said huskily. "And the pink strikes a perfect contrast—putting me in mind of raspberries and cream."

He drew away the towel and let it drop into the sink. Then he settled his hands at her waist. Smiling at her over the top of her curly head, he said, "Molly, meet Molly, one of the prettiest ladies I've ever clapped eyes on."

Another flush crept up her neck to pool in her cheeks. Jake met her gaze in the mirror. "There isn't an unmarried man in my acquaintance who could have resisted kissing you this morning. I guess maybe I should apologize for letting it get out of hand, but I'm not going to. I'll do it again if I get half a chance, so consider yourself warned."

She lowered her gaze to stare at the faucet.

Jake checked his watch. "I've got seven minutes left. Since I asked you to trust me, I'll behave myself, and I won't kiss you again tonight. I am going to take liberty with words, though, and tell you a couple of things that are probably going to embarrass you and make you hate me just a little. But they're things you need to hear, so I'll take my chances."

He braced his hands on the edge of the vanity and leaned down to smell her hair. The scent of shampoo and soap and Molly filled his head, making him feel a little dizzy.

"You have *gorgeous* breasts." He felt her stiffen. "I'll say that again. You have gorgeous, perfect breasts."

"You haven't seen them," she whispered tautly and tried to slip out from between his body and the vanity.

Jake blocked her way with his braced arm. "You're not going any-where, Molly. Not until I've finished."

Her expression pinched, she met his gaze in the mirror. "Don't do this."

"Don't do what? I'm only telling you the truth. Granted, maybe it's not a subject for polite conversation, but we went beyond polite when I had you pressed up against that tree this morning. At which point, I might add, I held your breasts in my hands and kissed them through your blouse." He winked at her again. "You can tell yourself that I really don't know what's under the clothing. I beg to correct you. I have the touch."

"The what?"

"The touch." He lifted his hand to rub his fingers and thumb together. "These hands know gorgeous breasts when they feel them." He studied her face for a moment. "I'd venture a guess that it was good old Rodney who told you that your body is less than perfect."

She glanced quickly away.

"I thought so." Jake gripped down hard on the edge of the vanity. "I've never met the man. But I've only to look at what he did to his horse and wife to know that he's a pissant."

She threw him another startled look, which he answered with a grin.

"A *lying* pissant," he revised. "You're a short, sweetly rounded lady. You want to know my take on Rodney? I think he's a limp-dick excuse for a man, an even poorer excuse for a husband, and an all-around lying bastard, if you'll excuse my French. He didn't want his wife to read his-torical romances because it might give her unrealistic expectations. *Hello?* That screams inferiority complex to me. I think he did his damnedest to make you feel ugly because it gave him more control. He was probably afraid you'd discover what a loser you were married to and trade him in for a better model."

Jake pushed erect.

"If I had been him, I would have been reading your books every time you laid them down to see how I could improve my skills and please you. Sec-ond warning of the night." He moved to the doorway. "I bought a couple."

She turned from the sink. "You bought a couple of what?"

Jake looked her dead in the eye. "Historical romances. I'm three-quarters through the first one." He flashed her a slow grin. "All I can say is, I like the way your mind works."

❦ CHAPTER THIRTEEN ❦

After Jake left, Molly turned back to regard her reflection in the mirror. Touching a hand to her hair, she stared at the masses of uncontrollable curls, which she'd never liked and had grown to hate after she married Rodney. Now, after listening to Jake wax poetic about how glorious her hair was, she wondered if she should start wearing it loose. Maybe he was right, and it was one of her best features, not one of her worst.

Gathering up the towel he'd dropped in the sink, she draped it across her chest again and studied herself critically. Could it be that she really had been hiding her light under a bushel for a decade? She'd always loved the color pink, but Rodney had convinced her it made her complexion look ruddy. Holding the terry close to her face, she leaned toward the glass and trailed a fingertip over her cheek. As hard as she tried, she could detect no increased reddish tones in her skin. Maybe Rodney had lied to her all those years, just as Jake insisted.

According to him, pink was her color. Though he hadn't come right out and said as much, she knew he wished she would stop wearing only neutral shades and become a bit more daring in her dress. A vision of herself in tight jeans and a figure-hugging, outrageous pink knit top spun through her mind. Just the *thought* of exposing her shape that way brought an embarrassed blush to her cheeks.

Reddish tones, she thought as she took in her heightened color. She had always flushed very easily—from exertion, heat, or embarrassment. Maybe her tendency to turn red at the drop of a hat was what Rodney had been talking about. She pressed even closer to the mirror to stare hard at her skin. The pink in her cheeks didn't seem to clash or look particularly ruddy against the towel. Did it? Jake had likened the contrast to raspberries and cream.

Rodney—Jake. Jake—Rodney. Whom was she supposed to believe?

Who was right, and who was wrong? As she pondered the questions, an ache took up throbbing residence in her temples. She didn't know what to believe anymore. Should she listen to Jake or continue as she had been, dressing and wearing her hair the way Rodney had suggested?

At the thought, the pain in her head became knifelike. *Dear God.* It was absolutely true; she was still living her life according to the guidelines Rodney had set down. Every stitch of clothing in her closet had been selected with his advice in mind. *"Loose, concealing garments and neutral colors,"* he'd always preached. *"You don't have the figure or the complexion to carry anything else off."* Because of him, she wore no makeup, afraid of looking like a trollop. Because of him, most of the time she wore platform-soled shoes that she detested in an attempt to look taller. She no longer even *laughed* naturally because of him.

Was it any wonder she couldn't find herself when she looked in a mirror? Molly pressed a hand to her throat as an even more alarming revelation came to her. Now, instead of following Rodney's rules, she was seriously thinking about complying with Jake's.

Shaken, she sank down on the toilet, not knowing what to think anymore. Only one thing seemed clear to her in that moment. Ten years ago, she'd bent over backward, trying to please Rodney, wearing the kinds of clothes that he preferred, doing her hair the way he liked. Now, after surviving a hellish marriage and coming out on the other side, she was listening to another man and about to do the same thing all over again.

She knotted her hands into fists and pressed them hard against her knees. She was so tired, so sick to death *tired,* of being told what to do. If she wanted to shave her head and wear a bodysuit of bright purple spandex, it was nobody's business but hers. It no longer mattered what Rodney thought. And she wasn't about to start living her life according to Jake Coulter's dictates. She was single, almost thirty, and this was a free country. No one was going to tell her what to do, how to behave, or how to look.

From this moment forward, she was going to do what *she* wanted, to hell with everyone else.

Leaping to her feet, Molly spun to take in her reflection. *Hair.* That was all she saw. She had a small face, and it was barely visible in the cloud.

Trembling violently, she threw open the cupboard door and searched frantically for the scissors. When she found them, she whirled back to the sink, grabbed a hank of hair, and whacked it off about two inches from her scalp. *Snip, snip, snip.* As she sheared off the hated curls, she refused to assess the damage she was doing. She didn't care. *Snip, snip.*

Take *that*, Jake Coulter. *Snip, snip.* She wasn't a stupid sheep, to be pushed and prodded and led around. Maybe she'd start wearing fire-engine red lipstick and gaudy earrings that dangled down past her shoulders. Why not?

When she ran out of curls to whack off, she felt limp with exhaustion. She let the scissors slip from her fingers and clatter into the sink with the towel and all her shorn locks. Almost afraid to look at herself, she forced her gaze to the mirror. The instant she saw her reflection, tears flooded her eyes.

Rodney hadn't lied. He'd been telling the absolute truth. She looked like Bozo the Clown.

"Molly's running late," Hank said grumpily.

Jake merely smiled as he poured himself a second cup of coffee. "Yeah, she is."

"She's never late," Hank pointed out. "Aren't you worried something's wrong?"

Jake chuckled. "She'll be along any time now."

"I was going to help her fix sandwiches."

Jake turned from the coffeepot. Lifting his steaming mug to his lips, he took a slow sip of brew, eyeing his brother over the porcelain rim. "We don't want to overwhelm her with too much the first morning. Why don't you go ahead with milking and gathering the eggs?"

"You going to help her fix breakfast?"

Jake nodded.

"What are you going to make?"

"A country-style breakfast with all the trimmings," Jake said.

"Biscuits from scratch?"

"Yes."

"Fried potatoes and pan gravy?"

Jake grinned. "Yes."

"Bacon and sausage and eggs?"

"Maybe even some ham as well," Jake assured him.

Hank looked as if he were about to drool. He went to the utility room for the egg basket and milk bucket.

As Molly left the cabin, her gaze was caught by something lying just over the threshold on the porch. She looked down and focused bewilderedly on a paperback novel and a nosegay of maiden pinks. She crouched down to stare. The delicate flowers were bound together at the stems with an old strip of leather.

Jake.

Tears stung Molly's eyes. Aside from her father, no man had ever given her flowers, not even her husband of ten years. Hand trembling, she picked up the nosegay and touched the blossoms to her nose, inhaling their delicate scent. How *sweet*. She imagined Jake traipsing through the woods in the predawn gloom to pick her a bouquet, and the sting of tears in her eyes became a flood.

With her free hand, she swiped at her cheeks, disgusted with herself for being so emotional. It was only a nosegay, after all, and had cost him nothing. Women received gorgeous hothouse roses all the time and didn't weep all over them.

Only somehow this nosegay with its smashed stems held fast by a leather thong seemed far more special than a delivery from a florist. Jake had invested a good chunk of his time in the endeavor. Then he'd bound the stems and made the delivery himself.

She'd never been the weepy type. Now, all of sudden, her tear ducts seemed to be turning off and on at will. Fresh tears sprang to her eyes, and no matter how fast she blinked, she couldn't dispel them.

It was just so sweet of him. *Flowers*. Finding them here brought back so many wonderful memories of her father. He'd always left her surprises. *"Little I-love-yous,"* he'd called them, and they'd often been flowers he'd picked from the garden. Nothing expensive, really. She'd wake up in the morning to find roses in a drinking glass on her nightstand or a nosegay of pansies next to her cheek on the pillow. It had been a lovely way to wake up and an even lovelier way to start her day, knowing her dad cared about her in a special way.

After she married, there had been no more sweet surprises on her pillow, only tear stains from where she'd lain awake crying while she waited for her husband to come home to her from the arms of another woman. She'd yearned for Rodney to give her flowers, just once, but he never had.

Remembering those times now, Molly knew that was nine-tenths why she'd tried so hard to please him. She'd been constantly competing with faceless rivals for his love, and she'd fallen into the trap of thinking she was the one at fault, that if she just tried hard enough, she might win his affection. She'd changed her appearance and altered her behavior in order to seem more sophisticated. Though it had happened slowly, she'd eventually changed herself so much that she could no longer recognize the person she had become.

Smiling sadly through her tears, Molly sniffed the maiden pinks again and then picked up the paperback. She wasn't surprised to see that it was a historical romance. She'd mentioned in passing that she'd once loved them, and in a very subtle way, Jake was calling her back to that, not to be the woman he wanted her to be, but to simply be herself again.

"Who are you now, Molly?" he'd asked her. At the time, she'd been so disturbed by the question that she'd resented him for asking it. In the days since, she'd often felt cornered and believed he was playing some vicious game, trying to seduce her, not because he really wanted her, but simply because she was there.

Now this.

She sighed and hugged the book to her heart, accepting now what she should have realized from the start. Jake Coulter was nothing like Rodney Wells. He was his antithesis in practically every way, the only similarity being that he was male.

Touching a hand to her hair, Molly wished now that she'd thought twice before cutting it. After ten endless years, a man had told her she was pretty, and instead of taking the compliment, she'd thrown it back in his face.

He was going to *hate* what she'd done to herself, and he'd probably be furious. By cutting off her hair, she'd told him she didn't value his opinion, plain and simple. He wasn't a stupid man. He'd get the message. Big problem. After finding the flowers and book, she wasn't sure that was the message she wanted to send.

Jake was wondering if Molly would be wearing her hair in that dreadful braid again this morning. On the one hand, he was reluctant to influence her too much. He had a feeling she'd gotten enough of that from her ex-husband to last her a lifetime. But another big part of him yearned to see her cut loose and be a free spirit for a change—to literally let her hair down and thumb her nose at the world.

He was imagining how she might look with all those fabulous curls falling in a riotous cascade to her shoulders when he heard her enter the house. He smiled smugly, keeping his back to the archway. The last thing he wanted was for her to think he was expecting her hair to be down. If by chance it was, the trick would be to act surprised. Then, after he collected himself, he'd shower her with compliments, pretending it had been all her idea.

"Hi," she said from behind him.

Her voice was shaky and faint. His smile deepened. He'd been around females enough to know when a woman was waiting on tenterhooks for a man's reaction to her appearance. Taking a last sip of coffee, he slowly turned, determined not to disappoint her.

The instant he saw her, he choked. Coffee went up his nose and down his windpipe. A harsh whistling sound erupted from his mouth. Molly's eyes went huge. She touched a hand to her hair, looking stricken.

"Jesus H. *Christ*," Jake rasped when he finally got his breath. "What the *hell* did you *do*?"

All the color drained from her face. Plucking at a short tendril of hair, she just stared at him, offering no explanation. Not that he needed one. He'd gone out of his way last night to tell her how gorgeous he thought her hair was, and now it was—*gone*. He'd been told to shove it a few times, but this took the prize.

Anger was his first reaction. Deep hurt quickly followed. And then he just felt stunned. She looked—*beautiful*. The short cap of amber curls feathered forward over her temples and cheeks, creating a perfect show-case for her delicate features. The cut was shaggy, and on someone else, it might have been unattractive, but the tousled, carefree style suited Molly perfectly, giving her a sassy look that was adorable.

Collecting himself, Jake set his mug of coffee on the counter and walked slowly toward her, barely able to take his eyes off her face. She shifted her feet, pushed self-consciously at her hair, and then dropped her chin as if she were ashamed to let him look at her.

"I'm sorry," she said faintly. "I know it was a dumb thing to do and that I look awful."

Jake slowly circled her. He really hated to be wrong, and he hated hav-ing to admit it even more. "Don't be silly. I think it's cute." He no sooner spoke than he wished he'd thought to use another word. Cute was sort of lukewarm. Gorgeous, on the other hand, would probably be suspect. What was a guy supposed to say? That it was darling? That was a femi-nine word, and he'd feel ridiculous. "I, um . . . " He came to stand in front of her. "It's perfect on you. Really. As pretty as I thought it was long, I like it this way even more."

She shoved at her hair again. The light glanced off the disturbed wisps of amber, making him want to touch them himself. "Right," she said. "There's no need to lie to save my feelings. I know it looks *awful*. Maybe I can go to a shop and get it evened up."

Jake liked it wispy and tousled. "Don't even think about it. No beauti-cian on earth can improve on it."

She flashed him a miserable look. "It grows pretty fast. It'll be long again before I know it."

Jake laughed and caught her face between his hands. "I didn't mean that it's beyond repair, Molly. I meant that it's not possible to improve on perfection."

An incredulous expression slipped into her lovely eyes. "You mean you really like it?"

"I really, really do. I thought it was beautiful long, but this is even better." Crooking a finger under her chin, he lifted her face to the light. "I'm no expert on hairstyles, but wearing it short brings out your eyes and draws attention to your face."

"Oh."

He couldn't help but smile. "With fine features like yours, that's a plus."

She lifted a dubious gaze to his. "Do you really think so?"

Still holding her face between his hands, Jake thought he'd never seen anyone so sweetly beautiful. Looking down at her, he could only wonder what he'd ever found attractive about tall, leggy blondes and redheads who wore gobs of makeup. Molly was what he'd wanted all along, but he'd been too dumb to realize it.

"I really think so," he whispered huskily.

For the remainder of the day, Jake grinned every time he recalled Molly's new hairstyle. She was turning out to be the most unpredictable female he'd ever met. What would come next, spike heels and black net stockings? He hoped not. Molly was more the Madonna type, and he hated to see her change that.

On the other hand, he'd been wrong about the hair. She'd probably knock his eyes out in black fishnet. Maybe the best thing for him to do was butt out entirely and let her create her own look.

The thought no sooner entered his brain than Jake knew he'd just experienced a rare moment of genius. *Of course* he needed to butt out. Molly had been pushed around too much already. *"I can't find myself anymore,"* she'd whispered to him last night. He had a very bad feeling that was because she'd buried herself to please her husband. Jake didn't want to make the same mistake.

It was high time that she should discover who she really was, and she didn't need his help to do that. When all was said and done, he'd take her in a heartbeat, be she in fishnet or a nun's habit. He wasn't sure when it had happened—or even exactly how—but he'd fallen head over heels in love with her. Done deal, no turning back.

Rationally, Jake knew it had happened way too fast and probably made little sense. Love and marriage weren't things an intelligent man jumped into. It was only smart to wait, to test the waters. Only somehow that didn't seem smart at all with Molly. She was running from the law.

He couldn't shake the feeling that time was short and might soon run out, that he might forever lose his chance with her if he didn't move quickly.

He couldn't let her slip through his fingers. He was damned near thirty-three. He'd been waiting for the right lady to come along ever since he'd grown mature enough to realize that love and sex were two entirely different things. If he didn't snatch her up while he had the chance, what were the odds that he'd ever meet anyone like her again?

That night, after cooking a meal under Jake's direction that was, in Molly's opinion, large enough to feed and clog the arteries of half the population of Crystal Falls, she set herself to the task of cleaning the kitchen. As always, Jake rolled up his sleeves to help. He took his usual position at the sink to wash while she dried.

"I've gotten the impression that the men you've known weren't much for helping with domestic tasks," he said.

She put a dinner plate in the cupboard. "My dad always helped in the kitchen on Cook's night off."

"Ah, so you had a cook, did you?"

Molly shot him a wary look. She glimpsed a twinkle in his eyes before he returned his attention to the pot he was scrubbing. "You have a cook," she pointed out.

"I also have a ranch and a lot of extra mouths to feed, which makes it a necessity rather than a luxury. We both know your father didn't own a cattle ranch. I'll venture a guess you've never been on a ranch or farm before in your life."

Molly's cheeks burned with embarrassment over all the lies and half-truths she'd told him. Now that he was calling her on it, she couldn't think what to say. "I'm sorry, Jake," she murmured.

"For what?"

"For lying to you. I can only say I don't make a habit of it."

He smiled. "You've only done what you felt you had to."

Molly couldn't think what to say. She drew a skillet from the drainer.

"So," he mused aloud, "if you had a cook while you were growing up, your father must have been wealthy then?"

"Well off. He wasn't a billionaire or anything."

"That leaves a lot of room for supposition. A millionaire, then?"

Molly's pulse escalated, and her fingers grew stiff and clumsy. She tightened her grip on the skillet handle. If she answered that question, Jake would be one step closer to learning her true identity. There weren't that many millionaires in Oregon, and she'd narrowed the search down considerably by telling him that she'd worked at an investment firm. She cast him an uneasy glance. She guessed it all boiled down to whether or not she trusted him.

Only it wasn't that simple. While she had come to trust that Jake would never deliberately hurt her, he was operating under a cloud of ignorance she didn't dare dispel. Her freedom and Sunset's future hung in the balance. So did her need to seek justice for her father's death. How might he react if she told him she was recently released from a mental ward and was still supposed to be under a doctor's care?

Under other circumstances, she might have taken a calculated risk and told him everything. But she wasn't like other women. Until a judge rapped his gavel and said otherwise, she was vulnerable in a way that terrified her. She'd been married to Rodney when she'd been deemed legally incompetent, and he had been appointed her guardian by the court. Because of the firm and all the related business entanglements, Rodney's attorney had been able to keep much of the arrangement status quo after the divorce, arguing that Rodney and Molly's financial future and all their marital assets hung in the balance. She'd still been at the clinic then. What judge worth his salt granted a mental ward patient the right to handle her own affairs when millions of dollars and the future of a financial empire were at stake?

As a result, Rodney might no longer be her husband, but he still had power over her. It was Rodney who had doled out money to her each month from the firm's coffers, Rodney who still had access to all those accounts, Rodney who could hire all the big-shot attorneys. She couldn't even scrape up a retainer fee, and if she managed, what lawyer in his right mind would take her on? There were the liability factors no attorney in his right mind could ignore. Representing a legally incompetent individual gave rise to a host of difficulties and possible legal infractions they preferred to avoid.

What had happened once could happen again, and if Molly forgot that, even for an instant, her fate would be sealed. The very thought filled her with cold fear. Rodney hated Sam Banks, the doctor who'd become her champion. If her ex-husband and mother had her committed again, it was highly unlikely that they would put her back in a clinic where she already had an ally. Oh, no. She'd be handed over to strangers, individuals who'd be predisposed to disbelieve everything she said.

After her release from the clinic, she'd tried once to get a restraining order against Rodney, and all she'd earned for her trouble was a pat on the arm. In short, crazy people weren't taken seriously, and nothing she'd said had carried any weight with the police. Harrassment? Stalking? Legally, she didn't have a leg to stand on.

Jake had no idea what a tangle her life was in. All it would take was for him to grow curious and make a few phone calls to the wrong people. If word of his inquiries filtered back to Rodney, she might be tracked down. It was anyone's guess what might happen then. It certainly wouldn't be pleasant.

"Okay," he said with a laugh when her reluctance to answer became obvious. "I guess that wasn't a fair question. Let's move on from there. So your dad helped in the kitchen on Cook's night off. Is that what you called her, Cook?"

"How do you know Cook wasn't a man?"

He laughed again and flicked suds at her. "I'm a redneck cowboy. I think the ERA is a real estate company. Don't burst my bubble."

She smiled in spite of herself. Jake was as far from being a male chauvinist as any man could get. "Yes, we called her Cook."

"How was Rodney for helping in the kitchen?"

"He didn't."

"Never?"

"Never. That was woman's work, amen."

Jake grinned and winked at her. "Like I said, a pissant."

A few minutes later, Jake was walking her home. As he'd taken to doing quite frequently, he detoured toward the creek. Molly almost gave in to the urge to simply follow along. Then she thought better of it and drew to a stop.

"I think I'll forgo the walk tonight."

He swung around to look at her questioningly. In the moonlight, he looked so tall and sturdy and handsome that Molly stood her ground with some regret. It was so tempting to bid common sense good-bye and grab this opportunity with both hands.

"Coward," he said softy.

She didn't prevaricate. "Yes, I'm afraid so." She scrunched her shoulders and hugged her parka closer, feeling suddenly cold. "I told you last night, Jake. I'm very attracted to you. In return, you issued a warning, if you'll recall. I'm just heeding it."

The brim of his hat cast a shadow over his face. It was testimony to the brilliance of his blue eyes that they gleamed at her through the gloom. "You afraid I'll kiss you?"

"And more."

He stood on a slight slope, one boot at a slightly higher level than the other, his long, denim-sheathed leg bent. Placing his hands on his hips, he regarded her as though she were a complicated puzzle. "Molly, nothing will ever happen between us that you don't want to happen. You do know that, I hope."

"Yes, well, that's the problem, isn't it? We don't always want what's good for us." She bent her head. "I've done a lot of thinking today, Jake. I'm not confident in my ability to tell you no a second time."

"That's good to hear."

She laughed and then groaned, her gaze returning to his dark face. "I'm not interested in a steamy interlude. I'm sorry. I know it's not a contemporary attitude. But I'm not the type to engage in casual sex and emerge from the experience whole."

"I never thought you were, and casual sex isn't what I have in mind. There's nothing casual about my feelings for you."

She had to smile. "I suppose it all boils down to one's definition of casual. I understand that a lot of people nowadays have what they call meaningful relationships outside of marriage with individuals they care about, but that's just not how I'm made." She shrugged and swallowed. "I'm not real sure about a lot of things right now, but I do know that much about myself. I'm an all or nothing kind of person. If I give my body to a man, my heart will be part of the package. I suppose it's a silly way to think, but we can't change our stripes."

"Do you see me laughing? I think it's a charming way to be."

"Yes, well, women who take these things less seriously have a lot more fun, I'm sure. I wish I were more like that." She dragged in a bracing breath. "If I thought for a minute that I could have an affair with you and watch you walk away later without it breaking my heart, I'd do it in a blink. But I'd get hurt, sure as the world, because I'd fall in love with you. I know I would. That being the case, I'm going to be a smart girl and say good night."

She turned to walk away. She only got two steps when his softly spoken, "Molly," jerked her to a halt. She looked back at him over her shoulder.

"Don't go." He hadn't moved, but even in the semidarkness, she could feel the pull of his gaze. "Are you wanting a ring and promises? Is that it? If so, I'll happily give them to you."

"Oh, Jake," she whispered, so touched by the offer she wanted to weep.

"I'm falling in love with you. I'd marry you in a heartbeat. If you think I'm bluffing, try me."

She sighed and shook her head. "Marriage isn't the answer for me, either. Aren't I a mess?" She dug her heel in the dirt. "Lucky for you. You haven't known me long enough to make a commitment like that."

"I know you as well as I need to." Absolute certainty rang in his voice. "You're a wonderful person, Molly. I knew that the second I saw you."

She rolled her eyes.

"Seriously. There you stood, no bigger than a minute, with that horse trailer rocking behind you and lifting the tires of your Toyota off the ground. I thought, 'There's a lady with a heart twice as big as she is.' And guess what? You haven't proved me wrong since. There isn't a male on the ranch who isn't a little bit in love with you, poor old Bart included. I'm just a whole lot more in love with you than the others."

She fixed her gaze on the tree line at the far side of the creek where pine boughs were etched in silhouette against a dark-blue velvet sky. She fancied them to be dancers, poised in a graceful ballet, the stars forming the diamonds in their delicate coronets. "I don't want any more entanglements. I'm free for the first time in ten years, Jake, and I'd like to stay that way. There are so many things I want to do. You know?" She thought of her stalled career and lost dreams. Some of those dreams could never be recaptured, she knew, but others might still be possible. More important, she needed to seek justice for her father's death so she could finally lay him to rest. "There are things I have to do. I know you don't understand. I wish I were free to explain. Just know that there are unresolved issues in my life, and I'll never be able to make a commitment to you or anyone until they're settled to my satisfaction."

"Let me help you then. Marriage is a partnership, honey, not a prison."

"Maybe not for a man, maybe not for most women, but it was for me."

"It won't be that way again."

"Yes. At least it could. Down deep, parts of the Molly I used to be still exist. I was a devout Catholic. I'll bet you never guessed that."

"I've got nothing against Catholics."

"You're missing the point. I didn't believe in divorce. I was trapped in a marriage that was a nightmare with a man who took advantage of my sacramental bondage at every turn. I'll never sucker in for that again."

"Sacramental bondage," he repeated. "That's heavy."

Molly doubted he had any idea just how heavy. "Like being buried alive under a thousand pounds of ice."

He moved slowly up the bank. "I'd never infringe on your personal freedoms, Molly."

"You'll never get a chance," she said lightly.

They fell into a slow walk together. He shoved his hands deeply into his jeans pockets. "So where does this leave us?"

"With friendship. If you touch me again with anything more than that in mind, I won't be here when you wake up the next morning. I'll leave your watch on the table, and as soon as I find work of some kind, I'll send you all the money I can to cover Sunset's expenses. But you'll never see me again."

"You don't leave a man much negotiating room," he said with a dry laugh.

"I don't intend to. This isn't negotiable."

"I don't want you to go away, Molly."

"You've heard my terms."

He drew to a stop, tugged his hands from his pockets to rest them at his hips, and leveled a look at her that made her heart do a funny little skip inside her chest. "And here are mine," he said softly. "I'll honor your stipulations—for a time. There's not a damned thing wrong with being good friends before we become lovers. I've got no quarrel with that. Just understand that I want more, and the day will come when I'll press you for more."

"When you do, I'll leave."

He flashed her a slow grin that turned the skip of her heart into leaps and somersaults. "We'll see."

"I'll never give another man control over my life."

He shrugged, looking totally unruffled by the proclamation. "Fine by me. I don't want control. I see marriage as a fifty-fifty proposition. My wife will be my partner, not a possession."

"That's what they all say until the ink dries on the marriage certificate."

He chuckled. "Now *that* is an archaic outlook. Have you checked the calendar lately?"

Molly shoved her hands into her jacket pockets and made tight fists. "Once burned, twice shy."

"I can see I've got my work cut out for me."

Molly sighed. "Have you heard anything I've said? All I'm interested in is friendship."

His teeth gleamed in the moonlight as he flashed her another grin. "As long as that's all you're interested in, that's all you'll get. That doesn't stop me from trying to convince you otherwise." As if he read her feelings in her expression, he quickly added, "In a completely hands-off way, of course. I'll never touch you unless you want me to."

Molly relaxed slightly. She could keep her head around him as long as he didn't kiss her or anything. No matter how much she might sometimes wish he would, that would be her secret. "Fine. Then we have a clear understanding?"

His eyes twinkled mischievously. "Crystal clear."

Why was it she had a feeling he found this entire situation vastly amusing?

He thrust out his hand to her. "That said, how about if we shake on it to seal our agreement?"

Molly was no longer totally sure what their agreement was. Nevertheless, she drew one hand from her pocket to place it across his broad palm. His long fingers closed around hers. His thumb traced light circles over the back of her wrist, sending little shocks of awareness up her arm.

"Fine, then," she said stupidly.

His grin broadened. "Now that we have that settled, will you come for a walk with me?"

He was still caressing her wrist. That didn't exactly strike her as being a good omen. Did he know how his touch tied her insides into knots? She had an awful feeling he did.

"Come on," he cajoled huskily. "Take a walk with me. You still trust me, don't you?"

Molly swallowed, her throat feeling suddenly dry and sticky. She did trust him. Excluding her father, she trusted him more than she'd ever trusted any man. On the other hand . . .

"I just agreed to your terms," he reminded her. "Friendship only. What can possibly happen?"

"Nothing, I don't suppose." She dragged in a breath for courage and nodded. "All right. Sure. Why not?"

Never releasing her hand, he turned and tucked it over the bend of his other arm. Then he began leading her back toward the creek. As Molly walked beside him, she found herself remembering a nursery rhyme from childhood.

Welcome to my parlor said the spider to the fly.

৯ CHAPTER FOURTEEN ৬

Over the next few days, Molly began to feel as if Jake were spinning a magical web and luring her ever deeper into its silken bonds. It was as if he sensed the emptiness within her and had set himself to the task of filling her up with a daily measure of beauty.

Practically every morning as she left the cabin, she found a gift lying on her doorstep. One morning, it might be a pretty rock or a feather from a wild bird. Another, she would find flowers. One morning, he left her a posy of spring clover blossoms, and for some reason, that was her favorite surprise of all, representative of all Jake Coulter was and everything he stood for, a man as earthy and elemental as this land from which he had sprung.

His habit of leaving her silly gifts reminded her so much of her father, leading her to begin assessing him in other ways and measuring him against Marshal Sterling. Jake looked nothing like her dad. As far as their mannerisms went, the two men were light years apart. But there were other similarities Molly couldn't deny, traits that ran deep and true, making them stand apart from all the rest of the men she knew.

When White Star had her foal, Jake insisted that Molly attend the birthing. It turned out to be the most amazing event she'd ever witnessed, followed by a bonding ritual called imprinting that she would never forget.

Over the first hour of the foal's life, she helped Jake desensitize the newborn to a host of stimuli that might otherwise frighten him later in life. They performed a mock shoeing and handled every part of the foal's body. When he was finally allowed to stand, Molly had the honor of introducing him to his first halter. "Surely he won't remember all this," she commented.

"Precocious newborns are programmed by nature to bond over the first hour of life with their mothers and any creatures hovering nearby, thus the herd instinct. It's necessary to their survival in the wild. So, yes, on some level, he'll remember everything he experiences today, and he'll be far more inclined to trust people." Jake ran the back of a vibrating clipper over the foal's hip. "Over the next few weeks, we'll repeat all this a few times to better imprint the lessons. At three months, this little guy will stand calmly for his first hoof trimming, he won't be frightened by a halter, rope, or slight weight on his back, and he'll come when he sees us, anxious for a scratch behind his ears. When he's old enough to ride, it will be an uneventful transition that he's been prepared to accept all his life."

Taking in Jake's lean, muscular body, Molly said, "You could break a horse the old-fashioned way. That would take much less time, wouldn't it? Why imprint?"

He frowned as he considered his reply. " 'Break' is the key word in your question, and it means just what it implies, that the horse's spirit or will is broken. Sometimes it's done gently, sometimes not. I've trained horses that way, and I've trained them this way. You can end up with a fine horse using old-fashioned methods, but what's to say that the same horse couldn't have been extraordinary?" He shrugged. "Have you ever seen a twitch, Molly?"

She shook her head, prompting him to lead her from the birthing stall to a spot midway up the central aisle of the stable. "That is a twitch," he said, pointing to an apparatus hanging on the wall that reminded Molly of a huge nutcracker. Indicating the circular end, he explained, "This part is clamped over the horse's nose. The resultant pain becomes the focus of his attention, enabling his handler to do pretty much whatever he likes to some other part of his body."

Molly shivered. "How awful."

Jake chuckled. "Not really. Necessary is the word when you're trying to work with a powerful animal that could make mincemeat out of you." He took the twitch from the wall. "Sometimes, for the horse's own good, we have to use a twitch." He pressed the circular end close to her face. "It's usually safer than a sedative." His voice dipped low. "So we pinch the tender flesh midway between upper lip and nose, do what's necessary, and then release the pressure."

"Your point?"

He smiled slowly. "A question, not a point. Bearing in mind that twitching is extremely uncomfortable, if not downright painful, if you were one of my horses, would you want me to use a twitch routinely when I had to work on you?"

"Definitely not."

He chuckled and hung the twitch back on its hook. "Point made. If imprinting makes a horse easier to handle and doctor, eliminating the use of a twitch in many situations, it's worth all the time and effort I put into it."

"You really love your animals, don't you?" she said softly.

"Yeah, I really do. I'd much rather befriend than conquer."

Molly had never met anyone like Jake Coulter, and she doubted she ever would again. He was the extraordinary one, in her estimation, a rare individual with such a depth of caring that he amazed her with some new revelation every time she was with him.

"Walk with me," he said at least once a day. It sounded like such a harmless pastime, a simple matter of placing one foot in front of the other and carrying on a friendly conversation. But Molly soon discovered that nothing about Jake was simple—and while in his company, things that seemed harmlessly mundane could suddenly become treacherously complicated.

"We've discussed what colors you feel you look best in," he said one evening, "but as I recall, you've never said what your favorite color is."

As a girl, she'd done her bedroom in varying shades of mauve with all four walls papered in roses. Practically every article of clothing she'd worn back then had been pink or sported touches of the color somewhere. For her eighteenth birthday, her dad had even bought her a pink car, and he'd presented her with the keys on a resin key ring that encased a miniature rosebud.

"I don't have a strong preference for any particular color anymore," she said.

"Aw, come on."

How could she explain that she'd stopped thinking in terms of what she liked years ago? "I used to love pink," she confessed.

"Past tense again," he chided. "Do you *still* like pink, Molly?"

"I tend to go overboard with things I like. Pink can be a very gaudy color if you overdo it, and I never had any restraint."

He chuckled. "Is that what life is about, restraint? What's wrong with gaudy if you like gaudy?"

Her limbs went tense. "Nothing, I suppose. But with a brilliant color like pink, one runs a risk of appearing gauche."

"Gauche?" He assumed an expression of mock horror. "God forbid."

Molly's cheeks burned. "Rodney hated me in pink. Now you're laughing because I've learned moderation. *Men.* Why not just leave me alone?"

He smiled thoughtfully. "I'm not laughing at you, Molly, and I'll be happy to see you wear whatever color or style you like. I'm just concerned because it seems to me you're still hanging back."

"Hanging back from what?"

"Being yourself." He reached over to ruffle her curls. "I *love* what you've done with your hair. You know what that tells me?"

"No, what?"

"That you should go with your instincts. You say you've learned moderation, but it seems to me you're practicing self-denial instead. I don't want to influence you. I think you need to make your own choices. But you aren't doing that. Where's the moderate amount of pink in your life? Even if it were true that you don't look good in it, what would be wrong with decorating your world in that color?"

"I'll paint the cabin pink tomorrow."

He laughed and shook his head. "Fine. Make jokes. Pink logs might be a bit much. Even I have to concede that point. But you could use pink to dress the place up."

"Pink doesn't lend itself well to quiet dignity."

"The world according to Rodney?"

Molly set her jaw and stared straight ahead. She wished he would just drop the subject. Discussing Rodney made her stomach upset. But Jake never backed off from subjects that disturbed her. He just kept digging and pressing until she forgot herself and said too much.

This time, he suddenly broke stride to step behind her and grasp her shoulders. "Look at that," he said in an oddly fierce tone.

"At what?" Molly asked, her gaze darting to the tree line, her nerves jangling. She half expected to see a bear or cougar lurking in the forest.

"At the *sky*," he whispered near her ear. When she glanced up, he tightened his hold on her shoulders. "Just *look* at that sunset, Molly. Have you ever seen such incredible shades of pink in all your life?"

Molly could scarcely believe she hadn't noticed the sunset on her own. Jake was right; it was absolutely breathtaking. "Oh, how lovely," she whispered.

"Is God gauche?"

The question took her off guard, and she snorted with laughter. "No, of course not."

"Would you say He practices restraint?"

The sky was a veritable pallet of rose shades, so beautiful, so perfect, that she could scarcely believe it was real. "No, He hasn't practiced restraint," she replied tautly.

"Would you say He lacks dignity?"

She laughed in spite of herself. "*No.*"

"Well then?" He rested his jaw against her hair to study the sky with her. "It appears to me that Rodney, the pissant, was wrong. *Dead* wrong. Pink is a beautiful, very dignified color, and the bastard wouldn't recognize gauche if it ran up and bit him on the ass." He massaged her shoulders, forcing the last bit of tension from her muscles. "Forget being restrained. Forget moderation. Forget self-denial. Celebrate life and drown yourself in pink if you want. It's perfectly okay."

On another evening, Molly confessed to Jake that she had no fashion sense and had always deferred to her husband's impeccable taste in clothing.

"Who said you have no fashion sense?" Jake asked.

Molly thought back, and as she did, her head started to ache, the pain sharp and centered directly behind her eyes. "Rodney," she admitted tautly.

"Ah," Jake chuckled dryly. "Who elected him fashion guru of the century?"

"Rodney," she whispered.

"Hmm," was all Jake said, but that one word conveyed such disgust, it was unnecessary for him to say more.

Two days later, Molly was in town to go grocery shopping and pick up some fluorescent tubes for Jake. As she hurried along the sidewalk toward the electric supply, she passed a ladies' apparel shop. There in the window was a gorgeous pink top.

Molly stopped dead in her tracks and stared at it. Never in her recollection had she wanted anything quite so much. She wasn't sure why, but in that top, she saw freedom. It was *her*, the Molly she'd lost, exactly the sort of thing she would have loved back in high school.

Of course, she'd weighed thirty pounds less back then, a spindly girl with an oversized bust. In her twenties, she'd grown thick at the waist and hippy. Something like that probably wouldn't look good on her anymore.

Even as she told herself that, Molly entered the shop. A pretty blond clerk came from behind the register. She wore a navy blue dress with red piping and sassy red sandals. Her shoulder-length hair was salon-conditioned perfect. Molly felt dowdy and plain by comparison.

"Hello," she managed to say. Gesturing at the window display, she added, "I noticed that pink top as I was walking by. Now that I'm closer, I can see it's not my color or style."

The blonde smiled. "You think not?" She stepped to a rack and pulled out a pink top like the one in the window. Holding it up against Molly, she grinned mischievously. "Wrong. It's perfect on you."

Molly glimpsed the price tag and nearly fainted. It was almost forty dollars. She'd spent less than two hundred of the thousand dollars she'd brought with her from Portland, but even so, blowing forty bucks on something so frivolous wasn't wise. Fingering the knit, she thought of a time in the not-so-distant past when she'd have spent three times more without blinking. She had Rodney to thank for her present financial straits.

Oh, how that burned. And suddenly she wanted that pink top beyond all reason.

"It's a little expensive," she said.

The clerk laughed. "Not at the prices these days. Live a little. At least try it on."

Molly couldn't resist. She grinned and stripped off her parka. When the other woman saw her clothes, she raised her eyebrows. "Have you lost weight?"

For a moment, Molly couldn't think why she asked. Then she glanced down. Her khaki slacks hung from her hips like tent canvas, and her blouse could have served as a maternity smock. "Yeah, I have," she lied. "Nothing fits right anymore."

"We have a huge sale going," the clerk said with a mischievous wink. Before Molly could protest, she was descending on a rack of jeans. "Aren't these darling?" she said as she turned to assess Molly's size. She drew out a pair of pants. "These are half off."

A fifty-percent discount was a really great deal if one had the money to take advantage of it. Molly didn't. She kept telling herself that as the clerk herded her to a dressing room. Leaving the door ajar while Molly changed, the woman kept bringing different outfits for her to try on.

"*This* would look marvelous on you," she said. Or, "This is so *you!*"

"I really can't afford a new wardrobe right now," Molly kept insisting, not sure who she was trying to convince, the clerk or herself.

"Any woman who loses that much weight owes herself a whole new look!" was the clerk's retort.

Molly knew she should leave, but trying on the clothes was so much fun she couldn't bring herself to run. The blonde had no idea of Molly's history. She didn't rave about how nice Molly looked just to bolster her confidence. Best of all, she had a flair for fashion. Anyone with eyes could see that by the way she was dressed. She might have stepped off the cover of a magazine.

Before Molly knew quite how it happened, she'd selected tons of clothes. The large discounts aside, she knew the total would be astronomical. She had to be out of her mind to even consider blowing so much money when she had absolutely no way of replacing it. All her wages at the ranch went toward Sunset's care and training.

"I really, *really* can't afford all this," she confessed.

The blonde winked. "Come on up front. Let's run it up on the calculator and see what we're looking at."

The total was over six hundred dollars, including the large sale discounts. Molly glanced down at the outfit she was wearing, a pair of snug jeans and a snappy red sweater. It was so totally outlandish, something she never would have considered wearing less than an hour ago, but she liked the way it made her look, transforming her in some magical way from dowdy old Molly into someone colorful, daring, and maybe even a little sexy in a plump sort of way.

"I really shouldn't."

The clerk winked at her. "I don't offer to do this for just anyone, but for you, I'll make an exception. I get a twenty-five-percent discount, working here. I'll take that off the total as well. Does that make the cost a little more manageable?"

Molly could scarcely believe she'd offered. "Don't you work on commission?"

"Yes. But I've done well this week with the clearance sale. And, hey, what's the use in having a job like this if I can't have fun once in a while? It's not every day that I can totally make someone over." She leaned closer and grinned conspiratorially. "I haven't used my discount all winter. The old battle-ax who owns this place is getting off cheap." She straightened and ran her gaze over Molly. "You look *so* great in that outfit. That's all the commission I need."

Molly left the store with so many outfits that the bags were difficult to carry, forcing her to return to the truck before she went on to the parts store. She'd changed back into her old clothes, and when she saw herself in the store windows as she hurried along the sidewalk, she cringed. The new Molly was in Jake's truck, and she couldn't wait to get home to try her back on.

When Jake walked into the kitchen that night, his eyes nearly popped from his head. Molly stood at the stove, only she looked nothing like the Molly he knew. She wore a pair of snug jeans and a bright red sweater that clung to her ample breasts. Jake's blood pressure shot clear off the chart before he knew what hit him.

When she turned fully toward him, he could only gawk. *Holy hell*. If he had this much trouble keeping his mouth closed, how were his men going to react? She was mouthwatering. Every delicious curve of her body was showcased.

He'd known she was sumptuously built, but he'd never in his wildest dreams imagined her to be this curvaceous. Ample didn't describe her breasts. A little bit of her cleavage was showing, and with breasts as generous as hers, a little bit of cleavage went a hell of a long way.

His gaze shot from there to her slender waist, which flowed gently into delightfully round hips and full thighs. Until now, he'd never realized the stretching properties of denim.

"You can't wear that."

The words no sooner popped from Jake's mouth than he wanted to call them back. It was just—sweet Lord above, didn't she realize how she looked? She had a body that made a man think about hot sex on silk sheets. He'd suggested a little more color in her wardrobe, not formfitting brilliance.

Didn't she understand that she was a lone female, working on a ranch with a bunch of horny men? Even the older ones still had some fire in their ovens. The younger fellows might get ideas, and if they did, a pass at Molly wouldn't be long in following. Jake would kill the first man who so much as made an off-color remark to her.

Jake saw that she'd gone as pale as a moonbeam. For a long moment, she just stood there looking at him with her heart in her eyes. Then, glancing down, she murmured, "I guess it is a little much." She plucked at the front of the sweater. "You're right, Jake. I'm sorry. I don't know what I was thinking. Can you, um, watch dinner while I run over to change?"

Jake wanted to kick himself. Only he couldn't until he removed his size twelve boot from his mouth. "Molly, I didn't mean that you don't look nice."

Her stricken expression remained.

"You look *fantastic*," he rushed to add. *Too* fantastic. *Shit*. She didn't believe him. He could tell that by her pallor and the injured look in her eyes. He hadn't meant to hurt her feelings. "I was, um, just—startled when I first saw you, is all."

"Yes, well." Her eyes went all shiny, giving him reason to suspect she was about to cry. Instead she laughed and flashed an overbright smile. "Startling people wasn't my aim when I got the outfit." She shrugged. "I never should have listened to that clerk. I told you my taste in clothes is atrocious."

Before Jake could collect himself and think of something else to say, she rushed from the room, so upset she didn't even stop at the coat rack to grab her parka.

Jake was at the stove, turning the chicken and cursing to turn the air blue, when Hank walked in the back door. "What's wrong?"

"Everything!" Jake handed his brother the fork. "Watch the chicken, would you? I have some fences to go mend."

"We just rode fence line yesterday. Everything looked pretty good."

"Not *that* kind of fence. Damn, Hank, I've really screwed up this time. Molly finally got up the courage to get some new clothes, and I ruined it for her."

"Why'd you do that? If anybody needs some new clothes, she does."

Jake passed a hand over his eyes. "She was wearing a sweater and jeans."

"Nothing wrong with that."

"There is with Molly packed into them. Bright red." Jake gestured help-lessly at his chest. "Holy hell. I can't have her looking like that out here on the ranch. The men won't be able to keep their eyes off her."

"No harm in looking as long as they don't touch."

"And what if one of them decides he isn't satisfied with just looking?" Jake shot back. "I'd kill him. I don't need the hassle."

Hank lifted the lid off the skillet to check the chicken. "Hmm. Sounds like a bad case of the green monster to me. Molly's perfectly capable of deflecting any unwanted advances. Trust her to handle it."

Jake ground his teeth. Molly was *not* capable of handling unwanted advances. She was too sweet to tell a man where to get off, for one thing, and too unsure of herself for another.

"You afraid somebody'll trespass on your turf, bro?" Hank asked softly.

"That's a cheap shot. I've never had a jealous bone in my body, and you know it."

"You've never cared enough about a woman before to get jealous," Hank pointed out. "What about all the gals you've dated who paraded around out here in halter tops and shorts that left little to the imagination? You never got bent out of shape when the men looked at them."

"That was different. They knew the score."

"And Molly doesn't? Give me a break. She's been married. I'm sure she's got a pretty good understanding of the birds and the bees, which is undoubtedly why she chose to wear jeans and a sweater, which are pretty modest compared to the two patches of material held together by strings that I've seen a few of your bimbos wear."

"I never dated any bimbos."

Hank grinned. "Exhibitionists, then. Remember that blond gal—Veronica, I think her name was—who teetered around out in the yard in spike heels and short shorts last September? When she bent over, it wasn't only her hairdresser who knew for sure. When the guys came on to her, you never so much as blinked."

Jake's blood pressure was rising again. "Where are you going with this?"

"I'm just trying to point out that jeans and a sweater can't be that risqué by comparison, even if they are skintight. We're all big boys. If we can't handle ourselves any better than that, we deserve a good ass kicking, and it sure as hell won't be Molly's fault."

Jake had heard enough. Hank had never been in love. He didn't understand anything about anything. He grabbed Molly's parka from the coat rack. Though spring was making its debut, it still got freezing cold after the sun went down, and he didn't want her taking a chill. "I'll be back in a bit."

Once outside, Jake sat on the porch. Clutching Molly's parka in his fists, he pressed the nylon shell to his face and breathed in the sweet scent of her that lingered on the cloth. Her smell made him think of wildflowers and sunshine, an essence as fresh and unpretentious as she was. *Jealous?* Damn Hank for saying that. Jake had never been the possessive type. If a woman wanted to be with him, then she wanted to be with him, end of story. If someone else caught her eye, he was perfectly willing to say adios without a hassle, no skin off his nose. He was *not* jealous.

He pressed the jacket harder against his face, repeating the refrain to assure himself it was so. He just didn't want Molly to get herself into a sticky situation. She was on her own out here, and he was her employer. That made him responsible for her, right?

Wrong. Jake knew he was bullshitting himself. As much as he hated to admit it, Hank was right. He was green with jealousy, and he felt possessive as hell. Just the thought of other men ogling Molly's body made him do a slow burn. Even worse, deep down, there was a part of him that was afraid she might find someone else. That was a scary thought.

He *loved* her, damn it. He didn't want to lose her to some jerk who wouldn't appreciate her or treat her the way she deserved to be treated.

Sighing, Jake pushed to his feet. He needed to go talk to her. What he meant to say, he had no idea. But somehow he had to fix the mess he'd made of things.

She didn't answer when he knocked on the cabin door. He knocked again. Again no answer. Since he figured he couldn't screw up any worse than he had already, Jake walked right in.

"Molly?"

He heard a gasp and a rush of movement in the bedroom. Clenching his teeth, he tossed her parka on the couch and made a beeline for the open doorway. She stood before the closet, holding the red sweater to her chest. He'd caught her changing.

Jake almost turned away. Instead he bent his head and stared at the floor. "Can you slip that sweater back on so we can talk?"

"There's nothing that needs saying. Give me a minute. I'll be right out."

"There's a lot that needs saying."

Jake lifted his gaze. The wad of red knit pressed to her breasts brought out the flawlessness of her skin. Her short-cropped curls shone in the overhead light like molten brass. And her eyes—oh, *God*—those eyes. They were dark with shadows that he knew he'd put there. Ever since meeting her, he had reviled Rodney. Now who was the bastard?

"I owe you an apology," he said hoarsely. "You look beautiful in that outfit, Molly, and I need my butt kicked for making you think otherwise."

She dipped her chin. The way her fingertips caressed the soft knit told Jake how very important the sweater was to her. He recalled telling her once that marriage to him wouldn't be a prison, that he'd never dream of infringing on her personal rights.

If choosing her clothing wasn't a personal right, what the hell was?

"Ah, Molly, sweetheart, I'm sorry."

She shook her head. "I'm afraid you don't understand." She met his gaze again. "I'm changing into something else for one reason and only one reason, because you're my employer and I'm still on shift." Her quivering chin came up. "In my free time, I'll dress however I like." She clutched the sweater more tightly to her chest. "If you don't approve, that's your problem."

Looking into her eyes, Jake realized that he'd misread her. That wasn't only hurt there but a strong dose of anger as well. He wanted to smile. Her outrage was a very good sign, and it told him more than she could possibly know, namely that she was finally starting to heal and find herself again.

"I see," he said carefully.

"No, you don't, and you probably never will. How could you?" Her larynx bobbed as she struggled to swallow. "No one's ever owned you."

Jake's heart caught at her choice of words. Was that really what her marriage had been like?

"Before my divorce, I couldn't even *vote* the way I wanted," she rushed to add. "Not unless I was prepared to lie about it afterward, and as I'm sure you've noticed, I'm a rotten liar. If Rodney found out I'd gone against him, he made my life hell for days, sometimes weeks, depending upon the seriousness of my transgression."

"Oh, Molly," he whispered.

"You have no idea what that was like," she continued in a taut, tremulous voice. "No idea at *all*. For ten years, I did everything I could to please him." She knotted her fist and pressed it hard against her chest. "I was only eighteen when we married. He was older and seemed so sophisticated. Whenever he wasn't happy, about anything, it was always my fault. *I* was the problem. Therefore I was the one who had to change. After a while, it becomes a mindset. You fall into a trap without even realizing it, and pretty soon you don't even think about what you're doing."

Jake had no clue what to say.

"Maybe I don't look good in this outfit. Maybe I look *awful* in it. But you know what, Jake?"

He wanted to refute those last two statements, but seeing that she needed to get this off her chest, he merely said, "No, what?"

"How I look doesn't matter. What counts is how I feel."

He couldn't have agreed more.

"From this point forward," she went on, "things are going to change." With one hand, she released her hold on the sweater to jab her chest. "I'm going to do what *I* want from now on. If you don't like my clothes, that's too bad. If I don't look good in them, tough. When I'm not working, I'm going to dress however I like." She flashed him a defiant glare. "When it's on your dime, I'll respect your wishes, but after hours, how I look is nobody else's business."

Jake only nodded. She was fighting for her freedom, trying desperately to be an individual again and find definition. If she fell into the trap of trying to please him as she once had Rodney, she was afraid she'd end up in the same situation all over again.

The insight enabled Jake to understand her in a way he hadn't before. Little wonder she was reluctant to make another emotional commitment. She was only recently divorced. He was a direct, straight-shooting man with a forceful personality. It was only natural that she might dread the thought of his having any control over her.

Jake had no intention of trying to control her. He'd tried to tell her that. Now he guessed it was time to put his money where his mouth was. He rubbed his jaw, acutely conscious of the faint rasping sound his fingers made on the stubble of whiskers.

"Dress however you like after hours, Molly. I think that's only fair."

"I will," she said stubbornly.

Jake couldn't help but smile. "May I make one suggestion?"

"Of course. I won't necessarily follow it, but feel free."

"If I were you, I'd wear the outfit now."

She flashed him a wary look.

"It's not as if there's a dress code. You're you. Dress however you want."

"But you don't like—"

"I never said that," he cut in. "I think that's a great outfit, and you look beautiful in it. *Too* beautiful."

Her delicate brows drew together in a scowl.

He cleared his throat and searched for words. "I didn't object to the outfit because I don't like it. The truth is, I like it a lot, and I'm afraid all the other men will as well. In short, I'm feeling a little jealous." He swallowed. "Strike that. I'm feeling a lot jealous."

"Of whom?"

"Anybody, everybody." Glimpsing the bewilderment in her eyes, he added, "I know it's stupid, but there it is. I don't want other men looking at you." That sounded so absurd that he felt heat crawling up his neck. He scratched his temple, groping for some way he might better explain. He came up blank. There was no rational explanation for the way he was feeling. "I know it's wrong of me, and I'm sorry for reacting before I took time to recognize my feelings for what they are. My only excuse is that I've never felt this way before. Given time, I'm sure I'll get a handle on it."

The bewilderment in her eyes had turned to incredulity.

"It's true," he said gruffly. He inclined his head at the sweater. "You looked so beautiful, Molly. You about knocked my eyes out. I knew if I felt that way, some of the other men would, too. As much as it pains me to admit it, I felt threatened."

"Oh, please."

"I'm not lying, I swear. Deep down, I'm afraid I'll lose out if a bunch of other men start coming on to you. It's not as if I'm any grand prize."

He scuffed the sole of his boot over the floor, noticing how clean the boards were. After working all the hours she did at the house, he had no idea how she found time to tidy up here. But then, he didn't know how she found time to brush Bart's teeth and give him baths, mend clothes, and fuss over all of them like she did, either. All and all, she was an amazing lady, her finest quality being that she always thought of others before she thought of herself.

He noticed some plastic shopping bags lying on the bed just then. The sleeve of a pretty yellow top protruded from one of them. He realized that she'd been on a shopping spree, that the jeans and sweater weren't all she'd bought. He remembered how her eyes had sparkled when she turned to face him in the kitchen, how she'd stood with her chin high and her shoulders straight. For the first time in a very long while, she had felt pretty, and in two seconds flat, he had crushed her.

He would never make that mistake again.

A few minutes later, Molly stood on the porch, rubbing her clammy palms on the legs of her new jeans. From inside, she heard voices, the deep timbre of a familiar one in particular. *Jake.* He'd convinced her to wear the sweater, not because she believed for a minute that he really thought she looked good in it, but simply because she wanted to.

The girl who had married Rodney Wells had been too young to know who she really was. For ten endless years, she'd drifted along, never fighting the changes because she hadn't realized her loss. She'd been Mrs. Rodney Wells, and in that role, she'd found definition, which had seemed enough.

Now the marriage was over, and she was faced with making choices for herself. She was supposed to be someone in her own right. Only she wasn't. Without Rodney to give her direction, she had to think for herself, and that was frightening.

Now she'd come to a crossroads, all because of an impulsive shopping spree and a silly red sweater. Only it wasn't just a sweater, not to her. She'd committed mutiny in that ladies' apparel shop today, breaking all of Rodney's rules and spending nearly her last dime to do it. She couldn't chicken out now. If she did, Rodney won.

As she opened Jake's front door and moved into the entryway, Molly had an awful feeling of impending doom. She placed one foot before the other, heading for the kitchen. She could tell by all the voices that most of the men had come in from the fields. She'd forgotten her coat at the cabin, and when she entered the room, they would see her.

She imagined startled gasps and raised eyebrows. Her insides shriveled in a tight knot of humiliation. Her face went red hot. Her skin felt as if it were shrinking and was suddenly a size too small for her body.

At the archway, she paused. Jake was turning from the stove and saw her first. He flashed a welcoming smile. As much as she appreciated that, it was the look in his eyes that lent her courage, a twinkling challenge that seemed to say, *"You've come this far. Don't stop now."*

Holding her arms rigid at her sides, she took another step. Then another. Sitting at the table, Danno glanced up. His red eyebrows lifted as his hazel eyes moved slowly over her. Following his gaze, Nate turned to look at her as well.

"Wow!" Nate said. "What happened to you?"

Molly gulped. "I, um . . . went shopping."

Nate gave her a slow, head-to-toe assessment, his laughing blue eyes warm with appreciation. "A paycheck has never been better spent. You look great!"

Levi followed that with, "You sure do, darlin'. Red is your color."

Shorty chimed in next. "Well, ain't you pretty as a speckled pup."

Given the fact that Shorty loved dogs, Molly decided to take that as a compliment. The other men nodded to her and smiled, but no one offered further comment. That was it? No gasps of shock, no derogatory remarks? She moved to help with the final meal preparations, feeling stiff and self-conscious. The conversation quickly shifted to a discussion about horse training, and her new outfit was forgotten.

As she began dishing up the mashed potatoes, Jake came to help hold the large pot. When she glanced up, he looked deeply into her eyes. Then he moved his gaze slowly downward. When he had finished his assessment, in a husky whisper for her ears alone, he said, "I don't know what that outfit cost, but it was worth every cent. You look absolutely beautiful."

⸙ CHAPTER FIFTEEN ⸙

The following morning, it was already half past six by the time Jake grabbed a shower, a quarter to seven before he'd gathered his clothes to get dressed. Still half asleep and groggy as hell because he'd been up half the night tending a gelding with a spasm of the diaphragm, called the "thumps," he yawned and tried to blink himself awake as he dragged on a clean pair of Wranglers.

What the Sam Hill? There was something in the right front pocket of his clean pants. He dived his hand inside and closed his fingers over a familiar shape, his grandfather's watch. His blood ran cold. Molly had promised to return it to him if she ever decided to leave. Now it had mysteriously appeared in a clean pair of his jeans where he would be sure to find it.

Jake swore under his breath and tugged on his boots. He grabbed a shirt, not bothering to put it on before he dashed from the bedroom. As he sprinted down the stairs, he imagined her out on the highway, driving aimlessly. He knew for a fact that she had only a little money and nowhere to go. Even worse, she'd been afraid the police might have an APB out on her car. What was she thinking? *Damn.* He had to find her before she drove too far, had to convince her it wasn't necessary for her to go at all. Had he spooked her with his references to jealousy? Maybe his autocratic, "You can't wear that," had been too reminiscent of Rodney. *Sweet Lord.* If the son of a bitch caught her off alone—Jake cut the thought short, unable to bear thinking about it.

His pickup keys were kept on a hook in the kitchen. He raced through the house, trying to dress as he ran, and had one arm shoved down a sleeve by the time he reached the archway.

"Jake? My goodness, where's the fire?"

He braked to a stop so suddenly that his boots skidded on the floor. Molly stood at the stove, scrubbing a burner plate. As he said her name, a piece of bread popped up from the toaster, making her jump. She flapped her hand. "My breakfast. Yours is warming in the oven. Shorty and Levi told me about the sick gelding. Bless their hearts, they volunteered their services and helped me in the kitchen this morning." She reassembled the burner. "I saved you some eggs, bacon, and pancakes. They were like kids in a candy store, and I was their short-order cook." She smiled. "Not that I minded. They helped a lot."

All the starch went out of Jake's spine. He'd never been so glad to see anyone in all his life. This morning, she was wearing that pretty yellow top he'd glimpsed last night and the same pair of jeans. The yellow cotton knit skimmed her figure like sunshine. The scoop neckline dipped low, revealing the tantalizing swell of her breasts. She looked young and beautiful and so sweet she made his heart catch.

He shoved his other arm into the sleeve of his shirt. "I thought you were gone."

A bewildered look came into her eyes. "Gone where?"

Jake couldn't help himself. He was across the kitchen in three strides. "Don't even think about leaving. Do you hear me, Molly?" He grabbed her up into his arms. "You scared the sand right out of me."

She gave a startled squeak as her feet cleared the floor. Jake felt the wet rag flop against his nape as she grabbed hold of his neck.

"My watch. You put it in my jeans. I thought you'd left." Jake hugged her close, so relieved to know she was still there and safe that he wanted to squeeze the breath right out of her. "You're not going anywhere, lady. Get that thought straight out of your head."

"But, Jake, I—"

"I mean it. I'll dismantle the whole damned Toyota and scatter the parts from hell to breakfast. You're staying put." He pressed his face to the curve of her neck, loving the smell of her, a blend of lotion, talc, and feminine essence that was exclusively her own. Sunshine and wildflowers. God, how he loved her. With each passing day, the feeling grew more intense. It was almost frightening to care so much about someone. "No arguments."

"I'm not arguing." She laughed shakily. "I didn't return the watch because I plan to leave. Not any time soon, anyway."

Jake went still. "You didn't?"

She leaned her head back, trying to see his face. "No. I just don't need to keep it anymore, and I figured you'd feel better if you had it back. A family heirloom like that is irreplaceable."

Jake straightened to search her eyes. "It was your only guarantee that

I'd keep my word and not contact the authorities. Your collateral, remember? If you aren't planning to leave, why don't you need it anymore?"

Steadying herself by gripping his shoulders, she arched her spine to put distance between their chests. The rag, still in her right hand, trailed wetly down his sleeve. Jake didn't care. All that mattered was that she was there, that he could hold her like this and protect her if it became necessary.

She was everything he'd ever wanted. Absolutely everything.

"I don't need collateral anymore. Your word alone is enough." A suspicious shimmer came into her eyes. "I realize that now. You aren't the kind of man who breaks his promises."

Her expression told him more than she could know. He wasn't the only one who'd fallen in love.

"Thank you. That's one of the nicest things anyone's ever said to me."

He wanted so badly to kiss her then. Memories of that day in the woods hurtled through his mind—how sweetly she had responded to him, how she had melted against him, offering no resistance. Not three feet away, the kitchen counter beckoned, offering a perfect stage for another seduction. The other men were already out working. They were alone in the house. He could deposit her on the edge of the counter, kiss her until she went boneless, and then peel away all those clothes. He yearned to kiss her beautiful breasts, this time without two layers of cotton to shield her nipples, and hear her gasp with pleasure. And, oh, God, how he wished he could curl his hands over her bare bottom. He could feel the sweet warmth of her skin even through her jeans.

"I thought maybe—I don't know—that something I said yesterday had upset you, and you'd decided to leave."

"Nothing upset me *that* much."

He was beginning to feel a little foolish, but he was loath to release her now that he had her in his arms again. "Promise me something?"

"What?"

"That you'll never leave without telling me, no matter what happens."

"I won't," she said solemnly.

"Do you promise?"

"I promise. I'll at least tell you I'm going first."

In which case, he would do everything in his power to stop her, he thought fiercely.

"I'm sorry I frightened you," she said. "I couldn't think how to explain about the watch, so yesterday morning when I did laundry, I just slipped it into your clean jeans where I knew you'd be sure to find it."

She had explained herself quite eloquently. *"Your word alone is enough."* That she had come to trust him so much meant more to him than he could say. He threw a last, yearning look at the counter, then loosened his hold on her, letting her slide down his body until her feet touched the floor. The feeling of all her ample softness abrading his hardness almost snapped his control.

Ah, but he was a patient man, and some things were better if you waited. When he made love to this lady, he wanted everything to be perfectly right.

After cleaning the kitchen and doing her household chores, which took her until well past noon, Molly started washing the windows, a task she'd been putting off in favor of more pressing jobs. She had moved outside and completed about half of the lower-story panes when she heard Jake saying, "Whoa. Easy boy." Her heart caught, for she knew the instant she heard his voice that he was working with Sunset.

Molly descended the ladder and sneaked around the corner of the house to watch. Man and horse stood stock-still, facing each other, like two pugilists waiting for the bell to ring. Until now, Jake had always sat quietly in one corner of the pen. Since that first day, he hadn't tried to approach the stallion again.

Fascinated, she climbed the steps and leaned against the porch post to watch. On the afternoon breeze, she could hear the rise and fall of Jake's voice but couldn't make out all he said. Sunset cocked his ears, then snorted and shook his head. Jake only smiled and kept talking.

After a moment, Molly gave up trying to hear exactly what he said. The words themselves didn't matter. The unthreatening way he stood was eloquent, his tone of voice conveying everything.

Sunset was nervous. The muscles in his flanks quivered, and he lowered his head, a sign of equine subservience, according to what Jake had told her. Glancing at the man, Molly decided she would surrender, too, if she were Sunset. Jake looked tall, strong, and ready for anything, a fearful opponent, indeed.

Keeping up a steady stream of assurances, Jake slowly sidled up to the horse. It was a beautiful, warm afternoon that made the thought of lazing about in the sunshine sound far more appealing than window washing. Molly considered the half-finished pane she'd so abruptly abandoned and told herself she really should go back to work. Fascination with the man, the horse, and the bonding that was about to take place had her sinking down onto a step instead.

After watching Jake for a moment, she knew he meant to touch Sunset today. Gaze fixed, heart pounding, she hugged her knees. He stood with his head bent, his face slightly averted, his arms spread. As he raised his hand toward Sunset's neck, the stallion quivered from chest to rump, and his snorts turned to a plaintive nickering.

"I know," she heard Jake say.

And then he was touching the horse's neck, his palm barely grazing the glistening black coat. Molly held her breath.

"I know," Jake said again. "But it's okay, Sunset. That's all over. No one is going to hurt you again."

Sunset whickered and shifted. Slipping his hand under the stallion's neck, Jake stepped in closer until they stood shoulder to shoulder. As if the contact were simply too much, Sunset wheeled away. Jake let him go, turning to keep the horse in sight. After circling the corral several times, Sunset stopped and turned to face him again.

And Jake began the entire process over.

An hour later, Molly still huddled on the step, watching. She had long since lost count of how many times Jake had approached the stallion, touched him, and then lost him again. She'd never seen anyone with such patience. One tiny step forward, a gigantic step back. He'd told her once that horse training was very like a courtship, and she saw now that it was true. Jake didn't seem to mind that he was making no progress. He was content to repeat the same steps as many times as Sunset needed him to repeat them.

Tears filled Molly's eyes. *Jake.* She thought of all the nosegays and other little surprises he'd left on her doorstep. Her fireplace mantel was cluttered with pretty stones, colorful feathers, and parched blossoms. *"Sweet nothings,"* he always said with a shrug when she thanked him. Molly disagreed. Those silly sweet nothings meant the world to her.

He was like no other individual she'd ever known. Horse whisperer or ordinary man, it no longer mattered. As he approached Sunset, she could almost feel his gentleness and concern. He had a very special gift, an air about him that worked past barriers and touched in a way that even a terrified horse couldn't resist.

"Come down here, Molly," he suddenly called.

She snapped erect. She hadn't realized he knew she was there.

"Come on," he called again.

Her legs had grown stiff. She pushed slowly up from the step. By the time she reached the corral, Jake had scaled the fence and stood outside. He smiled when she walked up to him.

"You've seen how it's done. Now you try it."

"Oh, no, I—"

He caught her chin on the edge of his hand, his gaze locking with hers. "You said this morning that you trust my word. Do you?"

"Yes, of course, but—"

"He won't hurt you. You've got my word on it."

"How can you know?"

Jake released her chin and turned his gaze toward the horse. "I feel it."

"You *feel* it?" Molly was tempted to laugh, only then she recalled the many times she'd seen him out in the fields, working with other horses. A silent communication seemed to take place between him and a horse that couldn't be explained by everyday standards, but was no less real.

Molly searched his gaze, all her senses suddenly acute. *Trust*. She'd sworn to never give hers blindly again.

"The whole time I've been working with him, I've caught him looking your way. That horse worships you, honey."

Molly gulped. She had come to trust Jake Coulter in a way she hadn't imagined might be possible when she first arrived, but she wasn't sure she trusted him so much she was willing to put her life on the line.

Molly was trembling so badly, she could barely climb over the fence. Sunset didn't help matters any. The moment she invaded his pen, he began grunting and sidestepping. Molly hung halfway down the inside rails, looking over her shoulder at the stallion, convinced he would trample her the instant her feet touched the ground.

"He's only talking to you," Jake assured her.

"What's he saying?" she asked shrilly.

Jake came to rest his arms on a rail and gazed over the fence at the horse. "He's saying it's about time you came in to visit him. He's been waiting and waiting. Isn't it just like a woman to drag her feet?"

Molly didn't believe for a minute that Jake knew what the horse was thinking, but she drew strength from the twinkling amusement in his eyes. If she knew nothing else about him, she believed he was a good and kind man. He wouldn't be laughing if he thought she were about to get hurt.

Trust. It kept coming back to that. Where men were involved, it didn't come easily to her. When she had awakened from a drug-induced stupor to find herself in a clinic for the emotionally ill, she'd lost her faith in the benevolent nature of the male of her species.

Now, here she was, at another crossroads. Jake was asking her to trust him with her safety, possibly even her life. If he was wrong—oh, God, if he was wrong—she would never be fleet enough of foot to escape before the stallion did her serious injury.

Her feet connected with the dirt. Molly gulped. It was all she could do to relax her grip on the fence rail. On legs that threatened to buckle, she turned to face the horse.

"His h-head is up," she said in a wobbly voice. "He's not subservient."

"No," Jake agreed softly. "Would you just look at that?"

Molly was looking, and she almost wet her pants. The stallion whickered, threw his massive head, and pawed the dirt with a front hoof. "Oh, God!"

"Sweetheart, he isn't afraid of you. *Look* at him. That's a welcome sight, if ever I saw one. He's just telling you hello."

"Oh." Molly struggled to swallow. "Hello, Sunset."

The stallion grunted and high-stepped in a figure eight at his end of the pen, his tail lifted high. When he wheeled to a stop, he whickered and threw his head again.

"Ah, Molly," Jake murmured. "Go to him."

She groped behind her for the fence rail. . . . *Nothing.* "I, um . . . maybe it'd be better if I wait for him to come to me."

"Just take it slow. You watched me. You know how to do it."

"Sort of sideways?"

"If you like. I'm not sure that's necessary. That's my signal to him that I mean him no harm. I think he already knows that you don't."

Molly figured the stallion probably wasn't afraid of her because she was so pathetically unthreatening, a plump woman of diminutive stature who tripped over her own feet.

"One slow step at a time," Jake whispered. "Go to him."

Molly took one step. Sunset blew through his nose and scared her half to death. "What's that mean?"

"Nothing. He's just talking to you."

"What's he saying this time?" She took another step. "I'm really not cut out for this, you know. What'll I do when I reach him?"

"Just pet him."

"Don't horses bite?"

"He won't bite you."

Molly prayed not. Sunset had gigantic teeth. She took another step, then another. The horse stopped prancing and stood stock-still, his head still lifted high, his ears cocked forward.

"Talk to him," Jake instructed. "Reassure him."

"Hello, Sunset," Molly called in a quivery trill. "Don't kill me. Okay?"

She took another step. "I, um . . . don't know anything about horses, you know. Make my first experience a pleasant one." She took several more steps and ran out of courage. "I can't, Jake. I just can't. He's so *big*."

"You're better than halfway. You can do it."

"No. I think maybe . . . " The horse took a step toward her. "Oh, dear. *Jake?*"

"I'll be damned," he said when the horse took another step. "Will you just look at that. Stand tight, Molly. He's as wary as you are. Don't frighten him by making any sudden movements."

Molly seriously doubted the horse was as wary as she was. He outweighed her by a goodly amount, and he had hooves and teeth.

Step by hesitant step, Sunset closed the remaining distance. When he reached Molly, he sniffed her chest. Then he simply stood there with his great head hanging.

Molly was no expert on horses, but even she could interpret this body language. Inexpressible weariness rolled off the stallion in waves. Her gaze shifted to his poor, abused body. From close range, she could see where the whip had sliced deeply into his flesh. Some of the wounds would leave vicious scars, and she knew the deep ones that hadn't yet healed must still hurt terribly.

"Oh, Sunset," she whispered. "I'm so sorry he did this. I'm so sorry."

The horse grunted and nudged her hand. His nose felt as soft as velvet. Molly turned her wrist to touch his muzzle with her fingertips. Sunset wiggled his lip, tickling her skin.

Just like that, the fear left Molly. Sunset wanted her as his friend. Not Jake, but *her*. Trembling, she ran her fingers up the center of his nose. She hadn't realized until now that horses had eyelashes. Sunset had long, sooty ones, and soulful brown eyes that pleaded with her. She touched the silky tufts at the base of his ears, then fingered his mane, which was coarse and heavy, the texture of the strands reminding her of raw silk.

"You're beautiful," she whispered in awe. "You're so beautiful, Sunset." Growing braver, Molly stretched out a hand to touch his neck, then she stepped closer to gently stroke his shoulder, taking care to avoid his lacerations. "Good boy. You're such a love."

From behind her, Jake said, "You've got your work cut out for you today. Those cuts need disinfectant and salve. The ones that haven't healed are starting to ooze puss."

Molly could see that they were, a sign that mild infection had set in. "He needs antibiotics."

"I have some penicillin in the stable fridge. Maybe later, when you're feeling more at ease, you can give him an injection. For now, it'll be a step forward just to clean them."

"You want *me* to do it?" she asked incredulously.

"No one else can touch him," was Jake's reply. "His vote carries the day, honey, and he's chosen you."

Molly had never been chosen for much of anything. In grade school, she'd been thin and undersized. None of the other kids had ever called her name when they were teaming up for sports. As she'd grown older, she'd become a bookworm, exacerbating the problem.

Warmth spread through her—a wonderful, uplifting feeling of warmth. Sunset had chosen *her*. Jake was far more qualified. He knew how to doctor horses, how to give injections. He was an all-around expert, while she knew absolutely nothing. But Sunset had chosen *her*.

"I'm going to run and get you some disinfectant and cotton. Two things for you to remember. Don't step behind him, ever. Horses can't see behind them, and they sometimes kick out. Another thing to bear in mind, always, is that he's got binocular vision in front, monocular to the side. When you stand near his rump, it's hard for him to see you unless he turns his head. Keep a hand on him so he knows where you are and talk to him a lot so he can keep track of your voice. A large percentage of the time when horses injure humans, it's because the humans do something stupid."

That sounded reasonable. "Are you sure it's safe to leave me then? I'm a master at stupidity."

He chuckled. "I'll only be gone a couple of minutes. Just continue as you are, Molly. Pet him, talk to him. That's the best medicine for what ails him right now, what he needs the very most."

"What do I say?"

Jake hesitated before replying. "What would you want someone to say to you?"

Keeping her voice pitched low so as not to be overheard, Molly spent the next few minutes speaking from her heart to Sunset, saying all the things she felt he needed to hear because she needed to hear them herself.

"It wasn't your fault," she whispered. "You gave him all you had and tried your hardest. That was never enough for him. He just kept pressing you for more, and then for more, pitting you against older, faster horses, wanting the fatter purse. It was never your fault, Sunset."

Sunset whinnied softly and thrust his nose in Molly's armpit. She stiffened, uncertain what to do, but when the horse only stood there, keeping his muzzle pressed against her, she realized he was only frightened and wanted to be as close to her as possible. A dog might have crawled on her lap. Being too large for that, Sunset sought comfort in the only way he could, by surrounding himself with her smell.

Taking care not to hurt him, she rested her other arm over the crest of his neck and pressed her cheek to his forehead. "Oh, Sunset, life is so unfair. I wish I could have stopped this. If only I had known, I would have stolen you sooner."

Jake returned with the medication just then. He waited with it at the opposite side of the fence, hesitant to enter for fear he might frighten the horse. "This stuff doesn't sting, and it has anesthetic properties to ease his discomfort," he said as she came to the fence for the bottle. "All you do is soak the cotton balls with it, then gently swab the lacerations, cleaning them as thoroughly as you can. Afterward you can apply salve, which will keep dirt out of the cuts and help them heal."

Molly nodded. Jake held her gaze, his dark face creasing in a smile. "You're doing great so far," he told her warmly.

"I'm not so scared now." She blinked and glanced quickly away. "Oh, Jake, he's so—broken. I remember how proud he used to look whenever I saw him, and now he's so broken."

"Nothing is irreversible," he assured her.

"I pray you're right. It would be such a shame if he never got over it."

"He will. If you love him enough, he will."

Molly met his gaze again, no longer caring if he saw the tears in her eyes.

"The pride is still there in him," he said. "That's why this has been so hard on him, because he's got pride and an inner strength that Rodney couldn't beat out of him. You know that saying, 'The bigger they are, the harder they fall.' Sunset took a painful tumble, Molly, but he's got it in him to get back up."

"I don't know," Molly said, remembering how the stallion had thrust his nose under her arm. "I really don't know if he has that kind of strength left."

Jake gazed solemnly at the horse. When at last he spoke, his voice had gone thick. "You have to believe in him, honey. Right now, he's so lost, and his world has been turned topsy-turvy. You have to help him believe in himself again." His mouth tipped into a sad smile. "You're his mirror. How you see him is how he'll eventually come to see himself. Do you understand what I'm saying?"

A lump came to Molly's throat. "That we see ourselves as others do?"

He reached through the fence to cup her cheek. After regarding each of her features as if to commit them to memory, he said, "Exactly. We see ourselves as others do."

When he turned and walked away, Molly gazed after him, unable to shake the feeling that he'd been referring to far more than just the horse.

We see ourselves as others do. Over the next two hours, as Molly worked with Sunset, those words circled endlessly in her mind.

Arms resting on a fence rail, Jake listened to Molly reassure the horse. In the not so distant past, she'd questioned her ability to be Sunset's mistress, claiming that her feelings for the stallion ran closer to pity than to love.

That wasn't what he heard now. Every word, every inflection of her voice, rang deep with caring. Jake relaxed slightly, confident that he'd done the right thing. He could easily have hooked on with Sunset himself, but when he'd felt Molly watching him, he'd started pulling back. She needed this, maybe even more than Sunset did. As she talked to the horse, she was talking to herself as well, whether she realized it or not.

"It wasn't your fault, Sunset. Never yours."

Nor had it ever been Molly's fault. Jake was absolutely sure of that.

"He's a vicious, cruel *monster* for doing this to you."

Rodney had been just as cruel to Molly, and it was only a matter of time before she began to realize it.

"He made you lose faith in yourself."

Molly's faith in herself had been destroyed as well.

"You're so beautiful, Sunset. So very, very beautiful."

Jake looked at Molly and thought how very beautiful she was. The sassy haircut and new clothes had transformed her. More important, he had completely lost his heart to the person she was within. All his life he'd been told that beauty was only skin deep, but he'd never really understood what that meant until now. He was going to love this woman forever, not just while she was young and pretty but when she grew old. Fifty years from now, when he looked at her, he would love every gray hair on her head and every wrinkle on her sweet face.

We see ourselves as others do.

Now that she'd said the words, how long would it be before the truth of them was driven home? How long would it be before she looked in the mirror and saw herself instead of the distorted image that Rodney had created in her mind?

Sweet, beautiful Molly, who believed she was plain.

Sweet, beautiful Molly, who constantly dieted in a futile attempt to alter the glorious figure that nature had bestowed on her.

Sweet, beautiful Molly, who looked but couldn't see.

"I'll never forgive him for what he's done to you," she whispered to the horse.

Jake heard the words and closed his eyes, thinking that he, too, would never forgive. He didn't know exactly what Rodney had done to her, but the results had been devastating, and, like the horse, she had a very long journey still ahead of her to reach wellness.

It was Jake's hope that woman and horse would make the journey together.

§ CHAPTER SIXTEEN §

Molly dreamed that night of Sarah and her father. Their faces haunted her in slumber as she never allowed them to during the day. *"Molly, help us!"* they cried, imploring her, reaching out to her.

Molly met with countless obstacles as she struggled to reach them. The world went dark with shifting shadows that drifted like sooty smoke, the tendrils seeming almost alive as they curled around her. She didn't know where she was, and nothing looked familiar.

She came to a deep, yawning chasm spanned by a rickety footbridge. When she looked across the fissure, she saw Sarah and her father standing on the other side, both of them reaching out to her. Molly called out that she was coming and hurried onto the bridge. Running, running . . . No matter how she tried, she seemed to get nowhere. With growing terror, she saw that the footbridge was becoming narrower and narrower until she was balanced on a quivering strip of wood little wider than a ruler. Afraid of falling, she turned back to find another way across, only the bridge behind her had vanished.

She fell then, head over heels and endlessly, plunging ever downward, the echoes of Sarah's and her father's screams becoming so faint they were barely whispers in her mind. When she hit bottom, she sank into a fathomless blackness as thick as crude oil. Drowning in it and frantic to breathe, she struggled upward. When at last she broke the surface, she treaded in place, searching the edge of the chasm for her father and her friend.

Finally she spotted them, arms thrown wide as they pleaded with her to save them. When she tried to swim, the thick coldness nearly sucked her under. She pressed onward, gasping for air, her heart slamming. I'm coming, *she thought.* I hear you this time, and I'm coming.

One minute it seemed to be Sarah's voice calling to her, the next her father's. Molly struggled onward, frantic to reach them. She couldn't let them die. Not this time. She wouldn't fail them again.

At last she saw Sarah just ahead. Her friend seemed to be standing under a spotlight, its harsh brilliance illuminating every detail of her person. Dressed in an oversized nightshirt, she looked frightened and confused, much as she had in the days before her death. In her right hand, she held a razor blade. "Help me," she cried, and then with a sob, she slashed her wrists.

"No!" *Molly screamed.* "Please, no! Wait for me, Sarah. I'm almost there! Don't, please, don't!"

Only it was too late. Sarah sank to her knees, crimson splashing over her white nightshirt and down her legs. Horrified, Molly realized the black slime all around her had turned to blood. Sarah began to scream, long, high-pitched cries of agony—and still Molly couldn't reach her. Not again. *It couldn't happen like this again.*

Molly jerked awake.

For a frozen instant, she stared blankly upward, her body rigid. Then she sat bolt upright in bed, her skin beaded with sweat, her legs tangled in the sheets. She covered her face with her hands, unable to get the screams out of her head. Shrill and piercing, they seemed so real.

Molly dropped her hands to listen, her horror growing as she realized the screaming wasn't part of a dream. She leaped from the bed and dashed to the open window. Flickering orange light played over the upper panes of glass. Grabbing the sill, Molly thrust her head out the opening and looked through the trees. *Fire.* The stable. Oh, dear God, the *stable.*

She never gave a thought to a robe as she raced from the bedroom. Once at the front door, she stumbled to a stop, bewildered to find it standing ajar. She would have sworn she locked it before going to bed.

The screams jerked the thought from her mind. The horses. All those poor horses. Was Jake already out there? Did he even realize that the stable was on fire?

Light from the flames reached into the darkness, enabling Molly to see. As she ran, she barely felt the pricks and jabs to the bottoms of her feet. She thought of White Star's brand-new baby, then of the mare herself and all the other horses. What a horrible way to die, trapped in a raging inferno. If Jake wasn't already awake, she had to raise an alarm.

When Molly drew near the burning building, she heard shouts and saw the dark silhouettes of men rushing about, some manning water hoses, others trying to calm the panicked animals they'd led from the building. The commotion was confusing. Horses shrieked and fought their leads, trying desperately to escape both the men and the fire. She saw Shorty and Tex struggling to free a hose from beneath the animals' churning hooves. Then she spotted Hank and Bill, tending to White Star's new foal, which looked more frightened than hurt.

Relieved not to be the first person on the scene, Molly ran to check on Sunset. The stallion stood at the far end of his pen, rump pressed to the rails, his attention riveted to the flames. When he saw Molly, he grunted nervously and swung his head. She skirted the corral and reached through the rails to pet him.

"It's okay, boy. You're safe here."

Almost as if he understood, the stallion nodded his massive head and pawed the dirt.

Convinced Sunset would be fine, Molly left him to go find Jake. Later she never knew how she managed to pick him out of the melee, but she spotted him almost instantly. Wielding a flashlight, he was moving from horse to horse, checking them for injuries. As Molly drew closer, she glanced at the burning stable, thinking that Jake's time might be better spent trying to help put out the blaze. A few of his hired hands were trying, but it looked as if they were losing the battle.

"Are all the horses okay?" she asked as she reached him.

He glanced up, then snaked out a hand to grab her wrist and draw her to his side. "Never do that, Molly! You'll get the shit kicked out of you."

Molly realized she'd run up behind the gelding. The long fingers of flickering amber that played over them suddenly flared more brightly, followed by a crashing sound and a burst of fiery orange against the night sky. Molly jumped with a start. The gelding wheeled and whinnied, panicked by the blast of heat.

Still holding Molly's wrist, Jake sprang erect and shoved hard against the animal's rump to keep it from sidestepping onto her feet. Glancing past his shoulder, she saw that the stable roof had just caved in.

"Oh, God," she cried, raising her voice to be heard over the din. "The stable, Jake. How did this start? Are all the horses out?"

"The horses are all fine." He jerked her hard against him, releasing her hand to slip an arm around her. "Damn, Molly, what are you doing out here half dressed and barefoot?"

Without waiting for an answer, he thrust the flashlight under his belt and shouldered his way through the milling horses and men, protecting her with his bulk as he drew her along. Only at the edge of the stable yard did he allow her to escape his embrace.

"What the hell were you thinking?" he asked sharply. "You don't come around panicked horses without shoes. Do you have any idea the damage their hooves can do?"

Molly hugged her waist, suddenly and acutely aware that she wore only an oversized T-shirt and a pair of white lace panties. Jake skimmed her with a glittering gaze, his attention lingering for a split second on her bare legs. "Go get some clothes on," he bit out.

She retreated a step. "I'm sorry. I just—" She broke off, the words to explain eluding her. "I wasn't sure if you knew. About the fire, I mean. So I just ran out here without thinking."

She turned to walk away. She took only two steps before he checked her flight with a steely hand on her shoulder.

"Molly."

Just that. *Molly*. Yet the way he said her name told her everything. She stopped to look back at him. In the play of firelight, she could see streaks of soot on his face. For the first time since she'd known him, his broad shoulders were slumped. He looked so defeated.

"I'm sorry," he ground out. Still grasping her shoulder, he glanced back toward the fire. "I shouldn't have snapped at you like that."

A horse screamed, and his grip on her shoulder tightened. Molly reached up to pry his fingers away. "Go, Jake. They need you, and I'm fine."

"I'm sorry," he said again. "I was just afraid you'd get hurt, and I—" He broke off and swallowed. "I'm sorry."

Molly managed a smile. "I'll get dressed and come back."

He gave her shoulder a gentle squeeze. "Stay away from the horses until they've calmed down. I've lost enough for one night."

Molly gazed after him, admiring the easy, sure strength of his movements as he broke into a run. When he reached the horses, he slipped the flashlight from his belt and resumed his task of checking them for burns.

Molly stood there for a time, observing him. He seemed totally focused on the animals. The shouts of the men fighting the fire didn't seem to penetrate his consciousness. When more timbers inside the burning building collapsed, he barely glanced in that direction, more concerned with the welfare of the horses than with the loss of his property. Seeing that tugged at Molly's heart. She had already come to admire Jake Coulter, but never more so than now.

The collapse of the timbers spooked a mare that had been tethered to an outside front corner of Sunset's pen. She reared and fought the rope, her front hooves slashing wildly at the fence rails. Jake hurried over to grab her halter.

"Whoa, whoa," Molly heard him say. Using his strength and weight, he hauled down hard on the frantic horse's head to prevent her from rearing again. She whinnied and trembled, sidestepping nervously. Jake ran a hand over her withers and leaned close to whisper something. The mare made plaintive grunting sounds, but she quieted under his touch. Jake untied her rope and led her to the opposite end of the corral where she would be away from the fire.

Molly smiled, remembering how he had denied being a horse whisperer. Far be it from her to argue the point, but she could testify to one thing. He had a way about him that soothed horses and gained their trust.

Her smile deepened. He had a way with women as well.

A few minutes later, as Molly ascended the porch steps to the cabin, she recalled the front door being ajar when she first woke up. *Strange*. She could have sworn she'd locked it before going to bed.

Feeling a need to hurry, she didn't allow herself to wonder about it. She wanted to get dressed as quickly as possible and return to the stable. She might be a total loss when it came to helping with the horses, but there were surely other things she could do.

She flipped on the overhead light as she stepped into the bedroom. Halfway across the room, she lurched to a stop, her gaze riveted to her rumpled bed. The white sheets were smeared with dirt and peppered with pine needles. Bewildered, Molly stepped closer for a better look. Her heart flipped and fluttered. She picked up a pine needle and stared stupidly at it. How on earth had debris gotten on her sheets? They'd been clean when she went to bed.

Feeling numb, she sank onto the edge of the mattress. A cold feeling washed over her. The pine needle slipped from her fingers and drifted to the floor. Once again, she recalled finding the front door ajar when she first woke up, a door she felt sure she had locked before going to bed.

Oh, God. Had she been sleepwalking?

The mere thought made Molly's stomach drop. Though she tried never to think of those days, she *did* have a history of somnambulism.

She turned to stare at the sheets. Then she looked down at her feet. They were filthy from running outdoors barefoot. If she climbed back into bed right now, she would rub dirt off on the linen, leaving smears much like the ones already there.

Oh, no . . . please, no.

Molly clamped a hand over her mouth, remembering her bouts of somnambulism in college. Had she sleepwalked and left the cabin when she wasn't aware of it? She'd been so certain that her more recent sleepwalking episodes had been staged by Rodney to make her look crazy. But maybe she'd been wrong.

Someone had left the front door standing open.

Someone had gotten dirt all over her sheets.

This couldn't be Rodney's handiwork. He was nowhere around.

She glanced at the window where light from the fire still played over the glass. An awful, sick feeling moved through her. She thought of White Star's sweet little foal. He might have died in that fire, and all the other horses could have as well.

Dear God. What had she done?

Pressing her hands over her face, Molly struggled to calm down. *Don't jump to conclusions.* Back in her college days, she'd had difficulty coming to grips with her best friend Sarah's suicide, and after her death, she had sleepwalked for a time. Once, she had wandered into the dormitory kitchen during the breakfast rush and awakened to find herself on display in nothing but a nightgown. Another time, she'd gone outside and awakened standing in a busy intersection. Those incidents had been alarming and undeniably bizarre, but she'd never done anything destructive or violent during the sleepwalking episodes until a year ago, shortly after her dad's death. And she had reason to believe Rodney had staged those episodes for his own nefarious reasons.

Why, then, should she automatically assume that she was responsible for setting that fire?

Molly dropped her hands and hauled in a deep, bracing breath. There was really no reason for her to believe she'd been sleepwalking. There was another explanation for the open front door and the dirt on her sheets.

There had to be.

By midafternoon the next day, Molly was so tired she could barely move. Since breakfast she'd been helping the men build emergency pens and lean-tos for the horses. Despite the chill air, the sun felt hot on her shoulders, and sweat trickled down her spine. Each time she raised the ax, her muscles quivered and jerked. For what felt like the millionth time, she swung at the base of a branch, her aim to denude a young lodgepole pine so it could be used as a fence rail.

At the edge of the forest, Bill manned a chainsaw to fell more trees. A woody smell drifted on the breeze along with particles of sawdust that coated her nostrils. Occasional puffs of smoke from the smoldering fire stung her eyes.

"Here's another one, Molly." Danno heaved a tree onto the growing pile that awaited her attention. "If you need a rest, holler. I'll take over for you."

As much as Molly appreciated the offer, she couldn't accept. Danno was needed to drag the fallen trees over to the pile, a job she lacked the strength to do. At least she was helping here. Sort of, anyway. No matter how fast she worked, she was unable to keep up with the men who labored behind her.

Each time they ran out of poles, one of the older hands helped Molly catch up, his skill and speed at wielding an ax putting hers to shame. They all seemed to appreciate her willingness to help, though, and that was what mattered.

"Got it!" Nate yelled to Ben. "Hold her steady." That directive was punctuated with loud hammering. "Okay, she's sturdy!"

Molly tried to swing the ax again, but her arms refused to cooperate. Accepting the fact that she had to rest for a few seconds, she propped the ax handle against the log, pressed a fist to the small of her back, and stood up straight. Pain. She could have sworn she heard every joint in her body pop.

She stared at the remains of the stable to her left. Warped and blackened by the extreme heat, the sheets of corrugated steel had collapsed helter-skelter, reminding her of a flattened house of cards. She remembered how the structure had once looked, a mammoth green pole building with tidy paddocks. Now the interior had been reduced to chunks of charred timber and ash.

"Pretty sad, isn't it?" Hank commented as he came to get another pole. "Why anyone would do such a thing is beyond me."

According to the Crystal County fire chief, who had concluded his investigation and left only a couple of hours ago, the stable blaze had been deliberately set. After dousing the back of the building with diesel taken from Jake's machine shop, someone had ignited the fuel with a match.

"I can't imagine it, either." Parched with thirst, the walls of Molly's throat rasped together. "At least you got all the horses out."

"That's true." Hefting a pole onto his shoulder, Hank walked away.

After he left, Molly wanted to just stand there for a few minutes. She checked the position of the sun. There wasn't much daylight left. Of the horses now grazing in the front pastures, two of the mares were due to foal soon, one of the geldings had a respiratory infection, another had been suffering with diaphragm spasms, and White Star's new baby still needed shelter at night when the temperature dropped. They *had* to get the lean-tos up before dark.

She clenched her teeth and bent to grab the ax. Just then she heard the front door of the house slam shut, the sound cutting through the air like a rifle shot. She glanced over her shoulder to see Jake coming down the porch steps. The erect set of his shoulders and the brisk way he moved told her he was angry.

In the middle of notching a pole, Hank stopped and swept off his hat to wipe sweat from his brow. "Well?" he called. "What'd the insurance guy say?"

Jake kicked a charred board from his path. "Son of a bitch is trying to renege. Says the machine shop should've been locked, that they aren't liable."

Hank slapped his Stetson back on his head. "That is such bullshit. Name me one working ranch where they keep all the outbuildings locked."

As Jake drew closer, he cut Molly a glance. Then he settled his hands at his hips. "If I have to, I'll hire a lawyer. There isn't a single clause in my policy that says the outbuildings have to be locked." Looking bone weary, he rubbed the back of his neck. "I spoke to the sheriff as well. He thinks kids set the fire."

"Kids?" Tex leaned over to spit. "This wasn't the work of youngsters."

Jake sighed as he surveyed the devastation. "Maybe the sheriff has a point. A sane adult would draw the line at setting fire to a stable full of horses."

Molly's stomach clenched. A *sane* adult? Sweat beaded her face. She resumed her task of hacking off branches. With every swing, the ax grew heavier. Half the time, she missed her mark and left big gouges in the log.

"The fuel cans were full and handy," Jake went on. "You take a bunch of drugged-up kids out on the prowl, and they might think setting a fire was fun."

"Oh, horse puckey," Levi said as he hammered a nail. "Even dopey kids have more sense than that. He gonna check for fingerprints on those cans?"

"Sure. Problem is, they may not match up with anything on file. If it was kids, they may never have been fingerprinted."

Molly was about to take another swing with the ax when a brown hand locked over her forearm. Startled, she glanced up into Jake's brilliant blue eyes. "You're finished," he said softly.

Molly gestured at the poles she still needed to strip. "I've got at least—"

"You're finished," he said again. "Go on up to the house and have a cup of coffee. You're so tuckered you can't spit. That ax could jump back at you."

Molly had narrowly missed hitting her shin a few minutes ago, so she didn't argue the point. She really *was* exhausted.

As she started away, Jake called, "Why are you limping?"

She paused to stare stupidly at her filthy sneakers. Recalling her race to the stable last night, she shrugged and said, "Stickers, I guess."

No sooner had she reached the kitchen than she heard the front door open and close. The thud of heavy boots followed her path through the house. She was about to pour a cup of coffee when Jake appeared in the archway. Without a word, he settled his hands on her shoulders and steered her to a chair.

Molly sank down, too weary to protest when he hunkered before her and lifted her foot onto his knee. Off went her shoe, then her sock. Turning her ankle, he bent to examine her sole. "Holy hell. Why didn't you get these out right away? Now they're all inflamed."

Molly craned her neck to see. The bottom of her foot was dotted with red spots. "I was so upset I didn't really notice the tenderness."

He lowered her foot back to the floor and went to a drawer for the kitchen matches. When he returned a moment later, he fished his pocketknife from his jeans, struck a match, and sterilized the blade. Molly watched him dubiously.

"If you plan to dig stickers from my feet with that, think again."

He chuckled and hunkered back down in front of her. Curling a warm hand over her ankle, he lifted her foot back onto his knee. "Trust me. This is the best sliver picker you've ever seen. Hold still, okay?"

"I don't dare move. I could lose a leg."

He smiled, his ministrations so gentle that Molly barely felt them. She sighed and relaxed. Well, almost. It was difficult to completely relax with his long fingers curled over her foot.

When he finished extracting all the stickers, he kept her left foot on his knee, his big, calloused hand wrapped over her ankle. His pinky found its way under her pant leg and lightly caressed her calf, setting her skin afire. He gazed solemnly up at her, the expression on his face unreadable.

"I guess you'll live," he said softly.

This was the first opportunity they'd really had to talk since the fire. "I'm so sorry about your stable, Jake."

"No need for you to be sorry. It wasn't your doing."

Molly prayed not. "I'm pleased that all the horses are okay."

He nodded. "They're all that really matters."

Molly gripped the edges of the chair. "I know it's none of my business, but you've said things that lead me to believe you may be in difficult financial straits."

"Now there's a nice, fancy way of putting it."

"So I haven't misread it?"

He lowered her foot to the floor, then reached for her shoes. "I'm in hock up to my gonads and feeling the squeeze."

Molly thought of the huge amounts of money that would be hers when she regained control of her inheritance. It didn't seem fair, somehow, that she should have so much when someone like Jake had so little. "I'm so sorry."

His mouth twitched. "You have a bad habit of saying you're sorry for things that aren't your fault. No one twisted my arm to make me buy this ranch back."

"Why did you then?" Again Molly realized she was asking a question about something that was none of her business. "You've been to college. You could probably make a far better living working for someone else."

He nodded. "Without a doubt, but money isn't everything. I grew up here." He shrugged. "It's hard to explain what that means to me. I thought us boys would take it over one day, that we'd live on this land, raise our families here like generations of Coulters had before." His mouth curved in another slight smile. "From the time I was a little guy, I was good with horses. When I grew older, I dreamed of raising my own line, of training them from birth. I always thought I'd be able to do it here, that one day I'd make the Lazy J famous, in its way. When I got the chance to buy it back, it wasn't a decision I made with my head, but with my heart."

Molly knew how that went. Helping Sunset had been a decision of the heart. "How did your dad lose the place?" She imagined him drinking or gambling himself into deep debt. "Or is that too personal a question?"

"He went bankrupt and lost everything," Jake said solemnly. "Everything but the dream, anyway."

By his husky tone of voice, Molly knew that had been a painful time for him.

"As soon as I got out of college, I started working and saving to buy another place," he went on. "It took me a few years to scrape up a down payment and the working capital, but I finally managed. I was watching the market, never dreaming the Lazy J might be available. One day, after looking at a spread out this way, Hank and I stopped by here on impulse to take a stroll down memory lane. The man who owned the place was ready to sell. I leaped at the chance."

Molly dug her nails into the underside of the chair seat. "What caused your dad to go bankrupt?"

He ran a hand over his rumpled hair. He'd scrubbed the soot from his face, but he still looked tired. "My sister Bethany was paralyzed in a riding accident. She underwent three surgeries, and our health insurance wasn't that good. My dad went into hock, hoping she might walk again. She never did."

Some men might resent that, but not Jake. She'd seen his disregard for the burning stable last night, his sole concern for the welfare of his horses. He undoubtedly would have sacrificed anything for his sister. "If the insurance company won't cover the fire damage, what will you do?"

"There's no way I can scrape up the money to rebuild the stable by myself." He pushed wearily to his feet. "They'll cover it. I won't take no for an answer."

Molly couldn't let it go at that. "But if it happens that they don't?"

His brows pleated in a frown. He stared out the kitchen window. Voice husky, he said, "Then I'll be back to square one, with only a dream in my pocket."

Molly fixed supper alone that night. Jake was far too busy working outside to help her cook. At his suggestion, she made a tuna-and-rice casserole, a simple concoction of rice, canned tuna, and cream of mushroom soup, which she sprinkled with cheddar cheese and baked. Two huge pans of cornbread and a giant mixing bowl filled with canned corn complemented the meal. High starch, high fat. Molly felt sure the men would love it.

She was about to call them in to eat when the kitchen wall-phone rang. Grabbing a towel to wipe her hands, she hurried to answer it. "The Lazy J."

"Howdy. This is Sheriff Dexter. Is Jake handy?"

Molly had steered clear of the sheriff that morning. Knowing it was he on the phone made her nerves leap. "I, um—yes. Can you hold for just a moment?"

She raced through the house and out onto the front porch. "Jake?" she called. "The sheriff is on the line."

He abandoned the section of fence he was building and came loping up to the house. Molly preceded him as they made their way to the kitchen. While Jake conversed on the phone, she put glasses on the table, along with two gallons of milk. She'd just finished when he broke the connection.

"Bad news?"

He nodded. "There were no prints on the fuel cans. Chances are the person or persons responsible will never be caught."

"No prints? That doesn't sound like the work of kids to me."

Jake scowled. "Not to me, either. Seems strange that a bunch of kids would have thought to wear gloves."

"Yes, it does." It also struck Molly as highly unlikely that a sleepwalker would have the presence of mind to be that clever.

The relief that coursed through her made her bones watery.

Directly after supper, the men went back outside to work on the lean-tos, using halogen floodlights to see in the deepening darkness. By the time Molly had finished all her kitchen chores, only half of the needed shelters were done. Jake was busy moving horses in from the pastures to put them in the few available lean-tos. The moment he saw Molly, he turned over the task to one of his men and walked to meet her.

"How can I help?" Molly asked.

He shook his head. "You've done enough for one day."

"Some of the horses need shelter, and the work still isn't done."

"But you are." He took her arm. "I want you to get a good night's rest."

"While you stay up half the night, finishing the lean-tos?"

"I'm used to losing sleep. You aren't."

As they fell into a walk, Molly realized he was heading for her cabin. "You don't need to see me home tonight, Jake." Gesturing toward the lights, she smiled. "I'll be able to see well enough. It's as bright as day out here."

"Not away from the lights, it isn't." He jerked off his soiled leather gloves and tucked them over his belt. "Besides, I'm due for a short break."

Molly saw no point in arguing. She'd come to know Jake well over the past three weeks. No matter what she said, he was going to walk her home.

"No detours tonight. You've got work to do, and my feet are sore."

Shortening his strides to match her pace, he chuckled and cast her an inquiring look. Light from behind them illuminated one side of his face, casting the other in shadow, which served to delineate the sharp bridge of his nose, the muscular line of his jaw, and the nearly perfect bow shape of his hard mouth.

"How's the rest of you doing?" he asked. "Any muscles screaming yet?"

Her muscles had started screaming hours ago, but she wasn't about to complain. Everyone else had worked hard, too. "I'm sturdier than most women."

The corner of his mouth twitched, telling her he was trying hard not to smile. "A veritable Amazon, that's you."

Molly shivered at the cold and drew her jacket closer around her. "Laugh if you like. I may not be well toned and athletic, but I *am* stout."

He said nothing to contradict her. As they walked along, Molly stared at their shadows, which danced like dark specters ahead of them, his tall and lean, hers short and squat. There was no denying that she was solidly built. Next to Jake's, the outline of her legs put her in mind of tree stumps.

Once at the house, he insisted on going in to check the rooms. Though touched by his concern for her safety, Molly couldn't resist teasing him when he entered the small, U-shaped kitchen to open the broom closet.

"That's barely big enough to hide a midge," she observed. When that didn't deter him, she laughed and added, "Don't forget to look under the sink."

"Go ahead, make fun. Anyone who'd set fire to a stable has a screw loose. Every last one of those horses could have burned to death. The person who did it has no conscience, and mercy is a word beyond his understanding."

Molly immediately sobered. "You're right. I'm sorry for giving you a hard time. I just—" She glanced at the broom closet. "I think a man would have a difficult time hiding in there, is all."

He nodded. "I'm not necessarily looking for a man." He closed the closet. "I'm not entirely convinced the sheriff's right, but on the off chance it was kids, caution is in order." He winked at her and looked under the sink, which made her laugh. "All secure," he said. "If you lock up tight, you should be safe enough." He arched a questioning eyebrow. "Will you feel comfortable staying over here alone? If not, you're more than welcome at the house. You do realize that."

Molly noticed a pair of brown cotton gloves lying on the counter behind him. She had no idea how they'd gotten there. Last night when she'd raced back here to dress, she hadn't come in the kitchen. The only other time she'd been in the cabin since the fire was this morning when she'd grabbed a shower.

"I-I'll be fine," she murmured. "I appreciate the offer, though."

His gaze sharpened on her face. "Is something wrong?"

Molly fiddled with a button on her new pink blouse. His eyes always unnerved her, making her feel as easy to read as an open book. "I'm just tired and need sleep."

His expression turned amused. "Sleep? What's that?"

"I'll think of you when I'm snuggled down in my warm, comfortable bed."

He grinned. "You do that."

Molly realized what she'd just said and blushed. Seeing her embarrassment, he chuckled and moved past her. Heart pounding, she followed him to the door.

Before stepping out, he cupped a hand to her cheek. "Get a good rest," he said.

For a fleeting instant, Molly thought he might kiss her. Instead he stepped out and closed the door firmly behind him. "Lock up tight, honey. If you need anything, just holler. I'll be here in two shakes of a lamb's tail."

"I'll do that," Molly called. "Good night, Jake."

As his steps faded away, she locked up and returned to the kitchen. When she found the courage to pick up the gloves, she saw dark splotches on the knit. The rank smell of diesel burned her nostrils.

Molly sucked in a sharp breath. With a shudder of revulsion, she opened the broom closet and flung the gloves inside. After slamming the door, she held it closed with the press of her palms, knowing on some level that it was silly. Out of sight, out of mind? She couldn't hide from this.

"There were no prints on the fuel cans," Jake had told her after speaking on the phone with the sheriff earlier. At the time, Molly had been relieved to hear the news, convinced it vindicated her.

Those gloves were glaring proof of her guilt.

It hadn't been kids who'd started that fire. It had been *her*.

All this time, she'd been so convinced that her illness of a few months ago had been induced, that Rodney had drugged her and staged all her bizarre behavior to make her look crazy. Now she had to face the terrible truth, that she might be as nuts as everyone deemed her to be.

She had to tell Jake. If she had sleepwalked and set that fire, there was no telling what she might do next.

She had reached the front door and was about to unfasten the bolt when sanity returned. If she told him she had reason to believe she might have set the fire, there was no predicting how he would react, except that he would want her off his ranch. To that end, if he contacted Rodney, she could soon find herself in an asylum again.

Memories flashed through her mind—awful memories of ice baths, shock treatments, and mind-numbing sedatives. In the early days of her treatment, she'd been a screaming recalcitrant, pounding on the door, begging to be let out, and refusing to eat. Her attendants had thought she was crazy. Even Sam Banks had believed that at first.

She would rather die than go through a similar experience again.

There was also Sunset to consider. If Rodney learned where she was, what would become of the horse? Her ex-husband would take his stallion back to Portland. If Sunset acted up, which he surely would, Rodney's solution would be to whip him. She couldn't bear the thought of that happening. No matter what became of her, she had to save Sunset from enduring any more abuse.

Think, Molly. Laying the truth out before Jake was the obvious course of action, but that didn't mean it was her only option. There had to be a way to protect herself and Sunset while safeguarding the ranch as well.

Trembling with nerves, Molly turned from the door to survey the cabin. She couldn't prevent herself from sleepwalking, but she could take measures to make sure she did nothing destructive.

She went to work. After locking all the windows, she used a roll of masking tape she'd brought from Portland to seal them shut. Then she located the sack of wind chimes that she'd stowed in the closet. After dismantling them, she used yarn from her crochet satchel to string the noisemakers over the windows and front door. Hopefully, the loud tinkling sound would awaken her if she tried to leave the cabin. As an added precaution, she scooted the heavy old easy chair and the antique trunk in front of the door to form a barricade.

Only then could she bring herself to go to bed and try to sleep, *try* being the operative word—she was afraid to close her eyes. Despite all her precautions, what if she left the cabin?

Madness. Every conceivable exit was either taped shut or barricaded, and she'd booby-trapped every opening with noisemakers. She was bound to jerk awake the instant she touched those wind chimes.

Molly had nearly convinced herself that it was safe to close her eyes when a knock came at the door. "Molly, it's me, Jake."

She sprang from bed, thinking of the furniture and wind chimes in front of the door. Grabbing her white chenille robe, she thrust her arms down the sleeves and knotted the sash as she dashed to the living room. She grabbed the chair to move it, cringing when the wooden feet scraped loudly over the floor.

"Coming!" she cried when Jake rapped the door again. "Just a sec."

"Are you all right in there?"

Evidently she hadn't been all right for a very long time, and she'd been too blind to see it. The wind chimes tinkled loudly as she ripped the string away from the door. She dropped them on the chair before opening up. Jake's expression was bewildered as he took in the furniture behind her.

"Sweetheart, I said you were welcome at the house. You don't have to stay over here alone if you're afraid."

Molly's mind raced for an explanation. "I, um, just felt better, knowing I'd wake up if anyone tried the door. That's all."

He leaned a shoulder against the frame, his gaze dark with worry. "Come up to the house. There are plenty of spare beds."

Molly didn't dare do that. She needed the chimes and barricade to ensure that she didn't wander in her sleep. She pushed at her loose hair, which was already tangled from tossing and turning. "No, really. I was already dozing off."

He straightened to reach for something tucked under his belt. Eyes widening, Molly saw that it was a pearl-handled, nickel-plated revolver. He thrust the weapon at her, handle first. "I want you to have this. Just in case."

Her father had died of a gunshot to the head. Even now, she couldn't forget the way the pistol had looked, loosely grasped in his blood-splattered hand. Molly recoiled. "Oh, no. I don't like guns."

Pointing the barrel at the floor, Jake spun the chamber. "This is an old .357 and very simple to use, the only drawback being that it's got a hell of a kick."

Molly shook her head. "No, thank you. I couldn't bring myself to shoot anyone, so what's the point?"

"You don't need to shoot anyone," he assured her. "If there's trouble, just aim at the ceiling. Call me a worrywart. I'm afraid I won't hear you calling for help. If you fire off a round, I know it'll get my attention."

He grasped her wrist and slipped the gun into her hand. Then, bending forward, he quickly showed her how to cock the hammer and take it off safety. "Just point and pull the trigger," he said. "It's as easy as that. If you won't come stay at the house, please keep it here with you. I'll feel better if you do."

Put like that, how could she refuse? She lowered the weapon, acutely aware of how cold and heavy it was. "Thank you. I'll keep it next to my bed."

"See that you do, and don't be afraid to use it. If you even *think* someone's trying to break in, fire off a round." He glanced up. "We're going to patch the roof this summer, anyway. You won't be hurting anything."

A moment later, Molly was bidding him farewell through the locked door again. After hanging the chimes and replacing the barricade, she took the gun to the bedroom. Fearful of what she might do in her sleep with a loaded weapon at her disposal, she took all the bullets from the cylinder and hid them at the bottom of her underwear drawer.

Only then did she feel it was safe for her to sleep.

❦ CHAPTER SEVENTEEN ❦

Molly hadn't even reached the main house the next morning when she heard Jake cursing. Following the sound of his voice, she circled the machine shop and found him crouched beside an old yellow tractor. Peering over his shoulder, she saw that the tire was flat as a fritter.

"What on *earth* happened?"

"It's slashed!" he fairly snarled. "Every damned tire on the place, *slashed*."

Staring in horrified fascination at the tire, she recalled all the times she and Rodney had awakened to find their house in disarray, gouged sofa cushions vomiting stuffing, expensive paintings hanging in ribbons from their frames.

"Oh, no," she said hollowly.

"Oh, no, is right." Jake's face looked gray as he pushed to his feet. "First my stable, now all the tires." He jerked off his hat and thrust a taut hand into his sable hair. "*Damn!* Tractor tires cost a fortune. Someone's out to ruin me."

Molly gulped and directed another glance at the tire. Her fingers and toes felt suddenly numb. "I didn't do it," she said shakily.

He gave her a curious look. "Of course you didn't."

Embarrassment washed through Molly for having said something so stupid. It was just—*oh, God*—always before, everyone had blamed her.

Jake swept past her, the heels of his boots sending up puffs of dust.

"Where are you going?"

"To call the sheriff! I'll be damned if he'll blame this one on kids. It took a man's strength to do that."

A man's strength? She wanted to believe him, but her conscience wouldn't allow it. Seven months ago, she'd seen her handiwork. While sleepwalking, she had slashed Rodney's paintings with such force that the butcher knife had penetrated the backs of the frames and gouged the walls. She'd heard that people could exhibit extraordinary strength when their adrenaline was up. Maybe that held true for sleepwalkers.

She retraced her steps to the cabin. Once inside, she checked the windows for the second time that morning. None of the tape or chimes looked disturbed, and the front door had still been barricaded when she first woke up. If she had sleepwalked, she supposed she might have pushed the furniture back in front of the door when she returned to the cabin, but it didn't seem probable. How exacting was a sleepwalker likely to be?

Still concerned, Molly drew back the covers on the bed to check the sheets. She'd changed the linen last night before retiring, and it still looked clean, no smudges of dirt or debris. If she had gone outside last night, she'd either worn shoes or washed her feet before returning to bed.

Suddenly exhausted, she sank onto the mattress and rested her head in her hands. Oh, God . . . oh, God. Had she slashed all those tires? There was no evidence that she'd left the cabin during the night. But what if she had?

All the while she washed the breakfast dishes later that morning, Molly circled the possibility that she had slashed the tires, a part of her convinced she was the culprit, another part of her unable to believe it. But if not her, then who? Rodney couldn't be blamed for this, not unless he'd somehow managed to track her down and was perpetrating the vandalism to convince Jake she was crazy.

The thought made her freeze. About to put a large frying pan into the drying rack, she stood there, staring at nothing, her fingers clenched over the wooden handle. What if Rodney *had* found her? Until now, that possibility hadn't occurred to her.

Her skin went icy. She glanced uneasily out the kitchen window, searching the line of trees that grew at the edge of the yard. For months now, she'd been convinced that her ex-husband had deliberately made her look crazy so he could gain control of the investment firm. Given her rapid recovery after she'd entered the clinic, it had been the only explanation that made sense. In less than seventy-two hours after she'd escaped Rodney, her head had cleared and she'd stopped feeling dizzy and nauseated. The sleepwalking incidents, about which her husband had complained so bitterly, never occurred in the clinic at all.

Sam had theorized that Molly's rapid improvement was due to the abrupt cessation of stress in her life. She was far removed from her overbearing husband's influence. She had escaped the tension at work. Lastly, he argued that the change of scenery had distanced her from all reminders of her father's suicide. No stress, no symptoms, it was as simple as that, he'd assured her in the beginning.

Molly had never bought into that explanation. Granted, stress had been known to make people dizzy and unable to think clearly, but her symptoms had been extreme. Toward the last, she'd been too weak and disoriented even to walk from her bed to the adjoining bathroom. One night Rodney had come home to find her lying half-conscious on the floor. After carrying her back to bed and helping her into a clean nightgown, he'd descended on her with yet more pills. *"Take your medicine, darling."* She had tried to tell him the drug was making her sick. He'd refused to listen, and when she wouldn't open her mouth to take the pills, he had poked them down her throat.

It had been a nightmare, a nightmare that had only grown more horrible when she awoke at the clinic. Molly shuddered at the memories. It had been glaringly obvious to her, if not to her doctor, that her husband had been drugging her and that her illness had been chemically induced. It followed that the recent sleepwalking incidents had been staged as well. Until Sam had finally come around, she'd tried frantically to make someone listen to her, experiencing a gamut of emotions when she failed—rage, fear, frustration, and an awful sense of helplessness.

Now, suddenly, it was all happening again. She was apparently sleepwalking, and this time Rodney couldn't be blamed. She was frightened, starting to question her own sanity, and mere inches away from losing her grip.

Rodney would be so pleased.

Oh, God, it would be just like him to wage an insidious attack, chipping away at her self-confidence until she began doubting herself at every turn. Even worse, such tactics would eventually lead Jake and everyone else on the ranch to doubt her sanity as well, robbing her of the only friends and support she had.

Poor, crazy Molly. An awful weak feeling attacked her legs as she recalled the stable fire. Until that night, she'd always slept with her bedroom window open so she could hear Sunset in case he needed her. Wasn't it possible that after setting the fire, Rodney could have slipped into her cabin through that window? Was she out of her mind to think he might have hidden somewhere in the house until she left so he could put debris in her bed and plant the gloves in the kitchen?

Molly remembered the nightmare she'd had that night about Sarah and her dad. Rodney knew all about her past. In movies, she'd seen people whisper suggestively to a sleeping person to induce a terrible dream. It would be very like Rodney to enjoy the risk of that, not knowing for sure when she might wake up. *"Molly, help us."* A shudder coursed over her. She could almost hear his whispering voice in her mind.

She could easily imagine him showing up at the ranch. He could be so convincing when he chose. He'd pretend to be concerned about her welfare even as he regretfully informed Jake that she was emotionally ill and undoubtedly responsible for all the vandalism on the Lazy J. Poor, crazy Molly, who sleepwalked. Poor, crazy Molly, who was a danger to herself and everyone around her. He would tell Jake that she needed constant supervision.

Molly felt as if she might vomit. *Rodney.* There had been a time when she never would have believed him capable of such heinous behavior, but no more. After her father's death, her rose-colored glasses had been ripped away, and she'd begun to see her husband not as she wished him to be, but as he truly was, a man who would stop at nothing.

Terror sluiced through her. If Rodney had found her, she didn't have a prayer of escaping him. The tires on her Toyota were flat. Until they were replaced, she didn't even have transportation.

Oh, God. With Claudia and Jared's help, he might be able to get her committed again, and once that happened, no telling how long it might be before she was released.

Molly sank down at the table and covered her face with her hands. She'd been on the Lazy J for about three weeks. She hadn't heard a word on the television or radio about a stolen horse. It was possible Rodney hadn't even reported the theft, choosing instead to track her down and deal with her himself.

Only how had he found her? She'd told no one where she was going, not even her mom. Without the help of law enforcement, how on earth could he have pinpointed her exact location?

The trainer.

Lowering her hands, Molly clutched the edge of the table with such force her knuckles began to ache. The *trainer.* Of course, that was it. Somehow, Rodney had coerced the man into revealing her whereabouts.

Molly leaped up from the chair and advanced to the wall phone. A few minutes later, she'd spoken to an information operator and was ringing Shamrock Greens, the Portland stable where Sonora Sunset had been boarded. A woman answered the call.

"Yes, I'd like to speak with Keith Sandusky, please," Molly said shakily. "Would you mind having him paged for me?"

"Oh, I'm sorry," the woman said. "Keith no longer works here."

"He doesn't?" Molly flattened a hand against the wall. "Are you certain of that?"

"Quite certain. I make out the payroll here."

Sandusky had told Molly that he'd worked at Shamrock Greens for thirty years and hoped to retire from there, which was why he hadn't wanted any kind of trouble with Rodney. He'd been afraid her ex-husband would have him blackballed from the racing circuit if he dared to cross swords with him. An odd-turned, funny-looking little man, Sandusky had worn riding silks even when he wasn't on the track. *"These horses are my life,"* he'd informed Molly. *"No wife, no children. This job is all I've got. That's why I didn't call you after the first whipping, why I waited until it got so bad. I was afraid of losing my job. That's no excuse, I know. The horse has suffered for my cowardice."*

Remembering the passion in Sandusky's voice, Molly couldn't believe he had suddenly left the stable. "When exactly did Mr. Sandusky quit?" she asked.

There was a long silence. Then the woman said, "Are you a friend?"

"Yes." The man had lent her his horse trailer, after all, so Molly didn't feel that was really a lie. They were friends, of sorts.

"Well, I suppose I won't be speaking out of school, then. Keith didn't exactly quit, he just up and left about three weeks ago. Not a word to the owners, no forwarding address. He didn't even collect his pay."

Molly frowned. "Isn't it strange that he didn't come by to get his check?"

The woman sighed. "There's just no figuring people sometimes. I keep expecting him to call or to find a note from him in the mail. So far, nothing. If he should get in touch, would you like me to give him a message?"

"No, thank you."

Molly hung up the phone. She doubted anyone at Shamrock Greens would hear from Keith Sandusky again. Something had happened. Maybe Rodney had grown so furious when he'd found Sunset missing that he'd threatened Sandusky, and the trainer had become so frightened that he'd pulled up stakes rather than stay and face the music. Molly just hoped Rodney hadn't actually harmed the man. Maybe Keith was down in Kentucky somewhere, happily working with expensive purebreds at a high-falutin stable where Rodney would never think to look for him.

The thought comforted Molly even though the news of the trainer's sudden departure from Portland left her with more questions than answers. Had Sandusky revealed her whereabouts to Rodney before he left, or had he run before Rodney could force the information out of him?

Molly had no way of knowing. There was still a possibility that Rodney had learned of her whereabouts and was responsible for all the vandalism on the Lazy J. There was also a strong possibility that Sandusky had told Rodney nothing, which took her back to square one. Rodney couldn't be responsible for the vandalism if Sandusky hadn't told him where she was.

The blame for the fire and those slashed tires might be hers, after all.

"Where's Jake?" Molly asked Hank a few minutes later.

Jake's brother turned from the pile of poles they'd stripped for fencing. Beneath the brim of his hat, his burnished face glistened with sweat. "He went to town to buy tires and have it out with the insurance company."

Molly had hoped to talk to Jake before she lost her courage. "I thought all the trucks had flats." She glanced to the right of the house where the vehicles were parked. Jake's battered green Ford was there. "How did he get to town?"

"He went up the road and borrowed the neighbor's truck." Hank's gaze sharpened on her face. "Are you okay? You're pale as milk."

Molly wasn't okay. She wasn't sure if she'd ever be okay again. *"Someone's out to ruin me,"* Jake had cried this morning. She gazed out across his ranch. This was no longer about just her and Sunset. Jake Coulter's heritage was at stake. If she didn't take immediate steps to stop herself from doing any more damage, he could lose everything he owned.

Jake was gone until late afternoon, and immediately upon his return, he went to work building corrals with feverish determination. Since it was time for her to start cooking the evening meal, Molly decided to postpone talking to him until after dinner. He always saw her home once the kitchen was put to rights. That would be a perfect time to confess her sins to him.

Molly had no idea what she meant to say, only that somehow she had to get it said. She would leave nothing out. She'd tell him that she'd been lying to him from the start, that she'd brought this trouble to his door, and that she was sorry, so very sorry, for unintentionally hurting him.

Knowing what lay ahead, Molly could barely eat supper. Occasionally, she caught Jake watching her, his eyes dark with concern. She avoided his gaze, so upset and ashamed that it was all she could do to remain sitting at the table.

When dinner was over, Jake didn't stay to help her clean up as he usually did, and when the dishes were done, it was Hank who grabbed his hat and jacket to walk her home.

"Where's Jake?" Molly asked, scarcely able to believe he'd altered their usual routine. Not tonight when she most needed to see him.

"He crashed," Hank told her softly. "I don't think he's slept more than two hours, all totaled, since the fire. He's been running on nerves and caffeine."

As Molly passed through the living room, she saw Jake sprawled on the log-frame sofa. One arm angled over his eyes, he was snoring softly. He looked absolutely exhausted, and she was glad he was getting some rest. At the same time, she wanted to run over and shake him awake. She was desperately afraid she might lose her courage if she postponed talking to him.

Hank gently ushered her from the house. Once on the porch, he flashed her a grin. "I'm glad he didn't wake up. He'd insist on walking you himself."

Disheartened, Molly allowed Hank to guide her down the steps. Unlike Jake, he didn't detour to take her for a stroll, but headed directly for the cabin. Not that she wanted to go walking. She was too worried to appreciate the beauty of the stars tonight.

Once on her porch, Hank said, "If you don't mind, I'll do a quick walk-through." He stepped inside ahead of her. "When Jake wakes up, he's bound to ask if I made sure you were safe before I left."

Molly waited just inside the front door while Jake's brother made a fast tour of the cabin. When he returned to the living room, he said, "All clear."

"Thank you. I really don't think anyone would hide in here, but it's nice to have you check."

He stopped beside her and flipped the wall switch to turn on the floor lamp. "Three days ago, I wouldn't have believed anyone would hide in here, either. Now nothing would surprise me. Better to be safe than sorry."

"Right." Molly turned to watch him step out. As she pushed the door closed, she called, "Good night, Hank. Thanks for walking me over."

"Not a problem. G'night."

Molly shoved the dead bolt home. Then she pressed her forehead against the sturdy planks, weariness weighing heavily on her shoulders. What an awful day it had been.

The chill of the room seeped through her jacket, making her shiver. Grabbing the afghan that lay over the back of the sofa, she hurried over to lay a fire. A moment later, when the flames sprang to life, she stared vacantly at the licking tongues of orange, remembering the stable fire two nights before.

Tomorrow, she promised herself. She would take Jake aside first thing in the morning, and she would tell him everything.

Morning dawned bright and cold, a layer of frost dusting everything with silvery white in the first faint light of day. Molly bundled up in a jacket before she left the cabin, but even so, she shivered in the chill air. As she drew abreast of Sunset's pen, the stallion whickered and trotted over to the fence, clearly pleased to see her. Unable to walk by without stopping to say hello, Molly stepped up onto a rail and reached over to scratch between the horse's ears.

"I'm sorry," she whispered. "We no sooner make friends, and now I'm neglecting you. I just haven't had any time."

The stallion sniffed her jacket. Molly pressed her cheek to his velvety muzzle, wishing she could spend time with him that afternoon. Unfortunately, it might be impossible. Once she spoke to Jake, he could send her packing. He wasn't going to be happy when she told him her story.

Lifting her gaze, she looked out over the pastureland that bordered both sides of the creek for as far as she could see. This was Jake's heritage, a dream of his great-grandfather's that had been passed down through generations. He'd played here as a little boy, as his father had before him. Molly knew all about heritage and tradition, how the sentiment of it became even more important than the business itself. Wasn't that a large part of the reason she'd remained here, to give herself time to heal so she might return to Portland and reclaim her share of the firm her dad had built?

Now, because of her, Jake could lose the Lazy J. All his dreams and aspirations would be little more than dust in the wind, and it would be her fault. The thought brought tears to her eyes.

It was tempting to linger at Sunset's pen rather than go face him. She had dreaded doing a few things in her life, but this took the prize.

Swinging off the fence, she hurried across the stretch of gravel to the house. She kept her gaze carefully averted from the charred remains of the stable. About halfway up the front steps, Molly saw a brownish-red lump lying on the porch. Her knees almost buckled. It was a dead chicken. The poor thing's head had been chopped off. Crimson neck tendons straggled from the gaping wound.

She rushed to the edge of the porch, grabbed the rail, and promptly lost what little was in her stomach. When the spasms passed, she slowly straightened. A quick glance over her shoulder verified that it was a beheaded chicken, all right, or what was left of it, anyway. The poor creature's feathers were half gone, as if it had been mauled.

She gulped, fighting back another wave of nausea. Then she raced for the front door. Once inside the entry hall, she leaned against the log wall, hoping to calm down before she proceeded to the kitchen.

"How the *hell* should I know?" she heard Hank say. "Damn, Jake, I can't believe you're trying to pin all this on me."

Curious, Molly followed the voice toward the downstairs bathroom, situated to the left just off the hall. Halfway there, she heard Jake say, "Well, I sure as hell don't know her." A loud thump and what sounded like water splashing punctuated the statement. "If I find out that this is all the result of some fatal attraction, Hank, I swear, I'll kick your ass clear into next week."

"I haven't gone out with a woman in months, let alone some fruitcake who'd do something like this. Why automatically blame me, anyway? Like you never dated any women? I'll bet there's a Sarah somewhere in your black book."

"*What* black book? If I had one, I've long since lost track of it, and I've *never* dated a woman named Sarah." Silence. "Well, maybe one. But that was almost two years ago. If she was pissed because I stopped seeing her, why the hell did she wait until now to do something about it?"

Molly reached the bathroom just then. She stared bewilderedly through the open doorway. For an instant, her brain couldn't assimilate what her eyes were seeing. *Blood.* It was everywhere, all over the floor, all over the sink and commode. Her gaze jerked to the bathtub where Jake knelt on one knee, wringing out a crimson-stained cleaning rag. Above his shoulder, she saw writing of some kind on the white ceramic tile. She stared incredulously as the letters came into focus. *Sarah.* Someone had written the name in blood.

Molly heard the ocean in her ears. Black spots danced before her eyes. *Sarah.* Memories hit her, hard and fast. She gasped and whirled away, covering her face with her hands. *Sarah.* Oh, dear God.

She broke into a run, not sure where she was going, only knowing she had to get out.

"Molly!" Jake called.

She kept going. When she reached the front door, she remembered the dead chicken on the porch. Wheeling, she raced back through the house into the great room. From there, she spilled into the kitchen. She aimed her lurching steps for the back door. *Out*. She had to get out. Fresh air. She needed to *breathe*.

Once outside, she nearly fell down the back steps in her haste to escape.

After searching high and low, Jake finally found Molly sitting by the creek several minutes later. Arms wrapped around her upraised knees, she sat on the grassy bank, staring off at nothing, her face so pale it frightened him. He started to speak. Then he thought better of it and simply joined her instead.

When she made no offer to say anything, he ventured a soft, "Hi."

"Hi," she said thinly.

She sounded perilously close to tears. Believing she was upset about the chicken, Jake tucked one leg under his rump and bent the other, using his raised knee as a rest for his arm. He joined her in staring across the creek.

"If it's any consolation, honey, the chicken didn't suffer. Beheading is a quick and merciful way to kill them. I know it looked bad, but I think that was a result of someone swinging it around the bathroom after it was dead to spread its blood every damned place."

It took her a moment to respond. Her voice was faint and quavering. "I need to tell you something, Jake, and I don't know how to start."

Jake angled her a searching look. "Start with the first thing that comes to mind, honey. I won't critique your delivery."

She tried to smile, but the attempt was ruined by a tremulous wobble of her chin. Her big, butterscotch-brown eyes went luminous with tears. "I've been lying to you. From the very first, I've done nothing but lie."

Jake rubbed a hand over his face and blinked. That came as no surprise. He'd always known she was lying to him about certain things.

"My last name, for instance. It isn't Houston like I said. It's really Sterling Wells. It'll be just Sterling when I legally drop my married name."

Jake arched an eyebrow. "Is that what this is about, honey? The fact that you've lied about a few things?"

"Not just a few things," she protested shakily. "About practically *everything*. And all of this"—she swung her hand to indicate the ranch—"has been my fault, if not directly, then indirectly, and the end result is the same, either way. You've been pushed to the edge of bankruptcy."

He wanted so badly to hug her. Seeing her cry nearly broke his heart. "I thought you were upset over the silly chicken."

Another rush of tears filled her eyes. "It upsets me, all right. I didn't think I had it in me to kill anything. Now just look at what I may have done."

"What?" Jake said carefully, convinced his ears had deceived him.

"You heard me." With trembling hands, she wiped her cheeks and sniffed. Then she bent her head. "I may have done this. I could have done all of it." She cupped a hand over her eyes. "I'm so *sorry*. Please, forgive me, Jake. I'm so very, very sorry. I'll make it up to you one day, I swear. I'll pay you for all the damages."

"Whoa. Back up. I'm getting confused. Why do you think you might have done all this? The deputy who came out when we called seemed pretty sure some gal named Sarah did it." Heat crawled up Jake's neck. "A scorned lover of mine or Hank's who's come back to haunt us."

She looked at him as if he'd lost his mind. "First kids set fire to your stable and slash all the tires, and now a scorned lover paints her name all over your bathroom in blood?"

Jake knew it sounded far-fetched. The local law enforcement officials seemed more interested in offering explanations for all the bizarre incidents than in actually catching the perpetrator. "If someone named Sarah didn't do it, who did?"

Molly steepled her fingers. "Trust me, Sarah didn't write her name on your tile. She couldn't have." Her chin wobbled again. "She's been dead for almost eleven years."

Jake was growing more confused by the moment. He was about to make her back up and start all over when he heard Hank shout his name. He glanced up to see his brother waving at him from across the creek.

"You need to come up to the house!" he yelled. "We've got trouble."

Jake could believe it. Lately trouble had been raining buckets. He groaned and pushed to his feet. "I'm sorry, honey. I'd better go see what the hell has happened now." He leaned down to offer her a hand. "Come back with me. As soon as I get a minute, we'll find a quiet place to talk."

As he drew her to her feet, she threw a worried look toward the house. "Oh, God, I wonder what it is this time."

He flashed what he hoped was a reassuring grin. "Unless the house is burning down, it can't be too bad. Right?"

She didn't return his smile. "I'm so sorry, Jake." She lifted a tear-filled gaze to his, her expression filled with hopeless resignation. "Please believe that. I never meant to hurt you."

Jake cupped a hand to her cheek. Thumbing away a tear, he said, "Sweetheart, you don't even need to say it. I know you didn't."

After all the recent vandalism on the Lazy J, Molly wasn't surprised to see the sheriff's Bronco parked out front when they drew near the house.

What did stop her cold was the cream-colored Lexus nosed in behind the county vehicle. She'd been half expecting Rodney to show up, but seeing his car was still a shock.

Her stomach dropped when the driver door opened and her ex-husband climbed out, looking just as she remembered him. Impeccably dressed, as always, he seemed taller to her as he unfolded to his full height. Walking toward them, he brushed the wrinkles from the sleeves of his expensive gray suit jacket, then straightened his tie and ran a hand over his perfectly groomed blond hair. Even at a distance, Molly could see the gleam of cunning and intelligence in his hazel eyes.

In that instant she knew, almost beyond a shadow of a doubt, that he'd been behind every awful incident at the ranch. There was no mistaking that little smirk. She'd seen it a hundred times—when he lied to her about his women, when he was trying to cover up his gambling. It was a smirk that said, *"I'm so phenomenal, and you are so incredibly stupid."*

Her first thought was to run. "Oh, God," she whispered to Jake, her footsteps faltering again.

He gave her a sharp look then snaked out a hand to grab her arm. Even through the sleeve of her jacket, she could feel the steely strength of his fingers. "Rodney?" he asked.

Molly nodded stupidly, shudders racking her body as she reached to dislodge his grip. He tightened his hold. She cast a frantic glance around her.

"Please, Jake? You have no idea what he'll do!"

"Don't," he whispered when she tried to jerk away. "He can't hurt you, honey. Not here. There's no reason to be afraid."

There was every reason, Molly thought wildly. She knotted her hands into fists. Had Rodney enlisted the help of law enforcement agencies to find her? Or had he coerced Keith Sandusky into telling him her whereabouts? Mingled with the jumble of questions in Molly's mind was one clear thought, that she hated Rodney Wells with a virulence to last a lifetime.

Recalling the blood in Jake's bathroom, she quaked with trepidation. Always before, there had been a dual purpose behind Rodney's pranks, the primary one being to frighten her and make her doubt her own sanity, while at the same time convincing others she was crazy. Now he'd shifted his focus, his chief purpose to cast her in as bad a light as possible. The *bastard*. He'd staged that bathroom mess entirely for Jake's benefit, trying to make her look crazier than a loon.

Pain lanced behind her eyes. The truth would come out now. She had hoped to tell Jake herself. Now he would hear Rodney's version of the story instead.

An awful feeling of resignation settled in her chest. The taste of defeat was as bitter as gall at the back of her throat. Rodney was a silver-tongued liar, and nothing she said or did was going to stop him from talking. He would tell Jake everything, putting his own wicked spin on the story. Jake would hand her over into his care, and she would soon be staring at bare white walls again. It was as simple as that.

Rodney flashed an oily smile as he neared them. His spit-shined Italian loafers glinted in the morning sunlight. "Molly," he said softly. "I've been worried about you, darling. What a relief it is to see that you're all right."

It was all Molly could do not to fly at him with her claws bared. Oh, how she detested him. Her eyes dry and burning, she stared at him. She was effectively trapped, and there was nothing she could do. *Nothing*. Even worse, he knew it. She didn't miss the mocking gleam in his eyes as he turned his smile on Jake.

Sheriff Dexter avoided looking at Molly as he stepped forward. "Good morning, Jake," he said softly, as if he hoped Molly wouldn't overhear if he kept his voice pitched low. "I've got bad news, I'm afraid."

"What's that?" Jake asked. He shot a glittering glance at Rodney before shifting his gaze back to the lawman.

The sheriff darted a glance at Molly. "You're not going to like it."

Molly felt Jake's hand stiffen on her arm.

The sheriff cleared his throat. "This young woman hasn't been up front with you, I'm afraid. Are you aware that she was only recently released from a mental hospital?"

Jake glanced at Molly, then back at the sheriff. "There's very little about Molly that I don't know."

"I see. Can I take that to mean you're also aware that she left Portland in defiance of a court order mandating that she see her therapist twice a week?" The lawman narrowed his eyes. "Be careful how you answer that." He hooked a thumb toward Sunset's pen. "Not only have you been harboring an emotionally disturbed young woman who needs treatment, but you've aided and abetted her in grand theft."

A muscle in Jake's cheek started to tic. "Grand theft?" he said softly. "Call it what you like, Dexter, but in my opinion, it was a grand rescue. I've every confidence the Humane Society will agree with me."

"Don't draw a line in the dirt, son," the sheriff advised. "I've got no real quarrel with you, and I'd like to keep it that way." He inclined his head at Molly, no longer bothering to keep his voice down. "This woman is an emotional powder keg with a documented history of committing violent acts while sleepwalking. I'm convinced now that she has been responsible for all the vandalism out here—not juveniles, like we thought." The sheriff gestured toward Rodney. "The lady's husband has come to collect her and take her back home so she can get the treatment she needs."

Silence. Molly died a little with each passing second. There was nothing she could do but stand there while her fate was decided. Jake would undoubtedly hand her over to Rodney now. Why wouldn't he? He was probably absolutely furious with her. And who could blame him?

Jake bent his head, his expression thoughtful. When he finally lifted his gaze back to the sheriff, he was frowning. "I'm sorry. You say this man's her husband? You've got it all wrong." Jake glanced at Rodney. "Molly is divorced from Mr. Wells. He no longer has any control over her."

Rodney stepped forward. Just as Molly had imagined he might, he gave Jake a charming smile. "You're right. We are divorced, but that doesn't mean I no longer care about what happens to her—or that I'm completely cut out of the picture. Things aren't quite that cut and dry with a woman in Molly's condition. She never should have been granted a divorce in the first place. She wasn't thinking clearly when she made that decision. By court order, I'm also, to all intents and purposes, her legal guardian. And we still have strong family ties as well." He glanced over his shoulder and crooked a finger, beckoning to someone in his car. "Her adoptive mother, Claudia, is now my dad's wife."

Molly glanced over just as the rear doors of the Lexus opened. Out stepped Jared Wells on one side, Claudia on the other. Jared looked just as he always had, an older version of his handsome son with a touch of steel gray in his blond hair. But the same couldn't be said for Claudia. Always impeccably dressed, she looked uncharacteristically rumpled in her expensive beige suit. As she picked her way closer on wobbly high heels, Molly saw that she had tears in her blue eyes, which were underscored with dark circles.

Being a Judas was obviously interfering with her sleep.

Molly knew then that she was lost. Only a miracle could help her now. Her ex-husband, her mom, and her new stepfather were all in cahoots against her. *Poor little Molly. It's time to lock her away.* It was the only kind and responsible thing to do.

When Claudia drew abreast of Rodney, she fixed an aching gaze on Molly. Her mouth trembled into a tearful smile. "You changed your hair," she said in a squeaky voice. Her face twisted, and she pressed her fingers to her mouth, looking at Molly through swimming tears. "My little girl. You're so beautiful. I love it done that way."

Rodney curled a comforting arm around Claudia's shoulders and drew her close to his body. He sent a commiserating look at his dad. To Jake, he said, "Have a heart, Mr. Coulter. By resisting the inevitable, you're only putting innocent people through a lot of unnecessary pain. As you can see, Molly is deeply loved. We're only trying to get her home to Portland so we can get her some help. She hasn't been herself for a very long while, I'm afraid." He turned his smile on Molly and reached to take her arm. "Come along, darling. Let us get you in the car."

Before Rodney could touch her, Jake shot out a hand and grabbed his wrist. "Keep your hands to yourself, buddy."

Molly threw an incredulous look at Jake. She'd never seen him truly angry until now, and the sight was frightening. His blue eyes glittered like chipped ice, and a ruddy flush had darkened his burnished features. "The lady isn't going anywhere she doesn't choose to go. Got it?"

Hank, who'd moved up onto the porch, descended the steps to stand behind his brother. From the corner of her eye, Molly saw the hired hands gathering around as well. Their message was clear. She had more than one man to defend her. Even Tex, with his bad shoulder, had joined the ranks.

She stared up at Jake's dark face through a blur of tears. *Trust.* She had vowed never to give hers easily again, but she hadn't known Jake Coulter then. Was he real, this man? She didn't deserve this kind of loyalty, not from him or his men. From the very start, she'd lied to him and kept things from him. Now, instead of abandoning her, he was protecting her. She could scarcely believe it.

Rodney looked imploringly at Molly. "Don't involve these nice people in this, Molly. Haven't you caused them enough grief?"

Molly couldn't have spoken if she tried.

"You need treatment," Rodney went on gently. "Let us take you home to see the doctor." He gave her a cajoling smile. "I know you blame me for everything. But, Molly, *think.* Is that really reasonable? Surely you can't believe that I set you up this time." He shook his head slightly. "You've been cut off from Sam Banks for only three weeks, and just look what you've done. You don't want to stay here and do anything more. What will it be next time, the house?"

Molly knew that she had caused Jake more than enough trouble. Even though she no longer believed she'd been directly responsible, she'd set him up as Rodney's target by staying here.

"One way or another, we have to take you back," Rodney went on. "Like it or not, you've been deemed legally incompetent, and we're responsible for you."

Claudia sent Molly an imploring look. "It's true, sweetie." She swung her hand toward the burned stable. "Until a judge reverses that decision, we're both responsible for you, which makes us liable. If you won't think of us, think of the firm and all that your father worked for. Do you really want to jeopardize that?" A single tear slid down Claudia's cheek. "If I were sick, wouldn't you do everything you could to make sure I got help? That's all we want to do, darling, just get you some help. Soon, you'll be well, and then you can come home. Won't that be nice?"

"You know we love you, Molly," Jared inserted. "Trust us to do what's best for you."

They spoke as if they were addressing a very small child. Molly's head hurt. Their voices bounced around inside her mind. She wanted to scream at them to go away, to just leave her alone. With relatives like these, who needed enemies?

"We can do it the easy way, or we can do it the hard way," Rodney interjected. "It's your choice, Molly. Just bear in mind that your friends may get in a lot of Dutch if they run afoul of the law, trying to help you."

"Don't listen to him, Molly," Jake interrupted.

Molly threw him an agonized look. "I've caused you enough grief, Jake."

"And you'll cause me even more if you listen to this bullshit and go with them," Jake retorted. "You're no crazier than I am."

Molly cupped a hand over her eyes. "Oh, *God*. I don't know anymore. I just don't know."

Jake's grip firmed over her arm. "You're just upset right now. Fortunately, I'm thinking quite clearly."

"Stay out of this, Mr. Coulter," Rodney warned.

Claudia drew away from Rodney and stepped closer. She fixed Jake with an imploring look. "I'm her mother. I sat up with her when she was sick. I was the one who put money under her pillow for the tooth fairy. Do you really believe I have anything but her best interests at heart?"

"No, I don't think that," Jake replied softly. "I'm sure you believe you're doing the right thing. Nevertheless, you're not taking her anywhere, not without a court order, which you obviously don't have. If you did, you'd be waving it under my nose."

Bright spots of angry red flagged Rodney's cheeks. "You're making a grave mistake, buster."

Sheriff Dexter scratched his jaw. "There's no point in this, Jake. Why is a court order necessary? We all have the same aim in mind, to do what's best for the lady. She's ill, and she needs help. You aren't doing her any favors by preventing her family from taking her back where she belongs."

"You're right about one thing," Jake agreed. "I have only Molly's best interests at heart, and the way I see it, she's best off remaining here on the Lazy J with people who truly care about her."

"Just one moment," Rodney interrupted coolly. "Are you suggesting that her own mother doesn't care about her? Or that I don't? She's my wife, damn it."

"Ex-wife," Jake reminded him. "And your feelings for her don't count for squat. She doesn't care about you. That's the bottom line."

Rodney's eyes sparked with fury. "Only because she's hopelessly confused right now. Stop and think. She needs hospital care, which can be very expensive. We can afford to give her that care. Can you?" Rodney shook his head. "We know Molly's history. We understand her as no one else does, and we'll take excellent care of her. You needn't worry on that score. She'll be in good hands."

"I know she'll be in good hands," Jake replied, "because she'll be staying here with me, end of discussion." He shot a look at the sheriff. "I don't believe she's sick. What's more, I know for a fact she wasn't responsible for the vandalism here." He glanced apologetically at Molly. "I've never been one to kiss and tell, but in this instance, I'll make an exception. Molly has been sharing my bed since shortly after she came here. I sleep with one eye open, and I know for a fact that she never left my side on the nights the vandalism occurred."

Molly's heart caught. She gaped at Jake, scarcely able to believe he would tell such a bald-faced lie to protect her.

The sheriff shifted his weight, angled Molly an appalled glance, and said, "Begging your pardon, ma'am. I never meant to falsely accuse you. I was told that—" He broke off and shot an accusing look at Rodney. "Well, never mind that. If you weren't responsible for the trouble, I apologize."

Molly swallowed to steady her voice. "That's all right, Sheriff. I know you're only trying to do your job."

"That's right." The lawman rubbed beside his nose and coughed. "Well, Mr. Wells? It would appear that you'll need a court order to remove the lady from the premises. Until you've obtained one, our business here is finished."

Rodney jabbed a finger at Jake. "I'll be back. Count on it. Not just for my wife, but my horse as well."

If Jake was intimidated by Rodney's threatening manner, he didn't reveal it by so much as a flicker of an eyelid. Instead he smiled. "You don't even want to open that can of worms, Wells. The horse stays right where he is."

"We'll see about that."

Jake's grin broadened. "My brother and I had the foresight to take dated photographs of that stallion when it first arrived to document his deplorable condition. He was one big, bloody lash mark, as you very well know, and the snapshots developed out in sharp detail. We also had the good sense to call out a vet who's willing to testify that it took a man's strength to cut the animal that deeply with a whip. You want to take it to court, Mr. Wells? Fine by me. In fact, it would do my heart good. I'm of the opinion that no man should be able to abuse an animal like that without paying the price. There are laws against that sort of thing, you know, and you'll find yourself in more trouble than you can handle if you make any for me."

"You have no proof whatsoever that I've ever lifted a hand to that stallion."

"There's where you're wrong." Jake glanced toward Sunset's pen. "In this instance, the proof will come straight from the horse's mouth. Walk over and climb in that corral."

Rodney followed Jake's gaze and paled visibly. "What kind of game is this?"

"Go on," Jake said sharply. "Say hello to your horse, Mr. Wells. If you never lifted a hand to him, he should be glad to see you."

Rodney bit out a curse. He leveled a long, hot glare at Molly before he spun on his heel and stalked back to his car, brushing past Claudia and Jared as if they weren't there. "You haven't seen the last of me!" he vowed. "Get your bags packed, Molly. I'll have that court order when you see me next. Don't think I won't. Your big, tough cowboy will find himself on the wrong side of the law if he interferes then!"

Claudia wrung her hands, her tearful gaze clinging to Molly's accusing one. "I know you question my love for your father now, Molly. That's a discussion for another day. But surely you have no doubt that I love you."

Molly ached to throw herself in her mom's arms. But this woman had remarried only a few months after her father's suspicious death and then abandoned her when she needed her the most. How could she be sure Claudia wasn't part of the plot to rob her of her inheritance? Any right-thinking person would seriously question her sincerity.

Rodney climbed inside the Lexus and slammed the door with such force that the side mirror vibrated. "Come on, Dad! We're wasting our time. We'll have to get the damned court order before we can do anything more."

Jared stepped over to take Claudia's arm. "Sweetheart?" he said gently.

Claudia nodded and curled a hand over Jared's, but her pleading gaze remained fixed on Molly. After a long moment, she shifted her attention to Jake. "If anything happens to her, Mr. Coulter, I will hold you personally responsible," she said shakily. "Do you understand me? If a single hair on her head has been hurt when we return, you'll rue the day you met me."

"I'll guard her with my life," Jake assured her.

"Come on, honey," Jared murmured.

Claudia allowed herself to be drawn away. Looking back over her shoulder as they drew near the Lexus, she called, "I love you, sweetie. Never doubt it."

Molly watched stonily as her adoptive mother and new stepfather disappeared into the back of the vehicle. The doors slammed simultaneously with a punctuation of finality. An instant later, the car engine roared to life. Tromping on the gas pedal, Rodney threw gravel with the tires as he backed up to turn around.

The sheriff sighed and shook his head as the Lexus disappeared over the rise. "Wells is right, you know," he told Jake. "You'll be on the wrong side of the law if you interfere when they show up with a court order."

"I'll cross that bridge when I come to it," Jake said softly.

Dexter nodded. "I have to do my job, Jake. Just so long as you understand that. If Wells gets a judge in his corner, this could get nasty."

"I know that, Dex." Jake extended a hand to him. "Just do what the taxpayer pays you to do. I'll worry about things at my end."

The sheriff nodded, his eyes reflecting displeasure with the entire situation. "Ma'am," he said, touching the brim of his hat and inclining his head. "Sorry to make your acquaintance under such unhappy circumstances. I hope our next meeting is more pleasant."

Molly hoped so, too. But somehow, knowing Rodney, she doubted it would be.

The sheriff left, and in less time than it took to draw a deep breath, Molly found herself being propelled up the steps to the house by her "big, tough cowboy." Jake's grip on her elbow didn't exactly hurt, but she could tell by the taut dig of his fingertips that he was furious.

Feeling like flotsam carried forth on a wave, she was pushed through the house and into the kitchen, where he jerked out a chair, pressed her onto the seat, and proceeded to lean down to glare at her, nose to nose. Molly inched her head back, intimidated in spite of herself. Under the best of circumstances, Jake Coulter was a lot of man to contend with. In a temper, he seemed to loom over her like a tree.

"Emotionally unstable, Molly? Sweet Christ. What else haven't you told me?"

There was so much she hadn't told him—so very much.

"What in God's name were you thinking?" he cried. "The bastard means to lock you up. Do you realize that? Why in the hell didn't you tell me?" He grasped her by the shoulders and gave her a little shake. "*Why?* If your mom backs him on this, you don't stand the chance of a snowball in hell. She's your closest living relative. You've already been in a clinic. There's a documented history of sleepwalking. They've already had you claimed legally incompetent. Who's going to believe they're lying if they say you need more treatment?"

"Nobody!" Molly cried. His anger had transmitted itself to her, and before she thought it through, she shot up from the chair, forcing him to rear back so their faces wouldn't collide. "Which is exactly why I was afraid to tell you. I was terrified you'd think I was nuts!"

"I never would have thought that."

"When should I have talked to you, Jake? The first night, maybe? 'Oh, by the way, please don't be alarmed, but I should probably mention that I was just released from a mental ward.' Or maybe later? Let me see. When would have been a good time? It's such an easy thing to tell someone, after all. I was afraid you'd think the worst and call Rodney."

His grip on her shoulders relaxed, and his eyes went dark with what looked like sadness. "You should have trusted me," he whispered. "They could have shown up a week ago, Molly. I could have come in from the fields and found you gone."

"They're going to take me back, anyway. What difference does it make?"

"They'll take you off this ranch over my dead body."

Molly stared up at him through a blur of tears. A thousand times over the last year, she'd wished for just one person besides her doctor whom she could trust, completely and without reservation. Now, here was Jake, willing to take on the world for her without even knowing for sure what he was up against.

"Oh, Jake," she said tremulously. "Who's the crazy one, you or me?"

He ran his big hands up and down her arms. "I'm crazy about you.

Does that work? I don't need to know what I'm biting off. He's not taking you anywhere."

Tears blurred her vision. "You won't be able to stop him," she said shakily. "You heard the sheriff. You'll only get in a lot of trouble if you try. Rodney will get his court order"—she snapped her fingers—"just like that, and he'll be back, probably with a police escort or the sheriff, to return me to Portland. I'm just his fruitcake ex-wife who, he'll be fast to inform a judge, obtained a divorce while she was institutionalized and not of sound mind. He has control of my father's half of the investment firm, control over my inheritance, and, by extension, control over *me*. My own mom has joined ranks against me. As much as I appreciate your wanting to, there's nothing you can do. They want my money, and to that end, they'll do anything to cut me out of the picture."

"No one can come onto my land and drag my wife away."

Molly blinked, convinced she hadn't heard him correctly. "I'm not your wife."

"Yet." He slipped his hands back up to her shoulders and firmed his grip. "Molly, how much do you trust me?"

Her heart lurched. "A lot, but not that much."

"Let me put it to you another way. Who do you trust more, me or Rodney?"

"That's not a fair question."

"Life isn't always fair, and right now, honey, it's throwing you a mean curve ball. I'm your only ace in the hole. We can be in Reno in five hours. As your husband, my legal rights will circumvent theirs. Even if they fight the legitimacy of the marriage in court, it'll take them months to do anything. Meanwhile, we can come up with another plan."

"Oh, *God*." The air suddenly seemed too thin. No matter how deeply Molly grabbed for breath, she couldn't get enough oxygen. "Reno?"

"When we get back, we'll be man and wife. Rodney's power over you will be history. Claudia's will be as well. From that point on, your only worry will be me."

Molly refocused on his dark face. "And you're a triviality?"

"Compared to them, I am."

ॐ CHAPTER EIGHTEEN ॐ

When Jake made up his mind to act, he didn't waste time second-guessing himself. Within thirty minutes, he had Molly bundled into his ranch truck and was breaking the speed limit to reach Reno. She sat in a huddle against the passenger-side door. There was a vacant look in her eyes that worried him.

"Sweetheart, you look scared to death." He gave her what he hoped was an understanding smile. "Am I such a bad proposition?" He glanced in the rearview mirror and swiped at his tousled hair. "I clean up fairly nice."

"It's nothing to do with you. I just don't want to be married again."

"Because I'll have control over your life?"

"That's one reason, plus a dozen others."

"Let's deal with one at a time. First the control issue. I have no intention of trying to control you. If that's how it was with Rodney, don't look for a repeat performance. Control isn't my thing." Taking in her sassy new hairstyle and the pretty pink blouse she was wearing, he could add with all honesty, "You've got good instincts. Within reason, you can do whatever the hell you want. I won't try to stop you."

"Within reason?"

Jake tamped down his annoyance at the question. "Yes, within reason. If you decide to walk a tightrope across the Grand Canyon without a safety net, I may have something to say about it."

She bent her head. When he glanced over, he thought he glimpsed a smile flirting at the corners of her mouth. When she finally looked up, she said, "I don't mean to be difficult. I should be thanking my lucky stars you've offered to do this. I'm sorry."

"I'm offering because I care about you, and for no other reason."

A distant look came into her eyes again.

Jake parted his lips to speak, then clamped his teeth closed, thinking long and hard before he said anything more, which was a virtue that didn't come easily for him. He'd spent most of his life speaking his mind.

He didn't blame Molly for being upset. She'd had a horrific morning, and though he still hadn't heard all the details, he had reason to believe the incident today was only the icing on the cake. He didn't want to say anything that might make matters worse.

Unfortunately, the way he saw it, there were matters they absolutely had to discuss. "Is it the sex that's worrying you?"

Her face drained of color. "Actually, I was hoping we might bypass that part. I have a really bad track record."

Jake shot her another look. "In your dreams. I want this to be a real marriage, Molly, not just a stopgap measure to hold Rodney at bay."

"I was afraid you were thinking that."

"Afraid? Your reasoning eludes me."

"I just don't want to go through all that again. I loved Rodney when I married him, and I believed he loved me. Then, in a twinkling, my fairy tale turned into a nightmare."

Jake mulled that over. The statement smacked of heartbreak. "Did your marriage to Rodney really go sour that fast?" he asked cautiously.

She laughed bitterly. "Our marriage went sour the first night. Rodney got drunk, deflowered his bride, and then passed out. And *that* was the highlight. After that, he mostly didn't bother. When he did, he had to charge his batteries by looking at porn magazines."

Jake felt sick. An awful, rolling nausea. He tightened his hands over the steering wheel, wishing it were Rodney Wells's neck.

"Remember that morning in the woods, Molly? How can you think it'll be anything less than wonderful between us?"

"Experience."

That was all she said, just that one word, but it conveyed a world of heartache. Jake wished he knew what to say to her—anything to take the wariness and apprehension from her eyes. But try as he might, he could think of nothing but platitudes. How could he assure her it would be different between them? How could he promise that he'd find her body attractive when he'd never actually seen it? More important, how could he guarantee that she'd enjoy intimacy with him? He could have all the best intentions and desire her with every fiber of his being, but unless she met him halfway with desire in equal measure, their lovemaking would fall far short of perfection.

Jake had never been a man to make promises he wasn't sure he could keep. He wasn't about to start now. Better to simply get a ring on her finger and deal with each issue as it presented itself, doing his best to make the marriage work.

That decided, he focused his attention on the road, hating the wall of silence between them, but feeling uncertain how to breach it.

Once in Reno, Jake made fast work of finding a parking place in a pay lot across from a supermarket. Just one block over was the main drag where casinos, hockshops, jewelry stores, and twenty-four-hour chapels lined the crowded sidewalks. He helped Molly from the truck, locked her door, and led her toward the street. She moved beside him like a well-programmed android, replying in a flat monotone when he asked a direct question, her movements rigid, her face pinched and pale. He felt like an executioner leading a condemned person to the guillotine.

Glancing at his watch, Jake decided he could afford to blow a little time before he herded her to a chapel. It was only shortly after noon. Maybe if he took her to lunch, she'd calm down a little and get some color back in her cheeks.

He found a nice café in the Eldorado casino, which had been remodeled since his last visit several years ago. He guided Molly to a booth, helped her out of her parka, and then took a seat across from her. Avoiding his gaze, she toyed nervously with the Keno cards and then pretended intense interest in the game rules.

"Would you like to try your luck?" he asked.

She shook her head and put the instructions back into the plastic holder. "No, thanks. I'm not very lucky. I've never won anything in my life."

Wrong. She'd won his heart. Jake studied her pale face, aching to see her smile. He was starting to feel like the world's biggest jerk for pushing her into this. Only, when he considered the alternatives, he honestly couldn't think of any other way to help her. With both Rodney and Claudia joined against her, she was in an extremely precarious legal position, vulnerable in a way that frightened him. By marrying her, he could protect her, at least temporarily. She'd be his wife. He would be able to block any attempts to have her institutionalized.

Jake realized he was mindlessly stirring his coffee, the spoon clacking loudly against the cup. He froze, staring stupidly into the black liquid. Normally, he used no sweetener, and he couldn't think why he'd chosen to now. Nerves, he guessed.

The waitress came for their order. Molly requested only a green salad with blue cheese dressing on the side. Since she'd eaten no breakfast, Jake didn't feel a salad was enough to sustain her until dinner that night.

After placing his own order, he asked, "Do you have a good garden burger?" When the waitress assured him that they did, he said, "In addition to the salad, the lady will have a garden burger and a bowl of fresh fruit as well, please."

As the waitress walked away, Molly fixed Jake with a sparking gaze made all the more vivid by her pallor. The tendons along her throat swelled to form pulsating cords at each side of her larynx. "Why did you do that?" she asked tautly.

"You need to eat, sweetheart."

Before Jake could guess her intent, she swept her arm across the table, sending the silverware flying and catching her coffee cup with the back of her hand. Hot liquid sprayed up and outward, a good measure of it spilling onto his lap. He shot up from his seat.

"Holy *hell*!" He swiped at his fly with his napkin, barely managing to bite back a string of colorful expletives. "What on earth possessed you to do that?"

She leaped to her feet as well. Hands knotted into fists at her sides, she jutted her chin and gave him a wild-eyed look. "How dare you? We aren't even married yet, and already you're taking over. If I wanted a garden burger, I would have ordered one."

Jake could scarcely believe his ears. "You just doused me with scalding hot coffee over a stupid *sandwich*?" He resisted the urge to dance and grab his crotch. *Pain*. No more worries about sex tonight. He wouldn't be functional for a week. "Don't you think you're overreacting just a little?"

"Go ahead. Make light of it." She jabbed his chest with her finger. "It's only a sandwich, after all. Why should it upset me that you consider it your right to decide what I'm going to eat?"

Jake realized they were causing a scene. He glanced uneasily around. People were gaping. An old lady to his left held a forkful of food poised before her parted lips, her eyes wide with stunned amazement.

"Keep your voice down," he whispered to Molly. "People are staring."

"Let them!" she cried. "Who cares?" To Jake's horror, she whirled around. "If any of you women are here to get married," she cried in a shrill, hysterical voice, "think twice! It may be the biggest mistake of your life!"

After screaming that pronouncement, she swept past Jake as if all the demons of hell were nipping at her heels. He barely managed to catch hold of her arm. "Where the Sam Hill do you think you're going?"

"To the ladies' room!" She tried to free her arm. When Jake tightened his hold, she turned up her volume. "Or are you going to start telling me when I can use the bathroom, too?"

That cut it. Jake turned her loose. Keeping an eye on her as she stormed from the café so he'd know in which direction she went, he tossed some money on the table, took a final swipe at his jeans with the soaked napkin, and made a fast exit himself.

The silence in the ladies' lounge soothed Molly's frazzled nerves. She sat forward on the sofa, elbows on her knees, head in her hands. The multicolored pattern of the carpet blurred in her vision, and tears tickled her nostrils as they dripped from the end of her nose. She was shaking, and no matter how hard she tried, she couldn't seem to stop.

Marriage. She couldn't go through with it. She just couldn't. No matter what Jake said, she'd feel like a prison inmate, and for her, it would be a lifelong sentence. Be it in a Reno chapel or a church, she couldn't make vows before God when she had no intention of keeping them.

Until death do us part.

Love, honor, and obey.

How many times had Rodney reminded her of the promises she had made when she married him? It hadn't mattered that he was breaking all the rules himself. It hadn't mattered if his disregard of those marital tenets was making her miserably unhappy. Rodney had never given a flip about anyone but himself. She'd been left to preserve the union as best she could, which had boiled down to swallowing her pride countless times each day, looking the other way, and smiling when she wanted to scream, all to save a marriage that shouldn't have happened in the first place.

Never again. Molly clenched her fingers into tight fists over her hair. If she wanted salad for lunch, she would damned well eat salad. She was finished with being pushed around.

Reaching that decision made her feel somewhat better. She wiped her cheeks and gazed blankly at the flocked paper on the opposite wall. One question circled endlessly in her head. If marriage was out of the question, what exactly was she going to do? No ideas came to her mind. Her adoptive mother was apparently in cahoots with her ex-husband, and there was every possibility that the two of them could manipulate the court system to have her put back in a sanitarium. To avoid that, Molly needed a champion in her corner, someone who could legally circumvent the court process already in play. As her husband, Jake would have the clout to do that.

A swimmy, disoriented feeling came over Molly. Back to square one. Always back to square one. Did other people find themselves in situations where there seemed to be no way out? Or was it just her? *Jake*. He was her only ace in the hole, as he'd so aptly put it.

For a moment, she considered running. She had no doubt that Jake would care for Sunset. He was nothing if not an animal lover. A surge of hope filled her. The casino was crammed with people. She could easily slip out of the lounge, get lost in the crowd, and exit the building by a back door. There was probably a bus depot nearby. She could buy a one-way ticket to anywhere, change her identity, and leave the past forever behind.

The thought was wonderfully appealing, but then Molly thought of all she would be abandoning, not only the firm, half of which was her birthright, but her dad's estate as well, which he'd worked all his life to acquire. She'd also be abandoning the few precious dreams she still had—to one day sit behind her father's desk, to gain recognition in the field of finance and carry on the Sterling tradition. And what of her determination to see Rodney punished? If she bailed out now, her father's death would be swept under the rug as a suicide. Even worse, his killer would gain control of his assets. That would be the final and ultimate insult to Marshal Sterling's memory, forever tarnishing everything he'd stood for all his life.

Molly couldn't allow that to happen. Besides, even if she did want to run, what could she buy a bus ticket with, her good looks? She glanced down at her pretty new blouse, thinking of all the money she'd so foolishly spent on clothes. She was all but broke now. The little money she had left was in her purse. At last count, there'd been just over a hundred dollars.

Her heart caught as she glanced stupidly around her. Where *was* her purse, anyway?

Oh, dear God. She'd left it in the café.

A hysterical urge to laugh came over her. She wasn't just broke; she was *penniless*. She didn't have the money to buy a cup of coffee, let alone a bus ticket.

The realization brought her staggering to her feet. Jake was undoubtedly furious over her behavior in the eatery. What if he had left? That was exactly what Rodney would do, she knew. Bad behavior was always punished. What better way to punish someone than to leave her stranded for a few days? No money equated to no lodging and no food.

Oh, God—oh, God. Molly imagined herself wandering the streets, digging in dumpsters for morsels of nourishment. If she sought shelter in the casinos at night, she'd be tossed out on her ear by security guards the instant she fell asleep. Inside of two days, she'd be half-starved, dead on her feet, and ready to kiss Jake Coulter's boots while she begged for forgiveness. If he took a page out of Rodney's book, he would grant her absolution only under certain terms.

Molly's heart was pounding so loudly that her eardrums felt as if they might burst. She had to find Jake and apologize before he took off and left her. Even now, he could be back at the truck, preparing to leave. *No, no, no.* She was better off getting married. Facing penury in Reno was not a pretty picture. She doubted it was a city that was kind to the homeless. People were far too involved with gambling and counting their losses to be in a charitable mood.

Molly hit the swinging door with such force, her shoulder thudded against the wood. Her legs felt curiously disconnected from her brain as she spilled from the lounge into the casino area. The noise of the slots immediately pummeled her, jackpot bells ringing loudly, the whirring sounds of the machines and soft blips of music compounding to create a computerized cacophony.

She tried to blank it out. *Jake.* Where would he have gone? She had to find him. If she apologized, maybe he would forgive her and go ahead with the marriage.

"Molly?"

About to plunge through the milling crowd to go in search of him, Molly was jerked up short by his deep voice. She whirled around, scarcely able to believe her eyes when she saw him sitting on a padded bench just outside the ladies' lounge. One long leg extended, the opposite knee raised, he was slumped on the seat, his Stetson settled low over his eyes.

In that lazy, slow-as-molasses way of his, he pushed to his feet. As he sauntered toward her, she saw that he held her purse clutched in one big fist. She pressed a hand to the base of her throat to slow her galloping heart.

"I was afraid you had left."

He arched a dark eyebrow. "Why the hell would I do that?"

He thrust the purse at her. When she took it, he clamped a hand over her arm. Molly braced for the cruel bite of his fingers, expecting him to exert unneeded pressure in his anger. Instead, his grip was only firm, not bruising.

"Call me bossy and overbearing if you want, but don't you *ever* run off like that again. Not without telling me *exactly* where you're going first. Do you have any idea the kind of creeps who hang around these joints?"

After imagining him leaving her, Molly was so relieved to be scolded instead that tears nearly came to her eyes. "No, what kind of creeps?"

His hold on her arm tightened. "The kind who wouldn't hesitate to back you against a wall and put a knife to your throat. That's what kind. I was worried sick."

Not three minutes ago, she had envisioned herself digging through dumpsters to stave off hunger. The throbbing anger in his voice told her how wrongly she'd judged him. For all his faults, which were admittedly few, Jake was nothing like Rodney, and she never should have painted him with the same brush.

What was wrong with her? All he'd done was order her a sandwich, and she'd gone clear over the edge. It was as if venomous spiders were caged in some dark, secluded part of her mind, and every once in a while, a few escaped to inject poison into her thoughts.

"Didn't you know I was inside the lounge?" she asked.

He drew her around a woman who'd just won a jackpot and was hopping about in celebratory glee. "Not for certain." He ground the words out, his jaw muscle ticking. "I had to go back for your purse and lost sight of you in the crowd. I hoped you had ducked in there. It was the only restroom I could find on this side of the casino, so waiting for you there seemed like my best bet."

He was leading her toward the front exit. Beyond the glass doors, she could see people milling about on the sidewalk in a wash of brilliant sunlight. "Where are we going?"

"Somewhere to talk."

"About what?"

He shot her a hard look. "What the hell we're going to do. What do you think?"

Molly supposed it had been a stupid question. Following the pull of his hand, she walked obediently beside him, feeling like a recalcitrant child being taken to the woodshed. Oddly, though, she wasn't apprehensive. Jake was nothing like Rodney. The fact that he'd waited outside the lounge for her was irrefutable proof of that. No games, no coercion tactics. Jake was just Jake, always up front with his thoughts and feelings. He'd told her that the very first night. *"I'm not much good at beating around the bush."*

Molly felt so small. His only sin had been to try his best to help her. Shame washed through her in waves. In that moment, every word Sam Banks had ever said to her came rushing back. He'd cautioned her dozens of times not to let the past influence her decisions now. *"Turn loose of it, Molly. Your life with Rodney is over. It's a whole new game from this point forward, with totally new players and completely new rules. Embrace that. Move ahead and don't look back."*

Sadly, it wasn't that easy, Molly thought as they exited the casino onto the crowded sidewalk. In so many ways, she was almost well. But in others, she wasn't, and she was starting to fear she might never be. Jake was nothing like Rodney, yet she constantly drew comparisons. As far as she knew, he'd never lied to her, yet she examined everything he said and did, analyzing his motives and reading between the lines. He'd never really tried to exert his will over her, either, but that hadn't stopped her from thinking he was.

It was fear that was trying to control her now, she realized, not the man who walked beside her. Jake had only been worried because she hadn't eaten breakfast, and he'd been thoughtful enough to make sure she got lunch. Even worse, he hadn't ordered her the kind of food he preferred himself, as Rodney would have done. No, he'd asked for vegetarian fare—a garden burger and fresh fruit. To someone else, that might be a small thing, but to Molly, it meant more than she could say.

"Oh, Jake, I'm so sorry. I behaved unconscionably. I'm so sorry."

Never breaking stride, he sighed and released his hold on her to slip his arm around her shoulders. After giving her a jostling hug, he said, "I'm the one who's sorry."

Just that. No explanation, no flowery words. As they drew up at the corner, Molly searched his dark face. "You're sorry? For what?"

He moved his hand lightly over her sleeve, the warmth of the caress seeping through the cotton. "For everything," he said huskily. The crosswalk light changed just then. He drew her out onto the street, his riding boots tapping out a sharp tattoo on the asphalt as he led her to the opposite curb. "For being a self-centered jerk. For railroading you into this. For treating you like a child at the café. You name it, I'm sorry for it. Hell, I even lost your coat."

Her coat? Molly realized her parka was missing. That he would even care about that at a time like this brought a wobbly smile to her lips.

"I was so upset when I went back to the café for your purse, I totally forgot it," he elaborated. "When I went back a second time, it was gone."

"You got my purse, at least. That's better than I can say for myself."

"Only because your identification is in it." He drew her toward the outer edge of the sidewalk to circle an approaching elderly couple. "Classic. I knew you couldn't marry me without ID. That's me, always focused on my own agenda."

As they crossed yet another street, she realized he was taking her back to the truck. She knew then that he'd done an about-face. The marriage was off.

Twenty minutes ago, she would have been relieved. Now her emotions were a crazy mix of relief and apprehension. If he backed out and refused to marry her, what on earth was she going to do?

After depositing her inside the vehicle, he circled to climb in on the driver's side. The report of the slamming door preceded a heavy silence broken only by the sound of their breathing. The window glass began to fog. Molly fixed her gaze on the windshield, stupidly watching the steam collect in an uneven line above the dusty dash.

Jake finally released a weary breath, folded his arms over the steering wheel, and rested his forehead on his wrists. The brim of his hat shadowed his features, making it difficult to read his expression, but the defeated slump of his broad shoulders spoke volumes.

"Ah, Molly." He sighed again. "I'm so sorry, honey. I should never have insisted on this. I don't know what I was thinking." He followed that with a self-deprecating laugh. "Strike that. I know what I was thinking. I just can't believe I was thinking it."

Molly traced a circle on her jeans, hating the dejected tone in his voice. This was her fault, not his. She was the one who'd gone berserk in the café.

"You only offered to help me, Jake. I don't think that's such a terrible thing."

"Yeah, I was a real prince. I offered you help, but only for a price. And for you, it's a dear one." He straightened away from the steering wheel. His dark face was drawn, his eyes lackluster. He searched her gaze. "Do you remember the night I told you an animal can't be owned, that it chooses its master?"

"Yes," she said faintly.

"The same holds true for people. Love can't be bought. You can't finagle your way into someone's heart. More important, though we may sign documents to make it legal, marriage isn't a contractual agreement. At least it shouldn't be." A suspicious shine came into his eyes. He swiped a hand over his mouth and directed his gaze out the windshield. "I want you as my wife, Molly. This morning, that wanting and my good intentions started riding double. You know what I'm saying?"

"I think so."

He smiled slightly. "I lost sight of the really important things for a while, namely that no one should ever be pushed into marriage, no matter how sound the reasons behind it." He drew his gaze back to her. "You aren't ready for marriage. When you are, I'll be first in line to pop the question and pray you'll say yes. But I don't want it to come about this way."

Molly hugged her waist. "So you're backing out, then?"

He huffed under his breath. "More like backing off. I guess I needed that douse of hot coffee in my lap to make me realize what I was doing. When ordering you a sandwich sends you into a tailspin, we've got some serious problems. They won't go away just because we get married."

Molly appreciated the fact that he'd said *they* had some problems. He wasn't pointing the finger or assigning blame. The fact that he wasn't prompted her to say, "I'm the one with the problems, Jake."

"Your problems are my problems," he said softly.

"I wish that—" She broke off, searching for words. "I can't explain what happened in there." Pressing a fist to her chest, she gave him an imploring look. "I'm all mixed up inside. It's like—I don't know—like an ignition of some kind. One minute, I'm fine, and the next, I'm losing it. I get so upset I can barely breathe, and reason flies out the window. The first thing I know, I'm doing and saying things I never would otherwise. Like the night you took my rotor. There was no excuse for the way I behaved. None at all. I felt trapped, and I couldn't get past that."

"Everyone loses it sometimes, Molly."

"Not in a restaurant."

"Yeah, even in restaurants. You just need time, honey. I'm sorry I lost sight of that and started pushing you." He drew in an unsteady breath. "We both need time, I think."

The way Molly saw it, there was no time. Rodney was closing in on her even as they spoke.

"You need to resolve a few issues in your mind," he went on. "And I need some time to show you I'm not the controlling bastard you think I am."

"I don't think that."

"Yeah. Yeah, you do." He held up a hand. "I don't blame you for that. Don't think it for a minute. You've been through a bad experience. Now I'm trying to herd you to the altar again." He puffed air into his cheeks and rubbed his forehead. "I can come off like a steamroller sometimes. I don't mean to, but there you have it. I don't stop to think before I speak, and even when I do, half the time I don't say what I mean."

Molly felt suddenly cold. She shivered and rubbed her arms. Jake swore under his breath and reached behind the seat.

"Here, honey. Put this on."

Molly accepted the denim jacket he handed her. Instead of slipping her arms down the sleeves, she pulled the wool lining over herself. "I'm scared, Jake."

He swore again, then dragged a hand over his face. "I know. Who wouldn't be? But, hey. We're going to lick this. Rodney isn't invincible, and there's always more than one way to skin a cat."

"Meaning?"

"Meaning that marriage isn't the only answer. Granted, it's the most surefire. But we've got options."

"Like what?" she asked thinly.

"I had some time to think while I was waiting outside the lounge for you. How about if I hire you a damned good lawyer? I'm sure my brother-in-law, Ryan Kendrick, can recommend a sharp one."

Given her legal incompetence, Molly doubted they could find a lawyer willing to take her case. "What would you hire a lawyer with? You're barely staying afloat financially as it is."

"I've still got some money in the bank."

"Isn't that your working capital?"

He shrugged. "I also have a few horses I can sell. I should be able to come up with enough for a hefty retainer fee. If not, I can always tap my sister Bethany for a loan." He flashed her a grin. "She married into money. Her old man's so rich, they'll never miss it."

Molly remembered that afternoon in the kitchen after the stable fire when he'd picked the slivers from her feet. He'd said nothing then about selling his stock or being able to borrow money to cover the cost of rebuilding. Instead, he'd stared out the window with a hollow-eyed hopelessness, saying he'd be left with only a dream in his pocket if the insurance company refused to cover the damages. By that, she knew that Jake Coulter was a man who believed in standing on his own two feet. Borrowing money wouldn't be easy for him.

"If you sell your horses, won't that seriously deplete your assets?"

The crease lines deepened at the corners of his intense blue eyes as he frowned past her out the window. "Nah."

Molly knew he was lying. Not because he didn't carry it off well, but because he couldn't look at her as he spoke. "Oh, Jake," she said shakily.

His gaze jerked back to hers. "What?"

She shook her head. "I can't let you do that. Besides, it's a long shot. Even if we can get a lawyer to take my case, there's no guarantee he can help me. I've got a documented history of emotional instability, I've already been institutionalized once, I've been judged legally incompetent, and my adoptive mother will testify in court that I'm a basket case. Realistically, what are my chances?"

"Will your doctor testify on your behalf?"

"I'm sure he would, but his professional opinion may be secondary if they put me in a different clinic. The attending doctor's testimony will carry the most weight with a judge."

"It's a chance we have to take. If we don't get married, hiring an attorney's your only hope."

"At what cost? The Lazy J means *everything* to you. If you deplete your funds and assets, you could end up losing the ranch."

This time, he was able to look her directly in the eye as he spoke. "The Lazy J doesn't mean everything to me, Molly. There are other things far more important."

Molly realized he was referring to her. An awful ache filled her chest. For a second, she was afraid she would burst into tears. That he would do this for her—that he would even *consider* doing it—nearly broke her heart.

"I won't let you throw away your dream," she finally managed to say. "Rodney's already destroyed most of mine. I won't let him take yours, too. I won't."

"Sweetheart, let's be reasonable."

"I am being reasonable. That ranch has been in your family for generations. It was a miracle you ever got it back in the first place. If you lose it a second time, chances are you'll never get your hands on it again."

"It's only a patch of dirt," he said. "I can always get another spread." His gaze trailed slowly over her face, as if he were committing every line to memory. "The same can't be said for a certain lady I know. She's one of a kind."

Molly felt her chin start to quiver. Then, as if an invisible hand nudged her from behind, she launched herself across the seat and into his arms. "Oh, Jake," she cried, nearly strangling on a suppressed sob as she hugged his neck. "I'm so sorry. So very sorry."

He was clearly startled by her embrace. She felt his body snap taut. Then the starch suddenly went out of him, and he tightened his arms around her. A hundred times, Molly had tried to imagine how it might feel to seek sanctuary in his strong arms. He'd held her twice, once out in the woods and another time in the kitchen, but both those times, her thoughts had been fragmented by other emotions, not allowing her to really absorb the essence of him.

Such was not the case now. All her senses were focused on how he felt. The breadth of his chest—the steely strength of his arms—the gentle brush of his big hand over her back. Molly closed her eyes and pressed closer to him, heedless of the gearshift that jabbed her thigh, heedless of everything but him. *Jake.* This was how it was supposed to be, she thought nonsensically. Two people, holding each other, with nothing but feelings between them.

"I can't let you lose your ranch," she murmured against his neck.

"Did I ask your permission? Done deal, lady. It's the only way I can think of to help you."

"*No.* Just marry me. I've resolved all my conflicts. Really. Getting married is the simplest way."

She felt his lips curve in a smile. "That was a mighty fast turnaround."

"If I can't trust you, who can I trust?"

He ran his big hand slowly up her spine. "No one," he admitted huskily. "As much as I love you, Molly, if you can't trust me, you're sunk."

She laughed, the sound shrill and a little hysterical. "So marry me. I'd rather do that than gamble with the Lazy J."

She could feel his hesitance. "Such unbridled enthusiasm."

"I'm sorry. I didn't mean it like that."

He fell silent for a moment. "I just don't feel right about it now. I'm afraid you're getting pushed into something you'll regret later, and I don't want to be one of your regrets. You know?" He ran a hand into her hair. "You're not ready for a real marriage. Not yet."

Molly wished with all her heart that she could deny that charge. But the truth was, she wasn't ready. She'd come a very long way since that fateful morning when she'd awakened at the clinic. With Sam's help, she'd been going through a healing process ever since, taking giant strides toward emotional wellness. But she hadn't made it to the finish line yet. She felt that she was nearly there—that she was poised on an edge and about to take that last, freeing leap. But until she did, she wouldn't be whole.

She was functional. She could take care of herself and get by. But a healthy relationship demanded more than that from a person. She wasn't the only one with needs. Jake had them, too—needs she wasn't yet ready to fulfill. And, like it or not, she had fears he couldn't dispel. She wished that he could. Oh, how she wished that he could. But that wasn't the way of things in real life. Knights in shining armor existed only in fairy tales, and to slay her dragons, she needed to deal the killing blows herself.

"I guess we could go for a marriage in name only," he whispered. "Unless we go ahead and have sex, it won't be valid."

She stirred to look up at him. "I thought you wanted this to be a real marriage. No stopgap measure, you said."

He tucked in his chin to smile ruefully down at her. "Yeah, well, I don't always get my druthers." He smoothed a hand over her hair. "Maybe in time, huh? For now, the important thing is to stonewall Rodney. We can deal with the other stuff later. Preferably sooner than later." He bent to kiss her forehead. "Hope springs eternal, and all that. I'll keep a positive outlook and work on you every chance I get."

Molly searched his expression. "You'll be happy with that arrangement?"

"Hell, no. I want more, Molly. A lot more. I love you."

She knew he did. After his willingness to sacrifice his ranch for her, how could she doubt it? Sadly, though, love wasn't always enough. Molly had learned that bitter lesson the hard way.

He waited a beat, his gaze still holding hers. "So, what do you say, Stir-Houston? You willing to take on a cowboy for a while?"

Molly stared hard at his chin. "I feel uncomfortable, making vows I'm not sure I can keep. To me, it's the worst kind of sin."

A twinkle slipped into his eyes. "We'll make up our own vows then. You can promise to stay with me as long as you can stand me. I'll promise to stay with you until your tread starts to wear and you need an oil change."

Molly gave a startled laugh. "Surely we can't be legally married, saying stuff like that."

He assumed a mock frown. "Why not? This is Reno, darlin'. Anything goes."

❦ CHAPTER NINETEEN ❦

Two hours later, they were headed back to Crystal Falls. For the first half hour, Jake left Molly to her thoughts. Except for the engine noise and the occasional rattling sound, the inside of the truck was as silent as a sepulcher. Arms folded at her waist, eyes straight ahead, Molly huddled against her door. Every once in a while, he saw her thumb the wedding band that he'd placed on her finger.

As rings went, it wasn't much. Using his charge card, he had purchased it at a jewelry store near the chapel where they'd gotten married. Chances were good that the gold would flake off later. Someday soon, he would buy her a nicer band and a pretty diamond to boot, he promised himself. For now, though, chintzy was all he could afford.

Not that Molly seemed to notice the quality of the ring. He had a feeling it was the meaning behind it that had her worried. He'd done his best to modify the set of vows they'd chosen from the chapel's selection of canned ceremonies. Unfortunately, he and the JP had been working at cross-purposes. Toward the end of the ceremony, the man had thrown in, "Do you, Molly Sterling, take this man to be your lawful husband, to love, honor, and cherish him, keeping yourself only unto him, until death do you part?" Molly had flashed Jake a panicked look. Then, before he could intervene, she'd said, "I do," in a thin, tremulous voice. After that, Jake had followed her lead. What else could he do without embarrassing her half to death?

Now they were hitched, with a string of promises behind them that Molly hadn't wanted to make. On the one hand, Jake wished she wouldn't take it all so seriously, but in another way, he was damned glad she did. Who wanted to be married to a woman who took her vows lightly? He sure as hell didn't.

His hands were slick with sweat on the steering wheel. His guts felt tied in knots. He found himself wanting to talk to her, about anything and everything. He loved the sound of her voice. He loved the way she wrinkled her nose in thought before she said something.

Damn. He just loved her, he guessed. Even when she grew difficult and unreasonable as she had in the café, he found himself stepping back to analyze the situation, rather than getting mad. He grinned to himself, remembering the scene she'd caused. That was a meal a number of people would never forget, himself included. In twenty years, he had a hunch it would be one of his fondest memories. Someday, he and Molly would tell their kids the tale, and they'd all laugh together about it.

That she might not be a part of his life in twenty years was a possibility Jake refused to contemplate. Somehow, some way, he would work past all her reservations, he assured himself. He had to. Otherwise he would lose her, and that simply couldn't happen.

He glanced over at her. "You okay?"

She pushed at her hair and nodded. "Yes, fine. Just tired."

Jake swallowed and tightened his grip on the wheel. "Can you tell me about it, Molly? I'm not real keen on walking into this blind."

She might have asked him to elaborate on his question. He'd left her that room. But, instead, she proved herself to be as courageous as he'd judged her to be from the start and began telling him about her marriage—about what she termed her foolish girlhood fantasies, which had died a sudden death after the marriage—about the endless string of other women in Rodney's life from the very beginning.

"I wasn't enough," she admitted hollowly. "No matter what I did, I wasn't enough."

That statement made Jake's heart twist. She was so damned pretty, so sweet and pure of heart. How could any man think she wasn't enough?

He took his gaze from the road for a moment to look at her. "Some people should never get married. That's the truth of it. Nothing is enough. No one is enough."

"I wanted to be," she said shakily. "I tried so hard to be."

Jake had already guessed that much. In fact, he believed her sense of commitment and loyalty had nearly destroyed her. "And nothing you did pleased him."

"Nothing," she admitted.

"It wasn't you, Molly. Never you."

"Yes. I think there's something lacking in me, Jake."

"Is there something lacking in Sunset?"

She closed her eyes. "That's different."

"Bullshit. That horse gave Rodney everything he had, and it wasn't enough. Your words, not mine. I heard you talking to him that afternoon. What applies to him applies to you. He's a beautiful animal, and I'll wager he's pure magic on the track. He's also got a heart as big as Texas, and then some. How is he lacking, Molly?"

She shook her head. "He isn't. He's perfect."

"Damned straight, and so are you." He reached up to adjust his visor to block out the setting sun. "That's a subject for later, though. Your marriage—or more specifically, what wasn't a marriage—is past history. Let's move on to the more pertinent details, namely what landed you in this mess."

"I'm almost afraid to tell you."

"Don't be silly."

"No, really. I'm terrified I'm doing the wrong thing by getting you mixed up in it."

Jake patted his shirt pocket, wishing to hell he still smoked. At times like this, he always craved a cigarette. "I can handle Rodney. Don't worry about it."

"You could handle Rodney in a confrontation. Unfortunately, Rodney won't be confrontational. He'll get you when your back is turned."

"I'm not afraid of him, and I don't want you to be. He can't hurt you now. You're my wife. If he lays a hand on you, I'll kill him."

"Rodney is treacherous, Jake. He lets nothing stand in the way of what he wants. Nothing. Now that you've married me, you'll be in his way."

"Short of murder, what the hell can he do about it?"

"That's just it," she said tremulously. "He may not stop at murder."

Jake was so shocked that he almost had to pull off the road. Surely he hadn't heard her right. "Say what?"

"I think Rodney may have killed my father."

"Dear God. *Why?*"

"I'm not sure. Rodney was gambling heavily, and Sonora Sunset was losing more races than he won. Maybe he was embezzling funds to cover his losses. I don't know. But I think Dad found out about it, and Rodney killed him to shut him up."

"Jesus Christ," Jake whispered. He seldom took the Lord's name in vain, but right now, he wasn't sure if he was cursing or praying. Murder? He'd known the instant he looked into Rodney Wells's eyes that the guy was a snake, but murder was beyond his comprehension. "What makes you think he killed him?"

"My dad was very upset about something the last few days before his death, and uncharacteristically of him, he refused to discuss it with anyone, not even Claudia. They were always very close, so that was strange. It was doubly strange that he refused to talk to me." She lifted her hands. "My dad was an honorable man and didn't make accusations lightly. If he found something suspicious, he would have kept it to himself until he had absolute proof. I think he may have been checking into it, trying to get the goods on Rodney, and Rodney found out."

"And your father ended up dead? How did he die?"

"A gunshot wound to the head. I'd gone in early that morning to try to talk to him and see if I could find out what was wrong. I was the one who found him."

Jake's heart caught at the expression on her face, which told him how desperately she was hanging on to her self-control. "Oh, honey. That must have been a nightmare."

"A nightmare, yes." She fixed her gaze on the dash. "It was especially hard because that was the second time for me. In college, my best friend Sarah slashed her wrists. We roomed together, and I was the one who discovered her body. You can't imagine how I felt when I found my father. It was like a replay of my worst memories, only worse because I loved him so much. I'd failed Sarah, and then I failed my dad. You just can't fathom how I felt. Right before both of them died, I knew something was horribly wrong, and I didn't *do* anything. After finding Dad, I grew completely hysterical."

"Of course, you did."

She hauled in a shaky breath and tidied her hair with nervous fingers. Then she dropped her hands to her lap and went back to staring out the glass. "The police said it was suicide. My dad had been acting strangely for about a week. They found evidence that the gun had been purchased in his name only a few days before." She shot him a meaningful look. "It was purchased with ID, but Rodney is so clever with computers, he could whip up a picture ID in thirty minutes. The police didn't think of that, of course, and neither did I at the time. The investigating officers told me that older men often get depressed for no apparent reason. A chemical imbalance, possibly. Or maybe just feeling that life is essentially over, and their dreams haven't been realized. They said suicide wasn't uncommon in men his age."

"But you didn't believe that."

"My father was a noble man, not the type to take the coward's way out unless there were some horrific, extenuating circumstances. No, I couldn't accept it. At that point, of course, I was still in shock, so I wasn't thinking in terms of murder. I thought maybe he'd lost a bunch of money on the stock market, or that he'd made a string of bad investments for his clients. I needed—" She broke off and passed a hand over her eyes. "I don't know. I needed an explanation, I guess. A *reason*. Before I could lay him to rest, I had to know why he'd taken his life."

"If that happened to my father, I'd feel exactly the same way," Jake assured her.

"Anyway, Jared and Rodney—"

"Jared?"

"He was the man with Claudia this morning. He's Rodney's father."

"Ah, the plot thickens."

She nodded. "He was my dad's partner and best friend. They went through college together, worked at the same firm to get their licenses after they graduated, and then opened Sterling and Wells. Until recently, I always called him Uncle Jared. My dad had no siblings, and I always thought of Jared as my only other male relative." She grabbed for breath again, giving Jake the impression she was feeling oxygen deprived. "Anyway, right after the funeral, Jared and Rodney removed all my dad's personal effects from our family home. I was afraid they'd clear out his office next, and I wanted to go through his business records before anyone tampered with them."

"So you went to the firm to do that?"

"It seemed like a perfectly natural thing to me. My dad was dead, and I needed to know why. Rodney didn't see it that way. When he found me in my father's office, he got upset. He said he would go through Dad's files, but he didn't want me to do it myself because it was too stressful. He was afraid I'd have another nervous breakdown."

Jake shot her a questioning look. "You'd had a nervous breakdown before that?"

Her face had gone deathly pale. "No, that's the whole point. When my friend Sarah killed herself, I had a rough time handling her death. I knew she was depressed, and I encouraged her to seek counseling. But when she refused, I didn't insist upon it. I should have, and she paid for that with her life."

"Ah, honey. You can't blame yourself for that. You were only eighteen."

"Seventeen, actually. I entered grade school when I was five, so I was only seventeen my freshman year. I realize now that I was simply too young to recognize how deeply troubled Sarah was, but at the time, I blamed myself. My dad had me moved to a new dorm, but you can't escape something like that. The memories followed me. I started having nightmares. Worry over my grades added to the stress. Pretty soon, between dread of the dreams and concerns about school, I could scarcely sleep at all, and when exhaustion did win out, I began sleepwalking."

The puzzle pieces began to fall together for Jake.

"The episodes were bizarre and alarming, but never violent. When my parents got wind of them, they insisted I drop out of school and come home for grief counseling. At about that time, Rodney had just returned to Portland after working for several years in Silicon Valley. He and his dad, who was recently divorced, were frequent dinner guests at our house. Rodney was privy to the problems I had over Sarah's death."

"And he called that a nervous breakdown?"

Her mouth tightened, and she flashed him a dark look. Jake returned his attention to the road, waiting for her answer.

"Until that morning at the firm, he had never called it a nervous breakdown. I think he only did so then because other people were within earshot."

Jake flipped on the turn signal to pass a slow-moving vehicle. "My God, he was setting you up."

He heard her release a pent-up breath and realized he was parroting her thoughts. "At the time, I was just incredulous and horribly embarrassed that he'd say such a thing in front of other people. Suddenly I was, in his words, 'emotionally fragile.' I refuted the statement. He patted me on the head and mollified me, playing the concerned husband. In my opinion, it was a performance deserving of an Oscar."

Jake mulled that over. "He was running scared. There was something in those files he didn't want you to see, and on the off chance that you had, he needed a backup plan to cast doubt on your credibility."

Silence. Jake glanced over and saw that she had bent her head and closed her eyes. When seconds passed, he grew concerned. "Are you okay?"

She covered her face with trembling hands. "I'm sorry. It's just—except for talks with my doctor, I've been dealing with this alone for a good long while, and to be perfectly truthful, there have been times when I've doubted my sanity." She wiped her cheeks and sniffed. "You can't know what a relief it is to hear you mirror my thoughts."

"You aren't crazy, honey. Get that notion straight out of your head."

She nodded. "It's just that—well, these last few days, I haven't been so sure a couple of times." She haltingly told him about finding the debris in her bed and the deisel-soaked gloves in her kitchen. "Until Rodney showed up this morning, I was half convinced it was *me* doing it all."

"You booby-trapped the cabin so you wouldn't sleepwalk? That's why you had all that crap in front of the door that night?"

"Yes, and then the tires got slashed. I realized you were in danger of losing the ranch. At that point, I felt so awful that I knew I had to tell you."

"Why didn't you?"

She reminded him that he hadn't been accessible for a couple of days. "I meant to tell you, wanted to tell you, but the moment didn't present itself."

She went on to tell him of the weeks following her father's death, how bizarre incidents began occurring in her and Rodney's home. "It always appeared that I had done it. You know? We found the bloodstained jacket my dad was wearing when he died, hanging on a dining room chair. Rodney asked why I had kept such a gruesome memento." She shook her head. "I never saw the clothes Dad died in after they took him away in the ambulance. I tried to tell Rodney that, but he didn't believe me."

"He was trying to make you think you were losing it."

"I *did* think I was losing it. Shortly after that, I began sleepwalking again, and the incidents had violent undertones. I had no recollection of them, but I'd wake up to find the house in a shambles. Slashed cushions, slashed pictures, overturned garbage. Red lipstick or catsup smeared on the bathroom walls to look like blood, with Sarah's name written in the mess. I didn't own a lipstick, but Rodney insisted I must have bought one and simply didn't remember."

Jake's heart caught at the agonizing trace of doubt he heard in her voice. "That must have been scary, thinking you had done things you couldn't recall."

"It was. Rodney was so convincing. You saw him today, how calm and gentle he seems. I thought I was going mad."

"But, of course, you weren't. That's only what he wanted you to think."

She nodded. "Finally, after one particularly bizarre sleepwalking incident, he called my mom in a panic early one morning."

"In a well-staged panic," Jake corrected. "Let's keep this story on track."

She flashed him another grateful look. "Claudia is a general practitioner with a thriving practice. She rushed over. When she saw the house, she concluded that I was having a hard time with my dad's death and had started sleepwalking again. She wanted me to see a good psychologist for counseling. Rodney wanted to wait. He said a few sleepwalking incidents didn't make me crazy. He suggested that Claudia write me a prescription for sleeping pills, his hope being that if I slept deeply, the incidents would stop. She finally relented, though I think it went against her better judgment, and wrote a prescription. Rodney got it filled."

Jake sensed what was coming.

"The pills made me sick. Horribly dizzy and disoriented all the next day. Rodney asked Claudia for another prescription that might better agree with me. I just got sicker. Pretty soon he was giving me pills to cure the symptoms caused by pills. I couldn't function. I couldn't think. It got so I couldn't even make it to the bathroom without collapsing."

"Oh, my God. He was slipping you something."

Her eyes brimmed with tears. "Yes," she said shakily, "I believe he was. I think my illness was chemically induced, that he drugged me to make it appear I was having a breakdown. During that time, he kept trying to get me to sign some papers. My dad had stressed never to sign anything I hadn't read. I hadn't observed that rule during Rodney's and my marriage because he often wanted me to sign personal papers, and sometimes I was too busy to read the fine print. But the documents he wanted me to sign during my illness could have been firm related. I felt responsible for my dad's half of the business, which represented his life's work, and I refused to sign anything without reading it first. That created a problem. My vision was too blurred for me to make out the words."

"I'll bet Rodney was thrilled about that."

"He was furious." She gazed off at nothing. "To understand the shock element of that, you have to know how Rodney was before then. I know you think he was a jerk, but he was never overt about it. If I displeased him, he never yelled or hit me. He'd simply not speak to me for days on end. Or he'd humiliate me, often in front of other people. I always paid for my transgressions, but not in the ways you'd think."

"He was a calculating, vicious bastard, in other words."

She laughed tremulously. "Yes, and very good at hiding it. He never meant to humiliate me in public. He never *intentionally* hurt me. He was simply stating a fact, and I was being too sensitive." She shrugged. "I can't count the times he'd say something in front of people that left me bleeding. Then he'd thump himself on the forehead and apologize to me for putting it that way. It made him appear thoughtless, but not deliberately cruel, and people found it endearing, the way he apologized so profusely after he tripped over his own tongue. In the beginning, even I fell for it. Unfortunately, that didn't lessen the hurt any, and later on, it hurt even more because I knew he intended it to wound."

"What kind of things did he say to you, honey?" Jake asked softly.

Silence. Finally, she said, "Just stupid stuff. It doesn't matter now."

Jake thought it mattered a great deal. "Can you give me just one example?"

Another silence. And then, waving a hand as if to indicate the insignificance, she said, "Things like, 'My God, where did you get that dress? It makes you look like a fat cow.' Then he'd do his forehead-thumping routine, hand me money to go shopping, and be all over himself, trying to flatter me."

Jake ground his teeth. He needed to say something, but he couldn't think of a single thing. In the end, he remained silent. Words weren't what she needed. Not from him, at least. He did his best talking with his actions.

"Anyway," she went on. "That's water under the bridge. My point was that Rodney hides behind a mask most of the time and only shows his real self when it suits his purposes. Afterward, he's very talented at glossing it over and winning people back. My father was a great judge of character. He never liked Rodney very much, but I don't think he knew until the end what kind of man Rodney really is. I certainly never knew. Not in the beginning. In the early years, I never suspected that he was being unfaithful to me, for instance. He was gone a lot, but he always had an explanation, and I had no reason to think he might lie."

"You were going to make him rich someday. If he'd been a blatant adulterer, you might have divorced him, not to mention that your father would have been down his throat. Rodney may be a snake, but he's a smart snake."

"Anyway," she said with another wave of her hand, "one night, when I refused to sign the papers, his mask slipped completely, and I saw the real Rodney in all his ugly glory. It was the most *awful* feeling, Jake. Even doped up as I was, I reeled from the shock. I looked into his eyes and saw a stranger. I know that sounds overly dramatic, but that was exactly how I felt. It was Rodney's face, but the man wearing it was a *monster*. He looked as if he wanted to rip me apart with his bare hands, and in that moment, I thought sure he would. The worst part was, I was so sick and dizzy, I saw three of him. I didn't know which fist would plow into my face."

"Oh, honey." Jake was tempted to pull over again, this time because he wanted so badly to hug her. Rodney Wells was a fairly big man, and Molly, for all her ample curves, was a slip of a woman. She must have been terrified.

"He intimidated me that night. But after losing my dad the way I had, I couldn't betray everything he'd taught me."

Jake smiled slightly, not at all surprised to hear that. He was coming to know that Molly would stand firm on her convictions no matter what it cost her.

"I refused to sign the papers. The next morning, I woke up in a clinic. I was strapped to the bed. I had no idea where I was or how I'd gotten there. My first reaction was to scream for help."

"Of course it was."

"My attendants didn't see it that way. They thought I was a raving lunatic. It was so awful, Jake." Her voice went whispery. "It was the first time I'd been able to think clearly in weeks, and they pumped me full of sedatives again to calm me down."

"At least you had a few minutes of clarity. Rodney wasn't there to shove pills down you."

She smiled sadly and sighed. "It is so *good* to tell someone all this."

"And find out your take on everything wasn't so crazy, after all?"

"Yes," she admitted. "After waking up at the clinic, I didn't immediately put two and two together, but in moments of clarity after that, I began to. At first, I didn't play by the clinic rules. I was so enraged. You know? My father was dead. I was locked up, and I wasn't crazy. I wanted to tell anyone who'd listen and try to get help. That only made me look crazier. It was a pretty outlandish story."

"Did they treat you kindly at the clinic?"

"Eventually. I had a fabulous doctor. His name is Sam Banks. In the beginning, he thought I was a certifiable basket case, but before long, he started to believe my story. After that, he became my champion. He petitioned the court to get me a divorce. He allowed Rodney to see me only when he was present. Rodney hated his guts and still does."

"I think I'll like Sam Banks."

"I know I do," she said. "With his help, I was able to recall details I had blocked out or forgotten, and eventually, I was able to pinpoint the exact moment everything started, the day I went to search my father's office. Rodney began a campaign then to make me look nuts. I think he slipped the debilitating drug into my prescription bottles just in case I read the labels. I don't know if he got it on the black market, or if Claudia helped him get it, but I'm convinced he gave me something that made me deathly ill."

"You really think Claudia may be involved?"

"She helped Rodney put me away. She took Jared into her bed shortly after my father's death. I can't rule it out. I'm suspicious of all of them. Maybe they want my share of the firm. A great deal of money will eventually be at stake. People have done more heinous things out of greed."

Right after meeting Molly, Jake had sensed how very lonely and lost she felt. Now he knew why. Even the woman she'd called mother may have betrayed her in the most horrible way.

"What kind of woman is Claudia?"

"I always believed she was wonderful. My mom died of ovarian cancer when I was only five. She was ill for a long time, and shortly after her death, my father met and fell in love with Claudia. She couldn't have children, and, after adopting me, she always treated me like her own." Her voice quaked as she added, "I would have trusted her with my life, Jake, and I never questioned her love for Dad. I truly thought she adored him."

Jake couldn't bear to hear that hollow, tortured ring in her voice. "Maybe she did, Molly. If you and your dad were fooled by Rodney, maybe she was as well. Let's not condemn her until we know for sure."

She flashed him a warm look, even though her eyes shimmered with tears. "That's exactly what Sam would say. And my dad, too, for that matter. You remind me so much of him sometimes."

"Sam or your dad?"

A glow warmed her eyes. "My dad."

Jake took that as the highest of compliments. "Thank you," he said huskily. He checked his speed, noted how much he'd slowed down while listening to her story, and sped back up a bit. "Maybe Claudia turned to Jared in her grief. From things you've said, she must have regarded him as a very good friend. Sometimes when we're hurting, we just need someone to hold us, and maybe Jared was there for her in a way no one else was because he loved your dad, too."

"I want to believe that," she said in a thin voice. "You can't know how much. But she never came to see me, Jake. Except for that one time when Rodney called her over to the house, she stayed away the entire time I was sick. I never saw her in the clinic until right before my release when she came to tell me she was marrying Jared."

Jake felt her pain like a knife in his gut. "That doesn't mean she didn't love your dad or that she was in on anything. It could very well be that Rodney was doing everything solo, and he said or did something to make Claudia stay away."

Keeping one eye on the road, he leaned over to open the glove box where he kept a roll of toilet paper. "My version of tissues," he said.

She sniffed and tore off a length of squares to blow her nose. "Claudia said Rodney told her I was furious about the thing between her and

Jared, and that I didn't want to see her. Knowing I was so ill, she didn't want to further upset me, so she honored my wishes. She came that one day to the clinic only because she felt I deserved to hear the news of her marriage directly from her."

"Sounds reasonable. Did you tell her of your suspicions about Rodney?"

Molly shook her head. "I'd worked so hard to get out of there. I was afraid to tell her anything for fear she and Rodney would have me moved to another clinic away from Sam. I didn't know if I could trust her."

"So the one time you could have talked with someone outside the clinic who might have believed your story, you were held back by fear."

"Yes."

"Did you ever see her again after that? Before today, I mean."

"Right after I was released from the clinic, but I was still on probation. Sam had warned me not to do or say anything to rock the boat, that they could go over his head and put me back in a ward." She shot him a worried look. "That could still happen. Stealing a horse will definitely strike a judge as being irrational."

Until that moment, Jake hadn't understood how greatly she had endangered herself to help that poor horse. She'd risked her freedom, her dreams, everything.

"Anyway," she went on, "I was afraid to tell Claudia anything. If she was in on it, and I started accusing Rodney of killing my dad, they could have claimed I was delusional."

"Why did you see her after you got out?" Jake asked, hoping she didn't feel as if he were grilling her.

"She'd heard about my divorce through Jared, and she knew I'd be out on the streets after my release until I found a place. She took it upon herself to get me an apartment, and working through Rodney's dad, she arranged to get my SUV returned to me so I'd have transportation. Except for the times Rodney showed up at the apartment after I was released to try to get me to sign those papers, I never had to see him."

Jake drew his brows together in a thoughtful scowl. The thing with the papers worried him. He had a bad feeling there might be far more to this than Molly realized. If Wells had her power of attorney, why did he need her signature on something? It just didn't figure.

Pulling himself back to the subject, Jake said, "It sounds to me as if Claudia did everything she could, outside of denying herself a relationship with Jared, to make sure her little girl was taken care of. As for her relationship with Jared, you can't condemn two grief-stricken people for clinging to each other."

"No," Molly whispered. "And if that's all it is, God forgive me for being so cold to her this morning."

Jake's throat went tight. "No self-recrimination allowed. You've been through a hell of a time. I don't think you've said or done anything that wasn't perfectly understandable, and if Claudia is half the woman I think she may be, she'll agree with me when she realizes what's been going on."

"You liked her, didn't you?"

Jake considered carefully before answering. He'd seen such pain in Claudia's eyes. "She was mighty upset. It's hard for me to believe it was all an act."

Molly sighed and began fiddling with the tissue. "I love her a lot. If she's innocent of any wrongdoing, I'd like very much to mend our relationship. I always loved Uncle Jared, too. He's a nice man." Her eyes darkened again. "At least I always thought so."

Jake fell quiet for a while, thinking about all that she'd told him. Then he said, "Okay, now I know all the facts. Right?"

Judging by the way she avoided his gaze, he guessed that she'd left out some of the grittier details about her marriage. He could understand that talking about something so personal wasn't easy. "You know all the really important things," she agreed.

"You come with some pretty serious trouble riding drag, lady."

She nodded. "Yes. If you want to annul the marriage and wash your hands of me, I won't blame you. You didn't create this mess, and it's not your job to fix it."

"I disagree. The moment I fell in love with you, Molly, everything about you became my problem."

"That's me, one big problem."

He winced. "I didn't mean it like that."

"I know you didn't. But it's the truth. I've been nothing but trouble, and if Rodney has his way, that won't end any time soon."

"I'll take you, trouble and all."

Molly thought she would have to start cooking dinner the moment they arrived at the ranch, but when she and Jake pulled up out front, four unfamiliar pickups were parked at the edge of the yard. Jake took one look at them and swore under his breath.

"Who is it?" Molly asked.

"Family," he muttered.

Molly's stomach dropped. "What are they doing here?"

"Hank must have called them." His eyes gleamed in the light from the porch. "I'm sorry. I know you're probably not keen on the idea of a big celebration."

Her hand flew to her hair. She glanced down at her clothes, which were wrinkled from traveling. "I'm a *mess*."

He grinned. "You look better than I do."

Molly stared at the house. "Are your parents here?"

Jake reached across the cab to touch her shoulder. "Don't bolt on me. My mom and dad are the salt of the earth."

Molly took that to mean yes. She gulped. At the moment, she didn't care how nice his parents were. She wasn't ready to meet them yet. They couldn't be happy about their eldest son's sudden decision to marry, not to mention that he'd chosen to elope without notifying anyone. The only thing this awful day needed to make it complete was familial discord and censure.

Jake piled out of the truck and came around to open her door. As he helped her down from the lofty four-wheel drive, he whispered, "Sweetheart, you look like you just swallowed a half-gallon carton of live guppies. Don't be nervous."

"They aren't going to like me."

"You're absolutely right. They're going to love you." He wrapped a strong arm around her shoulders as they set off for the house. "Just relax and be yourself. You'll have my dad wrapped around your finger in two seconds flat."

Molly wished she were confident of that. "Are they going to be upset with us for running off to Reno?"

He sighed. "Maybe. Under the circumstances, though, I'm sure they'll make allowances."

"You're going to tell them? About Rodney and the clinic, I mean?"

He started up the steps, drawing her firmly along, his embrace comforting on the one hand, yet unbreakable as well, the firmness of his hold a silent message that there was no avoiding this ordeal, no matter how much she might like to. "Hank probably told them already," he said. "The Kendrick brothers are here. It's my guess he called in the big guns just in case I need help handling Rodney or the law."

Molly cringed, so embarrassed she wanted to die. "Talk about having your dirty laundry aired in public."

"It's not your fault," he reminded her. "You have absolutely nothing to be ashamed of, Molly." Once on the porch, he paused to hold her gaze. "Head high, shoulders straight. I'll be right beside you."

For some insane reason, hearing him say that bolstered her confidence. She remembered how he'd stood beside her that morning, his booted feet spread wide, his big body braced for a fight. Jake Coulter was a man who could be counted on, no matter what. She had a feeling he would even take a stand against his family in defense of her, which made her chest ache with emotions she couldn't and didn't wish to name.

When they entered the house, they were greeted by the smell of food preparation and the sound of voices. Molly expected to find the great room crammed full of people, but to her surprise, all the noise seemed to be coming from the room beyond. Jake led her directly to the kitchen archway, then fell back a step to let her enter just ahead of him. The awful thought went through Molly's head that his lagging behind meant she would have to take the first bullet.

The kitchen brimmed over with people. In a glance, Molly picked out three dark-haired women—a slightly built brunette in a wheelchair who was holding a newborn baby; a short, plump older lady who was stirring something on the stove; and another woman standing by the refrigerator next to a tall, jet-haired cowboy in neatly creased Wranglers and a white Western shirt.

As curious as Molly was about the women, her attention became riveted to the men. To her wary gaze, they all seemed to have been poured from the same mold. Tall, lean, and dark, they were, to a man, impressive male specimens, but the most interesting thing she noticed was the marked resemblance they all bore to one another. Two of them were Kendricks, if Jake was to be believed, so why did they all look so much alike? Was it something in the water around Crystal Falls?

At first sight of Molly, Hank and the seven strangers turned in unison to stare. Then, as if by silent command, they all converged on her, crying, "Congratulations!" Molly was so startled by all the joyous shouts that she reared back against Jake. He caught her around the waist with one strong arm.

"Unko Jake!"

Molly glanced down to see a pint-sized cowboy barreling toward them. He was the most darling little guy she'd ever seen. Perched upon his dark head was a black Stetson bigger than he was. His brown eyes danced with delight.

Bypassing Molly, he grabbed Jake's leg. "Up high!" he cried.

Jake gave Molly a reassuring squeeze, then let go of her to scoop the child into his arms. "Who are you, partner? If this isn't a fine how-do-you-do. I leave for a while, and when I get back, my house is overtaken by strange cowboys."

The child grabbed Jake's ears, nearly knocking his hat off in the process. "I'm Jaimie. You know me."

Jake squinted as if to see the boy better. "Jaimie? Nah. It can't be. He's a little mite."

"I growed up!"

Jake grinned. "I'll be. It is Jaimie. What's your mama been feedin' you, boy? She needs to put a rock on your head. You're sprouting up too fast."

The older woman who'd been working at the stove stepped forward. Molly had a fleeting impression of friendly blue eyes, a radiant smile, and a sweet, very lovely countenance. "You must be Molly," she said, and then, with no further ado, gathered Molly into her plump arms for a hug. "She's lovely, Jake. I guess I'll have to forgive you for running off to Reno to get married. She's too pretty to toss back."

Jake hadn't relinquished his hold on the child, but he stepped closer, offering Molly his silent support. "There'll definitely be no tossing her back, Mom. I finally found a keeper. As for eloping, I'm sure Hank explained that it couldn't be helped." He leaned around to smile at Molly. "This is my mom, Mary, sweetheart. She's an incurable hugger, and she's never in her life met a stranger. All I can say is, you'll get used to her."

Mary flapped a hand. "Get away with you. If I can't hug my new daughter, who can I hug?"

Molly thought Jake's mother was delightful, and she found the unexpected hug reassuring, the thought going through her mind that she would have at least one friend in the Coulter camp. "I'm pleased to meet you, Mary."

"Just call me Mom," Mary chided. "Out of six kids, all I got was one daughter, and I had about given up on any of my sons bringing me home another one. This is one of the happiest days of my life."

A tall, dark-haired older man stepped forward just then. The family resemblance was so strong that Molly knew at a glance he had to be Jake's father. Aside from the silver at his temples and the lines that had been etched into his bronzed face by years of living, he looked so much like her husband and Hank that it was uncanny.

Nudging his wife aside, he grasped Molly by the hands to draw her away from Jake, whereupon he released her to give her a slow once-over with unsettling blue eyes. Molly felt a little like a mare on the auction block as he circled her. When he came to stand in front of her again, he caught her chin in his hand to turn her face this way and that. Molly half expected him to pry her mouth open and check her teeth.

His gaze warmed on hers. Then he flashed a grin at Jake. "She's a little on the short side, son."

Mary straightened her shoulders. "She's as tall as I am," she informed her big, burly husband.

Jake's father's eyes danced with laughter. "Like I said, she's a little on the short side, son."

Mary elbowed her husband in the stomach, making him grab for his midriff. He huffed and laughed even as his wife scolded him. "Leave off, Harv. The poor girl will think you don't approve of her."

Harv assumed an expression of mock dismay. "Well, we can't have that." He smiled at Molly. "I definitely approve."

Jake lowered Jaimie to the floor. The next instant, Molly felt his big hands settle warmly on her shoulders. "I thought you'd like her, Dad." To Molly, he said, "This is my father, by the way. He's a little on the short side himself when it comes to manners, but he's long on loyalty."

"Now we know where you got it, Jake!" Hank called out with a laugh. "You took after the old man."

Jake's father smiled at Molly. "Welcome to our family, honey." And with that, he followed his wife's example and caught her up in his arms for a hug, the crush of strength around her ribs threatening to rob her of breath.

As Molly slipped free from Harv Coulter's embrace, a tall, jet-haired man standing beside the brunette in the wheelchair said, "Run while you still can, Molly. The whole family's crazy. Worst of all, it's catching, and pretty soon, you start to think they're normal."

The woman in the wheelchair socked the man's thigh. Molly knew instantly she was Jake's sister. She had delicate features, but they bore the Coulter stamp, her eyes a blaze of blue, her small chin sporting just a hint of a cleft, her dainty jawline squared. "We are not crazy, just sort of— eccentric." She rolled her chair forward. Cuddling her baby in the crook of one arm, she extended only one hand, which Molly grasped to be polite. "Forgive us, Molly. They've already started on the champagne and forgotten their manners. I'm Bethany, Jake's sister." She wiggled a hand free to pat her newborn. "This is your new nephew, Sly. Sylvester, meet your aunt Molly."

Still trying to assimilate the fact that she was married, Molly was startled to hear Bethany refer to her as the baby's aunt. "He's darling," she found the presence of mind to say and leaned down to properly admire the infant. "What a handsome fellow."

"He's a preemie and still a little small, but the doctor says he'll catch up quickly. Judging by his appetite, I believe it." She shot the jet-haired man beside her a teasing look. "This big-mouthed fellow is his dad. May I introduce my husband, Ryan Kendrick? I'll warn you right up front not to believe a word he says. He delights in maligning my family."

Ryan laughed and extended a work-roughened palm. Pasting on a smile, Molly shook hands with him, whereupon she was somehow handed off to another tall, dark-haired man who caught her up for a second breath-robbing hug. "I'm Zeke, Jake's brother, the second oldest."

"Hi." Molly took in his cobalt blue eyes and chiseled features, which also bore the Coulter stamp. "I'm pleased to meet you."

Instead of releasing her after the hug, Zeke slipped an arm around her waist and led her across the room to where the third woman stood beside the jet-haired cowboy in the white Western shirt. Molly knew even before the introductions began that the man was Ryan Kendrick's brother. Upon closer inspection, she saw that the two looked enough alike to be twins. "Meet Rafe and Maggie Kendrick," Zeke said. "Rafe is Ryan's older brother. He and Maggie decided to crash our party."

Maggie laughed and rolled her sparkling brown eyes. "Don't believe him, Molly. We're family and don't need an invitation."

Drawing his arm from around Molly's waist, Zeke glanced over the top of her head at Jake, who stood just behind them. "I'm playing waiter. Would you and your bride like some champagne?"

Jake gave Molly a questioning look. Then he shook his head. "Thanks anyway, Zeke. We'll have some in a bit."

Maggie gave Molly a quick hug, then stepped past her to kiss Jake's cheek. "Congratulations, cowboy. It's about time someone got you snubbed down with a short rope."

"Shhh," Jake joked. "She thinks it's the other way around."

Maggie's cheek dimpled in a mischievous grin. She linked arms with Molly. "That won't last. Bethany and I will have her set straight in no time at all." Meeting Molly's gaze, she added, "I'm Jaimie's mom." She held out a hand to measure off the child's height. "The little guy with the big hat? He insisted on coming to Unko Jake's house. My sister Heidi is watching my daughter, Amanda."

"*Your* daughter, *your* son?" Rafe interrupted, his tone laced with teasing rebuttal. He winked lazily at Molly. "They're my kids, too. To hear Maggie talk, I'm nothing but a hat rack."

"Easy mistake. There's always a Stetson on your head," Maggie pointed out.

Touching the black brim of said Stetson, Rafe flashed his wife a wickedly sexy grin. "Not always. I take my hat off for one special lady on occasion."

Maggie's cheeks flamed. For a moment, Molly didn't get Rafe's meaning. Then her face grew as warm as Maggie's looked.

Jake stepped in to rescue her. "Don't mind Rafe," he said with a laugh. "His mama taught him manners, but they didn't stick."

Rafe slipped an arm around Maggie's shoulders and drew her back to his side. "Come back here, girl. I need a leanin' post."

His leaning post nailed him in the ribs with a sharp elbow. He pretended to struggle for breath. While he was hunched over, he took advantage of the opportunity to nibble on Maggie's neck. She leaped and squeaked. "Rafe Kendrick, be good."

"I'm always good. Sometimes excellent."

"Am I going to be the designated driver tonight?" Maggie demanded.

"Prob'ly." Rafe reached for the champagne he'd set atop the fridge. "This stuff has a kick like a sawed-off shotgun."

"That's only his second glass." Maggie sent Molly an apologetic look. "He seldom drinks. He had a problem with it a few years back, and—"

"I didn't have a problem," Rafe objected. "It's only a problem when you wanna quit and can't." He chuckled. "I never wanted to quit." He nearly spilled his champagne as he bent to nuzzle Maggie's ear. "Not until I met you, anyhow. Then I swore off."

"Maybe I'd better take him home." Maggie arched her eyebrows and looked inquisitively at Jake. "Do you think? I'm afraid he's a little drunk."

"Daddy, what's drunk?"

Everyone looked down to see Jaimie tugging on his father's jeans. Rafe immediately sobered. With exaggerated care, he returned the champagne to the top of the side-by-side, clinking the base of the glass against the porcelain with an air of finality. Then he crouched to loop an arm around his son. "Well, now," he said, frowning thoughtfully. "Drunk is one of the past tenses of drink." He ruffled the child's hair and hugged him close. "Your mama was just telling me I've reached the past-tense stage."

Jaimie climbed onto Rafe's knee. He smiled happily up at Jake. "I'm not all the way growed up yet, so my dad can still give me hugs."

"What d'ya mean, I can *still* give you hugs?" Rafe put both arms around Jaimie and gave him a fierce squeeze. "I'll always give you hugs, big guy."

"Even when I'm *great* big?"

"Even when."

Hank called out that it was time to toast the bride and groom. With a flourish, he uncorked another champagne bottle and began filling Jake's delicate crystal flutes, the ones that had been a housewarming gift. "Since I'm the best man who wasn't, I get to do the honors first."

A series of heartfelt good wishes followed, some humorous, some poignant. Molly noticed that Rafe Kendrick took only small sips from his glass after each toast. When he caught her watching him, he winked at her. The message was clear. For the remainder of the evening, he planned to be a past-tense imbiber.

Watching Rafe with Maggie, Molly felt a twinge of envy. They were clearly blissfully happy in their marriage. Jaimie and Amanda were very lucky children.

After the toasts, everyone began milling around to visit. Molly was a little overwhelmed, to say the least, not entirely sure how to interact with such a large, boisterous group. As if Jake sensed her discomfort, he kept an arm around her, moving from person to person to chat while everyone except Rafe and Bethany, the nursing mother, sipped champagne.

When dinner was finally ready, Molly was touched to discover that the meal was vegetarian, compliments of Hank and the hired hands, who'd informed Mary Coulter that Jake's new wife seldom ate meat.

The teasing banter, which was nonstop, helped Molly to relax. Evidently sensing that she felt better, Jake quietly excused himself and went to collect his newborn nephew. Molly couldn't help but notice the tender expression on his dark face as he took the baby from his sister's arms. Unlike many men, he seemed completely at ease holding an infant. When the baby tried to suckle the button on his breast pocket, he smiled and offered his knuckle as a substitute.

The conversation around Molly seemed to grow distant as she watched her new husband with the baby. Jake had removed his Stetson, and his dark hair fell over his forehead in lazy waves as he bent to kiss his nephew's temple. There was such love in the gesture, and unmistakable yearning. Molly recalled the morning when he'd confessed to wanting a family. At the time, she had scoffed, but after watching him with Jaimie and seeing him now, she knew it was true.

Jake Coulter ached to have a child of his own.

A lump came to Molly's throat. *Shattered dreams.* She, too, had always longed for a baby. After ten years with Rodney, she'd given up on it ever happening. Now, observing Jake, she felt a faint surge of hope.

What if? He claimed to love her. Incredible as it seemed, after his offer to sell his horses to hire her an attorney, Molly was half-convinced it might be true. Did she dare to hope that this marriage might actually last?

If it did, wasn't there every possibility that she and Jake might have a family?

The thought made Molly feel almost giddy, and because it did, she firmly shoved it from her mind. She'd walked that path once, and it had led to nothing but heartbreak. She was afraid to open herself up to that kind of hurt again. Jake Coulter was an extremely attractive, charming man. He could have almost any woman he wanted. Right now, he thought that woman was Molly, but she had no faith his feelings would last. She was too plain and dumpy to hold his interest for long, and if she let herself believe otherwise, it would nearly kill her when he developed a roving eye.

Despite the thought, she found herself smiling or laughing more times than not during the meal, which was served buffet style, allowing the diners to recline wherever they wished to enjoy their food. Molly sat in the great room with the women. By meal's end, she'd noted one marked similarity in all three of them. Whenever they mentioned their husbands, their eyes glowed. Molly couldn't help but feel envious. What must it be like to love so deeply and be loved in equal measure? She couldn't imagine it.

Feeling like the odd one out, she searched for Jake, who was chatting with Rafe Kendrick at the foot of the staircase. Still holding the baby, he stood with his dark head bent, his body relaxed against a banister. As if he sensed Molly's gaze on him, he glanced up, his blue eyes locking on hers. A faint smile played over his mouth. He murmured something to Rafe, then fell into a lazy saunter that carried him quickly across the room. After returning the infant to its mother, he took the empty plate Molly held on her lap and set it on the coffee table.

"We need to walk over to the cabin and grab a few of your things," he said softly.

Molly hadn't thought that far ahead. But, of course, he was right. If she meant to spend the night at the main house, she would need her toiletries, a fresh change of clothes, and something to sleep in. Her mind froze at the thought, for all she usually wore to bed was an oversized T-shirt and panties.

"I should stay until the kitchen is clean," she protested.

"A bride doesn't do dishes on her wedding night," Mary inserted. "Go with your husband. We'll handle the cleanup." Catching Harv's gaze, she smiled and added, "We should probably get to it. We've overstayed our welcome as it is. I'm sure the kids would like to be alone."

"Oh, no!" Molly assured her. "We're in no hurry for you to leave."

Ryan, who was hunkered by Bethany's chair, chuckled and glanced at Jake. "You hear that, Jake? You're in no hurry to get rid of us."

Jake only smiled, his warm gaze remaining fixed on Molly, his broad palm still outstretched. "Come on, honey."

It didn't seem to Molly that he was leaving her any option. Everyone in the room had turned to look at them. She took Jake's hand and let him pull her to her feet. After grabbing two denim jackets, they left the house, escaping all the staring eyes. Jake slipped an arm around her waist as they started down the steps, touching her with the same casual possessiveness he had all evening, as was his right now that they were married.

"You in there, girl?" He squeezed her hip through the lined denim. "Hank's coat damned near swallows you."

In Molly's opinion, it would be a mighty big gulp. As they walked along, she touched the wedding band on her finger. Wearing it felt odd after going without a ring for so many months, a silent reminder that she was no longer her own person. *Married.* The word rang in her mind like a key turning in a lock. She tried to remind herself that a life sentence with Jake might not be such a bad thing, but somehow that offered scant comfort.

Determined not to let panic get the best of her again as she had in Reno, she tried to push her concerns from her mind. Only she kept remembering her last wedding night, how Rodney had drunkenly groped her body, thrust into her with no thought for her pain, and then fallen into a stupor, crushing her with his limp weight. She'd been a possession to him, and nothing more. He'd had no regard for her feelings whatsoever, not that night or at any time thereafter. The thought of being treated that way again made her feel ill.

Jake wasn't like that, though, she assured herself. He *wasn't.* It was stupid to compare him to Rodney. Each time she made that mistake, he proved her dead wrong.

Though she'd walked this path with him many times, it seemed different tonight, more intimate somehow. He'd slipped his hand under the jacket, and his palm had found a resting place just above her left hip. The contact set her heart to skittering.

"You're tense," he observed dryly, his shimmering gaze finding hers in the moonlight.

Molly nodded. "It's been an eventful day. I feel as if I've climbed onto a roller coaster and can't get off."

He made a low sound at the base of his throat. "Things will calm down now. You'll feel better after a good night's sleep." He waited a beat. "I hope you don't mind my insisting that we come over to get your things. Under other circumstances, we could forgo appearances, and you could just stay at the cabin as you always have. But with Rodney lurking in the wings, that wouldn't be wise. I wouldn't put it past the bastard to sneak in on you during the night. I'd play hell getting you back once he got you to Portland."

Molly hadn't thought of Rodney's sneaking in on her. "You're right. We shouldn't put it past him."

"Trust me, I won't. I'm not letting you out of my sight. You can bunk with me."

Bunk with him? In the same bed? Molly threw him a startled look, which he didn't seem to notice. Her hip nudged his leg as they circled a fallen log. At the contact, it seemed to her that he drew her even closer. She fleetingly wondered if he hoped to consummate the marriage tonight. Then she discarded the concern. Jake would never take a woman without regard for how she felt about it. Besides that, he'd all but promised not to.

"It's a beautiful night." Molly heard the nervous edge in her voice and wanted to kick herself. "Just look at the stars."

"They are something," he agreed, his voice pitched low and husky.

When they reached the cabin, Molly hurriedly collected her things so they could return to the main house and their guests. While she was digging in her drawer for something suitable to serve as a nightshirt, he stepped up behind her, nearly startling her out of her skin. Grasping her upper arms, he drew her back against him and bent to feather his lips over her hair.

"Molly, would you relax? Just because we're married, it doesn't mean I'm going to jump you. Why are you so nervous?"

That was a question Molly couldn't readily answer. She certainly wasn't afraid of Jake. The very idea was preposterous. He was the kindest, most gentle man she'd ever known.

Unfortunately, he was also the most physically attractive man she'd ever known. The mere brush of his hands on her arms made her skin tingle. She had little faith in her ability to resist if he set his mind to seducing her. He made her want to forget everything. Just the thought of his touching her bare skin made her stomach do cartwheels.

"I don't know what's wrong with me," she said weakly. "I guess the reality of what we've done is starting to sink in. I just—getting married wasn't exactly on my agenda when I woke up this morning." His big hands massaged her arms, forcing the knots of tension from her muscles.

She leaned more of her weight against his chest, comforted by his sturdy hardness, yet unnerved by it as well. "I don't really know what to expect. I mean—well, we are married. I couldn't blame you for wanting to exercise your conjugal rights."

"Conjugal rights? Never in almost thirty-three years have I heard anyone use that term. It's hopelessly old-fashioned."

"Is it?" It didn't seem out of date to Molly, especially not now with Jake's big hands locked over her arms. "Men have always expected certain privileges in marriage. I don't think that has changed." She could feel that it hadn't in the way he touched her.

"I'm sorry the JP tossed in all the forever stuff during the ceremony," he murmured.

"It wasn't your fault."

"No," he agreed, "but it's worrying you."

"We ended up making all the traditional vows."

He feathered his lips over her temple. "True."

"Vows should be kept."

"I'll keep mine if you'll keep yours," he murmured with a teasing smile in his voice.

Molly squeezed her eyes closed. "I don't know that I have a choice. Maybe it was only a cheesy little chapel in Reno, but I feel that I made them before God, nevertheless."

"Me, too," he whispered. "That being the case, can I promise you one more thing?" At her nod of assent, he said, "You'll never regret marrying me. I'll spend the rest of my life making damned sure you've never got a reason."

Oh, how Molly wanted to believe that. She thought of how he'd looked holding his sister's baby, and she wanted to grab hold of the dream again with all her heart. "Does this mean you want to go ahead and have sex tonight?" she asked tautly.

"Molly, not everything in a relationship revolves around sex."

"You're thinking about it. Tell me you're not."

He went perfectly still. "Yes, I'm thinking about it. I want you so much that I ache. I won't lie to you about that." He ran his hands lightly downward until his fingertips found hers. He interlaced their hands. "I said I'd wait until you're ready, though. Do you think I was lying?"

Molly closed her eyes. "I think you know very well that in many ways I am ready."

He sighed, disentangled his hands from hers, and wrapped both arms around her, one large hand splayed and laying claim to the slope of her ribs just under her right breast. "In many ways, yes. I think I could kiss you and make you want me."

Molly almost denied it, but she'd told this man far too many lies already. "Yes," she admitted faintly. "You could."

He bent sideways to kiss the hollow just under her ear. "There's just one minor problem," he whispered. "You're afraid I won't want you. Until you're past that and start to feel better about a few other issues, it'll never be perfect between us. I think perfect is worth waiting for."

❧ CHAPTER TWENTY ❧

An hour later, Molly was alone with her new husband at the main house. Even Hank had left, abandoning his room at the opposite end of the landing from Jake's in favor of a cot in the bunkhouse. Knowing that he had left to give her and Jake privacy on their wedding night set Molly's nerves on edge even more. It seemed the whole world expected them to have sex at the first opportunity.

She was trembling as she mounted the stairs in front of Jake. He'd flipped off the lights on the main floor, leaving them with only the ceiling fixture above the landing to illuminate the way. Over the course of her employment at the Lazy J, Molly had ascended these stairs dozens of times to put away freshly laundered clothes or to clean the bedrooms. She didn't know why the climb unsettled her so badly now.

The thump of his boots resounded on the steps behind her, the plastic bag of her clothing that he carried rustling against his jeans. Once on the landing, he placed a hand at the small of her back and propelled her toward the master suite, which Molly already knew was a warm, rustically charming trio of rooms, a large sleeping area, a cozy reading nook, and a spacious four-section bath with an adjoining powder room, dressing room, and huge walk-in closet.

At the doorway, he grasped her shoulder to stop her from entering. Tossing the plastic bag in ahead of them, he said, "We can forego some of the traditions of a wedding night, but there's one custom I refuse to let slide."

He bent and caught her up in his arms. Afraid that he might drop her, she squeaked in surprise and grabbed hold of his neck. "Don't try to carry me!" she cried. "I'm way too heavy. You'll hurt your back."

He gave her a bounce. "Ah, bull. You're not so heavy."

"Almost a hundred and forty," she corrected.

"*That* much?"

She drew an arm from around his neck to slug his shoulder. He laughed and turned slightly sideways to move through the doorway so her feet wouldn't catch.

"At least this is an improvement," she observed.

"What is?"

"When Rodney carried me over the threshold, he bonked my head."

Jake winced and smiled. "Yeah, well, stick around. This isn't the only thing I'll improve upon, and greatly, I might add." He carried her to the bed, gently laid her on the mattress, and then, after bracing a hand on either side of her, moved back to gaze down at her. "Just as I thought," he said softly. "You look absolutely right, lying there." A twinkle of mischief entered his eyes. "How can a man get so lucky? I've never seen such a gorgeous compass."

Molly frowned bewilderedly. "Compass?"

He grinned and trailed a fingertip over her mouth. "That's north. I'll leave you to figure out the other pointers by yourself."

Molly groaned, which prompted him to laugh softly. Her cheeks went warm. Strike that, her whole body went warm. She stared up at him, dry mouthed. Keeping his gaze locked on hers, he bent his arms and lowered his head to gently kiss her. After tying her belly into tight knots and making practically every muscle in her body start to quiver, he drew back to gaze at the pointed tips of her breasts that peaked the cotton of her blouse.

"Those little beauties are definitely thrusting like sword points and stabbing my loins with desire," he whispered.

Recognizing that line from the romance he'd left on her porch, Molly gave a startled laugh.

"So you *did* read it," he teased.

"I leafed through it."

He nodded, his eyes gleaming. "To the best parts?"

She laughed again.

"That's better," he said approvingly. "Much better. You need to relax and take life just a little less seriously. Has anyone ever told you that?"

"Not that I recall, but I'll make note of it. Any other suggestions?"

He shoved with his hands to bounce up off the mattress. "Yeah, but they'll keep." He grabbed up the bag that he'd tossed on the floor and set it on the bed. "For now, just seeing you smile is a step in the right direction."

He began unbuttoning his shirt as he strode to the bathroom. Over his shoulder, he said, "You may as well get comfortable. I think it's going to be a very long night."

Molly sat up and opened the plastic bag. The T-shirt she'd elected to wear lay at the top, a wash-worn white thing that hung lower over her thighs than all her others. She sighed, wishing, not for the first time, that she had some flannel pajamas.

She was still sitting there staring at the shirt when Jake emerged from the bathroom a couple of minutes later. Bare from the waist up, he reminded her of the first time she'd ever seen him. Her initial thought was that she'd never seen any man more beautiful. Her mouth and throat suddenly felt as if she'd just gargled with Elmer's glue.

His upper body was burnished, every muscle and tendon that roped his torso standing out in sharp definition. His tousled dark hair gleamed in the lamplight, the tips ignited to gold. "Is something wrong?"

"I don't have any real pajamas, only a T-shirt."

He arched his dark eyebrows and stepped over to the bureau. "I'm going to dig out some sweats for me." After opening a drawer, he shot her a measuring glance. "I have some thermal underwear that would serve as pajamas. You want a top and bottoms?" At her surprised look, he grinned. "If I'm going to behave myself, I figure the less skin I see, the better. I really, really hate to break my word to a lady." He tossed the underwear onto the bed. "You in nothing but a T-shirt would be a little too tempting."

Molly gratefully grabbed the underwear. "Thank you."

"Not a problem." He winked at her. "If you need help getting it on, just holler. I promise to make a difficult situation impossible."

She laughed nervously and pushed to her feet. "I think I can manage."

"I was afraid you'd say that."

For the first five minutes, Jake waited patiently for Molly to come out of the bathroom. For the second five minutes, he waited, but not quite so patiently. When ten full minutes had elapsed, he started to worry. He heard none of the sounds people usually made while preparing for bed, no rush of water, no swish of a toothbrush, no flush of the toilet. What the hell was she doing in there, counting grout lines?

He swung off the bed, stood, and advanced on the closed bathroom door, which he felt pretty sure was locked. Even worse, he'd built it so sturdy he feared it would take two men and a small boy to break it down. If something was wrong, he might have to call on Hank to help him reach his wife.

Rapping lightly on the planks, he said, "You okay, sweetheart?"

"Not really," she called back. "Would you mind handing me in my T-shirt?"

"Why? What's wrong with my long johns?"

"Nothing's wrong with them. They just don't fit."

Jake frowned and flattened a hand against the door. The underwear fit him. Molly was much shorter and weighed over eighty pounds less. "Are they way too big?"

"In my dreams."

"Then how don't they fit?"

"It's more *where* they don't fit."

Jake grinned in spite of himself. Now that he came to think of it, she was more amply endowed in a couple of places than he was. "I'm sure they'll be fine. We're just going to sleep, not have a fashion show."

"If you think certain parts of me thrust like sword points under two layers of cotton, you ought see them under tight knit."

His smile broadening, Jake leaned a shoulder against the door. Delightful images sprang to his mind. "Honey, the shirt can't be that snug."

"It isn't—in most places. And excuse me, but it isn't just the shirt."

"Come on out. I won't look," he tried.

"Not a *chance*."

"I'll turn out the lights first. How's that?"

"No way. You can see in the dark."

Jake chuckled. She evidently heard him. "Hand me the blasted T-shirt."

He imagined cuddling up to her scantily clad butt and bare legs all night and knew he'd break his promise to her. "Molly, nothing but a T-shirt isn't a good plan."

"Trust me, my body vacuum packed in bubble wrap isn't a good plan, either."

Bubble wrap? Jake's eyebrows inched toward his hairline. The thermal knit was a little like bubble wrap. "Try stretching the stuff."

"How strong do you think I am?" Another silence. "The crotch hangs almost to my knees."

Jake pressed his forehead against the rough-hewn planks of wood. The images dancing through his head did not bode well for a celibate wedding night. "Molly?"

"What?"

"I love you."

"That's irrelevant."

It felt pretty damned relevant to him.

"I may as well parade out naked," she said crossly. "Do you have another pair of sweats?"

"No." And he wasn't about to part with the ones he was wearing. She'd run screaming from the room.

The bathroom door suddenly flew open, and Jake, caught off guard leaning against the planks, almost toppled onto his wife, who stood before him like a vertically challenged boxer, fists knotted at her sides, feet slightly apart, small chin jutting. His first thought was that his underwear had never had it so good. *Holy hell.* As much as he hated to admit it, he could see why she had been reluctant to come out. Every swell and dip of her body was revealed by the tight knit, some swells far more compelling to the male eye than others.

"Sweet mother of God."

She bent forward to tug at the apex of the underwear legs, which hung, just as she'd said, midway to her knees. Folds of extra knit were bunched around her slender ankles. The lady didn't measure up in height, but she sure had dimension.

Planting a hand in the center of his chest, she pushed him back a step and swept past him. "I told you to hand me my T-shirt."

Jake turned to watch her walk away. The fanny action was mind-boggling. She had the cutest butt he'd ever clapped eyes on, both cheeks jiggling with every step she took. He couldn't tell bubble knit from dimples. The part of him that was purely male and totally lacking in social graces sprang infuriatingly erect, poking eagerly against his sweats. He shoved himself down. The instant he turned loose, back up he went. Finally, he resorted to tucking himself between his legs, locking his knees together, and walking in awkward baby steps into the bedroom.

Molly, sitting with her back to him on the opposite side of the bed, had plopped all her glorious dimples down on the mattress, which had the spellbinding effect of magnifying her fullness. Above the temptingly plump swells of bottom and hip, her waist dipped in, making his hands ache to grab hold and never turn loose.

"I feel like a hippo stuffed into a knee-high stocking for a giraffe," she said crossly. Tugging the covers out of her way, she plopped onto her back. "Turn out the lights and stop staring at me. You're giving me a complex."

In Jake's opinion, she already had a complex, and he continued to stand there staring because he couldn't help himself. Never had east and west looked quite so good.

Molly was his exact opposite in every way, soft where he was hard, convex where he was concave, and temptingly full where he was streamlined. He couldn't look at her without aching to touch her, and his blood heated when he tried to imagine all that delicious softness pressed against him.

Her breasts were shaped like plump, delectably ripe melons. She'd once told him that they flopped. Not a problem. If her nipples tried to wander off during lovemaking, he would damned sure enjoy the chase and delight in the capture. Just looking at those sensitive peaks of flesh thrusting against tight knit got his juices flowing.

Oh, man. He was in trouble. A promise was a promise. He wouldn't touch her. But that didn't mean the temptation would be easy to resist. Her breasts did give way to gravity just a bit. The nipple pointed in his direction was nailing him right between the eyes.

He flipped off the lights. She was right; he could see in the dark. Relief flooded through him when she tugged the blankets up over herself. He picked his way to the bed, sat on the edge of the mattress, and stared at the eerily white outline of his feet. Funny. He'd never noticed how ugly his toes were before.

"What are you doing?" she asked in a faint voice.

Jake sighed. "Praying for fortitude."

She giggled. "Aw, come on. I've never overwhelmed anyone in my life."

Jake figured that was because she'd never paraded around in front of a man while wearing skintight thermal underwear. He wished he could see her nude. He didn't even know what color her nipples were yet. Pink, maybe? He clenched his teeth. The same color as her lips, probably.

"Lie down," she urged. "We'll talk until we feel sleepy."

Sleep would be a long time in coming. But he followed her advice and lifted the blankets to slip in beside her—flat on his back, arms crossed tightly over his chest so he wouldn't be tempted to touch her. He just hoped to hell she didn't suddenly develop decent night vision. Just below his waist, the sheet and blankets were having an uplifting experience.

She yawned. "It seems like forever since this morning."

"Yeah, it does."

Silence. Then she whispered, "What if he comes back with a court order, Jake? What if they discount our marriage as invalid because I'm legally incompetent?"

Hearing the fear in her voice tamped Jake's libido. He groped to find her hand. After enclosing her slender fingers in his, he whispered, "Don't worry about it, Molly. I won't let him take you away."

"What if you can't prevent it? He's got lots of money at his disposal, and he can hire the best lawyers."

"So can I," Jake assured her.

"No way are you selling any horses."

He squeezed her hand. "Rafe and Ryan offered to back me financially. Normally, I don't like to borrow money, but in this situation, I'll do it without batting an eye. The Kendricks are a powerful, very wealthy family with connections all over Oregon. Rafe told me this evening that if Rodney tries to cause any trouble, he'll hook me up with his attorney. The guy kicks ass and takes names."

He felt her body tense. "I hate for you to borrow money on my behalf."

Jake would have happily gone into debt for the rest of his life to keep her out of Rodney's clutches. He'd seen the coldness in the man's eyes. He never wanted her near the bastard again.

"Rafe and Ryan are relatives by marriage. I don't mind asking them for help. It's different when you tap family."

She sighed wearily. "Well," she said softly, "if it's any consolation, I'll be able to settle the debt one day. If the courts ever grant me control over my inheritance again, that is."

It was Jake's turn to grow tense. "Just how much was your dad worth exactly? You never really said."

"A lot. Not all of it is liquid, of course. Several million are tied up in the corporation. He left me his share of the firm. The rest of the estate was divided up equally between Claudia and me. I can't remember exact figures, but in stocks, bonds, and cash in the bank, I think I got around four, plus what my share of the firm is worth."

"Four what?"

"Million. Daddy started investing as soon as he got out of college. He was good at what he did."

"Dear God, I've married into money."

She giggled again. "Yes, well—it's nice that you didn't realize in advance. Being married for my future net worth was the pits." She fell quiet for a moment. Then, in a tremulous voice, she said, "It doesn't mean anything, you know. Money doesn't make you happy. If anything, it's only made my life difficult."

"Maybe it can't make you happy, but it sure as hell helps."

She laughed again. Then her fingers clutched his. "Does it bother you? My having money, I mean."

Jake tightened his hand over hers. "Money or the lack of it doesn't define us as individuals. I love you for who you are, not what you have."

She sighed. "And who do you think I am, Jake?"

A lump came into his throat. "A very special lady."

"I'm afraid you don't really know me. I barely know myself, so how can you?" He heard a hollow plunk and knew she'd swallowed to steady her voice. "Now I feel like I never will."

"Know yourself, you mean?" Her silence was all the answer he needed. "Molly, being married to me won't prevent you from achieving your own goals and chasing your own dreams."

"Yes. Yes, it will. Today, I became a rancher's wife. What did you become?"

He drew a blank at the question. "I'm not following."

"Exactly. I'll bet it never once occurred to you that you became a stockbroker's husband today." He felt her tension. It radiated from her like electronic waves. "That's who I am, Jake. Who I was raised to be, anyway. Being married to Rodney derailed my career. We were partners, he said, but in truth, I was little more than his girl Friday. He was the one with the impressive computer science degree. I dropped out of college and just took the state tests to get my license, which made me somehow less in his eyes, even though I'd teethed on finance and knew more about it than he did. I did all the legwork, he got all the recognition.

"After the divorce, I hoped to eventually return to the firm. I wanted to sit behind my dad's desk. You know? I wanted to take over my half of the business and carry on the Sterling tradition." A tremor ran through her. He felt the quiver in her hand. "I also wanted to investigate my father's death. Rodney did it. I'm almost *sure* of that. I wanted to prove it and make sure he paid."

"And you feel you can't do any of that now?"

"I'm married to a Central Oregon *rancher.* Been there, done that. I'll end up being an extension of you, just like it was with Rodney."

"Is that why you feel so lost sometimes?" he asked huskily.

"Yes." He could still feel her trembling. "It's not as bad now as it was, but yes."

"Ah, Molly. You just need time to rediscover yourself, that's all."

She went rigid. "How can I do that now? The cycle will just start all over again."

He tucked in his chin, trying to see her face. She pressed her thumb hard against his palm, and by that, he took measure of her agitation. "That's why I never wanted to be married again. They say we live in an enlightened age, but women still get absorbed into their husbands' lives, not the other way around. I'm not blaming you. I understand it's a societal condition, one that you didn't invent or perpetrate. You're the man. You don't have to change. I'm the woman, therefore I do."

"Do you dislike the idea of being a rancher's wife?"

She lay quietly beside him for a long while, saying nothing. When she finally spoke, her voice rang hollow. "I've become a rancher's wife. There's not much I can do to change it."

Jake smiled into the shadows. "I've become your husband as much as you've become my wife."

"No, you haven't. I'll bet it never once occurred to you all day that by marrying me, you'd changed from being a rancher into something else."

That was true. "It was a fast-paced day. I didn't have a lot of time to contemplate all the changes that are bound to occur in my life now."

"What changes?" she asked bitterly.

He chuckled.

"It isn't funny," she said tightly. "I told you why I didn't want to get married again, and you couldn't understand. I wanted to be me for a while. I needed to find out who I am again and just be me for a while."

The note of longing in her voice made Jake hurt for her.

"I gave up my freedom twelve hours ago, end of subject. I didn't have a choice, and I knew what I was doing when I did it. Now I just have to—" He heard her swallow again. "I just have to live with it, is all."

"No, you don't, Molly. That isn't what marriage is all about. I told you it won't be a prison, and I meant it. You want to be a stockbroker? Fine. Be the best damned stockbroker there is. Invest for me. Make me a rich man. I won't bitch."

"The firm is in Portland. If the court eventually rules in my favor, how can I work there and live here?" Her voice went thin. "Ever since I got out of the clinic, I've lived for the day when I could walk back into Sterling and Wells. Now I never will. I'll be the chief cook and bottle washer on the Lazy J, separating milk and making butter that will make me big as a barn if I eat it."

Jake disentangled his hand from hers, hooked an arm over her waist, and hauled her across the mattress into his arms. She gave a startled squeak, her body snapping taut. He pressed his face against her hair, hugging her fiercely.

"You listen up," he said huskily. When she started to speak, he gave her a squeeze to silence her. "You *will* walk back into Sterling and Wells again, and the first time you sit down behind your dad's desk, I'm going to be there to celebrate the moment with you. It's true that you've married a rancher, but that doesn't mean you have to wash my pots and pans. If you're working and I'm working, we can hire someone to do the domestic crap."

"You'd consider doing that?"

"I'll do better than just consider. As for living here, yeah, we'll have to at least part of the time. But what's to say we can't live in Portland part of the time as well? We're in a telecommunication age, Molly. When you're here, you can work out of a home office on a computer hooked up with the firm network. There are fax machines and telephones. And in case of an emergency, Portland isn't that far to drive. We can hop in a car and be there in three-and-a-half hours."

She sniffed. "You make it sound so simple, but it won't be. What'll you do with yourself if we stay for any period of time in Portland?"

He caught a silky curl between his teeth and gave it a gentle tug. "I'll be a stockbroker's husband. What else? If you can run a milk separator, I can run a calculator and become proficient on a computer."

He felt her mouth curve in a smile against his shoulder. "You'd really do that?"

"Damn straight." He ran a hand up her back, loving the way she felt in his arms. Now that he'd finally found her, he would move heaven and earth to make her happy. "During the winter, the snow gets so deep that the work here slacks off. Most cattlemen ship their cows down to California for winter grazing. I'll be able to break away and leave Hank in charge during that time, no sweat. Who knows? I may get a kick out of changing my occupation six months a year. It'll give us variety in our lives."

He felt her smile again. She sighed and slipped her arms around his neck. It felt wonderful to have her hug him back. "Jake Coulter in a suit. That I have to see."

"I look damned good in a suit, I'll have you know."

"When have you worn one?"

He grinned into the darkness. "I wore one—let me see. I went to a funeral last year. I wore one then. I smelled like mothballs, but I stayed downwind of everybody."

She rewarded him with a giggle. "You can't go to Sterling and Wells smelling like mothballs. We'll have to send the suit out for cleaning."

Jake gathered her closer, glad to hear that wondering, almost hopeful note in her voice. She still had a lot of reservations, but she was starting to believe it might be possible for them to make this work.

Jake had news for her. He'd make it work or die trying.

§ CHAPTER TWENTY-ONE §

The following day, Jake refused to let Molly out of his sight for fear Rodney might show up. She went with him while he fed the horses. She trudged beside him in oversized rubber boots while he changed sprinkler lines. That evening he insisted she accompany him in the pickup while he hayed the livestock.

"I never realized how hard you work all day," she commented when the last of the cattle had been fed.

He parked his truck near the house. After pocketing the keys, he looked over at her, his eyes as blue as sapphires as he traced her features. "Come for a walk with me."

"What about dinner?" She glanced at her watch. "It's after five, and I haven't started it yet."

"We're newlyweds. Screw dinner. We'll heat up leftovers. I'd like to spend a few quiet minutes with my bride. In lieu of a honeymoon, it's not much, but it's all I can offer for now, a walk by the creek."

It was a beautiful evening. Molly relented with a grin. "All right, but only if you'll help me fix something to eat. I'm tired from chasing after you all day."

"Done."

He held her hand as they walked along the stream. Their footsteps were slow, their bodies moving in lazy unison as they listened to the sounds that drifted on the air. Now early May, the days were growing longer, but even so, dusk was beginning to descend, forming pools of grayish gloom beneath the trees that fronted the woodlands. They startled a lone buck with beautiful antlers still in velvet.

Jake led her to sit on a grassy knoll by the stream. The valley narrowed there to only about a hundred yards wide, the north fence line across the creek running parallel with the encroaching forest. To the east, red Herefords dotted the landscape. Directly across the creek,

Molly saw a rabbit foraging for its supper, and at the edge of the woods, she glimpsed a doe and fawn.

"Uh-oh," she whispered. "I think we're preventing that mama and her baby from having their evening snack."

Jake followed her gaze. "They'll mosey along to find a more private spot."

Molly watched the deer bound away. "They're so lovely and graceful."

"They're quite something, all right." After a moment, he whispered, "Listen."

Molly went still. All around them, she heard a beautiful woodland symphony—the wind whispering in the trees, the call of a hawk in the distance, the chattering of the squirrels preparing for night.

"Isn't that fantastic?" he asked.

Molly agreed wholeheartedly. It was especially beautiful to be sharing it with him. Gazing at his dark profile, she felt her heart swell with emotions she didn't want to name or acknowledge, but there was no avoiding it. She'd done the unthinkable and let herself fall in love with him. *Oh, God.* The realization frightened her. He was such a strong-willed man—and so very handsome. Loving him could be dangerous.

He caught her studying him. His brilliant blue eyes went cloudy with tenderness, and he reached over to touch a fingertip to her nose. "Don't be afraid, Molly mine. I'm the best long-term investment you'll ever make."

She hugged her knees. "How can you know what I'm feeling?"

"I'm good at reading feelings. That's why I'm so good with horses." He gave her a slow smile. "When people love each other, they share all their feelings anyway. What's so wrong with my knowing how you feel without you telling me? On the bright side, it'll make me a better husband. I'll understand you and know straight off when I've stepped on your toes."

Silence. She sensed that he was searching for words. "You're only feeling the same thing I've been feeling for weeks," he pointed out gently. "It's scary when it first hits you, isn't it?" He trailed the back of a knuckle over her cheek. "Caring deeply leaves you so open to being hurt."

Molly glanced quickly away. "I don't think I could live through it again. I know it sounds pathetic, but I've been hurt enough to last me a lifetime."

"You won't ever be hurt again," he assured her. "Not by me."

She gnawed the inside of her lip. "I just—" A pent-up breath rushed from her. She turned her gaze back to him. "I know I'm not being fair to you, Jake. You're not Rodney. I'm very aware of that. But inside me—way down deep—there's this terrified *child*. She believed in fairy tales and he-roes once. Now, just thinking about buying into all of that again terrifies her. I try to tell her to grow up, that she's being stupid. But I think she's got the covers pulled over her head."

He grinned and nodded. "There's a child in all of us, Molly. You're not unique in that."

"Is there a child in you?"

"More a teenager, actually. High testosterone levels, horny as hell. And I'm pretty sure the little shit's wearing earplugs because he doesn't hear very good, either."

Molly laughed. She couldn't help herself. "What do you try to tell him?"

"To keep his damned hands off you, to keep his eyes where they be-long, and to keep his thoughts out of the gutter."

Molly smoothed her hands down the legs of her jeans. "I'm sorry I've done this to you."

"Do you realize how often you apologize for things that aren't your fault?"

"I'm nearly thirty years old. I should just sleep with you and get it over with. It's no big deal to other women."

"I didn't marry other women. I chose you."

"Hopefully, that wasn't a mistake. I know I'm being ridiculous, Jake, but deep down, I'm afraid, and I just can't shake it off."

"Of what?" he asked softly. "Not of me, I hope."

"Of course not. I'm coming to trust you more than I've ever trusted anyone. It's not that kind of fear."

"What kind is it, then?"

"I'm afraid you won't find my body attractive." The words came hard, and Molly dug her nails into the denim of her jeans as she forced each one out. "I'm afraid you'll pretend otherwise, but that I'll see the truth in your eyes. Just *thinking* about how humiliating that would be makes me cringe. I'd rather die."

He gazed off across the creek, his expression solemn. Molly expected him to comment on what she'd just told him. Instead, he surprised her by saying, "I played out here as a boy. I loved it here, and I still do." His voice had become hushed with something very like reverence. "When I want to remember the most important moments of my life, both good and bad, this is where I come. Aren't the trees beautiful?"

Baffled by the change of subject, she followed his gaze. The trees were indeed lovely, a grand mix of ponderosa and lodgepole pine that rose majestically against the darkening sky. "Yes, they are lovely."

"Which do you think is the prettiest one?"

Molly searched the tree line. "That's a hard one. They're all so beautiful in their own way. I can't really decide."

"That one's a beauty." He pointed to a ponderosa that stood straight and tall. "And just look at that one. Isn't it grand?"

Molly looked where he pointed next and smiled. "I've always loved trees of all kinds."

"Me, too." He inclined his head toward a half-dead, gnarled oak growing across the field at the forefront of the forest. "But that's the most special one of all to me. The most beautiful one, by far."

Bewildered, Molly stared at the tree he indicated. There was a split down the center of its once magnificent trunk, and half of its branches were dead. "What happened to it?"

"Lightning," he whispered. "And age, too, I guess. Time takes its toll."

"It looks as if it's dying, Jake."

"I don't notice that." He rested his folded arms on his upraised knees, staring at the dying oak with a dreamy expression on his face. "We're old friends, me and that tree. When I was little, I couldn't climb any of the ponderosas, and the junipers hardly seemed worth the effort because they were small. But I could climb that old oak."

Molly tried to picture him as a child. A likeness of little Jaimie slipped into her mind. "Did you ever fall?"

"Nah. Never once. That old tree has branches as big around as my waist. I built myself a fort up there. I think I was about six then. That poor old tree took a beating. I couldn't swing an ax or hammer very straight, and she's got scars all over her, way up high. Every single one of them is a memory for me. To this day, I can climb up there and go back in time, recalling a thousand afternoons and all-night sleep outs. It's like those times happened only yesterday. I spent a lot of happy hours up there, feeling like I was on top of the world and safe from everything. A lot of sad hours, too. Whenever anything bad happened, that was where I went. It was my secret place, apart from the world."

Molly sighed.

"One time, my dad nearly cut her down." He inclined his head. "If you look, you can see how close she grows to the fence. Her big old roots were pushing up a post."

"What stopped him from cutting it?"

"Me. I wrapped both arms around his leg and begged him not to. He tried to tell me there were other oaks growing on the place, that I'd never miss that silly old tree. But I finally convinced him that particular tree was special, that no other oak could take her place." He chuckled softly. "Dad put a jog in the fence and left her to stand."

Molly could see the jog in the fence now that he'd pointed it out. "How sweet of him."

"My dad's a good man. He has a heart of gold, for all his gruff ways." He grew solemn again, his gaze still fixed on the tree. "The night my sister was hurt in the barrel-racing accident, I came out here when I got home from the hospital. It was about four o'clock in the morning, still dark as pitch. All that evening, I had to be strong for my mom and dad, and my younger brothers. And for Bethany, too, when she woke up." His jaw muscle tightened. "She screamed when she realized. Just screamed and screamed. I had to hold her to the bed. I kept telling her it was going to be all right. The entire while, I knew I was lying, that nothing would ever be all right again. I loved her so much, and she was so damned beautiful. In a split second, her life had been destroyed, and there was nothing I could do to fix it. Being her big brother, I'd always fixed things for her, you know? And that night I couldn't."

His voice had gone gravelly with remembered pain. Molly closed her eyes. "Oh, Jake," she whispered.

"Seeing her like that really shook my faith in God. I kept asking myself *why*. How *could* He let that happen? To me, maybe, but not to someone like her. She'd never done a wrong thing to anybody, and she didn't deserve that." He sighed and ran a hand over his face. "I was so *angry*. I'd believed in God all my life, and suddenly it was all a lie, one great big *joke*. I needed to be alone."

"So you came out here."

He nodded. "My folks were a mess. My brothers, too. I felt like the world had ended. When I got out here, I climbed up to my old fort. The floor was rotting out, but I lay down on it anyway. It felt like home to me, a familiar, peaceful place when everything else had become a nightmare. After I cried myself dry, I cursed God and shook my fist at the sky, swearing I'd never believe in anything again. At that moment, I meant it with every fiber of my being."

"What changed your mind?" She had no doubt that something had. She'd never met anyone with more soul than Jake Coulter.

He turned his gaze eastward. "Dawn broke across the sky," he said softly. "You've never seen beautiful until you watch the sunrise from the top of my old tree. I sat up there, and I swear, it felt as if the light was moving clear through me. I knew then. I just *knew*. Me and my old tree were seeing the face of God, and He was saying 'good morning.'" He smiled at the memory. "The world hadn't ended, after all. I knew Bethany would somehow be all right eventually, and that no matter what happened, the sun would always rise again. Life goes on. We just have to find the strength to face it sometimes, and the only way we can do that is to reach deep for faith and believe with all our hearts."

The conviction in his voice brought a lump to Molly's throat. A peaceful silence fell over them. For a long while, they simply sat there, staring at the old oak. Hearing his story gave her a sense of place and history. It also revealed yet another side of this man she had grown to love. Just when she thought she'd learned all there was to know about him, he revealed another layer.

"When you look at my tree, you probably see the dead branches and that big split down her trunk."

"I see more than that now," she assured him. "I can understand why it'll always be the most beautiful tree in the woods to you."

He turned his gaze back to her. "Then why can't you understand that you'll always be the most beautiful woman in the world to me?"

Molly tried to look away, but she couldn't, and her eyes began filling with tears.

"I *love* you," he whispered. "I think I fell in love with you the first time I saw you, Molly mine. And when I look at you, that's all I'm ever going to see, the woman I love. It doesn't matter if you're perfect. To me, you will be, and that's all that counts. It'll be that way always. Even years from now, when you're old and withered, I'll see you with my heart, not my eyes. That's just the way it is when you love someone. The imperfections don't exist. If you see them at all, you think they're beautiful."

"Oh, Jake."

He cupped her chin in his hand. She squeezed her eyes closed as he gently kissed her cheek. Then he released her. A moment later, she heard his clothing rustle and knew he'd pushed to his feet. The wind whistled through the trees, its song lulling her and wrapping around her like an embrace.

"You gave the bastard ten years," he said huskily. "Don't let him ruin the rest of your life. Reach deep, Molly mine. Have some faith in me."

He left her then, his words replaying in her mind long after the sound of his footsteps faded away. *"Have some faith in me."* More tears welled in Molly's eyes. She stared across the clearing at the old oak, wanting so badly to go after him, but lacking the courage to do it.

When several minutes had passed, she pushed to her feet, scaled the fence, and walked across the pasture. When she reached the other stretch of wire, she gazed up into the oak, taking in the tangle of dead and living branches. The tree was huge, at least four feet in diameter at its base, with a towering height bearing testimony to its impressive age. Way up high, she could see the rotted remains of Jake's childhood tree fort. On the tree's massive trunk, she saw carvings in the rough bark, some of them weathered with age and others that looked fairly new. Slipping through the barbed wire, she moved closer to read the inscriptions.

A smile touched her mouth. Jake had chiseled a chronicle of his life on this old tree. One carving commemorated his graduation from college, reading, PIGSKIN, 1993, in painstakingly shaped, small block letters. Another inscription said, MY BEST FRIEND, PEDRO, 1976–1983. The letters weren't as even, indicating a boy's less accomplished skill with a knife. Counting back, Molly figured that Jake had been about thirteen at the time. Touching the dates, she wondered who Pedro had been. She guessed that he had died and that Jake had loved him so much he had tried to immortalize him in this special place.

It was the strangest feeling, reading those old inscriptions. Molly felt as if she were snooping through a personal journal that held all the secrets of Jake Coulter's heart. The freshest-looking inscription on that side of the tree recorded the birth of his nephew, SLY, APRIL, 2001. Molly touched that date as well, recalling the tenderness she'd seen on his dark face when he held the baby in his arms. A tight sensation filled her chest as she moved farther around the tree, taking in other inscriptions, some old, some new. Every major event of his life, both joyous and sad, had been recorded, including the dates of Bethany's accident and her marriage to Ryan Kendrick.

It was incredible, making her want to smile and cry, both at once. High in the network of huge branches, she could even see the crusted wounds that had been left in the bark by a little boy's ax blade. She pictured Jake as a child, struggling on a summer afternoon to drag boards up there and build a miniature mansion in the sky. From that point on, he'd spent much of his time in this place, and every mark on the tree was a memory.

As Molly turned to leave, she spied what looked like fresh cuts on the other side of the old oak's trunk. She stepped around to better examine them. What she saw nearly took her to her knees. It was a recently carved heart. Inside, he had chiseled out the words MOLLY, MY LOVE, 2001.

"Oh, Jake," she whispered shakily.

She lightly traced the engraving. Judging by the freshness of the cuts, he'd done this recently. She imagined him, laboring with his knife, recording yet another memory on his tree so he could come here years from now and remember the moment as if it were yesterday. *Molly, my love.* She could almost hear him whispering the words, his voice deep and raspy with emotion. If ever she had wished for irrefutable proof that he really loved her, this was it. She'd become part of the chronicle, her name inscribed in his secret place, never to be erased or forgotten.

Recalling the story he'd told her about the night of Bethany's accident, Molly wrapped her arms around herself and tipped her head back to gaze at the sky through the network of old branches. She couldn't say that she actually saw the face of God, but she did see and feel the incredible beauty of Creation all around her. And she came face-to-face with an undeniable truth.

Years from now, when Jake Coulter returned to this special place and looked at the carving that bore her name, she didn't want to be only a fond memory in his mind.

She wanted to be the woman who stood beside him.

True to his word, Jake helped Molly cook dinner that night, and after the meal was over, he rolled up his sleeves to wash the dishes. Standing beside him, Molly waited with a dish towel in her hands and butterflies in her stomach while he rinsed a large pot and slipped it in the drainer. Watching him, she tried to think how to best broach this conversation, but every idea she came up with seemed dumb, and she discarded it.

Finally she simply blurted, "I've reached a decision."

Scrubbing a blue Pyrex baking dish, he paused in his work to fix a questioning gaze on her. "You've reached a decision about what?"

Molly gulped. Her hands tightened on the dish towel. "That I'll have sex with you."

He almost dropped the baking dish. To his credit, he quickly recovered. "When?" he asked, his eyes glinting.

Molly hadn't planned the time and place. "I, um—whenever you'd like. Tonight, I guess. If you want to, that is."

"If I *want* to?" He grinned slowly. "Do I have to finish the dishes first?"

Molly. Jake had been in so many relationships that he'd forgotten what it was like to be with a woman who was shy and hesitant. After they finished up the dishes, she thought of last-minute tasks to delay the inevitable. The rug by the back door needed to be shaken out. She called Bart in and spent ten minutes chasing him around the kitchen to brush his teeth. A stove burner needed a quick scrub. Her hands were trembling so that she could barely hold on to the steel wool pad.

He thought about fetching the leftover bottle of champagne from the fridge and cracking it open, anything to help her relax, but he was afraid it would take a bathtub of bubbly to cure what ailed her. He didn't want her numb with drink the first time he made love to her.

"Molly, we don't have to do this tonight if you'd rather wait," he finally offered, praying to God and all His angels that she wouldn't take him up on it.

"Oh, no," she said shakily. "I want to."

Jake had seen people more enthusiastic about having major surgery. He schooled his expression, biting back a smile. The last thing he wanted was for her to think, even for a moment, that he was amused by her nervousness. Just the opposite was true. It caught at his heart and made him want to hug her.

Once upstairs, she stood by the bed, fixed worried eyes on him, and reached with violently trembling hands to unbutton her blouse.

"Sweetheart," he said cautiously, "this isn't how it's supposed to happen."

"It isn't?" Her voice was little more than a squeak.

"No, it isn't," he assured her. Stepping close, he caught her wrists and bent to kiss the corner of her mouth, which was also tremulous. Was she quivering this way all over? The thought ignited his imagination. "It's not an official unveiling. We're supposed to kiss and—" He pressed his face against her hair. "It's supposed to happen naturally."

"No," she said faintly. "Not this time, Jake. I, um—I need for you to see me first. That way, if you don't like me, we can just call it off."

Sweet Lord. She was so sweet and beautiful. How on earth could she believe that he could fail to like her? As if *like* were an appropriate word? He wanted her in a way he'd never wanted anyone. He also preferred to unwrap her himself. Nevertheless, he could tell by the determined ring in her voice that she needed to do this. In some convoluted reasoning, she had concluded that this was the only way she could slay her demons.

Sighing, Jake stepped back, lifting his hands in defeat. "All right. Have it your way."

She nodded decisively and resumed her struggle with the buttons. Never in Jake's memory had a blouse had so many. *One . . . fumble, fumble . . . two.* She was killing him. His hands itched to rip the damned thing off her.

Instead, he leaned against the door, crossing his arms and ankles. *Waiting.* The cotton slowly parted. Once in college, he'd gone to a strip show. All the other guys had whooped and hollered and made asses of themselves, tucking money under the performer's G-string and copping feels. Not him. He'd found the entire display disgusting, giving him cause to wonder if he was abnormal. *Not.* He knew now, beyond a shadow of a doubt, that watching a woman slowly, ever so *slowly,* remove her clothing could turn him on. She just had to be the *right* woman.

Molly. God, how he loved her. He leaned more heavily against the door, thankful for the constraints of denim, which made his arousal less apparent. He could do this. It might be the death of him, but he could do this.

Finally the damned blouse was unbuttoned. Her cheeks turned a painful pink as she peeled the cotton down her arms. *Plop.* The sound of the cloth hitting the floor went off in his head like a bomb. He hoped, *prayed,* that the bra would be next. But, oh, no, she reached for the waistband of her slacks instead, driving him nuts as she endeavored to unfasten the catch.

What the *hell* was the holdup? She jerked and fussed, then bent her head. The girl had fifty thumbs. He could have had that fastener undone in a blink. He settled his gaze on the swell of her breasts above the lacy edge of her bra and damned near swallowed his tongue.

After unfastening her slacks, she kicked off her shoes and bent to tug off her socks. His gaze dropped. He knew he was losing it when he got turned on looking at her toes. They were itty-bitty, the nails an iridescent pink. He imagined nibbling on each one.

With a wiggle of her hips, the slacks slid down her legs, pooling at her ankles. She stepped away, giving the garment a little kick. Jake wondered what would go next, bra or panties. She looked like a vision standing there, her most feminine parts still covered with bits of white nylon and lace.

He was a saint. No question. His shoulder blades had drilled holes through the door.

Next she pulled down her panties. As the nylon slid past her hips, she sucked in her tummy. The moment the underwear puddled at her feet, she pressed a hand over the abdominal roundness she obviously thought was a less than attractive feature. Jake liked her belly just fine. He honestly did. But it was that nest of butterscotch curls just below that made his eyes feel as if they might part company with their sockets.

"I, um . . . " Her voice trailed away, the sound reminding him of a tremulous note on a reed whistle. "My stomach is fat."

Jake's stomach was somewhere around his knees. He stared at her well-rounded hips and thighs. Her skin was as flawless as cream, and her shape was what men's dreams were made of—every inch of her soft and enticing.

The *bra*. He wanted it *off*. But, oh, no, those gorgeous breasts were the last things she wanted to unveil. She lifted trembling hands to the front clasp of the undergarment. Jake's brain snagged on the thought that there were probably four fasteners there for her to undo. His larynx was stuck at the back of his throat.

Patience was a virtue, he reminded himself. The bra would come off— eventually. Never in his memory had a clasp proved to be so stubborn. She jerked, she twisted, her breasts jiggling with every tug. He was going to have a coronary. He stared hard at the crests of her breasts, wondering what color her nipples were.

When the bra finally came open, she grasped either side of the front clasp, her body tense. A study in humiliation, she just stood there, not moving, her nipples still shielded by lace. Her eyes had gone dark. Bright slashes of crimson rode high on her cheeks. She looked so miserable, nearly naked, but not quite, her arms frozen in a torture of embarrassment.

He felt ashamed of himself for ogling her. He never should have allowed her to do this. He stepped toward her. He was about to grasp her wrists and force the issue when warning bells went off in his mind. She'd come this far. He sensed that she needed to go the remainder of the way, that somehow it was important to her that he stand back and see her. Really see her.

"Let me look at you, Molly love."

She gulped and stared at him. Damn, she was so pretty. How could she not realize that? In the faint light coming through the window, her skin shimmered like creamy satin. He wanted to kiss every sweet curve, every delicious hollow—to taste and nibble on her until she sobbed for more. In that moment, Jake could have killed Rodney Wells with his bare hands. The *bastard*. He'd hurt her so deeply, leaving wounds that still bled.

His voice grated like sandpaper over a knife blade. "Molly, let me look at you."

The tendons along her throat stood out. Her shoulders went taut. He felt her struggle. Bless her heart.

With a tug, she drew the cups of the bra from her breasts, and then she just stood there, trembling. Oddly, now that her lovely bosom was bare to his gaze, he hardly noticed the rose-pink nipples he'd been fantasizing about for so long. How could he enjoy looking at them when she was cringing? Without the heat of passion to ease her shyness, this was awful for her.

Jake wanted so badly to take her into his arms, to reassure her with whispers and soothing strokes of his hands. Even he might feel embarrassed to stand there naked while someone stared at him.

But, no, comfort wasn't what she needed from him right now. For her, these next few seconds—and his reaction—were pivotal.

Instead of embracing her, he slid the bra straps down her arms and let the undergarment fall to the floor. Then, grasping her by the wrist, he drew her away from the bed so there was room for him to walk a full circle around her. When this was finished, he vowed, she would know that he had examined every inch of her and looked closely at every imagined flaw.

And imagined flaws they were. She was exquisite—sweetly ample, but perfectly formed. The curve of her back was smooth without a hint of ribcage to mar the effect, the layer of feminine flesh over bone just generous enough to give her a lush softness that made his hands itch to touch her.

For the life of him, he couldn't see why she was so self-conscious about her breasts. Granted, they were large and heavy. She'd never pass a pencil test, that was for damned sure, but few full-figured women could. For all of that, her breasts were beautifully shaped. If that downward dip was a sag, he'd take her, sag and all, and count himself the luckiest man on earth.

Molly was dying. Each time she tried to draw breath, her lungs hitched. An airless pounding had started in her temples, making her afraid she might faint, a fear compounded by the violent slugging of her heart against her ribs. Her skin felt both cold and hot at once, pebbling from the chill air but burning wherever Jake's gaze touched.

When she could bear the agony of it no longer, she crossed her arms over her chest and forced herself to meet his gaze. He was staring back, only not at her face. She wanted to disappear. Under the bed, through a crack in the floor, anywhere, just so long as he couldn't look at her like that. Much as his father had done the evening before, he walked a slow circle around her, making her feel like an object up for bid on an auction block.

Coming to stand behind her, he lightly grazed a hand over the right cheek of her butt. "Dear God, that's the cutest fanny I've ever seen in my life."

Molly squeezed her eyes closed. *Cute?* Oh, God. That fell short. She needed him to think she was pretty even if she wasn't. Anything less simply wouldn't do.

He curled big, work-roughed hands over the sides of her waist, making her jump. His shirt grazed her shoulder blades. She felt his warm breath feathering over her neck just below her ear. He moved his hands down to rest them on her hips, his long, thick fingers pressing gently into her softness.

He moved in closer, sliding a palm from her hip to her tummy, where he explored the swell she so detested. His fingertips lightly traced the roundness, making her belly muscles quiver and jerk. "Oh, Molly," he murmured, "you feel so wonderful. Your skin is like silk. Are you this soft all over?"

She gulped and a low mewling sound she couldn't squelch came up her throat. He bent his head, kissing the line of her collarbone, his big hand pressing in hard against her abdomen to force her posterior against his hard thighs. The denim of his jeans felt warm and abrasive as he moved against her.

He suddenly released her to step around and face her again. His eyes a blaze of blue in his dark face, he ran his gaze the length of her, ending at her toes. On the return journey back up her body, his attention lingered at her knees, and a slight smile slanted across his mouth. Moving up from there, he spent a moment appraising her thighs, one of her worst features. Next, he settled a burning gaze at their apex.

When his eyes finally flicked back up to hers, he said, "Drop your arms, sweetheart."

They felt frozen across her chest, and Molly couldn't have moved them for anything. He stepped closer, curled his fingers over her wrists, and forced her hands down to her sides. Moving back, he stared at her breasts, his eyes an intense, piercing blue that seemed to touch and caress in an almost physical way. Seconds crawled by. Molly tried to cover herself again, but he braced against her.

"Don't," he whispered. *"Don't."*

She was shaking, shaking horribly. She wanted to stop, tried to stop, but her jerking muscles seemed to have a will of their own. With every shudder that ran through her body, her breasts jiggled.

He said nothing. And she needed him to say *something*. Instead he freed her hands to slide his palms up her sides and cup her fullness. She jerked and mewled again when he circled her nipples with his thumbs, torturing the pebbled areolas with feathery passes but avoiding the sensitive, hardened centers. A throbbing ache filled her breasts. Her breathing abated to soft, shallow pants that didn't reach her lungs. Her peripheral vision blurred until only his face was visible, dark and chiseled of feature.

"Dear God," he finally said in a throaty whisper, "you are so pretty, Molly. I knew you would be, but my imagination didn't come close to the reality."

Tears rushed to Molly's eyes. Her mouth suddenly felt as if it was all over her face, twisting every which way. Jake bent to kiss the quivering corners, every brush of his lips incredibly light.

"Don't cry, Molly love. Please don't cry. I'm sorry this has been so embarrassing for you. You are *so* beautiful, Molly. So very beautiful." He gathered her into his arms, his body taut, his hold vibrant with emotion and fiercely possessive. "There's not a spot on you that isn't perfect. From the top of your head to the tips of your toes, you're glorious. I love those little dimples on your butt."

"You do?"

"I do," he assured her.

"You don't think I'm fat?"

He grabbed one of her hands and shoved it between their bodies to press her palm over his fly. "Does that feel like I think you're fat?"

Molly felt throbbing hardness under the denim. Relief made her bones feel as soft as pudding. If not for the support of his arms, she felt sure she couldn't remain erect. Pressing her face against his shirt, she said in a muffled voice, "No."

"I told you, I think you're beautiful. I *like* the way you're made, Molly. If I wanted a woman built like a railroad tie, I could go find one. That's not what I want." He cupped a hand over her bottom, squeezing and releasing. "I love the way you feel, so soft everywhere. And I love the way you look. You have gorgeous breasts, I love all your dimples, and I've never seen prettier legs."

He slipped his hands to her hips then embarked on a slow, burning journey upward from there to cup his palms under her breasts again. This time, after tormenting the areolas with feathery caresses, he drew his thumbs over her nipples, teasing the tips until they budded and throbbed. "I want to kiss those little beauties. Will you let me?"

Molly was trembling—trembling so hard she feared her legs were going to buckle. All the way up the stairs and the entire while she'd been undressing, she'd imagined him turning way in disgust. Now, despite his reassurances, she couldn't quite believe he hadn't—or that he wouldn't yet.

"Are you sure you really want me?"

"Am I sure?" he asked with a husky laugh. "Molly, I want you so much I'm about to die." His voice was so low and throbbing it seemed to move clear through her.

He flicked her nipples again and tickled the inside of her ear with his tongue. With every drag of his thumbs, fiery shocks ribboned through her breasts, making her whole body jerk. Low in her belly, her muscles turned to a quivery mass of heat that made everything tingle and ache. Oh, God, he made her *want*. She'd never in her life wanted anything so much as she wanted Jake Coulter.

He trailed kisses down her neck. His breath wafted hot and steamy over the uplifted swells of her breasts. Molly moaned and clutched the sleeves of his shirt. With darting passes of his tongue, he traced the line of her cleavage, his dark hair whispery soft against her arched throat. Beneath her fingers, she could feel the bunched power in his arms, and his coiled hardness called together everything within her that was feminine to form a fiery, twisting ache at her center.

Lifting one breast, he touched the very tip of his tongue to her nipple. The wet heat sent a jolt of sensation clear to her toes, and her breath whistled in her throat. "I want you so much," he said in a gruff, imploring voice that hummed over her nerve endings.

Molly locked a fist over his hair so he couldn't get away. She wanted his mouth on her there. He licked her again, making her cry out. He moaned and blew softly on her moist flesh, the sudden shock of coolness making her crave his heat even more.

He abandoned her breasts to catch her face between his hands. His long fingers stretched to her hairline, the padded tips pressing possessively against her scalp, his roughened palms warm on her cheeks.

She struggled to focus on his burnished features. He rubbed the pads of his thumbs along her cheekbones. She felt him trembling slightly, and by that she knew he really did want her, and badly.

"Oh, Jake," she said shakily. In these moments of sensual respite, her head had started to clear a bit. She looked into his beautiful eyes and saw need burning in their depths, hot, raw, gut-clenching need. It was the first time in her life any man had ever looked at her that way. The most wonderful feelings coursed through her—a light, airy joy that made her want to laugh and dance about the room—a sense of relief that drained the awful tension from her muscles. "I want you, too. So much I can't bear it."

"Do you, now?" He gave a low chuckle and moved his hands to her shoulders. Pushing her back a step, he said, "Well, never let it be said that I kept a lady waiting."

Molly really, really liked having him look at her that way. The front of his shirt teased her nipples, making her ache to have his mouth on her again. Her legs butted up against the bed just then. With a little push, he sent her sprawling. Before she could gather her wits, he'd followed her down to the mattress, his hands braced at her shoulders to suspend his upper body over hers.

His face moved slightly closer. "When I'm done with you, lady, there won't be a place on you I haven't tasted."

Molly gulped. His shoulders were nearly twice the breadth of hers, the bunched muscles in his arms and chest stretching the cloth of his blue shirt taut to showcase his powerful build. His sable hair lay in tousled waves over his forehead. One dark eyebrow was arched in mischievous challenge. He grinned, the flash of his teeth against his coppery skin making her heart do a funny little jig at the base of her throat.

Before she could start to feel truly nervous, he settled his mouth over hers. *Moist heat, the brush of silk.* His lips were soft yet firm, and he used them with mastery, forcing hers apart to gain entry with his tongue. With long, searching thrusts, he tasted the deepest recesses of her mouth, tickling the roof, grazing the inside of her cheeks, teasing her lips. Molly's head swam. He shared his breath with her, slipping an arm under her waist to lock her against him. *Jake.* As had happened before, she forgot everything but how he made her feel. She arched against him, made fists in his hair, and trembled at the sensations that stormed through her.

This time when he broke off the kiss to trail his lips to her breasts, she didn't want him to stop. His mouth closed over a nipple. Her spine arched of its own accord, her breath snagged in her throat, and she cried out at the sheer pleasure of it. With every flick of his tongue, with every draw on her flesh, her muscles jerked and her toes curled.

He loved her there like a starving man until he was finally sated, and then he stayed to lazily tease her with his teeth, catching her sensitive flesh in a gentle vise and tormenting it with laps of his tongue. Molly moaned. She cried out. And still he teased her.

The need within her mounted, becoming an ache that bordered on pain. Only dimly aware, she wrapped her legs around his thigh and drove her hips against all that deliciously hard male muscle, mindlessly seeking release in a grind of passion as old as womankind.

"Oh, no, you don't," he whispered. "I'll get to that little sweetheart later."

He reared up onto his knees to strip off his shirt. She stared at his chest and upper arms, her heart locked in a struggle to keep its rhythm, her lungs grabbing frantically for oxygen. He was so beautiful. In the dusky light coming in the window, his skin looked shades darker than usual, his eyes an intense sky blue as he looked into hers. She wanted to run her hands over the bulge of muscle in his shoulders, skim her fingertips down his powerfully roped arms, and discover the texture of his skin.

"Jake?" she said tremulously. "I want you."

He flashed her a slow grin. She remembered thinking the first time she met him that he had the dark countenance of a wicked angel. He looked more than a little wicked now—a man who knew what he was about and had no intention of straying off course.

He cast his shirt aside and bent his dark head to lap at her navel. The shock of sensation jerked Molly's hips off the mattress. "Is there anything special you'd like—or anything in particular that you don't like?"

Molly could scarcely think, let alone formulate a coherent response. "I, um—I don't—with Rodney, I never . . . " Her voice trailed away as he flicked his tongue in a widening circle around her belly button. "Jake?"

He raised his head to stare at her, his eyes suddenly sharp and relentlessly intent. "With Rodney, you never what?" he asked softly.

Molly searched her muddled brain, trying to recall what she'd been about to say. He moved up, bringing his face closer to hers, his gaze filled with question.

"I never liked any of it," she found the presence of mind to say.

"It won't be that way with me," he whispered.

Molly knew it wouldn't. The beauty of what had happened so far assured her of that.

He bent to settle his mouth over hers again. After kissing her until she felt dizzy, he lifted his head to trail his lips over her cheek, then down the bridge of her nose. Then he kissed his way down her throat, lingering at the V of her collarbone. "If I do anything you don't like, you just tell me, all right?"

Molly couldn't imagine not liking anything. "All right," she managed to say.

He grazed his lips down her sternum. When he reached her belly again, Molly made fists on the bedspread and stared blindly at the knotty pine ceiling. She'd read about this kind of thing in romances and guessed his intention, but she'd never experienced it herself.

Jake circled lower to the nest of butterscotch curls at the apex of her thighs. She quivered and gulped, her insides clenching. He traced a teasing trail over her pelvis with his lips and tongue. When her stomach convulsed, he chuckled, the hot waft of his breath and the vibration of his chest against her thigh making her moan.

He circled out to her hip and took a lazy journey south, the hot skin of his chest grazing hers as he moved down. He kissed her toes. He made her ankles tingle. He trailed the tip of his tongue up her shins, tantalizing her with the titillating strokes until she felt sure she would go mad. By the time he moved higher, Molly thought she would die when he delved his tongue between her knees and licked his way up her inner thigh.

"Are you okay with this?" he asked huskily.

Molly couldn't have answered if her life had depended on it. He reached his target and dipped past her curls with the tip of his tongue, sending electrical shocks coursing through her whole body. What little breath remained in her lungs came rushing out. The ceiling did a slow revolution. He tickled her there again.

"Sweetheart, answer me. Is this all right with you?"

Molly's throat strained. She arched up, trembling so badly she felt the mattress shiver. "Yes," she managed to say breathlessly.

He thrust his tongue in, laving her with shocking heat. "Are you sure?" he murmured against her. "If it's too much, too fast, I'll understand."

The movement of his lips made bright spots dance before her eyes. Her only fear was that he might stop. "I'm—sure."

He closed his mouth over her then. Molly bucked and sobbed. It was the most incredible sensation. Far better than anything she'd ever read about in books. It was—she arched up. He teased her so gently that she held her breath until her temples pounded. She sobbed again and made fists in his hair, trying to press him closer. Still he tormented her with light strokes, making her insides twist and knot, making the urgency build.

When she thought she would die with the wanting, he shocked her by drawing hard on her with his mouth. Molly felt as if every nerve in her body had converged to that one spot. He dragged the rough of his tongue across her in rhythmic passes, pressing harder, taking complete possession, and sending her body into helpless spasms. When release finally caught her in its throes, Molly shrieked—shrill bleats of sound emitted with every convulsive expulsion of breath. He stayed with her until her throbbing flesh could stand no more, and then he brought her down with gentle strokes, soothing the pulsating nerve endings that he had just teased so mercilessly.

Afterward Molly felt as if she'd melted into a puddle. She couldn't move, couldn't think or focus clearly. She heard boots thump on the floor, followed by the plop of denim and pocket change rolling across the hardwood floor. Jake moved over her in a dark blur. He gently kissed her. Then he curled his hands over her hips and lifted her to him. Molly didn't think she could bear to feel anything more, didn't think the finale could possibly compare to what he'd just given her.

But she was wrong.

When the hard, hot heat of him pushed into her, she felt as if starbursts were going off low in her belly. He pressed forward gently at first, testing his way as if she were made of fragile silk. When he was buried to the hilt, he eased back and then carefully moved forward again.

"You okay?" he asked in a strangely tight voice.

Molly curled her hands over his rippling shoulders. "Oh, *yes*."

He picked up the tempo then, increasing the force of his thrusts. Pleasure bursts exploded inside her. She cried out and started to move with him, locking her legs around him to better gauge his strokes. Up, up. She felt as if he were lifting her toward a fiery crest. Her heart slugged against her ribs. Her breath came in sharp gasps. Black spots danced before her eyes. He increased the power of his thrusts, sliding her over the mattress with each impact until all that kept them joined was the clutch of her legs.

Heaven. Just when she felt his body snap taut, Molly reached her second climax. Through a dizzying blur, she focused on his dark face, loving him as she'd never loved anyone. *Jake*. She felt a rush of electrical heat spill into her. His hardness went into spasms deep within her. And then there was only spiraling delirium as they went over the edge together.

ᔰ CHAPTER TWENTY–TWO ᔱ

Jake held his world in his arms. Molly cuddled against him like a delectably shaped body pillow, so soft that he was sorely tempted to have her again, even though he knew she was still exhausted from last time. Completely without inhibition in slumber as she never was awake, she pressed so close that one full breast rested on his chest. Her relaxed tummy, which she'd tried to suck in earlier, pressed into the hollow above his hip, and one plump thigh angled across his as though to anchor him in place.

He smiled into the darkness that had descended over the bedroom. As if he was going anywhere? Not a chance. God, she was precious. If he ever saw her eating nothing but salad for lunch again, he'd turn her over his knee. He *liked* her round. There wasn't a place on her he could touch without going rock hard. He wanted to squeeze and kiss and fondle every soft inch of her, and doubted he would ever tire of the experience.

He toyed with her hair, loving the way the short tendrils curled over his fingers. He pressed close to inhale the scent of shampoo and feminine essence that were exclusively her own. *Damn.* Letting her hair slip from his hand, he ran his palm over her fanny. His fingertips searched out the dimples, and he grinned.

He couldn't help but marvel over how fantastic she felt. Everything in his life was hard. He got up of a morning and endured the harsh elements. He bucked hay. He wrestled bulls. He pitted his strength against recalcitrant horses. It was so incredibly arousing to feel satiny softness for a change. He cupped a hand over her shoulder and felt for bones. They were in there, but he had to search to find them, and that suited him just fine.

Molly moaned in her sleep. *Uh-oh.* He kissed her forehead and whispered, "It's all right, Molly mine."

"Mmm," she murmured and snuggled closer. Her body went limp again.

Jake ran his hand down her arm, testing for muscle. He found only a cute little dimple above her elbow. He made a mental note to trace it with his tongue the next time he made love to her. He touched the small knob of her elbow. Next he explored her wrist and hand. Under all the softness, there wasn't a whole lot to her.

Journeying south, he ran his hand over her bent leg. On the inside of her thigh, he found squishy little lumps under her skin that he guessed were cellulite. *Warm,* squishy little lumps. His dick went hard and stood at attention.

He sighed. Determined not to wake her, he closed his eyes and moved his hand to his chest. Only instead of chest, he found breast. He was lost. He wanted her again, and if he meant to get any sleep at all, he had to have her. He cupped his hand over the silky fullness of her. The instant he grazed her nipple with his thumb, her flesh went hard. Pushing her upward, he dipped his chin to flick her with his tongue. Her body flinched. She sighed in her sleep. He pushed her a little higher to take her into his mouth.

That sensitive rivet of flesh swelled and thrust eagerly against his tongue. He grazed it with his teeth, then suckled, teasing the crest to a throbbing rigidity. Molly moaned. Her slender fingers tightened over his ribs. He saw her lashes flutter. He nipped her lightly and felt her muscles jerk.

"Jake?" She fluttered her lashes again. "What are you doing?"

"Nothing. Just go back to sleep, sweetheart." Like he would let her? Ah, but she was so sweet like this, all relaxed and unguarded. He pushed her onto her back, following her over to keep her nipple caught between his teeth. He dragged his tongue over the tip. Once, twice. Her eyes came wide open. He lifted his head to grin at her. "Hi."

She sighed and arched her back. Her slender hands threaded into his hair. "Oh, my."

"I want you again. Do you mind?"

Her only answer was a dreamy sigh. Jake took that as a positive response and made love to her, this time paying special attention to all the dimples he'd missed during the first round.

Happiness. Molly realized now that she'd never really experienced it before. Being in love, being loved . . . it was such an incredible joy, and it was made all the more special by Jake's penchant for laughter. With him, Molly quickly learned that lovemaking would always be something to be enjoyed, not only during the act itself but before and after. He joked, he teased, he played with her. Sometimes he had Molly laughing so hard that when he finally kissed her the passion she felt came as a shock.

There was only one cloud on their horizon. *Rodney.* It worried Molly that her ex-husband had not returned with a court order as he'd threatened. She knew him. When he thought he had the upper hand, he moved in with merciless intent.

Why hadn't he come back? Molly knew he could easily have gotten his court order. He had no way of knowing she and Jake were married. Something wasn't right. Jake was worried about it, too, Molly knew. She often saw shadows in his eyes and knew he was pondering the situation.

On the third evening after their marriage, Jake invited her to take one of their frequent walks along the creek. Hand in hand, they strolled in silence for a long while. Then he finally said, "I feel like there's a bomb hanging over us by a slender thread and any little thing may bring it crashing down."

Molly squeezed his hand, knowing exactly what he meant. Not even in her most blissful moments with Jake could she forget that there would be unpleasantness to face. The possible outcome terrified her. She could never return to a clinic now—and stay sane. Jake had shown her what magic was like, and now anything less would equate to unbearable misery. She didn't think she could live without him.

"He wants something," Jake said softly. "If he once killed over it, Molly, it stands to reason he won't give up. He'll be back."

"I know."

His hand tightened over hers. "I hate waiting like a sitting duck. It's not in my nature." He sighed wearily. "I keep circling back to those papers he wanted you to sign. I think that's why he drugged you—why he had you locked away. He hoped to break you down, to reduce you to such a helpless mess, you'd do whatever he said, even if it meant signing papers you couldn't review first."

Molly's stomach clenched when she recalled how very close she'd come to being beaten. There had been times during her illness when she'd been so terrified, she would have done anything, *anything*, to escape the nightmare her life had become.

"If he's got your power of attorney, that makes no sense," Jake pointed out. "He should be able to sign in your stead, so why does he need your signature on something?"

Molly had been thinking about that as well. "Maybe the documents aren't covered by my power of attorney. Something he can't sign for me."

"What, though? A good attorney would draw up an all-inclusive power of attorney that would cover your business affairs in all fifty states."

Molly's heart caught as a horrible thought occurred to her. "Maybe it involves something outside the states."

Jake's eyes narrowed. "Damn it, I hate playing these guessing games."

Molly did as well. "I need to go through the firm records," she whispered.

She felt his body go still. He cast her a worried look. "How?"

"I could return to Portland, breach building security, and get on one of the network computers."

"No way! That'd be dangerous."

"Waiting for him to make a move is dangerous, too," she argued. "I know him, Jake. He's scheming and planning. If we wait for him to make his move, we may find ourselves in more trouble than we can worm out of."

"Forget it. You're not going."

A week ago, his authoritarian manner would have struck terror into Molly's heart. Now she looked into his eyes and saw only the fear he felt for her. Control wasn't the issue with Jake. Keeping her safe was his only concern.

"You could come with me."

He gazed off at nothing, his jaw muscle rippling as he clenched his teeth. "I guess I could, at that. At least then I'd know if something happened. You wouldn't have to face the son of a bitch alone."

Molly took both his hands in hers. "I'd feel a lot better if you were there, that's for sure."

His gaze locked on hers. "Deal. We'll go together."

Molly's heart started to gallop as she considered all that they'd have to do, most of it illegal. "We need to make plans."

He startled her half to death by releasing her hand, bending his legs, and locking an arm around her knees. Just that quickly, Molly found herself upended over his shoulder, her head dangling. She grabbed his belt to lever herself up. "*What* on *earth*? Jake, have you lost your *mind*?"

"Hell, no. I had a reason for bringing you out here, and I'll be damned if I'll let Rodney Wells screw it up. This is your one evening of the week off, and I'm going to enjoy every second of it."

He set off through the woods with Molly draped over his shoulder. She shrieked and playfully pummeled his back. He retaliated by smacking her upturned rump.

"*Ouch!*" she cried, even though it didn't hurt.

He cupped a hand over her butt and gave it a squeeze. "Damn, that was fun. I'm kinky and didn't even know it."

She giggled. "Forget it."

He jostled her to get a better hold and veered right. "Ah, come on. Let a guy have some fun."

"Have fun with someone else's fanny."

"I can't. Only yours will do." He suddenly braked and crouched to settle her feet on the ground. When she'd gained her balance, he grinned and patted the ponderosa pine beside them. "Remember this tree?"

Molly threw a startled look at the tree in question. "Is this the one?"

He patted the bark again. "Trust me, this is it. I'd know this tree anywhere. I've seen it in my dreams a hundred times."

Molly giggled. "Forget it. I'd get slivers in my already abused posterior."

His eyes began to twinkle, and he reached into his pocket to flash his pocketknife. "I brought my sliver picker. Afterward, I'll lay you over my knees and—" His eyes filled with an ominous glint. "Holy hell. That'd never work. I'd forget what I was about and make love to you again."

He slipped an arm around her waist. Dipping his head, he nibbled on her ear.

"*No!*" she cried halfheartedly. "Not against a *tree,* Jake."

"Please?" He nibbled some more. "I have to do this just once and get it out of my system. Otherwise it'll never leave me alone." He tightened his arm suddenly. The next instant, Molly found herself pinned against the tree trunk. "Wrap your legs around my hips."

She did as he told her. Her blood began to slog through her veins when she saw the heat in his eyes. Pressing in with his lower body to support her weight, he reached to touch her hair. The love she saw in his expression made her feel gloriously beautiful—so beautiful that she felt not a twinge of embarrassment when he started to unfasten her blouse. His gaze moved lightly over her face like lambent tongues of flame.

"Did you bring a rope?" she couldn't resist asking.

Surprise flickered across his dark countenance, and then he barked with laughter. "The love scene in the romance, right?" Before she could reply, he was kissing her—deeply, passionately, his tongue claiming hers in a rhythmic parry and thrust that made her think of the way he possessed her body. Molly gave herself up to the sensations. Oh, how she loved him. The feelings that coursed through her were indescribable—delicious, sweet, her yearning for him so sharp she thought she'd never feel sated.

She was wrong, of course. Jake never left her on the edge. He drew her over into the abyss with him, taking all she had to give, giving all she could take. When the moment came, he jerked off his shirt to wedge it between her bottom and the bark, protecting her even in the throes of passion.

He then proceeded to make one of her wildest fantasies come true. He flattened her against the tree, thrust himself into her eager body, and took her with a forceful urgency that made her heart soar.

One short month ago, Molly had never envisioned herself as a criminal sort. Then she'd stolen a sixty-five thousand dollar racehorse, and her moral character had deteriorated from there. Now she found herself breaking and entering. It was one of the most terrifying experiences of her life. All during the drive up from Crystal Falls, she'd dreaded this moment.

Her hands shook violently as she groped in her purse for her firm keys, one of the few things Rodney had forgotten to strip from her possession. Jake stood beside her in the shadows, one side of his face illuminated by the parking lot lights. In honor of their foray to the city, he'd doffed his Stetson and wore a white shirt and sport coat over his Wrangler jeans. He still looked every inch a cowboy. Molly figured he probably would even in an expensive three-piece suit, but she wouldn't have changed him for the world. He looked so big and sturdy and wonderfully dependable. Having him there made her feel less terrified.

"Oh, Jake," she whispered, staring down at the alarm key on her palm. "What if they've changed the system and I set off the alarm?"

"Then, Molly mine, we run like hell."

She giggled. "A big help you are. Criminals never outrun the cops. They always get caught."

"Most criminals don't have four-wheel-drive trucks with all-terrain tread," he said jokingly. "I'll leave them to eat our dust."

Gaining courage from the confidence in his voice, Molly took a deep breath and thrust the odd-shaped, tubular key into its niche. She held her breath as she gave it a turn. The little red light on the panel went out. Her shoulders sagged with relief. "Thank you, God."

"Amen." The moment Molly unlocked the door, he opened it. "Hurry, Molly girl. We're sore thumbs out here."

They stepped inside. Darkness enveloped them when he closed and relocked the door behind them. Molly knew her surroundings by memory. They stood in a carpeted hallway. On the right just a few feet away was the coffee lounge. To the left was the janitorial supply room where she'd once caught Rodney banging a girl Friday. The memory no longer hurt. It didn't even rankle. That rude shock had marked the beginning of her awakening, which had eventually led her into Jake Coulter's arms.

"Follow me," she whispered.

"Try to lose me," he said near her ear. "I'm joined to you at the hip."

Molly went directly to her dad's office, waiting until they were inside with the door closed before she flipped on the lights. *Memories.* They hit her hard and fast, so gruesome and clear they hurt like physical blows. Her dad's desk, where she'd found him with half his head blown off. The chair that she'd so often occupied as a girl while he worked.

Jake's arms came around her from behind. He drew her back against him. "Ah, Molly, honey. Talk to me. Don't remember alone."

Her voice quavered. "I can almost see him. All the blood." Her body started to shake. "I loved him so much, Jake. He was so *good.* So wonderful. No one ever had a better dad. I always knew he loved me, no matter what. During the worst times, knowing that was all that held me together. And then, just like that, he was dead, and in such a horrible way."

His embrace tightened. It was as if he knew how desperately she needed his strength right then. "I love you that way now, Molly mine. No matter what, and forever." He lifted his head to scan the room. "Remember past it, Molly. You must have had good times in here."

"Oh, yes," she said softly. Oddly, it wasn't the joyful memories that rushed to her mind, but those that were bittersweet, the things that had defined her relationship with her dad. Being eleven and heartbroken over not getting the lead part in a play. Developing breasts before all the other girls did and feeling acutely self-conscious. "My dad was always my rock," she whispered. "Somehow, no matter how upset I was, he could make me laugh, and he always made me feel special."

"That's what you should remember, all those special times. Death is our final scene, not the one that comprises our life. Remember your dad as he was, not the way he ended."

A feeling of peace settled over Molly. She hugged all the good memories close and leaned her weight against Jake's solid chest, closing her eyes for a moment. When she opened them again, she felt restored and knew she had the strength to face anything as long as this man was beside her.

When she said as much, Jake whispered, "You can face anything even without me. You've got steel in your spine, Molly. I've seen it a hundred times. You don't need me. You don't need anyone. If you did, you never would have made it this far."

Molly straightened away from him. Dropping her purse onto an upholstered Victorian chair along the wall, she stepped forward. One foot in front of the other. Not allowing herself to think of that morning when she'd found her father's body, she walked to his desk.

As she lowered herself onto his chair, tears stung her eyes. *This* was who she was. From infancy, she'd teethed on investment journals. *This* was her destiny, what she'd been groomed to do all her life.

"You look transformed sitting there," Jake whispered.

Her gaze clung to his. It pleased her to know that he understood exactly how she felt without her saying a word.

"Hello, Molly Sterling," he said softly. His eyes searched hers, delving deep. Then he held out a big, brown hand to her. "I've been waiting a hell of a long time to meet you."

Molly took his hand. An electrical surge seemed to run from his arm up hers. She slowly smiled. "How do you feel about being a stockbroker's husband?"

"Like the luckiest man alive. How do you feel about being a rancher's wife?"

Molly took a moment to reply. "Blessed," she said softly. "I feel so blessed."

He grinned and inclined his head at the computer. "Go to work, lady. Get the son of a bitch by the balls."

"Can I have them freeze-dried and hang them on our living room wall as a trophy?" she asked as she flipped on the computer.

"Hell, darlin', I'll make you a special display case."

She giggled and went to work. The computer was connected to the mainframe, giving her access to all the firm's files. Jake watched with keen interest over her shoulder as she invaded the firm's system. "Damn, you're good at what you do."

Molly's chin came up. A feeling of purpose surged through her. "Damn straight, Mr. Coulter. I was taught by one of the best."

For all of Molly's renewed confidence and sense of purpose, her search of the computer files revealed nothing. "Oh, Jake, there's nothing here. I can't find a single thing that looks out of the ordinary." She logged into her dad's personal files. Still, nothing. "Now, what?"

"We take a break and calm down," he said sagely. "Get all worked up, and you won't be able to think straight." He leaned a hip on the edge of the desk and grinned down at her. "How do you feel about sex on a Victorian chair?"

She giggled. "Not in *here*. It's a shrine."

He sighed and raked a hand through his hair. Glancing around, he said, "When we move up here six months out of the year, where'll I grab my afternoon fix if we can't do it in here?"

Molly grinned. "Maybe we could partition off one corner and designate it a nonshrine area."

"Done."

She ran her hands lovingly over her father's mahogany desk. Just touching it brought back so many memories. "When I was growing up, Daddy left me surprises in his secret compartment."

"What secret compartment?"

Molly leaned back in her chair and gave him a challenging look. "The one in his desk. Bet you can't find it."

He crouched beside her to study the desk's structure. He ran a hand over the left side panel.

"Nope, not even warm," she teased.

He flattened his hand against the opposite panel. "Cold, cold," she said. "Try north."

He reached up, feeling the panel beneath the center drawer. His gaze suddenly sharpened on hers. Then he grinned. The next instant, an invisible drawer beneath the center one popped open. "Voilà!" he said.

"Every time my dad went away, he'd buy me a little something and hide it in here for me," she said softly. "I'd come racing in here after school to—" Molly broke off and stared. Inside the drawer lay a computer disk. The hair on her nape prickled. Her skin developed goose bumps. "Oh, my God, Jake."

He twisted around. "What?" he said, and then he saw the disk. "Sweet Christ, Molly, I think he left you a final sweet nothing."

Molly liked that. *A sweet nothing*. It reminded her of all the little gifts Jake had left her on the cabin porch. With trembling fingers, she picked up the square of plastic. It gave her the oddest feeling to know her father had touched it last. Possibly right before he died. Her heart kicked in excitement.

"Let's not get ahead of ourselves," Jake whispered. "Have a look at what's on it first."

She nodded. "You're right. Daddy said secret panels were a joke because all desks have them. He never hid anything of importance in there."

"Maybe he broke that rule just once," Jake suggested huskily. "If you're right and Rodney shot him, it could be he didn't have time to hide it else-where. Or maybe he knew you'd be sure to look in there eventually, for old time's sake if nothing else, and he felt it was a sure way to get infor-mation to you."

"I thought we weren't going to get ahead of ourselves."

He smiled. "Just look at the damned disk," he urged, his tone edged with excitement.

Molly was shaking so hard, she had to take two stabs at inserting the disk into the drive. Telling herself not to get her hopes up, she began viewing the files.

"Oh, my God, Jake. Oh, my *God*!"

"What? It's all Greek. Talk to me."

"He used dummy corporations as a cover to invest heavily in stock, hedging his bets with insider information, which is against the law."

"Your father?"

"No," Molly whispered. "Daddy would never have done this. It was done under his name, though. Rodney's machination, I feel sure."

"That miserable son of a bitch," Jake said softly. "He couldn't even make his dirty money without setting up someone else to take the fall."

Molly opened another file. Again all she could think to say was, "Oh, my God." After the first shock wore off, she whispered, "He must have raked in millions, Jake. *Millions*." She anxiously opened another file. "Email messages. Oh, dear God, Jake, just look at this. Information from other companies about new products, upcoming mergers, swings in the mar-ket." Molly's heart caught when she saw that every message had been ad-dressed to Marshal Sterling. "Using insider information like this, Rodney was making a killing, all under dummy corporations and in Daddy's name so it wouldn't appear that the gains came to him."

As Molly continued to search through the files, her alarm mounted. "It's all under my father's name, Jake. If I go to the authorities with this, the blame for it will be pinned on him." She fell back in the chair and looked at her new husband with sick apprehension. "Rodney did this. I know it. But there's no way I can prove it." Her heart twisted in her chest. She glanced back at the computer screen. In a hollow voice, she said, "Maybe my dad killed himself after all. Maybe he was so devastated when he saw this that he decided to take the easy way out, rather than face the scandal."

Jake shook his head. "I never had the honor of meeting Marshal Ster-ling, but I know his daughter. No faint heart who would blow his brains out over a patch of trouble could have raised a woman of your caliber."

"Oh, Jake, thank you."

He stared hard at the computer display. "Why is it that all these files aren't on the main network?" he asked. "It's as if your dad copied them from a separate hard drive or something."

A chill zipped down Molly's spine. "Oh, Jake, I've been so upset I wasn't thinking straight. You're right. You're absolutely *right*." She jumped up from the chair. "These are records of company transactions, alleged activity in accounts of my father's. That being the case, they should be on the main system like all his other firm accounts, not hidden away on a disk."

Jake stood beside her.

"My father was worried sick about something for about a week before he died. Maybe he was suspicious of Rodney. The morning of his death, he came in early. He seldom did that, choosing instead to enjoy the mornings with Claudia before she left for the clinic. What if he came in early that day, expressly to get here before Rodney to have a look at his computer? Rodney came to the firm early that morning, too. At least he was supposed to. When I arrived, he still wasn't here, and I thought it strange. But what if he'd been here already and left?"

Jake nodded. "Go on. It's making sense to me so far."

Molly was trembling. "Maybe he caught Daddy in his office *after* he'd copied this information onto a disk and put it in his pocket. Rodney may have been angry and followed him back here. Dad would have sat at his desk while they talked. Maybe he sensed that things were turning lethal, and he slipped the disk into the secret compartment right before Rodney shot him."

Molly swung around the desk to go to Rodney's office, Jake fast on her heels. "Knowing my ex-husband, he's still investing heavily in stock illegally. Rodney, the gambler. Investing turns his crank. He says it's a sophisticated way of betting. Only he found a way to swing the odds in his favor."

"Let's just hope we can find some proof to nail the bastard."

"He *knew* Dad had gotten the goods on him," she cried shrilly as they raced along the corridor. "Don't you see, Jake? *That's* why he was so upset that day when he caught me searching Daddy's office. He didn't know where my father had stashed the evidence, and he was terrified I'd find it if I hadn't already. That's why he immediately started trying to make me look nuts. He *had* to cast doubt on my credibility so no matter what I found, I couldn't have him thrown in prison."

After sitting at Rodney's desk, Molly closed her eyes and reached deep within herself for calm. Justice would be served, she promised herself. Rodney would pay dearly for the lives he'd ruined. She lifted her lashes, focused on Rodney's computer screen, and determinedly went to work.

Jake folded his arms on the back of the chair to watch over her shoulder. "Your scenario all figures except for one thing," he mused aloud. "It doesn't explain why Rodney needs your signature on something so desperately."

"Maybe the answers are here," Molly said.

"If he's made millions, why the hell doesn't he just take his profits and scat?" Jake asked. "He could go to a foreign country, assume a new identity. If those account records we just saw are any indication, he made some huge profits."

"True, but Rodney's never satisfied. Greed is his middle name. He'll stay and rake in cash as long as he can. It's gambling to him. He's compulsive about it."

"If that's the case, why not just let you remain on the ranch, well out of his way, while he hauls in dough for the next few months? Until the power of attorney expires, he can run this place without any input from you." Jake growled low in his chest. "I smell a rat. I'm not sure what it is, but this stinks to high heaven."

Molly had barely gotten into Rodney's system before she hit a brick wall. "A bunch of these files are protected."

"Go for it. That's where he'll hide the good stuff."

"I need the password!" Molly cried in frustration. "Oh, God, Jake. Rodney is a genius with computers. The Silicon Valley guru, remember. I'm a babe in the woods by comparison. I'll never be able to crack a system he protected."

Jake laid a hand on her shoulder. Just his touch served to calm her. "Molly Sterling Coulter, you can do anything you set out to do. Didn't you steal a horse and put your whole life on the line?"

"Yes," she said weakly. The memory of that horrific day made her grin. "I did."

"Shhh." Jake's hand convulsed on her shoulder. "What the frigging hell is that?"

Molly's heart leaped at a shrill sound, pealing in the outside corridor. She almost jumped out of the chair, thinking they'd been caught and the alarm was going off. Then she laughed and went limp with relief. "It's the grandfather clock."

Jake listened and chuckled. "Damn. I thought our asses were grass for a second."

Molly relaxed and went back to password guessing. She tried everything she could think of—Rodney's name, his initials, his birth date, his social security number. Nothing gave her access to the protected files.

"What we need is a little blind luck," Jake whispered.

Luck. Rodney was a gambler. Molly typed in the word. It didn't work. "Well, that wasn't it." She thought for a moment. Then a thrill of excitement coursed through her. Going on a hunch, she typed in Sonora Sunset, the name of the horse Rodney had placed so many bets on.

"Bingo," Jake whispered. "That's it, Molly."

"I'm in," she said joyously. "I'm *in*, Jake."

"Holy Toledo," Jake said as she began opening files. "Rodney has been a very busy boy."

Molly found records of several illegal stock transactions. Then she stumbled upon entries of her ex-husband's betting at the track. "Now I understand why he whipped poor Sunset. Luck has not been Rodney's friend. Just look at this, Jake. He's suffered some very heavy losses, the largest when he last wagered on Sunset and the poor horse lost."

Jake whistled at the huge amounts of money Rodney had tossed away. "He's crazy. No wonder the bastard isn't lounging on an exotic beach somewhere. He's been betting at the track like a lord. Is that his present bottom line? How the hell can that be? It looks like he's damned near broke."

It made no sense to Molly, either. All those millions that Rodney had made illegally appeared to be gone. "I guess gambling finally got the upper hand," she whispered.

"Blowing money like that makes no sense at all to me," Jake said. "He has to know he can't continue with the insider trading forever without being caught. He should be using this window of time to make a killing, and then run when the heat turns up."

Molly sadly reviewed the accounting of all Sonora Sunset's losses at the track. The poor horse. He'd run his heart out for Rodney, but he just hadn't had what it took to win. He'd been too young, too green. His failures had earned him his owner's rage. "Oh, Jake, do you think Rodney whipped Sunset every time he lost?" she asked thinly. "It breaks my heart to think of it."

"I just thank God he managed to control his mean nature with you," Jake murmured.

"Sunset was just an animal. He had no recourse, and Rodney knew that I did. My dad would have been enraged if he'd laid a hand on me." Coldness filled her. "He killed my father, Jake. Looking at all this just drives home to me how very ruthless he actually is. I know he killed him. He probably did it without a twinge of conscience. He has no stops. No compassion for anyone or anything."

"Sonora Sunset, his password to a life of luxury," Jake said softly. "Who's the animal—the horse or him?"

"I'm just so glad I'm free of him," she whispered.

"Free, yes. It's time to heal and move on, Molly mine."

She smiled. "Yes, but to do that, I have to bring the bastard to justice."

"Is this enough to take to the Securities and Exchange Commission?" Jake asked.

Molly nodded and began copying all the protected files onto disks. "More than enough. The dates of the more recent transactions prove that my father had nothing to do with it. Dead men can't do insider trading, and thanks to Rodney, I've been effectively cut out of the picture for months, so he can't pin it on me, either."

When she'd finished making the copies and pushed up from the desk, Jake glanced around the plush office. "Do you have bad memories of this room?"

"A host of them," she admitted.

A twinkle slipped into his eyes. "Is it a shrine?"

"More like a horror chamber."

He caught her chin on the edge of his hand. "Do you think he ever screwed around on you with someone in here?"

"Undoubtedly."

He grinned. "Wanna get even?"

Molly giggled. "I think we'd better save it for later, Mr. Coulter. If we get caught, you could have difficulty running with your Wranglers around your ankles."

"Good point."

But he kissed her anyway. For Molly, the magic of that was enough to dispel all the bad memories and fill her mind with glorious new ones. Rodney Wells no longer had any power over her life.

On the way out of the city, Molly asked Jake to make just one stop— at the cemetery. She hadn't visited her father's grave since the day she buried him. It was time. High time. She felt ready now to face the pain.

Typical of Portland, it was raining by the time Jake parked near her dad's grave. Huddling inside her trench coat, which she hadn't had occasion to wear since that fateful morning when she'd left the city, Molly soon got soaked standing beside the headstone. Her short hair was plastered to her head and dripping wet. Still she just stood there, staring down at the stone. It seemed so sad, so terribly sad that a man's entire life could be synopsized with a dash between two dates. It was as if he'd never existed. It reminded her of the inscription on Jake's tree, PEDRO, 1976–1983. Life was so short, death so final.

"I'll be contacting the authorities on Monday, Daddy," she explained quietly. "Tomorrow being Sunday, I can't do anything sooner, but I promise you, I won't rest until it's done. I pray that I can present a convincing case against Rodney. Regardless, it's a risk I have to take to bring him to justice. If I fail, I could end up dragging your good name through the mud, and by extension, the reputation of Sterling and Wells may suffer. I know how much the firm meant to you."

Molly swallowed and closed her eyes. "If that happens, I'll be so sorry, Daddy. But this is something I have to do. I hope you can understand and that you'll forgive me if it all turns sour."

Jake, who'd been standing nearby without her realizing it, joined Molly just then and wrapped her in his strong arms. "You have to stop torturing yourself like this," he whispered. "Why do you think your father made a copy of Rodney's files? To turn the bastard in, of course. Under the same circumstances, I know I would have, and I'm beginning to think your dad was like me in many ways."

Molly smiled through the raindrops and tears, knowing Jake was right. Though she knew it was an inappropriate moment for the question, she shakily asked, "Who was Pedro, Jake?"

He stiffened. "What?" The tension slowly slipped from him. "You visited my tree."

"Yes." Inclining her head at the stone, she said, "Seeing the dates reminded me."

He rested his cheek against her hair. "Pedro was my dog. He got killed trying to protect me from a charging bull."

Molly's heart caught at the sadness in his voice. "He must have been a very special dog."

"My one and only. When I buried him, I swore I'd never get another one to take his place."

"And you never did?" Molly smiled through her tears and the raindrops, for it wasn't really a question. She was coming to realize that this man loved with his whole heart and soul. It comforted her to know that Pedro lived on in his memory. The dates on her father's headstone weren't just numbers chiseled in stone; they commemorated his life, and the dash was representative of the most important parts, all the events that had transpired between his opening scene and the final act. She would never forget him, and because she wouldn't, he would never really be gone. "May I ask a favor?"

"What's that?"

"Can I carve Daddy's name on your tree?"

He tightened his arms around her. "It's our tree now, Molly mine. I think your father's name belongs there."

Their tree. Oh, yes. She loved the sound of that. One day, she would carve the name of her father's first grandchild on that beautiful old oak. Marshal Sterling would live on in her, and in her and Jake's children.

For the first time in so long, Molly felt as if she were coming close to being the woman her father had raised her to be. "I can feel him here," she said. "I think he's looking down on us right now. And you know what?"

She felt his mouth tip in a smile. "No, what?"

"I think he's celebrating in heaven with the angels right now to see his daughter in the arms of such a fine man." She turned to frame his face between her hands. "You know what else, Jake? Nothing can stop us. Together, you and I are going to bring Rodney Wells to his knees and make him pay dearly for all that he's done. To Sunset, to me, to my father. He's going to pay. I'm going to see that he does."

CHAPTER TWENTY–THREE

Morning sunlight streamed in the kitchen window, bathing the log walls and wooden floors in a wash of gold. Sitting catty-corner together at the table, Jake and Molly fed each other breakfast, vegetarian fare aside from the eggs in the garden omelet. Licking the juice of a fresh ripe peach from her lips, Molly guided a forkful of fruit to her husband's mouth, giggling when he dodged the food and nipped at her knuckles instead.

"I'd much rather have you," he said huskily. "Come back upstairs with me."

"It's morning," Molly protested, glancing toward the window. "My day off as well, I might add. I don't want to spend all of it in bed."

He waggled his dark eyebrows at her. "Come on up, and I'll have brunch, Jake Coulter style."

She curled her toes inside the oversized wool socks she'd borrowed from his drawer. "Brunch?" Her gaze moved to his mouth. She imagined his lips trailing over her skin, and a delicious shiver ran up her spine. In a voice gone oddly thick, she said, "I might be convinced. Tell me more."

He took the piece of peach between his teeth, barely skimming the ripe flesh, then flicking it with his tongue. "Come upstairs," he whispered. "I do my best convincing with my actions."

Molly laid down the fork and pushed up from her chair. Jake trailed his gaze over her T-shirt to the hem, where he spent a moment admiring her bare legs. "Did you know you have cute little dimples in your knees?"

She bent to look. When she glanced back at him, she wrinkled her nose impishly. "Some men are wild for dimples."

"I'm one of them."

Five minutes later, Jake was intent on showing her just how wild he was for dimples, and Molly felt like a smorgasbord, created expressly for his enjoyment. He nibbled the dimples on her bottom. Then he moved to kiss the dimples at the small of her back. Then he slowly licked his way up her spine. Her skin was tingling everywhere by the time he turned her over to kiss her front.

"Have I told you this morning how much I love you?" he asked.

"Not for at least twenty minutes or so."

He grinned. "I love you more than words can say. You know what that means, don't you? I guess I'll just have to show you."

He was much better at showing than telling, Molly decided some thirty minutes later. He also knew how to totally monopolize a lady's day off. When he was done with her, she only wanted to snuggle up against him and sleep.

"Take a nap with me," she coaxed.

He frowned. "I have things to do today."

"Like what?"

"Work, as much as I hate to say the word. It's the men's day off. Hank and I have to carry the load on Saturday and Sunday."

Molly huffed under her breath and nipped his chest. "Well, then, I demand a change in my schedule. I want days off that you can enjoy with me."

"Speak to the lady of the manor. I don't handle the domestic crap anymore. I got smart and found myself a wife."

She playfully punched his ribs. Then she decided to change tactics and kissed them instead. "Take a nap with me, and I'll make it worth your while when we wake up."

He grinned and closed his eyes. "I might be convinced. Tell me more."

Molly rose to her knees. "I'd much rather give you a preview. I'm much more convincing with my actions than I am with words."

Jake chuckled. "It's a losing proposition. We just finished. I need some recharge time."

"Wanna bet?"

"How much are we talking?"

Molly giggled. "Who said anything about money?" She whispered in his ear what she wanted him to do to her if she won. "What do you say?"

He gave her a heavy-lidded look. "You're on, and I just lost the bet thinking about it."

Molly glanced down, saw the proof of his words, and burst out laughing. He didn't allow her to gloat for long. Before she knew it, he was making love to her again. Slow, languorous lovemaking that ended with snuggling and a snooze.

"Jake!"

Molly jerked awake to the sound of Hank shouting her husband's name. An instant later, she heard booted feet on the stairs. Jake sat up in bed, rubbing his eyes. Molly jerked the sheets up over herself just before the bedroom door flew open.

"Hurry up and get dressed," Hank cried. "Somehow the horses got loose. They're scattered from hell to Texas. The rancher down the road just called, and two are clear down at his place."

"That's two miles away!" Jake swore under his breath. "Damn it. How did they get out?"

"Beats me, but we've got to get them home before one of them gets run over."

The instant his brother exited the bedroom, Jake threw back the covers and swung out of bed. "Well, that shoots the nap all to hell."

Molly pushed up on her elbow. "Can I help catch them?"

He leaned back to kiss her, then pushed to his feet and jerked on his pants. "It'll be more time consuming than anything else." He winked at her as he bent to pull on his socks and boots. "I'd much rather you wait here. I haven't gotten to pay up on that bet I lost yet."

Molly sighed and snuggled back down, feeling deliciously lazy and content. "I'll be here then, waiting."

He grabbed his Stetson off the bedpost and put it on his head. "Stop looking at me like that, or I'll let the damned horses go to the devil."

She giggled sleepily. "Go on and do your cowboy thing. I need some recharging time myself now."

A moment later when he left the bedroom, Molly snuggled back down, hugging his pillow close so she could drift back to sleep with the scent of him all around her. *Jake*. She drifted in lazy contentment, half asleep and caught in that shadowy world between wakefulness and dreams. Oh, how she loved him. She felt as if some magical fairy godmother had waved her magic wand and made all her wishes come true.

She had just fallen back to sleep when a sound awakened her. She blinked sleepily and tried to focus. Lifting her lashes, she was surprised to see that the bedroom door stood ajar. She knew her husband had shut it when he left. She propped herself up on one arm.

"Jake? Did you catch the horses already?"

From behind her, a hand clamped over her hair. Molly screamed as pain exploded over her scalp. The next thing she knew she was being dragged off the bed. She glimpsed gray slacks and shiny loafers.

"No, you fat bitch, he hasn't caught the horses already."

Rodney. Molly's brain went cold with terror. She grabbed frantically at his hand to ease the pull on her hair. He hauled her out onto the floor and jerked her head back with such force she feared her neck might snap.

"God, you're disgusting." He pressed his face close to hers. "The poor bastard is so used to cows, he doesn't know udders when he sees them."

Molly stared up into her ex-husband's hazel eyes. Oddly, his words had no effect on her. He'd hurt her all he could. Nothing he could dish out now was going to bruise her feelings. Jake had given her a beautiful memory for every cruel thing Rodney had said. "What do you want, Rodney?"

Something cold pressed against her temple. She knew instantly that it was a gun. Her stomach clenched.

"One sound, and I'll pull the trigger," he whispered. "Get your fat ass dressed. We're going to have a little party."

Molly scrambled away from him the moment he released her. Keeping the weapon pointed at her, he followed her to the dresser where Jake had emptied some of his drawers to make room for her clothes. With fear-numbed fingers, she took out underwear and hurriedly put it on. Then she went into the walk-in closet for jeans and a blouse, Rodney following close behind her.

"Where are the computer disks?" he said as she put on the blouse.

Molly gave him what she hoped was a bewildered look. "What computer dis—"

He backhanded her across the mouth. The force of the blow sent her reeling into the wall, her head cracking against a log. Her legs suddenly rubbery, she slid down to the floor and then just sat there, staring stupidly up at him.

Pressing the barrel of the gun between her eyes, Rodney said, "Don't fuck with me, Molly. I blew your father's head off. I sure as hell won't hesitate to blow off yours."

That came as no surprise to Molly. She blinked, trying to regain her senses. Her jaw throbbed where he'd struck her, and her head was whirling.

"Did you really think I wouldn't know if someone messed with my computer?" he asked acidly. "You're as stupid as your father." He jabbed his chest. "My system is inviolate. No one can touch it that I don't immediately know when I log on. You left your fingerprints all over it, and I want the copies you made."

Molly was afraid to defy him. She staggered to her feet and withdrew the computer disks from the pocket of Jake's sport coat. Rodney snatched them from her hand. After looking at them, he shoved them in his suit pocket.

"Thank you," he said softly. "Now finish getting dressed."

While Molly drew on some jeans and leaned against the closet wall to tug on her sneakers, Rodney talked. "It's too damned bad your big, tough cowboy didn't listen to me and stay out of this," he bragged. "Instead he kept a crazy woman on his ranch, and now she's going to commit a final, crazy act, costing him dearly."

Molly had no idea what he meant until he forced her at gunpoint out onto the landing. A five-gallon can of diesel sat just outside the bedroom door.

"Start dousing the floors." Smiling one of those oily smiles she'd come to detest so much, he added, "I'd lend you my gloves, but it's extremely important that your fingerprints be all over the can later. I'm sure you understand."

Molly understood all right. *Oh, God, oh, God.* He meant to burn down Jake's house. As sick as the thought made her, she couldn't help but be even more afraid for herself. Rodney had just openly admitted to killing her father. He wouldn't have done that if he meant to let her live to tell about it.

With Rodney following behind her, Molly doused the floors with fuel. When she had emptied the five-gallon can, Rodney motioned her downstairs. "Take the can down with you. We'll be leaving it outside as evidence for the police."

As Molly started down the stairs, she prayed mindlessly, imploring God to intervene somehow. Rodney meant to kill her. She saw it in his eyes. Terror sluiced through her veins like ice water.

Once on the ground floor, Rodney smiled again, inclining his head to indicate yet another gas can. "You know the routine. Don't drag your feet. If your cowboy comes back, he'll end up being a very dead hero. You wouldn't want that, now would you?"

Molly imagined Jake's rage if he were to walk in on this scene. Her heart gave a painful twist, for she knew very well it wouldn't be the house that her husband would fight to protect. Helpless anger welled up within Molly. She'd spent all her adult life believing herself to be second rate. Now, for the first time in eleven years, she was happy. Meeting Jake Coulter had transformed her life. She loved him so, and he loved her. Somehow he'd done the impossible and made her feel beautiful. Not just so-so, not just pretty, but absolutely beautiful. Now Rodney meant to end it all, and in the most horrible of ways, making it appear that she had been responsible for the misdeed.

As she poured diesel over the great room floor, she remembered all the evenings she'd walked through the room with Jake. Tears nearly blinded her when she recalled the night Hank had teased her about the cougar threat. She had a *family* now. Jake's parents, who'd both called her daughter and taken her into their hearts. Jake's brothers and sister. She didn't want to die and miss out on that feeling of belonging.

"Now the kitchen," Rodney said in a low, venomous voice.

Molly swallowed hard to steady her voice before saying, "You're going to murder me, aren't you?"

"All in good time. First, we have business to conclude."

Molly flung diesel onto the middle of the floor. The fuel pooled around the cross-buck legs of the table Jake had built. *Oh, God.* She thought of the horseshoe clock. Then her mind conjured pictures of the downstairs bathroom where an antique Jack Daniel's barrel served as a sink vanity and horseshoes had been welded together as towel hooks. In the great room, all the furniture had been crafted from trees felled on this ranch. Every nook and cranny of this beautiful house bore Jake Coulter's stamp. He'd fashioned it all with those big, capable hands, making each room unique.

Rodney, who'd spent his whole life greedily taking and destroying, couldn't conceive what he was about to incinerate—not just a house, but Jake Coulter's dream.

"If you're going to kill me, I'm going to make good use of the minutes I have left." Molly straightened and turned to glare at the man who'd nearly destroyed her. "I want to make sure you know how much I detest you."

Rodney only smiled. "You weren't even a blip on my radar screen, Molly dear. Like I care?"

"No," Molly said, her voice quivering with revulsion. "You never cared. You've never cared about anyone but yourself. I look at you, and do you know what I see, Rodney? There's nothing to you. Not even the despicable parts amount to anything."

His beautifully drawn mouth, which she'd once admired, twisted into a sneer. "Shut up and just pour the damned gas."

"Diesel," she corrected. Molly had no choice but to do as he said. A feeling of separateness came over her. She fleetingly wondered if it was some sort of God-given protective device inside of her kicking in. *Numbness.* She was about to die, and she felt so apart from it, not really afraid any longer, just numb.

When she finished dousing the house, Rodney instructed her to carry the fuel cans outside and throw them over the porch railing into the front yard. Then, keeping the gun trained on her, he withdrew a cigarette lighter from his suit pocket.

"Don't do this, Rodney," she tried. "Jake's never harmed you. He's an innocent player. If you torch his house, you'll ruin him. Can't you accomplish whatever it is you need to without involving him?"

"Oh," he said in a falsely sympathetic tone, "be still, my heart. I think dumpy little Molly has fallen in love. *Again*. Don't cry for him, dear heart. How long do you think it would have been before he got tired of you? Not long, that's guaranteed. Trust me to know. You're the most unbearably boring woman I've ever met."

Molly glanced at the doorway, where diesel lay in pools just beyond the threshold. Rodney moved sideways in a half-crouch, extending the flame toward the fuel. "Be ready to move," he said.

"Please, *don't*!" Molly cried.

Rodney only laughed. The fuel ignited in a *whoosh* of fire. He leaped back, his hazel eyes glittering madly. "You're so crazy, Molly. Why in God's *name* would you burn down your lover's house? People will shake their heads. They're even Lazy J gas cans, which makes it perfect. They'll think you got them from the shed."

He grabbed her by the arm and flung her ahead of him down the steps. From out in his pen, Sunset shrieked. Molly knew by the sound that the stallion recognized Rodney. She stumbled as Rodney dragged her away toward the woods. He drew to a stop in approximately the same area where she'd first seen Jake, sawing up the fallen pine. *Jake*. It broke her heart that the house he'd built might burn to the ground. She could only thank God that he had cleared off most of the trees near the dwelling, just as he had around the stable, forming a fire break. He'd done it to protect the buildings in case of a forest fire, she felt sure. Hopefully, the safety precaution would work in reverse, preventing the flames from catching on the trees.

Grabbing her viciously by the hair, Rodney forced her to her knees. Rocks jabbed into her shins. Sharp pain lanced her thighs. The next instant, he shoved a pen and some papers in front of her face. "This time, you'll by God sign."

Molly blinked and tried to focus. "The papers again?" Her hands shook violently as she took them. "If you're going to kill me, at least tell me what they are."

"Just sign the damned thing!" He rammed the barrel of the gun against her temple, making her see stars. "So help me, if you don't, I'll blow your gray matter from here to hell. I have nothing left to lose. *Nothing*."

"Of course you don't. You've gambled it all away."

Turning his wrist, he struck her on the head with the weapon. The front sight cut into her scalp, the sting bringing tears to her eyes. She tried to focus on the papers. The roar of the house fire snarled in her ears like a ravenous beast. She didn't need to look back to know that Jake's home would soon be an inferno. The print blurred, making it impossible for her to tell where the signature line was located.

"Sign it!" Rodney cried.

"I'm trying, damn you. Stop hitting me. I can't see."

He shoved the barrel of the gun against her temple again. "Toward the bottom. Sign it." He gave her a hard nudge. "Your refusal to do it before fucked everything up for me. *Everything*. Why, all of a sudden, did you have to get stubborn. A hundred times, at least, I brought home papers, and you always signed them without a question. Why, the one time it really counted, did you have to get so goddamned righteous on me?"

"It didn't matter before!" she cried, still trying to focus on the page. "After Daddy died, it did. I was in charge of the firm. I had to be responsible."

"Responsible. Jesus Christ. You caused yourself no end of heartache, you stupid bitch. I would have split town and left you alone if only you had signed off. But, oh no, you had to be difficult for the first time in our marriage."

"What am I signing off?" Molly asked, struggling to hold the pen in her shaking fingers.

"An offshore account! *Millions* of dollars, Molly. All of it automatically deposited by the dummy corporations under your name. That way, the profits never came to me, and if anyone ever found out, you and your dad would take the fall. I thought having your power of attorney would enable me to make withdrawals, only that jerkwater foreign country doesn't recognize it as a legal document! All that money, and I couldn't touch a cent of it. I was almost broke, and you refused to sign. The only way I could survive was to bet on the races with what money I had here, hoping for a win."

"Only Sunset kept losing," she inserted hollowly.

"The goddamned horse has four left feet," Rodney retorted bitterly.

"I was locked up over this?" Molly wanted to fly at him, claw out his eyes, bite him, kick him. "You deprived me of my freedom for *money*?"

"It wasn't by choice. You forced my hand. What was I supposed to do, let you waltz away before you signed this, and let millions of dollars turn to dust in a bank account I couldn't touch? I had to make you sign. I figured you would eventually, that sooner or later, you'd break down and see reason."

"Why on *earth* did you bank your dirty money under *my* name?" Molly cried.

"Why not? If something went sour, I had it set up so your father and you would take the heat, and I'd walk away without being implicated."

"To amass another fortune?"

He smiled. "I profited by my own genius. So hang me. You and your father were both so stupid, lending yourself so easily to be used. Why not?"

Molly pressed the pen to the paper, remembering all the many times she'd refused to do this. "So it was all for money. You consigned me to hell for money."

"You could have ended it any time. I asked you, time and again, to sign this for me, and you refused." He crouched beside her, leveling the gun between her eyes. "Do you realize how brilliant I am, Molly? You have a brain the size of a pea, compared to mine. You saw all those emails I received under your father's name. Do you think those companies voluntarily sent me all that insider information? Hell, no. I developed a worm virus when I was working in the valley. No antivirus software on the market today can detect it. I can attach it to any email message I send out from my computer. When the recipients open the file, the worm infiltrates their system's email program, creating an automatic alias mailing address that's executed any time electronic mail is sent or received by that system."

Molly stared along the blue-black barrel of the gun at his face. His features were contorted with feverish intensity. In his irises, reflections of the flames behind her danced like tiny demons caught up in the throes of evil. "So all those companies unwittingly sent you copies of all their electronic correspondence," she whispered.

"Exactly. The perfect insider-trading setup. I sent them introductory email brochures about our firm, and after that, I got all the upcoming information about their products, their business dealings. My own little crystal ball to show me the future and enable me to make millions."

Her vision was beginning to clear from the rap on her head. Molly lowered her gaze to the document he wanted her to sign. She saw that it was a withdrawal form to an offshore bank account. She thought of all the movies she'd watched where the imperiled heroine got the villain to keep talking and thereby bought herself precious seconds of time. Fat chance. Rodney had said all there was to say. Time had run out.

She thought about defying him. Oh, how appealing that thought was. As if he guessed her thoughts, Rodney smiled coldly. "I can make it painful. Is that what you want? Before I'm done, you'll beg me to die. For once in your misbegotten life, do it the easy way."

Molly considered her options. Jake was out there somewhere. Even if it was painful for her, any delay might save her life. Her husband and Hank would surely see the smoke. At this very moment, they might be racing back to the ranch. How long did it take to cover two miles on horseback? She had no idea, absolutely none, but any chance she might have to live was one she couldn't ignore.

Molly looked Rodney dead in the eye. "If I sign this, I'm signing my death warrant."

A diabolical glint slipped into Rodney's eyes. "And if you don't sign it, you're signing his death warrant."

He smiled and pushed to his feet, aiming the gun away from her. For a moment, Molly couldn't think what he meant to shoot. Then her gaze followed the direction of the gun barrel—to Sunset. Her heart caught. She bit down hard on the inside of her cheek to keep from crying out and stared with burning eyes at the beautiful black horse.

Rodney sighted in, smiling evilly. "A knee first, don't you think? That's sure death for a horse. Slow, excruciating." The gun clicked ominously. "If you think I can't hit him from here, don't delude yourself. I've been practicing weekly at a shooting range for almost five years. I can pick my target. And I assure you, darling, I'll make it very painful for him."

Molly told herself that Sunset was only an animal, that her life was far more precious. But, somehow, when she looked at that magnificent black stallion, knowing how horribly he'd already suffered at Rodney's hands, it wasn't that simple. The bond that had developed between her and the horse ran deep, and she'd risked so much to save him. If she allowed Rodney to kill him now, all her efforts would be for nothing.

The thought washed her mouth with bitterness. Rodney Wells had taken so very much from her. He couldn't have Sunset, too.

Rodney would probably kill her anyway. It took only a split second to fire a bullet. How much time could she conceivably buy for herself? A minute, maybe? Looking at Sunset, she couldn't bring herself to sacrifice his life on the off chance that Jake might return in time to save her.

"No, *don't*!" she cried. "I'll sign, Rodney. Don't hurt him. Please, don't."

Rodney turned the gun back on her. "Then do it, damn you."

Her hands trembling so that she could barely move the pen, Molly scrawled her signature on the appropriate line, knowing as she did that she might be signing her life away. She thrust the paper at him. "There, you bastard. You've got your money. Now why don't you just go?"

"And have you blow the whistle on me? Not a chance, darling. When I walk away, there'll be no evidence to haunt me. That means I have to shut your trap, make it look like you went over the edge and did all this." He tucked the withdrawal form safely inside his suit jacket, then grabbed Molly's arm and jerked her to her feet. "Come on. Let's finish this before your cowboy rounds up his beasts and comes back to complicate matters."

Molly stumbled along beside him, wincing at the pain of his grip on her arm. "How will you kill me, Rodney? Not with the gun, surely. Or is it registered in my name like the one you killed my father with was registered in his?"

"I seldom repeat a stroke of genius," he said with a laugh. "It worked once. Repeat performances are risky."

He led her to Sunset's pen. When he suddenly released her at the gate, Molly stared stupidly at him, not registering what he meant to do until she glanced down to see a large rock and a whip lying near her feet. She threw him an appalled glance. He kept the gun trained on her as he bent to pick up the rock.

"Open the gate," he whispered.

Molly glanced back at the whip. "What are you—?"

"Just do it!"

She jerked away from the thrusting gun barrel and turned to open the gate. Against her back, she could feel the intensifying heat of the house fire. She wondered if Jake might see the smoke. Prayed he might.

"Step inside," Rodney ordered.

Molly did as he said.

"Stop!" he said. "And don't turn around. Things always hurt less if you don't look."

Molly braced, trying frantically to think of something she could do to save herself. The next instant, her head exploded with agony. In that split second between consciousness and oblivion, she knew he'd struck her with the rock. Then—*blessed blackness.*

Jake cut his horse in behind the gelding, clicking his tongue and softly talking to keep the animal from panicking. Fifty yards up the road, Hank was going through similar motions with a frightened mare.

"It's all right, boy," Jake crooned. "Let's head home and have some oats."

Hank was already dogging the mare in that direction. He waved his Stetson at Jake in silent communication. Jake lifted a hand to let his brother know he'd be right behind him. He was shifting in the saddle, thinking of his wife and wishing he were back in bed with her already, when he saw what looked like smoke in the distance. He stared at it stupidly for a moment. Then alarm bells clanged in his brain. It was coming from the Lazy J.

He tensed, standing rigid in the stirrups, his heart freezing in his chest. "Hank!" he yelled. "There's a fire back at the ranch!"

Hank wheeled his horse, following Jake's gaze. His whole body snapped to attention when he saw the smoke. "Holy hell! It's the house!"

Sweet Christ. Jake had thought the same thing, but it had frightened him so that he'd pushed it away. The house. Molly was in there. She was sleeping. Oh, sweet Christ.

Jake left the horse he'd been dogging to race his mount along the edge of the drainage ditch toward his brother. "Molly!" he cried when he got close enough to Hank to make himself heard clearly. "She's upstairs asleep!"

Hank leaned sharply forward in the saddle and dug in with his heels, urging his horse into a flat-out run. Jake fell in beside him in a breakneck dash for home.

Molly blinked dazedly. *Dirt.* In her mouth, in her eyes. She coughed and spat. Her fingers dug into the earth, the grit pushing up under her nails. Her head hurt. The pain was so excruciating, it was almost blinding. She didn't know where she was. There was a roaring in her ears, a loud snapping sound, and shrill bursts of noise that sounded like someone shrieking.

She moaned and rolled onto her side. In her blurry vision, black legs danced. She focused, blinked. *Hooves.* They flashed near her face with dizzying unpredictability, dust flying every time they impacted with the ground. Molly stared stupidly at them for a moment. Then it all came rushing back. *Rodney.* He'd hit her on the head. She was inside Sunset's pen.

She tried to push up on her elbow. Her body felt leaden, as if her limbs had become detached from her brain. She fell back onto the dirt, too disoriented to move or think clearly. She saw Rodney on the fence. He sat astride the top rail, and he was swinging one arm. As her vision cleared a bit, she realized he was snapping a whip.

Her brain froze with horror. She glanced up at Sunset, the source of all the shrieking sounds. The stallion danced in terror, trying to avoid the leather that whined in the air all around him. But there was no escape in the small corral.

"Trample her, you son of a bitch!" Rodney yelled. "Do something right, just once in your miserable life!"

Sunset screamed and sidestepped, narrowly avoiding the lacerating bite of the whip. Rodney laughed as the horse danced perilously close to Molly's legs. She tried frantically to move her feet, to escape the stallion's hooves, but her body ignored the commands. *Oh, God*. Rodney meant to make Sunset kill her. It would look like an unfortunate accident, Sunset would pay the price, and Rodney would waltz away scot-free.

To Molly's disbelief, Sunset didn't step on her. Coincidence? She threw another frightened look at the horse. The whip sliced through the air again, almost connecting with the stallion's nose. He threw up his head. Molly saw the whites of his eyes. He danced sideways—away from her.

Sunset. He'd looked at her. She'd seen the flash of his eyes. Even with Rodney terrorizing him, he was trying to avoid stepping on her.

"He won't hurt you, honey. I feel it," Jake had told her once.

Tears of sheer outrage sprang to Molly's eyes. She riveted a glare on Rodney, hating him as she'd never hated anyone. Fury sent a rush of adrenalin coursing through her body. She struggled up onto her elbows and knees. *Damn him, damn him.* He was a bastard without a heart. How could he do this?

"Step on her, you stupid beast!" The whip sang in the air again. "Do it, or I'll cut you. Do it, you son of a bitch!"

Sunset screamed again. Swaying dizzily on her knees, Molly looked up, and all she could see was the rearing horse and flashing hooves. *Dear God*. She threw up an arm to shield her face, knowing she was about to die. Only somehow Sunset wheeled at the last second, bringing his front feet down beside her instead of on her. Molly sobbed, her body quivering with relief.

Sunset tried to move away from her. Rodney cut him off with a snap of the whip. The horse circled the other way, and again, Rodney blocked his path. Molly knew the horse could only avoid stepping on her for so long. Eventually terror would blind him, and he'd kill her.

A snarl crawled up Molly's throat. She focused sharply on Rodney, despising him with a virulence that made her whole body tremble. *Enough.* He'd contaminated her life with his evilness, twisting and transforming everything into an ugly travesty, robbing her of everything precious. She wouldn't let him destroy Sunset as well. She *wouldn't*.

A sudden calm settled over her brain, even as she tensed her body to spring. She waited until Rodney swung the whip again. Then, with a speed and strength she didn't know she possessed, she vaulted from a crouch, throwing up her arms to catch the snaking leather in her hands. Dimly, she felt the whip cut into her palms. She tightened her grip, snapped her wrists to wrap the leather around her arms, and with all the force of her weight, she jerked.

With a surprised yelp, Rodney toppled off the fence rail into the pen. He hit the dirt in a facedown sprawl and shook his head as if to clear it.

"You bastard!" Molly cried, throwing the whip with all her strength through the rails of the fence. "You leave my horse alone!"

Rodney shook his head again. Then he tried to push to his knees. He fixed Molly with a dazed, bewildered look, as if his senses hadn't quite righted themselves yet. When his gaze cleared, he thrust a hand inside his jacket.

"Plan B," he said, and pulled out the gun. "It's registered in your name, darling. I lied."

Molly tensed, knowing a bullet would plow into her body at any second. This was it. She was dead.

Only she'd forgotten the third player in this scene. *Sunset.* The horse came from behind her like an avenging angel, mane flying, tail raised like a cavalry flag behind his gigantic black body. He advanced on Rodney, never slowing. Rodney screamed and tried to throw himself out of the stallion's path, but Sunset ran his heart out to reach him.

"Oh, God!" Rodney yelled.

The next instant, Sunset ran right over the top of him. Molly almost whooped. *Yes!* Rodney wasn't such a big man when he didn't have a whip in his hand.

Molly raced forward. The gun had slipped from Rodney's grasp and lay in the dirt. She kicked the weapon outside the pen, beyond Rodney's reach. Sunset circled to the far end of the corral. Molly, intent on Rodney, didn't realize the horse was racing back until she saw hooves flash. She glanced up. Sunset stood on his hind legs. Eyes wild, mane flying, his powerful body a sculpture of magnificent jet in the sunlight, the horse seemed poised there for endless seconds, a vengeful beast bent on destroying his tormentor.

With a scream of rage, the stallion brought his front hooves down on the man who had scarred him for life. Stupefied, Molly watched, a part of her cheering Sunset on. The horse deserved his moment of revenge. Rodney deserved to die. For seconds that seemed to last a short eternity,

Molly felt smug satisfaction and sincerely hoped the stallion delivered a lethal blow. What a fitting ending to a totally misbegotten life.

Sunset shrieked again and crouched on his rear legs to pummel Rodney with his front hooves. In that instant, Molly regained her sanity. *Sunset*. The stallion was intent on killing Rodney, and she didn't blame him. But what would happen to the horse if she allowed it? No matter what the provocation, a stallion that turned killer would be destroyed.

She darted forward, afraid the crazed horse might turn on her if she interfered. "Sunset, *no*! Sunset, stop!" Molly leaped in to grab the stallion's halter, knowing even as she did that she lacked the strength to pull him off. "Sunset, please. Please!"

The instant the horse felt her hands on him, he grunted and backed away to stand motionless over the man he hated so much, blowing, snorting, every muscle in his glorious body tensed. Molly sobbed and hugged the stallion's neck. "I *know*," she whispered. "I know just how you feel, Sunset, but it's better this way. It's better this way."

Rodney moaned and rolled over. Molly could tell by the way he moved that he wasn't seriously hurt. For Sunset's sake, she was glad of that. The stallion had already suffered enough because of this man. Keeping an arm around her horse's neck, she gazed down at her ex-husband, feeling detached. His suit was ripped and in a few places she thought she could see a little blood. Compared to the wounds he'd inflicted on Sunset, his injuries were mere scratches.

"Dare to move, and I'll turn him loose on you," Molly warned.

Rodney angled her a hate-filled glare. "And I'll see him shot!"

"No, you won't, because I'll let him kill you." Molly looked him dead in the eye. "I'll tell the authorities I bludgeoned you myself before I allow anyone to touch this animal."

Rodney came up on one knee. Sunset snorted and started to prance. Rodney froze, cast a wary glance at the stallion, and lay back down. "Hold him, for Christ's sake!"

Molly smiled. "I'm feeling very weak and dizzy from the blow to my head. Lie still, Rodney. If he starts to act up, I may not be able to keep him off you."

Rodney's hazel eyes went dark with fear. He flattened himself to the ground. "You bitch!" he whispered.

"Yes, and don't forget it."

Over the roar of the house fire, Molly thought she heard something. Before she could identify the sound, she heard Jake's voice. "Molly. Oh, sweet Jesus!"

Glancing around, she saw Jake swinging off his horse, dust billowing around him. He emerged from the rust-red cloud at a dead run, a blur of blue and burnished skin that sailed over the fence as if it wasn't there. Molly felt as if a locomotive had plowed into her when her husband snatched her up in his arms. Sunset whinnied and backed up a few inches, but he didn't run.

"Dear God, dear God." Jake turned in a half circle with her locked against his trembling body. Molly wanted to tell him she was okay, but he was hugging her so fiercely, she couldn't talk. "You're bleeding. You're hurt." He loosened his embrace to catch her face between his hands. "Oh, sweet Lord, your head's cut."

"He hit me with a rock." Molly reached to feel, wincing when her fingertips grazed the deep gash.

She was about to say that she was okay when Rodney rose to his knees. Molly staggered dizzily when Jake suddenly released her and whirled around.

"You son of a *bitch*!" He plucked Rodney up from the dirt and shook him like a rag doll. "I'll kill you. I swear to God, you're a dead man."

Rodney took a wild swing, grazing Jake's jaw. Jake retaliated by drawing back his fist and hitting Rodney squarely in the face. The blow sent the other man reeling back against the fence. Molly could only gape. She'd always known Jake was strong, but she hadn't realized he had the strength to lift a large man clear off his feet with one punch.

"My *nose*," Rodney cried, cupping his hands over his eyes. "You bastard, you broke my nose!"

"That's not all I'm going to break!" Face contorted with rage, big body taut, Jake advanced.

"Jake, no!" Molly cried.

It was as if Jake didn't hear her. He leaped on Rodney again, hauled him erect by the front of his jacket, and proceeded to rap his head against the fence post. Molly grabbed her husband's arm, screaming for him to stop. He paid her no heed.

"You miserable, worthless piece of trash!" Jake shook Molly off as if she weighed nothing and plowed his fist into Rodney's stomach, once again lifting him clear off his feet with the blow and bending him double. "Keep your filthy hands *off* my wife! Touch her—even *look* at her again—and I swear on all that's holy, I'll snap your neck."

Molly was afraid Jake might kill Rodney. She'd never seen him like this. His face was drawn. His eyes glittered. With every word he spoke, he bared his teeth in a snarl.

Suddenly Hank was there. He leaped on his brother's back, locked Jake's arms behind his waist in an unbreakable hold, and then rode it out, with Jake cursing a blue streak, staggering under his weight, and trying futilely to shake him off.

"Stop it, Jake!" Hank yelled. "He's not worth it. Let the law punish the bastard."

With a mighty roar of anger, Jake tried again to free his arms. "Get *off* me, damn you. He hurt my *wife*!"

Hank didn't unlock his hold on his brother's arms. "She's all right, Jake. She's going to be all right."

Jake stood with his legs braced apart to bear the extra two hundred pounds draped over his shoulders. He heaved for air, his fiery gaze riveted on Rodney, who had slumped to the ground with his back against the fence, one arm angled over his stomach.

"He's down," Hank said. "You got your message across. If you pound it home when he can't fight back, you'll hate yourself for it later!"

"Like *hell* I will!" Jake cried. "Why show him mercy? Did he show Sunset any? Damn him! He bashed my wife's head with a *rock*!"

"I'm all right, Jake," Molly said shakily. "See?" She waved a hand in front of her husband's face. "Would you look at me? I'm fine. It's only a little bump. I'm okay."

Jake cut her a glance. Some of the wildness went out of his eyes. "Nobody touches my wife," he bit out.

"He'll pay for it," Hank assured him. "He'll pay, Jake. But not this way. You could end up in prison. Is that what you want?"

Jake staggered sideways. Then he suddenly stopped fighting. Heaving for breath, he bent forward to better support Hank's weight. Molly saw sanity returning to his eyes. "No, of course, it's not what I want," he ground out. "Get off me, little brother, before I beat the sass out of you."

Hank grinned at Molly and released his brother's arms. Patting Jake on the shoulder, he said, "You need to watch that temper of yours, bro. It could get you in trouble."

Jake straightened, leveled a burning look at Rodney, and then, cursing vilely under his breath, he kicked dirt into the other man's face. Molly almost laughed when Rodney sputtered and coughed. Since she'd eaten her own share of dirt only a few minutes ago, she felt it was just punishment.

"This is your lucky day," Jake told Rodney through clenched teeth. "You're not worth going to prison over, so I'll spare your worthless hide."

He came to Molly then. With shaking hands, he checked her for injuries, his touch so careful and gentle, she might have been made of fragile glass.

"I'm all right," she whispered. "I'm all right, Jake."

She looked up and couldn't believe what she was seeing. Jake Coulter's vivid blue eyes were swimming with tears. A muscle in his cheek bunched as he cautiously examined the wound on the crown of her head, his fingertips barely grazing the edges of the gash. "He could have killed you," he said in a husky voice that shook slightly.

"But he didn't. Sunset wouldn't step on me, no matter what Rodney did, and together, we took him down."

Jake slipped an arm around her waist and drew her against him. She could hear his heart pounding and felt his body trembling. By that, she took measure of how very much he loved her. She closed her eyes and pressed her face against his shirt. Never had anyone's arms felt so wonderful. To love and be loved truly was such a fabulous feeling.

"Your house," she whispered shakily. "All I've done is bring you heartbreak, from start to finish, Jake. I'm so sorry."

His embrace tightened around her. He didn't even look toward the burning house. "Never that, Molly girl. Never that. A spot of trouble, here and there, but no heartbreak. Don't you know how much I love you?"

Molly did know. How could she not? She went up on her tiptoes to hug his neck. "Oh, Jake, I love you, too. But what of the ranch? He's destroyed everything."

"Not everything," he whispered against her hair. "Not even close. We have each other, sweetheart. Nothing can keep us down for long."

Sunset nickered just then. Molly opened her eyes to see that the horse was sniffing her husband's sleeve. Jake chuckled and reached out to curl a hand over the horse's halter. "So you've finally decided I'm okay, have you?" He tugged on the leather. "Come ahead. Love on her all you want."

Sunset nickered again and moved in closer to sniff Molly's clothing, then her hair. When the stallion smelled her blood, he snorted and pawed the dirt.

"I know," Jake muttered, tightening his grip on the horse's halter. "I'd like to stomp him, too. But we better not."

Molly grinned in spite of herself. In that moment, she knew Jake was absolutely right. Everything wasn't lost. They still had each other, and they still had Sunset.

Where there was enough love, anything was possible. The three of them formed a winner's circle, and together, they would start over. Sunset hadn't yet run his last race, and what had been razed by fire could be rebuilt. She would get her inheritance now. Money wouldn't be a problem.

Molly turned in her husband's arms to press her back against his chest.

She barely saw Hank, who was bent over Rodney, relieving him of the computer disks and the papers he'd forced her to sign. She gazed instead at the burning house. Beyond the flames, the pastureland and forests of the Lazy J stretched like a promise, offering grazing land for the horses, timber for reconstruction, and an endless playground for all the little Coulters who'd someday be born. Molly meant to make sure that they grew up right there, on Coulter land, with their father's dream a reality around them.

She straightened her shoulders and took a deep, cleansing breath. She remembered all the many times she'd heard a voice whisper in her mind. *Who are you, Molly? Where are you?* Now, she could answer both questions unequivocally.

She was Molly Sterling Coulter, and she was right where she belonged, in her husband's loving arms.

❧ EPILOGUE ❧

Seven months later:

Snowflakes drifted gently through the air, flocking the Douglas fir trees with white and lending the gray-blue gloaming of twilight a magical feeling of Christmas. Pulling his very pregnant wife on a sled behind him, Jake trudged more deeply into the forest, keeping an eye out for the "perfect" tree. So far, nothing he'd found suited Molly. He glanced at his watch. If he didn't find a Christmas tree soon, they wouldn't get back to the house in time to greet their guests. Unfortunately, he couldn't tell Molly that. He didn't want to ruin her surprise.

With a sigh of resignation, he forged onward. It was rough going in places, the snowdrifts so deep they came to his knees. The coarse towrope bit through his lined denim jacket, making his shoulder ache, and his legs were growing weary from the strain of pulling the extra weight.

"What about that one?" he asked hopefully, pointing to a small fir.

Molly gazed critically at the tree he indicated. After a moment, she shook her head. "It's too scrawny."

The last one had been too fat. Beginning to wonder if there was any such thing as a perfectly proportioned Christmas tree, Jake set off again. He walked only a short way before he had to stop for a breather.

"You're getting tired," Molly called in a worried voice. "I *knew* this was a bad idea. Just let me get off and walk. A little exercise will be good for me."

"No way," he managed to say between gulps of air. Though he'd already told her his reasons for pulling her behind him on the sled, he added, "Not in this deep snow. You could fall and hurt yourself."

"I'm not made of fragile glass, and neither is the baby." She pouted prettily and gave her head a shake to rid her curly hair of snowflakes. "It'd be like falling on a pillow." She dragged her gloved fingers through the fluffy whiteness beside the sled. "I couldn't possibly get hurt."

"You could fall on a stump hidden by a drift," Jake pointed out. "Or on a big rock we can't see. Besides, I'm not that tired."

"Yes, you are. Please let me walk? Just for a while, then I'll let you pull me again."

Jake narrowed an eye at her. "You promised, no arguments. When it comes to the safety of my wife and son, I don't want to take any chances." Hoping to distract her, Jake scanned the small stand of evergreen trees around them. His dad had planted them as seedlings years ago, and now they were finally large enough to harvest. "Do you see one that you like?"

She frowned slightly. "You know what I think my problem is? They're all too beautiful. I've never found it difficult to choose a Christmas tree from a tree lot. I'm in and out in ten minutes. Here, I can't seem to make up my mind."

"You know what they say. Give a woman too many choices, and all it does is confuse her."

Her laughing gaze met his, and she poked out her tongue. "Yes, well, most men wouldn't recognize symmetry if it ran up and bit them on the behind."

Jake laughed and stepped around the sled to steal a quick kiss. Her warm, moist mouth tasted of Christmas toffee, and he was sorely tempted to forgo tree hunting to join her under the wool blankets he'd tucked so carefully around her.

"Have I told you lately how much I love you?" he asked huskily.

"Not for at least twenty minutes. I'm feeling ne-glected."

Jake reclaimed her lips, deepening the kiss this time until she pressed close and put her arms around his neck. Unable to resist the invitation, he sank onto the sled beside her and drew her across his lap. When the kiss ended, they sat in silence, taking in the beauty of the forest around them. The falling snow seemed to absorb sound, creating an almost mystical silence that made Jake feel as if they were the only two people in the world. He rested his chin atop Molly's head and sighed.

"Happy?" he asked.

"I've never been so happy," she murmured. "And I can barely wait for Christmas." She rested a hand over the front of her new parka where her swollen tummy stretched the nylon taut. "I still can't believe you managed to get the house rebuilt in time. Our very first Christmas together, and we get to celebrate it in our home. I can almost see the great room, with lights twinkling on the tree and garland draped over the river rock."

When Jake tried to envision it, all he could picture was Molly's smile brightening the room. He was so glad that fate had led her to him.

"Thank you, Jake," she said softly.

He stirred to glance down at her. "For what?"

"For working so hard to get the house finished. It wasn't really necessary, you know. I would have been just as happy to celebrate Christmas at the cabin."

He bent to kiss the tip of her nose. "I didn't want to bring our baby boy home to that drafty old cabin. I knew that if I didn't get all the work done before Christmas, the holidays would set me back."

She sighed and snuggled closer. "Yes, well, thank you. Because of you, the last of my pregnancy is going to be what dreams are made of."

Even as she spoke, Jake heard the trace of sadness in her voice and knew there was still one very important element missing in her life. "I couldn't have done it without help. Hank and the men worked almost as hard as I did. And you contributed, too. What about all those cushions for the furniture that you helped Mom and Bethany make?"

"That was nothing. While we sat around sewing, you were working the ranch all day and making log furniture at night."

He cupped his hands protectively over her swollen middle. It would have been a lie to say that he hadn't burned his candle at both ends to get the house finished in time for the birth of their child in February. But all the long hours had been worth it.

"Right after New Year's, we'll start getting the nursery decorated and furnished," he promised. "I found a great pattern for a cradle. It looks like Noah's ark."

She giggled. "You're kidding."

"You do still want to go with the Noah's ark theme, right? Or have you changed your mind again?"

"Nope, Noah's ark it is. Growing up on a ranch, our little boy will be surrounded by animals. We may as well get him acclimated to the lifestyle early on." She brushed her cheek against his jacket. "Oh, Jake, I love you so. A cradle that's shaped like an ark? It'll be darling. You're making all my wishes come true."

Not all of them, he thought, and glanced at his watch again. It was almost five o'clock, and Molly's most meaningful Christmas present was due to arrive soon. Jake hoped to hell they didn't have an accident. There was a full-fledged snowstorm occurring in the mountains, making the highway conditions between there and Portland treacherous. He felt certain that traction devices were being required on the passes.

"It's all pretty perfect, isn't it?" he whispered, struggling to stay on track with his side of the conversation.

Molly rested quietly against him for a moment, saying nothing. When she finally spoke, she injected a note of blissful happiness into her voice. "Oh, yes, absolutely perfect."

Jake grinned against her curls. *Sweet Molly*. She would never dream of admitting that her happiness wasn't complete and would never be complete until her relationship with one very important person was mended. Jake understood, though, without her expressing her feelings. Every young woman wanted and needed her mother with her when she gave birth to her first child.

Rodney's had been a nasty, emotional trial, and Molly had given the most damaging testimony, which had ended with her ex-husband receiving two sentences, one for life, the other for forty years. The justice system being what it was, Jake figured the bastard would probably get paroled eventually to enjoy his golden years as a free man, but that was the way of things in this country. There seemed little point in letting the unpleasant inequities ruin his and Molly's happiness.

What bothered Jake—what he absolutely could not and would not accept—was the lack of communication between Molly and her adoptive mother. It had come out during the trial that Jared Wells, Rodney's father, had suspected that his son was involved in insider trading. Not realizing the extent of Rodney's depravity, Jared had done what many fathers might have done under the same circumstances. He had turned a blind eye, telling himself that Rodney would hurt only himself.

Wrong. Jared's error in good judgment had caused a great deal of harm to others, costing his best friend and partner his life and putting Molly through untold hardships in a sanitarium. Jared Wells would bear the guilt of that for the rest of his days, and a terrible guilt it was. He had hung his head at the trial and been unable to look Molly in the eye, thinking she despised him and would never forgive him for his failure to come forward. Claudia, being the loving, loyal woman she was, had stood by her new husband, her eyes revealing a world of heartbreak and regret every time she looked across the courtroom at her daughter.

What a mess. It was a situation Jake was determined to rectify for Molly's sake. He couldn't count the times he'd found her standing by the phone with a wistful expression clouding her features. When he'd asked her what was wrong, she'd only shaken her head and said nothing.

Jake had known what was bothering her. She wanted to call her mother, but fearful of rejection, she couldn't quite muster the courage. He understood how she felt. After all the ugliness of the trial, it wouldn't be easy for anyone to make the first overture.

Oddly—or perhaps not so oddly, considering that she'd been raised by a fine person like Claudia—Molly didn't blame Jared Wells for loving and protecting his son. From the first, she had understood why her surrogate uncle had chosen to keep silent. What father worth his salt could turn his child in to the authorities without it tearing his heart out? Jared hadn't known the extent of Rodney's illegal activities, and the man had no way of predicting how foul his son's deeds would become before it was all over. Murder, betrayal. Such things were beyond the comprehension of normal, decent people, and Jared Wells was nothing if not a decent, caring man. Jake had picked up on that the first time he spoke with him on the phone.

No, aside from Rodney, Molly blamed no one—not Jared, and certainly not Claudia. But as often happened in complicated situations such as this, Molly believed with all her heart that Claudia and Jared resented her because she had been instrumental in sending Rodney to prison. Not only that, but Molly had been understandably joyous when the jury had found Rodney guilty on all counts.

After seeing that justice was served, however, Molly had gone into a holding pattern, reluctant to make the first contact with her mother and stepfather. *"No matter how wrong Rodney was, you know how Jared must be grieving over this. If they want to see me, it's up to them to make the first phone call!"* she'd cried to Jake after the trial.

As a result, she hadn't even returned to Sterling and Wells to take her rightful place behind her father's desk. Out of respect and concern for her mother's feelings, she probably never would, and that would be a shame. Molly had been raised to follow in Marshal Sterling's footsteps. The investment firm was important to her, and until she took up the reins, she would never be the woman she was meant to be—or the woman she needed to be. That couldn't be allowed to happen, and it wouldn't if Jake had any say in the matter. Six months out of the year, he wanted to see his wife helping to run the firm her father had worked all his life to build. The way Jake saw things, it was not only Molly's heritage, but that of their future children as well, and he meant to make damned sure Marshal Sterling's legacy was passed down to them.

On the outside looking in, Jake saw three people who had once loved one another deeply, and still did. It was time for all of them to talk, shed their tears, and get on with life. Molly and Claudia especially needed to patch up their relationship. A child was on the way. Jake wasn't about to let his son grow up without knowing his maternal grandmother.

To that end, he had telephoned Claudia and insisted that she and

Jared come for a pre-Christmas dinner at the Lazy J. Claudia, concerned about how Molly might feel, had been reluctant to accept the invitation, but Jake had finally prevailed after a man-to-man talk with Jared. It would only be for an evening, after all. If things went well, Molly could ask her parents to stay longer. If the visit went badly, the misery would be over quickly.

"You feel tense," Molly whispered, jerking Jake from his reverie. She rubbed a hand over his arm. "Are you worried about something? You're all tied in knots."

Jake was praying to hear the faint sound of a car out on the main road. If Molly's parents had had an accident en route to the ranch, all his plans for a happy reunion might be forever spoiled. He didn't even want to think how Molly would react if something happened to her mother. At the very least, she'd probably be thrown into early labor.

"No, honey, I'm not worried. What's there to worry about? The insurance paid off on all the fire damage. The stable and house are rebuilt. Since the fall auction, we're actually operating in the black." He gave her shoulder a gentle squeeze. "And best of all, we're about to have a beautiful, healthy little boy. I've never been so content."

"Me, neither." Her gaze suddenly caught on a tree off to the right, and a delighted smile swept over her face. "Oh, Jake, look at that one. It's *gorgeous!*"

Jake turned to peruse the tree. His heart sank when he noted how huge it was. "Honey, that thing must be ten feet tall."

"We need a really tall one to go in front of the vaulted windows. A short tree will be dwarfed."

Setting her carefully off his lap, he stifled a sigh and pushed to his feet. He wanted their first Christmas together to be memorable for her in every way, and if that meant dragging a ten-foot tree all the way home, he'd do it without complaint. He grabbed the saw from where he'd stashed it on the sled and went to work. Minutes later, he jumped out of the way as the huge Douglas fir plummeted to the ground.

She struggled up from the sled in that awkward, tummy-first way of all pregnant ladies. Once standing, she appeared delightfully round in the parka and thick fleece pants he'd insisted she wear. Her hair fluffed in a brilliant cloud of curls around her head. "It'll be so beautiful, all decorated with lights."

"Not half as beautiful as you are." Jake meant that with all his heart. All his life he'd been told how radiant some women were during pregnancy, and Molly was one of them. Her eyes sparkled, and her skin seemed to glow.

After dragging the huge tree over and securing it across the sled with ropes, he and Molly began the homeward trek through the woods. "If you're not too tired, maybe we can get this monster decorated tonight after dinner."

"I won't be too tired," she insisted, her voice ringing with enthusiasm. "I haven't done anything but sit on the sled. You did all the work."

Jake guessed that was true.

As they drew near the house, he saw a beige Buick sedan coming up the drive. Relief flooded through him. Jared and Claudia had arrived safely. He drew the sled over the boards he'd laid out to bridge the creek. Then he stopped and glanced back at Molly. "It looks like we've got company."

She squinted to see through the falling snow. When she spied the slender woman stepping from the Buick, her eyes widened with incredulity, and her face drained of color. For an awful moment, Jake wondered if he'd made a mistake by inviting Claudia there without asking Molly in advance. But then his wife let out a glad little cry.

"It's my *mom*! Oh, Jake, it's my mom."

"Looks that way."

Her questioning gaze jerked to his. Then, before he could guess what she meant to do, she threw herself into his arms, their bodies connecting belly first. "You called her for me! Oh, Jake, *thank* you!" She rained kisses along his jaw. "I love you. You're the most wonderful husband who ever lived. I love you, love you, *love* you!"

Before he could think of a response, she shoved from his arms and whirled toward the house. Not wanting her to take a spill in the snow, Jake almost grabbed her hand. But then he thought better of it and let her go. This close to the house, there were no fallen logs or rocks hidden beneath the drifts. If she slipped and fell, the deep snow would provide her with a soft landing.

For a lady heavy with child, she ran with amazing agility. Pulling the tree-laden sled behind him, Jake followed at a much slower pace. This was Molly and Claudia's moment. He preferred to hang back until they said their hellos.

As Jake neared the barn, Hank emerged from the doorway. He tipped back his hat, his eyes twinkling with amusement as he watched Molly launch herself into her mother's arms. He flicked a knowing look at Jake. "You're going to be her hero for at least a month."

Jake observed the emotional reunion. Then he grinned. "I just set things in motion, that's all."

"You want me to run in the house and get a stack of towels?" Hank asked.

"What for?"

"To mop up all the tears." Hank rested his gloved hands at his hips, his dark face creased in a grin. "It's going to be ugly. She's been really weepy the last few days. Once the spigot gets turned on, she can't seem to shut it off."

Jake glanced at the women, who were locked in each other's arms and sobbing with joy as they swayed back and forth. "Most women cry easily during pregnancy. It's something to do with their hormone levels."

"I told her how big her stomach was yesterday, and she burst into tears," Hank said. "I felt terrible, but nothing I said made it better. I never meant to hurt her feelings. She's such a sweetheart, and she's cute as a button with that big tummy poking out."

"She feels fat and unattractive right now. I think most women do at this stage."

"She doesn't look fat," Hank observed. "I think it's cute, the way she waddles."

Jake shot his brother a warning look. "Do *not* say the word *waddle* in front of her. She'll be upset until after the baby's born."

Hank huffed. "Do I look that stupid?"

"Yes."

Another shrill wailing sound drifted to them. Jake turned to peer at his wife through the thickening downfall of snowflakes. His heart caught when he saw that Jared had joined the women and was now participating in a three-way embrace. Molly buried her face against her mother's shoulder, and then she turned to press her cheek to Jared's chest. Even from a distance, Jake could see the happiness in her expression.

He was glad—so very glad. From the start, he'd sensed Molly's loneliness. To someone like Jake, who'd grown up with so much love to sustain him, it seemed tragic that other people weren't so fortunate.

Smiling, he watched Claudia cup Molly's face between her hands. The tenderness in the older woman's actions spoke volumes, making Jake recall the afternoon he'd told Molly that everyone, both humans and animals, saw themselves as others did. He also remembered with a twinge of sadness how Molly had once gazed at her reflection in the bathroom mirror and told him she couldn't find herself anymore, that the person she'd once been was gone.

Jake had assured her then that the real Molly still existed, that she only needed time to rediscover herself. This reunion was the final step in that process, a reclaiming of childhood memories and a reestablishment of family bonds that defined who she really was and how deeply and unconditionally she was loved.

A lump came to Jake's throat. Eventually Molly and Claudia would have ironed things out on their own. The love between them ran too deep for it to happen otherwise. Nevertheless, he stood a little taller, knowing he'd been instrumental in making it happen today—before Christmas and before their son was born. What better gift could he give his wife?

As if Molly felt his gaze on her, she turned to search him out. The radiant smile she flashed his way was all the invitation Jake needed. He dropped the sled rope and started toward her. Breaking away from her parents, Molly ran to him.

Jake met her halfway and caught her up in his arms. She laughed tearfully and leaned back to search his eyes. Jake allowed her to look deeply, hoping to convey his message without words.

Judging by her radiant smile, he knew she understood—that, in his opinion, she was and would always be the most beautiful woman in the world.

❦ ABOUT THE AUTHOR ❧

Catherine Anderson lives in the pristine woodlands of Central Oregon. She is married to her high school sweetheart, Sid, and is the author of more than twenty bestselling and award-winning historical and contemporary romances.